Lourdes

Lourdes

Émile Zola

MINT EDITIONS

Lourdes was first published in 1894.

This edition published by Mint Editions 2021.

ISBN 9781513281063 | E-ISBN 9781513286082

Published by Mint Editions®

 MINT
EDITIONS

minteditionbooks.com

Publishing Director: Jennifer Newens
Design & Production: Rachel Lopez Metzger
Project Manager: Micaela Clark
Translated by Ernest A. Vizetelly
Typesetting: Westchester Publishing Services

Contents

The First Day

    I. Pilgrims and Patients   9

    II. Pierre and Marie   26

    III. Poitiers   44

    IV. Miracles   63

    V. Bernadette   84

The Second Day

    I. The Train Arrives   109

    II. Hospital and Grotto   126

    III. Fountain and Piscina   144

    IV. Verification   162

    V. Bernadette's Trials   181

The Third Day

    I. Bed and Board   203

    II. The "Ordinary"   220

    III. The Night Procession   241

IV. The Vigil   258

V. The Two Victims   277

The Fourth Day

I. The Bitterness of Death   297

II. The Service at the Grotto   313

III. Marie's Cure   330

IV. Triumph—Despair   347

V. Cradle and Grave   367

The Fifth Day

I. Egotism and Love   387

II. Pleasant Hours   403

III. Departure   424

IV. Marie's Vow   446

V. The Death of Bernadette—The New Religion   469

THE FIRST DAY

I

Pilgrims and Patients

The pilgrims and patients, closely packed on the hard seats of a third-class carriage, were just finishing the "Ave maris Stella," which they had begun to chant on leaving the terminus of the Orleans line, when Marie, slightly raised on her couch of misery and restless with feverish impatience, caught sight of the Paris fortifications through the window of the moving train.

"Ah, the fortifications!" she exclaimed, in a tone which was joyous despite her suffering. "Here we are, out of Paris; we are off at last!"

Her delight drew a smile from her father, M. de Guersaint, who sat in front of her, whilst Abbe Pierre Froment, who was looking at her with fraternal affection, was so carried away by his compassionate anxiety as to say aloud: "And now we are in for it till to-morrow morning. We shall only reach Lourdes at three-forty. We have more than two-and-twenty hours' journey before us."

It was half-past five, the sun had risen, radiant in the pure sky of a delightful morning. It was a Friday, the 19th of August. On the horizon, however, some small, heavy clouds already presaged a terrible day of stormy heat. And the oblique sunrays were enfilading the compartments of the railway carriage, filling them with dancing, golden dust.

"Yes, two-and-twenty hours," murmured Marie, relapsing into a state of anguish. "*Mon Dieu*! what a long time we must still wait!"

Then her father helped her to lie down again in the narrow box, a kind of wooden gutter, in which she had been living for seven years past. Making an exception in her favour, the railway officials had consented to take as luggage the two pairs of wheels which could be removed from the box, or fitted to it whenever it became necessary to transport her from place to place. Packed between the sides of this movable coffin, she occupied the room of three passengers on the carriage seat; and for a moment she lay there with eyes closed. Although she was three-and-twenty; her ashen, emaciated face was still delicately infantile, charming despite everything, in the midst of her marvellous fair hair, the hair of a queen, which illness had respected. Clad with the utmost simplicity in a gown of thin woollen stuff, she wore, hanging from her neck, the card bearing her name and number, which entitled her to *hospitalisation*, or free treatment. She herself had insisted on making the journey in this humble fashion, not wishing to be a source of expense to her relatives, who little by little had fallen into very straitened circumstances. And thus it was that she found herself in a third-class carriage of the "white train," the train which carried the greatest sufferers, the most woeful of the fourteen trains going to Lourdes that day, the one in which, in addition to five hundred healthy pilgrims, nearly three hundred unfortunate wretches, weak to the point of exhaustion, racked by suffering, were heaped together, and borne at express speed from one to the other end of France.

Sorry that he had saddened her, Pierre continued to gaze at her with the air of a compassionate elder brother. He had just completed his thirtieth year, and was pale and slight, with a broad forehead. After busying himself with all the arrangements for the journey, he had been desirous of accompanying her, and, having obtained admission among the Hospitallers of Our Lady of Salvation as an auxiliary member, wore on his cassock the red, orange-tipped cross of a bearer. M. de Guersaint on his side had simply pinned the little scarlet cross of the pilgrimage on his grey cloth jacket. The idea of travelling appeared to delight him; although he was over fifty he still looked young, and, with his eyes ever wandering over the landscape, he seemed unable to keep his head still—a bird-like head it was, with an expression of good nature and absent-mindedness.

However, in spite of the violent shaking of the train, which constantly drew sighs from Marie, Sister Hyacinthe had risen to her feet in the adjoining compartment. She noticed that the sun's rays were streaming in the girl's face.

"Pull down the blind, Monsieur l'Abbe," she said to Pierre. "Come, come, we must install ourselves properly, and set our little household in order."

Clad in the black robe of a Sister of the Assumption, enlivened by a white coif, a white wimple, and a large white apron, Sister Hyacinthe smiled, the picture of courageous activity. Her youth bloomed upon her small, fresh lips, and in the depths of her beautiful blue eyes, whose expression was ever gentle. She was not pretty, perhaps, still she was charming, slender, and tall, the bib of her apron covering her flat chest like that of a young man; one of good heart, displaying a snowy complexion, and overflowing with health, gaiety, and innocence.

"But this sun is already roasting us," said she; "pray pull down your blind as well, madame."

Seated in the corner, near the Sister, was Madame de Jonquiere, who had kept her little bag on her lap. She slowly pulled down the blind. Dark, and well built, she was still nice-looking, although she had a daughter, Raymonde, who was four-and-twenty, and whom for motives of propriety she had placed in the charge of two lady-hospitallers, Madame Desagneaux and Madame Volmar, in a first-class carriage. For her part, directress as she was of a ward of the Hospital of Our Lady of Dolours at Lourdes, she did not quit her patients; and outside, swinging against the door of her compartment, was the regulation placard bearing under her own name those of the two Sisters of the Assumption who accompanied her. The widow of a ruined man, she lived with her daughter on the scanty income of four or five thousand francs a year, at the rear of a courtyard in the Rue Vanneau. But her charity was inexhaustible, and she gave all her time to the work of the Hospitality of Our Lady of Salvation, an institution whose red cross she wore on her gown of carmelite poplin, and whose aims she furthered with the most active zeal. Of a somewhat proud disposition, fond of being flattered and loved, she took great delight in this annual journey, from which both her heart and her passion derived contentment.

"You are right, Sister," she said, "we will organise matters. I really don't know why I am encumbering myself with this bag."

And thereupon she placed it under the seat, near her.

"Wait a moment," resumed Sister Hyacinthe; "you have the water-can between your legs—it is in your way."

"No, no, it isn't, I assure you. Let it be. It must always be somewhere."

Then they both set their house in order as they expressed it, so that for a day and a night they might live with their patients as comfortably as possible. The worry was that they had not been able to take Marie into their compartment, as she wished to have Pierre and her father near her; however neighbourly intercourse was easy enough over the low partition. Moreover the whole carriage, with its five compartments of ten seats each, formed but one moving chamber, a common room as it were which the eye took in at a glance from end to end. Between its wooden walls, bare and yellow, under its white-painted panelled roof, it showed like a hospital ward, with all the disorder and promiscuous jumbling together of an improvised ambulance. Basins, brooms, and sponges lay about, half-hidden by the seats. Then, as the train only carried such luggage as the pilgrims could take with them, there were valises, deal boxes, bonnet boxes, and bags, a wretched pile of poor worn-out things mended with bits of string, heaped up a little bit everywhere; and overhead the litter began again, what with articles of clothing, parcels, and baskets hanging from brass pegs and swinging to and fro without a pause.

Amidst all this frippery the more afflicted patients, stretched on their narrow mattresses, which took up the room of several passengers, were shaken, carried along by the rumbling gyrations of the wheels; whilst those who were able to remain seated, leaned against the partitions, their faces pale, their heads resting upon pillows. According to the regulations there should have been one lady-hospitaller to each compartment. However, at the other end of the carriage there was but a second Sister of the Assumption, Sister Claire des Anges. Some of the pilgrims who were in good health were already getting up, eating and drinking. One compartment was entirely occupied by women, ten pilgrims closely pressed together, young ones and old ones, all sadly, pitifully ugly. And as nobody dared to open the windows on account of the consumptives in the carriage, the heat was soon felt and an unbearable odour arose, set free as it were by the jolting of the train as it went its way at express speed.

They had said their chaplets at Juvisy; and six o'clock was striking, and they were rushing like a hurricane past the station of Bretigny, when Sister Hyacinthe stood up. It was she who directed the pious exercises, which most of the pilgrims followed from small, blue-covered books.

"The Angelus, my children," said she with a pleasant smile, a maternal air which her great youth rendered very charming and sweet.

Then the "Aves" again followed one another, and were drawing to an end when Pierre and Marie began to feel interested in two women who occupied the other corner seats of their compartment. One of them, she who sat at Marie's feet, was a blonde of slender build and *bourgeoise* appearance, some thirty and odd years of age, and faded before she had grown old. She shrank back, scarcely occupying any room, wearing a dark dress, and showing colourless hair, and a long grief-stricken face which expressed unlimited self-abandonment, infinite sadness. The woman in front of her, she who sat on the same seat as Pierre, was of the same age, but belonged to the working classes. She wore a black cap and displayed a face ravaged by wretchedness and anxiety, whilst on her lap she held a little girl of seven, who was so pale, so wasted by illness, that she scarcely seemed four. With her nose contracted, her eyelids lowered and showing blue in her waxen face, the child was unable to speak, unable to give utterance to more than a low plaint, a gentle moan, which rent the heart of her mother, leaning over her, each time that she heard it.

"Would she eat a few grapes?" timidly asked the lady, who had hitherto preserved silence. "I have some in my basket."

"Thank you, madame," replied the woman, "she only takes milk, and sometimes not even that willingly. I took care to bring a bottleful with me."

Then, giving way to the desire which possesses the wretched to confide their woes to others, she began to relate her story. Her name was Vincent, and her husband, a gilder by trade, had been carried off by consumption. Left alone with her little Rose, who was the passion of her heart, she had worked by day and night at her calling as a dressmaker in order to bring the child up. But disease had come, and for fourteen months now she had had her in her arms like that, growing more and more woeful and wasted until reduced almost to nothingness. She, the mother, who never went to mass, entered a church, impelled by despair to pray for her daughter's cure; and there she had heard a voice which had told her to take the little one to Lourdes, where the Blessed Virgin would have pity on her. Acquainted with nobody, not knowing even how the pilgrimages were organised, she had had but one idea—to work, save up the money necessary for the journey, take a ticket, and start off with the thirty sous remaining to her, destitute of all supplies save a bottle of milk for the child, not having even thought of purchasing a crust of bread for herself.

"What is the poor little thing suffering from?" resumed the lady.

"Oh, it must be consumption of the bowels, madame! But the doctors have names they give it. At first she only had slight pains in the stomach. Then her stomach began to swell and she suffered, oh, so dreadfully! it made one cry to see her. Her stomach has gone down now, only she's worn out; she has got so thin that she has no legs left her, and she's wasting away with continual sweating."

Then, as Rose, raising her eyelids, began to moan, her mother leant over her, distracted and turning pale. "What is the matter, my jewel, my treasure?" she asked. "Are you thirsty?"

But the little girl was already closing her dim eyes of a hazy sky-blue hue, and did not even answer, but relapsed into her torpor, quite white in the white frock she wore—a last coquetry on the part of her mother, who had gone to this useless expense in the hope that the Virgin would be more compassionate and gentle to a little sufferer who was well dressed, so immaculately white.

There was an interval of silence, and then Madame Vincent inquired: "And you, madame, it's for yourself no doubt that you are going to Lourdes? One can see very well that you are ill."

But the lady, with a frightened look, shrank woefully into her corner, murmuring: "No, no, I am not ill. Would to God that I were! I should suffer less."

Her name was Madame Maze, and her heart was full of an incurable grief. After a love marriage to a big, gay fellow with ripe, red lips, she had found herself deserted at the end of a twelvemonth's honeymoon. Ever travelling, following the profession of a jeweller's bagman, her husband, who earned a deal of money, would disappear for six months at a stretch, deceive her from one frontier to the other of France, at times even carrying creatures about with him. And she worshipped him; she suffered so frightfully from it all that she had sought a remedy in religion, and had at last made up her mind to repair to Lourdes, in order to pray the Virgin to restore her husband to her and make him amend his ways.

Although Madame Vincent did not understand the other's words, she realised that she was a prey to great mental affliction, and they continued looking at one another, the mother, whom the sight of her dying daughter was killing, and the abandoned wife, whom her passion cast into throes of death-like agony.

However, Pierre, who, like Marie, had been listening to the conversation, now intervened. He was astonished that the dressmaker had not sought free treatment for her little patient. The Association of Our Lady of Salvation had been founded by the Augustine Fathers of the Assumption after the Franco-German war, with the object of contributing to the salvation of France and the defence of the Church by prayer in common and the practice of charity; and it was this association which had promoted the great pilgrimage movement, in particular initiating and unremittingly extending the national pilgrimage which every year, towards the close of August, set out for Lourdes. An elaborate organisation had been gradually perfected, donations of considerable amounts were collected in all parts of the world, sufferers were enrolled in every parish, and agreements were signed with the railway companies, to say nothing of the active help of the Little Sisters of the Assumption and the establishment of the Hospitality of Our Lady of Salvation, a widespread brotherhood of the benevolent, in which one beheld men and women, mostly belonging to society, who, under the orders of the pilgrimage managers, nursed the sick, helped to transport them, and watched over the observance of good discipline. A written request was needed for the sufferers to obtain hospitalisation, which dispensed them from making the smallest payment in respect either of their journey or their sojourn; they were fetched from their homes and conveyed back thither; and they simply had to provide a few provisions for the road. By far the greater number were recommended by priests or benevolent persons, who superintended the inquiries concerning them and obtained the needful papers, such as doctors' certificates and certificates of birth. And, these matters being settled, the sick ones had nothing further to trouble about, they became but so much suffering flesh, food for miracles, in the hands of the hospitallers of either sex.

"But you need only have applied to your parish priest, madame," Pierre explained. "This poor child is deserving of all sympathy. She would have been immediately admitted."

"I did not know it, monsieur l'Abbe."

"Then how did you manage?"

"Why, Monsieur l'Abbe, I went to take a ticket at a place which one of my neighbours, who reads the newspapers, told me about."

She was referring to the tickets, at greatly reduced rates, which were issued to the pilgrims possessed of means. And Marie, listening to her, felt great pity for her, and also some shame; for she who was not entirely destitute of resources had succeeded in obtaining *hospitalisation*, thanks to Pierre, whereas that mother and her sorry child, after exhausting their scanty savings, remained without a copper.

However, a more violent jolt of the carriage drew a cry of pain from the girl. "Oh, father," she said, "pray raise me a little! I can't stay on my back any longer."

When M. de Guersaint had helped her into a sitting posture, she gave a deep sigh of relief. They were now at Etampes, after a run of an hour and a half from Paris, and what with the increased warmth of the sun, the dust, and the noise, weariness was becoming apparent already. Madame de Jonquiere had got up to speak a few words of kindly encouragement to Marie over the partition; and Sister Hyacinthe moreover again rose, and gaily clapped her hands that she might be heard and obeyed from one to the other end of the carriage.

"Come, come!" said she, "we mustn't think of our little troubles. Let us pray and sing, and the Blessed Virgin will be with us."

She herself then began the rosary according to the rite of Our Lady of Lourdes, and all the patients and pilgrims followed her. This was the first chaplet—the five joyful mysteries, the Annunciation, the Visitation, the Nativity, the Purification, and Jesus found in the Temple. Then they all began to chant the canticle: "Let us contemplate the heavenly Archangel!" Their voices were lost amid the loud rumbling of the wheels; you heard but the muffled surging of that human wave, stifling within the closed carriage which rolled on and on without a pause.

Although M. de Guersaint was a worshipper, he could never follow a hymn to the end. He got up, sat down again, and finished by resting his elbow on the partition and conversing in an undertone with a patient who sat against this same partition in the next compartment. The patient in question was a thick-set man of fifty, with a good-natured face and a large head, completely bald. His name was Sabathier, and for fifteen years he had been stricken with ataxia. He only suffered pain by fits and starts, but he had quite lost the use of his legs, which his wife, who accompanied him, moved for him as though they had been dead legs, whenever they became too heavy, weighty like bars of lead.

"Yes, monsieur," he said, "such as you see me, I was formerly fifth-class professor at the Lycee Charlemagne. At first I thought that it was mere sciatica, but afterwards I was seized with sharp, lightning-like pains, red-hot sword thrusts, you know, in the muscles. For nearly ten years the disease kept on mastering me more and more. I consulted all the doctors, tried every imaginable mineral spring, and now I suffer less, but I can no longer move from my seat. And then, after long living without a thought of religion, I was led back to God by the idea that I was too wretched, and that Our Lady of Lourdes could not do otherwise than take pity on me."

Feeling interested, Pierre in his turn had leant over the partition and was listening.

"Is it not so, Monsieur l'Abbe?" continued M. Sabathier. "Is not suffering the best awakener of souls? This is the seventh year that I am going to Lourdes without despairing of cure. This year the Blessed Virgin will cure me, I feel sure of it. Yes, I expect to be able to walk about again; I now live solely in that hope."

M. Sabathier paused, he wished his wife to push his legs a little more to the left; and Pierre looked at him, astonished to find such obstinate faith in a man of intellect, in one of those university professors who, as a rule, are such Voltairians. How could the belief in miracles have germinated and taken root in this man's brain? As he himself said, great suffering alone explained this need of illusion, this blossoming of eternal and consolatory hope.

"And my wife and I," resumed the ex-professor, "are dressed, you see, as poor folks, for I wished to go as a mere pauper this year, and applied for *hospitalisation* in a spirit of humility in order that the Blessed Virgin might include me among the wretched, her children—only, as I did not wish to take the place of a real pauper, I gave fifty francs to the Hospitalite, and this, as you are aware, gives one the right to have a patient of one's own in the pilgrimage. I even know my patient. He was introduced to me at the railway station. He is suffering from tuberculosis, it appears, and seemed to me very low, very low."

A fresh interval of silence ensued. "Well," said M. Sabathier at last, "may the Blessed Virgin save him also, she who can do everything. I shall be so happy; she will have loaded me with favours."

Then the three men, isolating themselves from the others, went on conversing together, at first on medical subjects, and at last diverging into a discussion on romanesque architecture, *a propos* of a steeple which they had perceived on a hillside, and which every pilgrim had saluted with a sign of the cross. Swayed once more by the habits of cultivated intellect, the young priest and his two companions forgot themselves together in the midst of their fellow-passengers, all those poor, suffering, simple-minded folk, whom wretchedness stupefied. Another hour went by, two more canticles had just been sung, and the stations of Toury and Les Aubrais had been left behind, when, at Beaugency, they at last ceased their chat, on hearing Sister Hyacinthe clap her hands and intonate in her fresh, sonorous voice:

"*Parce, Domine, parce populo tuo.*"

And then the chant went on; all voices became mingled in that ever-surging wave of prayer which stilled pain, excited hope, and little by little penetrated the entire being, harassed by the haunting thought of the grace and cure which one and all were going to seek so far away.

However, as Pierre sat down again, he saw that Marie was very pale, and had her eyes closed. By the painful contraction of her features he could tell that she was not asleep. "Are you in great suffering?" he asked.

"Yes, yes, I suffer dreadfully. I shall never last to the end. It is this incessant jolting."

She moaned, raised her eyelids, and, half-fainting, remained in a sitting posture, her eyes turned on the other sufferers. In the adjoining compartment, La Grivotte, hitherto stretched out, scarce breathing, like a corpse, had just raised herself up in front of M. Sabathier. She was a tall, slip-shod, singular-looking creature of over thirty, with a round, ravaged face, which her frizzy hair and flaming eyes rendered almost pretty. She had reached the third stage of phthisis.

"Eh, mademoiselle," she said, addressing herself in a hoarse, indistinct voice to Marie, "how nice it would be if we could only doze off a little. But it can't be managed; all these wheels keep on whirling round and round in one's head."

Then, although it fatigued her to speak, she obstinately went on talking, volunteering particulars about herself. She was a mattress-maker, and with one of her aunts had long gone from yard to yard at Bercy to comb and sew up mattresses. And, indeed, it was to the pestilential wool which she had combed in her youth that she ascribed her malady. For five years she had been making the round of the hospitals of Paris, and she spoke familiarly of all the great doctors. It was the Sisters of Charity, at the Lariboisiere hospital, who, finding that she had a passion for religious ceremonies, had completed her conversion, and convinced her that the Virgin awaited her at Lourdes to cure her.

"I certainly need it," said she. "The doctors say that I have one lung done for, and that the other one is scarcely any better. There are great big holes you know. At first I only felt bad between the shoulders and spat up some froth. But then I got thin, and became a dreadful sight. And now I'm always in a sweat, and cough till I think I'm going to bring my heart up. And I can no longer spit. And I haven't the strength to stand, you see. I can't eat."

A stifling sensation made her pause, and she became livid.

"All the same I prefer being in my skin instead of in that of the Brother in the compartment behind you. He has the same complaint as I have, but he is in a worse state that I am."

She was mistaken. In the farther compartment, beyond Marie, there was indeed a young missionary, Brother Isidore, who was lying on a mattress and could not be seen, since he was unable to raise even a finger. But he was not suffering from phthisis. He was dying of inflammation of the liver, contracted in Senegal. Very long and lank, he had a yellow face, with skin as dry and lifeless as parchment. The abscess which had formed in his liver had ended by breaking out externally, and amidst the continuous shivering of fever, vomiting, and delirium, suppuration was exhausting him. His eyes alone were still alive, eyes full of unextinguishable love, whose flame lighted up his expiring face, a peasant face such as painters have given to the crucified Christ, common, but rendered sublime at moments by its expression of faith and passion. He was a Breton, the last puny child of an over-numerous family, and had left his little share of land to his elder brothers. One of his sisters, Marthe, older than himself by a couple of years, accompanied him. She had been in service in Paris, an insignificant maid-of-all-work, but withal so devoted to her brother that she had left her situation to follow him, subsisting scantily on her petty savings.

"I was lying on the platform," resumed La Grivotte, "when he was put in the carriage. There were four men carrying him—"

But she was unable to speak any further, for just then an attack of coughing shook her and threw her back upon the seat. She was suffocating, and the red flush on her cheek-bones turned blue. Sister Hyacinthe, however, immediately raised her head and wiped her lips with a linen cloth, which became spotted with blood. At the same time Madame de Jonquiere gave her attention to a patient in front of her, who had just fainted. She was called Madame Vetu, and was the wife of a petty clockmaker of the Mouffetard district, who had not been able to shut up his shop in order to accompany her to Lourdes. And to make sure that she would be cared for she had sought and obtained *hospitalisation*. The fear of death was bringing her back to religion, although she had not set foot in church since her first communion. She knew that she was lost, that a cancer in the chest was eating into her; and she already had the haggard, orange-hued mark of the cancerous patient. Since the beginning of the journey she had not spoken a word, but, suffering terribly, had remained with her lips tightly closed. Then all at once, she had swooned away after an attack of vomiting.

"It is unbearable!" murmured Madame de Jonquiere, who herself felt faint; "we must let in a little fresh air."

Sister Hyacinthe was just then laying La Grivotte to rest on her pillows, "Certainly," said she, "we will open the window for a few moments. But not on this side, for I am afraid we might have a fresh fit of coughing. Open the window on your side, madame."

The heat was still increasing, and the occupants of the carriage were stifling in that heavy evil-smelling atmosphere. The pure air which came in when the window was opened brought relief however. For a moment there were other duties to be attended to, a clearance and cleansing. The Sister emptied the basins out of the window, whilst the lady-hospitaller wiped the shaking floor with a sponge. Next, things had to be set in order; and then came a fresh anxiety, for the fourth patient, a slender girl whose face was entirely covered by a black fichu, and who had not yet moved, was saying that she felt hungry.

With quiet devotion Madame de Jonquiere immediately tendered her services. "Don't you trouble, Sister," she said, "I will cut her bread into little bits for her."

Marie, with the need she felt of diverting her mind from her own sufferings, had already begun to take an interest in that motionless sufferer whose countenance was so thickly veiled, for she not unnaturally suspected that it was a case of some distressing facial sore. She had merely been told that the patient was a servant, which was true, but it happened that the poor creature, a native of Picardy, named Elise Rouquet, had been obliged to leave her situation, and seek a home with a sister who ill-treated her, for no hospital would take her in. Extremely devout, she had for many months been possessed by an ardent desire to go to Lourdes.

While Marie, with dread in her heart, waited for the fichu to be moved aside, Madame de Jonquiere, having cut some bread into small pieces, inquired maternally: "Are they small enough? Can you put them into your mouth?"

Thereupon a hoarse voice growled confused words under the black fichu: "Yes, yes, madame." And at last the veil fell and Marie shuddered with horror.

It was a case of lupus which had preyed upon the unhappy woman's nose and mouth. Ulceration had spread, and was hourly spreading—in short, all the hideous peculiarities of this terrible disease were in full process of development, almost obliterating the traces of what once were pleasing womanly lineaments.

"Oh, look, Pierre!" Marie murmured, trembling. The priest in his turn shuddered as he beheld Elise Rouquet cautiously slipping the tiny pieces of bread into her poor shapeless mouth. Everyone in the carriage had turned pale at sight of the awful apparition. And the same thought ascended from all those hope-inflated souls. Ah! Blessed Virgin, Powerful Virgin, what a miracle indeed if such an ill were cured!

"We must not think of ourselves, my children, if we wish to get well," resumed Sister Hyacinthe, who still retained her encouraging smile.

And then she made them say the second chaplet, the five sorrowful mysteries: Jesus in the Garden of Olives, Jesus scourged, Jesus crowned with thorns, Jesus carrying the cross, and Jesus crucified. Afterwards came the canticle: "In thy help, Virgin, do I put my trust."

They had just passed through Blois; for three long hours they had been rolling onward; and Marie, who had averted her eyes from Elise Rouquet, now turned them upon a man who occupied a corner seat in the compartment on her left, that in which Brother Isidore was lying. She had noticed this man several times already. Poorly clad in an old black frock-coat, he looked still young, although his sparse beard was already turning grey; and, short and emaciated, he seemed to experience great suffering, his fleshless, livid face being covered with sweat. However, he remained motionless, ensconced in his corner, speaking to nobody, but staring straight before him with dilated eyes. And all at once Marie noticed that his eyelids were falling, and that he was fainting away.

She thereupon drew Sister's Hyacinthe's attention to him: "Look, Sister! One would think that that gentleman is dangerously ill."

"Which one, my dear child?"

"That one, over there, with his head thrown back."

General excitement followed, all the healthy pilgrims rose up to look, and it occurred to Madame de Jonquiere to call to Marthe, Brother Isidore's sister, and tell her to tap the man's hands.

"Question him," she added; "ask what ails him."

Marthe drew near, shook the man, and questioned him.

But instead of an answer only a rattle came from his throat, and his eyes remained closed.

Then a frightened voice was heard saying, "I think he is going to die."

The dread increased, words flew about, advice was tendered from one to the other end of the carriage. Nobody knew the man. He had certainly not obtained *hospitalisation*, for no white card was hanging from his neck. Somebody related, however, that he had seen him arrive, dragging himself along, but three minutes or so before the train started; and that he had remained quite motionless, scarce breathing, ever since he had flung himself with an air of intense weariness into that corner, where he was now apparently dying. His ticket was at last seen protruding from under the band of an old silk hat which was hung from a peg near him.

"Ah, he is breathing again now!" Sister Hyacinthe suddenly exclaimed. "Ask him his name."

However, on being again questioned by Marthe, the man merely gave vent to a low plaint, an exclamation scarcely articulated, "Oh, how I suffer!"

And thenceforward that was the only answer that could be obtained from him. With reference to everything that they wished to know, who he was, whence he came, what his illness was, what could be done for him, he gave no information, but still and ever continued moaning, "Oh, how I suffer—how I suffer!"

Sister Hyacinthe grew restless with impatience. Ah, if she had only been in the same compartment with him! And she resolved that she would change her seat at the first station they should stop at. Only there would be no stoppage for a long time. The position was becoming terrible, the more so as the man's head again fell back.

"He is dying, he is dying!" repeated the frightened voice.

What was to be done, *mon Dieu*? The Sister was aware that one of the Fathers of the Assumption, Father Massias, was in the train with the Holy Oils, ready to administer extreme unction to the dying; for every year some of the patients passed away during the journey. But she did not dare to have recourse to the alarm signal. Moreover, in the *cantine* van where Sister Saint Francois officiated, there was a doctor with a little medicine chest. If the sufferer should survive until they reached Poitiers, where there would be half an hour's stoppage, all possible help might be given to him.

But on the other hand he might suddenly expire. However, they ended by becoming somewhat calmer. The man, though still unconscious, began to breathe in a more regular manner, and seemed to fall asleep.

"To think of it, to die before getting there," murmured Marie with a shudder, "to die in sight of the promised land!" And as her father sought to reassure her she added: "I am suffering—I am suffering dreadfully myself."

"Have confidence," said Pierre; "the Blessed Virgin is watching over you."

She could no longer remain seated, and it became necessary to replace her in a recumbent position in her narrow coffin. Her father and the priest had to take every precaution in doing so, for the slightest hurt drew a moan from her. And she lay there breathless, like one dead, her face contracted by suffering, and surrounded by her regal fair hair. They had now been rolling on, ever rolling on for nearly four hours. And if the carriage was so greatly shaken, with an unbearable spreading tendency, it was from its position at the rear part of the train. The coupling irons shrieked, the wheels growled furiously; and as it was necessary to leave the windows partially open, the dust came in, acrid and burning; but it was especially the heat which grew terrible, a devouring, stormy heat falling from a tawny sky which large hanging clouds had slowly covered. The hot carriages, those rolling boxes where the pilgrims ate and drank, where the sick lay in a vitiated atmosphere, amid dizzying moans, prayers, and hymns, became like so many furnaces.

And Marie was not the only one whose condition had been aggravated; others also were suffering from the journey. Resting in the lap of her despairing mother, who gazed at her with large, tear-blurred eyes, little Rose had ceased to stir, and had grown so pale that Madame Maze had twice leant forward to feel her hands, fearful lest she should find them cold. At each moment also Madame Sabathier had to move her husband's legs, for their weight was so great, said he, that it seemed as if his hips were being torn from him. Brother Isidore too had just begun to cry out, emerging from his wonted torpor; and his sister had only been able to assuage his sufferings by raising him, and clasping him in her arms. La Grivotte seemed to be asleep, but a continuous hiccoughing shook her, and a tiny streamlet of blood dribbled from her mouth. Madame Vetu had again vomited, Elise Rouquet no longer thought of hiding the frightful sore open on her face. And from the man yonder, breathing hard, there still came a lugubrious rattle, as though he were at every moment on the point of expiring. In vain did Madame de Jonquiere and Sister Hyacinthe lavish their attentions on the patients, they could but slightly assuage so much suffering. At times it all seemed like an evil dream—that carriage of wretchedness and pain, hurried along at express speed, with a continuous shaking and jolting which made everything hanging from the pegs—the old clothes, the worn-out baskets mended with bits of string—swing to and fro incessantly. And in the compartment at the far end, the ten female pilgrims, some old, some young, and all pitifully ugly, sang on without a pause in cracked voices, shrill and dreary.

Then Pierre began to think of the other carriages of the train, that white train which conveyed most, if not all, of the more seriously afflicted patients; these carriages were rolling along, all displaying similar scenes of suffering among the three hundred sick and five hundred healthy pilgrims crowded within them. And afterwards he thought of the other trains which were leaving Paris that day, the grey train and the blue train* which had preceded the white one, the green train, the yellow train, the pink train, the orange train which were following it. From hour to hour trains set out from one to the other end of France. And he thought, too, of those which that same morning had started from Orleans, Le Mans, Poitiers, Bordeaux, Marseilles, and Carcassonne. Coming from all parts, trains were rushing across that land of France at the same hour, all directing their course yonder towards the holy Grotto, bringing thirty thousand patients and pilgrims to the Virgin's feet. And he reflected that other days of the year witnessed a like rush of human beings, that not a week went by without Lourdes beholding the arrival of some pilgrimage; that it was not merely France which set out on the march, but all Europe, the whole world; that in certain years of great religious fervour there had been three hundred thousand, and even five hundred thousand, pilgrims and patients streaming to the spot.

Pierre fancied that he could hear those flying trains, those trains from everywhere, all converging towards the same rocky cavity where the tapers were blazing. They all rumbled loudly amid the cries of pain and snatches of hymns wafted from their carriages. They were the rolling hospitals of disease at its last stage, of human suffering rushing to the hope of cure, furiously seeking consolation between attacks of increased severity, with the ever-present threat of death—death hastened, supervening under awful conditions, amidst the mob-like scramble. They rolled on, they rolled on again and again, they rolled on without a pause, carrying the wretchedness of the world on its way to the divine illusion, the health of the infirm, the consolation of the afflicted.

And immense pity overflowed from Pierre's heart, human compassion for all the suffering and all the tears that consumed weak and naked men. He was sad unto death and ardent charity burnt within him, the unextinguishable flame as it were of his fraternal feelings towards all things and beings.

When they left the station of Saint Pierre des Corps at half-past ten, Sister Hyacinthe gave the signal, and they recited the third chaplet, the five glorious mysteries, the Resurrection of Our Lord, the Ascension of Our Lord, the Mission of the Holy Ghost, the Assumption of the Most Blessed Virgin, the Crowning of the Most Blessed Virgin. And

---

* Different-coloured tickets are issued for these trains; it is for this reason that they are called the white, blue, and grey trains, etc.—Trans.

ÉMILE ZOLA

afterwards they sang the canticle of Bernadette, that long, long chant, composed of six times ten couplets, to which the ever recurring Angelic Salutation serves as a refrain—a prolonged lullaby slowly besetting one until it ends by penetrating one's entire being, transporting one into ecstatic sleep, in delicious expectancy of a miracle.

II

Pierre and Marie

The green landscapes of Poitou were now defiling before them, and Abbe Pierre Froment, gazing out of the window, watched the trees fly away till, little by little, he ceased to distinguish them. A steeple appeared and then vanished, and all the pilgrims crossed themselves. They would not reach Poitiers until twelve-thirty-five, and the train was still rolling on amid the growing weariness of that oppressive, stormy day. Falling into a deep reverie, the young priest no longer heard the words of the canticle, which sounded in his ears merely like a slow, wavy lullaby.

Forgetfulness of the present had come upon him, an awakening of the past filled his whole being. He was reascending the stream of memory, reascending it to its source. He again beheld the house at Neuilly, where he had been born and where he still lived, that home of peace and toil, with its garden planted with a few fine trees, and parted by a quickset hedge and palisade from the garden of the neighbouring house, which was similar to his own. He was again three, perhaps four, years old, and round a table, shaded by the big horse-chestnut tree he once more beheld his father, his mother, and his elder brother at *dejeuner*. To his father, Michel Froment, he could give no distinct lineaments; he pictured him but faintly, vaguely, renowned as an illustrious chemist, bearing the title of Member of the Institute, and leading a cloistered life in the laboratory which he had installed in that secluded, deserted suburb. However he could plainly see his first brother Guillaume, then fourteen years of age, whom some holiday had brought from college that morning, and then and even more vividly his mother, so gentle and so quiet, with eyes so full of active kindliness. Later on he learnt what anguish had racked that religious soul, that believing woman who, from esteem and gratitude, had resignedly accepted marriage with an unbeliever, her senior by fifteen years, to whom her relatives were indebted for great services. He, Pierre, the tardy offspring of this union, born when his father was already near his fiftieth year, had only known his mother as a respectful, conquered woman in the presence of her husband, whom she had learnt to love passionately, with the frightful torment of knowing, however, that he was doomed to perdition. And, all at once, another memory flashed upon the young priest, the terrible memory of the day when his father had died, killed in his laboratory by an accident, the explosion of a retort. He, Pierre, had then been five years old, and he remembered the slightest incidents—his mother's cry when she had found the shattered body among the remnants of the chemical appliances, then her terror, her sobs, her prayers at the idea that God had slain the unbeliever, damned him for evermore. Not daring to burn his books and papers, she had contented herself with locking up the laboratory, which henceforth nobody entered. And from that moment, haunted by a vision of hell, she had had but one idea, to possess herself of her second son, who was still so young, to give him a strictly religious training, and through him to ransom her husband—secure his forgiveness from God. Guillaume, her elder boy, had already ceased to belong to her, having grown up at college, where he had been won over by the ideas of the century; but she resolved that the other, the younger one, should not leave the house, but should have a priest as tutor; and her secret dream, her consuming hope, was that she might some day see him a priest himself, saying his first mass and solacing souls whom the thought of eternity tortured.

Then between green, leafy boughs, flecked with sunlight, another figure rose vividly before Pierre's eyes. He suddenly beheld Marie de Guersaint as he had seen her one morning through a gap in the hedge dividing the two gardens. M. de Guersaint, who belonged to the petty Norman *noblesse*, was a combination of architect and inventor; and he was at that time busy with a scheme of model dwellings for the poor, to which churches and schools were to be attached; an affair of considerable magnitude, planned none too well, however, and in which, with his customary impetuosity, the lack of foresight of an imperfect artist, he was risking the three hundred thousand francs that he possessed. A similarity of religious faith had drawn Madame de Guersaint and Madame Froment together; but the former was altogether a superior woman, perspicuous and rigid, with an iron hand which alone prevented her household from gliding to a catastrophe; and she was bringing up her two daughters, Blanche and Marie, in principles of narrow piety, the elder one already being as grave as herself, whilst the younger, albeit very devout, was still fond of play, with an intensity of life within her which found vent in gay peals of sonorous laughter. From their early childhood Pierre and Marie played together, the hedge was ever being crossed, the two families constantly mingled. And on that clear sunshiny morning, when he pictured her parting the leafy branches she was already ten years old. He, who was sixteen, was to enter the seminary on the following Tuesday. Never had she seemed to him so pretty. Her hair, of a pure golden hue, was so long that when it was let down it sufficed to clothe her. Well did he remember her face as it had been, with round cheeks, blue eyes, red mouth, and skin of dazzling, snowy whiteness. She was indeed as gay and brilliant as the sun itself, a transplendency. Yet there were tears at the corners of her eyes, for she was aware of his coming departure. They sat down together at the far end of the garden, in the shadow cast by the hedge. Their hands mingled, and their hearts were very heavy. They had, however, never exchanged any vows amid their pastimes, for their innocence was absolute. But now, on the eve of separation, their mutual tenderness rose to their lips, and they spoke without knowing, swore that they would ever think of one another, and find one another again, some day, even as one meets in heaven to be very, very happy. Then, without understanding how it happened, they clasped each other tightly, to the point of suffocation, and kissed each other's face, weeping, the while, hot tears. And it was that delightful memory which Pierre had ever carried with him, which he felt alive within him still, after so many years, and after so many painful renunciations.

Just then a more violent shock roused him from his reverie. He turned his eyes upon the carriage and vaguely espied the suffering beings it contained—Madame Maze motionless, overwhelmed with grief; little Rose gently moaning in her mother's lap; La Grivotte, whom a hoarse cough was choking. For a moment Sister Hyacinthe's gay face shone out amidst the whiteness of her coif and wimple, dominating all the others. The painful journey was continuing, with a ray of divine hope still and ever shining yonder. Then everything slowly vanished from Pierre's eyes as a fresh wave of memory brought the past back from afar; and nothing of the present remained save the lulling hymn, the indistinct voices of dreamland, emerging from the invisible.

Henceforth he was at the seminary. The classrooms, the recreation ground with its trees, rose up clearly before him. But all at once he only beheld, as in a mirror, the youthful face which had then been his, and he contemplated it and scrutinised it, as though it had been the face of a stranger. Tall and slender, he had an elongated visage, with an unusually developed forehead, lofty and straight like a tower; whilst his jaws tapered, ending in a small refined chin. He seemed, in fact, to be all brains; his mouth, rather large, alone retained an expression of tenderness. Indeed, when his usually serious face relaxed, his mouth and eyes acquired an exceedingly soft expression, betokening an unsatisfied, hungry desire to love, devote oneself, and live. But immediately afterwards, the look of intellectual passion would come back again, that intellectuality which had ever consumed him with an anxiety to understand and know. And it was with surprise that he now recalled those years of seminary life. How was it that he had so long been able to accept the rude discipline of blind faith, of obedient belief in everything without the slightest examination? It had been required of him that he should absolutely surrender his reasoning faculties, and he had striven to do so, had succeeded indeed in stifling his torturing need of truth. Doubtless he had been softened, weakened by his mother's tears, had been possessed by the sole desire to afford her the great happiness she dreamt of. Yet now he remembered certain quiverings of revolt; he found in the depths of his mind the memory of nights which he had spent in weeping without knowing why, nights peopled with vague images, nights through which galloped the free, virile life of the world, when Marie's face incessantly returned to him, such as he had seen it one morning, dazzling and bathed in tears, while she embraced him with her whole soul. And that alone now remained; his years of religious study with their monotonous lessons, their ever similar exercises and ceremonies, had flown away into the same haze, into a vague half-light, full of mortal silence.

Then, just as the train had passed though a station at full speed, with the sudden uproar of its rush there arose within him a succession of confused visions. He had noticed a large deserted enclosure, and fancied that he could see himself within it at twenty years of age. His reverie was wandering. An indisposition of rather long duration had, however, at one time interrupted his studies, and led to his being sent into the country. He had remained for a long time without seeing Marie; during his vacations spent at Neuilly he had twice failed to meet her, for she was almost always travelling. He knew that she was very ill, in consequence of a fall from a horse when she was thirteen, a critical moment in a girl's life; and her despairing mother, perplexed by the contradictory advice of medical men, was taking her each year to a different watering-place. Then he learnt the startling news of the sudden tragical death of that mother, who was so severe and yet so useful to her kin. She had been carried off in five days by inflammation of the lungs, which she had contracted one evening whilst she was out walking at La Bourboule, through having taken off her mantle to place it round the shoulders of Marie, who had been conveyed thither for treatment. It had been necessary that the father should at once start off to fetch his daughter, who was mad with grief, and the corpse of his wife, who had been so suddenly torn from him. And unhappily, after losing her, the affairs of the family went from bad to worse in the hands of this architect, who, without counting, flung his fortune into the yawning gulf of his unsuccessful enterprises. Marie no longer stirred from her couch; only Blanche remained to manage the household, and she had matters of her own to attend to, being busy with the last examinations which she had to pass, the diplomas which she was obstinately intent on securing, foreseeing as she did that she would someday have to earn her bread.

All at once, from amidst this mass of confused, half-forgotten incidents, Pierre was conscious of the rise of a vivid vision. Ill-health, he remembered, had again compelled him to take a holiday. He had just completed his twenty-fourth year, he was greatly behindhand, having so far only secured the four minor orders; but on his return a sub-deaconship would be conferred on him, and an inviolable vow would bind him for evermore. And the Guersaints' little garden at Neuilly, whither he had formerly so often gone to play, again distinctly appeared before him. Marie's couch had been rolled under the tall trees at the far end of the garden near the hedge, they were alone together in the sad peacefulness of an autumnal afternoon, and he saw Marie, clad in deep mourning for her mother and reclining there with legs inert; whilst he, also clad in black, in a cassock already, sat near her on an iron garden chair. For five years she had been suffering. She was now eighteen, paler and thinner than formerly, but still adorable with her regal golden hair, which illness respected. He believed from what he had heard that she was destined to remain infirm, condemned never to become a woman, stricken even in her sex. The doctors, who failed to agree respecting her case, had abandoned her. Doubtless it was she who told him these things that dreary afternoon, whilst the yellow withered leaves rained upon them. However, he could not remember the words that they had spoken; her pale smile, her young face, still so charming though already dimmed by regretfulness for life, alone remained present with him. But he realised that she had evoked the far-off day of their parting, on that same spot, behind the hedge flecked with sunlight; and all that was already as though dead—their tears, their embrace, their promise to find one another some day with a certainty of happiness. For although they had found one another again, what availed it, since she was but a corpse, and he was about to bid farewell to the life of the world? As the doctors condemned her, as she would never be woman, nor wife, nor mother, he, on his side, might well renounce manhood, and annihilate himself, dedicate himself to God, to whom his mother gave him. And he still felt within him the soft bitterness of that last interview: Marie smiling painfully at memory of their childish play and prattle, and speaking to him of the happiness which he would assuredly find in the service of God; so penetrated indeed with emotion at this thought, that she had made him promise that he would let her hear him say his first mass.

But the train was passing the station of Sainte-Maure, and just then a sudden uproar momentarily brought Pierre's attention back to the carriage and its occupants. He fancied that there had been some fresh seizure or swooning, but the suffering faces that he beheld were still the same, ever contracted by the same expression of anxious waiting for the divine succour which was so slow in coming. M. Sabathier was vainly striving to get his legs into a comfortable position, whilst Brother Isidore raised a feeble continuous moan like a dying child, and Madame Vetu, a prey to terrible agony, devoured by her disease, sat motionless, and kept her lips tightly closed, her face distorted, haggard, and almost black. The noise which Pierre had heard had been occasioned by Madame de Jonquiere, who whilst cleansing a basin had dropped the large zinc water-can. And, despite their torment, this had made the patients laugh, like the simple souls they were, rendered puerile by suffering. However, Sister Hyacinthe, who rightly called them her children, children whom she governed with a word, at once set them saying the chaplet again, pending the Angelus, which would only be said at Chatellerault, in accordance with the predetermined programme. And thereupon the "Aves" followed one after the other, spreading into a confused murmuring and mumbling amidst the rattling of the coupling irons and noisy growling of the wheels.

Pierre had meantime relapsed into his reverie, and beheld himself as he had been at six-and-twenty, when ordained a priest. Tardy scruples had come to him a few days before his ordination, a semi-consciousness that he was binding himself without having clearly questioned his heart and mind. But he had avoided doing so, living in the dizzy bewilderment of his decision, fancying that he had lopped off all human ties and feelings with a voluntary hatchet-stroke. His flesh had surely died with his childhood's innocent romance, that white-skinned girl with golden hair, whom now he never beheld otherwise than stretched upon her couch of suffering, her flesh as lifeless as his own. And he had afterwards made the sacrifice of his mind, which he then fancied even an easier one, hoping as he did that determination would suffice to prevent him from thinking. Besides, it was too late, he could not recoil at the last moment, and if when he pronounced the last solemn vow he felt a secret terror, an indeterminate but immense regret agitating him, he forgot everything, saving a divine reward for his efforts on the day when he afforded his mother the great and long-expected joy of hearing him say his first mass.

He could still see the poor woman in the little church of Neuilly, which she herself had selected, the church where the funeral service for his father had been celebrated; he saw her on that cold November morning, kneeling almost alone in the dark little chapel, her hands hiding her face as she continued weeping whilst he raised the Host. It was there that she had tasted her last happiness, for she led a sad and lonely life, no longer seeing her elder son, who had gone away, swayed by other ideas than her own, bent on breaking off all family intercourse since his brother intended to enter the Church. It was said that Guillaume, a chemist of great talent, like his father, but at the same time a Bohemian, addicted to revolutionary dreams, was living in a little house in the suburbs, where he devoted himself to the dangerous study of explosive substances; and folks added that he was living with a woman who had come no one knew whence. This it was which had severed the last tie between himself and his mother, all piety and propriety. For three years Pierre had not once seen Guillaume, whom in his childhood he had worshipped as a kind, merry, and fatherly big brother.

But there came an awful pang to his heart—he once more beheld his mother lying dead. This again was a thunderbolt, an illness of scarce three days' duration, a sudden passing away, as in the case of Madame de Guersaint. One evening, after a wild hunt for the doctor, he had found her motionless and quite white. She had died during his absence; and his lips had ever retained the icy thrill of the last kiss that he had given her. Of everything else—the vigil, the preparations, the funeral—he remembered nothing. All that had become lost in the black night of his stupor and grief, grief so extreme that he had almost died of it—seized with shivering on his return from the cemetery, struck down by a fever which during three weeks had kept him delirious, hovering between life and death. His brother had come and nursed him and had then attended to pecuniary matters, dividing the little inheritance, leaving him the house and a modest income and taking his own share in money. And as soon as Guillaume had found him out of danger he had gone off again, once more vanishing into the unknown. But then through what a long convalescence he, Pierre, had passed, buried as it were in that deserted house. He had done nothing to detain Guillaume, for he realised that there was an abyss between them. At first the solitude had brought him suffering, but afterwards it had grown very pleasant, whether in the deep silence of the rooms which the rare noises of the street did not disturb, or under the screening, shady foliage of the little garden, where he could spend whole days without seeing a soul. His favourite place of refuge, however, was the old laboratory, his father's cabinet, which his mother for twenty years had kept carefully locked up, as though to immure within it all the incredulity and damnation of the past. And despite the gentleness, the respectful submissiveness which she had shown in former times, she would perhaps have some day ended by destroying all her husband's books and papers, had not death so suddenly surprised her. Pierre, however, had once more had the windows opened, the writing-table and the bookcase dusted; and, installed in the large leather arm-chair, he now spent delicious hours there, regenerated as it were by his illness, brought back to his youthful days again, deriving a wondrous intellectual delight from the perusal of the books which he came upon.

The only person whom he remembered having received during those two months of slow recovery was Doctor Chassaigne, an old friend of his father, a medical man of real merit, who, with the one ambition of curing disease, modestly confined himself to the *role* of the practitioner. It was in vain that the doctor had sought to save Madame Froment, but he flattered himself that he had extricated the young priest from grievous danger; and he came to see him from time to time, to chat with him and cheer him, talking with him of his father, the great chemist, of whom he recounted many a charming anecdote, many a particular, still glowing with the flame of ardent friendship. Little by little, amidst the weak languor of convalescence, the son had thus beheld an embodiment of charming simplicity, affection, and good nature rising up before him. It was his father such as he had really been, not the man of stern science whom he had pictured whilst listening to his mother. Certainly she had never taught him aught but respect for that dear memory; but had not her husband been the unbeliever, the man who denied, and made the angels weep, the artisan of impiety who sought to change the world that God had made? And so he had long remained a gloomy vision, a spectre of damnation prowling about the house, whereas now he became the house's very light, clear and gay, a worker consumed by a longing for truth, who had never desired anything but the love and happiness of all. For his part, Doctor Chassaigne, a Pyrenean by birth, born in a far-off secluded village where folks still believed in sorceresses, inclined rather towards religion, although he had not set his foot inside a church during the forty years he had been living in Paris. However, his conviction was absolute: if there were a heaven somewhere, Michel Froment was assuredly there, and not merely there, but seated upon a throne on the Divinity's right hand.

Then Pierre, in a few minutes, again lived through the frightful torment which, during two long months, had ravaged him. It was not that he had found controversial works of an anti-religious character in the bookcase, or that his father, whose papers he sorted, had ever gone beyond his technical studies as a *savant*. But little by little, despite himself, the light of science dawned upon him, an *ensemble* of proven phenomena, which demolished dogmas and left within him nothing of the things which as a priest he should have believed. It seemed, in fact, as though illness had renewed him, as though he were again beginning to live and learn amidst the physical pleasantness of convalescence, that still subsisting weakness which lent penetrating lucidity to his brain. At the seminary, by the advice of his masters, he had always kept the spirit of inquiry, his thirst for knowledge, in check. Much of that which was taught him there had surprised him; however, he had succeeded in making the sacrifice of his mind required of his piety. But now, all the laboriously raised scaffolding of dogmas was swept away in a revolt of that sovereign mind which clamoured for its rights, and which he could no longer silence. Truth was bubbling up and overflowing in such an irresistible stream that he realised he would never succeed in lodging error in his brain again. It was indeed the total and irreparable ruin of faith. Although he had been able to kill his flesh by renouncing the romance of his youth, although he felt that he had altogether mastered carnal passion, he now knew that it would be impossible for him to make the sacrifice of his intelligence. And he was not mistaken; it was indeed his father again springing to life in the depths of his being, and at last obtaining the mastery in that dual heredity in which, during so many years, his mother had dominated. The upper part of his face, his straight, towering brow, seemed to have risen yet higher, whilst the lower part, the small chin, the affectionate mouth, were becoming less distinct. However, he suffered; at certain twilight hours when his kindliness, his need of love awoke, he felt distracted with grief at no longer believing, distracted with desire to believe again; and it was necessary that the lighted lamp should be brought in, that he should see clearly around him and within him, before he could recover the energy and calmness of reason, the strength of martyrdom, the determination to sacrifice everything to the peace of his conscience.

Then came the crisis. He was a priest and he no longer believed. This had suddenly dawned before him like a bottomless abyss. It was the end of his life, the collapse of everything. What should he do? Did not simple rectitude require that he should throw off the cassock and return to the world? But he had seen some renegade priests and had despised them. A married priest with whom he was acquainted filled him with disgust. All this, no doubt, was but a survival of his long religious training. He retained the notion that a priest cannot, must not, weaken; the idea that when one has dedicated oneself to God one cannot take possession of oneself again. Possibly, also, he felt that he was too plainly branded, too different from other men already, to prove otherwise than awkward and unwelcome among them. Since he had been cut off from them he would remain apart in his grievous pride; And, after days of anguish, days of struggle incessantly renewed, in which his thirst for happiness warred with the energies of his returning health, he took the heroic resolution to remain a priest, and an honest one. He would find the strength necessary for such abnegation. Since he had conquered the flesh, albeit unable to conquer the brain, he felt sure of keeping his vow of chastity, and that would be unshakable; therein lay the pure, upright life which he was absolutely certain of living. What mattered the rest if he alone suffered, if nobody in the world suspected that his heart was reduced to ashes, that nothing remained of his faith, that he was agonising amidst fearful falsehood? His rectitude would prove a firm prop; he would follow his priestly calling like an honest man, without breaking any of the vows he had taken; he would, in due accordance with the rites, discharge his duties as a minister of the Divinity, whom he would praise and glorify at the altar, and distribute as the Bread of Life to the faithful. Who, then, would dare to impute his loss of faith to him as a crime, even if this great misfortune should some day become known? And what more could be asked of him than lifelong devotion to his vow, regard for his ministry, and the practice of every charity without the hope of any future reward? In this wise he ended by calming himself, still upright, still bearing his head erect, with the desolate grandeur of the priest who himself no longer believes, but continues watching over the faith of others. And he certainly was not alone; he felt that he had many brothers, priests with ravaged minds, who had sunk into incredulity, and who yet, like soldiers without a fatherland, remained at the altar, and, despite, everything, found the courage to make the divine illusion shine forth above the kneeling crowds.

On recovering his health Pierre had immediately resumed his service at the little church of Neuilly. He said his mass there every morning. But he had resolved to refuse any appointment, any preferment. Months and years went by, and he obstinately insisted on remaining the least known and the most humble of those priests who are tolerated in a parish, who appear and disappear after discharging their duty. The acceptance of any appointment would have seemed to him an aggravation of his falsehood, a theft from those who were more deserving than himself. And he had to resist frequent offers, for it was impossible for his merits to remain unnoticed. Indeed, his obstinate modesty provoked astonishment at the archbishop's palace, where there was a desire to utilise the power which could be divined in him. Now and again, it is true, he bitterly regretted that he was not useful, that he did not co-operate in some great work, in furthering the purification of the world, the salvation and happiness of all, in accordance with his own ardent, torturing desire. Fortunately his time was nearly all his own, and to console himself he gave rein to his passion for work by devouring every volume in his father's bookcase, and then again resuming and considering his studies, feverishly preoccupied with regard to the history of nations, full of a desire to explore the depths of the social and religious crisis so that he might ascertain whether it were really beyond remedy.

It was at this time, whilst rummaging one morning in one of the large drawers in the lower part of the bookcase, that he discovered quite a collection of papers respecting the apparitions of Lourdes. It was a very complete set of documents, comprising detailed notes of the interrogatories to which Bernadette had been subjected, copies of numerous official documents, and police and medical reports, in addition to many private and confidential letters of the greatest interest. This discovery had surprised Pierre, and he had questioned, Doctor Chassaigne concerning it. The latter thereupon remembered that his friend, Michel Froment, had at one time passionately devoted himself to the study of Bernadette's case; and he himself, a native of the village near Lourdes, had procured for the chemist a portion of the documents in the collection. Pierre, in his turn, then became impassioned, and for a whole month continued studying the affair, powerfully attracted by the visionary's pure, upright nature, but indignant with all that had subsequently sprouted up—the barbarous fetishism, the painful superstitions, and the triumphant simony. In the access of unbelief which had come upon him, this story of Lourdes was certainly of a nature to complete the collapse of his faith. However, it had also excited his curiosity, and he would have liked to investigate it, to establish beyond dispute what scientific truth might be in it, and render pure Christianity the service of ridding it of this scoria, this fairy tale, all touching and childish as it was. But he had been obliged to relinquish his studies, shrinking from the necessity of making a journey to the Grotto, and finding that it would be extremely difficult to obtain the information which he still needed; and of it all there at last only remained within him a tender feeling for Bernadette, of whom he could not think without a sensation of delightful charm and infinite pity.

The days went by, and Pierre led a more and more lonely life. Doctor Chassaigne had just left for the Pyrenees in a state of mortal anxiety. Abandoning his patients, he had set out for Cauterets with his ailing wife, who was sinking more and more each day, to the infinite distress of both his charming daughter and himself. From that moment the little house at Neuilly fell into deathlike silence and emptiness. Pierre had no other distraction than that of occasionally going to see the Guersaints, who had long since left the neighbouring house, but whom he had found again in a small lodging in a wretched tenement of the district. And the memory of his first visit to them there was yet so fresh within him, that he felt a pang at his heart as he recalled his emotion at sight of the hapless Marie.

That pang roused him from his reverie, and on looking round he perceived Marie stretched on the seat, even as he had found her on the day which he recalled, already imprisoned in that gutter-like box, that coffin to which wheels were adapted when she was taken out-of-doors for an airing. She, formerly so brimful of life, ever astir and laughing, was dying of inaction and immobility in that box. Of her old-time beauty she had retained nothing save her hair, which clad her as with a royal mantle, and she was so emaciated that she seemed to have grown smaller again, to have become once more a child. And what was most distressing was the expression on her pale face, the blank, frigid stare of her eyes which did not see, the ever haunting absent look, as of one whom suffering overwhelmed. However, she noticed that Pierre was gazing at her, and at once desired to smile at him; but irresistible moans escaped her, and when she did at last smile, it was like a poor smitten creature who is convinced that she will expire before the miracle takes place. He was overcome by it, and, amidst all the sufferings with which the carriage abounded, hers were now the only ones that he beheld and heard, as though one and all were summed up in her, in the long and terrible agony of her beauty, gaiety, and youth.

Then by degrees, without taking his eyes from Marie, he again reverted to former days, again lived those hours, fraught with a mournful and bitter charm, which he had often spent beside her, when he called at the sorry lodging to keep her company. M. de Guersaint had finally ruined himself by trying to improve the artistic quality of the religious prints so widely sold in France, the faulty execution of which quite irritated him. His last resources had been swallowed up in the failure of a colour-printing firm; and, heedless as he was, deficient in foresight, ever trusting in Providence, his childish mind continually swayed by illusions, he did not notice the awful pecuniary embarrassment of the household; but applied himself to the study of aerial navigation, without even realising what prodigious activity his elder daughter, Blanche, was forced to display, in order to earn the living of her two children, as she was wont to call her father and her sister. It was Blanche who, by running about Paris in the dust or the mud from morning to evening in order to give French or music lessons, contrived to provide the money necessary for the unremitting attentions which Marie required. And Marie often experienced attacks of despair—bursting into tears and accusing herself of being the primary cause of their ruin, as for years and years now it had been necessary to pay for medical attendance and for taking her to almost every imaginable spring—La Bourboule, Aix, Lamalou, Amelie-les-Bains, and others. And the outcome of ten years of varied diagnosis and treatment was that the doctors had now abandoned her.

Some thought her illness to be due to the rupture of certain ligaments, others believed in the presence of a tumour, others again to paralysis due to injury to the spinal cord, and as she, with maidenly revolt, refused to undergo any examination, and they did not even dare to address precise questions to her, they each contented themselves with their several opinions and declared that she was beyond cure. Moreover, she now solely relied upon the divine help, having grown rigidly pious since she had been suffering, and finding her only relief in her ardent faith. Every morning she herself read the holy offices, for to her great sorrow she was unable to go to church. Her inert limbs indeed seemed quite lifeless, and she had sunk into a condition of extreme weakness, to such a point, in fact, that on certain days it became necessary for her sister to place her food in her mouth.

Pierre was thinking of this when all at once he recalled an evening he had spent with her. The lamp had not yet been lighted, he was seated beside her in the growing obscurity, and she suddenly told him that she wished to go to Lourdes, feeling certain that she would return cured. He had experienced an uncomfortable sensation on hearing her speak in this fashion, and quite forgetting himself had exclaimed that it was folly to believe in such childishness. He had hitherto made it a rule never to converse with her on religious matters, having not only refused to be her confessor, but even to advise her with regard to the petty uncertainties of her pietism. In this respect he was influenced by feelings of mingled shame and compassion; to lie to her of all people would have made him suffer, and, moreover, he would have deemed himself a criminal had he even by a breath sullied that fervent pure faith which lent her such strength against pain. And so, regretting that he had not been able to restrain his exclamation, he remained sorely embarrassed, when all at once he felt the girl's cold hand take hold of his own. And then, emboldened by the darkness, she ventured in a gentle, faltering voice, to tell him that she already knew his secret, his misfortune, that wretchedness, so fearful for a priest, of being unable to believe.

Despite himself he had revealed everything during their chats together, and she, with the delicate intuition of a friend, had been able to read his conscience. She felt terribly distressed on his account; she deemed him, with that mortal moral malady, to be more deserving of pity than herself. And then as he, thunderstruck, was still unable to find an answer, acknowledging the truth of her words by his very silence, she again began to speak to him of Lourdes, adding in a low whisper that she wished to confide him as well as herself to the protection of the Blessed Virgin, whom she entreated to restore him to faith. And from that evening forward she did not cease speaking on the subject, repeating again and again, that if she went to Lourdes she would be surely cured. But she was prevented from making the journey by lack of means and she did not even dare to speak to her sister of the pecuniary question. So two months went by, and day by day she grew weaker, exhausted by her longing dreams, her eyes ever turned towards the flashing light of the miraculous Grotto far away. Pierre then experienced many painful days. He had at first told Marie that he would not accompany her. But his decision was somewhat shaken by the thought that if he made up his mind to go, he might profit by the journey to continue his inquiries with regard to Bernadette, whose charming image lingered in his heart. And at last he even felt penetrated by a delightful feeling, an unacknowledged hope, the hope that Marie was perhaps right, that the Virgin might take pity on him and restore to him his former blind faith, the faith of the child who loves and does not question. Oh! to believe, to believe with his whole soul, to plunge into faith for ever! Doubtless there was no other possible happiness. He longed for faith with all the joyousness of his youth, with all the love that he had felt for his mother, with all his burning desire to escape from the torment of understanding and knowing, and to slumber forever in the depths of divine ignorance. It was cowardly, and yet so delightful; to exist no more, to become a mere thing in the hands of the Divinity. And thus he was at last possessed by a desire to make the supreme experiment.

A week later the journey to Lourdes was decided upon. Pierre, however, had insisted on a final consultation of medical men in order to ascertain if it were really possible for Marie to travel; and this again was a scene which rose up before him, with certain incidents which he ever beheld whilst others were already fading from his mind. Two of the doctors who had formerly attended the patient, and one of whom believed in the rupture of certain ligaments, whilst the other asserted the case to be one of medullary paralysis, had ended by agreeing that this paralysis existed, and that there was also, possibly, some ligamentary injury. In their opinion all the symptoms pointed to this diagnosis, and the nature of the case seemed to them so evident that they did not hesitate to give certificates, each his own, agreeing almost word for word with one another, and so positive in character as to leave no room for doubt. Moreover, they thought that the journey was practicable, though it would certainly prove an exceedingly painful one. Pierre thereupon resolved to risk it, for he had found the doctors very prudent, and very desirous to arrive at the truth; and he retained but a confused recollection of the third medical man who had been called in, a distant cousin of his named De Beauclair, who was young, extremely intelligent, but little known as yet, and said by some to be rather strange in his theories. This doctor, after looking at Marie for a long time, had asked somewhat anxiously about her parents, and had seemed greatly interested by what was told him of M. de Guersaint, this architect and inventor with a weak and exuberant mind. Then he had desired to measure the sufferer's visual field, and by a slight discreet touch had ascertained the locality of the pain, which, under certain pressure, seemed to ascend like a heavy shifting mass towards the breast. He did not appear to attach importance to the paralysis of the legs; but on a direct question being put to him he exclaimed that the girl ought to be taken to Lourdes and that she would assuredly be cured there, if she herself were convinced of it. Faith sufficed, said he, with a smile; two pious lady patients of his, whom he had sent thither during the preceding year, had returned in radiant health. He even predicted how the miracle would come about; it would be like a lightning stroke, an awakening, an exaltation of the entire being, whilst the evil, that horrid, diabolical weight which stifled the poor girl would once more ascend and fly away as though emerging by her mouth. But at the same time he flatly declined to give a certificate. He had failed to agree with his two *confreres*, who treated him coldly, as though they considered him a wild, adventurous young fellow. Pierre confusedly remembered some shreds of the discussion which had begun again in his presence, some little part of the diagnosis framed by Beauclair. First, a dislocation of the organ, with a slight laceration of the ligaments, resulting from the patient's fall from her horse; then a slow healing, everything returning to its place, followed by consecutive nervous symptoms, so that the sufferer was now simply beset by her original fright, her attention fixed on the injured part, arrested there amidst increasing pain, incapable of acquiring fresh notions unless it were under the lash of some violent emotion. Moreover, he also admitted the probability of accidents due to nutrition, as yet unexplained, and on the course and importance of which he himself would not venture to give an opinion. However, the idea that Marie *dreamt* her disease, that the fearful sufferings torturing her came from an injury long since healed, appeared such a paradox to Pierre when he gazed at her and saw her in such agony, her limbs already stretched out lifeless on her bed of misery, that he did not even pause to consider it; but at that moment felt simply happy in the thought that all three doctors agreed in authorising the journey to Lourdes. To him it was sufficient that she *might* be cured, and to attain that result he would have followed her to the end of the world.

Ah! those last days of Paris, amid what a scramble they were spent! The national pilgrimage was about to start, and in order to avoid heavy expenses, it had occurred to him to obtain *hospitalisation* for Marie. Then he had been obliged to run about in order to obtain his own admission, as a helper, into the Hospitality of Our Lady of Salvation. M. de Guersaint was delighted with the prospect of the journey, for he was fond of nature, and ardently desired to become acquainted with the Pyrenees. Moreover, he did not allow anything to worry him, but was perfectly willing that the young priest should pay his railway fare, and provide for him at the hotel yonder as for a child; and his daughter Blanche, having slipped a twenty-franc piece into his hand at the last moment, he had even thought himself rich again. That poor brave Blanche had a little hidden store of her own, savings to the amount of fifty francs, which it had been absolutely necessary to accept, for she became quite angry in her determination to contribute towards her sister's cure, unable as she was to form one of the party, owing to the lessons which she had to give in Paris, whose hard pavements she must continue pacing, whilst her dear ones were kneeling yonder, amidst the enchantments of the Grotto. And so the others had started on, and were now rolling, ever rolling along.

As they passed the station of Chatellerault a sudden burst of voices made Pierre start, and drove away the torpor into which his reverie had plunged him. What was the matter? Were they reaching Poitiers? But it was only half-past twelve o'clock, and it was simply Sister Hyacinthe who had roused him, by making her patients and pilgrims say the Angelus, the three "Aves" thrice repeated. Then the voices burst forth, and the sound of a fresh canticle arose, and continued like a lamentation. Fully five and twenty minutes must elapse before they would reach Poitiers, where it seemed as if the half-hour's stoppage would bring relief to every suffering! They were all so uncomfortable, so roughly shaken in that malodorous, burning carriage! Such wretchedness was beyond endurance. Big tears coursed down the cheeks of Madame

ÉMILE ZOLA

Vincent, a muttered oath escaped M. Sabathier usually so resigned, and Brother Isidore, La Grivotte, and Madame Vetu seemed to have become inanimate, mere waifs carried along by a torrent. Moreover, Marie no longer answered, but had closed her eyes and would not open them, pursued as she was by the horrible vision of Elise Rouquet's face, that face with its gaping cavities which seemed to her to be the image of death. And whilst the train increased its speed, bearing all this human despair onward, under the heavy sky, athwart the burning plains, there was yet another scare in the carriage. The strange man had apparently ceased to breathe, and a voice cried out that he was expiring.

III

Poitiers

As soon as the train arrived at Poitiers, Sister Hyacinthe alighted in all haste, amidst the crowd of porters opening the carriage doors, and of pilgrims darting forward to reach the platform. "Wait a moment, wait a moment," she repeated, "let me pass first. I wish to see if all is over."

Then, having entered the other compartment, she raised the strange man's head, and seeing him so pale, with such blank eyes, she did at first think him already dead. At last, however, she detected a faint breathing. "No, no," she then exclaimed, "he still breathes. Quick! there is no time to be lost." And, perceiving the other Sister, she added: "Sister Claire des Anges, will you go and fetch Father Massias, who must be in the third or fourth carriage of the train? Tell him that we have a patient in very great danger here, and ask him to bring the Holy Oils at once."

Without answering, the other Sister at once plunged into the midst of the scramble. She was small, slender, and gentle, with a meditative air and mysterious eyes, but withal extremely active.

Pierre, who was standing in the other compartment watching the scene, now ventured to make a suggestion: "And would it not be as well to fetch the doctor?" said he.

"Yes, I was thinking of it," replied Sister Hyacinthe, "and, Monsieur l'Abbe, it would be very kind of you to go for him yourself."

It so happened that Pierre intended going to the cantine carriage to fetch some broth for Marie. Now that she was no longer being jolted she felt somewhat relieved, and had opened her eyes, and caused her father to raise her to a sitting posture. Keenly thirsting for fresh air, she would have much liked them to carry her out on to the platform for a moment, but she felt that it would be asking too much, that it would be too troublesome a task to place her inside the carriage again. So M. de Guersaint remained by himself on the platform, near the open door, smoking a cigarette, whilst Pierre hastened to the cantine van, where he knew he would find the doctor on duty, with his travelling pharmacy.

Some other patients, whom one could not think of removing, also remained in the carriage. Amongst them was La Grivotte, who was stifling and almost delirious, in such a state indeed as to detain Madame de Jonquiere, who had arranged to meet her daughter Raymonde, with Madame Volmar and Madame Desagneaux, in the refreshment-room, in order that they might all four lunch together. But that unfortunate creature seemed on the point of expiring, so how could she leave her all alone, on the hard seat of that carriage? On his side, M. Sabathier, likewise riveted to his seat, was waiting for his wife, who had gone to fetch a bunch of grapes for him; whilst Marthe had remained with her brother the missionary, whose faint moan never ceased. The others, those who were able to walk, had hustled one another in their haste to alight, all eager as they were to escape for a moment from that cage of wretchedness where their limbs had been quite numbed by the seven hours' journey which they had so far gone. Madame Maze had at once drawn apart, straying with melancholy face to the far end of the platform, where she found herself all alone; Madame Vetu, stupefied by her sufferings, had found sufficient strength to take a few steps, and sit down on a bench, in the full sunlight, where she did not even feel the burning heat; whilst Elise Rouquet, who had had the decency to cover her face with a black wrap, and was consumed by a desire for fresh water, went hither and thither in search of a drinking fountain. And meantime Madame Vincent, walking slowly, carried her little Rose about in her arms, trying to smile at her, and to cheer her by showing her some gaudily coloured picture bills, which the child gravely gazed at, but did not see.

Pierre had the greatest possible difficulty in making his way through the crowd inundating the platform. No effort of imagination could enable one to picture the living torrent of ailing and healthy beings which the train had here set down—a mob of more than a thousand persons just emerging from suffocation, and bustling, hurrying hither and thither. Each carriage had contributed its share of wretchedness, like some hospital ward suddenly evacuated; and it was now possible to form an idea of the frightful amount of suffering which this terrible white train carried along with it, this train which disseminated a legend of horror wheresoever it passed. Some infirm sufferers were dragging themselves about, others were being carried, and many remained in a heap on the platform. There were sudden pushes, violent calls, innumerable displays of distracted eagerness to reach the refreshment-room and the *buvette*. Each and all made haste, going wheresoever their wants called them. This stoppage of half an hour's duration, the only stoppage there would be before reaching Lourdes, was, after all, such a short one. And the only gay note, amidst all the black cassocks and the threadbare garments of the poor, never of any precise shade of colour, was supplied by the smiling whiteness of the Little Sisters of the Assumption, all bright and active in their snowy coifs, wimples, and aprons.

When Pierre at last reached the cantine van near the middle of the train, he found it already besieged. There was here a petroleum stove, with a small supply of cooking utensils. The broth prepared from concentrated meat-extract was being warmed in wrought-iron pans, whilst the preserved milk in tins was diluted and supplied as occasion required. There were some other provisions, such as biscuits, fruit, and chocolate, on a few shelves. But Sister Saint-Francois, to whom the service was entrusted, a short, stout woman of five-and-forty, with a good-natured fresh-coloured face, was somewhat losing her head in the presence of all the hands so eagerly stretched towards her. Whilst continuing her distribution, she lent ear to Pierre, as he called the doctor, who with his travelling pharmacy occupied another corner of the van. Then, when the young priest began to explain matters, speaking of the poor unknown man who was dying, a sudden desire came to her to go and see him, and she summoned another Sister to take her place.

"Oh! I wished to ask you, Sister, for some broth for a passenger who is ill," said Pierre, at that moment turning towards her.

"Very well, Monsieur l'Abbe, I will bring some. Go on in front."

The doctor and the abbe went off in all haste, rapidly questioning and answering one another, whilst behind them followed Sister Saint-Francois, carrying the bowl of broth with all possible caution amidst the jostling of the crowd. The doctor was a dark-complexioned man of eight-and-twenty, robust and extremely handsome, with the head of a young Roman emperor, such as may still be occasionally met with in the sunburnt land of Provence. As soon as Sister Hyacinthe caught sight of him, she raised an exclamation of surprise: "What! Monsieur Ferrand, is it you?" Indeed, they both seemed amazed at meeting in this manner.

It is, however, the courageous mission of the Sisters of the Assumption to tend the ailing poor, those who lie in agony in their humble garrets, and cannot pay for nursing; and thus these good women spend their lives among the wretched, installing themselves beside the sufferer's pallet in his tiny lodging, and ministering to every want,

ÉMILE ZOLA

attending alike to cooking and cleaning, and living there as servants and relatives, until either cure or death supervenes. And it was in this wise that Sister Hyacinthe, young as she was, with her milky face, and her blue eyes which ever laughed, had installed herself one day in the abode of this young fellow, Ferrand, then a medical student, prostrated by typhoid fever, and so desperately poor that he lived in a kind of loft reached by a ladder, in the Rue du Four. And from that moment she had not stirred from his side, but had remained with him until she cured him, with the passion of one who lived only for others, one who when an infant had been found in a church porch, and who had no other family than that of those who suffered, to whom she devoted herself with all her ardently affectionate nature. And what a delightful month, what exquisite comradeship, fraught with the pure fraternity of suffering, had followed! When he called her "Sister," it was really to a sister that he was speaking. And she was a mother also, a mother who helped him to rise, and who put him to bed as though he were her child, without aught springing up between them save supreme pity, the divine, gentle compassion of charity. She ever showed herself gay, sexless, devoid of any instinct excepting that which prompted her to assuage and to console. And he worshipped her, venerated her, and had retained of her the most chaste and passionate of recollections.

"O Sister Hyacinthe!" he murmured in delight.

Chance alone had brought them face to face again, for Ferrand was not a believer, and if he found himself in that train it was simply because he had at the last moment consented to take the place of a friend who was suddenly prevented from coming. For nearly a twelvemonth he had been a house-surgeon at the Hospital of La Pitie. However, this journey to Lourdes, in such peculiar circumstances, greatly interested him.

The joy of the meeting was making them forget the ailing stranger. And so the Sister resumed: "You see, Monsieur Ferrand, it is for this man that we want you. At one moment we thought him dead. Ever since we passed Amboise he has been filling us with fear, and I have just sent for the Holy Oils. Do you find him so very low? Could you not revive him a little?"

The doctor was already examining the man, and thereupon the sufferers who had remained in the carriage became greatly interested and began to look. Marie, to whom Sister Saint-Francois had given the bowl of broth, was holding it with such an unsteady hand that Pierre had to take it from her, and endeavour to make her drink; but she could not swallow, and she left the broth scarce tasted, fixing her eyes upon the man waiting to see what would happen like one whose own existence is at stake.

"Tell me," again asked Sister Hyacinthe, "how do you find him? What is his illness?"

"What is his illness!" muttered Ferrand; "he has every illness."

Then, drawing a little phial from his pocket, he endeavoured to introduce a few drops of the contents between the sufferer's clenched teeth. The man heaved a sigh, raised his eyelids and let them fall again; that was all, he gave no other sign of life.

Sister Hyacinthe, usually so calm and composed, so little accustomed to despair, became impatient.

"But it is terrible," said she, "and Sister Claire des Anges does not come back! Yet I told her plainly enough where she would find Father Massias's carriage. *Mon Dieu!* what will become of us?"

Sister Saint-Francois, seeing that she could render no help, was now about to return to the cantine van. Before doing so, however, she inquired if the man were not simply dying of hunger; for such cases presented themselves, and indeed she had only come to the compartment with the view of offering some of her provisions. At last, as she went off, she promised that she would make Sister Claire des Anges hasten her return should she happen to meet her; and she had not gone twenty yards when she turned round and waved her arm to call attention to her colleague, who with discreet short steps was coming back alone.

Leaning out of the window, Sister Hyacinthe kept on calling to her, "Make haste, make haste! Well, and where is Father Massias?"

"He isn't there."

"What! not there?"

"No. I went as fast as I could, but with all these people about it was not possible to get there quickly. When I reached the carriage Father Massias had already alighted, and gone out of the station, no doubt."

She thereupon explained, that according to what she had heard, Father Massias and the priest of Sainte-Radegonde had some appointment together. In other years the national pilgrimage halted at Poitiers for four-and-twenty hours, and after those who were ill had been placed in the town hospital the others went in procession to

Sainte-Radegonde.* That year, however, there was some obstacle to this course being followed, so the train was going straight on to Lourdes; and Father Massias was certainly with his friend the priest, talking with him on some matter of importance.

"They promised to tell him and send him here with the Holy Oils as soon as they found him," added Sister Claire.

However, this was quite a disaster for Sister Hyacinthe. Since Science was powerless, perhaps the Holy Oils would have brought the sufferer some relief. She had often seen that happen.

"O Sister, Sister, how worried I am!" she said to her companion. "Do you know, I wish you would go back and watch for Father Massias and bring him to me as soon as you see him. It would be so kind of you to do so!"

"Yes, Sister," compliantly answered Sister Claire des Anges, and off she went again with that grave, mysterious air of hers, wending her way through the crowd like a gliding shadow.

Ferrand, meantime, was still looking at the man, sorely distressed at his inability to please Sister Hyacinthe by reviving him. And as he made a gesture expressive of his powerlessness she again raised her voice entreatingly: "Stay with me, Monsieur Ferrand, pray stay," she said. "Wait till Father Massias comes—I shall be a little more at ease with you here."

He remained and helped her to raise the man, who was slipping down upon the seat. Then, taking a linen cloth, she wiped the poor fellow's face which a dense perspiration was continually covering. And the spell of waiting continued amid the uneasiness of the patients who had remained in the carriage, and the curiosity of the folks who had begun to assemble on the platform in front of the compartment.

All at once however a girl hastily pushed the crowd aside, and, mounting on the footboard, addressed herself to Madame de Jonquiere:

---

* The church of Sainte-Radegonde, built by the saint of that name in the sixth century, is famous throughout Poitou. In the crypt between the tombs of Ste. Agnes and St. Disciole is that of Ste. Radegonde herself, but it now only contains some particles of her remains, as the greater portion was burnt by the Huguenots in 1562. On a previous occasion (1412) the tomb had been violated by Jean, Duc de Berry, who wished to remove both the saint's head and her two rings. Whilst he was making the attempt, however, the skeleton is said to have withdrawn its hand so that he might not possess himself of the rings. A greater curiosity which the church contains is a footprint on a stone slab, said to have been left by Christ when He appeared to Ste. Radegonde in her cell. This attracts pilgrims from many parts.—Trans.

"What is the matter, mamma?" she said. "They are waiting for you in the refreshment-room."

It was Raymonde de Jonquiere, who, already somewhat ripe for her four-and-twenty years, was remarkably like her mother, being very dark, with a pronounced nose, large mouth, and full, pleasant-looking face.

"But, my dear, you can see for yourself. I can't leave this poor woman," replied the lady-hospitaller; and thereupon she pointed to La Grivotte, who had been attacked by a fit of coughing which shook her frightfully.

"Oh, how annoying, mamma!" retorted Raymonde, "Madame Desagneaux and Madame Volmar were looking forward with so much pleasure to this little lunch together."

"Well, it can't be helped, my dear. At all events, you can begin without waiting for me. Tell the ladies that I will come and join them as soon as I can." Then, an idea occurring to her, Madame de Jonquiere added: "Wait a moment, the doctor is here. I will try to get him to take charge of my patient. Go back, I will follow you. As you can guess, I am dying of hunger."

Raymonde briskly returned to the refreshment-room whilst her mother begged Ferrand to come into her compartment to see if he could do something to relieve La Grivotte. At Marthe's request he had already examined Brother Isidore, whose moaning never ceased; and with a sorrowful gesture he had again confessed his powerlessness. However, he hastened to comply with Madame de Jonquiere's appeal, and raised the consumptive woman to a sitting posture in the hope of thus stopping her cough, which indeed gradually ceased. And then he helped the lady-hospitaller to make her swallow a spoonful of some soothing draught. The doctor's presence in the carriage was still causing a stir among the ailing ones. M. Sabathier, who was slowly eating the grapes which his wife had been to fetch him, did not, however, question Ferrand, for he knew full well what his answer would be, and was weary, as he expressed it, of consulting all the princes of science; nevertheless he felt comforted as it were at seeing him set that poor consumptive woman on her feet again. And even Marie watched all that the doctor did with increasing interest, though not daring to call him herself, certain as she also was that he could do nothing for her.

Meantime, the crush on the platform was increasing. Only a quarter of an hour now remained to the pilgrims. Madame Vetu, whose eyes were open but who saw nothing, sat like an insensible being in the broad sunlight, in the hope possibly that the scorching heat would deaden her pains; whilst up and down, in front of her, went Madame Vincent ever with the same sleep-inducing step and ever carrying her little Rose, her poor ailing birdie, whose weight was so trifling that she scarcely felt her in her arms. Many people meantime were hastening to the water tap in order to fill their pitchers, cans, and bottles. Madame Maze, who was of refined tastes and careful of her person, thought of going to wash her hands there; but just as she arrived she found Elise Rouquet drinking, and she recoiled at sight of that disease-smitten face, so terribly disfigured and robbed of nearly all semblance of humanity. And all the others likewise shuddered, likewise hesitated to fill their bottles, pitchers, and cans at the tap from which she had drunk.

A large number of pilgrims had now begun to eat whilst pacing the platform. You could hear the rhythmical taps of the crutches carried by a woman who incessantly wended her way through the groups. On the ground, a legless cripple was painfully dragging herself about in search of nobody knew what. Others, seated there in heaps, no longer stirred. All these sufferers, momentarily unpacked as it were, these patients of a travelling hospital emptied for a brief half-hour, were taking the air amidst the bewilderment and agitation of the healthy passengers; and the whole throng had a frightfully woeful, poverty-stricken appearance in the broad noontide light.

Pierre no longer stirred from the side of Marie, for M. de Guersaint had disappeared, attracted by a verdant patch of landscape which could be seen at the far end of the station. And, feeling anxious about her, since she had not been able to finish her broth, the young priest with a smiling air tried to tempt her palate by offering to go and buy her a peach; but she refused it; she was suffering too much, she cared for nothing. She was gazing at him with her large, woeful eyes, on the one hand impatient at this stoppage which delayed her chance of cure, and on the other terrified at the thought of again being jolted along that hard and endless railroad.

Just then a stout gentleman whose full beard was turning grey, and who had a broad, fatherly kind of face, drew near and touched Pierre's arm: "Excuse me, Monsieur l'Abbe," said he, "but is it not in this carriage that there is a poor man dying?"

And on the priest returning an affirmative answer, the gentleman became quite affable and familiar.

"My name is Vigneron," he said; "I am the head clerk at the Ministry of Finances, and applied for leave in order that I might help my wife to take our son Gustave to Lourdes. The dear lad places all his hope in the Blessed Virgin, to whom we pray morning and evening on his behalf. We are in a second-class compartment of the carriage just in front of yours."

Then, turning round, he summoned his party with a wave of the hand. "Come, come!" said he, "it is here. The unfortunate man is indeed in the last throes."

Madame Vigneron was a little woman with the correct bearing of a respectable *bourgeoise*, but her long, livid face denoted impoverished blood, terrible evidence of which was furnished by her son Gustave. The latter, who was fifteen years of age, looked scarcely ten. Twisted out of shape, he was a mere skeleton, with his right leg so wasted, so reduced, that he had to walk with a crutch. He had a small, thin face, somewhat awry, in which one saw little excepting his eyes, clear eyes, sparkling with intelligence, sharpened as it were by suffering, and doubtless well able to dive into the human soul.

An old puffy-faced lady followed the others, dragging her legs along with difficulty; and M. Vigneron, remembering that he had forgotten her, stepped back towards Pierre so that he might complete the introduction. "That lady," said he, "is Madame Chaise, my wife's eldest sister. She also wished to accompany Gustave, whom she is very fond of." And then, leaning forward, he added in a whisper, with a confidential air: "She is the widow of Chaise, the silk merchant, you know, who left such an immense fortune. She is suffering from a heart complaint which causes her much anxiety."

The whole family, grouped together, then gazed with lively curiosity at what was taking place in the railway carriage. People were incessantly flocking to the spot; and so that the lad might be the better able to see, his father took him up in his arms for a moment whilst his aunt held the crutch, and his mother on her side raised herself on tip-toe.

The scene in the carriage was still the same; the strange man was still stiffly seated in his corner, his head resting against the hard wood. He was livid, his eyes were closed, and his mouth was twisted by suffering; and every now and then Sister Hyacinthe with her linen cloth wiped away the cold sweat which was constantly covering his face. She no longer spoke, no longer evinced any impatience, but had recovered her serenity and relied on Heaven. From time to time she would simply glance towards the platform to see if Father Massias were coming.

"Look at him, Gustave," said M. Vigneron to his son; "he must be consumptive."

The lad, whom scrofula was eating away, whose hip was attacked by an abscess, and in whom there were already signs of necrosis of the vertebrae, seemed to take a passionate interest in the agony he thus beheld. It did not frighten him, he smiled at it with a smile of infinite sadness.

"Oh! how dreadful!" muttered Madame Chaise, who, living in continual terror of a sudden attack which would carry her off, turned pale with the fear of death.

"Ah! well," replied M. Vigneron, philosophically, "it will come to each of us in turn. We are all mortal."

Thereupon, a painful, mocking expression came over Gustave's smile, as though he had heard other words than those—perchance an unconscious wish, the hope that the old aunt might die before he himself did, that he would inherit the promised half-million of francs, and then not long encumber his family.

"Put the boy down now," said Madame Vigneron to her husband. "You are tiring him, holding him by the legs like that."

Then both she and Madame Chaise bestirred themselves in order that the lad might not be shaken. The poor darling was so much in need of care and attention. At each moment they feared that they might lose him. Even his father was of opinion that they had better put him in the train again at once. And as the two women went off with the child, the old gentleman once more turned towards Pierre, and with evident emotion exclaimed: "Ah! Monsieur l'Abbe, if God should take him from us, the light of our life would be extinguished—I don't speak of his aunt's fortune, which would go to other nephews. But it would be unnatural, would it not, that he should go off before her, especially as she is so ill? However, we are all in the hands of Providence, and place our reliance in the Blessed Virgin, who will assuredly perform a miracle."

Just then Madame de Jonquiere, having been reassured by Doctor Ferrand, was able to leave La Grivotte. Before going off, however, she took care to say to Pierre: "I am dying of hunger and am going to the refreshment-room for a moment. But if my patient should begin coughing again, pray come and fetch me."

When, after great difficulty, she had managed to cross the platform and reach the refreshment-room, she found herself in the midst of another scramble. The better-circumstanced pilgrims had taken the tables by assault, and a great many priests were to be seen hastily lunching amidst all the clatter of knives, forks, and crockery. The three or four waiters were not able to attend to all the requirements, especially as they were hampered in their movements by the crowd purchasing fruit, bread, and cold meat at the counter. It was at a little table at the far end of the room that Raymonde was lunching with Madame Desagneaux and Madame Volmar.

"Ah! here you are at last, mamma!" the girl exclaimed, as Madame de Jonquiere approached. "I was just going back to fetch you. You certainly ought to be allowed time to eat!"

She was laughing, with a very animated expression on her face, quite delighted as she was with the adventures of the journey and this indifferent scrambling meal. "There," said she, "I have kept you some trout with green sauce, and there's a cutlet also waiting for you. We have already got to the artichokes."

Then everything became charming. The gaiety prevailing in that little corner rejoiced the sight.

Young Madame Desagneaux was particularly adorable. A delicate blonde, with wild, wavy, yellow hair, a round, dimpled, milky face, a gay, laughing disposition, and a remarkably good heart, she had made a rich marriage, and for three years past had been wont to leave her husband at Trouville in the fine August weather, in order to accompany the national pilgrimage as a lady-hospitaller. This was her great passion, an access of quivering pity, a longing desire to place herself unreservedly at the disposal of the sick for five days, a real debauch of devotion from which she returned tired to death but full of intense delight. Her only regret was that she as yet had no children, and with comical passion, she occasionally expressed a regret that she had missed her true vocation, that of a sister of charity.

"Ah! my dear," she hastily said to Raymonde, "don't pity your mother for being so much taken up with her patients. She, at all events, has something to occupy her." And addressing herself to Madame de Jonquiere, she added: "If you only knew how long we find the time in our fine first-class carriage. We cannot even occupy ourselves with a little needlework, as it is forbidden. I asked for a place with the patients, but all were already distributed, so that my only resource will be to try to sleep tonight."

She began to laugh, and then resumed: "Yes, Madame Volmar, we will try to sleep, won't we, since talking seems to tire you?" Madame Volmar, who looked over thirty, was very dark, with a long face and

ÉMILE ZOLA

delicate but drawn features. Her magnificent eyes shone out like brasiers, though every now and then a cloud seemed to veil and extinguish them. At the first glance she did not appear beautiful, but as you gazed at her she became more and more perturbing, till she conquered you and inspired you with passionate admiration. It should be said though that she shrank from all self-assertion, comporting herself with much modesty, ever keeping in the background, striving to hide her lustre, invariably clad in black and unadorned by a single jewel, although she was the wife of a Parisian diamond-merchant.

"Oh! for my part," she murmured, "as long as I am not hustled too much I am well pleased."

She had been to Lourdes as an auxiliary lady-helper already on two occasions, though but little had been seen of her there—at the hospital of Our Lady of Dolours—as, on arriving, she had been overcome by such great fatigue that she had been forced, she said, to keep her room.

However, Madame de Jonquiere, who managed the ward, treated her with good-natured tolerance. "Ah! my poor friends," said she, "there will be plenty of time for you to exert yourselves. Get to sleep if you can, and your turn will come when I can no longer keep up." Then addressing her daughter, she resumed: "And you would do well, darling, not to excite yourself too much if you wish to keep your head clear."

Raymonde smiled and gave her mother a reproachful glance: "Mamma, mamma, why do you say that? Am I not sensible?" she asked.

Doubtless she was not boasting, for, despite her youthful, thoughtless air, the air of one who simply feels happy in living, there appeared in her grey eyes an expression of firm resolution, a resolution to shape her life for herself.

"It is true," the mother confessed with a little confusion, "this little girl is at times more sensible than I am myself. Come, pass me the cutlet—it is welcome, I assure you. Lord! how hungry I was!"

The meal continued, enlivened by the constant laughter of Madame Desagneaux and Raymonde. The latter was very animated, and her face, which was already growing somewhat yellow through long pining for a suitor, again assumed the rosy bloom of twenty. They had to eat very fast, for only ten minutes now remained to them. On all sides one heard the growing tumult of customers who feared that they would not have time to take their coffee.

All at once, however, Pierre made his appearance; a fit of stifling had again come over La Grivotte; and Madame de Jonquiere hastily finished her artichoke and returned to her compartment, after kissing her daughter, who wished her "good-night" in a facetious way. The priest, however, had made a movement of surprise on perceiving Madame Volmar with the red cross of the lady-hospitallers on her black bodice. He knew her, for he still called at long intervals on old Madame Volmar, the diamond-merchant's mother, who had been one of his own mother's friends. She was the most terrible woman in the world, religious beyond all reason, so harsh and stern, moreover, as to close the very window shutters in order to prevent her daughter-in-law from looking into the street. And he knew the young woman's story, how she had been imprisoned on the very morrow of her marriage, shut up between her mother-in-law, who tyrannised over her, and her husband, a repulsively ugly monster who went so far as to beat her, mad as he was with jealousy, although he himself kept mistresses. The unhappy woman was not allowed out of the house excepting it were to go to mass. And one day, at La Trinite, Pierre had surprised her secret, on seeing her behind the church exchanging a few hasty words with a well-groomed, distinguished-looking man.

The priest's sudden appearance in the refreshment-room had somewhat disconcerted Madame Volmar.

"What an unexpected meeting, Monsieur l'Abbe!" she said, offering him her long, warm hand. "What a long time it is since I last saw you!" And thereupon she explained that this was the third year she had gone to Lourdes, her mother-in-law having required her to join the Association of Our Lady of Salvation. "It is surprising that you did not see her at the station when we started," she added. "She sees me into the train and comes to meet me on my return."

This was said in an apparently simple way, but with such a subtle touch of irony that Pierre fancied he could guess the truth. He knew that she really had no religious principles at all, and that she merely followed the rites and ceremonies of the Church in order that she might now and again obtain an hour's freedom; and all at once he intuitively realised that someone must be waiting for her yonder, that it was for the purpose of meeting him that she was thus hastening to Lourdes with her shrinking yet ardent air and flaming eyes, which she so prudently shrouded with a veil of lifeless indifference.

"For my part," he answered, "I am accompanying a friend of my childhood, a poor girl who is very ill indeed. I must ask your help for her; you shall nurse her."

Thereupon she faintly blushed, and he no longer doubted the truth of his surmise. However, Raymonde was just then settling the bill with the easy assurance of a girl who is expert in figures; and immediately afterwards Madame Desagneaux led Madame Volmar away. The waiters were now growing more distracted and the tables were fast being vacated; for, on hearing a bell ring, everybody had begun to rush towards the door.

Pierre, on his side, was hastening back to his carriage, when he was stopped by an old priest. "Ah! Monsieur le Cure," he said, "I saw you just before we started, but I was unable to get near enough to shake hands with you."

Thereupon he offered his hand to his brother ecclesiastic, who was looking and smiling at him in a kindly way. The Abbe Judaine was the parish priest of Saligny, a little village in the department of the Oise. Tall and sturdy, he had a broad pink face, around which clustered a mass of white, curly hair, and it could be divined by his appearance that he was a worthy man whom neither the flesh nor the spirit had ever tormented. He believed indeed firmly and absolutely, with a tranquil godliness, never having known a struggle, endowed as he was with the ready faith of a child who is unacquainted with human passions. And ever since the Virgin at Lourdes had cured him of a disease of the eyes, by a famous miracle which folks still talked about, his belief had become yet more absolute and tender, as though impregnated with divine gratitude.

"I am pleased that you are with us, my friend," he gently said; "for there is much in these pilgrimages for young priests to profit by. I am told that some of them at times experience a feeling of rebellion. Well, you will see all these poor people praying,—it is a sight which will make you weep. How can one do otherwise than place oneself in God's hands, on seeing so much suffering cured or consoled?"

The old priest himself was accompanying a patient; and he pointed to a first-class compartment, at the door of which hung a placard bearing the inscription: "M. l'Abbe Judaine, Reserved." Then lowering his voice, he said: "It is Madame Dieulafay, you know, the great banker's wife. Their chateau, a royal domain, is in my parish, and when they learned that the Blessed Virgin had vouchsafed me such an undeserved favour, they begged me to intercede for their poor sufferer. I have already said several masses, and most sincerely pray for her. There, you see her yonder on the ground. She insisted on being taken out of the carriage, in spite of all the trouble which one will have to place her in it again."

On a shady part of the platform, in a kind of long box, there was, as the old priest said, a woman whose beautiful, perfectly oval face, lighted up by splendid eyes, denoted no greater age than six-and-twenty. She was suffering from a frightful disease. The disappearance from her system of the calcareous salts had led to a softening of the osseous framework, the slow destruction of her bones. Three years previously, after the advent of a stillborn child, she had felt vague pains in the spinal column. And then, little by little, her bones had rarefied and lost shape, the vertebrae had sunk, the bones of the pelvis had flattened, and those of the arms and legs had contracted. Thus shrunken, melting away as it were, she had become a mere human remnant, a nameless, fluid thing, which could not be set erect, but had to be carried hither and thither with infinite care, for fear lest she should vanish between one's fingers. Her face, a motionless face, on which sat a stupefied imbecile expression, still retained its beauty of outline, and yet it was impossible to gaze at this wretched shred of a woman without feeling a heart-pang, the keener on account of all the luxury surrounding her; for not only was the box in which she lay lined with blue quilted silk, but she was covered with valuable lace, and a cap of rare valenciennes was set upon her head, her wealth thus being proclaimed, displayed, in the midst of her awful agony.

"Ah! how pitiable it is," resumed the Abbe Judaine in an undertone. "To think that she is so young, so pretty, possessed of millions of money! And if you knew how dearly loved she was, with what adoration she is still surrounded. That tall gentleman near her is her husband, that elegantly dressed lady is her sister, Madame Jousseur."

Pierre remembered having often noticed in the newspapers the name of Madame Jousseur, wife of a diplomatist, and a conspicuous member of the higher spheres of Catholic society in Paris. People had even circulated a story of some great passion which she had fought against and vanquished. She also was very prettily dressed, with marvellously tasteful simplicity, and she ministered to the wants of her sorry sister with an air of perfect devotion. As for the unhappy woman's husband, who at the age of five-and-thirty had inherited his father's colossal business, he was a clear-complexioned, well-groomed, handsome man, clad in a closely buttoned frock-coat. His eyes, however, were full of tears, for he adored his wife, and had left his business in order to take her to Lourdes, placing his last hope in this appeal to the mercy of Heaven.

Ever since the morning, Pierre had beheld many frightful sufferings in that woeful white train. But none had so distressed his soul as did that wretched female skeleton, slowly liquefying in the midst of its lace and its millions. "The unhappy woman!" he murmured with a shudder.

The Abbe Judaine, however, made a gesture of serene hope. "The Blessed Virgin will cure her," said he; "I have prayed to her so much."

Just then a bell again pealed, and this time it was really the signal for starting. Only two minutes remained. There was a last rush, and folks hurried back towards the train carrying eatables wrapped in paper, and bottles and cans which they had filled with water. Several of them quite lost their heads, and in their inability to find their carriages, ran distractedly from one to the other end of the train; whilst some of the infirm ones dragged themselves about amidst the precipitate tapping of crutches, and others, only able to walk with difficulty, strove to hasten their steps whilst leaning on the arms of some of the lady-hospitallers. It was only with infinite difficulty that four men managed to replace Madame Dieulafay in her first-class compartment. The Vignerons, who were content with second-class accommodation, had already reinstalled themselves in their quarters amidst an extraordinary heap of baskets, boxes, and valises which scarcely allowed little Gustave enough room to stretch his poor puny limbs—the limbs as it were of a deformed insect. And then all the women appeared again: Madame Maze gliding along in silence; Madame Vincent raising her dear little girl in her outstretched arms and dreading lest she should hear her cry out; Madame Vetu, whom it had been necessary to push into the train, after rousing her from her stupefying torment; and Elise Rouquet, who was quite drenched through her obstinacy in endeavouring to drink from the tap, and was still wiping her monstrous face. Whilst each returned to her place and the carriage filled once more, Marie listened to her father, who had come back delighted with his stroll to a pointsman's little house beyond the station, whence a really pleasant stretch of landscape could be discerned.

"Shall we lay you down again at once?" asked Pierre, sorely distressed by the pained expression on Marie's face.

"Oh no, no, by-and-by!" she replied. "I shall have plenty of time to hear those wheels roaring in my head as though they were grinding my bones."

Then, as Ferrand seemed on the point of returning to the cantine van, Sister Hyacinthe begged him to take another look at the strange man before he went off. She was still waiting for Father Massias, astonished at the inexplicable delay in his arrival, but not yet without hope, as Sister Claire des Anges had not returned.

"Pray, Monsieur Ferrand," said she, "tell me if this unfortunate man is in any immediate danger."

The young doctor again looked at the sufferer, felt him, and listened to his breathing. Then with a gesture of discouragement he answered in a low voice, "I feel convinced that you will not get him to Lourdes alive."

Every head was still anxiously stretched forward. If they had only known the man's name, the place he had come from, who he was! But it was impossible to extract a word from this unhappy stranger, who was about to die there, in that carriage, without anybody being able to give his face a name!

It suddenly occurred to Sister Hyacinthe to have him searched. Under the circumstances there could certainly be no harm in such a course. "Feel in his pockets, Monsieur Ferrand," she said.

The doctor thereupon searched the man in a gentle, cautious way, but the only things that he found in his pockets were a chaplet, a knife, and three sous. And nothing more was ever learnt of the man.

At that moment, however, a voice announced that Sister Claire des Anges was at last coming back with Father Massias. All this while the latter had simply been chatting with the priest of Sainte-Radegonde in one of the waiting-rooms. Keen emotion attended his arrival; for a moment all seemed saved. But the train was about to start, the porters were already closing the carriage doors, and it was necessary that extreme unction should be administered in all haste in order to avoid too long a delay.

"This way, reverend Father!" exclaimed Sister Hyacinthe; "yes, yes, pray come in; our unfortunate patient is here."

Father Massias, who was five years older than Pierre, whose fellow-student however he had been at the seminary, had a tall, spare figure with an ascetic countenance, framed round with a light-coloured beard and vividly lighted up by burning eyes, He was neither the priest harassed by doubt, nor the priest with childlike faith, but an apostle carried away by his passion, ever ready to fight and vanquish for the pure glory of the Blessed Virgin. In his black cloak with its large hood,

ÉMILE ZOLA

and his broad-brimmed flossy hat, he shone resplendently with the perpetual ardour of battle.

He immediately took from his pocket the silver case containing the Holy Oils, and the ceremony began whilst the last carriage doors were being slammed and belated pilgrims were rushing back to the train; the station-master, meantime, anxiously glancing at the clock, and realising that it would be necessary for him to grant a few minutes' grace.

"*Credo in unum Deum*," hastily murmured the Father.

"*Amen*," replied Sister Hyacinthe and the other occupants of the carriage.

Those who had been able to do so, had knelt upon the seats, whilst the others joined their hands, or repeatedly made the sign of the cross; and when the murmured prayers were followed by the Litanies of the ritual, every voice rose, an ardent desire for the remission of the man's sins and for his physical and spiritual cure winging its flight heavenward with each successive *Kyrie eleison*. Might his whole life, of which they knew nought, be forgiven him; might he enter, stranger though he was, in triumph into the Kingdom of God!

"*Christe, exaudi nos.*"

"*Ora pro nobis, sancta Dei Genitrix.*"

Father Massias had pulled out the silver needle from which hung a drop of Holy Oil. In the midst of such a scramble, with the whole train waiting—many people now thrusting their heads out of the carriage windows in surprise at the delay in starting—he could not think of following the usual practice, of anointing in turn all the organs of the senses, those portals of the soul which give admittance to evil.

He must content himself, as the rules authorised him to do in pressing cases, with one anointment; and this he made upon the man's lips, those livid parted lips from between which only a faint breath escaped, whilst the rest of his face, with its lowered eyelids, already seemed indistinct, again merged into the dust of the earth.

"*Per istam sanctam unctionem*," said the Father, "*et suam piissimam misericordiam indulgeat tibi Dominus quidquid per visum, auditum, odoratum, gustum, tactum, deliquisti.*"*

The remainder of the ceremony was lost amid the hurry and scramble of the departure. Father Massias scarcely had time to wipe off the oil

---

* Through this holy unction and His most tender mercy may the Lord pardon thee whatever sins thou hast committed by thy sight, hearing, etc.

with the little piece of cotton-wool which Sister Hyacinthe held in readiness, before he had to leave the compartment and get into his own as fast as possible, setting the case containing the Holy Oils in order as he did so, whilst the pilgrims finished repeating the final prayer.

"We cannot wait any longer! It is impossible!" repeated the station-master as he bustled about. "Come, come, make haste everybody!"

At last then they were about to resume their journey. Everybody sat down, returned to his or her corner again. Madame de Jonquiere, however, had changed her place, in order to be nearer La Grivotte, whose condition still worried her, and she was now seated in front of M. Sabathier, who remained waiting with silent resignation. Moreover, Sister Hyacinthe had not returned to her compartment, having decided to remain near the unknown man so that she might watch over him and help him. By following this course, too, she was able to minister to Brother Isidore, whose sufferings his sister Marthe was at a loss to assuage. And Marie, turning pale, felt the jolting of the train in her ailing flesh, even before it had resumed its journey under the heavy sun, rolling onward once more with its load of sufferers stifling in the pestilential atmosphere of the over-heated carriages.

At last a loud whistle resounded, the engine puffed, and Sister Hyacinthe rose up to say: The *Magnificat*, my children!

IV

Miracles

J ust as the train was beginning to move, the door of the compartment in which Pierre and Marie found themselves was opened and a porter pushed a girl of fourteen inside, saying: "There's a seat here—make haste!"

The others were already pulling long faces and were about to protest, when Sister Hyacinthe exclaimed: "What, is it you, Sophie? So you are going back to see the Blessed Virgin who cured you last year!"

And at the same time Madame de Jonquiere remarked: "Ah! Sophie, my little friend, I am very pleased to see that you are grateful."

"Why, yes, Sister; why, yes, madame," answered the girl, in a pretty way.

The carriage door had already been closed again, so that it was necessary that they should accept the presence of this new pilgrim who had fallen from heaven as it were at the very moment when the train, which she had almost missed, was starting off again. She was a slender damsel and would not take up much room. Moreover these ladies knew her, and all the patients had turned their eyes upon her on hearing that the Blessed Virgin had been pleased to cure her. They had now got beyond the station, the engine was still puffing, whilst the wheels increased their speed, and Sister Hyacinthe, clapping her hands, repeated: "Come, come, my children, the *Magnificat*."

Whilst the joyful chant arose amidst the jolting of the train, Pierre gazed at Sophie. She was evidently a young peasant girl, the daughter of some poor husbandman of the vicinity of Poitiers, petted by her parents, treated in fact like a young lady since she had become the subject of a miracle, one of the elect, whom the priests of the district flocked to see. She wore a straw hat with pink ribbons, and a grey woollen dress trimmed with a flounce. Her round face although not pretty was a very pleasant one, with a beautifully fresh complexion and clear, intelligent eyes which lent her a smiling, modest air.

When the *Magnificat* had been sung, Pierre was unable to resist his desire to question Sophie. A child of her age, with so candid an air, so utterly unlike a liar, greatly interested him.

"And so you nearly missed the train, my child?" he said.

"I should have been much ashamed if I had, Monsieur l'Abbe," she replied. "I had been at the station since twelve o'clock. And all at once I saw his reverence, the priest of Sainte-Radegonde, who knows me well and who called me to him, to kiss me and tell me that it was very good of me to go back to Lourdes. But it seems the train was starting and I only just had time to run on to the platform. Oh! I ran so fast!"

She paused, laughing, still slightly out of breath, but already repenting that she had been so giddy.

"And what is your name, my child?" asked Pierre.

"Sophie Couteau, Monsieur l'Abbe."

"You do not belong to the town of Poitiers?"

"Oh no! certainly not. We belong to Vivonne, which is seven kilometres away. My father and mother have a little land there, and things would not be so bad if there were not eight children at home—I am the fifth,—fortunately the four older ones are beginning to work."

"And you, my child, what do you do?"

"I, Monsieur l'Abbe! Oh! I am no great help. Since last year, when I came home cured, I have not been left quiet a single day, for, as you can understand, so many people have come to see me, and then too I have been taken to Monseigneur's,* and to the convents and all manner of other places. And before all that I was a long time ill. I could not walk without a stick, and each step I took made me cry out, so dreadfully did my foot hurt me."

"So it was of some injury to the foot that the Blessed Virgin cured you?"

Sophie did not have time to reply, for Sister Hyacinthe, who was listening, intervened: "Of caries of the bones of the left heel, which had been going on for three years," said she. "The foot was swollen and quite deformed, and there were fistulas giving egress to continual suppuration."

On hearing this, all the sufferers in the carriage became intensely interested. They no longer took their eyes off this little girl on whom a miracle had been performed, but scanned her from head to foot as though seeking for some sign of the prodigy. Those who were able to stand rose up in order that they might the better see her, and the others, the infirm ones, stretched on their mattresses, strove to raise

---

* The Bishop's residence.

themselves and turn their heads. Amidst the suffering which had again come upon them on leaving Poitiers, the terror which filled them at the thought that they must continue rolling onward for another fifteen hours, the sudden advent of this child, favoured by Heaven, was like a divine relief, a ray of hope whence they would derive sufficient strength to accomplish the remainder of their terrible journey. The moaning had abated somewhat already, and every face was turned towards the girl with an ardent desire to believe.

This was especially the case with Marie, who, already reviving, joined her trembling hands, and in a gentle supplicating voice said to Pierre, "Question her, pray question her, ask her to tell us everything—cured, O God! cured of such a terrible complaint!"

Madame de Jonquiere, who was quite affected, had leant over the partition to kiss the girl. "Certainly," said she, "our little friend will tell you all about it. Won't you, my darling? You will tell us what the Blessed Virgin did for you?"

"Oh, certainly! madame—as much as you like," answered Sophie with her smiling, modest air, her eyes gleaming with intelligence. Indeed, she wished to begin at once, and raised her right hand with a pretty gesture, as a sign to everybody to be attentive. Plainly enough, she had already acquired the habit of speaking in public.

She could not be seen, however, from some parts of the carriage, and an idea came to Sister Hyacinthe, who said: "Get up on the seat, Sophie, and speak loudly, on account of the noise which the train makes."

This amused the girl, and before beginning she needed time to become serious again. "Well, it was like this," said she; "my foot was past cure, I couldn't even go to church any more, and it had to be kept bandaged, because there was always a lot of nasty matter coming from it. Monsieur Rivoire, the doctor, who had made a cut in it, so as to see inside it, said that he should be obliged to take out a piece of the bone; and that, sure enough, would have made me lame for life. But when I got to Lourdes and had prayed a great deal to the Blessed Virgin, I went to dip my foot in the water, wishing so much that I might be cured that I did not even take the time to pull the bandage off. And everything remained in the water, there was no longer anything the matter with my foot when I took it out."

A murmur of mingled surprise, wonder, and desire arose and spread among those who heard this marvellous tale, so sweet and soothing to all who were in despair. But the little one had not yet finished. She had simply paused. And now, making a fresh gesture, holding her arms somewhat apart, she concluded: "When I got back to Vivonne and Monsieur Rivoire saw my foot again, he said: 'Whether it be God or the Devil who has cured this child, it is all the same to me; but in all truth she *is* cured.'"

This time a burst of laughter rang out. The girl spoke in too recitative a way, having repeated her story so many times already that she knew it by heart. The doctor's remark was sure to produce an effect, and she herself laughed at it in advance, certain as she was that the others would laugh also. However, she still retained her candid, touching air.

But she had evidently forgotten some particular, for Sister Hyacinthe, a glance from whom had foreshadowed the doctor's jest, now softly prompted her "And what was it you said to Madame la Comtesse, the superintendent of your ward, Sophie?"

"Ah! yes. I hadn't brought many bandages for my foot with me, and I said to her, 'It was very kind of the Blessed Virgin to cure me the first day, as I should have run out of linen on the morrow.'"

This provoked a fresh outburst of delight. They all thought her so nice, to have been cured like that! And in reply to a question from Madame de Jonquiere, she also had to tell the story of her boots, a pair of beautiful new boots which Madame la Comtesse had given her, and in which she had run, jumped, and danced about, full of childish delight. Boots! think of it, she who for three years had not even been able to wear a slipper.

Pierre, who had become grave, waxing pale with the secret uneasiness which was penetrating him, continued to look at her. And he also asked her other questions. She was certainly not lying, and he merely suspected a slow distortion of the actual truth, an easily explained embellishment of the real facts amidst all the joy she felt at being cured and becoming an important little personage. Who now knew if the cicatrisation of her injuries, effected, so it was asserted, completely, instantaneously, in a few seconds, had not in reality been the work of days? Where were the witnesses?

Just then Madame de Jonquiere began to relate that she had been at the hospital at the time referred to. "Sophie was not in my ward," said she, "but I had met her walking lame that very morning—"

Pierre hastily interrupted the lady-hospitaller. "Ah! you saw her foot before and after the immersion?"

"No, no! I don't think that anybody was able to see it, for it was bound round with bandages. She told you that the bandages had fallen into the piscina." And, turning towards the child, Madame de Jonquiere added, "But she will show you her foot—won't you, Sophie? Undo your shoe."

The girl took off her shoe, and pulled down her stocking, with a promptness and ease of manner which showed how thoroughly accustomed she had become to it all. And she not only stretched out her foot, which was very clean and very white, carefully tended indeed, with well-cut, pink nails, but complacently turned it so that the young priest might examine it at his ease. Just below the ankle there was a long scar, whose whity seam, plainly defined, testified to the gravity of the complaint from which the girl had suffered.

"Oh! take hold of the heel, Monsieur l'Abbe," said she. "Press it as hard as you like. I no longer feel any pain at all."

Pierre made a gesture from which it might have been thought that he was delighted with the power exercised by the Blessed Virgin. But he was still tortured by doubt. What unknown force had acted in this case? Or rather what faulty medical diagnosis, what assemblage of errors and exaggerations, had ended in this fine tale?

All the patients, however, wished to see the miraculous foot, that outward and visible sign of the divine cure which each of them was going in search of. And it was Marie, sitting up in her box, and already feeling less pain, who touched it first. Then Madame Maze, quite roused from her melancholy, passed it on to Madame Vincent, who would have kissed it for the hope which it restored to her. M. Sabathier had listened to all the explanations with a beatific air; Madame Vetu, La Grivotte, and even Brother Isidore opened their eyes, and evinced signs of interest; whilst the face of Elise Rouquet had assumed an extraordinary expression, transfigured by faith, almost beatified. If a sore had thus disappeared, might not her own sore close and disappear, her face retaining no trace of it save a slight scar, and again becoming such a face as other people had? Sophie, who was still standing, had to hold on to one of the iron rails, and place her foot on the partition, now on the right, now on the left. And she did not weary of it all, but felt exceedingly happy and proud at the many exclamations which were raised, the quivering admiration and religious respect which were bestowed on that little piece of her person, that little foot which had now, so to say, become sacred.

"One must possess great faith, no doubt," said Marie, thinking aloud. "One must have a pure unspotted soul." And, addressing herself to M. de Guersaint, she added: "Father, I feel that I should get well if I were ten years old, if I had the unspotted soul of a little girl."

"But you are ten years old, my darling! Is it not so, Pierre? A little girl of ten years old could not have a more spotless soul."

Possessed of a mind prone to chimeras, M. de Guersaint was fond of hearing tales of miracles. As for the young priest, profoundly affected by the ardent purity which the young girl evinced, he no longer sought to discuss the question, but let her surrender herself to the consoling illusions which Sophie's tale had wafted through the carriage.

The temperature had become yet more oppressive since their departure from Poitiers, a storm was rising in the coppery sky, and it seemed as though the train were rushing through a furnace. The villages passed, mournful and solitary under the burning sun. At Couhe-Verac they had again said their chaplets, and sung another canticle. At present, however, there was some slight abatement of the religious exercises. Sister Hyacinthe, who had not yet been able to lunch, ventured to eat a roll and some fruit in all haste, whilst still ministering to the strange man whose faint, painful breathing seemed to have become more regular. And it was only on passing Ruffec at three o'clock that they said the vespers of the Blessed Virgin.

"*Ora pro nobis, sancta Dei Genitrix.*"

"*Ut digni efficiamur promissionibus Christi.*"*

As they were finishing, M. Sabathier, who had watched little Sophie while she put on her shoe and stocking, turned towards M. de Guersaint.

"This child's case is interesting, no doubt," he remarked. "But it is a mere nothing, monsieur, for there have been far more marvellous cures than that. Do you know the story of Pierre de Rudder, a Belgian working-man?"

Everybody had again begun to listen.

"This man," continued M. Sabathier, "had his leg broken by the fall of a tree. Eight years afterwards the two fragments of the bone had not yet joined together again—the two ends could be seen in the depths of a sore which was continually suppurating; and the leg hung down quite limp, swaying in all directions. Well, it was sufficient for this man to drink a glassful of the miraculous water, and his leg was made whole again. He was able to walk without crutches, and the doctor said to

---

* "Pray for us, O holy Mother of God, That we may be made worthy of the promises of Christ."

him: 'Your leg is like that of a new-born child.' Yes, indeed, a perfectly new leg."

Nobody spoke, but the listeners exchanged glances of ecstasy.

"And, by the way," resumed M. Sabathier, "it is like the story of Louis Bouriette, a quarryman, one of the first of the Lourdes miracles. Do you know it? Bouriette had been injured by an explosion during some blasting operations. The sight of his right eye was altogether destroyed, and he was even threatened with the loss of the left one. Well, one day he sent his daughter to fetch a bottleful of the muddy water of the source, which then scarcely bubbled up to the surface. He washed his eye with this muddy liquid, and prayed fervently. And, all at once, he raised a cry, for he could see, monsieur, see as well as you and I. The doctor who was attending him drew up a detailed narrative of the case, and there cannot be the slightest doubt about its truth."

"It is marvellous," murmured M. de Guersaint in his delight.

"Would you like another example, monsieur? I can give you a famous one, that of Francois Macary, the carpenter of Lavaur. During eighteen years he had suffered from a deep varicose ulcer, with considerable enlargement of the tissues in the mesial part of the left leg. He had reached such a point that he could no longer move, and science decreed that he would forever remain infirm. Well, one evening he shuts himself up with a bottle of Lourdes water. He takes off his bandages, washes both his legs, and drinks what little water then remains in the bottle. Then he goes to bed and falls asleep; and when he awakes, he feels his legs and looks at them. There is nothing left; the varicose enlargement, the ulcers, have all disappeared. The skin of his knee, monsieur, had become as smooth, as fresh as it had been when he was twenty."

This time there was an explosion of surprise and admiration. The patients and the pilgrims were entering into the enchanted land of miracles, where impossibilities are accomplished at each bend of the pathways, where one marches on at ease from prodigy to prodigy. And each had his or her story to tell, burning with a desire to contribute a fresh proof, to fortify faith and hope by yet another example.

That silent creature, Madame Maze, was so transported that she spoke the first. "I have a friend," said she, "who knew the Widow Rizan, that lady whose cure also created so great a stir. For four-and-twenty years her left side had been entirely paralysed. Her stomach was unable to retain any solid food, and she had become an inert bag of bones which had to be turned over in bed, The friction of the sheets, too, had ended by rubbing her skin away in parts. Well, she was so low one evening that the doctor announced that she would die during the night. An hour later, however, she emerged from her torpor and asked her daughter in a faint voice to go and fetch her a glass of Lourdes water from a neighbour's. But she was only able to obtain this glass of water on the following morning; and she cried out to her daughter: 'Oh! it is life that I am drinking—rub my face with it, rub my arm and my leg, rub my whole body with it!' And when her daughter obeyed her, she gradually saw the huge swelling subside, and the paralysed, tumefied limbs recover their natural suppleness and appearance. Nor was that all, for Madame Rizan cried out that she was cured and felt hungry, and wanted bread and meat—she who had eaten none for four-and-twenty years! And she got out of bed and dressed herself, whilst her daughter, who was so overpowered that the neighbours thought she had become an orphan, replied to them: 'No, no, mamma isn't dead, she has come to life again!'"

This narrative had brought tears to Madame Vincent's eyes. Ah! if she had only been able to see her little Rose recover like that, eat with a good appetite, and run about again! At the same time, another case, which she had been told of in Paris and which had greatly influenced her in deciding to take her ailing child to Lourdes, returned to her memory.

"And I, too," said she, "know the story of a girl who was paralysed. Her name was Lucie Druon, and she was an inmate of an orphan asylum. She was quite young and could not even kneel down. Her limbs were bent like hoops. Her right leg, the shorter of the two, had ended by becoming twisted round the left one; and when any of the other girls carried her about you saw her feet hanging down quite limp, like dead ones. Please notice that she did not even go to Lourdes. She simply performed a novena; but she fasted during the nine days, and her desire to be cured was so great that she spent her nights in prayer. At last, on the ninth day, whilst she was drinking a little Lourdes water, she felt a violent commotion in her legs. She picked herself up, fell down, picked herself up again and walked. All her little companions, who were astonished, almost frightened at the sight, began to cry out 'Lucie can walk! Lucie can walk!' It was quite true. In a few seconds her legs had become straight and strong and healthy. She crossed the courtyard and was able to climb up the steps of the chapel, where the whole sisterhood, transported with gratitude, chanted the *Magnificat*. Ah! the dear child, how happy, how happy she must have been!"

As Madame Vincent finished, two tears fell from her cheeks on to the pale face of her little girl, whom she kissed distractedly.

The general interest was still increasing, becoming quite impassioned. The rapturous joy born of these beautiful stories, in which Heaven invariably triumphed over human reality, transported these childlike souls to such a point that those who were suffering the most grievously sat up in their turn, and recovered the power of speech. And with the narratives of one and all was blended a thought of the sufferer's own ailment, a belief that he or she would also be cured, since a malady of the same description had vanished like an evil dream beneath the breath of the Divinity.

"Ah!" stammered Madame Vetu, her articulation hindered by her sufferings, "there was another one, Antoinette Thardivail, whose stomach was being eaten away like mine. You would have said that dogs were devouring it, and sometimes there was a swelling in it as big as a child's head. Tumours indeed were ever forming in it, like fowl's eggs, so that for eight months she brought up blood. And she also was at the point of death, with nothing but her skin left on her bones, and dying of hunger, when she drank some water of Lourdes and had the pit of her stomach washed with it. Three minutes afterwards, her doctor, who on the previous day had left her almost in the last throes, scarce breathing, found her up and sitting by the fireside, eating a tender chicken's wing with a good appetite. She had no more tumours, she laughed as she had laughed when she was twenty, and her face had regained the brilliancy of youth. Ah! to be able to eat what one likes, to become young again, to cease suffering!"

"And the cure of Sister Julienne!" then exclaimed La Grivotte, raising herself on one of her elbows, her eyes glittering with fever. "In her case it commenced with a bad cold as it did with me, and then she began to spit blood. And every six months she fell ill again and had to take to her bed. The last time everybody said that she wouldn't leave it alive. The doctors had vainly tried every remedy, iodine, blistering, and cauterising. In fact, hers was a real case of phthisis, certified by half a dozen medical men. Well, she comes to Lourdes, and Heaven alone knows amidst what awful suffering—she was so bad, indeed, that at Toulouse they thought for a moment that she was about to die! The Sisters had to carry her in their arms, and on reaching the piscina the lady-hospitallers wouldn't bathe her. She was dead, they said. No matter! she was undressed at last, and plunged into the water, quite unconscious and covered with perspiration. And when they took her out she was so pale that they laid her on the ground, thinking that it was certainly all over with her at last. But, all at once, colour came back to her cheeks, her eyes opened, and she drew a long breath. She was cured; she dressed herself without any help and made a good meal after she had been to the Grotto to thank the Blessed Virgin. There! there's no gainsaying it, that was a real case of phthisis, completely cured as though by medicine!"

Thereupon Brother Isidore in his turn wished to speak; but he was unable to do so at any length, and could only with difficulty manage to say to his sister: "Marthe, tell them the story of Sister Dorothee which the priest of Saint-Sauveur related to us."

"Sister Dorothee," began the peasant girl in an awkward way, "felt her leg quite numbed when she got up one morning, and from that time she lost the use of it, for it got as cold and as heavy as a stone. Besides which she felt a great pain in the back. The doctors couldn't understand it. She saw half a dozen of them, who pricked her with pins and burnt her skin with a lot of drugs. But it was just as if they had sung to her. Sister Dorothee had well understood that only the Blessed Virgin could find the right remedy for her, and so she went off to Lourdes, and had herself dipped in the piscina. She thought at first that the water was going to kill her, for it was so bitterly cold. But by-and-by it became so soft that she fancied it was warm, as nice as milk. She had never felt so nice before, it seemed to her as if her veins were opening and the water were flowing into them. As you will understand, life was returning into her body since the Blessed Virgin was concerning herself in the case. She no longer had anything the matter with her when she came out, but walked about, ate the whole of a pigeon for her dinner, and slept all night long like the happy woman she was. Glory to the Blessed Virgin, eternal gratitude to the most Powerful Mother and her Divine Son!"

Elise Rouquet would also have liked to bring forward a miracle which she was acquainted with. Only she spoke with so much difficulty owing to the deformity of her mouth, that she had not yet been able to secure a turn. Just then, however, there was a pause, and drawing the wrap, which concealed the horror of her sore, slightly on one side, she profited by the opportunity to begin.

"For my part, I wasn't told anything about a great illness, but it was a very funny case at all events," she said. "It was about a woman, Celestine Dubois, as she was called, who had run a needle right into her hand while she was washing. It stopped there for seven years, for no doctor was able to take it out. Her hand shrivelled up, and she could no longer open it. Well, she got to Lourdes, and dipped her hand into the piscina. But as soon as she did so she began to shriek, and took it out again. Then they caught hold of her and put her hand into the water by force, and kept it there while she continued sobbing, with her face covered with sweat. Three times did they plunge her hand into the piscina, and each time they saw the needle moving along, till it came out by the tip of the thumb. She shrieked, of course, because the needle was moving though her flesh just as though somebody had been pushing it to drive it out. And after that Celestine never suffered again, and only a little scar could be seen on her hand as a mark of what the Blessed Virgin had done."

This anecdote produced a greater effect than even the miraculous cures of the most fearful illnesses. A needle which moved as though somebody were pushing it! This peopled the Invisible, showed each sufferer his Guardian Angel standing behind him, only awaiting the orders of Heaven in order to render him assistance. And besides, how pretty and childlike the story was—this needle which came out in the miraculous water after obstinately refusing to stir during seven long years. Exclamations of delight resounded from all the pleased listeners; they smiled and laughed with satisfaction, radiant at finding that nothing was beyond the power of Heaven, and that if it were Heaven's pleasure they themselves would all become healthy, young, and superb. It was sufficient that one should fervently believe and pray in order that nature might be confounded and that the Incredible might come to pass. Apart from that there was merely a question of good luck, since Heaven seemed to make a selection of those sufferers who should be cured.

"Oh! how beautiful it is, father," murmured Marie, who, revived by the passionate interest which she took in the momentous subject, had so far contented herself with listening, dumb with amazement as it were. "Do you remember," she continued, "what you yourself told me of that poor woman, Joachine Dehaut, who came from Belgium and made her way right across France with her twisted leg eaten away by an ulcer, the awful smell of which drove everybody away from her? First of all the ulcer was healed; you could press her knee and she felt nothing, only a slight redness remained to mark where it had been. And then came the turn of the dislocation. She shrieked while she was in the water, it seemed to her as if somebody were breaking her bones, pulling her leg away from her; and, at the same time, she and the woman who was bathing her, saw her deformed foot rise and extend into its natural shape with the regular movement of a clock hand. Her leg also straightened itself, the muscles extended, the knee replaced itself in its proper position, all amidst such acute pain that Joachine ended by fainting. But as soon as she recovered consciousness, she darted off, erect and agile, to carry her crutches to the Grotto."

M. de Guersaint in his turn was laughing with wonderment, waving his hand to confirm this story, which had been told him by a Father of the Assumption. He could have related a score of similar instances, said he, each more touching, more extraordinary than the other. He even invoked Pierre's testimony, and the young priest, who was unable to believe, contented himself with nodding his head. At first, unwilling as he was to afflict Marie, he had striven to divert his thoughts by gazing though the carriage window at the fields, trees, and houses which defiled before his eyes. They had just passed Angouleme, and meadows stretched out, and lines of poplar trees fled away amidst the continuous fanning of the air, which the velocity of the train occasioned.

They were late, no doubt, for they were hastening onward at full speed, thundering along under the stormy sky, through the fiery atmosphere, devouring kilometre after kilometre in swift succession. However, despite himself, Pierre heard snatches of the various narratives, and grew interested in these extravagant stories, which the rough jolting of the wheels accompanied like a lullaby, as though the engine had been turned loose and were wildly bearing them away to the divine land of dreams, They were rolling, still rolling along, and Pierre at last ceased to gaze at the landscape, and surrendered himself to the heavy, sleep-inviting atmosphere of the carriage, where ecstasy was growing and spreading, carrying everyone far from the world of reality across which they were so rapidly rushing, The sight of Marie's face with its brightened look filled the young priest with sincere joy, and he let her retain his hand, which she had taken in order to acquaint him, by the pressure of her fingers, with all the confidence which was reviving in her soul. And why should he have saddened her by his doubts, since he was so desirous of her cure? So he continued clasping her small, moist hand, feeling infinite affection for her, a dolorous brotherly love which distracted him, and made him anxious to believe in the pity of the spheres, in a superior kindness which tempered suffering to those who were plunged in despair, "Oh!" she repeated, "how beautiful it is, Pierre! How beautiful it is! And what glory it will be if the Blessed Virgin deigns to disturb herself for me! Do you really think me worthy of such a favour?"

"Assuredly I do," he exclaimed; "you are the best and the purest, with a spotless soul as your father said; there are not enough good angels in Paradise to form your escort."

But the narratives were not yet finished. Sister Hyacinthe and Madame de Jonquiere were now enumerating all the miracles with which they were acquainted, the long, long series of miracles which for more than thirty years had been flowering at Lourdes, like the uninterrupted budding of the roses on the Mystical Rose-tree. They could be counted by thousands, they put forth fresh shoots every year with prodigious verdancy of sap, becoming brighter and brighter each successive season. And the sufferers who listened to these marvellous stories with increasing feverishness were like little children who, after hearing one fine fairy tale, ask for another, and another, and yet another. Oh! that they might have more and more of those stories in which evil reality was flouted, in which unjust nature was cuffed and slapped, in which the Divinity intervened as the supreme healer, He who laughs at science and distributes happiness according to His own good pleasure.

First of all there were the deaf and the dumb who suddenly heard and spoke; such as Aurelie Bruneau, who was incurably deaf, with the drums of both ears broken, and yet was suddenly enraptured by the celestial music of a harmonium; such also as Louise Pourchet, who on her side had been dumb for five-and-twenty years, and yet, whilst praying in the Grotto, suddenly exclaimed, "Hail, Mary, full of grace!" And there were others and yet others who were completely cured by merely letting a few drops of water fall into their ears or upon their tongues. Then came the procession of the blind: Father Hermann, who felt the Blessed Virgin's gentle hand removing the veil which covered his eyes; Mademoiselle de Pontbriant, who was threatened with a total loss of sight, but after a simple prayer was enabled to see better than she had ever seen before; then a child twelve years old whose corneas resembled marbles, but who, in three seconds, became possessed of clear, deep eyes, bright with an angelic smile. However, there was especially an abundance of paralytics, of lame people suddenly enabled to walk upright, of sufferers for long years powerless to stir from their beds of misery and to whom the voice said: "Arise and walk!" Delannoy,* afflicted with ataxia, vainly cauterised and burnt, fifteen times an inmate of the Paris hospitals, whence he had emerged with the concurring diagnosis of twelve doctors, feels a strange force raising him up as the Blessed Sacrament goes by, and he begins to follow it, his legs strong and healthy once more. Marie Louise Delpon, a girl of fourteen, suffering from paralysis which had stiffened her legs, drawn back her hands, and twisted her mouth on one side, sees her limbs loosen and the distortion of her mouth disappear as though an invisible hand were severing the fearful bonds which had deformed her. Marie Vachier, riveted to her arm-chair during seventeen years by paraplegia, not only runs and flies on emerging from the piscina, but finds no trace even of the sores with which her long-enforced immobility had covered her body. And Georges Hanquet, attacked by softening of the spinal marrow, passes without transition from agony to perfect health; while Leonie Charton, likewise afflicted with softening of the medulla, and whose vertebrae bulge out to a considerable extent, feels her hump melting away as though by enchantment, and her legs rise and straighten, renovated and vigorous.

---

* This was one of the most notorious of the recorded cases and had a very strange sequel subsequent to the first publication of this work. Pierre Delannoy had been employed as a ward-assistant in one of the large Paris hospitals from 1877 to 1881, when he came to the conclusion that the life of an in-patient was far preferable to the one he was leading. He, therefore, resolved to pass the rest of his days inside different hospitals in the capacity of invalid. He started by feigning locomotor ataxia, and for six years deceived the highest medical experts in Paris, so curiously did he appear to suffer. He stayed in turn in all the hospitals in the city, being treated with every care and consideration, until at last he met with a doctor who insisted on cauterisation and other disagreeable remedies. Delannoy thereupon opined that the time to be cured had arrived, and cured he became, and was discharged. He next appeared at Lourdes, supported by crutches, and presenting every symptom of being hopelessly crippled. With other infirm and decrepid people he was dipped in the piscina and so efficacious did this treatment prove that he came out another man, threw his crutches to the ground and walked, as an onlooker expressed it, "like a rural postman." All Lourdes rang with the fame of the miracle, and the Church, after starring Delannoy round the country as a specimen of what could be done at the holy spring, placed him in charge of a home for invalids. But this was too much like hard work, and he soon decamped with all the money he could lay his hands on. Returning to Paris he was admitted to the Hospital of Ste. Anne as suffering from mental debility, but this did not prevent him from running off one night with about $300 belonging to a dispenser. The police were put on his track and arrested him in May, 1895, when he tried to pass himself off as a lunatic; but he had become by this time too well known, and was indicted in due course. At his trial he energetically denied that he had ever shammed, but the Court would not believe him, and sentenced him to four years' imprisonment with hard labour.—Trans.

Then came all sorts of ailments. First those brought about by scrofula—a great many more legs long incapable of service and made anew. There was Margaret Gehier, who had suffered from coxalgia for seven-and-twenty years, whose hip was devoured by the disease, whose left knee was anchylosed, and who yet was suddenly able to fall upon her knees to thank the Blessed Virgin for healing her. There was also Philomene Simonneau, the young Vendeenne, whose left leg was perforated by three horrible sores in the depths of which her carious bones were visible, and whose bones, whose flesh, and whose skin were all formed afresh.

Next came the dropsical ones: Madame Ancelin, the swelling of whose feet, hands, and entire body subsided without anyone being able to tell whither all the water had gone; Mademoiselle Montagnon, from whom, on various occasions, nearly twenty quarts of water had been drawn, and who, on again swelling, was entirely rid of the fluid by the application of a bandage which had been dipped in the miraculous source. And, in her case also, none of the water could be found, either in her bed or on the floor. In the same way, not a complaint of the stomach resisted, all disappeared with the first glass of water. There was Marie Souchet, who vomited black blood, who had wasted to a skeleton, and who devoured her food and recovered her flesh in two days' time! There was Marie Jarlaud, who had burnt herself internally through drinking a glass of a metallic solution used for cleansing and brightening kitchen utensils, and who felt the tumour which had resulted from her injuries melt rapidly away. Moreover, every tumour disappeared in this fashion, in the piscina, without leaving the slightest trace behind. But that which caused yet greater wonderment was the manner in which ulcers, cancers, all sorts of horrible, visible sores were cicatrised as by a breath from on high. A Jew, an actor, whose hand was devoured by an ulcer, merely had to dip it in the water and he was cured. A very wealthy young foreigner, who had a wen as large as a hen's egg, on his right wrist, *beheld* it dissolve. Rose Duval, who, as a result of a white tumour, had a hole in her left elbow, large enough to accommodate a walnut, was able to watch and follow the prompt action of the new flesh in filling up this cavity! The Widow Fromond, with a lip half decoyed by a cancerous formation, merely had to apply the miraculous water to it as a lotion, and not even a red mark remained. Marie Moreau, who experienced fearful sufferings from a cancer in the breast, fell asleep, after laying on it a linen cloth soaked in some water of Lourdes, and when she awoke, two hours later, the pain had disappeared, and her flesh was once more smooth and pink and fresh.

At last Sister Hyacinthe began to speak of the immediate and complete cures of phthisis, and this was the triumph, the healing of that terrible disease which ravages humanity, which unbelievers defied the Blessed Virgin to cure, but which she did cure, it was said, by merely raising her little finger. A hundred instances, more extraordinary one than the other, pressed forward for citation.

Marguerite Coupel, who had suffered from phthisis for three years, and the upper part of whose lungs is destroyed by tuberculosis, rises up and goes off, radiant with health. Madame de la Riviere, who spits blood, who is ever covered with a cold perspiration, whose nails have already acquired a violet tinge, who is indeed on the point of drawing her last breath, requires but a spoonful of the water to be administered to her between her teeth, and lo! the rattles cease, she sits up, makes the responses to the litanies, and asks for some broth. Julie Jadot requires four spoonfuls; but then she could no longer hold up her head, she was of such a delicate constitution that disease had reduced her to nothing; and yet, in a few days, she becomes quite fat. Anna Catry, who is in the most advanced stage of the malady, with her left lung half destroyed by a cavity, is plunged five times into the cold water, contrary to all the dictates of prudence, and she is cured, her lung is healthy once more. Another consumptive girl, condemned by fifteen doctors, has asked nothing, has simply fallen on her knees in the Grotto, by chance as it were, and is afterwards quite surprised at having been cured *au passage*, through the lucky circumstance of having been there, no doubt, at the hour when the Blessed Virgin, moved to pity, allows miracles to fall from her invisible hands.

Miracles and yet more miracles! They rained down like the flowers of dreams from a clear and balmy sky. Some of them were touching, some of them were childish. An old woman, who, having her hand anchylosed, had been incapable of moving it for thirty years, washes it in the water and is at once able to make the sign of the Cross. Sister Sophie, who barked like a dog, plunges into the piscina and emerges from it with a clear, pure voice, chanting a canticle. Mustapha, a Turk, invokes the White Lady and recovers the use of his right eye by applying a compress to it. An officer of Turcos was protected at Sedan; a cuirassier of Reichsoffen would have died, pierced in the heart by a bullet, if this bullet after passing though his pocket-book had not stayed its flight on reaching a little picture of Our Lady of Lourdes! And, as with the men and women, so did the children, the poor, suffering little ones, find mercy; a paralytic boy of five rose and walked after being held for five minutes under the icy jet of the spring; another one, fifteen years of age, who, lying in bed, could only raise an inarticulate cry, sprang out of the piscina, shouting that he was cured; another one, but two years old, a poor tiny fellow who had never been able to walk, remained for a quarter of an hour in the cold water and then, invigorated and smiling, took his first steps like a little man! And for all of them, the little ones as well as the adults, the pain was acute whilst the miracle was being accomplished; for the work of repair could not be effected without causing an extraordinary shock to the whole human organism; the bones grew again, new flesh was formed, and the disease, driven away, made its escape in a final convulsion. But how great was the feeling of comfort which followed! The doctors could not believe their eyes, their astonishment burst forth at each fresh cure, when they saw the patients whom they had despaired of run and jump and eat with ravenous appetites. All these chosen ones, these women cured of their ailments, walked a couple of miles, sat down to roast fowl, and slept the soundest of sleeps for a dozen hours. Moreover, there was no convalescence, it was a sudden leap from the death throes to complete health. Limbs were renovated, sores were filled up, organs were reformed in their entirety, plumpness returned to the emaciated, all with the velocity of a lightning flash! Science was completely baffled. Not even the most simple precautions were taken, women were bathed at all times and seasons, perspiring consumptives were plunged into the icy water, sores were left to their putrefaction without any thought of employing antiseptics. And then what canticles of joy, what shouts of gratitude and love arose at each fresh miracle! The favoured one falls upon her knees, all who are present weep, conversions are effected, Protestants and Jews alike embrace Catholicism—other miracles these, miracles of faith, at which Heaven triumphs. And when the favoured one, chosen for the miracle, returns to her village, all the inhabitants crowd to meet her, whilst the bells peal merrily; and when she is seen springing lightly from the vehicle which has brought her home, shouts and sobs of joy burst forth and all intonate the *Magnificat*: Glory to the Blessed Virgin! Gratitude and love for ever!

Indeed, that which was more particularly evolved from the realisation of all these hopes, from the celebration of all these ardent thanksgivings, was gratitude—gratitude to the Mother most pure and most admirable. She was the great passion of every soul, she, the Virgin most powerful, the Virgin most merciful, the Mirror of Justice, the Seat of Wisdom.* All hands were stretched towards her, Mystical Rose in the dim light of the chapels, Tower of Ivory on the horizon of dreamland, Gate of Heaven leading into the Infinite. Each day at early dawn she shone forth, bright Morning Star, gay with juvenescent hope. And was she not also the Health of the weak, the Refuge of sinners, the Comforter of the afflicted? France had ever been her well-loved country, she was adored there with an ardent worship, the worship of her womanhood and her motherhood, the soaring of a divine affection; and it was particularly in France that it pleased her to show herself to little shepherdesses. She was so good to the little and the humble; she continually occupied herself with them; and if she was appealed to so willingly it was because she was known to be the intermediary of love betwixt Earth and Heaven. Every evening she wept tears of gold at the feet of her divine Son to obtain favours from Him, and these favours were the miracles which He permitted her to work,—these beautiful, flower-like miracles, as sweet-scented as the roses of Paradise, so prodigiously splendid and fragrant.

But the train was still rolling, rolling onward. They had just passed Contras, it was six o'clock, and Sister Hyacinthe, rising to her, feet, clapped her hands together and once again repeated: "The Angelus, my children!"

Never had "Aves" impregnated with greater faith, inflamed with a more fervent desire to be heard by Heaven, winged their flight on high. And Pierre suddenly understood everything, clearly realised the meaning of all these pilgrimages, of all these trains rolling along through every country of the civilised world, of all these eager crowds, hastening towards Lourdes, which blazed over yonder like the abode of salvation for body and for mind. Ah! the poor wretches whom, ever since morning, he had heard groaning with pain, the poor wretches who exposed their sorry carcasses to the fatigues of such a journey! They were all condemned, abandoned by science, weary of consulting doctors, of having tried the torturing effects of futile remedies. And

---

* For the information of Protestant and other non-Catholic readers it may be mentioned that all the titles enumerated in this passage are taken from the Litany of the Blessed Virgin.—Trans.

ÉMILE ZOLA

how well one could understand that, burning with a desire to preserve their lives, unable to resign themselves to the injustice and indifference of Nature, they should dream of a superhuman power, of an almighty Divinity who, in their favour, would perchance annul the established laws, alter the course of the planets, and reconsider His creation! For if the world failed them, did not the Divinity remain to them? In their cases reality was too abominable, and an immense need of illusion and falsehood sprang up within them. Oh! to believe that there is a supreme Justiciar somewhere, one who rights the apparent wrongs of things and beings; to believe that there is a Redeemer, a consoler who is the real master, who can carry the torrents back to their source, who can restore youth to the aged, and life to the dead! And when you are covered with sores, when your limbs are twisted, when your stomach is swollen by tumours, when your lungs are destroyed by disease, to be able to say that all this is of no consequence, that everything may disappear and be renewed at a sign from the Blessed Virgin, that it is sufficient that you should pray to her, touch her heart, and obtain the favour of being chosen by her. And then what a heavenly fount of hope appeared with the prodigious flow of those beautiful stories of cure, those adorable fairy tales which lulled and intoxicated the feverish imaginations of the sick and the infirm. Since little Sophie Couteau, with her white, sound foot, had climbed into that carriage, opening to the gaze of those within it the limitless heavens of the Divine and the Supernatural, how well one could understand the breath of resurrection that was passing over the world, slowly raising those who despaired the most from their beds of misery, and making their eyes shine since life was itself a possibility for them, and they were, perhaps, about to begin it afresh.

Yes, 't was indeed that. If that woeful train was rolling, rolling on, if that carriage was full, if the other carriages were full also, if France and the world, from the uttermost limits of the earth, were crossed by similar trains, if crowds of three hundred thousand believers, bringing thousands of sick along with them, were ever setting out, from one end of the year to the other, it was because the Grotto yonder was shining forth in its glory like a beacon of hope and illusion, like a sign of the revolt and triumph of the Impossible over inexorable materiality. Never had a more impassionating romance been devised to exalt the souls of men above the stern laws of life. To dream that dream, this was the great, the ineffable happiness. If the Fathers of the Assumption had seen the success of their pilgrimages increase and spread from year to year, it was because they sold to all the flocking peoples the bread of consolation and illusion, the delicious bread of hope, for which suffering humanity ever hungers with a hunger that nothing will ever appease. And it was not merely the physical sores which cried aloud for cure, the whole of man's moral and intellectual being likewise shrieked forth its wretchedness, with an insatiable yearning for happiness. To be happy, to place the certainty of life in faith, to lean till death should come upon that one strong staff of travel—such was the desire exhaled by every breast, the desire which made every moral grief bend the knee, imploring a continuance of grace, the conversion of dear ones, the spiritual salvation of self and those one loved. The mighty cry spread from pole to pole, ascended and filled all the regions of space: To be happy, happy for evermore, both in life and in death!

And Pierre saw the suffering beings around him lose all perception of the jolting and recover their strength as league by league they drew nearer to the miracle. Even Madame Maze grew talkative, certain as she felt that the Blessed Virgin would restore her husband to her. With a smile on her face Madame Vincent gently rocked her little Rose in her arms, thinking that she was not nearly so ill as those all but lifeless children who, after being plunged in the icy water, sprang out and played. M. Sabathier jested with M. de Guersaint, and explained to him that, next October, when he had recovered the use of his legs, he should go on a trip to Rome—a journey which he had been postponing for fifteen years and more. Madame Vetu, quite calmed, feeling nothing but a slight twinge in the stomach, imagined that she was hungry, and asked Madame de Jonquiere to let her dip some strips of bread in a glass of milk; whilst Elise Rouquet, forgetting her sores, ate some grapes, with face uncovered. And in La Grivotte who was sitting up and Brother Isidore who had ceased moaning, all those fine stories had left a pleasant fever, to such a point that, impatient to be cured, they grew anxious to know the time. For a minute also the man, the strange man, resuscitated. Whilst Sister Hyacinthe was again wiping the cold sweat from his brow, he raised his eyelids, and a smile momentarily brightened his pallid countenance. Yet once again he, also, had hoped.

Marie was still holding Pierre's fingers in her own small, warm hand. It was seven o'clock, they were not due at Bordeaux till half-past seven; and the belated train was quickening its pace yet more and more, rushing along with wild speed in order to make up for the minutes it had lost. The storm had ended by coming down, and now a gentle light of infinite purity fell from the vast clear heavens.

"Oh! how beautiful it is, Pierre—how beautiful it is!" Marie again repeated, pressing his hand with tender affection. And leaning towards him, she added in an undertone: "I beheld the Blessed Virgin a little while ago, Pierre, and it was your cure that I implored and shall obtain."

The priest, who understood her meaning, was thrown into confusion by the divine light which gleamed in her eyes as she fixed them on his own. She had forgotten her own sufferings; that which she had asked for was his conversion; and that prayer of faith, emanating, pure and candid, from that dear, suffering creature, upset his soul. Yet why should he not believe some day? He himself had been distracted by all those extraordinary narratives. The stifling heat of the carriage had made him dizzy, the sight of all the woe heaped up there caused his heart to bleed with pity. And contagion was doing its work; he no longer knew where the real and the possible ceased, he lacked the power to disentangle such a mass of stupefying facts, to explain such as admitted of explanation and reject the others. At one moment, indeed, as a hymn once more resounded and carried him off with its stubborn importunate rhythm, he ceased to be master of himself, and imagined that he was at last beginning to believe amidst the hallucinatory vertigo which reigned in that travelling hospital, rolling, ever rolling onward at full speed.

V

BERNADETTE

T he train left Bordeaux after a stoppage of a few minutes, during which those who had not dined hastened to purchase some provisions. Moreover, the ailing ones were constantly drinking milk, and asking for biscuits, like little children. And, as soon as they were off again, Sister Hyacinthe clapped her hands, and exclaimed: "Come, let us make haste; the evening prayer."

Thereupon, during a quarter of an hour came a confused murmuring, made up of "Paters" and "Aves," self-examinations, acts of contrition, and vows of trustful reliance in God, the Blessed Virgin, and the Saints, with thanksgiving for protection and preservation that day, and, at last, a prayer for the living and for the faithful departed.

"In the name of the Father, the Son, and the Holy Ghost. Amen."

It was ten minutes past eight o'clock, the shades of night were already bedimming the landscape—a vast plain which the evening mist seemed to prolong into the infinite, and where, far away, bright dots of light shone out from the windows of lonely, scattered houses. In the carriage, the lights of the lamps were flickering, casting a subdued yellow glow on the luggage and the pilgrims, who were sorely shaken by the spreading tendency of the train's motion.

"You know, my children," resumed Sister Hyacinthe, who had remained standing, "I shall order silence when we get to Lamothe, in about an hour's time. So you have an hour to amuse yourselves, but you must be reasonable and not excite yourselves too much. And when we have passed Lamothe, you hear me, there must not be another word, another sound, you must all go to sleep."

This made them laugh.

"Oh! but it is the rule, you know," added the Sister, "and surely you have too much sense not to obey me."

Since the morning they had punctually fulfilled the programme of religious exercises specified for each successive hour. And now that all the prayers had been said, the beads told, the hymns chanted, the day's duties were over, and a brief interval for recreation was allowed before sleeping. They were, however, at a loss as to what they should do.

"Sister," suddenly said Marie, "if you would allow Monsieur l'Abbe to read to us—he reads extremely well,—and as it happens I have a little book with me—a history of Bernadette which is so interesting—"

The others did nor let her finish, but with the suddenly awakened desire of children to whom a beautiful story has been promised, loudly exclaimed: "Oh! yes, Sister. Oh! yes, Sister—"

"Of course I will allow it," replied Sister Hyacinthe, "since it is a question of reading something instructive and edifying."

Pierre was obliged to consent. But to be able to read the book he wished to be under the lamp, and it was necessary that he should change seats with M. de Guersaint, whom the promise of a story had delighted as much as it did the ailing ones. And when the young priest, after changing seats and declaring that he would be able to see well enough, at last opened the little book, a quiver of curiosity sped from one end of the carriage to the other, and every head was stretched out, lending ear with rapt attention. Fortunately, Pierre had a clear, powerful voice and made himself distinctly heard above the wheels, which, now that the train travelled across a vast level plain, gave out but a subdued, rumbling sound.

Before beginning, however, the young priest had examined the book. It was one of those little works of propaganda issued from the Catholic printing-presses and circulated in profusion throughout all Christendom. Badly printed, on wretched paper, it was adorned on its blue cover with a little wood-cut of Our Lady of Lourdes, a naive design alike stiff and awkward. The book itself was short, and half an hour would certainly suffice to read it from cover to cover without hurrying.

Accordingly, in his fine, clear voice, with its penetrating, musical tones, he began his perusal as follows:—

"It happened at Lourdes, a little town near the Pyrenees, on a Thursday, February 11, 1858. The weather was cold, and somewhat cloudy, and in the humble home of a poor but honest miller named Francois Soubirous there was no wood to cook the dinner. The miller's wife, Louise, said to her younger daughter Marie, 'Go and gather some wood on the bank of the Gave or on the common-land.' The Gave is a torrent which passes through Lourdes.

"Marie had an elder sister, named Bernadette, who had lately arrived from the country, where some worthy villagers had employed her as a shepherdess. She was a slender, delicate, extremely innocent child, and knew nothing except her rosary. Louise Soubirous hesitated to send her out with her sister, on account of the cold, but at last, yielding to the entreaties of Marie and a young girl of the neighbourhood called Jeanne Abadie, she consented to let her go.

"Following the bank of the torrent and gathering stray fragments of dead wood, the three maidens at last found themselves in front of the Grotto, hollowed out in a huge mass of rock which the people of the district called Massabielle."

Pierre had reached this point and was turning the page when he suddenly paused and let the little book fall on his knees. The childish character of the narrative, its ready-made, empty phraseology, filled him with impatience. He himself possessed quite a collection of documents concerning this extraordinary story, had passionately studied even its most trifling details, and in the depths of his heart retained a feeling of tender affection and infinite pity for Bernadette. He had just reflected, too, that on the very next day he would be able to begin that decisive inquiry which he had formerly dreamt of making at Lourdes. In fact, this was one of the reasons which had induced him to accompany Marie on her journey. And he was now conscious of an awakening of all his curiosity respecting the Visionary, whom he loved because he felt that she had been a girl of candid soul, truthful and ill-fated, though at the same time he would much have liked to analyse and explain her case. Assuredly, she had not lied, she had indeed beheld a vision and heard voices, like Joan of Arc; and like Joan of Arc also, she was now, in the opinion of the devout, accomplishing the deliverance of France— from sin if not from invaders. Pierre wondered what force could have produced her—her and her work. How was it that the visionary faculty had become developed in that lowly girl, so distracting believing souls as to bring about a renewal of the miracles of primitive times, as to found almost a new religion in the midst of a Holy City, built at an outlay of millions, and ever invaded by crowds of worshippers more numerous and more exalted in mind than had ever been known since the days of the Crusades?

And so, ceasing to read the book, Pierre began to tell his companions all that he knew, all that he had divined and reconstructed of that story which is yet so obscure despite the vast rivers of ink which it has already caused to flow. He knew the country and its manners and customs, through his long conversations with his friend Doctor Chassaigne. And he was endowed with charming fluency of language, an emotional power of exquisite purity, many remarkable gifts well fitting him to be a pulpit orator, which he never made use of, although he had known them to be within him ever since his seminary days. When the occupants of the carriage perceived that he knew the story, far better and in far greater detail than it appeared in Marie's little book, and that he related it also in such a gentle yet passionate way, there came an increase of attention, and all those afflicted souls hungering for happiness went forth towards him. First came the story of Bernadette's childhood at Bartres, where she had grown up in the abode of her foster-mother, Madame Lagues, who, having lost an infant of her own, had rendered those poor folks, the Soubirouses, the service of suckling and keeping their child for them. Bartres, a village of four hundred souls, at a league or so from Lourdes, lay as it were in a desert oasis, sequestered amidst greenery, and far from any frequented highway. The road dips down, the few houses are scattered over grassland, divided by hedges and planted with walnut and chestnut trees, whilst the clear rivulets, which are never silent, follow the sloping banks beside the pathways, and nothing rises on high save the small ancient romanesque church, which is perched on a hillock, covered with graves. Wooded slopes undulate upon all sides. Bartres lies in a hollow amidst grass of delicious freshness, grass of intense greenness, which is ever moist at the roots, thanks to the eternal subterranean expanse of water which is fed by the mountain torrents. And Bernadette, who, since becoming a big girl, had paid for her keep by tending lambs, was wont to take them with her, season after season, through all the greenery where she never met a soul. It was only now and then, from the summit of some slope, that she saw the far-away mountains, the Pic du Midi, the Pic de Viscos, those masses which rose up, bright or gloomy, according to the weather, and which stretched away to other peaks, lightly and faintly coloured, vaguely and confusedly outlined, like apparitions seen in dreams.

Then came the home of the Lagueses, where her cradle was still preserved, a solitary, silent house, the last of the village. A meadow planted with pear and apple trees, and only separated from the open country by a narrow stream which one could jump across, stretched out in front of the house. Inside the latter, a low and damp abode, there were, on either side of the wooden stairway leading to the loft, but two spacious rooms, flagged with stones, and each containing four or five beds. The girls, who slept together, fell asleep at even, gazing at the fine pictures affixed to the walls, whilst the big clock in its pinewood case gravely struck the hours in the midst of the deep silence.

Ah! those years at Bartres; in what sweet peacefulness did Bernadette live them! Yet she grew up very thin, always in bad health, suffering from a nervous asthma which stifled her in the least veering of the wind; and on attaining her twelfth year she could neither read nor write, nor speak otherwise than in dialect, having remained quite infantile, behindhand in mind as in body. She was a very good little girl, very gentle and well behaved, and but little different from other children, except that instead of talking she preferred to listen. Limited as was her intelligence, she often evinced much natural common-sense, and at times was prompt in her *reparties*, with a kind of simple gaiety which made one smile. It was only with infinite trouble that she was taught her rosary, and when she knew it she seemed bent on carrying her knowledge no further, but repeated it all day long, so that whenever you met her with her lambs, she invariably had her chaplet between her fingers, diligently telling each successive "Pater" and "Ave." For long, long hours she lived like this on the grassy slopes of the hills, hidden away and haunted as it were amidst the mysteries of the foliage, seeing nought of the world save the crests of the distant mountains, which, for an instant, every now and then, would soar aloft in the radiant light, as ethereal as the peaks of dreamland.

Days followed days, and Bernadette roamed, dreaming her one narrow dream, repeating the sole prayer she knew, which gave her amidst her solitude, so fresh and naively infantile, no other companion and friend than the Blessed Virgin. But what pleasant evenings she spent in the winter-time in the room on the left, where a fire was kept burning! Her foster-mother had a brother, a priest, who occasionally read some marvellous stories to them—stories of saints, prodigious adventures of a kind to make one tremble with mingled fear and joy, in which Paradise appeared upon earth, whilst the heavens opened and a glimpse was caught of the splendour of the angels. The books he brought with him were often full of pictures—God the Father enthroned amidst His glory; Jesus, so gentle and so handsome with His beaming face; the Blessed Virgin, who recurred again and again, radiant with splendour, clad now in white, now in azure, now in gold, and ever so amiable that Bernadette would see her again in her dreams. But the book which was read more than all others was the Bible, an old Bible which had been in the family for more than a hundred years, and which time and usage had turned yellow. Each winter evening Bernadette's foster-father, the only member of the household who had learnt to read, would take a pin, pass it at random between the leaves of the book, open the latter, and then start reading from the top of the right-hand page, amidst the deep attention of both the women and the children, who ended by knowing the book by heart, and could have continued reciting it without a single mistake.

However, Bernadette, for her part, preferred the religious works in which the Blessed Virgin constantly appeared with her engaging smile. True, one reading of a different character amused her, that of the marvellous story of the Four Brothers Aymon. On the yellow paper cover of the little book, which had doubtless fallen from the bale of some peddler who had lost his way in that remote region, there was a naive cut showing the four doughty knights, Renaud and his brothers, all mounted on Bayard, their famous battle charger, that princely present made to them by the fairy Orlanda. And inside were narratives of bloody fights, of the building and besieging of fortresses, of the terrible swordthrusts exchanged by Roland and Renaud, who was at last about to free the Holy Land, without mentioning the tales of Maugis the Magician and his marvellous enchantments, and the Princess Clarisse, the King of Aquitaine's sister, who was more lovely than sunlight. Her imagination fired by such stories as these, Bernadette often found it difficult to get to sleep; and this was especially the case on the evenings when the books were left aside, and some person of the company related a tale of witchcraft. The girl was very superstitious, and after sundown could never be prevailed upon to pass near a tower in the vicinity, which was said to be haunted by the fiend. For that matter, all the folks of the region were superstitious, devout, and simple-minded, the whole countryside being peopled, so to say, with mysteries—trees which sang, stones from which blood flowed, cross-roads where it was necessary to say three "Paters" and three "Aves," if you did not wish to meet the seven-horned beast who carried maidens off to perdition. And what a wealth of terrifying stories there was! Hundreds of stories, so that there was no finishing on the evenings when somebody started them. First came the wehrwolf adventures, the tales of the unhappy men whom the demon forced to enter into the bodies of dogs, the great white dogs of the mountains. If you fire a gun at the dog and a single shot should strike him, the man will be delivered; but if the shot should fall on the dog's shadow, the man will immediately die. Then came the endless procession of sorcerers and sorceresses. In one of these tales Bernadette evinced a passionate interest; it was the story of a clerk of the tribunal of Lourdes who, wishing to see the devil, was conducted by a witch into an untilled field at midnight on Good Friday. The devil arrived clad in magnificent scarlet garments, and at once proposed to the clerk that he should buy his soul, an offer which the clerk pretended to accept. It so happened that the devil was carrying under his arm a register in which different persons of the town, who had already sold themselves, had signed their names. However, the clerk, who was a cunning fellow, pulled out of his pocket a pretended bottle of ink, which in reality contained holy water, and with this he sprinkled the devil, who raised frightful shrieks, whilst the clerk took to flight, carrying the register off with him. Then began a wild, mad race, which might last throughout the night, over the mountains, through the valleys, across the forests and the torrents. "Give me back my register!" shouted the fiend. "No, you sha'n't have it!" replied the clerk. And again and again it began afresh: "Give me back my register!"—"No, you sha'n't have it'!" And at last, finding himself out of breath, near the point of succumbing, the clerk, who had his plan, threw himself into the cemetery, which was consecrated ground, and was there able to deride the devil at his ease, waving the register which he had purloined so as to save the souls of all the unhappy people who had signed their names in it. On the evening when this story was told, Bernadette, before surrendering herself to sleep, would mentally repeat her rosary, delighted with the thought that hell should have been baffled, though she trembled at the idea that it would surely return to prowl around her, as soon as the lamp should have been put out.

Throughout one winter, the long evenings were spent in the church. Abbe Ader, the village priest, had authorised it, and many families came, in order to economise oil and candles. Moreover, they felt less cold when gathered together in this fashion. The Bible was read, and prayers were repeated, whilst the children ended by falling asleep. Bernadette alone struggled on to the finish, so pleased she was at being there, in that narrow nave whose slender nervures were coloured blue and red. At the farther end was the altar, also painted and gilded, with its twisted columns and its screens on which appeared the Virgin and Ste. Anne, and the beheading of St. John the Baptist—the whole of a gaudy and somewhat barbaric splendour. And as sleepiness grew upon her, the child must have often seen a mystical vision as it were of those crudely coloured designs rising before her—have seen the blood flowing from St. John's severed head, have seen the aureolas shining, the Virgin ever returning and gazing at her with her blue, living eyes, and looking as though she were on the point of opening her vermilion lips in order to speak to her. For some months Bernadette spent her evenings in this wise, half asleep in front of that sumptuous, vaguely defined altar, in the incipiency of a divine dream which she carried away with her, and finished in bed, slumbering peacefully under the watchful care of her guardian angel.

And it was also in that old church, so humble yet so impregnated with ardent faith, that Bernadette began to learn her catechism. She would soon be fourteen now, and must think of her first communion. Her foster-mother, who had the reputation of being avaricious, did not send her to school, but employed her in or about the house from morning till evening. M. Barbet, the schoolmaster, never saw her at his classes, though one day, when he gave the catechism lesson, in the place of Abbe Ader who was indisposed, he remarked her on account of her piety and modesty. The village priest was very fond of Bernadette and often spoke of her to the schoolmaster, saying that he could never look at her without thinking of the children of La Salette, since they must have been good, candid, and pious as she was, for the Blessed Virgin to have appeared to them.* On another occasion whilst the two men were walking one morning near the village, and saw Bernadette disappear with her little flock under some spreading trees in the distance, the Abbe repeatedly turned round to look for her, and again remarked "I cannot account for it, but every time I meet that child it seems to me as if I saw Melanie, the young shepherdess, little Maximin's companion." He was certainly beset by this singular idea, which became, so to say, a prediction. Moreover, had he not one day after catechism, or one evening, when the villagers were gathered in the church, related that marvellous story which was already twelve years old, that story of the Lady in the dazzling robes who walked upon the grass without even making it bend, the Blessed Virgin who

---

* It was on September 19, 1846, that the Virgin is said to have appeared in the ravine of La Sezia, adjacent to the valley of La Salette, between Corps and Eutraigues, in the department of the Isere. The visionaries were Melanie Mathieu, a girl of fourteen, and Maximin Giraud, a boy of twelve. The local clergy speedily endorsed the story of the miracle, and thousands of people still go every year in pilgrimage to a church overlooking the valley, and bathe and drink at a so-called miraculous source. Two priests of Grenoble, however, Abbe Deleon and Abbe Cartellier, accused a Mlle. de Lamerliere of having concocted the miracle, and when she took proceedings against them for libel she lost her case.—Trans.

showed herself to Melanie and Maximin on the banks of a stream in the mountains, and confided to them a great secret and announced the anger of her Son? Ever since that day a source had sprung up from the tears which she had shed, a source which cured all ailments, whilst the secret, inscribed on parchment fastened with three seals, slumbered at Rome! And Bernadette, no doubt, with her dreamy, silent air, had listened passionately to that wonderful tale and carried it off with her into the desert of foliage where she spent her days, so that she might live it over again as she walked along behind her lambs with her rosary, slipping bead by bead between her slender fingers.

Thus her childhood ran its course at Bartres. That which delighted one in this Bernadette, so poor-blooded, so slight of build, was her ecstatic eyes, beautiful visionary eyes, from which dreams soared aloft like birds winging their flight in a pure limpid sky. Her mouth was large, with lips somewhat thick, expressive of kindliness; her square-shaped head had a straight brow, and was covered with thick black hair, whilst her face would have seemed rather common but for its charming expression of gentle obstinacy. Those who did not gaze into her eyes, however, gave her no thought. To them she was but an ordinary child, a poor thing of the roads, a girl of reluctant growth, timidly humble in her ways. Assuredly it was in her glance that Abbe Ader had with agitation detected the stifling ailment which filled her puny, girlish form with suffering—that ailment born of the greeny solitude in which she had grown up, the gentleness of her bleating lambs, the Angelic Salutation which she had carried with her, hither and thither, under the sky, repeating and repeating it to the point of hallucination, the prodigious stories, too, which she had heard folks tell at her foster-mother's, the long evenings spent before the living altar-screens in the church, and all the atmosphere of primitive faith which she had breathed in that far-away rural region, hemmed in by mountains.

At last, on one seventh of January, Bernadette had just reached her fourteenth birthday, when her parents, finding that she learnt nothing at Bartres, resolved to bring her back to Lourdes for good, in order that she might diligently study her catechism, and in this wise seriously prepare herself for her first communion. And so it happened that she had already been at Lourdes some fifteen or twenty days, when on February 11, a Thursday, cold and somewhat cloudy—

But Pierre could carry his narrative no further, for Sister Hyacinthe had risen to her feet and was vigorously clapping her hands. "My children," she exclaimed, "it is past nine o'clock. Silence! silence!"

The train had indeed just passed Lamothe, and was rolling with a dull rumble across a sea of darkness—the endless plains of the Landes which the night submerged. For ten minutes already not a sound ought to have been heard in the carriage, one and all ought to have been sleeping or suffering uncomplainingly. However, a mutiny broke out.

"Oh! Sister!" exclaimed Marie, whose eyes were sparkling, "allow us just another short quarter of an hour! We have got to the most interesting part."

Ten, twenty voices took up the cry: "Oh yes, Sister, please do let us have another short quarter of an hour!"

They all wished to hear the continuation, burning with as much curiosity as though they had not known the story, so captivated were they by the touches of compassionate human feeling which Pierre introduced into his narrative. Their glances never left him, all their heads were stretched towards him, fantastically illumined by the flickering light of the lamps. And it was not only the sick who displayed this interest; the ten women occupying the compartment at the far end of the carriage had also become impassioned, and, happy at not missing a single word, turned their poor ugly faces now beautified by naive faith.

"No, I cannot!" Sister Hyacinthe at first declared; "the rules are very strict—you must be silent."

However, she weakened, she herself feeling so interested in the tale that she could detect her heart beating under her stomacher. Then Marie again repeated her request in an entreating tone; whilst her father, M. de Guersaint, who had listened like one hugely amused, declared that they would all fall ill if the story were not continued. And thereupon, seeing Madame de Jonquiere smile with an indulgent air, Sister Hyacinthe ended by consenting.

"Well, then," said she, "I will allow you another short quarter of an hour; but only a short quarter of an hour, mind. That is understood, is it not? For I should otherwise be in fault."

Pierre had waited quietly without attempting to intervene. And he resumed his narrative in the same penetrating voice as before, a voice in which his own doubts were softened by pity for those who suffer and who hope.

The scene of the story was now transferred to Lourdes, to the Rue des Petits Fosses, a narrow, tortuous, mournful street taking a downward course between humble houses and roughly plastered dead walls. The Soubirous family occupied a single room on the ground floor of one of these sorry habitations, a room at the end of a dark passage, in which seven persons were huddled together, the father, the mother, and five children. You could scarcely see in the chamber; from the tiny, damp inner courtyard of the house there came but a greenish light. And in that room they slept, all of a heap; and there also they ate, when they had bread. For some time past, the father, a miller by trade, could only with difficulty obtain work as a journeyman. And it was from that dark hole, that lowly wretchedness, that Bernadette, the elder girl, with Marie, her sister, and Jeanne, a little friend of the neighbourhood, went out to pick up dead wood, on the cold February Thursday already spoken of.

Then the beautiful tale was unfolded at length; how the three girls followed the bank of the Gave from the other side of the castle, and how they ended by finding themselves on the Ile du Chalet in front of the rock of Massabielle, from which they were only separated by the narrow stream diverted from the Gave, and used for working the mill of Savy. It was a wild spot, whither the common herdsman often brought the pigs of the neighbourhood, which, when showers suddenly came on, would take shelter under this rock of Massabielle, at whose base there was a kind of grotto of no great depth, blocked at the entrance by eglantine and brambles. The girls found dead wood very scarce that day, but at last on seeing on the other side of the stream quite a gleaning of branches deposited there by the torrent, Marie and Jeanne crossed over through the water; whilst Bernadette, more delicate than they were, a trifle young-ladyfied, perhaps, remained on the bank lamenting, and not daring to wet her feet. She was suffering slightly from humour in the head, and her mother had expressly bidden her to wrap herself in her *capulet*,* a large white *capulet* which contrasted vividly with her old black woollen dress. When she found that her companions would not help her, she resignedly made up her mind to take off her *sabots*, and pull down her stockings. It was then about noon, the three strokes of the Angelus rang out from the parish church, rising into the broad calm winter sky, which was somewhat veiled by fine fleecy clouds. And it was then that a great agitation arose within her, resounding in her ears with such a tempestuous roar that she fancied a hurricane had

---

* This is a kind of hood, more generally known among the Bearnese peasantry as a *sarot*. Whilst forming a coif it also completely covers the back and shoulders.—Trans.

ÉMILE ZOLA

descended from the mountains, and was passing over her. But she looked at the trees and was stupefied, for not a leaf was stirring. Then she thought that she had been mistaken, and was about to pick up her *sabots*, when again the great gust swept through her; but, this time, the disturbance in her ears reached her eyes, she no longer saw the trees, but was dazzled by a whiteness, a kind of bright light which seemed to her to settle itself against the rock, in a narrow, lofty slit above the Grotto, not unlike an ogival window of a cathedral. In her fright she fell upon her knees. What could it be, *mon Dieu?* Sometimes, during bad weather, when her asthma oppressed her more than usual, she spent very bad nights, incessantly dreaming dreams which were often painful, and whose stifling effect she retained on awaking, even when she had ceased to remember anything. Flames would surround her, the sun would flash before her face. Had she dreamt in that fashion during the previous night? Was this the continuation of some forgotten dream? However, little by little a form became outlined, she believed that she could distinguish a figure which the vivid light rendered intensely white. In her fear lest it should be the devil, for her mind was haunted by tales of witchcraft, she began to tell her beads. And when the light had slowly faded away, and she had crossed the canal and joined Marie and Jeanne, she was surprised to find that neither of them had seen anything whilst they were picking up the wood in front of the Grotto. On their way back to Lourdes the three girls talked together. So she, Bernadette, had seen something then? What was it? At first, feeling uneasy, and somewhat ashamed, she would not answer; but at last she said that she had seen something white.

From this the rumours started and grew. The Soubirouses, on being made acquainted with the circumstance, evinced much displeasure at such childish nonsense, and told their daughter that she was not to return to the rock of Massabielle. All the children of the neighbourhood, however, were already repeating the tale, and when Sunday came the parents had to give way, and allow Bernadette to betake herself to the Grotto with a bottle of holy water to ascertain if it were really the devil whom one had to deal with. She then again beheld the light, the figure became more clearly defined, and smiled upon her, evincing no fear whatever of the holy water. And, on the ensuing Thursday, she once more returned to the spot accompanied by several persons, and then for the first time the radiant lady assumed sufficient corporality to speak, and say to her: "Do me the kindness to come here for fifteen days."

Thus, little by little, the lady had assumed a precise appearance. The something clad in white had become indeed a lady more beautiful than a queen, of a kind such as is only seen in pictures. At first, in presence of the questions with which all the neighbours plied her from morning till evening, Bernadette had hesitated, disturbed, perhaps, by scruples of conscience. But then, as though prompted by the very interrogatories to which she was subjected, she seemed to perceive the figure which she had beheld, more plainly, so that it definitely assumed life, with lines and hues from which the child, in her after-descriptions, never departed. The lady's eyes were blue and very mild, her mouth was rosy and smiling, the oval of her face expressed both the grace of youth and of maternity. Below the veil covering her head and falling to her heels, only a glimpse was caught of her admirable fair hair, which was slightly curled. Her robe, which was of dazzling whiteness, must have been of some material unknown on earth, some material woven of the sun's rays. Her sash, of the same hue as the heavens, was fastened loosely about her, its long ends streaming downwards, with the light airiness of morning. Her chaplet, wound about her right arm, had beads of a milky whiteness, whilst the links and the cross were of gold. And on her bare feet, on her adorable feet of virgin snow, flowered two golden roses, the mystic roses of this divine mother's immaculate flesh.

Where was it that Bernadette had seen this Blessed Virgin, of such traditionally simple composition, unadorned by a single jewel, having but the primitive grace imagined by the painters of a people in its childhood? In which illustrated book belonging to her foster-mother's brother, the good priest, who read such attractive stories, had she beheld this Virgin? Or in what picture, or what statuette, or what stained-glass window of the painted and gilded church where she had spent so many evenings whilst growing up? And whence, above all things, had come those golden roses poised on the Virgin's feet, that piously imagined florescence of woman's flesh—from what romance of chivalry, from what story told after catechism by the Abbe Ader, from what unconscious dream indulged in under the shady foliage of Bartres, whilst ever and ever repeating that haunting Angelic Salutation?

Pierre's voice had acquired a yet more feeling tone, for if he did not say all these things to the simple-minded folks who were listening to him, still the human explanation of all these prodigies which the feeling of doubt in the depths of his being strove to supply, imparted to his narrative a quiver of sympathetic, fraternal love. He loved Bernadette the better for the great charm of her hallucination—that lady of such gracious access, such perfect amiability, such politeness in appearing and disappearing so appropriately. At first the great light would show itself, then the vision took form, came and went, leant forward, moved about, floating imperceptibly, with ethereal lightness; and when it vanished the glow lingered for yet another moment, and then disappeared like a star fading away. No lady in this world could have such a white and rosy face, with a beauty so akin to that of the Virgins on the picture-cards given to children at their first communions. And it was strange that the eglantine of the Grotto did not even hurt her adorable bare feet blooming with golden flowers.

Pierre, however, at once proceeded to recount the other apparitions. The fourth and fifth occurred on the Friday and the Saturday; but the Lady, who shone so brightly and who had not yet told her name, contented herself on these occasions with smiling and saluting without pronouncing a word. On the Sunday, however, she wept, and said to Bernadette, "Pray for sinners." On the Monday, to the child's great grief, she did not appear, wishing, no doubt, to try her. But on the Tuesday she confided to her a secret which concerned her (the girl) alone, a secret which she was never to divulge*; and then she at last told her what mission it was that she entrusted to her: "Go and tell the priests," she said, "that they must build a chapel here." On the Wednesday she frequently murmured the word "Penitence! penitence! penitence!" which the child repeated, afterwards kissing the earth. On the Thursday the Lady said to her: "Go, and drink, and wash at the spring, and eat of the grass that is beside it," words which the Visionary ended by understanding, when in the depths of the Grotto a source suddenly sprang up beneath her fingers. And this was the miracle of the enchanted fountain.

Then the second week ran its course. The lady did not appear on the Friday, but was punctual on the five following days, repeating her commands and gazing with a smile at the humble girl whom she had chosen to do her bidding, and who, on her side, duly told her beads at each apparition, kissed the earth, and repaired on her knees to the source, there to drink and wash. At last, on Thursday, March 4, the last

---

* In a like way, it will be remembered, the apparition at La Salette confided a secret to Melanie and Maximin (see *ante*, note). There can be little doubt that Bernadette was acquainted with the story of the miracle of La Salette.—Trans.

day of these mystical assignations, the Lady requested more pressingly than before that a chapel might be erected in order that the nations might come thither in procession from all parts of the earth. So far, however, in reply to all Bernadette's appeals, she had refused to say who she was; and it was only three weeks later, on Thursday, March 25, that, joining her hands together, and raising her eyes to Heaven, she said: "I am the Immaculate Conception." On two other occasions, at somewhat long intervals, April 7 and July 16, she again appeared: the first time to perform the miracle of the lighted taper, that taper above which the child, plunged in ecstasy, for a long time unconsciously left her hand, without burning it; and the second time to bid Bernadette farewell, to favour her with a last smile, and a last inclination of the head full of charming politeness. This made eighteen apparitions all told; and never again did the Lady show herself.

Whilst Pierre went on with his beautiful, marvellous story, so soothing to the wretched, he evoked for himself a vision of that pitiable, lovable Bernadette, whose sufferings had flowered so wonderfully. As a doctor had roughly expressed it, this girl of fourteen, at a critical period of her life, already ravaged, too, by asthma, was, after all, simply an exceptional victim of hysteria, afflicted with a degenerate heredity and lapsing into infancy. If there were no violent crises in her case, if there were no stiffening of the muscles during her attacks, if she retained a precise recollection of her dreams, the reason was that her case was peculiar to herself, and she added, so to say, a new and very curious form to all the forms of hysteria known at the time. Miracles only begin when things cannot be explained; and science, so far, knows and can explain so little, so infinitely do the phenomena of disease vary according to the nature of the patient! But how many shepherdesses there had been before Bernadette who had seen the Virgin in a similar way, amidst all the same childish nonsense! Was it not always the same story, the Lady clad in light, the secret confided, the spring bursting forth, the mission which had to be fulfilled, the miracles whose enchantments would convert the masses? And was not the personal appearance of the Virgin always in accordance with a poor child's dreams—akin to some coloured figure in a missal, an ideal compounded of traditional beauty, gentleness, and politeness. And the same dreams showed themselves in the naivete of the means which were to be employed and of the object which was to be attained—the deliverance of nations, the building of churches, the processional pilgrimages of the faithful! Then, too, all the words which fell from Heaven resembled one another, calls for penitence, promises of help; and in this respect, in Bernadette's case the only new feature was that most extraordinary declaration: "I am the Immaculate Conception," which burst forth—very usefully—as the recognition by the Blessed Virgin herself of the dogma promulgated by the Court of Rome but three years previously! It was not the Immaculate Virgin who appeared: no, it was the Immaculate Conception, the abstraction itself, the thing, the dogma, so that one might well ask oneself if really the Virgin had spoken in such a fashion. As for the other words, it was possible that Bernadette had heard them somewhere and stored them up in some unconscious nook of her memory. But these—"I am the Immaculate Conception"—whence had they come as though expressly to fortify a dogma—still bitterly discussed—with such prodigious support as the direct testimony of the Mother conceived without sin? At this thought, Pierre, who was convinced of Bernadette's absolute good faith, who refused to believe that she had been the instrument of a fraud, began to waver, deeply agitated, feeling his belief in truth totter within him.

The apparitions, however, had caused intense emotion at Lourdes; crowds flocked to the spot, miracles began, and those inevitable persecutions broke out which ensure the triumph of new religions. Abbe Peyramale, the parish priest of Lourdes, an extremely honest man, with an upright, vigorous mind, was able in all truth to declare that he did not know this child, that she had not yet been seen at catechism. Where was the pressure, then, where the lesson learnt by heart? There was nothing but those years of childhood spent at Bartres, the first teachings of Abbe Ader, conversations possibly, religious ceremonies in honour of the recently proclaimed dogma, or simply the gift of one of those commemorative medals which had been scattered in profusion. Never did Abbe Ader reappear upon the scene, he who had predicted the mission of the future Visionary. He was destined to remain apart from Bernadette and her future career, he who, the first, had seen her little soul blossom in his pious hands. And yet all the unknown forces that had sprung from that sequestered village, from that nook of greenery where superstition and poverty of intelligence prevailed, were still making themselves felt, disturbing the brains of men, disseminating the contagion of the mysterious. It was remembered that a shepherd of Argeles, speaking of the rock of Massabielle, had prophesied that great things would take place there. Other children, moreover, now fell in ecstasy with their eyes dilated and their limbs quivering with convulsions, but these only saw the devil. A whirlwind of madness seemed to be passing over the region. An old lady of Lourdes declared that Bernadette was simply a witch and that she had herself seen the toad's foot in her eye. But for the others, for the thousands of pilgrims who hastened to the spot, she was a saint, and they kissed her garments. Sobs burst forth and frenzy seemed to seize upon the souls of the beholders, when she fell upon her knees before the Grotto, a lighted taper in her right hand, whilst with the left she told the beads of her rosary. She became very pale and quite beautiful, transfigured, so to say. Her features gently ascended in her face, lengthened into an expression of extraordinary beatitude, whilst her eyes filled with light, and her lips parted as though she were speaking words which could not be heard. And it was quite certain that she had no will of her own left her, penetrated as she was by a dream, possessed by it to such a point in the confined, exclusive sphere in which she lived, that she continued dreaming it even when awake, and thus accepted it as the only indisputable reality, prepared to testify to it even at the cost of her blood, repeating it over and over again, obstinately, stubbornly clinging to it, and never varying in the details she gave. She did not lie, for she did not know, could not and would not desire anything apart from it.

Forgetful of the flight of time, Pierre was now sketching a charming picture of old Lourdes, that pious little town, slumbering at the foot of the Pyrenees. The castle, perched on a rock at the point of intersection of the seven valleys of Lavedan, had formerly been the key of the mountain districts. But, in Bernadette's time, it had become a mere dismantled, ruined pile, at the entrance of a road leading nowhere. Modern life found its march stayed by a formidable rampart of lofty, snow-capped peaks, and only the trans-Pyrenean railway—had it been constructed—could have established an active circulation of social life in that sequestered nook where human existence stagnated like dead water. Forgotten, therefore, Lourdes remained slumbering, happy and sluggish amidst its old-time peacefulness, with its narrow, pebble-paved streets and its bleak houses with dressings of marble. The old roofs were still all massed on the eastern side of the castle; the Rue de la Grotte, then called the Rue du Bois, was but a deserted and often impassable road; no houses stretched down to the Gave as now, and the scum-laden waters rolled through a perfect solitude of pollard willows and tall grass. On week-days but few people passed across the Place du Marcadal, such as housewives hastening on errands, and petty cits airing their leisure hours; and you had to wait till Sundays or fair days to find the inhabitants rigged out in their best clothes and assembled on the Champ Commun, in company with the crowd of graziers who had come down from the distant tablelands with their cattle. During the season when people resort to the Pyrenean-waters, the passage of the visitors to Cauterets and Bagneres also brought some animation; *diligences* passed through the town twice a day, but they came from Pau by a wretched road, and had to ford the Lapaca, which often overflowed its banks. Then climbing the steep ascent of the Rue Basse, they skirted the terrace of the church, which was shaded by large elms. And what soft peacefulness prevailed in and around that old semi-Spanish church, full of ancient carvings, columns, screens, and statues, peopled with visionary patches of gilding and painted flesh, which time had mellowed and which you faintly discerned as by the light of mystical lamps! The whole population came there to worship, to fill their eyes with the dream of the mysterious. There were no unbelievers, the inhabitants of Lourdes were a people of primitive faith; each corporation marched behind the banner of its saint, brotherhoods of all kinds united the entire town, on festival mornings, in one large Christian family. And, as with some exquisite flower that has grown in the soil of its choice, great purity of life reigned there. There was not even a resort of debauchery for young men to wreck their lives, and the girls, one and all, grew up with the perfume and beauty of innocence, under the eyes of the Blessed Virgin, Tower of Ivory and Seat of Wisdom.

And how well one could understand that Bernadette, born in that holy soil, should flower in it, like one of nature's roses budding in the wayside bushes! She was indeed the very florescence of that region of ancient belief and rectitude; she would certainly not have sprouted elsewhere; she could only appear and develop there, amidst that belated race, amidst the slumberous peacefulness of a childlike people, under the moral discipline of religion. And what intense love at once burst forth all around her! What blind confidence was displayed in her mission, what immense consolation and hope came to human hearts on the very morrow of the first miracles! A long cry of relief had greeted the cure of old Bourriette recovering his sight, and of little Justin Bouhohorts coming to life again in the icy water of the spring. At last, then, the Blessed Virgin was intervening in favour of those who despaired, forcing that unkind mother, Nature, to be just and charitable.

This was divine omnipotence returning to reign on earth, sweeping the laws of the world aside in order to work the happiness of the suffering and the poor. The miracles multiplied, blazed forth, from day to day more and more extraordinary, like unimpeachable proof of Bernadette's veracity. And she was, indeed, the rose of the divine garden, whose deeds shed perfume, the rose who beholds all the other flowers of grace and salvation spring into being around her.

Pierre had reached this point of his story, and was again enumerating the miracles, on the point of recounting the prodigious triumph of the Grotto, when Sister Hyacinthe, awaking with a start from the ecstasy into which the narrative had plunged her, hastily rose to her feet. "Really, really," said she, "there is no sense in it. It will soon be eleven o'clock."

This was true. They had left Morceux behind them, and would now soon be at Mont de Marsan. So Sister Hyacinthe clapped her hands once more, and added: "Silence, my children, silence!"

This time they did not dare to rebel, for they felt she was in the right; they were unreasonable. But how greatly they regretted not hearing the continuation, how vexed they were that the story should cease when only half told! The ten women in the farther compartment even let a murmur of disappointment escape them; whilst the sick, their faces still outstretched, their dilated eyes gazing upon the light of hope, seemed to be yet listening. Those miracles which ever and ever returned to their minds and filled them with unlimited, haunting, supernatural joy.

"And don't let me hear anyone breathe, even," added Sister Hyacinthe gaily, "or otherwise I shall impose penance on you."

Madame de Jonquiere laughed good-naturedly. "You must obey, my children," she said; "be good and get to sleep, so that you may have strength to pray at the Grotto to-morrow with all your hearts."

Then silence fell, nobody spoke any further; and the only sounds were those of the rumbling of the wheels and the jolting of the train as it was carried along at full speed through the black night.

Pierre, however, was unable to sleep. Beside him, M. de Guersaint was already snoring lightly, looking very happy despite the hardness of his seat. For a time the young priest saw Marie's eyes wide open, still full of all the radiance of the marvels that he had related. For a long while she kept them ardently fixed upon his own, but at last closed them, and then he knew not whether she was sleeping, or with eyelids simply closed was living the everlasting miracle over again. Some of the sufferers were dreaming aloud, giving vent to bursts of laughter which unconscious moans interrupted. Perhaps they beheld the Archangels opening their flesh to wrest their diseases from them. Others, restless with insomnia, turned over and over, stifling their sobs and gazing fixedly into the darkness. And, with a shudder born of all the mystery he had evoked, Pierre, distracted, no longer master of himself in that delirious sphere of fraternal suffering, ended by hating his very mind, and, drawn into close communion with all those humble folks, sought to believe like them. What could be the use of that physiological inquiry into Bernadette's case, so full of gaps and intricacies? Why should he not accept her as a messenger from the spheres beyond, as one of the elect chosen for the divine mystery? Doctors were but ignorant men with rough and brutal hands, and it would be so delightful to fall asleep in childlike faith, in the enchanted gardens of the impossible. And for a moment indeed he surrendered himself, experiencing a delightful feeling of comfort, no longer seeking to explain anything, but accepting the Visionary with her sumptuous *cortege* of miracles, and relying on God to think and determine for him. Then he looked out through the window, which they did not dare to open on account of the consumptive patients, and beheld the immeasurable night which enwrapped the country across which the train was fleeing. The storm must have burst forth there; the sky was now of an admirable nocturnal purity, as though cleansed by the masses of fallen water. Large stars shone out in the dark velvet, alone illumining, with their mysterious gleams, the silent, refreshed fields, which incessantly displayed only the black solitude of slumber. And across the Landes, through the valleys, between the hills, that carriage of wretchedness and suffering rolled on and on, over-heated, pestilential, rueful, and wailing, amidst the serenity of the august night, so lovely and so mild.

They had passed Riscle at one in the morning. Between the jolting, the painful, the hallucinatory silence still continued. At two o'clock, as they reached Vic-de-Bigorre, low moans were heard; the bad state of the line, with the unbearable spreading tendency of the train's motion, was sorely shaking the patients. It was only at Tarbes, at half-past two, that silence was at length broken, and that morning prayers were said, though black night still reigned around them. There came first the "Pater," and then the "Ave," the "Credo," and the supplication to God to grant them the happiness of a glorious day.

"O God, vouchsafe me sufficient strength that I may avoid all that is evil, do all that is good, and suffer uncomplainingly every pain."

And now there was to be no further stoppage until they reached Lourdes. Barely three more quarters of an hour, and Lourdes, with all its vast hopes, would blaze forth in the midst of that night, so long and cruel. Their painful awakening was enfevered by the thought; a final agitation arose amidst the morning discomfort, as the abominable sufferings began afresh.

Sister Hyacinthe, however, was especially anxious about the strange man, whose sweat-covered face she had been continually wiping. He had so far managed to keep alive, she watching him without a pause, never having once closed her eyes, but unremittingly listening to his faint breathing with the stubborn desire to take him to the holy Grotto before he died.

All at once, however, she felt frightened; and addressing Madame de Jonquiere, she hastily exclaimed, "Pray pass me the vinegar bottle at once—I can no longer hear him breathe."

For an instant, indeed, the man's faint breathing had ceased. His eyes were still closed, his lips parted; he could not have been paler, he had an ashen hue, and was cold. And the carriage was rolling along with its ceaseless rattle of coupling-irons; the speed of the train seemed even to have increased.

"I will rub his temples," resumed Sister Hyacinthe. "Help me, do!"

But, at a more violent jolt of the train, the man suddenly fell from the seat, face downward.

"Ah! *mon Dieu*, help me, pick him up!"

They picked him up, and found him dead. And they had to seat him in his corner again, with his back resting against the woodwork. He remained there erect, his torso stiffened, and his head wagging slightly at each successive jolt. Thus the train continued carrying him along, with the same thundering noise of wheels, while the engine, well pleased, no doubt, to be reaching its destination, began whistling shrilly, giving vent to quite a flourish of delirious joy as it sped through the calm night.

And then came the last and seemingly endless half-hour of the journey, in company with that wretched corpse. Two big tears had rolled down Sister Hyacinthe's cheeks, and with her hands joined she had begun to pray. The whole carriage shuddered with terror at sight of that terrible companion who was being taken, too late alas! to the Blessed Virgin.

Hope, however, proved stronger than sorrow or pain, and although all the sufferings there assembled awoke and grew again, irritated by overwhelming weariness, a song of joy nevertheless proclaimed the sufferers' triumphal entry into the Land of Miracles. Amidst the tears which their pains drew from them, the exasperated and howling sick began to chant the "Ave maris Stella" with a growing clamour in which lamentation finally turned into cries of hope.

Marie had again taken Pierre's hand between her little feverish fingers. "Oh, *mon Dieu!*" said she, "to think that poor man is dead, and I feared so much that it was I who would die before arriving. And we are there—there at last!"

The priest was trembling with intense emotion. "It means that you are to be cured, Marie," he replied, "and that I myself shall be cured if you pray for me—"

The engine was now whistling in a yet louder key in the depths of the bluish darkness. They were nearing their destination. The lights of Lourdes already shone out on the horizon. Then the whole train again sang a canticle—the rhymed story of Bernadette, that endless ballad of six times ten couplets, in which the Angelic Salutation ever returns as a refrain, all besetting and distracting, opening to the human mind the portals of the heaven of ecstasy:—

> *"It was the hour for ev'ning pray'r;*
> *Soft bells chimed on the chilly air.*
> *Ave, ave, ave Maria!*

> *"The maid stood on the torrent's bank,*
> *A breeze arose, then swiftly sank.*
> *Ave, ave, ave Maria!*

> *"And she beheld, e'en as it fell,*
> *The Virgin on Massabielle.*
> *Ave, ave, ave Maria!*

> *"All white appeared the Lady chaste,*
> *A zone of Heaven round her waist.*
> *Ave, ave, ave Maria!*

> *"Two golden roses, pure and sweet,*
> *Bloomed brightly on her naked feet.*
> *Ave, ave, ave Maria!*

"Upon her arm, so white and round,
Her chaplet's milky pearls were wound.
Ave, ave, ave Maria!

"The maiden prayed till, from her eyes,
The vision sped to Paradise.
Ave, ave, ave Maria!"

ÉMILE ZOLA

THE SECOND DAY

I

The Train Arrives

It was twenty minutes past three by the clock of the Lourdes railway station, the dial of which was illumined by a reflector. Under the slanting roof sheltering the platform, a hundred yards or so in length, some shadowy forms went to and fro, resignedly waiting. Only a red signal light peeped out of the black countryside, far away.

Two of the promenaders suddenly halted. The taller of them, a Father of the Assumption, none other indeed than the Reverend Father Fourcade, director of the national pilgrimage, who had reached Lourdes on the previous day, was a man of sixty, looking superb in his black cloak with its large hood. His fine head, with its clear, domineering eyes and thick grizzly beard, was the head of a general whom an intelligent determination to conquer inflames. In consequence, however, of a sudden attack of gout he slightly dragged one of his legs, and was leaning on the shoulder of his companion, Dr. Bonamy, the practitioner attached to the Miracle Verification Office, a short, thick-set man, with a square-shaped, clean-shaven face, which had dull, blurred eyes and a tranquil cast of features.

Father Fourcade had stopped to question the station-master whom he perceived running out of his office. "Will the white train be very late, monsieur?" he asked.

"No, your reverence. It hasn't lost more than ten minutes; it will be here at the half-hour. It's the Bayonne train which worries me; it ought to have passed through already."

So saying, he ran off to give an order; but soon came back again, his slim, nervous figure displaying marked signs of agitation. He lived, indeed, in a state of high fever throughout the period of the great pilgrimages. Apart from the usual service, he that day expected eighteen trains, containing more than fifteen thousand passengers. The grey and the blue trains which had started from Paris the first had already arrived at the regulation hour. But the delay in the arrival of the white train was very troublesome, the more so as the Bayonne express—which passed over the same rails—had not yet been signalled. It was easy to understand, therefore, what incessant watchfulness was necessary, not a second passing without the entire staff of the station being called upon to exercise its vigilance.

"In ten minutes, then?" repeated Father Fourcade.

"Yes, in ten minutes, unless I'm obliged to close the line!" cried the station-master as he hastened into the telegraph office.

Father Fourcade and the doctor slowly resumed their promenade. The thing which astonished them was that no serious accident had ever happened in the midst of such a fearful scramble. In past times, especially, the most terrible disorder had prevailed. Father Fourcade complacently recalled the first pilgrimage which he had organised and led, in 1875; the terrible endless journey without pillows or mattresses, the patients exhausted, half dead, with no means of reviving them at hand; and then the arrival at Lourdes, the train evacuated in confusion, no *materiel* in readiness, no straps, nor stretchers, nor carts. But now there was a powerful organisation; a hospital awaited the sick, who were no longer reduced to lying upon straw in sheds. What a shock for those unhappy ones! What force of will in the man of faith who led them to the scene of miracles! The reverend Father smiled gently at the thought of the work which he had accomplished.

Then, still leaning on the doctor's shoulder, he began to question him: "How many pilgrims did you have last year?" he asked.

"About two hundred thousand. That is still the average. In the year of the Coronation of the Virgin the figure rose to five hundred thousand. But to bring that about an exceptional occasion was needed with a great effort of propaganda. Such vast masses cannot be collected together every day."

A pause followed, and then Father Fourcade murmured: "No doubt. Still the blessing of Heaven attends our endeavours; our work thrives more and more. We have collected more than two hundred thousand francs in donations for this journey, and God will be with us, there will be many cures for you to proclaim to-morrow, I am sure of it." Then, breaking off, he inquired: "Has not Father Dargeles come here?"

Dr. Bonamy waved his hand as though to say that he did not know. Father Dargeles was the editor of the "Journal de la Grotte." He belonged to the Order of the Fathers of the Immaculate Conception whom the Bishop had installed at Lourdes and who were the absolute masters there; though, when the Fathers of the Assumption came to the town with the national pilgrimage from Paris, which crowds of faithful Catholics from Cambrai, Arras, Chartres, Troyes, Rheims, Sens, Orleans, Blois, and Poitiers joined, they evinced a kind of affectation in disappearing from the scene. Their omnipotence was no longer felt either at the Grotto or at the Basilica; they seemed to surrender every key together with every responsibility. Their superior, Father Capdebarthe, a tall, peasant-like man, with a knotty frame, a big head which looked as if it had been fashioned with a bill-hook, and a worn face which retained a ruddy mournful reflection of the soil, did not even show himself. Of the whole community you only saw little, insinuating Father Dargeles; but he was met everywhere, incessantly on the look-out for paragraphs for his newspaper. At the same time, however, although the Fathers of the Immaculate Conception disappeared in this fashion, it could be divined that they were behind the vast stage, like a hidden sovereign power, coining money and toiling without a pause to increase the triumphant prosperity of their business. Indeed, they turned even their humility to account.

"It's true that we have had to get up early—two in the morning," resumed Father Fourcade gaily. "But I wished to be here. What would my poor children have said, indeed, if I had not come?"

He was alluding to the sick pilgrims, those who were so much flesh for miracle-working; and it was a fact that he had never missed coming to the station, no matter what the hour, to meet that woeful white train, that train which brought such grievous suffering with it.

"Five-and-twenty minutes past three—only another five minutes now," exclaimed Dr. Bonamy repressing a yawn as he glanced at the clock; for, despite his obsequious air, he was at bottom very much annoyed at having had to get out of bed so early. However, he continued his slow promenade with Father Fourcade along that platform which resembled a covered walk, pacing up and down in the dense night which the gas jets here and there illumined with patches of yellow light. Little parties, dimly outlined, composed of priests and gentlemen in frock-coats, with a solitary officer of dragoons, went to and fro incessantly, talking together the while in discreet murmuring tones. Other people, seated on benches, ranged along the station wall, were also chatting or putting their patience to proof with their glances wandering away into the black stretch of country before them. The doorways of the offices and waiting-rooms, which were brilliantly lighted, looked like great holes in the darkness, and all was flaring in the refreshment-room, where you could see the marble tables and the counter laden with bottles and glasses and baskets of bread and fruit.

On the right hand, beyond the roofing of the platform, there was a confused swarming of people. There was here a goods gate, by which the sick were taken out of the station, and a mass of stretchers, litters, and hand-carts, with piles of pillows and mattresses, obstructed the broad walk. Three parties of bearers were also assembled here, persons of well-nigh every class, but more particularly young men of good society, all wearing red, orange-tipped crosses and straps of yellow leather. Many of them, too, had adopted the Bearnese cap, the convenient head-gear of the region; and a few, clad as though they were bound on some distant expedition, displayed wonderful gaiters reaching to their knees. Some were smoking, whilst others, installed in their little vehicles, slept or read newspapers by the light of the neighbouring gas jets. One group, standing apart, were discussing some service question.

Suddenly, however, one and all began to salute. A paternal-looking man, with a heavy but good-natured face, lighted by large blue eyes, like those of a credulous child, was approaching. It was Baron Suire, the President of the Hospitality of Our Lady of Salvation. He possessed a great fortune and occupied a high position at Toulouse.

"Where is Berthaud?" he inquired of one bearer after another, with a busy air. "Where is Berthaud? I must speak to him."

The others answered, volunteering contradictory information. Berthaud was their superintendent, and whilst some said that they had seen him with the Reverend Father Fourcade, others affirmed that he must be in the courtyard of the station inspecting the ambulance vehicles. And they thereupon offered to go and fetch him.

"No, no, thank you," replied the Baron. "I shall manage to find him myself."

Whilst this was happening, Berthaud, who had just seated himself on a bench at the other end of the station, was talking with his young friend, Gerard de Peyrelongue, by way of occupation pending the arrival of the train. The superintendent of the bearers was a man of forty, with a broad, regular-featured, handsome face and carefully trimmed whiskers of a lawyer-like pattern. Belonging to a militant Legitimist family and holding extremely reactionary opinions, he had been Procureur de la Republique (public prosecutor) in a town of the south of France from the time of the parliamentary revolution of the twenty-fourth of May[*] until that of the decree of the Religious Communities,[**] when he had

---

[*] The parliamentary revolution of May, 1873, by which M. Thiers was overthrown and Marshal MacMahon installed in his place with the object of restoring the Monarchy in France.—Trans.

[**] M. Grevy's decree by which the Jesuits were expelled.—Trans.

resigned his post in a blusterous fashion, by addressing an insulting letter to the Minister of Justice. And he had never since laid down his arms, but had joined the Hospitality of Our Lady of Salvation as a sort of protest, repairing year after year to Lourdes in order to "demonstrate"; convinced as he was that the pilgrimages were both disagreeable and hurtful to the Republic, and that God alone could re-establish the Monarchy by one of those miracles which He worked so lavishly at the Grotto. Despite all this, however, Berthaud possessed no small amount of good sense, and being of a gay disposition, displayed a kind of jovial charity towards the poor sufferers whose transport he had to provide for during the three days that the national pilgrimage remained at Lourdes.

"And so, my dear Gerard," he said to the young man seated beside him, "your marriage is really to come off this year?"

"Why yes, if I can find such a wife as I want," replied the other. "Come, cousin, give me some good advice."

Gerard de Peyrelongue, a short, thin, carroty young man, with a pronounced nose and prominent cheek-bones, belonged to Tarbes, where his father and mother had lately died, leaving him at the utmost some seven or eight thousand francs a year. Extremely ambitious, he had been unable to find such a wife as he desired in his native province—a well-connected young woman capable of helping him to push both forward and upward in the world; and so he had joined the Hospitality, and betook himself every summer to Lourdes, in the vague hope that amidst the mass of believers, the torrent of devout mammas and daughters which flowed thither, he might find the family whose help he needed to enable him to make his way in this terrestrial sphere. However, he remained in perplexity, for if, on the one hand, he already had several young ladies in view, on the other, none of them completely satisfied him.

"Eh, cousin? You will advise me, won't you?" he said to Berthaud. "You are a man of experience. There is Mademoiselle Lemercier who comes here with her aunt. She is very rich; according to what is said she has over a million francs. But she doesn't belong to our set, and besides I think her a bit of a madcap."

Berthaud nodded. "I told you so; if I were you I should choose little Raymonde, Mademoiselle de Jonquiere."

"But she hasn't a copper!"

"That's true—she has barely enough to pay for her board. But she is fairly good-looking, she has been well brought up, and she has no extravagant tastes. That is the really important point, for what is the use of marrying a rich girl if she squanders the dowry she brings you? Besides, I know Madame and Mademoiselle de Jonquiere very well, I meet them all through the winter in the most influential drawing-rooms of Paris. And, finally, don't forget the girl's uncle, the diplomatist, who has had the painful courage to remain in the service of the Republic. He will be able to do whatever he pleases for his niece's husband."

For a moment Gerard seemed shaken, and then he relapsed into perplexity. "But she hasn't a copper," he said, "no, not a copper. It's too stiff. I am quite willing to think it over, but it really frightens me too much."

This time Berthaud burst into a frank laugh. "Come, you are ambitious, so you must be daring. I tell you that it means the secretaryship of an embassy before two years are over. By the way, Madame and Mademoiselle de Jonquiere are in the white train which we are waiting for. Make up your mind and pay your court at once."

"No, no! Later on. I want to think it over."

At this moment they were interrupted, for Baron Suire, who had already once gone by without perceiving them, so completely did the darkness enshroud them in that retired corner, had just recognised the ex-public prosecutor's good-natured laugh. And, thereupon, with the volubility of a man whose head is easily unhinged, he gave him several orders respecting the vehicles and the transport service, deploring the circumstance that it would be impossible to conduct the patients to the Grotto immediately on their arrival, as it was yet so extremely early. It had therefore been decided that they should in the first instance be taken to the Hospital of Our Lady of Dolours, where they would be able to rest awhile after their trying journey.

Whilst the Baron and the superintendent were thus settling what measures should be adopted, Gerard shook hands with a priest who had sat down beside him. This was the Abbe des Hermoises, who was barely eight-and-thirty years of age and had a superb head—such a head as one might expect to find on the shoulders of a worldly priest. With his hair well combed, and his person perfumed, he was not unnaturally a great favourite among women. Very amiable and distinguished in his manners, he did not come to Lourdes in any official capacity, but simply for his pleasure, as so many other people did; and the bright, sparkling smile of a sceptic above all idolatry gleamed in the depths of his fine eyes. He certainly believed, and bowed to superior decisions; but the

ÉMILE ZOLA

Church—the Holy See—had not pronounced itself with regard to the miracles; and he seemed quite ready to dispute their authenticity. Having lived at Tarbes he was already acquainted with Gerard.

"Ah!" he said to him, "how impressive it is—isn't it?—this waiting for the trains in the middle of the night! I have come to meet a lady— one of my former Paris penitents—but I don't know what train she will come by. Still, as you see, I stop on, for it all interests me so much."

Then another priest, an old country priest, having come to sit down on the same bench, the Abbe considerately began talking to him, speaking of the beauty of the Lourdes district and of the theatrical effect which would take place by-and-by when the sun rose and the mountains appeared.

However, there was again a sudden alert, and the station-master ran along shouting orders. Removing his hand from Dr. Bonamy's shoulder, Father Fourcade, despite his gouty leg, hastily drew near.

"Oh! it's that Bayonne express which is so late," answered the station-master in reply to the questions addressed to him. "I should like some information about it; I'm not at ease."

At this moment the telegraph bells rang out and a porter rushed away into the darkness swinging a lantern, whilst a distant signal began to work. Thereupon the station-master resumed: "Ah! this time it's the white train. Let us hope we shall have time to get the sick people out before the express passes."

He started off once more and disappeared. Berthaud meanwhile called to Gerard, who was at the head of a squad of bearers, and they both made haste to join their men, into whom Baron Suire was already instilling activity. The bearers flocked to the spot from all sides, and setting themselves in motion began dragging their little vehicles across the lines to the platform at which the white train would come in—an unroofed platform plunged in darkness. A mass of pillows, mattresses, stretchers, and litters was soon waiting there, whilst Father Fourcade, Dr. Bonamy, the priests, the gentlemen, and the officer of dragoons in their turn crossed over in order to witness the removal of the ailing pilgrims. All that they could as yet see, far away in the depths of the black country, was the lantern in front of the engine, looking like a red star which grew larger and larger. Strident whistles pierced the night, then suddenly ceased, and you only heard the panting of the steam and the dull roar of the wheels gradually slackening their speed. Then the canticle became distinctly audible, the song of Bernadette with the ever-recurring "Aves" of its refrain, which the whole train was chanting in chorus. And at last this train of suffering and faith, this moaning, singing train, thus making its entry into Lourdes, drew up in the station.

The carriage doors were at once opened, the whole throng of healthy pilgrims, and of ailing ones able to walk, alighted, and streamed over the platform. The few gas lamps cast but a feeble light on the crowd of poverty-stricken beings clad in faded garments, and encumbered with all sorts of parcels, baskets, valises, and boxes. And amidst all the jostling of this scared flock, which did not know in which direction to turn to find its way out of the station, loud exclamations were heard, the shouts of people calling relatives whom they had lost, mingled with the embraces of others whom relatives or friends had come to meet. One woman declared with beatifical satisfaction, "I have slept well." A priest went off carrying his travelling-bag, after wishing a crippled lady "good luck!" Most of them had the bewildered, weary, yet joyous appearance of people whom an excursion train sets down at some unknown station. And such became the scramble and the confusion in the darkness, that they did not hear the railway *employes* who grew quite hoarse through shouting, "This way! this way!" in their eagerness to clear the platform as soon as possible.

Sister Hyacinthe had nimbly alighted from her compartment, leaving the dead man in the charge of Sister Claire des Anges; and, losing her head somewhat, she ran off to the cantine van in the idea that Ferrand would be able to help her. Fortunately she found Father Fourcade in front of the van and acquainted him with the fatality in a low voice. Repressing a gesture of annoyance, he thereupon called Baron Suire, who was passing, and began whispering in his ear. The muttering lasted for a few seconds, and then the Baron rushed off, and clove his way through the crowd with two bearers carrying a covered litter. In this the man was removed from the carriage as though he were a patient who had simply fainted, the mob of pilgrims paying no further attention to him amidst all the emotion of their arrival. Preceded by the Baron, the bearers carried the corpse into a goods office, where they provisionally lodged it behind some barrels; one of them, a fair-haired little fellow, a general's son, remaining to watch over it.

Meanwhile, after begging Ferrand and Sister Saint-Francois to go and wait for her in the courtyard of the station, near the reserved vehicle which was to take them to the Hospital of Our Lady of Dolours, Sister

Hyacinthe returned to the railway carriage and talked of helping her patients to alight before going away. But Marie would not let her touch her. "No, no!" said the girl, "do not trouble about me, Sister. I shall remain here the last. My father and Abbe Froment have gone to the van to fetch the wheels; I am waiting for their return; they know how to fix them, and they will take me away all right, you may be sure of it."

In the same way M. Sabathier and Brother Isidore did not desire to be moved until the crowd had decreased. Madame de Jonquiere, who had taken charge of La Grivotte, also promised to see to Madame Vetu's removal in an ambulance vehicle. And thereupon Sister Hyacinthe decided that she would go off at once so as to get everything ready at the hospital. Moreover, she took with her both little Sophie Couteau and Elise Rouquet, whose face she very carefully wrapped up. Madame Maze preceded them, while Madame Vincent, carrying her little girl, who was unconscious and quite white, struggled through the crowd, possessed by the fixed idea of running off as soon as possible and depositing the child in the Grotto at the feet of the Blessed Virgin.

The mob was now pressing towards the doorway by which passengers left the station, and to facilitate the egress of all these people it at last became necessary to open the luggage gates. The *employes*, at a loss how to take the tickets, held out their caps, which a downpour of the little cards speedily filled. And in the courtyard, a large square courtyard, skirted on three sides by the low buildings of the station, the most extraordinary uproar prevailed amongst all the vehicles of divers kinds which were there jumbled together. The hotel omnibuses, backed against the curb of the footway, displayed the most sacred names on their large boards—Jesus and Mary, St. Michel, the Rosary, and the Sacred Heart. Then there were ambulance vehicles, landaus, cabriolets, brakes, and little donkey carts, all entangled together, with their drivers shouting, swearing, and cracking their whips—the tumult being apparently increased by the obscurity in which the lanterns set brilliant patches of light.

Rain had fallen heavily a few hours previously. Liquid mud splashed up under the hoofs of the horses; the foot passengers sank into it to their ankles. M. Vigneron, whom Madame Vigneron and Madame Chaise were following in a state of distraction, raised Gustave, in order to place him in the omnibus from the Hotel of the Apparitions, after which he himself and the ladies climbed into the vehicle. Madame Maze, shuddering slightly, like a delicate tabby who fears to dirty the tips of her paws, made a sign to the driver of an old brougham, got into it, and quickly drove away, after giving as address the Convent of the Blue Sisters. And at last Sister Hyacinthe was able to install herself with Elise Rouquet and Sophie Couteau in a large *char-a-bancs*, in which Ferrand and Sisters Saint-Francois and Claire des Anges were already seated. The drivers whipped up their spirited little horses, and the vehicles went off at a breakneck pace, amidst the shouts of those left behind, and the splashing of the mire.

In presence of that rushing torrent, Madame Vincent, with her dear little burden in her arms, hesitated to cross over. Bursts of laughter rang out around her every now and then. Oh! what a filthy mess! And at sight of all the mud, the women caught up their skirts before attempting to pass through it. At last, when the courtyard had somewhat emptied, Madame Vincent herself ventured on her way, all terror lest the mire should make her fall in that black darkness. Then, on reaching a downhill road, she noticed there a number of women of the locality who were on the watch, offering furnished rooms, bed and board, according to the state of the pilgrim's purse.

"Which is the way to the Grotto, madame, if you please?" asked Madame Vincent, addressing one old woman of the party.

Instead of answering the question, however, the other offered her a cheap room. "You won't find anything in the hotels," said she, "for they are all full. Perhaps you will be able to eat there, but you certainly won't find a closet even to sleep in."

Eat, sleep, indeed! Had Madame Vincent any thought of such things; she who had left Paris with thirty sous in her pocket, all that remained to her after the expenses she had been put to!

"The way to the Grotto, if you please, madame?" she repeated.

Among the women who were thus touting for lodgers, there was a tall, well-built girl, dressed like a superior servant, and looking very clean, with carefully tended hands. She glanced at Madame Vincent and slightly shrugged her shoulders. And then, seeing a broad-chested priest with a red face go by, she rushed after him, offered him a furnished room, and continued following him, whispering in his ear.

Another girl, however, at last took pity on Madame Vincent and said to her: "Here, go down this road, and when you get to the bottom, turn to the right and you will reach the Grotto."

Meanwhile, the confusion inside the station continued. The healthy pilgrims, and those of the sick who retained the use of their legs could go off, thus, in some measure, clearing the platform; but the others, the more grievously stricken sufferers whom it was difficult to get out of the carriages and remove to the hospital, remained waiting. The bearers seemed to become quite bewildered, rushing madly hither and thither with their litters and vehicles, not knowing at what end to set about the profusion of work which lay before them.

As Berthaud, followed by Gerard, went along the platform, gesticulating, he noticed two ladies and a girl who were standing under a gas jet and to all appearance waiting. In the girl he recognised Raymonde, and with a sign of the hand he at once stopped his companion. "Ah! mademoiselle," said he, "how pleased I am to see you! Is Madame de Jonquiere quite well? You have made a good journey, I hope?" Then, without a pause, he added: "This is my friend, Monsieur Gerard de Peyrelongue."

Raymonde gazed fixedly at the young man with her clear, smiling eyes. "Oh! I already have the pleasure of being slightly acquainted with this gentleman," she said. "We have previously met one another at Lourdes."

Thereupon Gerard, who thought that his cousin Berthaud was conducting matters too quickly, and was quite resolved that he would not enter into any hasty engagement, contented himself with bowing in a ceremonious way.

"We are waiting for mamma," resumed Raymonde. "She is extremely busy; she has to see after some pilgrims who are very ill."

At this, little Madame Desagneaux, with her pretty, light wavy-haired head, began to say that it served Madame de Jonquiere right for refusing her services. She herself was stamping with impatience, eager to join in the work and make herself useful, whilst Madame Volmar, silent, shrinking back as though taking no interest in it at all, seemed simply desirous of penetrating the darkness, as though, indeed, she were seeking somebody with those magnificent eyes of hers, usually bedimmed, but now shining out like brasiers.

Just then, however, they were all pushed back. Madame Dieulafay was being removed from her first-class compartment, and Madame Desagneaux could not restrain an exclamation of pity. "Ah! the poor woman!"

There could in fact be no more distressing sight than this young woman, encompassed by luxury, covered with lace in her species of coffin, so wasted that she seemed to be a mere human shred, deposited on that platform till it could be taken away. Her husband and her sister, both very elegant and very sad, remained standing near her, whilst a man-servant and maid ran off with the valises to ascertain if the carriage which had been ordered by telegram was in the courtyard. Abbe Judaine also helped the sufferer; and when two men at last took her up he bent over her and wished her *au revoir*, adding some kind words which she did not seem to hear. Then as he watched her removal, he resumed, addressing himself to Berthaud, whom he knew: "Ah! the poor people, if they could only purchase their dear sufferer's cure. I told them that prayer was the most precious thing in the Blessed Virgin's eyes, and I hope that I have myself prayed fervently enough to obtain the compassion of Heaven. Nevertheless, they have brought a magnificent gift, a golden lantern for the Basilica, a perfect marvel, adorned with precious stones. May the Immaculate Virgin deign to smile upon it!"

In this way a great many offerings were brought by the pilgrims. Some huge bouquets of flowers had just gone by, together with a kind of triple crown of roses, mounted on a wooden stand. And the old priest explained that before leaving the station he wished to secure a banner, the gift of the beautiful Madame Jousseur, Madame Dieulafay's sister.

Madame de Jonquiere was at last approaching, however, and on perceiving Berthaud and Gerard she exclaimed: "Pray do go to that carriage, gentlemen—that one, there! We want some men very badly. There are three or four sick persons to be taken out. I am in despair; I can do nothing myself."

Gerard ran off after bowing to Raymonde, whilst Berthaud advised Madame de Jonquiere to leave the station with her daughter and those ladies instead of remaining on the platform. Her presence was in nowise necessary, he said; he would undertake everything, and within three quarters of an hour she would find her patients in her ward at the hospital. She ended by giving way, and took a conveyance in company with Raymonde and Madame Desagneaux. As for Madame Volmar, she had at the last moment disappeared, as though seized with a sudden fit of impatience. The others fancied that they had seen her approach a strange gentleman, with the object no doubt of making some inquiry of him. However, they would of course find her at the hospital.

Berthaud joined Gerard again just as the young man, assisted by two fellow-bearers, was endeavouring to remove M. Sabathier from the carriage. It was a difficult task, for he was very stout and very heavy,

ÉMILE ZOLA

and they began to think that he would never pass through the doorway of the compartment. However, as he had been got in they ought to be able to get him out; and indeed when two other bearers had entered the carriage from the other side, they were at last able to deposit him on the platform.

The dawn was now appearing, a faint pale dawn; and the platform presented the woeful appearance of an improvised hospital. La Grivotte, who had lost consciousness, lay there on a mattress pending her removal in a litter; whilst Madame Vetu had been seated against a lamp-post, suffering so severely from another attack of her ailment that they scarcely dared to touch her. Some hospitallers, whose hands were gloved, were with difficulty wheeling their little vehicles in which were poor, sordid-looking women with old baskets at their feet. Others, with stretchers on which lay the stiffened, woeful bodies of silent sufferers, whose eyes gleamed with anguish, found themselves unable to pass; but some of the infirm pilgrims, some unfortunate cripples, contrived to slip through the ranks, among them a young priest who was lame, and a little humpbacked boy, one of whose legs had been amputated, and who, looking like a gnome, managed to drag himself with his crutches from group to group. Then there was quite a block around a man who was bent in half, twisted by paralysis to such a point that he had to be carried on a chair with his head and feet hanging downward. It seemed as though hours would be required to clear the platform.

The dismay therefore reached a climax when the station-master suddenly rushed up shouting: "The Bayonne express is signalled. Make haste! make haste! You have only three minutes left!"

Father Fourcade, who had remained in the midst of the throng, leaning on Doctor Bonamy's arm, and gaily encouraging the more stricken of the sufferers, beckoned to Berthaud and said to him: "Finish taking them out of the train; you will be able to clear the platform afterwards!"

The advice was very sensible, and in accordance with it they finished placing the sufferers on the platform. In Madame de Jonquière's carriage Marie now alone remained, waiting patiently. M. de Guersaint and Pierre had at last returned to her, bringing the two pairs of wheels by means of which the box in which she lay was rolled about. And with Gerard's assistance Pierre in all haste removed the girl from the train. She was as light as a poor shivering bird, and it was only the box that gave them any trouble. However, they soon placed it on the wheels and made the latter fast, and then Pierre might have rolled Marie away had it not been for the crowd which hampered him.

"Make haste! make haste!" furiously repeated the station-master.

He himself lent a hand, taking hold of a sick man by the feet in order to remove him from the compartment more speedily. And he also pushed the little hand-carts back, so as to clear the edge of the platform. In a second-class carriage, however, there still remained one woman who had just been overpowered by a terrible nervous attack. She was howling and struggling, and it was impossible to think of touching her at that moment. But on the other hand the express, signalled by the incessant tinkling of the electric bells, was now fast approaching, and they had to close the door and in all haste shunt the train to the siding where it would remain for three days, until in fact it was required to convey its load of sick and healthy passengers back to Paris. As it went off to the siding the crowd still heard the cries of the suffering woman, whom it had been necessary to leave in it, in charge of a Sister, cries which grew weaker and weaker, like those of a strengthless child whom one at last succeeds in consoling.

"Good Lord!" muttered the station-master; "it was high time!"

In fact the Bayonne express was now coming along at full speed, and the next moment it rushed like a crash of thunder past that woeful platform littered with all the grievous wretchedness of a hospital hastily evacuated. The litters and little handcarts were shaken, but there was no accident, for the porters were on the watch, and pushed back the bewildered flock which was still jostling and struggling in its eagerness to get away. As soon as the express had passed, however, circulation was re-established, and the bearers were at last able to complete the removal of the sick with prudent deliberation.

Little by little the daylight was increasing—a clear dawn it was, whitening the heavens whose reflection illumined the earth, which was still black. One began to distinguish things and people clearly.

"Oh, by-and-by!" Marie repeated to Pierre, as he endeavoured to roll her away. "Let us wait till some part of the crowd has gone."

Then, looking around, she began to feel interested in a man of military bearing, apparently some sixty years of age, who was walking about among the sick pilgrims. With a square-shaped head and white bushy hair, he would still have looked sturdy if he had not dragged his left foot, throwing it inward at each step he took. With the left hand, too, he leant heavily on a thick walking-stick. When M. Sabathier, who had visited Lourdes for six years past, perceived him, he became quite gay. "Ah!" said he, "it is you, Commander!"

Commander was perhaps the old man's name. But as he was decorated with a broad red riband, he was possibly called Commander on account of his decoration, albeit the latter was that of a mere chevalier. Nobody exactly knew his story. No doubt he had relatives and children of his own somewhere, but these matters remained vague and mysterious. For the last three years he had been employed at the railway station as a superintendent in the goods department, a simple occupation, a little berth which had been given him by favour and which enabled him to live in perfect happiness. A first stroke of apoplexy at fifty-five years of age had been followed by a second one three years later, which had left him slightly paralysed in the left side. And now he was awaiting the third stroke with an air of perfect tranquillity. As he himself put it, he was at the disposal of death, which might come for him that night, the next day, or possibly that very moment. All Lourdes knew him on account of the habit, the mania he had, at pilgrimage time, of coming to witness the arrival of the trains, dragging his foot along and leaning upon his stick, whilst expressing his astonishment and reproaching the ailing ones for their intense desire to be made whole and sound again.

This was the third year that he had seen M. Sabathier arrive, and all his anger fell upon him. "What! you have come back *again*!" he exclaimed. "Well, you *must* be desirous of living this hateful life! But *sacrebleu*! go and die quietly in your bed at home. Isn't that the best thing that can happen to anyone?"

M. Sabathier evinced no anger, but laughed, exhausted though he was by the handling to which he had been subjected during his removal from the carriage. "No, no," said he, "I prefer to be cured."

"To be cured, to be cured! That's what they all ask for. They travel hundreds of leagues and arrive in fragments, howling with pain, and all this to be cured—to go through every worry and every suffering again. Come, monsieur, you would be nicely caught if, at your age and with your dilapidated old body, your Blessed Virgin should be pleased to restore the use of your legs to you. What would you do with them, *mon Dieu?* What pleasure would you find in prolonging the abomination of old age for a few years more? It's much better to die at once, while you are like that! Death is happiness!"

He spoke in this fashion, not as a believer who aspires to the delicious reward of eternal life, but as a weary man who expects to fall into nihility, to enjoy the great everlasting peace of being no more.

Whilst M. Sabathier was gaily shrugging his shoulders as though he had a child to deal with, Abbe Judaine, who had at last secured his banner, came by and stopped for a moment in order that he might gently scold the Commander, with whom he also was well acquainted. "Don't blaspheme, my dear friend," he said. "It is an offence against God to refuse life and to treat health with contempt. If you yourself had listened to me, you would have asked the Blessed Virgin to cure your leg before now."

At this the Commander became angry. "My leg! The Virgin can do nothing to it! I'm quite at my ease. May death come and may it all be over forever! When the time comes to die you turn your face to the wall and you die—it's simple enough."

The old priest interrupted him, however. Pointing to Marie, who was lying on her box listening to them, he exclaimed: "You tell all our sick to go home and die—even mademoiselle, eh? She who is full of youth and wishes to live."

Marie's eyes were wide open, burning with the ardent desire which she felt to *be*, to enjoy her share of the vast world; and the Commander, who had drawn near, gazed upon her, suddenly seized with deep emotion which made his voice tremble. "If mademoiselle gets well," he said, "I will wish her another miracle, that she be happy."

Then he went off, dragging his foot and tapping the flagstones with the ferrule of his stout stick as he continued wending his way, like an angry philosopher among the suffering pilgrims.

Little by little, the platform was at last cleared. Madame Vetu and La Grivotte were carried away, and Gerard removed M. Sabathier in a little cart, whilst Baron Suire and Berthaud already began giving orders for the green train, which would be the next one to arrive. Of all the ailing pilgrims the only one now remaining at the station was Marie, of whom Pierre jealously took charge. He had already dragged her into the courtyard when he noticed that M. de Guersaint had disappeared; but a moment later he perceived him conversing with the Abbe des Hermoises, whose acquaintance he had just made. Their admiration of the beauties of nature had brought them together. The daylight had now appeared, and the surrounding mountains displayed themselves in all their majesty.

"What a lovely country, monsieur!" exclaimed M. de Guersaint. "I have been wishing to see the Cirque de Gavarnie for thirty years past. But it is some distance away and the trip must be an expensive one, so that I fear I shall not be able to make it."

"You are mistaken, monsieur," said the Abbe; "nothing is more easily managed. By making up a party the expense becomes very slight. And as it happens, I wish to return there this year, so that if you would like to join us—"

"Oh, certainly, monsieur. We will speak of it again. A thousand thanks," replied M. de Guersaint.

His daughter was now calling him, however, and he joined her after taking leave of the Abbe in a very cordial manner. Pierre had decided that he would drag Marie to the hospital so as to spare her the pain of transference to another vehicle. But as the omnibuses, landaus, and other conveyances were already coming back, again filling the courtyard in readiness for the arrival of the next train, the young priest had some difficulty in reaching the road with the little chariot whose low wheels sank deeply in the mud. Some police agents charged with maintaining order were cursing that fearful mire which splashed their boots; and indeed it was only the touts, the young and old women who had rooms to let, who laughed at the puddles, which they crossed and crossed again in every direction, pursuing the last pilgrims that emerged from the station.

When the little car had begun to roll more easily over the sloping road Marie suddenly inquired of M. de Guersaint, who was walking near her: "What day of the week is it, father?"

"Saturday, my darling."

"Ah! yes, Saturday, the day of the Blessed Virgin. Is it to-day that she will cure me?"

Then she began thinking again; while, at some distance behind her, two bearers came furtively down the road, with a covered stretcher in which lay the corpse of the man who had died in the train. They had gone to take it from behind the barrels in the goods office, and were now conveying it to a secret spot of which Father Fourcade had told them.

II

Hospital and Grotto

B uilt, so far as it extends, by a charitable Canon, and left unfinished through lack of money, the Hospital of Our Lady of Dolours is a vast pile, four storeys high, and consequently far too lofty, since it is difficult to carry the sufferers to the topmost wards. As a rule the building is occupied by a hundred infirm and aged paupers; but at the season of the national pilgrimage these old folks are for three days sheltered elsewhere, and the hospital is let to the Fathers of the Assumption, who at times lodge in it as many as five and six hundred patients. Still, however closely packed they may be, the accommodation never suffices, so that the three or four hundred remaining sufferers have to be distributed between the Hospital of Salvation and the town hospital, the men being sent to the former and the women to the latter institution.

That morning at sunrise great confusion prevailed in the sand-covered courtyard of Our Lady of Dolours, at the door of which a couple of priests were mounting guard. The temporary staff, with its formidable supply of registers, cards, and printed formulas, had installed itself in one of the ground-floor rooms on the previous day. The managers were desirous of greatly improving upon the organisation of the preceding year. The lower wards were this time to be reserved to the most helpless sufferers; and in order to prevent a repetition of the cases of mistaken identity which had occurred in the past, very great care was to be taken in filling in and distributing the admission cards, each of which bore the name of a ward and the number of a bed. It became difficult, however, to act in accordance with these good intentions in presence of the torrent of ailing beings which the white train had brought to Lourdes, and the new formalities so complicated matters that the patients had to be deposited in the courtyard as they arrived, to wait there until it became possible to admit them in something like an orderly manner. It was the scene witnessed at the railway station all over again, the same woeful camping in the open, whilst the bearers and the young seminarists who acted as the secretary's assistants ran hither and thither in bewilderment.

"We have been over-ambitious, we wanted to do things too well!" exclaimed Baron Suire in despair.

There was much truth in his remark, for never had a greater number of useless precautions been taken, and they now discovered that, by some inexplicable error, they had allotted not the lower—but the higher-placed wards to the patients whom it was most difficult to move. It was impossible to begin the classification afresh, however, and so as in former years things must be allowed to take their course, in a haphazard way. The distribution of the cards began, a young priest at the same time entering each patient's name and address in a register. Moreover, all the *hospitalisation* cards bearing the patients' names and numbers had to be produced, so that the names of the wards and the numbers of the beds might be added to them; and all these formalities greatly protracted the *defile*.

Then there was an endless coming and going from the top to the bottom of the building, and from one to the other end of each of its four floors. M. Sabathier was one of the first to secure admittance, being placed in a ground-floor room which was known as the Family Ward. Sick men were there allowed to have their wives with them; but to the other wards of the hospital only women were admitted. Brother Isidore, it is true, was accompanied by his sister; however, by a special favour it was agreed that they should be considered as conjoints, and the missionary was accordingly placed in the bed next to that allotted to M. Sabathier. The chapel, still littered with plaster and with its unfinished windows boarded up, was close at hand. There were also various wards in an unfinished state; still these were filled with mattresses, on which sufferers were rapidly placed. All those who could walk, however, were already besieging the refectory, a long gallery whose broad windows looked into an inner courtyard; and the Saint-Frai Sisters, who managed the hospital at other times, and had remained to attend to the cooking, began to distribute bowls of coffee and chocolate among the poor women whom the terrible journey had exhausted.

"Rest yourselves and try to gain a little strength," repeated Baron Suire, who was ever on the move, showing himself here, there, and everywhere in rapid succession. "You have three good hours before you, it is not yet five, and their reverences have given orders that you are not to be taken to the Grotto until eight o'clock, so as to avoid any excessive fatigue."

Meanwhile, up above on the second floor, Madame de Jonquiere had been one of the first to take possession of the Sainte-Honorine

Ward of which she was the superintendent. She had been obliged to leave her daughter Raymonde downstairs, for the regulations did not allow young girls to enter the wards, where they might have witnessed sights that were scarcely proper or else too horrible for such eyes as theirs. Raymonde had therefore remained in the refectory as a helper; however, little Madame Desagneaux, being a lady-hospitaller, had not left the superintendent, and was already asking her for orders, in her delight that she should at last be able to render some assistance.

"Are all these beds properly made, madame?" she inquired; "perhaps I had better make them afresh with Sister Hyacinthe."

The ward, whose walls were painted a light yellow, and whose few windows admitted but little light from an inner yard, contained fifteen beds, standing in two rows against the walls.

"We will see by-and-by," replied Madame de Jonquiere with an absorbed air. She was busy counting the beds and examining the long narrow apartment. And this accomplished she added in an undertone: "I shall never have room enough. They say that I must accommodate twenty-three patients. We shall have to put some mattresses down."

Sister Hyacinthe, who had followed the ladies after leaving Sister Saint-Francois and Sister Claire des Anges in a small adjoining apartment which was being transformed into a linen-room, then began to lift up the coverlets and examine the bedding. And she promptly reassured Madame Desagneaux with regard to her surmises. "Oh! the beds are properly made," she said; "everything is very clean too. One can see that the Saint-Frai Sisters have attended to things themselves. The reserve mattresses are in the next room, however, and if madame will lend me a hand we can place some of them between the beds at once.

"Oh, certainly!" exclaimed young Madame Desagneaux, quite excited by the idea of carrying mattresses about with her weak slender arms.

It became necessary for Madame de Jonquiere to calm her. "By-and-by," said the lady-superintendent; "there is no hurry. Let us wait till our patients arrive. I don't much like this ward, it is so difficult to air. Last year I had the Sainte-Rosalie Ward on the first floor. However, we will organise matters, all the same."

Some other lady-hospitallers were now arriving, quite a hiveful of busy bees, all eager to start on their work. The confusion which so often arose was, in fact, increased by the excessive number of nurses, women of the aristocracy and upper-middle class, with whose fervent zeal some little vanity was blended. There were more than two hundred of them, and as each had to make a donation on joining the Hospitality of Our Lady of Salvation, the managers did not dare to refuse any applicants, for fear lest they might check the flow of alms-giving. Thus the number of lady-hospitallers increased year by year. Fortunately there were among them some who cared for nothing beyond the privilege of wearing the red cloth cross, and who started off on excursions as soon as they reached Lourdes. Still it must be acknowledged that those who devoted themselves were really deserving, for they underwent five days of awful fatigue, sleeping scarcely a couple of hours each night, and living in the midst of the most terrible and repulsive spectacles. They witnessed the death agonies, dressed the pestilential sores, cleaned up, changed linen, turned the sufferers over in their beds, went through a sickening and overwhelming labour to which they were in no wise accustomed. And thus they emerged from it aching all over, tired to death, with feverish eyes flaming with the joy of the charity which so excited them.

"And Madame Volmar?" suddenly asked Madame Desagneaux. "I thought we should find her here."

This was apparently a subject which Madame de Jonquiere did not care to have discussed; for, as though she were aware of the truth and wished to bury it in silence, with the indulgence of a woman who compassionates human wretchedness, she promptly retorted: "Madame Volmar isn't strong, she must have gone to the hotel to rest. We must let her sleep."

Then she apportioned the beds among the ladies present, allotting two to each of them; and this done they all finished taking possession of the place, hastening up and down and backwards and forwards in order to ascertain where the offices, the linen-room, and the kitchens were situated.

"And the dispensary?" then asked one of the ladies.

But there was no dispensary. There was no medical staff even. What would have been the use of any?—since the patients were those whom science had given up, despairing creatures who had come to beg of God the cure which powerless men were unable to promise them. Logically enough, all treatment was suspended during the pilgrimage. If a patient seemed likely to die, extreme unction was administered. The only medical man about the place was the young doctor who had come by the white train with his little medicine chest; and his intervention was limited to an endeavour to assuage the sufferings of those patients who chanced to ask for him during an attack.

As it happened, Sister Hyacinthe was just bringing Ferrand, whom Sister Saint-Francois had kept with her in a closet near the linen-room which he proposed to make his quarters. "Madame," said he to Madame de Jonquiere, "I am entirely at your disposal. In case of need you will only have to ring for me."

She barely listened to him, however, engaged as she was in a quarrel with a young priest belonging to the management with reference to a deficiency of certain utensils. "Certainly, monsieur, if we should need a soothing draught," she answered, and then, reverting to her discussion, she went on: "Well, Monsieur l'Abbe, you must certainly get me four or five more. How can we possibly manage with so few? Things are bad enough as it is."

Ferrand looked and listened, quite bewildered by the extraordinary behaviour of the people amongst whom he had been thrown by chance since the previous day. He who did not believe, who was only present out of friendship and charity, was amazed at this extraordinary scramble of wretchedness and suffering rushing towards the hope of happiness. And, as a medical man of the new school, he was altogether upset by the careless neglect of precautions, the contempt which was shown for the most simple teachings of science, in the certainty which was apparently felt that, if Heaven should so will it, cure would supervene, sudden and resounding, like a lie given to the very laws of nature. But if this were the case, what was the use of that last concession to human prejudices—why engage a doctor for the journey if none were wanted? At this thought the young man returned to his little room, experiencing a vague feeling of shame as he realised that his presence was useless, and even a trifle ridiculous.

"Get some opium pills ready all the same," said Sister Hyacinthe, as she went back with him as far as the linen-room. "You will be asked for some, for I feel anxious about some of the patients."

While speaking she looked at him with her large blue eyes, so gentle and so kind, and ever lighted by a divine smile. The constant exercise which she gave herself brought the rosy flush of her quick blood to her skin all dazzling with youthfulness. And like a good friend who was willing that he should share the work to which she gave her heart, she added: "Besides, if I should need somebody to get a patient in or out of bed, you will help me, won't you?"

Thereupon, at the idea that he might be of use to her, he was pleased that he had come and was there. In his mind's eye, he again beheld her at his bedside, at the time when he had so narrowly escaped death, nursing him with fraternal hands, with the smiling, compassionate grace of a sexless angel, in whom there was something more than a comrade, something of a woman left. However, the thought never occurred to him that there was religion, belief, behind her.

"Oh! I will help you as much as you like, Sister," he replied. "I belong to you, I shall be so happy to serve you. You know very well what a debt of gratitude I have to pay you."

In a pretty way she raised her finger to her lips so as to silence him. Nobody owed her anything. She was merely the servant of the ailing and the poor.

At this moment a first patient was making her entry into the Sainte-Honorine Ward. It was Marie, lying in her wooden box, which Pierre, with Gerard's assistance, had just brought up-stairs. The last to start from the railway station, she had secured admission before the others, thanks to the endless complications which, after keeping them all in suspense, now freed them according to the chance distribution of the admission cards. M. de Guersaint had quitted his daughter at the hospital door by her own desire; for, fearing the hotels would be very full, she had wished him to secure two rooms for himself and Pierre at once. Then, on reaching the ward, she felt so weary that, after venting her chagrin at not being immediately taken to the Grotto, she consented to be laid on a bed for a short time.

"Come, my child," repeated Madame de Jonquiere, "you have three hours before you. We will put you to bed. It will ease you to take you out of that case."

Thereupon the lady-superintendent raised her by the shoulders, whilst Sister Hyacinthe held her feet. The bed was in the central part of the ward, near a window. For a moment the poor girl remained on it with her eyes closed, as though exhausted by being moved about so much. Then it became necessary that Pierre should be readmitted, for she grew very fidgety, saying that there were things which she must explain to him.

"Pray don't go away, my friend," she exclaimed when he approached her. "Take the case out on to the landing, but stay there, because I want to be taken down as soon as I can get permission."

"Do you feel more comfortable now?" asked the young priest.

"Yes, no doubt—but I really don't know. I so much want to be taken yonder to the Blessed Virgin's feet."

However, when Pierre had removed the case, the successive arrivals of the other patients supplied her with some little diversion. Madame Vetu, whom two bearers had brought up-stairs, holding her under the arms, was laid, fully dressed, on the next bed, where she remained motionless, scarce breathing, with her heavy, yellow, cancerous mask. None of the patients, it should be mentioned, were divested of their clothes, they were simply stretched out on the beds, and advised to go to sleep if they could manage to do so. Those whose complaints were less grievous contented themselves with sitting down on their mattresses, chatting together, and putting the things they had brought with them in order. For instance, Elise Rouquet, who was also near Marie, on the other side of the latter's bed, opened her basket to take a clean fichu out of it, and seemed sorely annoyed at having no hand-glass with her. In less than ten minutes all the beds were occupied, so that when La Grivotte appeared, half carried by Sister Hyacinthe and Sister Claire des Anges, it became necessary to place some mattresses on the floor.

"Here! here is one," exclaimed Madame Desagneaux; "she will be very well here, out of the draught from the door."

Seven other mattresses were soon added in a line, occupying the space between the rows of beds, so that it became difficult to move about. One had to be very careful, and follow narrow pathways which had been left between the beds and the mattresses. Each of the patients had retained possession of her parcel, or box, or bag, and round about the improvised shakedowns were piles of poor old things, sorry remnants of garments, straying among the sheets and the coverlets. You might have thought yourself in some woeful infirmary, hastily organised after some great catastrophe, some conflagration or earthquake which had thrown hundreds of wounded and penniless beings into the streets.

Madame de Jonquiere made her way from one to the other end of the ward, ever and ever repeating, "Come, my children, don't excite yourselves; try to sleep a little."

However, she did not succeed in calming them, and indeed, she herself, like the other lady-hospitallers under her orders, increased the general fever by her own bewilderment. The linen of several patients had to be changed, and there were other needs to be attended to. One woman, suffering from an ulcer in the leg, began moaning so dreadfully that Madame Desagneaux undertook to dress her sore afresh; but she was not skilful, and despite all her passionate courage she almost fainted, so greatly was she distressed by the unbearable odour. Those patients who were in better health asked for broth, bowlfuls of which began to circulate amidst the calls, the answers, and the contradictory orders which nobody executed. And meanwhile, let loose amidst this frightful scramble, little Sophie Couteau, who remained with the Sisters, and was very gay, imagined that it was playtime, and ran, and jumped, and hopped in turn, called and petted first by one and then by another, dear as she was to all alike for the miraculous hope which she brought them.

However, amidst this agitation, the hours went by. Seven o'clock had just struck when Abbe Judaine came in. He was the chaplain of the Sainte-Honorine Ward, and only the difficulty of finding an unoccupied altar at which he might say his mass had delayed his arrival. As soon as he appeared, a cry of impatience arose from every bed.

"Oh! Monsieur le Cure, let us start, let us start at once!"

An ardent desire, which each passing minute heightened and irritated, was upbuoying them, like a more and more devouring thirst, which only the waters of the miraculous fountain could appease. And more fervently than any of the others, La Grivotte, sitting up on her mattress, and joining her hands, begged and begged that she might be taken to the Grotto. Was there not a beginning of the miracle in this—in this awakening of her will power, this feverish desire for cure which enabled her to set herself erect? Inert and fainting on her arrival, she was now seated, turning her dark glances in all directions, waiting and watching for the happy moment when she would be removed. And colour also was returning to her livid face. She was already resuscitating.

"Oh! Monsieur le Cure, pray do tell them to take me—I feel that I shall be cured," she exclaimed.

With a loving, fatherly smile on his good-natured face, Abbe Judaine listened to them all, and allayed their impatience with kind words. They would soon set out; but they must be reasonable, and allow sufficient time for things to be organised; and besides, the Blessed Virgin did not like to have violence done her; she bided her time, and distributed her divine favours among those who behaved themselves the best.

As he paused before Marie's bed and beheld her, stammering entreaties with joined hands, he again paused. "And you, too, my daughter, you are in a hurry?" he said. "Be easy, there is grace enough in heaven for you all."

"I am dying of love, Father," she murmured in reply. "My heart is so swollen with prayers, it stifles me—"

He was greatly touched by the passion of this poor emaciated child, so harshly stricken in her youth and beauty, and wishing to appease her, he called her attention to Madame Vetu, who did not move, though with her eyes wide open she stared at all who passed.

"Look at madame, how quiet she is!" he said. "She is meditating, and she does right to place herself in God's hands, like a little child."

However, in a scarcely audible voice, a mere breath, Madame Vetu stammered: "Oh! I am suffering, I am suffering."

At last, at a quarter to eight o'clock, Madame de Jonquiere warned her charges that they would do well to prepare themselves. She herself, assisted by Sister Hyacinthe and Madame Desagneaux, buttoned several dresses, and put shoes on impotent feet. It was a real toilette, for they all desired to appear to the greatest advantage before the Blessed Virgin. A large number had sufficient sense of delicacy to wash their hands. Others unpacked their parcels, and put on clean linen. On her side, Elise Rouquet had ended by discovering a little pocket-glass in the hands of a woman near her, a huge, dropsical creature, who was very coquettish; and having borrowed it, she leant it against the bolster, and then, with infinite care, began to fasten her fichu as elegantly as possible about her head, in order to hide her distorted features. Meanwhile, erect in front of her, little Sophie watched her with an air of profound interest.

It was Abbe Judaine who gave the signal for starting on the journey to the Grotto. He wished, he said, to accompany his dear suffering daughters thither, whilst the lady-hospitallers and the Sisters remained in the ward, so as to put things in some little order again. Then the ward was at once emptied, the patients being carried down-stairs amidst renewed tumult. And Pierre, having replaced Marie's box upon its wheels, took the first place in the *cortege*, which was formed of a score of little handcarts, bath-chairs, and litters. The other wards, however, were also emptying, the courtyard became crowded, and the *defile* was organised in haphazard fashion. There was soon an interminable train descending the rather steep slope of the Avenue de la Grotte, so that Pierre was already reaching the Plateau de la Merlasse when the last stretchers were barely leaving the precincts of the hospital.

It was eight o'clock, and the sun, already high, a triumphant August sun, was flaming in the great sky, which was beautifully clear. It seemed as if the blue of the atmosphere, cleansed by the storm of the previous night, were quite new, fresh with youth. And the frightful *defile*, a perfect "Cour des Miracles" of human woe, rolled along the sloping pavement amid all the brilliancy of that radiant morning. There was no end to the train of abominations; it appeared to grow longer and longer. No order was observed, ailments of all kinds were jumbled together; it seemed like the clearing of some inferno where the most monstrous maladies, the rare and awful cases which provoke a shudder, had been gathered together. Eczema, roseola, elephantiasis, presented a long array of doleful victims. Well-nigh vanished diseases reappeared; one old woman was affected with leprosy, another was, covered with impetiginous lichen like a tree which has rotted in the shade. Then came the dropsical ones, inflated like wine-skins; and beside some stretchers there dangled hands twisted by rheumatism, while from others protruded feet swollen by oedema beyond all recognition, looking, in fact, like bags full of rags. One woman, suffering from hydrocephalus, sat in a little cart, the dolorous motions of her head bespeaking her grievous malady. A tall girl afflicted with chorea—St. Vitus's dance— was dancing with every limb, without a pause, the left side of her face being continually distorted by sudden, convulsive grimaces. A younger one, who followed, gave vent to a bark, a kind of plaintive animal cry, each time that the tic douloureux which was torturing her twisted her mouth and her right cheek, which she seemed to throw forward. Next came the consumptives, trembling with fever, exhausted by dysentery, wasted to skeletons, with livid skins, recalling the colour of that earth in which they would soon be laid to rest; and there was one among them who was quite white, with flaming eyes, who looked indeed like a death's head in which a torch had been lighted. Then every deformity of the contractions followed in succession—twisted trunks, twisted arms, necks askew, all the distortions of poor creatures whom nature had warped and broken; and among these was one whose right hand was thrust back behind her ribs whilst her head fell to the left resting fixedly upon her shoulder. Afterwards came poor rachitic girls displaying waxen complexions and slender necks eaten away by sores, and yellow-faced women in the painful stupor which falls on those whose bosoms are devoured by cancers; whilst others, lying down with their mournful eyes gazing heavenwards, seemed to be listening to the throbs of the tumours which obstructed their organs. And still more and more went by; there was always something more frightful to come; this woman following that other one increased the general shudder of horror. From the neck of a girl of twenty who had a crushed, flattened head like a toad's, there hung so large a goitre that it fell even to her waist like the bib of an apron. A blind woman walked along, her head erect, her face pale like marble, displaying the acute inflammation of her poor, ulcerated eyes. An aged woman stricken with imbecility, afflicted with dreadful facial disfigurements, laughed aloud with a terrifying laugh. And all at once an epileptic was seized with convulsions, and began foaming on her stretcher, without, however, causing any stoppage of the procession, which never slackened its march, lashed onward as it was by the blizzard of feverish passion which impelled it towards the Grotto.

The bearers, the priests, and the ailing ones themselves had just intonated a canticle, the song of Bernadette, and all rolled along amid the besetting "Aves," so that the little carts, the litters, and the pedestrians descended the sloping road like a swollen and overflowing torrent of roaring water. At the corner of the Rue Saint-Joseph, near the Plateau de la Merlasse, a family of excursionists, who had come from Cauterets or Bagneres, stood at the edge of the footway, overcome with profound astonishment. These people were evidently well-to-do *bourgeois*, the father and mother very correct in appearance and demeanour, while their two big girls, attired in light-coloured dresses, had the smiling faces of happy creatures who are amusing themselves. But their first feeling of surprise was soon followed by terror, a growing terror, as if they beheld the opening of some pesthouse of ancient times, some hospital of the legendary ages, evacuated after a great epidemic. The two girls became quite pale, while the father and the mother felt icy cold in presence of that endless *defile* of so many horrors, the pestilential emanations of which were blown full in their faces. O God! to think that such hideousness, such filth, such suffering, should exist! Was it possible—under that magnificently radiant sun, under those broad heavens so full of light and joy whither the freshness of the Gave's waters ascended, and the breeze of morning wafted the pure perfumes of the mountains!

When Pierre, at the head of the *cortege*, reached the Plateau de la Merlasse, he found himself immersed in that clear sunlight, that fresh and balmy air. He turned round and smiled affectionately at Marie; and as they came out on the Place du Rosaire in the morning splendour, they were both enchanted with the lovely panorama which spread around them.

In front, on the east, was Old Lourdes, lying in a broad fold of the ground beyond a rock. The sun was rising behind the distant mountains, and its oblique rays clearly outlined the dark lilac mass of that solitary rock, which was crowned by the tower and crumbling walls of the ancient castle, once the redoubtable key of the seven valleys. Through the dancing, golden dust you discerned little of the ruined pile except some stately outlines, some huge blocks of building which looked as though reared by Cyclopean hands; and beyond the rock you but vaguely distinguished the discoloured, intermingled house-roofs of the old town. Nearer in than the castle, however, the new town—the rich and noisy city which had sprung up in a few years as though by miracle—spread out on either hand, displaying its hotels, its stylish shops, its lodging-houses all with white fronts smiling amidst patches of greenery. Then there was the Gave flowing along at the base of the rock, rolling clamorous, clear waters, now blue and now green, now deep as they passed under the old bridge, and now leaping as they careered under the new one, which the Fathers of the Immaculate Conception had built in order to connect the Grotto with the railway station and the recently opened Boulevard. And as a background to this delightful picture, this fresh water, this greenery, this gay, scattered, rejuvenated town, the little and the big Gers arose, two huge ridges of bare rock and low herbage, which, in the projected shade that bathed them, assumed delicate tints of pale mauve and green, fading softly into pink.

Then, upon the north, on the right bank of the Gave, beyond the hills followed by the railway line, the heights of La Buala ascended, their wooded slopes radiant in the morning light. On that side lay Bartres. More to the left arose the Serre de Julos, dominated by the Miramont. Other crests, far off, faded away into the ether. And in the foreground, rising in tiers among the grassy valleys beyond the Gave, a number of convents, which seemed to have sprung up in this region of prodigies like early vegetation, imparted some measure of life to the landscape. First, there was an Orphan Asylum founded by the Sisters of Nevers, whose vast buildings shone brightly in the sunlight. Next came the Carmelite convent, on the highway to Pau, just in front of the Grotto; and then that of the Assumptionists higher up, skirting the road to Poueyferre; whilst the Dominicans showed but a corner of their roofs, sequestered in the far-away solitude. And at last appeared the establishment of the Sisters of the Immaculate Conception, those who were called the Blue Sisters, and who had founded at the far end of the valley a home where they received well-to-do lady pilgrims, desirous of solitude, as boarders.

At that early hour all the bells of these convents were pealing joyfully in the crystalline atmosphere, whilst the bells of other convents, on the other, the southern horizon, answered them with the same silvery strains of joy. The bell of the nunnery of Sainte Clarissa, near the old bridge, rang a scale of gay, clear notes, which one might have fancied to be the chirruping of a bird. And on this side of the town, also, there were valleys that dipped down between the ridges, and mountains that upreared their bare sides, a commingling of smiling and of agitated nature, an endless surging of heights amongst which you noticed those of Visens, whose slopes the sunlight tinged ornately with soft blue and carmine of a rippling, moire-like effect.

However, when Marie and Pierre turned their eyes to the west, they were quite dazzled. The sun rays were here streaming on the large and the little Beout with their cupolas of unequal height. And on this side the background was one of gold and purple, a dazzling mountain on whose sides one could only discern the road which snaked between the trees on its way to the Calvary above. And here, too, against the sunlit background, radiant like an aureola, stood out the three superposed churches which at the voice of Bernadette had sprung from the rock to the glory of the Blessed Virgin. First of all, down below, came the church of the Rosary, squat, circular, and half cut out of the rock, at the farther end of an esplanade on either side of which, like two huge arms, were colossal gradient ways ascending gently to the Crypt church. Vast labour had been expended here, a quarryful of stones had been cut and set in position, there were arches as lofty as naves supporting the gigantic terraced avenues which had been constructed so that the processions might roll along in all their pomp, and the little conveyances containing sick children might ascend without hindrance to the divine presence. Then came the Crypt, the subterranean church within the rock, with only its low door visible above the church of the Rosary, whose paved roof, with its vast promenade, formed a continuation of the terraced inclines. And at last, from the summit sprang the Basilica, somewhat slender and frail, recalling some finely chased jewel of the Renascence, and looking very new and very white—like a prayer, a spotless dove, soaring aloft from the rocks of Massabielle. The spire, which appeared the more delicate and slight when compared with the gigantic inclines below, seemed like the little vertical flame of a taper set in the midst of the vast landscape, those endless waves of valleys and mountains. By the side, too, of the dense greenery of the Calvary hill, it looked fragile and candid, like childish faith; and at sight of it you instinctively thought of the little white arm, the little thin hand of the puny girl, who had here pointed to Heaven in the crisis of her human sufferings. You could not see the Grotto, the entrance of which was on the left, at the base of the rock. Beyond the Basilica, the only buildings which caught the eye were the heavy square pile where the Fathers of the Immaculate Conception had their abode, and the episcopal palace, standing much farther away, in a spreading, wooded valley. And the three churches were flaming in the morning glow, and the rain of gold scattered by the sun rays was sweeping the whole countryside, whilst the flying peals of the bells seemed to be the very vibration of the light, the musical awakening of the lovely day that was now beginning.

Whilst crossing the Place du Rosaire, Pierre and Marie glanced at the Esplanade, the public walk with its long central lawn skirted by broad parallel paths and extending as far as the new bridge. Here, with face turned towards the Basilica, was the great crowned statue of the Virgin. All the sufferers crossed themselves as they went by. And still passionately chanting its canticle, the fearful *cortege* rolled on, through nature in festive array. Under the dazzling sky, past the mountains of gold and purple, amidst the centenarian trees, symbolical of health, the running waters whose freshness was eternal, that *cortege* still and ever marched on with its sufferers, whom nature, if not God, had condemned, those who were afflicted with skin diseases, those whose flesh was eaten away, those who were dropsical and inflated like wine-skins, and those whom rheumatism and paralysis had twisted into postures of agony. And the victims of hydrocephalus followed, with the dancers of St. Vitus, the consumptives, the rickety, the epileptic, the cancerous, the goitrous, the blind, the mad, and the idiotic. "Ave, ave, ave, Maria!" they sang; and the stubborn plaint acquired increased volume, as nearer and nearer to the Grotto it bore that abominable torrent of human wretchedness and pain, amidst all the fright and horror of the passers-by, who stopped short, unable to stir, their hearts frozen as this nightmare swept before their eyes.

Pierre and Marie were the first to pass under the lofty arcade of one of the terraced inclines. And then, as they followed the quay of the Gave, they all at once came upon the Grotto. And Marie, whom Pierre wheeled as near to the railing as possible, was only able to raise herself in her little conveyance, and murmur: "O most Blessed Virgin, Virgin most loved!"

She had seen neither the entrances to the piscinas nor the twelve-piped fountain, which she had just passed; nor did she distinguish any better the shop on her left hand where crucifixes, chaplets, statuettes, pictures, and other religious articles were sold, or the stone pulpit on her right which Father Massias already occupied. Her eyes were dazzled by the splendour of the Grotto; it seemed to her as if a hundred thousand tapers were burning there behind the railing, filling the low entrance with the glow of a furnace and illuminating, as with star rays, the statue of the Virgin, which stood, higher up, at the edge of a narrow ogive-like cavity. And for her, apart from that glorious apparition, nothing existed there, neither the crutches with which a part of the vault had been covered, nor the piles of bouquets fading away amidst the ivy and the eglantine, nor even the altar placed in the centre near a little portable organ over which a cover had been thrown. However, as she raised her eyes above the rock, she once more beheld the slender white Basilica profiled against the sky, its slight, tapering spire soaring into the azure of the Infinite like a prayer.

"O Virgin most powerful—Queen of the Virgins—Holy Virgin of Virgins!"

Pierre had now succeeded in wheeling Marie's box to the front rank, beyond the numerous oak benches which were set out here in the open air as in the nave of a church. Nearly all these benches were already occupied by those sufferers who could sit down, while the vacant spaces were soon filled with litters and little vehicles whose wheels became entangled together, and on whose close-packed mattresses and pillows all sorts of diseases were gathered pell-mell. Immediately on arriving, the young priest had recognised the Vignerons seated with their sorry child Gustave in the middle of a bench, and now, on the flagstones, he caught sight of the lace-trimmed bed of Madame Dieulafay, beside whom her husband and sister knelt in prayer. Moreover, all the patients of Madame de Jonquiere's carriage took up position here—M. Sabathier and Brother Isidore side by side, Madame Vetu reclining hopelessly in a conveyance, Elise Rouquet seated, La Grivotte excited and raising herself on her clenched hands. Pierre also again perceived Madame Maze, standing somewhat apart from the others, and humbling herself in prayer; whilst Madame Vincent, who had fallen on her knees, still holding her little Rose in her arms, presented the child to the Virgin with ardent entreaty, the distracted gesture of a mother soliciting compassion from the mother of divine grace. And around this reserved space was the ever-growing throng of pilgrims, the pressing, jostling mob which gradually stretched to the parapet overlooking the Gave.

"O Virgin most merciful," continued Marie in an undertone, "Virgin most faithful, Virgin conceived without sin!"

Then, almost fainting, she spoke no more, but with her lips still moving, as though in silent prayer, gazed distractedly at Pierre. He thought that she wished to speak to him and leant forward: "Shall I remain here at your disposal to take you to the piscina by-and-by?" he asked.

But as soon as she understood him she shook her head. And then in a feverish way she said: "No, no, I don't want to be bathed this morning. It seems to me that one must be truly worthy, truly pure, truly holy before seeking the miracle! I want to spend the whole morning in imploring it with joined hands; I want to pray, to pray with all my strength and all my soul—" She was stifling, and paused. Then she added: "Don't come to take me back to the hospital till eleven o'clock. I will not let them take me from here till then."

However, Pierre did not go away, but remained near her. For a moment, he even fell upon his knees; he also would have liked to pray with the same burning faith, to beg of God the cure of that poor sick child, whom he loved with such fraternal affection. But since he had reached the Grotto he had felt a singular sensation invading him, a covert revolt, as it were, which hampered the pious flight of his prayer. He wished to believe; he had spent the whole night hoping that belief would once more blossom in his soul, like some lovely flower of innocence and candour, as soon as he should have knelt upon the soil of that land of miracle. And yet he only experienced discomfort and anxiety in presence of the theatrical scene before him, that pale stiff statue in the false light of the tapers, with the chaplet shop full of jostling customers on the one hand, and the large stone pulpit whence a Father of the Assumption was shouting "Aves" on the other. Had his soul become utterly withered then? Could no divine dew again impregnate it with innocence, render it like the souls of little children, who at the slightest caressing touch of the sacred legend give themselves to it entirely?

Then, while his thoughts were still wandering, he recognised Father Massias in the ecclesiastic who occupied the pulpit. He had formerly known him, and was quite stirred by his sombre ardour, by the sight of his thin face and sparkling eyes, by the eloquence which poured from his large mouth as he offered violence to Heaven to compel it to descend upon earth. And whilst he thus examined Father Massias, astonished at feeling himself so unlike the preacher, he caught sight of Father Fourcade, who, at the foot of the pulpit, was deep in conference with Baron Suire. The latter seemed much perplexed by something which Father Fourcade said to him; however he ended by approving it with a complaisant nod. Then, as Abbe Judaine was also standing there, Father Fourcade likewise spoke to him for a moment, and a scared expression came over the Abbe's broad, fatherly face while he listened; nevertheless, like the Baron, he at last bowed assent.

Then, all at once, Father Fourcade appeared in the pulpit, erect, drawing up his lofty figure which his attack of gout had slightly bent; and he had not wished that Father Massias, his well-loved brother, whom he preferred above all others, should altogether go down the narrow stairway, for he had kept him upon one of the steps, and was leaning on his shoulder. And in a full, grave voice, with an air of sovereign authority which caused perfect silence to reign around, he spoke as follows:

"My dear brethren, my dear sisters, I ask your forgiveness for interrupting your prayers, but I have a communication to make to you, and I have to ask the help of all your faithful souls. We had a very sad accident to deplore this morning, one of our brethren died in one of the trains by which you came to Lourdes, died just as he was about to set foot in the promised land."

A brief pause followed and Father Fourcade seemed to become yet taller, his handsome face beaming with fervour, amidst his long, streaming, royal beard.

"Well, my dear brethren, my dear sisters," he resumed, "in spite of everything, the idea has come to me that we ought not to despair. Who knows if God Almighty did not will that death in order that He might prove His Omnipotence to the world? It is as though a voice were speaking to me, urging me to ascend this pulpit and ask your prayers for this man, this man who is no more, but whose life is nevertheless in the hands of the most Blessed Virgin who can still implore her Divine Son in his favour. Yes, the man is here, I have caused his body to be brought hither, and it depends on you, perhaps, whether a brilliant miracle shall dazzle the universe, if you pray with sufficient ardour to touch the compassion of Heaven. We will plunge the man's body into the piscina and we will entreat the Lord, the master of the world, to resuscitate him, to give unto us this extraordinary sign of His sovereign beneficence!"

An icy thrill, wafted from the Invisible, passed through the listeners. They had all become pale, and though the lips of none of them had opened, it seemed as if a murmur sped through their ranks amidst a shudder.

"But with what ardour must we not pray!" violently resumed Father Fourcade, exalted by genuine faith. "It is your souls, your whole souls, that I ask of you, my dear brothers, my dear sisters, it is a prayer in which you must put your hearts, your blood, your very life with whatever may be most noble and loving in it! Pray with all your strength, pray till you no longer know who you are, or where you are; pray as one loves, pray as one dies, for that which we are about to ask is so precious, so rare, so astounding a grace that only the energy of our worship can induce God to answer us. And in order that our prayers may be the more efficacious, in order that they may have time to spread and ascend to the feet of the Eternal Father, we will not lower the body into the piscina until four o'clock this afternoon. And now my dear brethren, now my dear sisters, pray, pray to the most Blessed Virgin, the Queen of the Angels, the Comforter of the Afflicted!"

Then he himself, distracted by emotion, resumed the recital of the rosary, whilst near him Father Massias burst into sobs. And thereupon the great anxious silence was broken, contagion seized upon the throng, it was transported and gave vent to shouts, tears, and confused stammered entreaties. It was as though a breath of delirium were sweeping by, reducing men's wills to naught, and turning all these beings into one being, exasperated with love and seized with a mad desire for the impossible prodigy.

And for a moment Pierre had thought that the ground was giving way beneath him, that he was about to fall and faint. But with difficulty he managed to rise from his knees and slowly walked away.

III

FOUNTAIN AND PISCINA

As Pierre went off, ill at ease, mastered by invincible repugnance, unwilling to remain there any longer, he caught sight of M. de Guersaint, kneeling near the Grotto, with the absorbed air of one who is praying with his whole soul. The young priest had not seen him since the morning, and did not know whether he had managed to secure a couple of rooms in one or other of the hotels, so that his first impulse was to go and join him. Then, however, he hesitated, unwilling to disturb his meditations, for he was doubtless praying for his daughter, whom he fondly loved, in spite of the constant absent-mindedness of his volatile brain. Accordingly, the young priest passed on, and took his way under the trees. Nine o'clock was now striking, he had a couple of hours before him.

By dint of money, the wild bank where swine had formerly pastured had been transformed into a superb avenue skirting the Gave. It had been necessary to put back the river's bed in order to gain ground, and lay out a monumental quay bordered by a broad footway, and protected by a parapet. Some two or three hundred yards farther on, a hill brought the avenue to an end, and it thus resembled an enclosed promenade, provided with benches, and shaded by magnificent trees. Nobody passed along, however; merely the overflow of the crowd had settled there, and solitary spots still abounded between the grassy wall limiting the promenade on the south, and the extensive fields spreading out northward beyond the Gave, as far as the wooded slopes which the white-walled convents brightened. Under the foliage, on the margin of the running water, one could enjoy delightful freshness, even during the burning days of August.

Thus Pierre, like a man at last awakening from a painful dream, soon found rest of mind again. He had questioned himself in the acute anxiety which he felt with regard to his sensations. Had he not reached Lourdes that morning possessed by a genuine desire to believe, an idea that he was indeed again beginning to believe even as he had done in the docile days of childhood when his mother had made him join his hands, and taught him to fear God? Yet as soon as he had found himself at the Grotto, the idolatry of the worship, the violence of the display of faith, the onslaught upon human reason which he witnessed, had so disturbed him that he had almost fainted. What would become of him then? Could he not even try to contend against his doubts by examining things and convincing himself of their truth, thus turning his journey to profit? At all events, he had made a bad beginning, which left him sorely agitated, and he indeed needed the environment of those fine trees, that limpid, rushing water, that calm, cool avenue, to recover from the shock.

Still pondering, he was approaching the end of the pathway, when he most unexpectedly met a forgotten friend. He had, for a few seconds, been looking at a tall old gentleman who was coming towards him, dressed in a tightly buttoned frock-coat and broad-brimmed hat; and he had tried to remember where it was that he had previously beheld that pale face, with eagle nose, and black and penetrating eyes. These he had seen before, he felt sure of it; but the promenader's long white beard and long curly white hair perplexed him. However, the other halted, also looking extremely astonished, though he promptly exclaimed, "What, Pierre? Is it you, at Lourdes?"

Then all at once the young priest recognised Doctor Chassaigne, his father's old friend, his own friend, the man who had cured and consoled him in the terrible physical and mental crisis which had come upon him after his mother's death.

"Ah! my dear doctor, how pleased I am to see you!" he replied.

They embraced with deep emotion. And now, in presence of that snowy hair and snowy beard, that slow walk, that sorrowful demeanour, Pierre remembered with what unrelenting ferocity misfortune had fallen on that unhappy man and aged him. But a few years had gone by, and now, when they met again, he was bowed down by destiny.

"You did not know, I suppose, that I had remained at Lourdes?" said the doctor. "It's true that I no longer write to anybody; in fact, I am no longer among the living. I live in the land of the dead." Tears were gathering in his eyes, and emotion made his voice falter as he resumed: "There! come and sit down on that bench yonder; it will please me to live the old days afresh with you, just for a moment."

In his turn the young priest felt his sobs choking him. He could only murmur: "Ah! my dear doctor, my old friend, I can truly tell you that I pitied you with my whole heart, my whole soul."

Doctor Chassaigne's story was one of disaster, the shipwreck of a life. He and his daughter Marguerite, a tall and lovable girl of twenty, had gone to Cauterets with Madame Chassaigne, the model wife and mother, whose state of health had made them somewhat anxious. A fortnight had elapsed and she seemed much better, and was already planning several pleasure trips, when one morning she was found dead in her bed. Her husband and daughter were overwhelmed, stupefied by this sudden blow, this cruel treachery of death. The doctor, who belonged to Bartres, had a family vault in the Lourdes cemetery, a vault constructed at his own expense, and in which his father and mother already rested. He desired, therefore, that his wife should be interred there, in a compartment adjoining that in which he expected soon to lie himself. And after the burial he had lingered for a week at Lourdes, when Marguerite, who was with him, was seized with a great shivering, and, taking to her bed one evening, died two days afterwards without her distracted father being able to form any exact notion of the illness which had carried her off. And thus it was not himself, but his daughter, lately radiant with beauty and health, in the very flower of her youth, who was laid in the vacant compartment by the mother's side. The man who had been so happy, so worshipped by his two helpmates, whose heart had been kept so warm by the love of two dear creatures all his own, was now nothing more than an old, miserable, stammering, lost being, who shivered in his icy solitude. All the joy of his life had departed; he envied the men who broke stones upon the highways when he saw their barefooted wives and daughters bring them their dinners at noontide. And he had refused to leave Lourdes, he had relinquished everything, his studies, his practice in Paris, in order that he might live near the tomb in which his wife and his daughter slept the eternal sleep.

"Ah, my old friend," repeated Pierre, "how I pitied you! How frightful must have been your grief! But why did you not rely a little on those who love you? Why did you shut yourself up here with your sorrow?"

The doctor made a gesture which embraced the horizon. "I could not go away, they are here and keep me with them. It is all over, I am merely waiting till my time comes to join them again."

Then silence fell. Birds were fluttering among the shrubs on the bank behind them, and in front they heard the loud murmur of the Gave. The sun rays were falling more heavily in a slow, golden dust, upon the hillsides; but on that retired bench under the beautiful trees, the coolness was still delightful. And although the crowd was but a couple of hundred yards distant, they were, so to say, in a desert, for nobody tore himself away from the Grotto to stray as far as the spot which they had chosen.

They talked together for a long time, and Pierre related under what circumstances he had reached Lourdes that morning with M. de Guersaint and his daughter, all three forming part of the national pilgrimage. Then all at once he gave a start of astonishment and exclaimed: "What! doctor, so you now believe that miracles are possible? You, good heavens! whom I knew as an unbeliever, or at least as one altogether indifferent to these matters?"

He was gazing at M. Chassaigne quite stupefied by something which he had just heard him say of the Grotto and Bernadette. It was amazing, coming from a man with so strong a mind, a *savant* of such intelligence, whose powerful analytical faculties he had formerly so much admired! How was it that a lofty, clear mind, nourished by experience and method, had become so changed as to acknowledge the miraculous cures effected by that divine fountain which the Blessed Virgin had caused to spurt forth under the pressure of a child's fingers?

"But just think a little, my dear doctor," he resumed. "It was you yourself who supplied my father with memoranda about Bernadette, your little fellow-villager as you used to call her; and it was you, too, who spoke to me at such length about her, when, later on, I took a momentary interest in her story. In your eyes she was simply an ailing child, prone to hallucinations, infantile, but self-conscious of her acts, deficient of will-power. Recollect our chats together, my doubts, and the healthy reason which you again enabled me, to acquire!"

Pierre was feeling very moved, for was not this the strangest of adventures? He a priest, who in a spirit of resignation had formerly endeavoured to believe, had ended by completely losing all faith through intercourse with this same doctor, who was then an unbeliever, but whom he now found converted, conquered by the supernatural, whilst he himself was racked by the torture of no longer believing.

"You who would only rely on accurate facts," he said, "you who based everything on observation! Do you renounce science then?"

Chassaigne, hitherto quiet, with a sorrowful smile playing on his lips, now made a violent gesture expressive of sovereign contempt. "Science indeed!" he exclaimed. "Do I know anything? Can I accomplish anything? You asked me just now what malady it was that killed my poor Marguerite. But I do not know! I, whom people think so learned, so well armed against death, I understood nothing of it, and I could do nothing—not even prolong my daughter's life for a single hour! And my wife, whom I found in bed already cold, when on the previous evening she had lain down in much better health and quite gay—was I even capable of foreseeing what ought to have been done in her case? No, no! for me at all events, science has become bankrupt. I wish to know nothing; I am but a fool and a poor old man!"

He spoke like this in a furious revolt against all his past life of pride and happiness. Then, having become calm again, he added: "And now I only feel a frightful remorse. Yes, a remorse which haunts me, which ever brings me here, prowling around the people who are praying. It is remorse for not having in the first instance come and humbled myself at that Grotto, bringing my two dear ones with me. They would have knelt there like those women whom you see, I should have knelt beside them, and perhaps the Blessed Virgin would have cured and preserved them. But, fool that I was, I only knew how to lose them! It is my fault."

Tears were now streaming from his eyes. "I remember," he continued, "that in my childhood at Bartrès, my mother, a peasant woman, made me join my hands and implore God's help each morning. The prayer she taught me came back to my mind, word for word, when I again found myself alone, as weak, as lost, as a little child. What would you have, my friend? I joined my hands as in my younger days, I felt too wretched, too forsaken, I had too keen a need of a superhuman help, of a divine power which should think and determine for me, which should lull me and carry me on with its eternal prescience. How great at first was the confusion, the aberration of my poor brain, under the frightful, heavy blow which fell upon it! I spent a score of nights without being able to sleep, thinking that I should surely go mad. All sorts of ideas warred within me; I passed through periods of revolt when I shook my fist at Heaven, and then I lapsed into humility, entreating God to take me in my turn. And it was at last a conviction that there must be justice, a conviction that there must be love, which calmed me by restoring me my faith. You knew my daughter, so tall and strong, so beautiful, so brimful of life. Would it not be the most monstrous injustice if for her, who did not know life, there should be nothing beyond the tomb? She will live again, I am absolutely convinced of it, for I still hear her at times, she tells me that we shall meet, that we shall see one another again. Oh! the dear beings whom one has lost, my dear daughter, my dear wife, to see them once more, to live with them elsewhere, that is the one hope, the one consolation for all the sorrows of this world! I have given myself to God, since God alone can restore them to me!"

He was shaking with a slight tremor, like the weak old man he had become; and Pierre was at last able to understand and explain the conversion of this *savant*, this man of intellect who, growing old, had reverted to belief under the influence of sentiment. First of all, and this he had previously suspected, he discovered a kind of atavism of faith in this Pyrenean, this son of peasant mountaineers, who had been brought up in belief of the legend, and whom the legend had again mastered even when fifty years, of positive study had rolled over it. Then, too, there was human weariness; this man, to whom science had not brought happiness, revolted against science on the day when it seemed to him shallow, powerless to prevent him from shedding tears. And finally there was discouragement, a doubt of all things, ending in a need of certainty on the part of one whom age had softened, and who felt happy at being able to fall asleep in credulity.

Pierre did not protest, however; he did not jeer, for his heart was rent at sight of this tall, stricken old man, with his woeful senility. Is it not indeed pitiful to see the strongest, the clearest-minded become mere children again under such blows of fate? "Ah!" he faintly sighed, "if I could only suffer enough to be able to silence my reason, and kneel yonder and believe in all those fine stories."

The pale smile, which at times still passed over Doctor Chassaigne's lips, reappeared on them. "You mean the miracles?" said he. "You are a priest, my child, and I know what your misfortune is. The miracles seem impossible to you. But what do you know of them? Admit that you know nothing, and that what to our senses seems impossible is every minute taking place. And now we have been talking together for a long time, and eleven o'clock will soon strike, so that you must return to the Grotto. However, I shall expect you, at half-past three, when I will take you to the Medical Verification Office, where I hope I shall be able to show you some surprising things. Don't forget, at half-past three."

Thereupon he sent him off, and remained on the bench alone. The heat had yet increased, and the distant hills were burning in the furnace-like glow of the sun. However, he lingered there forgetfully, dreaming in the greeny half-light amidst the foliage, and listening to the continuous murmur of the Gave, as if a voice, a dear voice from the realms beyond, were speaking to him.

Pierre meantime hastened back to Marie. He was able to join her without much difficulty, for the crowd was thinning, a good many people having already gone off to *dejeuner*. And on arriving he perceived the girl's father, who was quietly seated beside her, and who at once wished to explain to him the reason of his long absence. For more than a couple of hours that morning he had scoured Lourdes in all directions, applying at twenty hotels in turn without being able to find the smallest closet where they might sleep. Even the servants' rooms were let and you could not have even secured a mattress on which to stretch yourself in some passage. However, all at once, just as he was despairing, he had discovered two rooms, small ones, it is true, and just under the roof, but in a very good hotel, that of the Apparitions, one of the best patronised in the town. The persons who had retained these rooms had just telegraphed that the patient whom they had meant to bring with them was dead. Briefly, it was a piece of rare good luck, and seemed to make M. de Guersaint quite gay.

Eleven o'clock was now striking and the woeful procession of sufferers started off again through the sunlit streets and squares. When it reached the hospital Marie begged her father and Pierre to go to the hotel, lunch and rest there awhile, and return to fetch her at two o'clock, when the patients would again be conducted to the Grotto. But when, after lunching, the two men went up to the rooms which they were to occupy at the Hotel of the Apparitions, M. de Guersaint, overcome by fatigue, fell so soundly asleep that Pierre had not the heart to awaken him. What would have been the use of it? His presence was not indispensable. And so the young priest returned to the hospital alone. Then the *cortege* again descended the Avenue de la Grotte, again wended its way over the Plateau de la Merlasse, again crossed the Place du Rosaire, past an ever-growing crowd which shuddered and crossed itself amid all the joyousness of that splendid August day. It was now the most glorious hour of a lovely afternoon.

When Marie was again installed in front of the Grotto she inquired if her father were coming. "Yes," answered Pierre; "he is only taking a little rest."

She waved her hand as though to say that he was acting rightly, and then in a sorely troubled voice she added: "Listen, Pierre; don't take me to the piscina for another hour. I am not yet in a state to find favour from Heaven, I wish to pray, to keep on praying."

After evincing such an ardent desire to come to Lourdes, terror was agitating her now that the moment for attempting the miracle was at hand. In fact, she began to relate that she had been unable to eat anything, and a girl who overheard her at once approached saying: "If you feel too weak, my dear young lady, remember we have some broth here."

Marie looked at her and recognised Raymonde. Several young girls were in this wise employed at the Grotto to distribute cups of broth and milk among the sufferers. Some of them, indeed, in previous years had displayed so much coquetry in the matter of silk, aprons trimmed with lace, that a uniform apron, of modest linen, with a small check pattern, blue and white, had been imposed on them. Nevertheless, in spite of this enforced simplicity, Raymonde, thanks to her freshness and her active, good-natured, housewifely air, had succeeded in making herself look quite charming.

"You will remember, won't you?" she added; "you have only to make me a sign and I will serve you."

Marie thanked her, saying, however, that she felt sure she would not be able to take anything; and then, turning towards the young priest, she resumed: "One hour—you must allow me one more hour, my friend."

Pierre wished at any rate to remain near her, but the entire space was reserved to the sufferers, the bearers not being allowed there. So he had to retire, and, caught in the rolling waves of the crowd, he found himself carried towards the piscinas, where he came upon an extraordinary spectacle which stayed his steps. In front of the low buildings where the baths were, three by three, six for the women and three for the men, he perceived under the trees a long stretch of ground enclosed by a rope fastened to the tree-trunks; and here, various sufferers, some sitting in their bath-chairs and others lying on the mattresses of their litters, were drawn up in line, waiting to be bathed, whilst outside the rope, a huge, excited throng was ever pressing and surging. A Capuchin, erect in the centre of the reserved space, was at that moment conducting the prayers. "Aves" followed one after the other, repeated by the crowd in a loud confused murmur. Then, all at once, as Madame Vincent, who, pale with agony, had long been waiting, was admitted to the baths, carrying her dear burden, her little girl who looked like a waxen image of the child Christ, the Capuchin let himself fall upon his knees with his arms extended, and cried aloud: "Lord, heal our sick!" He raised this cry a dozen, twenty times, with a growing fury, and each time the crowd repeated it, growing more and more excited at each shout, till it sobbed and kissed the ground in a state of frenzy. It was like a hurricane of delirium rushing by and laying every head in the dust. Pierre was utterly distracted by the sob of suffering which arose from the very bowels of these poor folks—at first a prayer, growing louder and louder, then bursting forth like a demand in impatient, angry, deafening, obstinate accents, as though to compel the help of Heaven. "Lord, heal our sick!"—"Lord, heal our sick!" The shout soared on high incessantly.

An incident occurred, however; La Grivotte was weeping hot tears because they would not bathe her. "They say that I'm a consumptive," she plaintively exclaimed, "and that they can't dip consumptives in cold water. Yet they dipped one this morning; I saw her. So why won't they dip me? I've been wearing myself out for the last half-hour in telling them that they are only grieving the Blessed Virgin, for I am going to be cured, I feel it, I am going to be cured!"

As she was beginning to cause a scandal, one of the chaplains of the piscinas approached and endeavoured to calm her. They would see what they could do for her, by-and-by, said he; they would consult the reverend Fathers, and, if she were very good, perhaps they would bathe her all the same.

Meantime the cry continued: "Lord, heal our sick! Lord, heal our sick!" And Pierre, who had just perceived Madame Vetu, also waiting at the piscina entry, could no longer turn his eyes away from her hope-tortured face, whose eyes were fixed upon the doorway by which the happy ones, the elect, emerged from the divine presence, cured of all their ailments. However, a sudden increase of the crowd's frenzy, a perfect rage of entreaties, gave him such a shock as to draw tears from his eyes. Madame Vincent was now coming out again, still carrying her little girl in her arms, her wretched, her fondly loved little girl, who had been dipped in a fainting state in the icy water, and whose little face, but imperfectly wiped, was as pale as ever, and indeed even more woeful and lifeless. The mother was sobbing, crucified by this long agony, reduced to despair by the refusal of the Blessed Virgin, who had remained insensible to her child's sufferings. And yet when Madame Vetu in her turn entered, with the eager passion of a dying woman about to drink the water of life, the haunting, obstinate cry burst out again, without sign of discouragement or lassitude: "Lord, heal our sick! Lord, heal our sick!" The Capuchin had now fallen with his face to the ground, and the howling crowd, with arms outstretched, devoured the soil with its kisses.

Pierre wished to join Madame Vincent to soothe her with a few kind, encouraging words; however, a fresh string of pilgrims not only prevented him from passing, but threw him towards the fountain which another throng besieged. There was here quite a range of low buildings, a long stone wall with carved coping, and it had been necessary for the people to form in procession, although there were twelve taps from which the water fell into a narrow basin. Many came hither to fill bottles, metal cans, and stoneware pitchers. To prevent too great a waste of water, the tap only acted when a knob was pressed with the hand. And thus many weak-handed women lingered there a long time, the water dripping on their feet. Those who had no cans to fill at least came to drink and wash their faces. Pierre noticed one young man who drank seven small glassfuls of water, and washed his eyes seven times without wiping them. Others were drinking out of shells, tin goblets, and leather cups. And he was particularly interested by the sight of Elise Rouquet, who, thinking it useless to go to the piscinas to bathe the frightful sore which was eating away her face, had contented herself with employing the water of the fountain as a lotion, every two hours since her arrival that morning. She knelt down, threw back her fichu, and for a long time applied a handkerchief to her face—a handkerchief which she had soaked with the miraculous fluid like a sponge; and the crowd around rushed upon the fountain in such fury that folks no longer noticed her diseased face, but washed themselves and drank from the same pipe at which she constantly moistened her handkerchief.

Just then, however, Gerard, who passed by dragging M. Sabathier to the piscinas, called to Pierre, whom he saw unoccupied, and asked him to come and help him, for it would not be an easy task to move and bathe this helpless victim of ataxia. And thus Pierre lingered with the sufferer in the men's piscina for nearly half an hour, whilst Gerard returned to the Grotto to fetch another patient. These piscinas seemed to the young priest to be very well arranged. They were divided into three compartments, three baths separated by partitions, with steps leading into them. In order that one might isolate the patient, a linen curtain hug before each entry, which was reached through a kind of waiting-room having a paved floor, and furnished with a bench and a couple of chairs. Here the patients undressed and dressed themselves with an awkward haste, a nervous kind of shame. One man, whom

Pierre found there when he entered, was still naked, and wrapped himself in the curtain before putting on a bandage with trembling hands. Another one, a consumptive who was frightfully emaciated, sat shivering and groaning, his livid skin mottled with violet marks. However, Pierre became more interested in Brother Isidore, who was just being removed from one of the baths. He had fainted away, and for a moment, indeed, it was thought that he was dead. But at last he began moaning again, and one's heart filled with pity at sight of his long, lank frame, which suffering had withered, and which, with his diseased hip, looked a human remnant on exhibition. The two hospitallers who had been bathing him had the greatest difficulty to put on his shirt, fearful as they were that if he were suddenly shaken he might expire in their arms.

"You will help me, Monsieur l'Abbe, won't you?" asked another hospitaller as he began to undress M. Sabathier.

Pierre hastened to give his services, and found that the attendant, discharging such humble duties, was none other than the Marquis de Salmon-Roquebert whom M. de Guersaint had pointed out to him on the way from the station to the hospital that morning. A man of forty, with a large, aquiline, knightly nose set in a long face, the Marquis was the last representative of one of the most ancient and illustrious families of France. Possessing a large fortune, a regal mansion in the Rue de Lille at Paris, and vast estates in Normandy, he came to Lourdes each year, for the three days of the national pilgrimage, influenced solely by his benevolent feelings, for he had no religious zeal and simply observed the rites of the Church because it was customary for noblemen to do so. And he obstinately declined any high functions. Resolved to remain a hospitaller, he had that year assumed the duty of bathing the patients, exhausting the strength of his arms, employing his fingers from morning till night in handling rags and re-applying dressings to sores.

"Be careful," he said to Pierre; "take off the stockings very slowly. Just now, some flesh came away when they were taking off the things of that poor fellow who is being dressed again, over yonder."

Then, leaving M. Sabathier for a moment in order to put on the shoes of the unhappy sufferer whom he alluded to, the Marquis found the left shoe wet inside. Some matter had flowed into the fore part of it, and he had to take the usual medical precautions before putting it on the patient's foot, a task which he performed with extreme care; and so as not to touch the man's leg, into which an ulcer was eating.

"And now," he said to Pierre, as he returned to M. Sabathier, "pull down the drawers at the same time I do, so that we may get them off at one pull."

In addition to the patients and the hospitallers selected for duty at the piscinas, the only person in the little dressing-room was a chaplain who kept on repeating "Paters" and "Aves," for not even a momentary pause was allowed in the prayers. Merely a loose curtain hung before the doorway leading to the open space which the rope enclosed; and the ardent clamorous entreaties of the throng were incessantly wafted into the room, with the piercing shouts of the Capuchin, who ever repeated "Lord, heal our sick! Lord, heal our sick!" A cold light fell from the high windows of the building and constant dampness reigned there, with the mouldy smell like that of a cellar dripping with water.

At last M. Sabathier was stripped, divested of all garments save a little apron which had been fastened about his loins for decency's sake.

"Pray don't plunge me," said he; "let me down into the water by degrees."

In point of fact that cold water quite terrified him. He was still wont to relate that he had experienced such a frightful chilling sensation on the first occasion that he had sworn never to go in again. According to his account, there could be no worse torture than that icy cold. And then too, as he put it, the water was scarcely inviting; for, through fear lest the output of the source should not suffice, the Fathers of the Grotto only allowed the water of the baths to be changed twice a day. And nearly a hundred patients being dipped in the same water, it can be imagined what a terrible soup the latter at last became. All manner of things were found in it, so that it was like a frightful *consomme* of all ailments, a field of cultivation for every kind of poisonous germ, a quintessence of the most dreaded contagious diseases; the miraculous feature of it all being that men should emerge alive from their immersion in such filth.

"Gently, gently," repeated M. Sabathier to Pierre and the Marquis, who had taken hold of him under the hips in order to carry him to the bath. And he gazed with childlike terror at that thick, livid water on which floated so many greasy, nauseating patches of scum. However, his dread of the cold was so great that he preferred the polluted baths of the afternoon, since all the bodies that were dipped in the water during the early part of the day ended by slightly warming it.

"We will let you slide down the steps," exclaimed the Marquis in an undertone; and then he instructed Pierre to hold the patient with all his strength under the arm-pits.

"Have no fear," replied the priest; "I will not let go."

M. Sabathier was then slowly lowered. You could now only see his back, his poor painful back which swayed and swelled, mottled by the rippling of a shiver. And when they dipped him his head fell back in a spasm, a sound like the cracking of bones was heard, and breathing hard, he almost stifled.

The chaplain, standing beside the bath, had begun calling with renewed fervour: "Lord, heal our sick! Lord, heal our sick!"

M. de Salmon-Roquebert repeated the cry, which the regulations required the hospitallers to raise at each fresh immersion. Pierre, therefore, had to imitate his companion, and his pitiful feelings at the sight of so much suffering were so intense that he regained some little of his faith. It was long indeed since he had prayed like this, devoutly wishing that there might be a God in heaven, whose omnipotence could assuage the wretchedness of humanity. At the end of three or four minutes, however, when with great difficulty they drew M. Sabathier, livid and shivering, out of the bath, the young priest fell into deeper, more despairing sorrow than ever at beholding how downcast, how overwhelmed the sufferer was at having experienced no relief. Again had he made a futile attempt; for the seventh time the Blessed Virgin had not deigned to listen to his prayers. He closed his eyes, from between the lids of which big tears began to roll while they were dressing him again.

Then Pierre recognised little Gustave Vigneron coming in, on his crutch, to take his first bath. His relatives, his father, his mother, and his aunt, Madame Chaise, all three of substantial appearance and exemplary piety, had just fallen on their knees at the door. Whispers ran through the crowd; it was said that the gentleman was a functionary of the Ministry of Finances. However, while the child was beginning to undress, a tumult arose, and Father Fourcade and Father Massias, suddenly arriving, gave orders to suspend the immersions. The great miracle was about to be attempted, the extraordinary favour which had been so ardently prayed for since the morning—the restoration of the dead man to life.

The prayers were continuing outside, rising in a furious appeal which died away in the sky of that warm summer afternoon. Two bearers came in with a covered stretcher, which they deposited in the middle of the dressing-room. Baron Suire, President of the Association, followed, accompanied by Berthaud, one of its principal officers, for the affair was causing a great stir among the whole staff, and before anything was done a few words were exchanged in low voices between the gentlemen and the two Fathers of the Assumption. Then the latter fell upon their knees, with arms extended, and began to pray, their faces illumined, transfigured by their burning desire to see God's omnipotence displayed.

"Lord, hear us! Lord, grant our prayer!"

M. Sabathier had just been taken away, and the only patient now present was little Gustave, who had remained on a chair, half-undressed and forgotten. The curtains of the stretcher were raised, and the man's corpse appeared, already stiff, and seemingly reduced and shrunken, with large eyes which had obstinately remained wide open. It was necessary, however, to undress the body, which was still fully clad, and this terrible duty made the bearers momentarily hesitate. Pierre noticed that the Marquis de Salmon-Roquebert, who showed such devotion to the living, such freedom from all repugnance whenever they were in question, had now drawn aside and fallen on his knees, as though to avoid the necessity of touching that lifeless corpse. And the young priest thereupon followed his example, and knelt near him in order to keep countenance.

Father Massias meanwhile was gradually becoming excited, praying in so loud a voice that it drowned that of his superior, Father Fourcade: "Lord, restore our brother to us!" he cried. "Lord, do it for Thy glory!"

One of the hospitallers had already begun to pull at the man's trousers, but his legs were so stiff that the garment would not come off. In fact the corpse ought to have been raised up; and the other hospitaller, who was unbuttoning the dead man's old frock coat, remarked in an undertone that it would be best to cut everything away with a pair of scissors. Otherwise there would be no end of the job.

Berthaud, however, rushed up to them, after rapidly consulting Baron Suire. As a politician he secretly disapproved of Father Fourcade's action in making such an attempt, only they could not now do otherwise than carry matters to an issue; for the crowd was waiting and had been entreating God on the dead man's behalf ever since the morning. The wisest course, therefore, was to finish with the affair at once, showing as much respect as possible for the remains of the deceased. In lieu, therefore, of pulling the corpse about in order to strip it bare, Berthaud was of opinion that it would be better to dip it in the piscina clad as it was. Should the man resuscitate, it would be easy to procure fresh clothes for him; and in the contrary event, no harm would have been done. This is what he hastily said to the bearers; and forthwith he helped them to pass some straps under the man's hips and arms.

Father Fourcade had nodded his approval of this course, whilst Father Massias prayed with increased fervour: "Breathe upon him, O Lord, and he shall be born anew! Restore his soul to him, O, Lord, that he may glorify Thee!"

Making an effort, the two hospitallers now raised the man by means of the straps, carried him to the bath, and slowly lowered him into the water, at each moment fearing that he would slip away from their hold. Pierre, although overcome by horror, could not do otherwise than look at them, and thus he distinctly beheld the immersion of this corpse in its sorry garments, which on being wetted clung to the bones, outlining the skeleton-like figure of the deceased, who floated like a man who has been drowned. But the repulsive part of it all was, that in spite of the *rigor mortis*, the head fell backward into the water, and was submerged by it. In vain did the hospitallers try to raise it by pulling the shoulder straps; as they made the attempt, the man almost sank to the bottom of the bath. And how could he have recovered his breath when his mouth was full of water, his staring eyes seemingly dying afresh, beneath that watery veil?

Then, during the three long minutes allowed for the immersion, the two Fathers of the Assumption and the chaplain, in a paroxysm of desire and faith, strove to compel the intervention of Heaven, praying in such loud voices that they seemed to choke.

"Do Thou but look on him, O Lord, and he will live again! Lord! may he rise at Thy voice to convert the earth! Lord! Thou hast but one word to say and all Thy people will acclaim Thee!"

At last, as though some vessel had broken in his throat, Father Massias fell groaning and choking on his elbows, with only enough strength left him to kiss the flagstones. And from without came the clamour of the crowd, the ever-repeated cry, which the Capuchin was still leading: "Lord, heal our sick! Lord, heal our sick!" This appeal seemed so singular at that moment, that Pierre's sufferings were increased. He could feel, too, that the Marquis was shuddering beside him. And so the relief was general when Berthaud, thoroughly annoyed with the whole business, curtly shouted to the hospitallers: "Take him out! Take him out at once!"

The body was removed from the bath and laid on the stretcher, looking like the corpse of a drowned man with its sorry garments

ÉMILE ZOLA

clinging to its limbs. The water was trickling from the hair, and rivulets began falling on either side, spreading out in pools on the floor. And naturally, dead as the man had been, dead he remained.

The others had all risen and stood looking at him amidst a distressing silence. Then, as he was covered up and carried away, Father Fourcade followed the bier leaning on the shoulder of Father Massias and dragging his gouty leg, the painful weight of which he had momentarily forgotten. But he was already recovering his strong serenity, and as a hush fell upon the crowd outside, he could be heard saying: "My dear brothers, my dear sisters, God has not been willing to restore him to us, doubtless because in His infinite goodness He has desired to retain him among His elect."

And that was all; there was no further question of the dead man. Patients were again being brought into the dressing-room, the two other baths were already occupied. And now little Gustave, who had watched that terrible scene with his keen inquisitive eyes, evincing no sign of terror, finished undressing himself. His wretched body, the body of a scrofulous child, appeared with its prominent ribs and projecting spine, its limbs so thin that they looked like mere walking-sticks. Especially was this the case as regards the left one, which was withered, wasted to the bone; and he also had two sores, one on the hip, and the other in the loins, the last a terrible one, the skin being eaten away so that you distinctly saw the raw flesh. Yet he smiled, rendered so precocious by his sufferings that, although but fifteen years old and looking no more than ten, he seemed to be endowed with the reason and philosophy of a grown man.

The Marquis de Salmon-Roquebert, who had taken him gently in his arms, refused Pierre's offer of service: "Thanks, but he weighs no more than a bird. And don't be frightened, my dear little fellow. I will do it gently."

"Oh, I am not afraid of cold water, monsieur," replied the boy; "you may duck me."

Then he was lowered into the bath in which the dead man had been dipped. Madame Vigneron and Madame Chaise, who were not allowed to enter, had remained at the door on their knees, whilst the father, M. Vigneron, who was admitted into the dressing-room, went on making the sign of the cross.

Finding that his services were no longer required, Pierre now departed. The sudden idea that three o'clock must have long since struck and that Marie must be waiting for him made him hasten his steps. However, whilst he was endeavouring to pierce the crowd, he saw the girl arrive in her little conveyance, dragged along by Gerard, who had not ceased transporting sufferers to the piscina. She had become impatient, suddenly filled with a conviction that she was at last in a frame of mind to find grace. And at sight of Pierre she reproached him, saying, "What, my friend, did you forget me?"

He could find no answer, but watched her as she was taken into the piscina reserved for women, and then, in mortal sorrow, fell upon his knees. It was there that he would wait for her, humbly kneeling, in order that he might take her back to the Grotto, cured without doubt and singing a hymn of praise. Since she was certain of it, would she not assuredly be cured? However, it was in vain that he sought for words of prayer in the depths of his distracted being. He was still under the blow of all the terrible things that he had beheld, worn out with physical fatigue, his brain depressed, no longer knowing what he saw or what he believed. His desperate affection for Marie alone remained, making him long to humble himself and supplicate, in the thought that when little ones really love and entreat the powerful they end by obtaining favours. And at last he caught himself repeating the prayers of the crowd, in a distressful voice that came from the depths of his being "Lord, heal our sick! Lord, heal our sick!"

Ten minutes, a quarter of an hour perhaps, went by. Then Marie reappeared in her little conveyance. Her face was very pale and wore an expression of despair. Her beautiful hair was fastened above her head in a heavy golden coil which the water had not touched. And she was not cured. The stupor of infinite discouragement hollowed and lengthened her face, and she averted her eyes as though to avoid meeting those of the priest who thunderstruck, chilled to the heart, at last made up his mind to grasp the handle of the little vehicle, so as to take the girl back to the Grotto.

And meantime the cry of the faithful, who with open arms were kneeling there and kissing the earth, again rose with a growing fury, excited by the Capuchin's shrill voice: "Lord, heal our sick! Heal our sick, O Lord!"

As Pierre was placing Marie in position again in front of the Grotto, an attack of weakness came over her and she almost fainted. Gerard, who was there, saw Raymonde quickly hurry to the spot with a cup of broth, and at once they began zealously rivalling each other in their attentions to the ailing girl. Raymonde, holding out the cup in a pretty way, and assuming the coaxing airs of an expert nurse, especially insisted that Marie should accept the bouillon; and Gerard, glancing at this portionless girl, could not help finding her charming, already expert in the business of life, and quite ready to manage a household with a firm hand without ceasing to be amiable. Berthaud was no doubt right, this was the wife that he, Gerard, needed.

"Mademoiselle," said he to Raymonde, "shall I raise the young lady a little?"

"Thank you, monsieur, I am quite strong enough. And besides I will give it to her in spoonfuls; that will be the better way."

Marie, however, obstinately preserving her fierce silence as she recovered consciousness, refused the broth with a gesture. She wished to be left in quietness, she did not want anybody to question her. And it was only when the others had gone off smiling at one another, that she said to Pierre in a husky voice: "Has not my father come then?"

After hesitating for a moment the priest was obliged to confess the truth. "I left him sleeping and he cannot have woke up."

Then Marie relapsed into her state of languid stupor and dismissed him in his turn, with the gesture with which she declined all succour. She no longer prayed, but remained quite motionless, gazing fixedly with her large eyes at the marble Virgin, the white statue amidst the radiance of the Grotto. And as four o'clock was now striking, Pierre with his heart sore went off to the Verification Office, having suddenly remembered the appointment given him by Doctor Chassaigne.

IV

VERIFICATION

The doctor was waiting for the young priest outside the Verification Office, in front of which a compact and feverish crowd of pilgrims was assembled, waylaying and questioning the patients who went in, and acclaiming them as they came out whenever the news spread of any miracle, such as the restoration of some blind man's sight, some deaf woman's hearing, or some paralytic's power of motion.

Pierre had no little difficulty in making his way through the throng, but at last he reached his friend. "Well," he asked, "are we going to have a miracle—a real, incontestable one I mean?"

The doctor smiled, indulgent despite his new faith. "Ah, well," said he, "a miracle is not worked to order. God intervenes when He pleases."

Some hospitallers were mounting guard at the door, but they all knew M. Chassaigne, and respectfully drew aside to let him enter with his companion. The office where the cures were verified was very badly installed in a wretched wooden shanty divided into two apartments, first a narrow ante-chamber, and then a general meeting room which was by no means so large as it should have been. However, there was a question of providing the department with better accommodation the following year; with which view some large premises, under one of the inclined ways of the Rosary, were already being fitted up.

The only article of furniture in the antechamber was a wooden bench on which Pierre perceived two female patients awaiting their turn in the charge of a young hospitaller. But on entering the meeting room the number of persons packed inside it quite surprised him, whilst the suffocating heat within those wooden walls on which the sun was so fiercely playing, almost scorched his face. It was a square bare room, painted a light yellow, with the panes of its single window covered with whitening, so that the pressing throng outside might see nothing of what went on within. One dared not even open this window to admit a little fresh air, for it was no sooner set ajar than a crowd of inquisitive heads peeped in. The furniture was of a very rudimentary kind, consisting simply of two deal tables of unequal height placed end to end and not even covered with a cloth; together with a kind of big "canterbury" littered with untidy papers, sets of documents, registers and pamphlets, and finally some thirty rush-seated chairs placed here and there over the floor and a couple of ragged arm-chairs usually reserved for the patients.

Doctor Bonamy at once hastened forward to greet Doctor Chassaigne, who was one of the latest and most glorious conquests of the Grotto. He found a chair for him and, bowing to Pierre's cassock, also made the young priest sit down. Then, in the tone of extreme politeness which was customary with him, he exclaimed: "*Mon cher confrere*, you will kindly allow me to continue. We were just examining mademoiselle."

He referred to a deaf peasant girl of twenty, who was seated in one of the arm-chairs. Instead of listening, however, Pierre, who was very weary, still with a buzzing in his head, contented himself with gazing at the scene, endeavouring to form some notion of the people assembled in the room. There were some fifty altogether, many of them standing and leaning against the walls. Half a dozen, however, were seated at the two tables, a central position being occupied by the superintendent of the piscinas, who was constantly consulting a thick register; whilst around him were a Father of the Assumption and three young seminarists who acted as secretaries, writing, searching for documents, passing them and classifying them again after each examination. Pierre, however, took most interest in a Father of the Immaculate Conception, Father Dargeles, who had been pointed out to him that morning as being the editor of the "Journal de la Grotte." This ecclesiastic, whose thin little face, with its blinking eyes, pointed nose, and delicate mouth was ever smiling, had modestly seated himself at the end of the lower table where he occasionally took notes for his newspaper. He alone, of the community to which he belonged, showed himself during the three days of the national pilgrimage. Behind him, however, one could divine the presence of all the others, the slowly developed hidden power which organised everything and raked in all the proceeds.

The onlookers consisted almost entirely of inquisitive people and witnesses, including a score of doctors and a few priests. The medical men, who had come from all parts, mostly preserved silence, only a few of them occasionally venturing to ask a question; and every now and then they would exchange oblique glances, more occupied apparently in watching one another than in verifying the facts submitted to their examination. Who could they be? Some names were mentioned, but they were quite unknown. Only one had caused any stir, that of a celebrated doctor, professor at a Catholic university.

That afternoon, however, Doctor Bonamy, who never sat down, busy as he was conducting the proceedings and questioning the patients, reserved most of his attentions for a short, fair-haired man, a writer of some talent who contributed to one of the most widely read Paris newspapers, and who, in the course of a holiday tour, had by chance reached Lourdes that morning. Was not this an unbeliever whom it might be possible to convert, whose influence it would be desirable to gain for advertisement's sake? Such at all events appeared to be M. Bonamy's opinion, for he had compelled the journalist to take the second arm-chair, and with an affectation of smiling good-nature was treating him to a full performance, again and again repeating that he and his patrons had nothing to hide, and that everything took place in the most open manner.

"We only desire light," he exclaimed. "We never cease to call for the investigations of all willing men."

Then, as the alleged cure of the deaf girl did not seem at all a promising case, he addressed her somewhat roughly: "Come, come, my girl, this is only a beginning. You must come back when there are more distinct signs of improvement." And turning to the journalist he added in an undertone: "If we were to believe them they would all be healed. But the only cures we accept are those which are thoroughly proven, which are as apparent as the sun itself. Pray notice moreover that I say cures and not miracles; for we doctors do not take upon ourselves to interpret and explain. We are simply here to see if the patients, who submit themselves to our examination, have really lost all symptoms of their ailments."

Thereupon he struck an attitude. Doubtless he spoke like this in order that his rectitude might not be called in question. Believing without believing, he knew that science was yet so obscure, so full of surprises, that what seemed impossible might always come to pass; and thus, in the declining years of his life, he had contrived to secure an exceptional position at the Grotto, a position which had both its inconveniences and its advantages, but which, taken for all in all, was very comfortable and pleasant.

And now, in reply to a question from the Paris journalist, he began to explain his mode of proceeding. Each patient who accompanied the pilgrimage arrived provided with papers, amongst which there was almost always a certificate of the doctor who had been attending the case. At times even there were certificates given by several doctors, hospital bulletins and so forth—quite a record of the illness in its various stages. And thus if a cure took place and the cured person came forward, it was only necessary to consult his or her set of documents in order to ascertain the nature of the ailment, and then examination would show if that ailment had really disappeared.

Pierre was now listening. Since he had been there, seated and resting himself, he had grown calmer, and his mind was clear once more. It was only the heat which at present caused him any inconvenience. And thus, interested as he was by Doctor Bonamy's explanations, and desirous of forming an opinion, he would have spoken out and questioned, had it not been for his cloth which condemned him to remain in the background. He was delighted, therefore, when the little fair-haired gentleman, the influential writer, began to bring forward the objections which at once occurred to him.* Was it not most unfortunate that one doctor should diagnose the illness and that another one should verify the cure? In this mode of proceeding there was certainly a source of frequent error. The better plan would have been for a medical commission to examine all the patients as soon as they arrived at Lourdes and draw up reports on every case, to which reports the same commission would have referred whenever an alleged cure was brought before it. Doctor Bonamy, however, did not fall in with this suggestion. He replied, with some reason, that a commission would never suffice for such gigantic labour. Just think of it! A thousand patients to examine in a single morning! And how many different theories there would be, how many contrary diagnoses, how many endless discussions, all of a nature to increase the general uncertainty! The preliminary examination of the patients, which was almost always impossible, would, even if attempted, leave the door open for as many errors as the present system. In practice, it was necessary to remain content with the certificates delivered by the medical men who had been in attendance on the patients, and these certificates accordingly acquired capital, decisive importance. Doctor Bonamy ran through the documents lying on one of the tables and gave the Paris journalist some of these certificates to read. A great many of them unfortunately were very brief. Others, more skilfully drawn up,

---

* The reader will doubtless have understood that the Parisian journalist is none other than M. Zola himself—Trans.

clearly specified the nature of the complaint; and some of the doctors' signatures were even certified by the mayors of the localities where they resided. Nevertheless doubts remained, innumerable and not to be surmounted. Who were these doctors? Who could tell if they possessed sufficient scientific authority to write as they did? With all respect to the medical profession, were there not innumerable doctors whose attainments were very limited? And, besides, might not these have been influenced by circumstances that one knew nothing of, in some cases by considerations of a personal character? One was tempted to ask for an inquiry respecting each of these medical men. Since everything was based on the documents supplied by the patients, these documents ought to have been most carefully controlled; for there could be no proof of any miracle if the absolute certainty of the alleged ailments had not been demonstrated by stringent examination.

Very red and covered with perspiration, Doctor Bonamy waved his arms. "But that is the course we follow, that is the course we follow!" said he. "As soon as it seems to us that a case of cure cannot be explained by natural means, we institute a minute inquiry, we request the person who has been cured to return here for further examination. And as you can see, we surround ourselves with all means of enlightenment. These gentlemen here, who are listening to us, are nearly every one of them doctors who have come from all parts of France. We always entreat them to express their doubts if they feel any, to discuss the cases with us, and a very detailed report of each discussion is drawn up. You hear me, gentlemen; by all means protest if anything occurs here of a nature to offend your sense of truth."

Not one of the onlookers spoke. Most of the doctors present were undoubtedly Catholics, and naturally enough they merely bowed. As for the others, the unbelievers, the *savants* pure and simple, they looked on and evinced some interest in certain phenomena, but considerations of courtesy deterred them from entering into discussions which they knew would have been useless. When as men of sense their discomfort became too great, and they felt themselves growing angry, they simply left the room.

As nobody breathed a word, Doctor Bonamy became quite triumphant, and on the journalist asking him if he were all alone to accomplish so much work, he replied: "Yes, all alone; but my functions as doctor of the Grotto are not so complicated as you may think, for, I repeat it, they simply consist in verifying cures whenever any take place." However, he corrected himself, and added with a smile: "All! I was forgetting, I am not quite alone, I have Raboin, who helps me to keep things a little bit in order here."

So saying, he pointed to a stout, grey-haired man of forty, with a heavy face and bull-dog jaw. Raboin was an ardent believer, one of those excited beings who did not allow the miracles to be called in question. And thus he often suffered from his duties at the Verification Office, where he was ever ready to growl with anger when anybody disputed a prodigy. The appeal to the doctors had made him quite lose his temper, and his superior had to calm him.

"Come, Raboin, my friend, be quiet!" said Doctor Bonamy. "All sincere opinions are entitled to a hearing."

However, the *defile* of patients was resumed. A man was now brought in whose trunk was so covered with eczema that when he took off his shirt a kind of grey flour fell from his skin. He was not cured, but simply declared that he came to Lourdes every year, and always went away feeling relieved. Then came a lady, a countess, who was fearfully emaciated, and whose story was an extraordinary one. Cured of tuberculosis by the Blessed Virgin, a first time, seven years previously, she had subsequently given birth to four children, and had then again fallen into consumption. At present she was a morphinomaniac, but her first bath had already relieved her so much, that she proposed taking part in the torchlight procession that same evening with the twenty-seven members of her family whom she had brought with her to Lourdes. Then there was a woman afflicted with nervous aphonia, who after months of absolute dumbness had just recovered her voice at the moment when the Blessed Sacrament went by at the head of the four o'clock procession.

"Gentlemen," declared Doctor Bonamy, affecting the graciousness of a *savant* of extremely liberal views, "as you are aware, we do not draw any conclusions when a nervous affection is in question. Still you will kindly observe that this woman was treated at the Salpetriere for six months, and that she had to come here to find her tongue suddenly loosened."

Despite all these fine words he displayed some little impatience, for he would have greatly liked to show the gentleman from Paris one of those remarkable instances of cure which occasionally presented themselves during the four o'clock procession—that being the moment of grace and exaltation when the Blessed Virgin interceded for those whom she had chosen. But on this particular afternoon there had apparently been none. The cures which had so far passed before them were doubtful ones, deficient in interest. Meanwhile, out-of-doors, you could hear the stamping and roaring of the crowd, goaded into a frenzy by repeated hymns, enfevered by its earnest desire for the Divine interposition, and growing more and more enervated by the delay.

All at once, however, a smiling, modest-looking young girl, whose clear eyes sparkled with intelligence, entered the office. "Ah!" exclaimed Doctor Bonamy joyously, "here is our little friend Sophie. A remarkable cure, gentlemen, which took place at the same season last year, and the results of which I will ask permission to show you."

Pierre had immediately recognized Sophie Couteau, the *miraculee* who had got into the train at Poitiers. And he now witnessed a repetition of the scene which had already been enacted in his presence. Doctor Bonamy began giving detailed explanations to the little fair-haired gentleman, who displayed great attention. The case, said the doctor, had been one of caries of the bones of the left heel, with a commencement of necrosis necessitating excision; and yet the frightful, suppurating sore had been healed in a minute at the first immersion in the piscina.

"Tell the gentlemen how it happened, Sophie," he added.

The little girl made her usual pretty gesture as a sign to everybody to be attentive. And then she began: "Well, it was like this; my foot was past cure, I couldn't even go to church any more, and it had to be kept bandaged because there was always a lot of matter coming from it. Monsieur Rivoire, the doctor, who had made a cut in it so as to see inside it, said that he should be obliged to take out a piece of the bone; and that, sure enough, would have made me lame for life. But when I got to Lourdes, and had prayed a great deal to the Blessed Virgin, I went to dip my foot in the water, wishing so much that I might be cured, that I did not even take the time to pull the bandages off. And everything remained in the water; there was no longer anything the matter with my foot when I took it out."

Doctor Bonamy listened, and punctuated each word with an approving nod. "And what did your doctor say, Sophie?" he asked.

"When I got back to Vivonne, and Monsieur Rivoire saw my foot again, he said: 'Whether it be God or the Devil who has cured this child, it is all the same to me; but in all truth, she is cured.'"

A burst of laughter rang out. The doctor's remark was sure to produce an effect.

"And what was it, Sophie, that you said to Madame la Comtesse, the superintendent of your ward?"

"Ah, yes! I hadn't brought many bandages for my foot with me, and I said to her, 'It was very kind of the Blessed Virgin to cure me the first day, as I should have run out of linen on the morrow.'"

Then there was fresh laughter, a general display of satisfaction at seeing her look so pretty, telling her story, which she now knew by heart, in too recitative a manner, but, nevertheless, remaining very touching and truthful in appearance.

"Take off your shoe, Sophie," now said Doctor Bonamy; "show your foot to these gentlemen. Let them feel it. Nobody must retain any doubt."

The little foot promptly appeared, very white, very clean, carefully tended indeed, with its scar just below the ankle, a long scar, whose whity seam testified to the gravity of the complaint. Some of the medical men had drawn near, and looked on in silence. Others, whose opinions, no doubt, were already formed, did not disturb themselves, though one of them, with an air of extreme politeness, inquired why the Blessed Virgin had not made a new foot while she was about it, for this would assuredly have given her no more trouble. Doctor Bonamy, however, quickly replied, that if the Blessed Virgin had left a scar, it was certainly in order that a trace, a proof of the miracle, might remain. Then he entered into technical particulars, demonstrating that a fragment of bone and flesh must have been instantly formed, and this, of course, could not be explained in any natural way.

"*Mon Dieu!*" interrupted the little fair-haired gentleman, "there is no need of any such complicated affair. Let me merely see a finger cut with a penknife, let me see it dipped in the water, and let it come out with the cut cicatrised. The miracle will be quite as great, and I shall bow to it respectfully." Then he added: "If I possessed a source which could thus close up sores and wounds, I would turn the world topsy-turvy. I do not know exactly how I should manage it, but at all events I would summon the nations, and the nations would come. I should cause the miracles to be verified in such an indisputable manner, that I should be the master of the earth. Just think what an extraordinary power it would be—a divine power. But it would be necessary that not a doubt should remain, the truth would have to be as patent, as apparent as the sun itself. The whole world would behold it and believe!"

Then he began discussing various methods of control with the doctor. He had admitted that, owing to the great number of patients, it would be difficult, if not impossible, to examine them all on their arrival. Only, why didn't they organise a special ward at the hospital, a ward which would be reserved for cases of visible sores? They would have thirty such cases all told, which might be subjected to the preliminary examination of a committee. Authentic reports would be drawn up, and the sores might even be photographed. Then, if a case of cure should present itself, the commission would merely have to authenticate it by a fresh report. And in all this there would be no question of any internal complaint, the diagnostication of which is difficult, and liable to be controverted. There would be visible evidence of the ailment, and cure could be proved.

Somewhat embarrassed, Doctor Bonamy replied: "No doubt, no doubt; all we ask for is enlightenment. The difficulty would be in forming the committee you speak of. If you only knew how little medical men agree! However, there is certainly an idea in what you say."

Fortunately a fresh patient now came to his assistance. Whilst little Sophie Couteau, already forgotten, was putting on, her shoes again, Elise Rouquet appeared, and, removing her wrap, displayed her diseased face to view. She related that she had been bathing it with her handkerchief ever since the morning, and it seemed to her that her sore, previously so fresh and raw, was already beginning to dry and grow paler in colour. This was true; Pierre noticed, with great surprise, that the aspect of the sore was now less horrible. This supplied fresh food for the discussion on visible sores, for the little fair-haired gentleman clung obstinately to his idea of organising a special ward. Indeed, said he, if the condition of this girl had been verified that morning, and she should be cured, what a triumph it would have been for the Grotto, which could have claimed to have healed a lupus! It would then have no longer been possible to deny that miracles were worked.

Doctor Chassaigne had so far kept in the background, motionless and silent, as though he desired that the facts alone should exercise their influence on Pierre. But he now leant forward and said to him in an undertone: "Visible sores, visible sores indeed! That gentleman can have no idea that our most learned medical men suspect many of these sores to be of nervous origin. Yes, we are discovering that complaints of this kind are often simply due to bad nutrition of the skin. These questions of nutrition are still so imperfectly studied and understood! And some medical men are also beginning to prove that the faith which heals can even cure sores, certain forms of lupus among others. And so I would ask what certainty that gentleman would obtain with his ward for visible sores? There would simply be a little more confusion and passion in arguing the eternal question. No, no! Science is vain, it is a sea of uncertainty."

He smiled sorrowfully whilst Doctor Bonamy, after advising Elise Rouquet to continue using the water as lotion and to return each day for further examination, repeated with his prudent, affable air: "At all events, gentlemen, there are signs of improvement in this case—that is beyond doubt."

But all at once the office was fairly turned topsy-turvy by the arrival of La Grivotte, who swept in like a whirlwind, almost dancing with delight and shouting in a full voice: "I am cured! I am cured!"

And forthwith she began to relate that they had first of all refused to bathe her, and that she had been obliged to insist and beg and sob in order to prevail upon them to do so, after receiving Father Fourcade's express permission. And then it had all happened as she had previously said it would. She had not been immersed in the icy water for three minutes—all perspiring as she was with her consumptive rattle—before she had felt strength returning to her like a whipstroke lashing her whole body. And now a flaming excitement possessed her; radiant, stamping her feet, she was unable to keep still.

"I am cured, my good gentlemen, I am cured!"

Pierre looked at her, this time quite stupefied. Was this the same girl whom, on the previous night, he had seen lying on the carriage seat, annihilated, coughing and spitting blood, with her face of ashen hue? He could not recognise her as she now stood there, erect and slender, her cheeks rosy, her eyes sparkling, upbuoyed by a determination to live, a joy in living already.

"Gentlemen," declared Doctor Bonamy, "the case appears to me to be a very interesting one. We will see."

Then he asked for the documents concerning La Grivotte. But they could not be found among all the papers heaped together on the tables. The young seminarists who acted as secretaries began turning everything over; and the superintendent of the piscinas who sat in their midst himself had to get up to see if these documents were in the "canterbury." At last, when he had sat down again, he found them under the register which lay open before him. Among them were three medical certificates which he read aloud. All three of them agreed in stating that the case was one of advanced phthisis, complicated by nervous incidents which invested it with a peculiar character.

Doctor Bonamy wagged his head as though to say that such an *ensemble* of testimony could leave no room for doubt. Forthwith, he subjected the patient to a prolonged auscultation. And he murmured: "I hear nothing—I hear nothing." Then, correcting himself, he added: "At least I hear scarcely anything."

Finally he turned towards the five-and-twenty or thirty doctors who were assembled there in silence. "Will some of you gentlemen," he asked, "kindly lend me the help of your science? We are here to study and discuss these questions."

At first nobody stirred. Then there was one who ventured to come forward and, in his turn subject the patient to auscultation. But instead of declaring himself, he continued reflecting, shaking his head anxiously. At last he stammered that in his opinion one must await further developments. Another doctor, however, at once took his place, and this one expressed a decided opinion. He could hear nothing at all, that woman could never have suffered from phthisis. Then others followed him; in fact, with the exception of five or six whose smiling faces remained impenetrable, they all joined the *defile*. And the confusion now attained its apogee; for each gave an opinion sensibly differing from that of his colleagues, so that a general uproar arose and one could no longer hear oneself speak. Father Dargeles alone retained the calmness of perfect serenity, for he had scented one of those cases which impassion people and redound to the glory of Our Lady of Lourdes. He was already taking notes on a corner of the table.

Thanks to all the noise of the discussion, Pierre and Doctor Chassaigne, seated at some distance from the others, were now able to talk together without being heard. "Oh! those piscinas!" said the young priest, "I have just seen them. To think that the water should be so seldom changed! What filth it is, what a soup of microbes! What a terrible blow for the present-day mania, that rage for antiseptic precautions! How is it that some pestilence does not carry off all these poor people? The opponents of the microbe theory must be having a good laugh—"

M. Chassaigne stopped him. "No, no, my child," said he. "The baths may be scarcely clean, but they offer no danger. Please notice that the temperature of the water never rises above fifty degrees, and that seventy-seven are necessary for the cultivation of germs.* Besides, scarcely any contagious diseases come to Lourdes, neither cholera, nor typhus, nor variola, nor measles, nor scarlatina. We only see certain organic affections here, paralysis, scrofula, tumours, ulcers and abscesses, cancers and phthisis; and the latter cannot be transmitted by the water of the baths. The old sores which are bathed have nothing to fear, and offer no risk of contagion. I can assure you that on this point there is even no necessity for the Blessed Virgin to intervene."

"Then, in that case, doctor," rejoined Pierre, "when you were practising, you would have dipped all your patients in icy water—women at no matter what season, rheumatic patients, people suffering from diseases of the heart, consumptives, and so on? For instance, that unhappy girl, half dead, and covered with sweat—would you have bathed her?"

"Certainly not! There are heroic methods of treatment to which, in practice, one does not dare to have recourse. An icy bath may undoubtedly kill a consumptive; but do we know, whether, in certain circumstances, it might not save her? I, who have ended by admitting that a supernatural power is at work here, I willingly admit that some cures must take place under natural conditions, thanks to that immersion in cold water which seems to us idiotic and barbarous. Ah! the things we don't know, the things we don't know!"

He was relapsing into his anger, his hatred of science, which he scorned since it had left him scared and powerless beside the deathbed of his wife and his daughter. "You ask for certainties," he resumed, "but assuredly it is not medicine which will give you them. Listen for a moment to those gentlemen and you will be edified. Is it not beautiful, all that confusion in which so many opinions clash together? Certainly there are ailments with which one is thoroughly acquainted, even to the most minute details of their evolution; there are remedies also, the effects of which have been studied with the most scrupulous care; but the thing that one does not know, that one cannot know, is the relation of the remedy to the ailment, for there are as many cases as there may be patients, each liable to variation, so that experimentation begins afresh every time. This is why the practice of medicine remains an art, for there can be no experimental finality in it. Cure always depends on chance, on some fortunate circumstance, on some bright idea of the doctor's. And so you will understand that all the people who come and

---

* The above are Fahrenheit degrees.—Trans.

discuss here make me laugh when they talk about the absolute laws of science. Where are those laws in medicine? I should like to have them shown to me."

He did not wish to say any more, but his passion carried him away, so he went on: "I told you that I had become a believer—nevertheless, to speak the truth, I understand very well why this worthy Doctor Bonamy is so little affected, and why he continues calling upon doctors in all parts of the world to come and study his miracles. The more doctors that might come, the less likelihood there would be of the truth being established in the inevitable battle between contradictory diagnoses and methods of treatment. If men cannot agree about a visible sore, they surely cannot do so about an internal lesion the existence of which will be admitted by some, and denied by others. And why then should not everything become a miracle? For, after all, whether the action comes from nature or from some unknown power, medical men are, as a rule, none the less astonished when an illness terminates in a manner which they have not foreseen. No doubt, too, things are very badly organised here. Those certificates from doctors whom nobody knows have no real value. All documents ought to be stringently inquired into. But even admitting any absolute scientific strictness, you must be very simple, my dear child, if you imagine that a positive conviction would be arrived at, absolute for one and all. Error is implanted in man, and there is no more difficult task than that of demonstrating to universal satisfaction the most insignificant truth."

Pierre had now begun to understand what was taking place at Lourdes, the extraordinary spectacle which the world had been witnessing for years, amidst the reverent admiration of some and the insulting laughter of others. Forces as yet but imperfectly studied, of which one was even ignorant, were certainly at work—auto-suggestion, long prepared disturbance of the nerves; inspiriting influence of the journey, the prayers, and the hymns; and especially the healing breath, the unknown force which was evolved from the multitude, in the acute crisis of faith. Thus it seemed to him anything but intelligent to believe in trickery. The facts were both of a much more lofty and much more simple nature. There was no occasion for the Fathers of the Grotto to descend to falsehood; it was sufficient that they should help in creating confusion, that they should utilise the universal ignorance. It might even be admitted that everybody acted in good faith—the doctors void of genius who delivered the certificates, the consoled patients who believed themselves cured, and the impassioned witnesses who swore that they had beheld what they described. And from all this was evolved the obvious impossibility of proving whether there was a miracle or not. And such being the case, did not the miracle naturally become a reality for the greater number, for all those who suffered and who had need of hope?

Then, as Doctor Bonamy, who had noticed that they were chatting apart, came up to them, Pierre ventured to inquire: "What is about the proportion of the cures to the number of cases?"

"About ten per cent.," answered the doctor; and reading in the young priest's eyes the words that he could not utter, he added in a very cordial way: "Oh! there would be many more, they would all be cured if we chose to listen to them. But it is as well to say it, I am only here to keep an eye on the miracles, like a policeman as it were. My only functions are to check excessive zeal, and to prevent holy things from being made ridiculous. In one word, this office is simply an office where a *visa* is given when the cures have been verified and seem real ones."

He was interrupted, however, by a low growl. Raboin was growing angry: "The cures verified, the cures verified," he muttered. "What is the use of that? There is no pause in the working of the miracles. What is the use of verifying them so far as believers are concerned? *They* merely have to bow down and believe. And what is the use, too, as regards the unbelievers? *They* will never be convinced. The work we do here is so much foolishness."

Doctor Bonamy severely ordered him to hold his tongue. "You are a rebel, Raboin," said he; "I shall tell Father Capdebarthe that I won't have you here any longer since you pass your time in sowing disobedience."

Nevertheless, there was truth in what had just been said by this man, who so promptly showed his teeth, eager to bite whenever his faith was assailed; and Pierre looked at him with sympathy. All the work of the Verification Office—work anything but well performed—was indeed useless, for it wounded the feelings of the pious, and failed to satisfy the incredulous. Besides, can a miracle be proved? No, you must believe in it! When God is pleased to intervene, it is not for man to try to understand. In the ages of real belief, Science did not make any meddlesome attempt to explain the nature of the Divinity. And why should it come and interfere here? By doing so, it simply hampered faith and diminished its own prestige. No, no, there must be no Science, you must throw yourself upon the ground, kiss it, and believe. Or else you must take yourself off. No compromise was possible. If examination once began it must go on, and must, fatally, conduct to doubt.

Pierre's greatest sufferings, however, came from the extraordinary conversations which he heard around him. There were some believers present who spoke of the miracles with the most amazing ease and tranquillity. The most stupefying stories left their serenity entire. Another miracle, and yet another! And with smiles on their faces, their reason never protesting, they went on relating such imaginings as could only have come from diseased brains. They were evidently living in such a state of visionary fever that nothing henceforth could astonish them. And not only did Pierre notice this among folks of simple, childish minds, illiterate, hallucinated creatures like Raboin, but also among the men of intellect, the men with cultivated brains, the *savants* like Doctor Bonamy and others. It was incredible. And thus Pierre felt a growing discomfort arising within him, a covert anger which would doubtless end by bursting forth. His reason was struggling, like that of some poor wretch who after being flung into a river, feels the waters seize him from all sides and stifle him; and he reflected that the minds which, like Doctor Chassaigne's, sink at last into blind belief, must pass though this same discomfort and struggle before the final shipwreck.

He glanced at his old friend and saw how sorrowful he looked, struck down by destiny, as weak as a crying child, and henceforth quite alone in life. Nevertheless, he was unable to check the cry of protest which rose to his lips: "No, no, if we do not know everything, even if we shall never know everything, there is no reason why we should leave off learning. It is wrong that the Unknown should profit by man's debility and ignorance. On the contrary, the eternal hope should be that the things which now seem inexplicable will some day be explained; and we cannot, under healthy conditions, have any other ideal than this march towards the discovery of the Unknown, this victory slowly achieved by reason amidst all the miseries both of the flesh and of the mind. Ah! reason—it is my reason which makes me suffer, and it is from my reason too that I await all my strength. When reason dies, the whole being perishes. And I feel but an ardent thirst to satisfy my reason more and more, even though I may lose all happiness in doing so."

Tears were appearing in Doctor Chassaigne's eyes; doubtless the memory of his dear dead ones had again flashed upon him. And, in his turn, he murmured: "Reason, reason, yes, certainly it is a thing to be very proud of; it embodies the very dignity of life. But there is love, which is life's omnipotence, the one blessing to be won again when you have lost it."

His voice sank in a stifled sob; and as in a mechanical way he began to finger the sets of documents lying on the table, he espied among them one whose cover bore the name of Marie de Guersaint in large letters. He opened it and read the certificates of the two doctors who had inferred that the case was one of paralysis of the marrow. "Come, my child," he then resumed, "I know that you feel warm affection for Mademoiselle de Guersaint. What should you say if she were cured here? There are here some certificates, bearing honourable names, and you know that paralysis of this nature is virtually incurable. Well, if this young person should all at once run and jump about as I have seen so many others do, would you not feel very happy, would you not at last acknowledge the intervention of a supernatural power?"

Pierre was about to reply, when he suddenly remembered his cousin Beauclair's expression of opinion, the prediction that the miracle would come about like a lightning stroke, an awakening, an exaltation of the whole being; and he felt his discomfort increase and contented himself with replying: "Yes, indeed, I should be very happy. And you are right; there is doubtless only a determination to secure happiness in all the agitation one beholds here."

However, he could remain in that office no longer. The heat was becoming so great that perspiration streamed down the faces of those present. Doctor Bonamy had begun to dictate a report of the examination of La Grivotte to one of the seminarists, while Father Dargeles, watchful with regard to the phraseology employed, occasionally rose and whispered some verbal alteration in the writer's ear. Meantime, the tumult around them was continuing; the discussion among the medical men had taken another turn and now bore on certain technical points of no significance with regard to the case in question. You could no longer breathe within those wooden walls, nausea was upsetting every heart and every head. The little fair-haired gentleman, the influential writer from Paris, had already gone away, quite vexed at not having seen a real miracle.

Pierre thereupon said to Doctor Chassaigne, "Let us go; I shall be taken ill if I stay here any longer."

They left the office at the same time as La Grivotte, who was at last being dismissed. And as soon as they reached the door they found themselves caught in a torrential, surging, jostling crowd, which was eager to behold the girl so miraculously healed; for the report of the miracle must have already spread, and one and all were struggling to see the chosen one, question her, and touch her. And she, with her empurpled cheeks, her flaming eyes, her dancing gait, could do nothing but repeat, "I am cured, I am cured!"

Shouts drowned her voice, she herself was submerged, carried off amidst the eddies of the throng. For a moment one lost sight of her as though she had sunk in those tumultuous waters; then she suddenly reappeared close to Pierre and the doctor, who endeavoured to extricate her from the crush. They had just perceived the Commander, one of whose manias was to come down to the piscinas and the Grotto in order to vent his anger there. With his frock-coat tightly girding him in military fashion, he was, as usual, leaning on his silver-knobbed walking-stick, slightly dragging his left leg, which his second attack of paralysis had stiffened. And his face reddened and his eyes flashed with anger when La Grivotte, pushing him aside in order that she might pass, repeated amidst the wild enthusiasm of the crowd, "I am cured, I am cured!"

"Well!" he cried, seized with sudden fury, "so much the worse for you, my girl!"

Exclamations arose, folks began to laugh, for he was well known, and his maniacal passion for death was forgiven him. However, when he began stammering confused words, saying that it was pitiful to desire life when one was possessed of neither beauty nor fortune, and that this girl ought to have preferred to die at once rather than suffer again, people began to growl around him, and Abbe Judaine, who was passing, had to extricate him from his trouble. The priest drew him away. "Be quiet, my friend, be quiet," he said. "It is scandalous. Why do you rebel like this against the goodness of God who occasionally shows His compassion for our sufferings by alleviating them? I tell you again that you yourself ought to fall on your knees and beg Him to restore to you the use of your leg and let you live another ten years."

The Commander almost choked with anger. "What!" he replied, "ask to live for another ten years, when my finest day will be the day I die! Show myself as spiritless, as cowardly as the thousands of patients whom I see pass along here, full of a base terror of death, shrieking aloud their weakness, their passion to remain alive! Ah! no, I should feel too much contempt for myself. I want to die!—to die at once! It will be so delightful to be no more."

He was at last out of the scramble of the pilgrims, and again found himself near Doctor Chassaigne and Pierre on the bank of the Gave. And he addressed himself to the doctor, whom he often met: "Didn't they try to restore a dead man to life just now?" he asked; "I was told of it—it almost suffocated me. Eh, doctor? You understand? That man was happy enough to be dead, and they dared to dip him in their water in the criminal hope to make him alive again! But suppose they had succeeded, suppose their water had animated that poor devil once more—for one never knows what may happen in this funny world—don't you think that the man would have had a perfect right to spit his anger in the face of those corpse-menders? Had he asked them to awaken him? How did they know if he were not well pleased at being dead? Folks ought to be consulted at any rate. Just picture them playing the same vile trick on me when I at last fall into the great deep sleep. Ah! I would give them a nice reception. 'Meddle with what concerns you,' I should say, and you may be sure I should make all haste to die again!"

He looked so singular in the fit of rage which had come over him that Abbe Judaine and the doctor could not help smiling. Pierre, however, remained grave, chilled by the great quiver which swept by. Were not those words he had just heard the despairing imprecations of Lazarus? He had often imagined Lazarus emerging from the tomb and crying aloud: "Why hast Thou again awakened me to this abominable life, O Lord? I was sleeping the eternal, dreamless sleep so deeply; I was at last enjoying such sweet repose amidst the delights of nihility! I had known every wretchedness and every dolour, treachery, vain hope, defeat, sickness; as one of the living I had paid my frightful debt to suffering, for I was born without knowing why, and I lived without knowing how; and now, behold, O Lord, Thou requirest me to pay my debt yet again; Thou condemnest me to serve my term of punishment afresh! Have I then been guilty of some inexpiable transgression that thou shouldst inflict such cruel chastisement upon me? Alas! to live again, to feel oneself die a little in one's flesh each day, to have no intelligence save such as is required in order to doubt; no will, save such as one must have to be unable; no tenderness, save such as is needed to weep over one's own sorrows. Yet it was passed, I had crossed the terrifying threshold of death, I had known that second which is so horrible that it sufficeth to poison the whole of life. I had felt the sweat of agony cover me with moisture, the blood flow back from my limbs, my breath forsake me, flee away in a last gasp. And Thou ordainest that

I should know this distress a second time, that I should die twice, that my human misery should exceed that of all mankind. Then may it be even now, O Lord! Yes, I entreat Thee, do also this great miracle; may I once more lay myself down in this grave, and again fall asleep without suffering from the interruption of my eternal slumber. Have mercy upon me, and forbear from inflicting on me the torture of living yet again; that torture which is so frightful that Thou hast never inflicted it on any being. I have always loved Thee and served Thee; and I beseech Thee do not make of me the greatest example of Thy wrath, a cause of terror unto all generations. But show unto me Thy gentleness and loving kindness, O Lord! restore unto me the slumber I have earned, and let me sleep once more amid the delights of Thy nihility."

While Pierre was pondering in this wise, Abbe Judaine had led the Commander away, at last managing to calm him; and now the young priest shook hands with Doctor Chassaigne, recollecting that it was past five o'clock, and that Marie must be waiting for him. On his way back to the Grotto, however, he encountered the Abbe des Hermoises deep in conversation with M. de Guersaint, who had only just left his room at the hotel, and was quite enlivened by his good nap. He and his companion were admiring the extraordinary beauty which the fervour of faith imparted to some women's countenances, and they also spoke of their projected trip to the Cirque de Gavarnie.

On learning, however, that Marie had taken a first bath with no effect, M. de Guersaint at once followed Pierre. They found the poor girl still in the same painful stupor, with her eyes still fixed on the Blessed Virgin who had not deigned to hear her. She did not answer the loving words which her father addressed to her, but simply glanced at him with her large distressful eyes, and then again turned them upon the marble statue which looked so white amid the radiance of the tapers. And whilst Pierre stood waiting to take her back to the hospital, M. de Guersaint devoutly fell upon his knees. At first he prayed with passionate ardour for his daughter's cure, and then he solicited, on his own behalf, the favour of finding some wealthy person who would provide him with the million francs that he needed for his studies on aerial navigation.

V

Bernadette's Trials

About eleven o'clock that night, leaving M. de Guersaint in his room at the Hotel of the Apparitions, it occurred to Pierre to return for a moment to the Hospital of Our Lady of Dolours before going to bed himself. He had left Marie in such a despairing state, so fiercely silent, that he was full of anxiety about her. And when he had asked for Madame de Jonquiere at the door of the Sainte-Honorine Ward he became yet more anxious, for the news was by no means good. The young girl, said the superintendent, had not even opened her mouth. She would answer nobody, and had even refused to eat. Madame de Jonquiere, insisted therefore that Pierre should come in. True, the presence of men was forbidden in the women's wards at night-time, but then a priest is not a man.

"She only cares for you and will only listen to you," said the worthy lady. "Pray come in and sit down near her till Abbe Judaine arrives. He will come at about one in the morning to administer the communion to our more afflicted sufferers, those who cannot move and who have to eat at daybreak. You will be able to assist him."

Pierre thereupon followed Madame de Jonquiere, who installed him at the head of Marie's bed. "My dear child," she said to the girl, "I have brought you somebody who is very fond of you. You will be able to chat with him, and you will be reasonable now, won't you?"

Marie, however, on recognising Pierre, gazed at him with an air of exasperated suffering, a black, stern expression of revolt.

"Would you like him to read something to you," resumed Madame de Jonquiere, "something that would ease and console you as he did in the train? No? It wouldn't interest you, you don't care for it? Well, we will see by-and-by. I will leave him with you, and I am sure you will be quite reasonable again in a few minutes."

Pierre then began speaking to her in a low voice, saying all the kind consoling things that his heart could think of, and entreating her not to allow herself to sink into such despair. If the Blessed Virgin had not cured her on the first day, it was because she reserved her for some conspicuous miracle. But he spoke in vain. Marie had turned her head away, and did not even seem to listen as she lay there with a bitter expression on her mouth and a gleam of irritation in her eyes, which wandered away into space. Accordingly he ceased speaking and began to gaze at the ward around him.

The spectacle was a frightful one. Never before had such a nausea of pity and terror affected his heart. They had long since dined, nevertheless plates of food which had been brought up from the kitchens still lay about the beds; and all through the night there were some who ate whilst others continued restlessly moaning, asking to be turned over or helped out of bed. As the hours went by a kind of vague delirium seemed to come upon almost all of them. Very few were able to sleep quietly. Some had been undressed and were lying between the sheets, but the greater number were simply stretched out on the beds, it being so difficult to get their clothes off that they did not even change their linen during the five days of the pilgrimage. In the semi-obscurity, moreover, the obstruction of the ward seemed to have increased. To the fifteen beds ranged along the walls and the seven mattresses filling the central space, some fresh pallets had been added, and on all sides there was a confused litter of ragged garments, old baskets, boxes, and valises. Indeed, you no longer knew where to step. Two smoky lanterns shed but a dim light upon this encampment of dying women, in which a sickly smell prevailed; for, instead of any freshness, merely the heavy heat of the August night came in through the two windows which had been left ajar. Nightmare-like shadows and cries sped to and fro, peopling the inferno, amidst the nocturnal agony of so much accumulated suffering.

However, Pierre recognised Raymonde, who, her duties over, had come to kiss her mother, before going to sleep in one of the garrets reserved to the Sisters of the hospital. For her own part, Madame de Jonquiere, taking her functions to heart, did not close her eyes during the three nights spent at Lourdes.

She certainly had an arm-chair in which to rest herself, but she never sat down in it for a moment with out being disturbed. It must be admitted that she was bravely seconded by little Madame Desagneaux, who displayed such enthusiastic zeal that Sister Hyacinthe asked her, with a smile: "Why don't you take the vows?" whereupon she responded, with an air of scared surprise: "Oh! I can't, I'm married, you know, and I'm very fond of my husband." As for Madame Volmar, she had not even shown herself; but it was alleged that Madame de Jonquiere had sent her to bed on hearing her complain of a frightful headache. And

ÉMILE ZOLA

this had put Madame Desagneaux in quite a temper; for, as she sensibly enough remarked, a person had no business to offer to nurse the sick when the slightest exertion exhausted her. She herself, however, at last began to feel her legs and arms aching, though she would not admit it, but hastened to every patient whom she heard calling, ever ready as she was to lend a helping hand. In Paris she would have rung for a servant rather than have moved a candlestick herself; but here she was ever coming and going, bringing and emptying basins, and passing her arms around patients to hold them up, whilst Madame de Jonquiere slipped pillows behind them. However, shortly after eleven o'clock, she was all at once overpowered. Having imprudently stretched herself in the armchair for a moment's rest, she there fell soundly asleep, her pretty head sinking on one of her shoulders amidst her lovely, wavy fair hair, which was all in disorder. And from that moment neither moan nor call, indeed no sound whatever, could waken her.

Madame de Jonquiere, however, had softly approached the young priest again. "I had an idea," said she in a low voice, "of sending for Monsieur Ferrand, the house-surgeon, you know, who accompanies us. He would have given the poor girl something to calm her. Only he is busy downstairs trying to relieve Brother Isidore, in the Family Ward. Besides, as you know, we are not supposed to give medical attendance here; our work consists in placing our dear sick ones in the hands of the Blessed Virgin."

Sister Hyacinthe, who had made up her mind to spend the night with the superintendent, now drew, near. "I have just come from the Family Ward," she said; "I went to take Monsieur Sabathier some oranges which I had promised him, and I saw Monsieur Ferrand, who had just succeeded in reviving Brother Isidore. Would you like me to go down and fetch him?"

But Pierre declined the offer. "No, no," he replied, "Marie will be sensible. I will read her a few consoling pages by-and-by, and then she will rest."

For the moment, however, the girl still remained obstinately silent. One of the two lanterns was hanging from the wall close by, and Pierre could distinctly see her thin face, rigid and motionless like stone. Then, farther away, in the adjoining bed, he perceived Elise Rouquet, who was sound asleep and no longer wore her fichu, but openly displayed her face, the ulcerations of which still continued to grow paler. And on the young priest's left hand was Madame Vetu, now greatly weakened, in a hopeless state, unable to doze off for a moment, shaken as she was by a continuous rattle. He said a few kind words to her, for which she thanked him with a nod; and, gathering her remaining strength together, she was at last able to say: "There were several cures to-day; I was very pleased to hear of them."

On a mattress at the foot of her bed was La Grivotte, who in a fever of extraordinary activity kept on sitting up to repeat her favourite phrase: "I am cured, I am cured!" And she went on to relate that she had eaten half a fowl for dinner, she who had been unable to eat for long months past. Then, too, she had followed the torchlight procession on foot during nearly a couple of hours, and she would certainly have danced till daybreak had the Blessed Virgin only been pleased to give a ball. And once more she repeated: "I am cured, yes, cured, quite cured!"

Thereupon Madame Vetu found enough strength to say with childlike serenity and perfect, gladsome abnegation: "The Blessed Virgin did well to cure her since she is poor. I am better pleased than if it had been myself, for I have my little shop to depend upon and can wait. We each have our turn, each our turn."

One and all displayed a like charity, a like pleasure that others should have been cured. Seldom, indeed, was any jealousy shown; they surrendered themselves to a kind of epidemical beatitude, to a contagious hope that they would all be cured whenever it should so please the Blessed Virgin. And it was necessary that she should not be offended by any undue impatience; for assuredly she had her reasons and knew right well why she began by healing some rather than others. Thus with the fraternity born of common suffering and hope, the most grievously afflicted patients prayed for the cure of their neighbours. None of them ever despaired, each fresh miracle was the promise of another one, of the one which would be worked on themselves. Their faith remained unshakable. A story was told of a paralytic woman, some farm servant, who with extraordinary strength of will had contrived to take a few steps at the Grotto, and who while being conveyed back to the hospital had asked to be set down that she might return to the Grotto on foot. But she had gone only half the distance when she had staggered, panting and livid; and on being brought to the hospital on a stretcher, she had died there, cured, however, said her neighbours in the ward. Each, indeed, had her turn; the Blessed Virgin forgot none of her dear daughters unless it were her design to grant some chosen one immediate admission into Paradise.

All at once, at the moment when Pierre was leaning towards her, again offering to read to her, Marie burst into furious sobs. Letting her head fall upon her friend's shoulder, she vented all her rebellion in a low, terrible voice, amidst the vague shadows of that awful room. She had experienced what seldom happened to her, a collapse of faith, a sudden loss of courage, all the rage of the suffering being who can no longer wait. Such was her despair, indeed, that she even became sacrilegious.

"No, no," she stammered, "the Virgin is cruel; she is unjust, for she did not cure me just now. Yet I felt so certain that she would grant my prayer, I had prayed to her so fervently. I shall never be cured, now that the first day is past. It was a Saturday, and I was convinced that I should be cured on a Saturday. I did not want to speak—and oh! prevent me, for my heart is too full, and I might say more than I ought to do."

With fraternal hands he had quickly taken hold of her head, and he was endeavouring to stifle the cry of her rebellion. "Be quiet, Marie, I entreat you! It would never do for anyone to hear you—you so pious! Do you want to scandalise every soul?"

But in spite of her efforts she was unable to keep silence. "I should stifle, I must speak out," she said. "I no longer love her, no longer believe in her. The tales which are related here are all falsehoods; there is *nothing*, she does not even exist, since she does not hear when one speaks to her, and sobs. If you only knew all that I said to her! Oh! I want to go away at once. Take me away, carry me away in your arms, so that I may go and die in the street, where the passers-by, at least, will take pity on my sufferings!"

She was growing weak again, and had once more fallen on her back, stammering, talking childishly. "Besides, nobody loves me," she said. "My father was not even there. And you, my friend, forsook me. When I saw that it was another who was taking me to the piscinas, I began to feel a chill. Yes, that chill of doubt which I often felt in Paris. And that is at least certain, I doubted—perhaps, indeed, that is why she did not cure me. I cannot have prayed well enough, I am not pious enough, no doubt."

She was no longer blaspheming, but seeking for excuses to explain the non-intervention of Heaven. However, her face retained an angry expression amidst this struggle which she was waging with the Supreme Power, that Power which she had loved so well and entreated so fervently, but which had not obeyed her. When, on rare occasions, a fit of rage of this description broke out in the ward, and the sufferers, lying on their beds, rebelled against their fate, sobbing and lamenting, and at times even swearing, the lady-hospitallers and the Sisters, somewhat shocked, would content themselves with simply closing the bed-curtains. Grace had departed, one must await its return. And at last, sometimes after long hours, the rebellious complaints would die away, and peace would reign again amidst the deep, woeful silence.

"Calm yourself, calm yourself, I implore you," Pierre gently repeated to Marie, seeing that a fresh attack was coming upon her, an attack of doubt in herself, of fear that she was unworthy of the divine assistance.

Sister Hyacinthe, moreover, had again drawn near. "You will not be able to take the sacrament by-and-by, my dear child," said she, "if you continue in such a state. Come, since we have given Monsieur l'Abbe permission to read to you, why don't you let him do so?"

Marie made a feeble gesture as though to say that she consented, and Pierre at once took out of the valise at the foot of her bed, the little blue-covered book in which the story of Bernadette was so naively related. As on the previous night, however, when the train was rolling on, he did not confine himself to the bald phraseology of the book, but began improvising, relating all manner of details in his own fashion, in order to charm the simple folks who listened to him. Nevertheless, with his reasoning, analytical proclivities, he could not prevent himself from secretly re-establishing the real facts, imparting, for himself alone, a human character to this legend, whose wealth of prodigies contributed so greatly to the cure of those that suffered. Women were soon sitting up on all the surrounding beds. They wished to hear the continuation of the story, for the thought of the sacrament which they were passionately awaiting had prevented almost all of them from getting to sleep. And seated there, in the pale light of the lantern hanging from the wall above him, Pierre little by little raised his voice, so that he might be heard by the whole ward.

"The persecutions began with the very first miracles. Called a liar and a lunatic, Bernadette was threatened with imprisonment. Abbe Peyramale, the parish priest of Lourdes, and Monseigneur Laurence, Bishop of Tarbes, like the rest of the clergy, refrained from all intervention, waiting the course of events with the greatest prudence; whilst the civil authorities, the Prefect, the Public Prosecutor, the Mayor, and the Commissary of Police, indulged in excessive anti-religious zeal."

Continuing his perusal in this fashion, Pierre saw the real story rise up before him with invincible force. His mind travelled a short distance backward and he beheld Bernadette at the time of the first apparitions, so candid, so charming in her ignorance and good faith, amidst all her sufferings. And she was truly the visionary, the saint, her face assuming an expression of superhuman beauty during her crises of ecstasy. Her brow beamed, her features seemed to ascend, her eyes were bathed with light, whilst her parted lips burnt with divine love. And then her whole person became majestic; it was in a slow, stately way that she made the sign of the cross, with gestures which seemed to embrace the whole horizon. The neighbouring valleys, the villages, the towns, spoke of Bernadette alone. Although the Lady had not yet told her name, she was recognised, and people said, "It is she, the Blessed Virgin." On the first market-day, so many people flocked into Lourdes that the town quite overflowed. All wished to see the blessed child whom the Queen of the Angels had chosen, and who became so beautiful when the heavens opened to her enraptured gaze. The crowd on the banks of the Gave grew larger each morning, and thousands of people ended by installing themselves there, jostling one another that they might lose nothing of the spectacle! As soon as Bernadette appeared, a murmur of fervour spread: "Here is the saint, the saint, the saint!" Folks rushed forward to kiss her garments. She was a Messiah, the eternal Messiah whom the nations await, and the need of whom is ever arising from generation to generation. And, moreover, it was ever the same adventure beginning afresh: an apparition of the Virgin to a shepherdess; a voice exhorting the world to penitence; a spring gushing forth; and miracles astonishing and enrapturing the crowds that hastened to the spot in larger and larger numbers.

Ah! those first miracles of Lourdes, what a spring-tide flowering of consolation and hope they brought to the hearts of the wretched, upon whom poverty and sickness were preying! Old Bourriette's restored eyesight, little Bouhohort's resuscitation in the icy water, the deaf recovering their hearing, the lame suddenly enabled to walk, and so many other cases, Blaise Maumus, Bernade Soubies,* Auguste Bordes, Blaisette Soupenne, Benoite Cazeaux, in turn cured of the most dreadful ailments, became the subject of endless conversations, and fanned the illusions of all those who suffered either in their hearts

---

* I give this name as written by M. Zola; but in other works on Lourdes I find it given as "Bernarde Loubie—a bed-ridden old woman, cured of a paralytic affection by drinking the water of the Grotto."—Trans.

or their flesh. On Thursday, March 4th, the last day of the fifteen visits solicited by the Virgin, there were more than twenty thousand persons assembled before the Grotto. Everybody, indeed, had come down from the mountains. And this immense throng found at the Grotto the divine food that it hungered for, a feast of the Marvellous, a sufficient meed of the Impossible to content its belief in a superior Power, which deigned to bestow some attention upon poor folks, and to intervene in the wretched affairs of this lower world, in order to re-establish some measure of justice and kindness. It was indeed the cry of heavenly charity bursting forth, the invisible helping hand stretched out at last to dress the eternal sores of humanity. Ah! that dream in which each successive generation sought refuge, with what indestructible energy did it not arise among the disinherited ones of this world as soon as it found a favourable spot, prepared by circumstances! And for centuries, perhaps, circumstances had never so combined to kindle the mystical fire of faith as they did at Lourdes.

A new religion was about to be founded, and persecutions at once began, for religions only spring up amidst vexations and rebellions. And even as it was long ago at Jerusalem, when the tidings of miracles spread, the civil authorities—the Public Prosecutor, the Justice of the Peace, the Mayor, and particularly the Prefect of Tarbes—were all roused and began to bestir themselves. The Prefect was a sincere Catholic, a worshipper, a man of perfect honour, but he also had the firm mind of a public functionary, was a passionate defender of order, and a declared adversary of fanaticism which gives birth to disorder and religious perversion. Under his orders at Lourdes there was a Commissary of Police, a man of great intelligence and shrewdness, who had hitherto discharged his functions in a very proper way, and who, legitimately enough, beheld in this affair of the apparitions an opportunity to put his gift of sagacious skill to the proof. So the struggle began, and it was this Commissary who, on the first Sunday in Lent, at the time of the first apparitions, summoned Bernadette to his office in order that he might question her. He showed himself affectionate, then angry, then threatening, but all in vain; the answers which the girl gave him were ever the same. The story which she related, with its slowly accumulated details, had little by little irrevocably implanted itself in her infantile mind. And it was no lie on the part of this poor suffering creature, this exceptional victim of hysteria, but an unconscious haunting, a radical lack of will-power to free herself from her original hallucination. She knew not how to exert any such will, she could not, she would not exert it. Ah! the poor child, the dear child, so amiable and so gentle, so incapable of any evil thought, from that time forward lost to life, crucified by her fixed idea, whence one could only have extricated her by changing her environment, by restoring her to the open air, in some land of daylight and human affection. But she was the chosen one, she had beheld the Virgin, she would suffer from it her whole life long and die from it at last!

Pierre, who knew Bernadette so well, and who felt a fraternal pity for her memory, the fervent compassion with which one regards a human saint, a simple, upright, charming creature tortured by her faith, allowed his emotion to appear in his moist eyes and trembling voice. And a pause in his narrative ensued. Marie, who had hitherto been lying there quite stiff, with a hard expression of revolt still upon her face, opened her clenched hands and made a vague gesture of pity. "Ah," she murmured, "the poor child, all alone to contend against those magistrates, and so innocent, so proud, so unshakable in her championship of the truth!"

The same compassionate sympathy was arising from all the beds in the ward. That hospital inferno with its nocturnal wretchedness, its pestilential atmosphere, its pallets of anguish heaped together, its weary lady-hospitallers and Sisters flitting phantom-like hither and thither, now seemed to be illumined by a ray of divine charity. Was not the eternal illusion of happiness rising once more amidst tears and unconscious falsehoods? Poor, poor Bernadette! All waxed indignant at the thought of the persecutions which she had endured in defence of her faith.

Then Pierre, resuming his story, related all that the child had had to suffer. After being questioned by the Commissary she had to appear before the judges of the local tribunal. The entire magistracy pursued her, and endeavoured to wring a retractation from her. But the obstinacy of her dream was stronger than the common sense of all the civil authorities put together. Two doctors who were sent by the Prefect to make a careful examination of the girl came, as all doctors would have done, to the honest opinion that it was a case of nervous trouble, of which the asthma was a sure sign, and which, in certain circumstances, might have induced visions. This nearly led to her removal and confinement in a hospital at Tarbes. But public exasperation was feared. A bishop had fallen on his knees before her. Some ladies had sought to buy favours from her for gold. Moreover she had found a refuge with the Sisters of Nevers, who tended the aged in the town asylum, and there she made her first communion, and was with difficulty taught to read and write. As the Blessed Virgin seemed to have chosen her solely to work the happiness of others, and she herself had not been cured, it was very sensibly decided to take her to the baths of Cauterets, which were so near at hand. However, they did her no good. And no sooner had she returned to Lourdes than the torture of being questioned and adored by a whole people began afresh, became aggravated, and filled her more and more with horror of the world. Her life was over already; she would be a playful child no more; she could never be a young girl dreaming of a husband, a young wife kissing the cheeks of sturdy children. She had beheld the Virgin, she was the chosen one, the martyr. If the Virgin, said believers, had confided three secrets to her, investing her with a triple armour as it were, it was simply in order to sustain her in her appointed course.

The clergy had for a long time remained aloof, on its own side full of doubt and anxiety. Abby Peyramale, the parish priest of Lourdes, was a man of somewhat blunt ways, but full of infinite kindness, rectitude, and energy whenever he found himself in what he thought the right path. On the first occasion when Bernadette visited him, he received this child who had been brought up at Bartres and had not yet been seen at Catechism, almost as sternly as the Commissary of Police had done; in fact, he refused to believe her story, and with some irony told her to entreat the Lady to begin by making the briars blossom beneath her feet, which, by the way, the Lady never did. And if the Abbe ended by taking the child under his protection like a good pastor who defends his flock, it was simply through the advent of persecution and the talk of imprisoning this puny child, whose clear eyes shone so frankly, and who clung with such modest, gentle stubbornness to her original tale. Besides, why should he have continued denying the miracle after merely doubting it like a prudent priest who had no desire to see religion mixed up in any suspicious affair? Holy Writ is full of prodigies, all dogma is based on the mysterious; and that being so, there was nothing to prevent him, a priest, from believing that the Virgin had really entrusted Bernadette with a pious message for him, an injunction to build a church whither the faithful would repair in procession. Thus it was that he began loving and defending Bernadette for her charm's sake, whilst still refraining from active interference, awaiting as he did the decision of his Bishop.

ÉMILE ZOLA

This Bishop, Monseigneur Laurence, seemed to have shut himself up in his episcopal residence at Tarbes, locking himself within it and preserving absolute silence as though there were nothing occurring at Lourdes of a nature to interest him. He had given strict instructions to his clergy, and so far not a priest had appeared among the vast crowds of people who spent their days before the Grotto. He waited, and even allowed the Prefect to state in his administrative circulars that the civil and the religious authorities were acting in concert. In reality, he cannot have believed in the apparitions of the Grotto of Massabielle, which he doubtless considered to be the mere hallucinations of a sick child. This affair, which was revolutionising the region, was of sufficient importance for him to have studied it day by day, and the manner in which he disregarded it for so long a time shows how little inclined he was to admit the truth of the alleged miracles, and how greatly he desired to avoid compromising the Church in a matter which seemed destined to end badly. With all his piety, Monseigneur Laurence had a cool, practical intellect, which enabled him to govern his diocese with great good sense. Impatient and ardent people nicknamed him Saint Thomas at the time, on account of the manner in which his doubts persisted until events at last forced his hand. Indeed, he turned a deaf ear to all the stories that were being related, firmly resolved as he was that he would only listen to them if it should appear certain that religion had nothing to lose.

However, the persecutions were about to become more pronounced. The Minister of Worship in Paris, who had been informed of what was going on, required that a stop should be put to all disorders, and so the Prefect caused the approaches to the Grotto to be occupied by the military. The Grotto had already been decorated with vases of flowers offered by the zeal of the faithful and the gratitude of sufferers who had been healed. Money, moreover, was thrown into it; gifts to the Blessed Virgin abounded. Rudimentary improvements, too, were carried out in a spontaneous way; some quarrymen cut a kind of reservoir to receive the miraculous water, and others removed the large blocks of stone, and traced a path in the hillside. However, in presence of the swelling torrents of people, the Prefect, after renouncing his idea of arresting Bernadette, took the serious resolution of preventing all access to the Grotto by placing a strong palisade in front of it. Some regrettable incidents had lately occurred; various children pretended that they had seen the devil, some of them being guilty of simulation in this respect, whilst others had given way to real attacks of hysteria, in the contagious nervous unhinging which was so prevalent. But what a terrible business did the removal of the offerings from the Grotto prove! It was only towards evening that the Commissary was able to find a girl willing to let him have a cart on hire, and two hours later this girl fell from a loft and broke one of her ribs. Likewise, a man who had lent an axe had one of his feet crushed on the morrow by the fall of a block of stone.[*] It was in the midst of jeers and hisses that the Commissary carried off the pots of flowers, the tapers which he found burning, the coppers and the silver hearts which lay upon the sand. People clenched their fists, and covertly called him "thief" and "murderer." Then the posts for the palisades were planted in the ground, and the rails were nailed to the crossbars, no little labour being performed to shut off the Mystery, in order to bar access to the Unknown, and put the miracles in prison. And the civil authorities were simple enough to imagine that it was all over, that those few bits of boarding would suffice to stay the poor people who hungered for illusion and hope.

But as soon as the new religion was proscribed, forbidden by the law as an offence, it began to burn with an inextinguishable flame in the depths of every soul. Believers came to the river bank in far greater numbers, fell upon their knees at a short distance from the Grotto, and sobbed aloud as they gazed at the forbidden heaven. And the sick, the poor ailing folks, who were forbidden to seek cure, rushed on the Grotto despite all prohibitions, slipped in whenever they could find an aperture or climbed over the palings when their strength enabled them to do so, in the one ardent desire to steal a little of the water. What! there was a prodigious water in that Grotto, which restored the sight to the blind, which set the infirm erect upon their legs again, which instantaneously healed all ailments; and there were officials cruel enough to put that water under lock and key so that it might not cure any more poor people! Why, it was monstrous! And a cry of hatred arose from all the humble ones, all the disinherited ones who had as much need of the Marvellous as of bread to live! In accordance with a municipal decree, the names of all delinquents were to be taken by the police, and thus one soon beheld a woeful *defile* of old women and lame men summoned before the Justice of the Peace for the sole offence of taking a little water from the fount of life! They stammered and entreated, at

---

[*] Both of these accidents were interpreted as miracles.—Trans.

ÉMILE ZOLA

their wit's end when a fine was imposed upon them. And, outside, the crowd was growling; rageful unpopularity was gathering around those magistrates who treated human wretchedness so harshly, those pitiless masters who after taking all the wealth of the world, would not even leave to the poor their dream of the realms beyond, their belief that a beneficent superior power took a maternal interest in them, and was ready to endow them with peace of soul and health of body. One day a whole band of poverty-stricken and ailing folks went to the Mayor, knelt down in his courtyard, and implored him with sobs to allow the Grotto to be reopened; and the words they spoke were so pitiful that all who heard them wept. A mother showed her child who was half-dead; would they let the little one die like that in her arms when there was a source yonder which had saved the children of other mothers? A blind man called attention to his dim eyes; a pale, scrofulous youth displayed the sores on his legs; a paralytic woman sought to join her woeful twisted hands: did the authorities wish to see them all perish, did they refuse them the last divine chance of life, condemned and abandoned as they were by the science of man? And equally great was the distress of the believers, of those who were convinced that a corner of heaven had opened amidst the night of their mournful existences, and who were indignant that they should be deprived of the chimerical delight, the supreme relief for their human and social sufferings, which they found in the belief that the Blessed Virgin had indeed come down from heaven to bring them the priceless balm of her intervention. However, the Mayor was unable to promise anything, and the crowd withdrew weeping, ready for rebellion, as though under the blow of some great act of injustice, an act of idiotic cruelty towards the humble and the simple for which Heaven would assuredly take vengeance.

The struggle went on for several months; and it was an extraordinary spectacle which those sensible men—the Minister, the Prefect, and the Commissary of Police—presented, all animated with the best intentions and contending against the ever-swelling crowd of despairing ones, who would not allow the doors of dreamland to be closed upon them, who would not be shut off from the mystic glimpse of future happiness in which they found consolation for their present wretchedness. The authorities required order, the respect of a discreet religion, the triumph of reason; whereas the need of happiness carried the people off into an enthusiastic desire for cure both in this world and in the next. Oh! to cease suffering, to secure equality in the comforts of life; to march on under the protection of a just and beneficent Mother, to die only to awaken in heaven! And necessarily the burning desire of the multitude, the holy madness of the universal joy, was destined to sweep aside the rigid, morose conceptions of a well-regulated society in which the ever-recurring epidemical attacks of religious hallucination are condemned as prejudicial to good order and healthiness of mind.

The Sainte-Honorine Ward, on hearing the story, likewise revolted. Pierre again had to pause, for many were the stifled exclamations in which the Commissary of Police was likened to Satan and Herod. La Grivotte had sat up on her mattress, stammering: "Ah! the monsters! To behave like that to the Blessed Virgin who has cured me!"

And even Madame Vetu—once more penetrated by a ray of hope amidst the covert certainty she felt that she was going to die—grew angry at the idea that the Grotto would not have existed had the Prefect won the day. "There would have been no pilgrimages," she said, "we should not be here, hundreds of us would not be cured every year."

A fit of stifling came over her, however, and Sister Hyacinthe had to raise her to a sitting posture. Madame de Jonquiere was profiting by the interruption to attend to a young woman afflicted with a spinal complaint, whilst two other women, unable to remain on their beds, so unbearable was the heat, prowled about with short, silent steps, looking quite white in the misty darkness. And from the far end of the ward, where all was black, there resounded a noise of painful breathing, which had been going on without a pause, accompanying Pierre's narrative like a rattle. Elise Rouquet alone was sleeping peacefully, still stretched upon her back, and displaying her disfigured countenance, which was slowly drying.

Midnight had struck a quarter of an hour previously, and Abbe Judaine might arrive at any moment for the communion. Grace was now again descending into Marie's heart, and she was convinced that if the Blessed Virgin had refused to cure her it was, indeed, her own fault in having doubted when she entered the piscina. And she, therefore, repented of her rebellion as of a crime. Could she ever be forgiven? Her pale face sank down among her beautiful fair hair, her eyes filled with tears, and she looked at Pierre with an expression of anguish. "Oh! how wicked I was, my friend," she said. "It was through hearing you relate how that Prefect and those magistrates sinned through pride, that I understood my transgression. One must believe, my friend; there is no happiness outside faith and love."

Then, as Pierre wished to break off at the point which he had reached, they all began protesting and calling for the continuation of his narrative, so that he had to promise to go on to the triumph of the Grotto.

Its entrance remained barred by the palisade, and you had to come secretly at night if you wished to pray and carry off a stolen bottle of water. Still, the fear of rioting increased, for it was rumoured that whole villages intended to come down from the hills in order to deliver God, as they naively expressed it. It was a *levee en masse* of the humble, a rush of those who hungered for the miraculous, so irresistible in its impetuosity that mere common sense, mere considerations of public order were to be swept away like chaff. And it was Monseigneur Laurence, in his episcopal residence at Tarbes, who was first forced to surrender. All his prudence, all his doubts were outflanked by the popular outburst. For five long months he had been able to remain aloof, preventing his clergy from following the faithful to the Grotto, and defending the Church against the tornado of superstition which had been let loose. But what was the use of struggling any longer? He felt the wretchedness of the suffering people committed to his care to be so great that he resigned himself to granting them the idolatrous religion for which he realised them to be eager. Some prudence remaining to him, however, he contented himself in the first instance with drawing up an *ordonnance*, appointing a commission of inquiry, which was to investigate the question; this implied the acceptance of the miracles after a period of longer or shorter duration. If Monseigneur Laurence was the man of healthy culture and cool reason that he is pictured to have been, how great must have been his anguish on the morning when he signed that *ordonnance*! He must have knelt in his oratory, and have begged the Sovereign Master of the world to dictate his conduct to him. He did not believe in the apparitions; he had a loftier, more intellectual idea of the manifestations of the Divinity. Only would he not be showing true pity and mercy in silencing the scruples of his reason, the noble prejudices of his faith, in presence of the necessity of granting that bread of falsehood which poor humanity requires in order to be happy? Doubtless, he begged the pardon of Heaven for allowing it to be mixed up in what he regarded as childish pastime, for exposing it to ridicule in connection with an affair in which there was only sickliness and dementia. But his flock suffered so much, hungered so ravenously for the marvellous, for fairy stories with which to lull the pains of life. And thus, in tears, the Bishop at last sacrificed his respect for the dignity of Providence to his sensitive pastoral charity for the woeful human flock.

Then the Emperor in his turn gave way. He was at Biarritz at the time, and was kept regularly informed of everything connected with this affair of the apparitions, with which the entire Parisian press was also occupying itself, for the persecutions would not have been complete if the pens of Voltairean newspaper-men had not meddled in them. And whilst his Minister, his Prefect, and his Commissary of Police were fighting for common sense and public order, the Emperor preserved his wonted silence—the deep silence of a day-dreamer which nobody ever penetrated. Petitions arrived day by day, yet he held his tongue. Bishops came, great personages, great ladies of his circle watched and drew him on one side, and still he held his tongue. A truceless warfare was being waged around him: on one side the believers and the men of fanciful minds whom the Mysterious strongly interested; on the other the unbelievers and the statesmen who distrusted the disturbances of the imagination;—and still and ever he held his tongue. Then, all at once, with the sudden decision of a naturally timid man, he spoke out. The rumour spread that he had yielded to the entreaties of his wife Eugenie. No doubt she did intervene, but the Emperor was more deeply influenced by a revival of his old humanitarian dreams, his genuine compassion for the disinherited.* Like the Bishop, he did not wish to close the portals of illusion to the wretched by upholding the unpopular decree which forbade despairing sufferers to go and drink life at the holy source. So he sent a telegram, a curt order to remove the palisade, so as to allow everybody free access to the Grotto.

Then came a shout of joy and triumph. The decree annulling the previous one was read at Lourdes to the sound of drum and trumpet. The Commissary of Police had to come in person to superintend the removal of the palisade. He was afterwards transferred elsewhere like the Prefect.** People flocked to Lourdes from all parts, the new *cultus*

---

* I think this view of the matter the right one, for, as all who know the history of the Second Empire are aware, it was about this time that the Emperor began taking great interest in the erection of model dwellings for the working classes, and the plantation and transformation of the sandy wastes of the Landes.—Trans.

** The Prefect was transferred to Grenoble, and curiously enough his new jurisdiction extended over the hills and valleys of La Salette, whither pilgrims likewise flocked to drink, pray, and wash themselves at a miraculous fountain. Warned by experience, however, Baron Massy (such was the Prefect's name) was careful to avoid any further interference in religious matters.—Trans.

was organised at the Grotto, and a cry of joy ascended: God had won the victory! God?—alas, no! It was human wretchedness which had won the battle, human wretchedness with its eternal need of falsehood, its hunger for the marvellous, its everlasting hope akin to that of some condemned man who, for salvation's sake, surrenders himself into the hands of an invisible Omnipotence, mightier than nature, and alone capable, should it be willing, of annulling nature's laws. And that which had also conquered was the sovereign compassion of those pastors, the merciful Bishop and merciful Emperor who allowed those big sick children to retain the fetich which consoled some of them and at times even cured others.

In the middle of November the episcopal commission came to Lourdes to prosecute the inquiry which had been entrusted to it. It questioned Bernadette yet once again, and studied a large number of miracles. However, in order that the evidence might be absolute, it only registered some thirty cases of cure. And Monseigneur Laurence declared himself convinced. Nevertheless, he gave a final proof of his prudence, by continuing to wait another three years before declaring in a pastoral letter that the Blessed Virgin had in truth appeared at the Grotto of Massabielle and that numerous miracles had subsequently taken place there. Meantime, he had purchased the Grotto itself, with all the land around it, from the municipality of Lourdes, on behalf of his see. Work was then begun, modestly at first, but soon on a larger and larger scale as money began to flow in from all parts of Christendom. The Grotto was cleared and enclosed with an iron railing. The Gave was thrown back into a new bed, so as to allow of spacious approaches to the shrine, with lawns, paths, and walks. At last, too, the church which the Virgin had asked for, the Basilica, began to rise on the summit of the rock itself. From the very first stroke of the pick, Abbe Peyramale, the parish priest of Lourdes, went on directing everything with even excessive zeal, for the struggle had made him the most ardent and most sincere of all believers in the work that was to be accomplished. With his somewhat rough but truly fatherly nature, he had begun to adore Bernadette, making her mission his own, and devoting himself, soul and body, to realising the orders which he had received from Heaven through her innocent mouth. And he exhausted himself in mighty efforts; he wished everything to be very beautiful and very grand, worthy of the Queen of the Angels who had deigned to visit this mountain nook. The first religious ceremony did not take place till six years after the apparitions. A marble statue of the Virgin was installed with great pomp on the very spot where she had appeared. It was a magnificent day, all Lourdes was gay with flags, and every bell rang joyously. Five years later, in 1869, the first mass was celebrated in the crypt of the Basilica, whose spire was not yet finished. Meantime, gifts flowed in without a pause, a river of gold was streaming towards the Grotto, a whole town was about to spring up from the soil. It was the new religion completing its foundations. The desire to be healed did heal; the thirst for a miracle worked the miracle. A Deity of pity and hope was evolved from man's sufferings, from that longing for falsehood and relief which, in every age of humanity, has created the marvellous palaces of the realms beyond, where an almighty Power renders justice and distributes eternal happiness.

And thus the ailing ones of the Sainte-Honorine Ward only beheld in the victory of the Grotto the triumph of their hopes of cure. Along the rows of beds there was a quiver of joy when, with his heart stirred by all those poor faces turned towards him, eager for certainty, Pierre repeated: "God had conquered. Since that day the miracles have never ceased, and it is the most humble who are the most frequently relieved."

Then he laid down the little book. Abbe Judaine was coming in, and the Sacrament was about to be administered. Marie, however, again penetrated by the fever of faith, her hands burning, leant towards Pierre. "Oh, my friend!" said she, "I pray you hear me confess my fault and absolve me. I have blasphemed, and have been guilty of mortal sin. If you do not succour me, I shall be unable to receive the Blessed Sacrament, and yet I so greatly need to be consoled and strengthened."

The young priest refused her request with a wave of the hand. He had never been willing to act as confessor to this friend, the only woman he had loved in the healthy, smiling days of youth. However, she insisted. "I beg you to do so," said she; "you will help to work the miracle of my cure."

Then he gave way and received the avowal of her fault, that impious rebellion induced by suffering, that rebellion against the Virgin who had remained deaf to her prayers. And afterwards he granted her absolution in the sacramental form.

Meanwhile Abbe Judaine had already deposited the ciborium on a little table, between two lighted tapers, which looked like woeful stars in the semi-obscurity of the ward. Madame de Jonquiere had just decided to open one of the windows quite wide, for the odour emanating from all the suffering bodies and heaped-up rags had become unbearable. But no air came in from the narrow courtyard into which the window opened; though black with night, it seemed like a well of fire. Having offered to act as server, Pierre repeated the "Confiteor." Then, after responding with the "Misereatur" and the "Indulgentiam," the chaplain, who wore his alb, raised the pyx, saying, "Behold the Lamb of God, who taketh away the sins of the world." All the women who, writhing in agony, were impatiently awaiting the communion, like dying creatures who await life from some fresh medicine which is a long time coming, thereupon thrice repeated, in all humility, and with lips almost closed: "Lord, I am not worthy that Thou shouldst enter under my roof; but only say the word and my soul shall be healed."

Abbe Judaine had begun to make the round of those woeful beds, accompanied by Pierre, and followed by Madame de Jonquiere and Sister Hyacinthe, each of whom carried one of the lighted tapers. The Sister designated those who were to communicate; and, murmuring the customary Latin words, the priest leant forward and placed the Host somewhat at random on the sufferer's tongue. Almost all were waiting for him with widely opened, glittering eyes, amidst the disorder of that hastily pitched camp. Two were found to be sound asleep, however, and had to be awakened. Several were moaning without being conscious of it, and continued moaning even after they had received the sacrament. At the far end of the ward, the rattle of the poor creature who could not be seen still resounded. And nothing could have been more mournful than the appearance of that little *cortege* in the semi-darkness, amidst which the yellow flames of the tapers gleamed like stars.

But Marie's face, to which an expression of ecstasy had returned, was like a divine apparition. Although La Grivotte was hungering for the bread of life, they had refused her the sacrament on this occasion, as it was to be administered to her in the morning at the Rosary; Madame Vetu, however, had received the Host on her black tongue in a hiccough. And now Marie was lying there under the pale light of the tapers, looking so beautiful amidst her fair hair, with her eyes dilated and her features transfigured by faith, that everyone admired her. She received the sacrament with rapture; Heaven visibly descended into her poor, youthful frame, reduced to such physical wretchedness. And, clasping Pierre's hand, she detained him for a moment, saying: "Oh! she will heal me, my friend, she has just promised me that she will do so. Go and take some rest. I shall sleep so soundly now!"

As he withdrew in company with Abbe Judaine, Pierre caught sight of little Madame Desagneaux stretched out in the arm-chair in which weariness had overpowered her. Nothing could awaken her. It was now half-past one in the morning; and Madame de Jonquiere and her assistant, Sister Hyacinthe, were still going backwards and forwards, turning the patients over, cleansing them, and dressing their sores. However, the ward was becoming more peaceful, its heavy darkness had grown less oppressive since Bernadette with her charm had passed through it. The visionary's little shadow was now flitting in triumph from bed to bed, completing its work, bringing a little of heaven to each of the despairing ones, each of the disinherited ones of this world; and as they all at last sank to sleep they could see the little shepherdess, so young, so ill herself, leaning over them and kissing them with a kindly smile.

THE THIRD DAY

I

BED AND BOARD

At seven o'clock on the morning of that fine, bright, warm August Sunday, M. de Guersaint was already up and dressed in one of the two little rooms which he had fortunately been able to secure on the third floor of the Hotel of the Apparitions. He had gone to bed at eleven o'clock the night before and had awoke feeling quite fresh and gay. As soon as he was dressed he entered the adjoining room which Pierre occupied; but the young priest, who had not returned to the hotel until past one in the morning, with his blood heated by insomnia, had been unable to doze off until daybreak and was now still slumbering. His cassock flung across a chair, his other garments scattered here and there, testified to his great weariness and agitation of mind.

"Come, come, you lazybones!" cried M. de Guersaint gaily; "can't you hear the bells ringing?"

Pierre awoke with a start, quite surprised to find himself in that little hotel room into which the sunlight was streaming. All the joyous peals of the bells, the music of the chiming, happy town, moreover, came in through the window which he had left open.

"We shall never have time to get to the hospital before eight o'clock to fetch Marie," resumed M. de Guersaint, "for we must have some breakfast, eh?"

"Of course, make haste and order two cups of chocolate. I will get up at once, I sha'n't be long," replied Pierre.

In spite of the fatigue which had already stiffened his joints, he sprang out of bed as soon as he was alone, and made all haste with his toilet. However, he still had his head in the washing basin, ducking it in the fresh, cool water, when M. de Guersaint, who was unable to remain alone, came back again. "I've given the order," said he; "they will bring it up. Ah! what a curious place this hotel is! You have of course seen the landlord, Master Majeste, clad in white from head to foot and looking so dignified in his office. The place is crammed, it appears; they have never had so many people before. So it is no wonder that there should be such a fearful noise. I was wakened up three times during the night.

People kept on talking in the room next to mine. And you, did you sleep well?"

"No, indeed," answered Pierre; "I was tired to death, but I couldn't close my eyes. No doubt it was the uproar you speak of that prevented me."

In his turn he then began to talk of the thin partitions, and the manner in which the house had been crammed with people until it seemed as though the floors and the walls would collapse with the strain. The place had been shaking all night long; every now and then people suddenly rushed along the passages, heavy footfalls resounded, gruff voices ascended nobody knew whence; without speaking of all the moaning and coughing, the frightful coughing which seemed to re-echo from every wall. Throughout the night people evidently came in and went out, got up and lay down again, paying no attention to time in the disorder in which they lived, amid shocks of passion which made them hurry to their devotional exercises as to pleasure parties.

"And Marie, how was she when you left her last night?" M. de Guersaint suddenly inquired.

"A great deal better," replied Pierre; "she had an attack of extreme discouragement, but all her courage and faith returned to her at last."

A pause followed; and then the girl's father resumed with his tranquil optimism: "Oh! I am not anxious. Things will go on all right, you'll see. For my own part, I am delighted. I had asked the Virgin to grant me her protection in my affairs—you know, my great invention of navigable balloons. Well, suppose I told you that she has already shown me her favour? Yes, indeed yesterday evening while I was talking with Abbe des Hermoises, he told me that at Toulouse he would no doubt be able to find a person to finance me—one of his friends, in fact, who is extremely wealthy and takes great interest in mechanics! And in this I at once saw the hand of God!" M. de Guersaint began laughing with his childish laugh, and then he added: "That Abbe des Hermoises is a charming man. I shall see this afternoon if there is any means of my accompanying him on an excursion to the Cirque de Gavarnie at small cost."

Pierre, who wished to pay everything, the hotel bill and all the rest, at once encouraged him in this idea. "Of course," said he, "you ought not to miss this opportunity to visit the mountains, since you have so great a wish to do so. Your daughter will be very happy to know that you are pleased."

Their talk, however, was now interrupted by a servant girl bringing the two cups of chocolate with a couple of rolls on a metal tray covered with a napkin. She left the door open as she entered the room, so that a glimpse was obtained of some portion of the passage. "Ah! they are already doing my neighbour's room!" exclaimed M. de Guersaint. "He is a married man, isn't he? His wife is with him?"

The servant looked astonished. "Oh, no," she replied, "he is quite alone!"

"Quite alone? Why, I heard people talking in his room this morning."

"You must be mistaken, monsieur," said the servant; "he has just gone out after giving orders that his room was to be tidied up at once." And then, while taking the cups of chocolate off the tray and placing them on the table, she continued: "Oh! he is a very respectable gentleman. Last year he was able to have one of the pavilions which Monsieur Majeste lets out to visitors, in the lane by the side of the hotel; but this year he applied too late and had to content himself with that room, which greatly worried him, for it isn't a large one, though there is a big cupboard in it. As he doesn't care to eat with everybody, he takes his meals there, and he orders good wine and the best of everything, I can tell you."

"That explains it all!" replied M. de Guersaint gaily; "he dined too well last night, and I must have heard him talking in his sleep."

Pierre had been listening somewhat inquisitively to all this chatter. "And on this side, my side," said he, "isn't there a gentleman with two ladies, and a little boy who walks about with a crutch?"

"Yes, Monsieur l'Abbe, I know them. The aunt, Madame Chaise, took one of the two rooms for herself; and Monsieur and Madame Vigneron with their son Gustave have had to content themselves with the other one. This is the second year they have come to Lourdes. They are very respectable people too."

Pierre nodded. During the night he had fancied he could recognise the voice of M. Vigneron, whom the heat doubtless had incommoded. However, the servant was now thoroughly started, and she began to enumerate the other persons whose rooms were reached by the same passage; on the left hand there was a priest, then a mother with three daughters, and then an old married couple; whilst on the right lodged another gentleman who was all alone, a young lady, too, who was unaccompanied, and then a family party which included five young children. The hotel was crowded to its garrets. The servants had had to give up their rooms the previous evening and lie in a heap in the washhouse. During the night, also, some camp bedsteads had even been set up on the landings; and one honourable ecclesiastic, for lack of other accommodation, had been obliged to sleep on a billiard-table.

When the girl had retired and the two men had drunk their chocolate, M. de Guersaint went back into his own room to wash his hands again, for he was very careful of his person; and Pierre, who remained alone, felt attracted by the gay sunlight, and stepped for a moment on to the narrow balcony outside his window. Each of the third-floor rooms on this side of the hotel was provided with a similar balcony, having a carved-wood balustrade. However, the young priest's surprise was very great, for he had scarcely stepped outside when he suddenly saw a woman protrude her head over the balcony next to him—that of the room occupied by the gentleman whom M. de Guersaint and the servant had been speaking of.

And this woman he had recognised: it was Madame Volmar. There was no mistaking her long face with its delicate drawn features, its magnificent large eyes, those brasiers over which a veil, a dimming *moire*, seemed to pass at times. She gave a start of terror on perceiving him. And he, extremely ill at ease, grieved that he should have frightened her, made all haste to withdraw into his apartment. A sudden light had dawned upon him, and he now understood and could picture everything. So this was why she had not been seen at the hospital, where little Madame Desagneaux was always asking for her. Standing motionless, his heart upset, Pierre fell into a deep reverie, reflecting on the life led by this woman whom he knew, that torturing conjugal life in Paris between a fierce mother-in-law and an unworthy husband, and then those three days of complete liberty spent at Lourdes, that brief bonfire of passion to which she had hastened under the sacrilegious pretext of serving the divinity. Tears whose cause he could not even explain, tears that ascended from the very depths of his being, from his own voluntary chastity, welled into his eyes amidst the feeling of intense sorrow which came over him.

"Well, are you ready?" joyously called M. de Guersaint as he came back, with his grey jacket buttoned up and his hands gloved.

"Yes, yes, let us go," replied Pierre, turning aside and pretending to look for his hat so that he might wipe his eyes.

Then they went out, and on crossing the threshold heard on their left hand an unctuous voice which they recognised; it was that of

M. Vigneron, who was loudly repeating the morning prayers. A moment afterwards came a meeting which interested them. They were walking down the passage when they were passed by a middle-aged, thick-set, sturdy-looking gentleman, wearing carefully trimmed whiskers. He bent his back and passed so rapidly that they were unable to distinguish his features, but they noticed that he was carrying a carefully made parcel. And immediately afterwards he slipped a key into the lock of the room adjoining M. de Guersaint's, and opening the door disappeared noiselessly, like a shadow.

M. de Guersaint had glanced round: "Ah! my neighbour," said he; "he has been to market and has brought back some delicacies, no doubt!"

Pierre pretended not to hear, for his companion was so light-minded that he did not care to trust him with a secret which was not his own. Besides, a feeling of uneasiness was returning to him, a kind of chaste terror at the thought that the world and the flesh were there taking their revenge, amidst all the mystical enthusiasm which he could feel around him.

They reached the hospital just as the patients were being brought out to be carried to the Grotto; and they found that Marie had slept well and was very gay. She kissed her father and scolded him when she learnt that he had not yet decided on his trip to Gavarnie. She should really be displeased with him, she said, if he did not go. Still with the same restful, smiling expression, she added that she did not expect to be cured that day; and then, assuming an air of mystery, she begged Pierre to obtain permission for her to spend the following night before the Grotto. This was a favour which all the sufferers ardently coveted, but which only a few favoured ones with difficulty secured. After protesting, anxious as he felt with regard to the effect which a night spent in the open air might have upon her health, the young priest, seeing how unhappy she had suddenly become, at last promised that he would make the application. Doubtless she imagined that she would only obtain a hearing from the Virgin when they were alone together in the slumbering peacefulness of the night. That morning, indeed, she felt so lost among the innumerable patients who were heaped together in front of the Grotto, that already at ten o'clock she asked to be taken back to the hospital, complaining that the bright light tired her eyes. And when her father and the priest had again installed her in the Sainte-Honorine Ward, she gave them their liberty for the remainder of the day. "No, don't come to fetch me," she said, "I shall not go back to the Grotto this afternoon—it would be useless. But you will come for me this evening at nine o'clock, won't you, Pierre? It is agreed, you have given me your word."

He repeated that he would endeavour to secure the requisite permission, and that, if necessary, he would apply to Father Fourcade in person.

"Then, till this evening, darling," said M. de Guersaint, kissing his daughter. And he and Pierre went off together, leaving her lying on her bed, with an absorbed expression on her features, as her large, smiling eyes wandered away into space.

It was barely half-past ten when they got back to the Hotel of the Apparitions; but M. de Guersaint, whom the fine weather delighted, talked of having *dejeuner* at once, so that he might the sooner start upon a ramble through Lourdes. First of all, however, he wished to go up to his room, and Pierre following him, they encountered quite a drama on their way. The door of the room occupied by the Vignerons was wide open, and little Gustave could be seen lying on the sofa which served as his bed. He was livid; a moment previously he had suddenly fainted, and this had made the father and mother imagine that the end had come. Madame Vigneron was crouching on a chair, still stupefied by her fright, whilst M. Vigneron rushed about the room, thrusting everything aside in order that he might prepare a glass of sugared-water, to which he added a few drops of some elixir. This draught, he exclaimed, would set the lad right again. But all the same, it was incomprehensible. The boy was still strong, and to think that he should have fainted like that, and have turned as white as a chicken! Speaking in this wise, M. Vigneron glanced at Madame Chaise, the aunt, who was standing in front of the sofa, looking in good health that morning; and his hands shook yet more violently at the covert idea that if that stupid attack had carried off his son, they would no longer have inherited the aunt's fortune. He was quite beside himself at this thought, and eagerly opening the boy's mouth he compelled him to swallow the entire contents of the glass. Then, however, when he heard Gustave sigh, and saw him open his eyes again, his fatherly good-nature reappeared, and he shed tears, and called the lad his dear little fellow. But on Madame Chaise drawing near to offer some assistance, Gustave repulsed her with a sudden gesture of hatred, as though he understood how this woman's money unconsciously perverted his parents, who, after all, were worthy folks. Greatly offended, the old lady turned on her heel, and seated herself in a corner, whilst the father and mother, at last freed from their anxiety, returned thanks to the Blessed Virgin for having preserved their darling, who smiled at them with his intelligent and infinitely sorrowful smile, knowing and understanding everything as he did, and no longer having any taste for life, although he was not fifteen.

"Can we be of any help to you?" asked Pierre in an obliging way.

"No, no, I thank you, gentlemen," replied M. Vigneron, coming for a moment into the passage. "But oh! we did have a fright! Think of it, an only son, who is so dear to us too."

All around them the approach of the *dejeuner* hour was now throwing the house into commotion. Every door was banging, and the passages and the staircase resounded with the constant pitter-patter of feet. Three big girls passed by, raising a current of air with the sweep of their skirts. Some little children were crying in a neighbouring room. Then there were old people who seemed quite scared, and distracted priests who, forgetting their calling, caught up their cassocks with both hands, so that they might run the faster to the dining-room. From the top to the bottom of the house one could feel the floors shaking under the excessive weight of all the people who were packed inside the hotel.

"Oh, I hope that it is all over now, and that the Blessed Virgin will cure him," repeated M. Vigneron, before allowing his neighbours to retire. "We are going down-stairs, for I must confess that all this has made me feel faint. I need something to eat, I am terribly hungry."

When Pierre and M. de Guersaint at last left their rooms, and went down-stairs, they found to their annoyance that there was not the smallest table-corner vacant in the large dining-room. A most extraordinary mob had assembled there, and the few seats that were still unoccupied were reserved. A waiter informed them that the room never emptied between ten and one o'clock, such was the rush of appetite, sharpened by the keen mountain air. So they had to resign themselves to wait, requesting the waiter to warn them as soon as there should be a couple of vacant places. Then, scarcely knowing what to do with themselves, they went to walk about the hotel porch, whence there was a view of the street, along which the townsfolk, in their Sunday best, streamed without a pause.

All at once, however, the landlord of the Hotel of the Apparitions, Master Majeste in person, appeared before them, clad in white from head to foot; and with a great show of politeness he inquired if the gentlemen would like to wait in the drawing-room. He was a stout man of five-and-forty, and strove to bear the burden of his name in a right royal fashion. Bald and clean-shaven, with round blue eyes in a waxy face, displaying three superposed chins, he always deported himself with much dignity. He had come from Nevers with the Sisters who managed the orphan asylum, and was married to a dusky little woman, a native of Lourdes. In less than fifteen years they had made their hotel one of the most substantial and best patronised establishments in the town. Of recent times, moreover, they had started a business in religious articles, installed in a large shop on the left of the hotel porch and managed by a young niece under Madame Majeste's Supervision.

"You can wait in the drawing-room, gentlemen," again suggested the hotel-keeper whom Pierre's cassock rendered very attentive.

They replied, however, that they preferred to walk about and wait in the open air. And thereupon Majeste would not leave them, but deigned to chat with them for a moment as he was wont to do with those of his customers whom he desired to honour. The conversation turned at first on the procession which would take place that night and which promised to be a superb spectacle as the weather was so fine. There were more than fifty thousand strangers gathered together in Lourdes that day, for visitors had come in from all the neighbouring bathing stations. This explained the crush at the *table d'hote*. Possibly the town would run short of bread as had been the case the previous year.

"You saw what a scramble there is," concluded Majeste, "we really don't know how to manage. It isn't my fault, I assure you, if you are kept waiting for a short time."

At this moment, however, a postman arrived with a large batch of newspapers and letters which he deposited on a table in the office. He had kept one letter in his hand and inquired of the landlord, "Have you a Madame Maze here?"

"Madame Maze, Madame Maze," repeated the hotel-keeper. "No, no, certainly not."

Pierre had heard both question and answer, and drawing near he exclaimed, "I know of a Madame Maze who must be lodging with the Sisters of the Immaculate Conception, the Blue Sisters as people call them here, I think."

The postman thanked him for the information and went off, but a somewhat bitter smile had risen to Majeste's lips. "The Blue Sisters," he muttered, "ah! the Blue Sisters." Then, darting a side glance at Pierre's cassock, he stopped short, as though he feared that he might say too much. Yet his heart was overflowing; he would have greatly liked to ease his feelings, and this young priest from Paris, who looked so liberal-minded, could not be one of the "band" as he called all those who discharged functions at the Grotto and coined money out of Our Lady of Lourdes. Accordingly, little by little, he ventured to speak out.

"I am a good Christian, I assure you, Monsieur l'Abbe," said he. "In fact we are all good Christians here. And I am a regular worshipper and take the sacrament every Easter. But, really, I must say that members of a religious community ought not to keep hotels. No, no, it isn't right!"

And thereupon he vented all the spite of a tradesman in presence of what he considered to be disloyal competition. Ought not those Blue Sisters, those Sisters of the Immaculate Conception, to have confined themselves to their real functions, the manufacture of wafers for sacramental purposes, and the repairing and washing of church linen? Instead of that, however, they had transformed their convent into a vast hostelry, where ladies who came to Lourdes unaccompanied found separate rooms, and were able to take their meals either in privacy or in a general dining-room. Everything was certainly very clean, very well organised and very inexpensive, thanks to the thousand advantages which the Sisters enjoyed; in fact, no hotel at Lourdes did so much business. "But all the same," continued Majeste, "I ask you if it is proper. To think of nuns selling victuals! Besides, I must tell you that the lady superior is really a clever woman, and as soon as she saw the stream of fortune rolling in, she wanted to keep it all for her own community and resolutely parted with the Fathers of the Grotto who wanted to lay their hands on it. Yes, Monsieur l'Abbe, she even went to Rome and gained her cause there, so that now she pockets all the money that her bills bring in. Think of it, nuns, yes nuns, *mon Dieu*! letting furnished rooms and keeping a *table d' hote*!"

He raised his arms to heaven, he was stifling with envy and vexation.

"But as your house is crammed," Pierre gently objected, "as you no longer have either a bed or a plate at anybody's disposal, where would you put any additional visitors who might arrive here?"

Majeste at once began protesting. "Ah! Monsieur l'Abbe!" said he, "one can see very well that you don't know the place. It's quite true that there is work for all of us, and that nobody has reason to complain during the national pilgrimage. But that only lasts four or five days, and in ordinary times the custom we secure isn't nearly so great. For myself, thank Heaven, I am always satisfied. My house is well known, it occupies the same rank as the Hotel of the Grotto, where two landlords have already made their fortunes. But no matter, it is vexing to see those Blue Sisters taking all the cream of the custom, for instance the ladies of the *bourgeoisie* who spend a fortnight and three weeks here at a stretch; and that, too, just in the quiet season, when there are not many people here. You understand, don't you? There are people of position who dislike uproar; they go by themselves to the Grotto, and pray there all day long, for days together, and pay good prices for their accommodation without any higgling."

Madame Majeste, whom Pierre and M. de Guersaint had not noticed leaning over an account-book in which she was adding up some figures, thereupon intervened in a shrill voice: "We had a customer like that, gentlemen, who stayed here for two months last year. She went to the Grotto, came back, went there again, took her meals, and went to bed. And never did we have a word of complaint from her; she was always smiling, as though to say that she found everything very nice. She paid her bill, too, without even looking at it. Ah! one regrets people of that kind."

Short, thin, very dark, and dressed in black, with a little white collar, Madame Majeste had risen to her feet; and she now began to solicit custom: "If you would like to buy a few little souvenirs of Lourdes before you leave, gentlemen, I hope that you will not forget us. We have a shop close by, where you will find an assortment of all the articles that are most in request. As a rule, the persons who stay here are kind enough not to deal elsewhere."

However, Majeste was again wagging his head, with the air of a good Christian saddened by the scandals of the time. "Certainly," said he, "I don't want to show any disrespect to the reverend Fathers, but it must in all truth be admitted that they are too greedy. You must have seen the shop which they have set up near the Grotto, that shop which is always crowded, and where tapers and articles of piety are sold. A bishop declared that it was shameful, and that the buyers and sellers ought to be driven out of the temple afresh. It is said, too, that the Fathers run that big shop yonder, just across the street, which supplies all the petty dealers in the town. And, according to the reports which circulate, they have a finger in all the trade in religious articles, and levy a percentage on the millions of chaplets, statuettes, and medals which are sold every year at Lourdes."

ÉMILE ZOLA

Majeste had now lowered his voice, for his accusations were becoming precise, and he ended by trembling somewhat at his imprudence in talking so confidentially to strangers. However, the expression of Pierre's gentle, attentive face reassured him; and so he continued with the passion of a wounded rival, resolved to go on to the very end: "I am willing to admit that there is some exaggeration in all this. But all the same, it does religion no good for people to see the reverend Fathers keeping shops like us tradesmen. For my part, of course, I don't go and ask for a share of the money which they make by their masses, or a percentage on the presents which they receive, so why should they start selling what I sell? Our business was a poor one last year owing to them. There are already too many of us; nowadays everyone at Lourdes sells 'religious articles,' to such an extent, in fact, that there will soon be no butchers or wine merchants left—nothing but bread to eat and water to drink. Ah! Monsieur l'Abbe, it is no doubt nice to have the Blessed Virgin with us, but things are none the less very bad at times."

A person staying at the hotel at that moment disturbed him, but he returned just as a young girl came in search of Madame Majeste. The damsel, who evidently belonged to Lourdes, was very pretty, small but plump, with beautiful black hair, and a round face full of bright gaiety.

"That is our niece Apolline," resumed Majeste. "She has been keeping our shop for two years past. She is the daughter of one of my wife's brothers, who is in poor circumstances. She was keeping sheep at Ossun, in the neighbourhood of Bartres, when we were struck by her intelligence and nice looks and decided to bring her here; and we don't repent having done so, for she has a great deal of merit, and has become a very good saleswoman."

A point to which he omitted to refer, was that there were rumours current of somewhat flighty conduct on Mademoiselle Apolline's part. But she undoubtedly had her value: she attracted customers by the power, possibly, of her large black eyes, which smiled so readily. During his sojourn at Lourdes the previous year, Gerard de Peyrelongue had scarcely stirred from the shop she managed, and doubtless it was only the matrimonial ideas now flitting through his head that prevented him from returning thither. It seemed as though the Abbe des Hermoises had taken his place, for this gallant ecclesiastic brought a great many ladies to make purchases at the repository.

"Ah! you are speaking of Apolline," said Madame Majeste, at that moment coming back from the shop. "Have you noticed one thing about her, gentlemen—her extraordinary likeness to Bernadette? There, on the wall yonder, is a photograph of Bernadette when she was eighteen years old."

Pierre and M. de Guersaint drew near to examine the portrait, whilst Majeste exclaimed: "Bernadette, yes, certainly—she was rather like Apolline, but not nearly so nice; she looked so sad and poor."

He would doubtless have gone on chattering, but just then the waiter appeared and announced that there was at last a little table vacant. M. de Guersaint had twice gone to glance inside the dining-room, for he was eager to have his *dejeuner* and spend the remainder of that fine Sunday out-of-doors. So he now hastened away, without paying any further attention to Majeste, who remarked, with an amiable smile, that the gentlemen had not had so very long to wait after all.

To reach the table mentioned by the waiter, the architect and Pierre had to cross the dining-room from end to end. It was a long apartment, painted a light oak colour, an oily yellow, which was already peeling away in places and soiled with stains in others. You realised that rapid wear and tear went on here amidst the continual scramble of the big eaters who sat down at table. The only ornaments were a gilt zinc clock and a couple of meagre candelabra on the mantelpiece. Guipure curtains, moreover, hung at the five large windows looking on to the street, which was flooded with sunshine; some of the fierce arrow-like rays penetrating into the room although the blinds had been lowered. And, in the middle of the apartment, some forty persons were packed together at the *table d'hote*, which was scarcely eleven yards in length and did not supply proper accommodation for more than thirty people; whilst at the little tables standing against the walls upon either side another forty persons sat close together, hustled by the three waiters each time that they went by. You had scarcely reached the threshold before you were deafened by the extraordinary uproar, the noise of voices and the clatter of forks and plates; and it seemed, too, as if you were entering a damp oven, for a warm, steamy mist, laden with a suffocating smell of victuals, assailed the face.

Pierre at first failed to distinguish anything, but, when he was installed at the little table—a garden-table which had been brought indoors for the occasion, and on which there was scarcely room for two covers—he felt quite upset, almost sick, in fact, at the sight presented by the *table d'hote*, which his glance now enfiladed from end to end. People had been eating at it for an hour already, two sets of customers had followed one upon the other, and the covers were strewn about in higgledy-piggledy fashion. On the cloth were numerous stains of wine and sauce, while there was no symmetry even in the arrangement of the glass fruit-stands, which formed the only decorations of the table. And one's astonishment increased at sight of the motley mob which was collected there—huge priests, scraggy girls, mothers overflowing with superfluous fat, gentlemen with red faces, and families ranged in rows and displaying all the pitiable, increasing ugliness of successive generations. All these people were perspiring, greedily swallowing, seated slantwise, lacking room to move their arms, and unable even to use their hands deftly. And amidst this display of appetite, increased tenfold by fatigue, and of eager haste to fill one's stomach in order to return to the Grotto more quickly, there was a corpulent ecclesiastic who in no wise hurried, but ate of every dish with prudent slowness, crunching his food with a ceaseless, dignified movement of the jaws.

"*Fichtre!*" exclaimed M. de Guersaint, "it is by no means cool in here. All the same, I shall be glad of something to eat, for I've felt a sinking in the stomach ever since I have been at Lourdes. And you—are you hungry?"

"Yes, yes, I shall eat," replied Pierre, though, truth to tell, he felt quite upset.

The *menu* was a copious one. There was salmon, an omelet, mutton cutlets with mashed potatoes, stewed kidneys, cauliflowers, cold meats, and apricot tarts—everything cooked too much, and swimming in sauce which, but for its grittiness, would have been flavourless. However, there was some fairly fine fruit on the glass stands, particularly some peaches. And, besides, the people did not seem at all difficult to please; they apparently had no palates, for there was no sign of nausea. Hemmed in between an old priest and a dirty, full-bearded man, a girl of delicate build, who looked very pretty with her soft eyes and silken skin, was eating some kidneys with an expression of absolute beatitude, although the so-called "sauce" in which they swam was simply greyish water.

"Hum!" resumed even M. de Guersaint, "this salmon is not so bad. Add a little salt to it and you will find it all right."

Pierre made up his mind to eat, for after all he must take sustenance for strength's sake. At a little table close by, however, he had just caught sight of Madame Vigneron and Madame Chaise, who sat face to face, apparently waiting. And indeed, M. Vigneron and his son Gustave soon appeared, the latter still pale, and leaning more heavily than usual on his crutch. "Sit down next to your aunt," said his father; "I will take the chair beside your mother." But just then he perceived his two neighbours, and stepping up to them, he added: "Oh! he is now all right again. I have been rubbing him with some eau-de-Cologne, and by-and-by he will be able to take his bath at the piscina."

Thereupon M. Vigneron sat down and began to devour. But what an awful fright he had had! He again began talking of it aloud, despite himself, so intense had been his terror at the thought that the lad might go off before his aunt. The latter related that whilst she was kneeling at the Grotto the day before, she had experienced a sudden feeling of relief; in fact, she flattered herself that she was cured of her heart complaint, and began giving precise particulars, to which her brother-in-law listened with dilated eyes, full of involuntary anxiety. Most certainly he was a good-natured man, he had never desired anybody's death; only he felt indignant at the idea that the Virgin might cure this old woman, and forget his son, who was so young. Talking and eating, he had got to the cutlets, and was swallowing the mashed potatoes by the forkful, when he fancied he could detect that Madame Chaise was sulking with her nephew. "Gustave," he suddenly inquired, "have you asked your aunt's forgiveness?" The lad, quite astonished, began staring at his father with his large clear eyes. "Yes," added M. Vigneron, "you behaved very badly, you pushed her back just now when she wanted to help you to sit up."

Madame Chaise said nothing, but waited with a dignified air, whilst Gustave, who, without any show of appetite, was finishing the *noix* of his cutlet, which had been cut into small pieces, remained with his eyes lowered on his plate, this time obstinately refusing to make the sorry show of affection which was demanded of him.

"Come, Gustave," resumed his father, "be a good boy. You know how kind your aunt is, and all that she intends to do for you."

But no, he would not yield. At that moment, indeed, he really hated that woman, who did not die quickly enough, who polluted the affection of his parents, to such a point that when he saw them surround him with attentions he no longer knew whether it were himself or the inheritance which his life represented that they wished to save. However, Madame Vigneron, so dignified in her demeanour, came to her husband's help. "You really grieve me, Gustave," said she; "ask your aunt's forgiveness, or you will make me quite angry with you."

Thereupon he gave way. What was the use of resisting? Was it not better that his parents should obtain that money? Would he not himself die later on, so as to suit the family convenience? He was aware of all that; he understood everything, even when not a word was spoken. So keen was the sense of hearing with which suffering had endowed him, that he even heard the others' thoughts.

"I beg your pardon, aunt," he said, "for not having behaved well to you just now."

Then two big tears rolled from his eyes, whilst he smiled with the air of a tender-hearted man who has seen too much of life and can no longer be deceived by anything. Madame Chaise at once kissed him and told him that she was not at all angry. And the Vignerons' delight in living was displayed in all candour.

"If the kidneys are not up to much," M. de Guersaint now said to Pierre, "here at all events are some cauliflowers with a good flavour."

The formidable mastication was still going on around them. Pierre had never seen such an amount of eating, amidst such perspiration, in an atmosphere as stifling as that of a washhouse full of hot steam. The odour of the victuals seemed to thicken into a kind of smoke. You had to shout to make yourself heard, for everybody was talking in loud tones, and the scared waiters raised a fearful clatter in changing the plates and forks; not to mention the noise of all the jaw-crunching, a mill-like grinding which was distinctly audible. What most hurt the feelings of the young priest, however, was the extraordinary promiscuity of the *table d'hote*, at which men and women, young girls and ecclesiastics, were packed together in chance order, and satisfied their hunger like a pack of hounds snapping at offal in all haste. Baskets of bread went round and were promptly emptied. And there was a perfect massacre of cold meats, all the remnants of the victuals of the day before, leg of mutton, veal, and ham, encompassed by a fallen mass of transparent jelly which quivered like soft glue. They had all eaten too much already, but these viands seemed to whet their appetites afresh, as though the idea had come to them that nothing whatever ought to be left. The fat priest in the middle of the table, who had shown himself such a capital knife-and-fork, was now lingering over the fruit, having just got to his third peach, a huge one, which he slowly peeled and swallowed in slices with an air of compunction.

All at once, however, the whole room was thrown into agitation. A waiter had come in and begun distributing the letters which Madame Majeste had finished sorting. "Hallo!" exclaimed M. Vigneron; "a letter for me! This is surprising—I did not give my address to anybody." Then, at a sudden recollection, he added, "Yes I did, though; this must have come from Sauvageot, who is filling my place at the Ministry." He opened the letter, his hands began to tremble, and suddenly he raised a cry: "The chief clerk is dead!"

Deeply agitated, Madame Vigneron was also unable to bridle her tongue: "Then you will have the appointment!"

This was the secret dream in which they had so long and so fondly indulged: the chief clerk's death, in order that he, Vigneron, assistant chief clerk for ten years past, might at last rise to the supreme post, the bureaucratic marshalship. And so great was his delight that he cast aside all restraint. "Ah! the Blessed Virgin is certainly protecting me, my dear. Only this morning I again prayed to her for a rise, and, you see, she grants my prayer!"

However, finding Madame Chaise's eyes fixed upon his own, and seeing Gustave smile, he realised that he ought not to exult in this fashion. Each member of the family no doubt thought of his or her interests and prayed to the Blessed Virgin for such personal favours as might be desired. And so, again putting on his good-natured air, he resumed: "I mean that the Blessed Virgin takes an interest in every one of us and will send us all home well satisfied. Ah! the poor chief, I'm sorry for him. I shall have to send my card to his widow."

In spite of all his efforts he could not restrain his exultation, and no longer doubted that his most secret desires, those which he did not even confess to himself, would soon be gratified. And so all honour was done to the apricot tarts, even Gustave being allowed to eat a portion of one.

"It is surprising," now remarked M. de Guersaint, who had just ordered a cup of coffee; "it is surprising that one doesn't see more sick people here. All these folks seem to me to have first-rate appetites."

After a close inspection, however, in addition to Gustave, who ate no more than a little chicken, he ended by finding a man with a goitre seated at the *table d'hote* between two women, one of whom certainly suffered from cancer. Farther on, too, there was a girl so thin and pale that she must surely be a consumptive. And still farther away there was a female idiot who had made her entry leaning on two relatives, and with expressionless eyes and lifeless features was now carrying her food to her mouth with a spoon, and slobbering over her napkin. Perhaps there were yet other ailing ones present who could not be distinguished among all those noisy appetites, ailing ones whom the journey had braced, and who were eating as they had not eaten for a long time past. The apricot tarts, the cheese, the fruits were all engulfed amidst the increasing disorder of the table, where at last there only remained the stains of all the wine and sauce which had been spilt upon the cloth.

It was nearly noon. "We will go back to the Grotto at once, eh?" said M. Vigneron.

Indeed, "To the Grotto! To the Grotto!" were well-nigh the only words you now heard. The full mouths were eagerly masticating and swallowing, in order that they might repeat prayers and hymns again with all speed. "Well, as we have the whole afternoon before us," declared M. de Guersaint, "I suggest that we should visit the town a little. I want to see also if I can get a conveyance for my excursion, as my daughter so particularly wishes me to make it."

Pierre, who was stifling, was glad indeed to leave the dining-room. In the porch he was able to breathe again, though even there he found a torrent of customers, new arrivals who were waiting for places. No sooner did one of the little tables become vacant than its possession was eagerly contested, whilst the smallest gap at the *table d'hote* was instantly filled up. In this wise the assault would continue for more than another hour, and again would the different courses of the *menu* appear in procession, to be engulfed amidst the crunching of jaws, the stifling heat, and the growing nausea.

II

The "Ordinary"

When Pierre and M. de Guersaint got outside they began walking slowly amidst the ever-growing stream of the Sundayfied crowd. The sky was a bright blue, the sun warmed the whole town, and there was a festive gaiety in the atmosphere, the keen delight that attends those great fairs which bring entire communities into the open air. When they had descended the crowded footway of the Avenue de la Grotte, and had reached the corner of the Plateau de la Merlasse, they found their way barred by a throng which was flowing backward amidst a block of vehicles and stamping of horses. "There is no hurry, however," remarked M. de Guersaint. "My idea is to go as far as the Place du Marcadal in the old town; for the servant girl at the hotel told me of a hairdresser there whose brother lets out conveyances cheaply. Do you mind going so far?"

"I?" replied Pierre. "Go wherever you like, I'll follow you."

"All right—and I'll profit by the opportunity to have a shave."

They were nearing the Place du Rosaire, and found themselves in front of the lawns stretching to the Gave, when an encounter again stopped them. Mesdames Desagneaux and Raymonde de Jonquiere were here, chatting gaily with Gerard de Peyrelongue. Both women wore light-coloured gowns, seaside dresses as it were, and their white silk parasols shone in the bright sunlight. They imparted, so to say, a pretty note to the scene—a touch of society chatter blended with the fresh laughter of youth.

"No, no," Madame Desagneaux was saying, "we certainly can't go and visit your 'ordinary' like that—at the very moment when all your comrades are eating."

Gerard, however, with a very gallant air, insisted on their accompanying him, turning more particularly towards Raymonde, whose somewhat massive face was that day brightened by the radiant charm of health.

"But it is a very curious sight, I assure you," said the young man, "and you would be very respectfully received. Trust yourself to me, mademoiselle. Besides, we should certainly find M. Berthaud there, and he would be delighted to do you the honours."

Raymonde smiled, her clear eyes plainly saying that she was quite agreeable. And just then, as Pierre and M. de Guersaint drew near in order to present their respects to the ladies, they were made acquainted with the question under discussion. The "ordinary" was a kind of restaurant or *table d'hote* which the members of the Hospitality of Our Lady of Salvation—the bearers, the hospitallers of the Grotto, the piscinas, and the hospitals—had established among themselves with the view of taking their meals together at small cost. Many of them were not rich, for they were recruited among all classes; however, they had contrived to secure three good meals for the daily payment of three francs apiece. And in fact they soon had provisions to spare and distributed them among the poor. Everything was in their own management; they purchased their own supplies, recruited a cook and a few waiters, and did not disdain to lend a hand themselves, in order that everything might be comfortable and orderly.

"It must be very interesting," said M, de Guersaint, when these explanations had been given him. "Let us go and see it, if we are not in the way."

Little Madame Desagneaux thereupon gave her consent. "Well, if we are going in a party," said she, "I am quite willing. But when this gentleman first proposed to take Raymonde and me, I was afraid that it might not be quite proper."

Then, as she began to laugh, the others followed her example. She had accepted M. de Guersaint's arm, and Pierre walked beside her on the other hand, experiencing a sudden feeling of sympathy for this gay little woman, who was so full of life and so charming with her fair frizzy hair and creamy complexion.

Behind them came Raymonde, leaning upon Gerard's arm and talking to him in the calm, staid voice of a young lady who holds the best principles despite her air of heedless youth. And since here was the husband whom she had so often dreamt of, she resolved that she would this time secure him, make him beyond all question her own. She intoxicated him with the perfume of health and youth which she diffused, and at the same time astonished him by her knowledge of housewifely duties and of the manner in which money may be economised even in the most trifling matters; for having questioned him with regard to the purchases which he and his comrades made for their "ordinary," she proceeded to show him that they might have reduced their expenditure still further.

Meantime M. de Guersaint and Madame Desagneaux were also chatting together: "You must be fearfully tired, madame," said the architect.

But with a gesture of revolt, and an exclamation of genuine anger, she replied: "Oh no, indeed! Last night, it is true, fatigue quite overcame me at the hospital; I sat down and dozed off, and Madame de Jonquiere and the other ladies were good enough to let me sleep on." At this the others again began to laugh; but still with the same angry air she continued: "And so I slept like a log until this morning. It was disgraceful, especially as I had sworn that I would remain up all night." Then, merriment gaining upon her in her turn, she suddenly burst into a sonorous laugh, displaying her beautiful white teeth. "Ah! a pretty nurse I am, and no mistake! It was poor Madame de Jonquiere who had to remain on her legs all the time. I tried to coax her to come out with us just now. But she preferred to take a little rest."

Raymonde, who overheard these words, thereupon raised her voice to say: "Yes, indeed, my poor mamma could no longer keep on her feet. It was I who compelled her to lie down, telling her that she could go to sleep without any uneasiness, for we should get on all right without her—"

So saying, the girl gave Gerard a laughing glance. He even fancied that he could detect a faint squeeze of the fresh round arm which was resting on his own, as though, indeed, she had wished to express her happiness at being alone with him so that they might settle their own affairs without any interference. This quite delighted him; and he began to explain that if he had not had *dejeuner* with his comrades that day, it was because some friends had invited him to join them at the railway-station refreshment-room at ten o'clock, and had not given him his liberty until after the departure of the eleven-thirty train.

"Ah! the rascals!" he suddenly resumed. "Do you hear them, mademoiselle?"

The little party was now nearing its destination, and the uproarious laughter and chatter of youth rang out from a clump of trees which concealed the old zinc and plaster building in which the "ordinary" was installed. Gerard began by taking the visitors into the kitchen, a very spacious apartment, well fitted up, and containing a huge range and an immense table, to say nothing of numerous gigantic cauldrons. Here, moreover, the young man called the attention of his companions to the circumstance that the cook, a fat, jovial-looking man, had the red cross pinned on his white jacket, being himself a member of the pilgrimage. Then, pushing open a door, Gerard invited his friends to enter the common room.

It was a long apartment containing two rows of plain deal tables; and the only other articles of furniture were numerous rush-seated tavern chairs, with an additional table which served as a sideboard. The whitewashed walls and the flooring of shiny, red tiles looked, however, extremely clean amidst this intentional bareness, which was similar to that of a monkish refectory. But, the feature of the place which more particularly struck you, as you crossed the threshold, was the childish gaiety which reigned there; for, packed together at the tables, were a hundred and fifty hospitallers of all ages, eating with splendid appetites, laughing, applauding, and singing, with their mouths full. A wondrous fraternity united these men, who had flocked to Lourdes from every province of France, and who belonged to all classes, and represented every degree of fortune. Many of them knew nothing of one another, save that they met here and elbowed one another during three days every year, living together like brothers, and then going off and remaining in absolute ignorance of each other during the rest of the twelvemonth. Nothing could be more charming, however, than to meet again at the next pilgrimage, united in the same charitable work, and to spend a few days of hard labour and boyish delight in common once more; for it all became, as it were, an "outing" of a number of big fellows, let loose under a lovely sky, and well pleased to be able to enjoy themselves and laugh together. And even the frugality of the table, with the pride of managing things themselves, of eating the provisions which they had purchased and cooked, added to the general good humour.

"You see," explained Gerard, "we are not at all inclined to be sad, although we have so much hard work to get through. The Hospitality numbers more than three hundred members, but there are only about one hundred and fifty here at a time, for we have had to organise two successive services, so that there may always be some of us on duty at the Grotto and the hospitals."

The sight of the little party of visitors assembled on the threshold of the room seemed to have increased the general delight; and Berthaud, the superintendent of the bearers, who was lunching at the head of one of the tables, gallantly rose up to receive the ladies.

"But it smells very nice," exclaimed Madame Desagneaux in her giddy way. "Won't you invite us to come and taste your cookery to-morrow?"

"Oh! we can't ask ladies," replied Berthaud, laughing. "But if you gentlemen would like to join us to-morrow we should be extremely pleased to entertain you."

He had at once noticed the good understanding which prevailed between Gerard and Raymonde, and seemed delighted at it, for he greatly wished his cousin to make this match. He laughed pleasantly, at the enthusiastic gaiety which the young girl displayed as she began to question him. "Is not that the Marquis de Salmon-Roquebert," she asked, "who is sitting over yonder between those two young men who look like shop assistants?"

"They are, in fact, the sons of a small stationer at Tarbes," replied Berthaud; "and that is really the Marquis, your neighbour of the Rue de Lille, the owner of that magnificent mansion, one of the richest and most noble men of title in France. You see how he is enjoying our mutton stew!"

It was true, the millionaire Marquis seemed delighted to be able to board himself for his three francs a day, and to sit down at table in genuine democratic fashion by the side of petty *bourgeois* and workmen who would not have dared to accost him in the street. Was not that chance table symbolical of social communion, effected by the joint practice of charity? For his part, the Marquis was the more hungry that day, as he had bathed over sixty patients, sufferers from all the most abominable diseases of unhappy humanity, at the piscinas that morning. And the scene around him seemed like a realisation of the evangelical commonalty; but doubtless it was so charming and so gay simply because its duration was limited to three days.

Although M. de Guersaint had but lately risen from table, his curiosity prompted him to taste the mutton stew, and he pronounced it perfect. Meantime, Pierre caught sight of Baron Suire, the director of the Hospitality, walking about between the rows of tables with an air of some importance, as though he had allotted himself the task of keeping an eye on everything, even on the manner in which his staff fed itself. The young priest thereupon remembered the ardent desire which Marie had expressed to spend the night in front of the Grotto, and it occurred to him that the Baron might be willing to give the necessary authorisation.

"Certainly," replied the director, who had become quite grave whilst listening to Pierre, "we do sometimes allow it; but it is always a very delicate matter! You assure me at all events that this young person is not consumptive? Well, well, since you say that she so much desires it I will mention the matter to Father Fourcade and warn Madame de Jonquiere, so that she may let you take the young lady away."

He was in reality a very good-natured fellow, albeit so fond of assuming the air of an indispensable man weighed down by the heaviest responsibilities. In his turn he now detained the visitors, and gave them full particulars concerning the organisation of the Hospitality. Its members said prayers together every morning. Two board meetings were held each day, and were attended by all the heads of departments, as well as by the reverend Fathers and some of the chaplains. All the hospitallers took the Sacrament as frequently as possible. And, moreover, there were many complicated tasks to be attended to, a prodigious rotation of duties, quite a little world to be governed with a firm hand. The Baron spoke like a general who each year gains a great victory over the spirit of the age; and, sending Berthaud back to finish his *dejeuner*, he insisted on escorting the ladies into the little sanded courtyard, which was shaded by some fine trees.

"It is very interesting, very interesting," repeated Madame Desagneaux. "We are greatly obliged to you for your kindness, monsieur."

"Don't mention it, don't mention it, madame," answered the Baron. "It is I who am pleased at having had an opportunity to show you my little army."

So far Gerard had not quitted Raymonde's side; but M. de Guersaint and Pierre were already exchanging glances suggestive of leave-taking, in order that they might repair by themselves to the Place du Marcadal, when Madame Desagneaux suddenly remembered that a friend had requested her to send her a bottle of Lourdes water. And she thereupon asked Gerard how she was to execute this commission. The young man began to laugh. "Will you again accept me as a guide?" said he. "And by the way, if these gentlemen like to come as well, I will show you the place where the bottles are filled, corked, packed in cases, and then sent off. It is a curious sight."

M. de Guersaint immediately consented; and all five of them set out again, Madame Desagneaux still between the architect and the priest, whilst Raymonde and Gerard brought up the rear. The crowd in the burning sunlight was increasing; the Place du Rosaire was now overflowing with an idle sauntering mob resembling some concourse of sight-seers on a day of public rejoicing.

The bottling and packing shops were situated under one of the arches on the left-hand side of the Place. They formed a suite of three apartments of very simple aspect. In the first one the bottles were filled in the most ordinary of fashions. A little green-painted zinc barrel, not unlike a watering-cask, was dragged by a man from the Grotto, and the light-coloured bottles were then simply filled at its tap, one by one; the blouse-clad workman entrusted with the duty exercising no particular watchfulness to prevent the water from overflowing. In fact there was quite a puddle of it upon the ground. There were no labels on the bottles; the little leaden capsules placed over the corks alone bore an inscription, and they were coated with a kind of ceruse, doubtless to ensure preservation. Then came two other rooms which formed regular packing shops, with carpenters' benches, tools, and heaps of shavings. The boxes, most frequently made for one bottle or for two, were put together with great care, and the bottles were deposited inside them, on beds of fine wood parings. The scene reminded one in some degree of the packing halls for flowers at Nice and for preserved fruits at Grasse.

Gerard went on giving explanations with a quiet, satisfied air. "The water," he said, "really comes from the Grotto, as you can yourselves see, so that all the foolish jokes which one hears really have no basis. And everything is perfectly simple, natural, and goes on in the broad daylight. I would also point out to you that the Fathers don't sell the water as they are accused of doing. For instance, a bottle of water here costs twenty centimes,* which is only the price of the bottle itself. If you wish to have it sent to anybody you naturally have to pay for the packing and the carriage, and then it costs you one franc and seventy centimes.** However, you are perfectly at liberty to go to the source and fill the flasks and cans and other receptacles that you may choose to bring with you."

Pierre reflected that the profits of the reverend Fathers in this respect could not be very large ones, for their gains were limited to what they made by manufacturing the boxes and supplying the bottles, which latter, purchased by the thousand, certainly did not cost them so much as twenty centimes apiece. However, Raymonde and Madame Desagneaux, as well as M. de Guersaint, who had such a lively imagination, experienced deep disappointment at sight of the little green barrel, the capsules, sticky with ceruse, and the piles of shavings lying around the benches. They had doubtless imagined all sorts of

---

* Four cents, U.S.A.
** About 32 cents, U.S.A.

ceremonies, the observance of certain rites in bottling the miraculous water, priests in vestments pronouncing blessings, and choir-boys singing hymns of praise in pure crystalline voices. For his part, Pierre, in presence of all this vulgar bottling and packing, ended by thinking of the active power of faith. When one of those bottles reaches some far-away sick-room, and is unpacked there, and the sufferer falls upon his knees, and so excites himself by contemplating and drinking the pure water that he actually brings about the cure of his ailment, there must truly be a most extraordinary plunge into all-powerful illusion.

"Ah!" exclaimed Gerard as they came out, "would you like to see the storehouse where the tapers are kept, before going to the offices? It is only a couple of steps away."

And then, not even waiting for their answer, he led them to the opposite side of the Place du Rosaire. His one desire was to amuse Raymonde, but, in point of fact, the aspect of the place where the tapers were stored was even less entertaining than that of the packing-rooms which they had just left. This storehouse, a kind of deep vault under one of the right-hand arches of the Place, was divided by timber into a number of spacious compartments, in which lay an extraordinary collection of tapers, classified according to size. The overplus of all the tapers offered to the Grotto was deposited here; and such was the number of these superfluous candles that the little conveyances stationed near the Grotto railing, ready to receive the pilgrims' offerings, had to be brought to the storehouse several times a day in order to be emptied there, after which they were returned to the Grotto, and were promptly filled again. In theory, each taper that was offered ought to have been burnt at the feet of the Virgin's statue; but so great was the number of these offerings, that, although a couple of hundred tapers of all sizes were kept burning by day and night, it was impossible to exhaust the supply, which went on increasing and increasing. There was a rumour that the Fathers could not even find room to store all this wax, but had to sell it over and over again; and, indeed, certain friends of the Grotto confessed, with a touch of pride, that the profit on the tapers alone would have sufficed to defray all the expenses of the business.

The quantity of these votive candles quite stupefied Raymonde and Madame Desagneaux. How many, how many there were! The smaller ones, costing from fifty centimes to a franc apiece, were piled up in fabulous numbers. M. de Guersaint, desirous of getting at the exact figures, quite lost himself in the puzzling calculation he attempted.

As for Pierre, it was in silence that he gazed upon this mass of wax, destined to be burnt in open daylight to the glory of God; and although he was by no means a rigid utilitarian, and could well understand that some apparent acts of extravagance yield an illusive enjoyment and satisfaction which provide humanity with as much sustenance as bread, he could not, on the other hand, refrain from reflecting on the many benefits which might have been conferred on the poor and the ailing with the money represented by all that wax, which would fly away in smoke.

"But come, what about that bottle which I am to send off?" abruptly asked Madame Desagneaux.

"We will go to the office," replied Gerard. "In five minutes everything will be settled."

They had to cross the Place du Rosaire once more and ascend the stone stairway leading to the Basilica. The office was up above, on the left hand, at the corner of the path leading to the Calvary. The building was a paltry one, a hut of lath and plaster which the wind and the rain had reduced to a state of ruin. On a board outside was the inscription: "Apply here with reference to Masses, Offerings, and Brotherhoods. Forwarding office for Lourdes water. Subscriptions to the 'Annals of O. L. of Lourdes.'" How many millions of people must have already passed through this wretched shanty, which seemed to date from the innocent days when the foundations of the adjacent Basilica had scarcely been laid!

The whole party went in, eager to see what might be inside. But they simply found a wicket at which Madame Desagneaux had to stop in order to give her friend's name and address; and when she had paid one franc and seventy centimes, a small printed receipt was handed her, such as you receive on registering luggage at a railway station.

As soon as they were outside again Gerard pointed to a large building standing two or three hundred yards away, and resumed: "There, that is where the Fathers reside."

"But we see nothing of them," remarked Pierre.

This observation so astonished the young man that he remained for a moment without replying. "It's true," he at last said, "we do not see them, but then they give up the custody of everything—the Grotto and all the rest—to the Fathers of the Assumption during the national pilgrimage."

Pierre looked at the building which had been pointed out to him, and noticed that it was a massive stone pile resembling a fortress. The windows were closed, and the whole edifice looked lifeless. Yet everything at Lourdes came from it, and to it also everything returned. It seemed, in fact, to the young priest that he could hear the silent, formidable rake-stroke which extended over the entire valley, which caught hold of all who had come to the spot, and placed both the gold and the blood of the throng in the clutches of those reverend Fathers! However, Gerard just then resumed in a low voice "But come, they do show themselves, for here is the reverend superior, Father Capdebarthe himself."

An ecclesiastic was indeed just passing, a man with the appearance of a peasant, a knotty frame, and a large head which looked as though carved with a billhook. His opaque eyes were quite expressionless, and his face, with its worn features, had retained a loamy tint, a gloomy, russet reflection of the earth. Monseigneur Laurence had really made a politic selection in confiding the organisation and management of the Grotto to those Garaison missionaries, who were so tenacious and covetous, for the most part sons of mountain peasants and passionately attached to the soil.

However, the little party now slowly retraced its steps by way of the Plateau de la Merlasse, the broad boulevard which skirts the inclined way on the left hand and leads to the Avenue de la Grotte. It was already past one o'clock, but people were still eating their *dejeuners* from one to the other end of the overflowing town. Many of the fifty thousand pilgrims and sight-seers collected within it had not yet been able to sit down and eat; and Pierre, who had left the *table d'hote* still crowded, who had just seen the hospitallers squeezing together so gaily at the "ordinary," found more and more tables at each step he took. On all sides people were eating, eating without a pause. Hereabouts, however, in the open air, on either side of the broad road, the hungry ones were humble folk who had rushed upon the tables set up on either footway— tables formed of a couple of long boards, flanked by two forms, and shaded from the sun by narrow linen awnings. Broth and coffee were sold at these places at a penny a cup. The little loaves heaped up in high baskets also cost a penny apiece. Hanging from the poles which upheld the awnings were sausages, chitterlings, and hams. Some of the open-air *restaurateurs* were frying potatoes, and others were concocting more or less savoury messes of inferior meat and onions. A pungent smoke, a violent odour, arose into the sunlight, mingling with the dust which was raised by the continuous tramp of the promenaders. Rows of people, moreover, were waiting at each cantine, so that each time a party rose from table fresh customers took possession of the benches ranged beside the oilcloth-covered planks, which were so narrow that there was scarcely room for two bowls of soup to be placed side by side. And one and all made haste, and devoured with the ravenous hunger born of their fatigue, that insatiable appetite which so often follows upon great moral shocks. In fact, when the mind had exhausted itself in prayer, when everything physical had been forgotten amidst the mental flight into the legendary heavens, the human animal suddenly appeared, again asserted itself, and began to gorge. Moreover, under that dazzling Sunday sky, the scene was like that of a fair-field with all the gluttony of a merrymaking community, a display of the delight which they felt in living, despite the multiplicity of their abominable ailments and the dearth of the miracles they hoped for.

"They eat, they amuse themselves; what else can one expect?" remarked Gerard, guessing the thoughts of his amiable companions.

"Ah! poor people!" murmured Pierre, "they have a perfect right to do so."

He was greatly touched to see human nature reassert itself in this fashion. However, when they had got to the lower part of the boulevard near the Grotto, his feelings were hurt at sight of the desperate eagerness displayed by the female vendors of tapers and bouquets, who with the rough fierceness of conquerors assailed the passers-by in bands. They were mostly young women, with bare heads, or with kerchiefs tied over their hair, and they displayed extraordinary effrontery. Even the old ones were scarcely more discreet. With parcels of tapers under their arms, they brandished the one which they offered for sale and even thrust it into the hand of the promenader. "Monsieur," "madame," they called, "buy a taper, buy a taper, it will bring you luck!" One gentleman, who was surrounded and shaken by three of the youngest of these harpies, almost lost the skirts of his frock-coat in attempting to escape their clutches. Then the scene began afresh with the bouquets—large round bouquets they were, carelessly fastened together and looking like cabbages. "A bouquet, madame!" was the cry. "A bouquet for the Blessed Virgin!" If the lady escaped, she heard muttered insults behind her. Trafficking, impudent trafficking, pursued the pilgrims to the very outskirts of the Grotto. Trade was not merely triumphantly installed in every one of the shops, standing close together and transforming each street into a bazaar, but it overran the footways and barred the road with hand-carts full of chaplets, medals, statuettes, and religious prints. On all sides people were buying almost to the same extent as they ate, in order that they might take away with them some souvenir of this holy Kermesse. And the bright gay note of this commercial eagerness, this scramble of hawkers, was supplied by the urchins who rushed about through the crowd, crying the "Journal de la Grotte." Their sharp, shrill voices pierced the ear: "The 'Journal de la Grotte,' this morning's number, two sous, the 'Journal de la Grotte.'"

Amidst the continual pushing which accompanied the eddying of the ever-moving crowd, Gerard's little party became separated. He and Raymonde remained behind the others. They had begun talking together in low tones, with an air of smiling intimacy, lost and isolated as they were in the dense crowd. And Madame Desagneaux at last had to stop, look back, and call to them: "Come on, or we shall lose one another!"

As they drew near, Pierre heard the girl exclaim: "Mamma is so very busy; speak to her before we leave." And Gerard thereupon replied: "It is understood. You have made me very happy, mademoiselle."

Thus the husband had been secured, the marriage decided upon, during this charming promenade among the sights of Lourdes. Raymonde had completed her conquest, and Gerard had at last taken a resolution, realising how gay and sensible she was, as she walked beside him leaning on his arm.

M. de Guersaint, however, had raised his eyes, and was heard inquiring: "Are not those people up there, on that balcony, the rich folk who made the journey in the same train as ourselves?—You know whom I mean, that lady who is so very ill, and whose husband and sister accompany her?"

He was alluding to the Dieulafays; and they indeed were the persons whom he now saw on the balcony of a suite of rooms which they had rented in a new house overlooking the lawns of the Rosary. They here occupied a first-floor, furnished with all the luxury that Lourdes could provide, carpets, hangings, mirrors, and many other things, without mentioning a staff of servants despatched beforehand from Paris. As the weather was so fine that afternoon, the large armchair on which lay the poor ailing woman had been rolled on to the balcony. You could see her there, clad in a lace *peignoir*. Her husband, always correctly attired in a black frock-coat, stood beside her on her right hand, whilst her sister, in a delightful pale mauve gown, sat on her left smiling and leaning over every now and then so as to speak to her, but apparently receiving no reply.

"Oh!" declared little Madame Desagneaux, "I have often heard people speak of Madame Jousseur, that lady in mauve. She is the wife of a diplomatist who neglects her, it seems, in spite of her great beauty; and last year there was a deal of talk about her fancy for a young colonel who is well known in Parisian society. It is said, however, in Catholic *salons* that her religious principles enabled her to conquer it."

They all five remained there, looking up at the balcony. "To think," resumed Madame Desagneaux, "that her sister, poor woman, was once her living portrait." And, indeed, there was an expression of greater kindliness and more gentle gaiety on Madame Dieulafay's face. And now you see her—no different from a dead woman except that she is above instead of under ground—with her flesh wasted away, reduced to a livid, boneless thing which they scarcely dare to move. Ah! the unhappy woman!

Raymonde thereupon assured the others that Madame Dieulafay, who had been married scarcely two years previously, had brought all the jewellery given her on the occasion of her wedding to offer it as a gift to Our Lady of Lourdes; and Gerard confirmed this assertion, saying that the jewellery had been handed over to the treasurer of the Basilica that very morning with a golden lantern studded with gems and a large sum of money destined for the relief of the poor. However, the Blessed Virgin could not have been touched as yet, for the sufferer's condition seemed, if anything, to be worse.

From that moment Pierre no longer beheld aught save that young woman on that handsome balcony, that woeful, wealthy creature lying there high above the merrymaking throng, the Lourdes mob which was feasting and laughing in the Sunday sunshine. The two dear ones who were so tenderly watching over her—her sister who had forsaken her society triumphs, her husband who had forgotten his financial business, his millions dispersed throughout the world—increased, by their irreproachable demeanour, the woefulness of the group which they thus formed high above all other heads, and face to face with the lovely valley. For Pierre they alone remained; and they were exceedingly wealthy and exceedingly wretched.

However, lingering in this wise on the footway with their eyes upturned, the five promenaders narrowly escaped being knocked down and run over, for at every moment fresh vehicles were coming up, for the most part landaus drawn by four horses, which were driven at a fast trot, and whose bells jingled merrily. The occupants of these carriages were tourists, visitors to the waters of Pau, Bareges, and Cauterets, whom curiosity had attracted to Lourdes, and who were delighted with the fine weather and quite inspirited by their rapid drive across the mountains. They would remain at Lourdes only a few hours; after hastening to the Grotto and the Basilica in seaside costumes, they would start off again, laughing, and well pleased at having seen it all. In this wise families in light attire, bands of young women with bright parasols, darted hither and thither among the grey, neutral-tinted crowd of pilgrims, imparting to it, in a yet more pronounced manner, the aspect of a fair-day mob, amidst which folks of good society deign to come and amuse themselves.

All at once Madame Desagneaux raised a cry "What, is it you, Berthe?" And thereupon she embraced a tall, charming brunette who had just alighted from a landau with three other young women, the whole party smiling and animated. Everyone began talking at once, and all sorts of merry exclamations rang out, in the delight they felt at meeting in this fashion. "Oh! we are at Cauterets, my dear," said the tall brunette. "And as everybody comes here, we decided to come all four together. And your husband, is he here with you?"

Madame Desagneaux began protesting: "Of course not," said she. "He is at Trouville, as you ought to know. I shall start to join him on Thursday."

"Yes, yes, of course," resumed the tall brunette, who, like her friend, seemed to be an amiable, giddy creature, "I was forgetting; you are here with the pilgrimage."

Then Madame Desagneaux offered to guide her friends, promising to show them everything of interest in less than a couple of hours; and turning to Raymonde, who stood by, smiling, she added "Come with us, my dear; your mother won't be anxious."

The ladies and Pierre and M. de Guersaint thereupon exchanged bows: and Gerard also took leave, tenderly pressing Raymonde's hand, with his eyes fixed on hers, as though to pledge himself definitively. The women swiftly departed, directing their steps towards the Grotto, and when Gerard also had gone off, returning to his duties, M. de Guersaint said to Pierre: "And the hairdresser on the Place du Marcadal, I really must go and see him. You will come with me, won't you?"

"Of course I will go wherever you like. I am quite at your disposal as Marie does not need us."

Following the pathways between the large lawns which stretch out in front of the Rosary, they reached the new bridge, where they had another encounter, this time with Abbe des Hermoises, who was acting as guide to two young married ladies who had arrived that morning from Tarbes. Walking between them with the gallant air of a society priest, he was showing them Lourdes and explaining it to them, keeping them well away, however, from its more repugnant features, its poor and its ailing folk, its odour of low misery, which, it must be admitted, had well-nigh disappeared that fine, sunshiny day. At the first word which M. de Guersaint addressed to him with respect to the hiring of a vehicle for the trip to Gavarnie, the Abbe was seized with a dread lest he should be obliged to leave his pretty lady-visitors: "As you please, my dear sir," he replied. "Kindly attend to the matter, and—you are quite right, make the cheapest arrangements possible, for I shall have two ecclesiastics of small means with me. There will be four of us. Let me know at the hotel this evening at what hour we shall start."

Thereupon he again joined his lady-friends, and led them towards the Grotto, following the shady path which skirts the Gave, a cool, sequestered path well suited for lovers' walks.

Feeling somewhat tired, Pierre had remained apart from the others, leaning against the parapet of the new bridge. And now for the first time he was struck by the prodigious number of priests among the crowd. He saw all varieties of them swarming across the bridge: priests of correct mien who had come with the pilgrimage and who could be recognised by their air of assurance and their clean cassocks; poor village priests who were far more timid and badly clothed, and who, after making sacrifices in order that they might indulge in the journey, would return home quite scared and, finally, there was the whole crowd of unattached ecclesiastics who had come nobody knew whence, and who enjoyed such absolute liberty that it was difficult to be sure whether they had even said their mass that morning. They doubtless found this liberty very agreeable; and thus the greater number of them, like Abbe des Hermoises, had simply come on a holiday excursion, free from all duties, and happy at being able to live like ordinary men, lost, unnoticed as they were in the multitude around them. And from the young, carefully groomed and perfumed priest, to the old one in a dirty cassock and shoes down at heel, the entire species had its representative in the throng—there were corpulent ones, others but moderately fat, thin ones, tall ones and short ones, some whom faith had brought and whom ardour was consuming, some also who simply plied their calling like worthy men, and some, moreover, who were fond of intriguing, and who were only present in order that they might help the good cause. However, Pierre was quite surprised to see such a stream of priests pass before him, each with his special passion, and one and all hurrying to the Grotto as one hurries to a duty, a belief, a pleasure, or a task. He noticed one among the number, a very short, slim, dark man with a pronounced Italian accent, whose glittering eyes seemed to be taking a plan of Lourdes, who looked, indeed, like one of those spies who come and peer around with a view to conquest; and then he observed another one, an enormous fellow with a paternal air, who was breathing hard through inordinate eating, and who paused in front of a poor sick woman, and ended by slipping a five-franc piece into her hand.

Just then, however, M. de Guersaint returned: "We merely have to go down the boulevard and the Rue Basse," said he.

Pierre followed him without answering. He had just felt his cassock on his shoulders for the first time that afternoon, for never had it seemed so light to him as whilst he was walking about amidst the scramble of the pilgrimage. The young fellow was now living in a state of mingled unconsciousness and dizziness, ever hoping that faith would fall upon him like a lightning flash, in spite of all the vague uneasiness which was growing within him at sight of the things which he beheld. However, the spectacle of that ever-swelling stream of priests no longer wounded his heart; fraternal feelings towards these unknown colleagues had returned to him; how many of them there must be who believed no more than he did himself, and yet, like himself, honestly fulfilled their mission as guides and consolers!

"This boulevard is a new one, you know," said M. de Guersaint, all at once raising his voice. "The number of houses built during the last twenty years is almost beyond belief. There is quite a new town here."

The Lapaca flowed along behind the buildings on their right and, their curiosity inducing them to turn into a narrow lane, they came upon some strange old structures on the margin of the narrow stream. Several ancient mills here displayed their wheels; among them one which Monseigneur Laurence had given to Bernadette's parents after the apparitions. Tourists, moreover, were here shown the pretended abode of Bernadette, a hovel whither the Soubirous family had removed on leaving the Rue des Petits Fosses, and in which the young girl, as she was already boarding with the Sisters of Nevers, can have but seldom slept. At last, by way of the Rue Basse, Pierre and his companion reached the Place du Marcadal.

This was a long, triangular, open space, the most animated and luxurious of the squares of the old town, the one where the cafes, the chemists, all the finest shops were situated. And, among the latter, one showed conspicuously, coloured as it was a lively green, adorned with lofty mirrors, and surmounted by a broad board bearing in gilt letters the inscription: "Cazaban, Hairdresser".

M. de Guersaint and Pierre went in, but there was nobody in the salon and they had to wait. A terrible clatter of forks resounded from the adjoining room, an ordinary dining-room transformed into a *table d'hote*, in which some twenty people were having *dejeuner* although it was already two o'clock. The afternoon was progressing, and yet people were still eating from one to the other end of Lourdes. Like every other householder in the town, whatever his religious convictions might be, Cazaban, in the pilgrimage season, let his bedrooms, surrendered his dining-room, end sought refuge in his cellar, where, heaped up with his family, he ate and slept, although this unventilated hole was no more than three yards square. However, the passion for trading and moneymaking carried all before it; at pilgrimage time the whole population disappeared like that of a conquered city, surrendering even the beds of its women and its children to the pilgrims, seating them at its tables, and supplying them with food.

"Is there nobody here?" called M. de Guersaint after waiting a moment.

At last a little man made his appearance, Cazaban himself, a type of the knotty but active Pyrenean, with a long face, prominent cheekbones, and a sunburned complexion spotted here and there with red. His big, glittering eyes never remained still; and the whole of his spare little figure quivered with incessant exuberance of speech and gesture.

"For you, monsieur—a shave, eh?" said he. "I must beg your pardon for keeping you waiting; but my assistant has gone out, and I was in there with my boarders. If you will kindly sit down, I will attend to you at once."

Thereupon, deigning to operate in person, Cazaban began to stir up the lather and strop the razor. He had glanced rather nervously, however, at the cassock worn by Pierre, who without a word had seated himself in a corner and taken up a newspaper in the perusal of which he appeared to be absorbed.

A short interval of silence followed; but it was fraught with suffering for Cazaban, and whilst lathering his customer's chin he began to chatter: "My boarders lingered this morning such a long time at the Grotto, monsieur, that they have scarcely sat down to *dejeuner*. You can hear them, eh? I was staying with them out of politeness. However, I owe myself to my customers as well, do I not? One must try to please everybody."

M. de Guersaint, who also was fond of a chat, thereupon began to question him: "You lodge some of the pilgrims, I suppose?"

"Oh! we all lodge some of them, monsieur; it is necessary for the town," replied the barber.

"And you accompany them to the Grotto?"

At this, however, Cazaban revolted, and, holding up his razor, he answered with an air of dignity "Never, monsieur, never! For five years past I have not been in that new town which they are building."

He was still seeking to restrain himself, and again glanced at Pierre, whose face was hidden by the newspaper. The sight of the red cross pinned on M. de Guersaint's jacket was also calculated to render him prudent; nevertheless his tongue won the victory. "Well, monsieur, opinions are free, are they not?" said he. "I respect yours, but for my part I don't believe in all that phantasmagoria! Oh I've never concealed it! I was already a republican and a freethinker in the days of the Empire. There were barely four men of those views in the whole town at that time. Oh! I'm proud of it."

He had begun to shave M. de Guersaint's left cheek and was quite triumphant. From that moment a stream of words poured forth from his mouth, a stream which seemed to be inexhaustible. To begin with, he brought the same charges as Majeste against the Fathers of the Grotto. He reproached them for their dealings in tapers, chaplets, prints, and crucifixes, for the disloyal manner in which they competed with those who sold those articles as well as with the hotel and lodging-house keepers. And he was also wrathful with the Blue Sisters of the Immaculate Conception, for had they not robbed him of two tenants, two old ladies, who spent three weeks at Lourdes each year? Moreover you could divine within him all the slowly accumulated, overflowing spite with which the old town regarded the new town—that town which had sprung up so quickly on the other side of the castle, that rich city with houses as big as palaces, whither flowed all the life, all the luxury, all the money of Lourdes, so that it was incessantly growing larger and wealthier, whilst its elder sister, the poor, antique town of the mountains, with its narrow, grass-grown, deserted streets, seemed near the point of death. Nevertheless the struggle still continued; the old town seemed determined not to die, and, by lodging pilgrims and opening shops on her side, endeavoured to compel her ungrateful junior to grant her a share of the spoils. But custom only flowed to the shops which were near the Grotto, and only the poorer pilgrims were willing to lodge so far away; so that the unequal conditions of the struggle intensified the rupture and turned the high town and the low town into two irreconcilable enemies, who preyed upon one another amidst continual intrigues.

"Ah, no! They certainly won't see me at their Grotto," resumed Cazaban, with his rageful air. "What an abusive use they make of that Grotto of theirs! They serve it up in every fashion! To think of such idolatry, such gross superstition in the nineteenth century! Just ask them if they have cured a single sufferer belonging to the town during the last twenty years! Yet there are plenty of infirm people crawling about our streets. It was our folk that benefited by the first miracles; but it would seem that the miraculous water has long lost all its power, so far as we are concerned. We are too near it; people have to come from a long distance if they want it to act on them. It's really all too stupid; why, I wouldn't go there even if I were offered a hundred francs!"

Pierre's immobility was doubtless irritating the barber. He had now begun to shave M. de Guersaint's right cheek; and was inveighing against the Fathers of the Immaculate Conception, whose greed for gain was the one cause of all the misunderstanding. These Fathers who were at home there, since they had purchased from the Municipality the land on which they desired to build, did not even carry out the stipulations of the contract they had signed, for there were two clauses in it forbidding all trading, such as the sale of the water and of religious articles. Innumerable actions might have been brought against them. But they snapped their fingers, and felt themselves so powerful that they no longer allowed a single offering to go to the parish, but arranged matters so that the whole harvest of money should be garnered by the Grotto and the Basilica.

And, all at once, Cazaban candidly exclaimed: "If they were only reasonable, if they would only share with us!" Then, when M. de

ÉMILE ZOLA

Guersaint had washed his face, and reseated himself, the hairdresser resumed: "And if I were to tell you, monsieur, what they have done with our poor town! Forty years ago all the young girls here conducted themselves properly, I assure you. I remember that in my young days when a young man was wicked he generally had to go elsewhere. But times have changed, our manners are no longer the same. Nowadays nearly all the girls content themselves with selling candles and nosegays; and you must have seen them catching hold of the passers-by and thrusting their goods into their hands! It is really shameful to see so many bold girls about! They make a lot of money, acquire lazy habits, and, instead of working during the winter, simply wait for the return of the pilgrimage season. And I assure you that the young men don't need to go elsewhere nowadays. No, indeed! And add to all this the suspicious floating element which swells the population as soon as the first fine weather sets in—the coachmen, the hawkers, the cantine keepers, all the low-class, wandering folk reeking with grossness and vice—and you can form an idea of the honest new town which they have given us with the crowds that come to their Grotto and their Basilica!"

Greatly struck by these remarks, Pierre had let his newspaper fall and begun to listen. It was now, for the first time, that he fully realised the difference between the two Lourdes—old Lourdes so honest and so pious in its tranquil solitude, and new Lourdes corrupted, demoralised by the circulation of so much money, by such a great enforced increase of wealth, by the ever-growing torrent of strangers sweeping through it, by the fatal rotting influence of the conflux of thousands of people, the contagion of evil examples. And what a terrible result it seemed when one thought of Bernadette, the pure, candid girl kneeling before the wild primitive grotto, when one thought of all the naive faith, all the fervent purity of those who had first begun the work! Had they desired that the whole countryside should be poisoned in this wise by lucre and human filth? Yet it had sufficed that the nations should flock there for a pestilence to break out.

Seeing that Pierre was listening, Cazaban made a final threatening gesture as though to sweep away all this poisonous superstition. Then, relapsing into silence, he finished cutting M. de Guersaint's hair.

"There you are, monsieur!"

The architect rose, and it was only now that he began to speak of the conveyance which he wished to hire. At first the hairdresser declined to enter into the matter, pretending that they must apply to his brother at the Champ Commun; but at last he consented to take the order. A pair-horse landau for Gavarnie was priced at fifty francs. However, he was so pleased at having talked so much, and so flattered at hearing himself called an honest man, that he eventually agreed to charge only forty francs. There were four persons in the party, so this would make ten francs apiece. And it was agreed that they should start off at about two in the morning, so that they might get back to Lourdes at a tolerably early hour on the Monday evening.

"The landau will be outside the Hotel of the Apparitions at the appointed time," repeated Cazaban in his emphatic way. "You may rely on me, monsieur."

Then he began to listen. The clatter of crockery did not cease in the adjoining room. People were still eating there with that impulsive voracity which had spread from one to the other end of Lourdes. And all at once a voice was heard calling for more bread.

"Excuse me," hastily resumed Cazaban, "my boarders want me." And thereupon he rushed away, his hands still greasy through fingering the comb.

The door remained open for a second, and on the walls of the dining-room Pierre espied various religious prints, and notably a view of the Grotto, which surprised him; in all probability, however, the hairdresser only hung these engravings there during the pilgrimage season by way of pleasing his boarders.

It was now nearly three o'clock. When the young priest and M. de Guersaint got outside they were astonished at the loud pealing of bells which was flying through the air. The parish church had responded to the first stroke of vespers chiming at the Basilica; and now all the convents, one after another, were contributing to the swelling peals. The crystalline notes of the bell of the Carmelites mingled with the grave notes of the bell of the Immaculate Conception; and all the joyous bells of the Sisters of Nevers and the Dominicans were jingling together. In this wise, from morning till evening on fine days of festivity, the chimes winged their flight above the house-roofs of Lourdes. And nothing could have been gayer than that sonorous melody resounding in the broad blue heavens above the gluttonous town, which had at last lunched, and was now comfortably digesting as it strolled about in the sunlight.

III

The Night Procession

As soon as night had fallen Marie, still lying on her bed at the Hospital of Our Lady of Dolours, became extremely impatient, for she had learnt from Madame de Jonquiere that Baron Suire had obtained from Father Fourcade the necessary permission for her to spend the night in front of the Grotto. Thus she kept on questioning Sister Hyacinthe, asking her: "Pray, Sister, is it not yet nine o'clock?"

"No, my child, it is scarcely half-past eight," was the reply. "Here is a nice woollen shawl for you to wrap round you at daybreak, for the Gave is close by, and the mornings are very fresh, you know, in these mountainous parts."

"Oh! but the nights are so lovely, Sister, and besides, I sleep so little here!" replied Marie; "I cannot be worse off out-of-doors. *Mon Dieu*, how happy I am; how delightful it will be to spend the whole night with the Blessed Virgin!"

The entire ward was jealous of her; for to remain in prayer before the Grotto all night long was the most ineffable of joys, the supreme beatitude. It was said that in the deep peacefulness of night the chosen ones undoubtedly beheld the Virgin, but powerful protection was needed to obtain such a favour as had been granted to Marie; for nowadays the reverend Fathers scarcely liked to grant it, as several sufferers had died during the long vigil, falling asleep, as it were, in the midst of their ecstasy.

"You will take the Sacrament at the Grotto tomorrow morning, before you are brought back here, won't you, my child?" resumed Sister Hyacinthe.

However, nine o'clock at last struck, and, Pierre not arriving, the girl wondered whether he, usually so punctual, could have forgotten her? The others were now talking to her of the night procession, which she would see from beginning to end if she only started at once. The ceremonies concluded with a procession every night, but the Sunday one was always the finest, and that evening, it was said, would be remarkably splendid, such, indeed, as was seldom seen. Nearly thirty thousand pilgrims would take part in it, each carrying a lighted taper:

the nocturnal marvels of the sky would be revealed; the stars would descend upon earth. At this thought the sufferers began to bewail their fate; what a wretched lot was theirs, to be tied to their beds, unable to see any of those wonders.

At last Madame de Jonquiere approached Marie's bed. "My dear girl," said she, "here is your father with Monsieur l'Abbe."

Radiant with delight, the girl at once forgot her weary waiting. "Oh! pray let us make haste, Pierre," she exclaimed; "pray let us make haste!"

They carried her down the stairs, and the young priest harnessed himself to the little car, which gently rolled along, under the star-studded heavens, whilst M. de Guersaint walked beside it. The night was moonless, but extremely beautiful; the vault above looked like deep blue velvet, spangled with diamonds, and the atmosphere was exquisitely mild and pure, fragrant with the perfumes from the mountains. Many pilgrims were hurrying along the street, all bending their steps towards the Grotto, but they formed a discreet, pensive crowd, with naught of the fair-field, lounging character of the daytime throng. And, as soon as the Plateau de la Merlasse was reached, the darkness spread out, you entered into a great lake of shadows formed by the stretching lawns and lofty trees, and saw nothing rising on high save the black, tapering spire of the Basilica.

Pierre grew rather anxious on finding that the crowd became more and more compact as he advanced. Already on reaching the Place du Rosaire it was difficult to take another forward step. "There is no hope of getting to the Grotto yet awhile," he said. "The best course would be to turn into one of the pathways behind the pilgrims' shelter-house and wait there."

Marie, however, greatly desired to see the procession start. "Oh! pray try to go as far as the Gave," said she. "I shall then see everything from a distance; I don't want to go near."

M. de Guersaint, who was equally inquisitive, seconded this proposal. "Don't be uneasy," he said to Pierre. "I am here behind, and will take care to let nobody jostle her."

Pierre had to begin pulling the little vehicle again. It took him a quarter of an hour to pass under one of the arches of the inclined way on the left hand, so great was the crush of pilgrims at that point. Then, taking a somewhat oblique course, he ended by reaching the quay beside the Gave, where there were only some spectators standing on the sidewalk, so that he was able to advance another fifty yards. At last he halted, and backed the little car against the quay parapet, in full view of the Grotto. "Will you be all right here?" he asked.

"Oh yes, thank you. Only you must sit me up; I shall then be able to see much better."

M. de Guersaint raised her into a sitting posture, and then for his part climbed upon the stonework running from one to the other end of the quay. A mob of inquisitive people had already scaled it in part, like sight-seers waiting for a display of fireworks; and they were all raising themselves on tiptoe, and craning their necks to get a better view. Pierre himself at last grew interested, although there was, so far, little to see.

Some thirty thousand people were assembled, and, every moment there were fresh arrivals. All carried candles, the lower parts of which were wrapped in white paper, on which a picture of Our Lady of Lourdes was printed in blue ink. However, these candles were not yet lighted, and the only illumination that you perceived above the billowy sea of heads was the bright, forge-like glow of the taper-lighted Grotto. A great buzzing arose, whiffs of human breath blew hither and thither, and these alone enabled you to realise that thousands of serried, stifling creatures were gathered together in the black depths, like a living sea that was ever eddying and spreading. There were even people hidden away under the trees beyond the Grotto, in distant recesses of the darkness of which one had no suspicion.

At last a few tapers began to shine forth here and there, like sudden sparks of light spangling the obscurity at random. Their number rapidly increased, eyots of stars were formed, whilst at other points there were meteoric trails, milky ways, so to say, flowing midst the constellations. The thirty thousand tapers were being lighted one by one, their beams gradually increasing in number till they obscured the bright glow of the Grotto and spread, from one to the other end of the promenade, the small yellow flames of a gigantic brasier.

"Oh! how beautiful it is, Pierre!" murmured Marie; "it is like the resurrection of the humble, the bright awakening of the souls of the poor."

"It is superb, superb!" repeated M. de Guersaint, with impassioned artistic satisfaction. "Do you see those two trails of light yonder, which intersect one another and form a cross?"

Pierre's feelings, however, had been touched by what Marie had just said. He was reflecting upon her words. There was truth in them. Taken singly, those slender flames, those mere specks of light, were modest and unobtrusive, like the lowly; it was only their great number that supplied the effulgence, the sun-like resplendency. Fresh ones were continually appearing, farther and farther away, like waifs and strays. "Ah!" murmured the young priest, "do you see that one which has just begun to flicker, all by itself, far away—do you see it, Marie? Do you see how it floats and slowly approaches until it is merged in the great lake of light?"

In the vicinity of the Grotto one could see now as clearly as in the daytime. The trees, illumined from below, were intensely green, like the painted trees in stage scenery. Above the moving brasier were some motionless banners, whose embroidered saints and silken cords showed with vivid distinctness. And the great reflection ascended to the rock, even to the Basilica, whose spire now shone out, quite white, against the black sky; whilst the hillsides across the Gave were likewise brightened, and displayed the pale fronts of their convents amidst their sombre foliage.

There came yet another moment of uncertainty. The flaming lake, in which each burning wick was like a little wave, rolled its starry sparkling as though it were about to burst from its bed and flow away in a river. Then the banners began to oscillate, and soon a regular motion set in.

"Oh! so they won't pass this way!" exclaimed M. de Guersaint in a tone of disappointment.

Pierre, who had informed himself on the matter, thereupon explained that the procession would first of all ascend the serpentine road—constructed at great cost up the hillside—and that it would afterwards pass behind the Basilica, descend by the inclined way on the right hand, and then spread out through the gardens.

"Look!" said he; "you can see the foremost tapers ascending amidst the greenery."

Then came an enchanting spectacle. Little flickering lights detached themselves from the great bed of fire, and began gently rising, without it being possible for one to tell at that distance what connected them with the earth. They moved upward, looking in the darkness like golden particles of the sun. And soon they formed an oblique streak, a streak which suddenly twisted, then extended again until it curved once more. At last the whole hillside was streaked by a flaming zigzag, resembling those lightning flashes which you see falling from black skies in cheap engravings. But, unlike the lightning, the luminous trail did not fade away; the little lights still went onward in the same slow, gentle, gliding manner. Only for a moment, at rare intervals, was there a sudden eclipse; the procession, no doubt, was then passing behind some clump of trees. But, farther on, the tapers beamed forth afresh, rising heavenward by an intricate path, which incessantly diverged and then started upward again. At last, however, the time came when the lights no longer ascended, for they had reached the summit of the hill and had begun to disappear at the last turn of the road.

Exclamations were rising from the crowd. "They are passing behind the Basilica," said one. "Oh! it will take them twenty minutes before they begin coming down on the other side," remarked another. "Yes, madame," said a third, "there are thirty thousand of them, and an hour will go by before the last of them leaves the Grotto."

Ever since the start a sound of chanting had risen above the low rumbling of the crowd. The hymn of Bernadette was being sung, those sixty couplets between which the Angelic Salutation, with its all-besetting rhythm, was ever returning as a refrain. When the sixty couplets were finished they were sung again; and that lullaby of "Ave, ave, ave Maria!" came back incessantly, stupefying the mind, and gradually transporting those thousands of beings into a kind of wide-awake dream, with a vision of Paradise before their eyes. And, indeed, at night-time when they were asleep, their beds would rock to the eternal tune, which they still and ever continued singing.

"Are we going to stop here?" asked M. de Guersaint, who speedily got tired of remaining in any one spot. "We see nothing but the same thing over and over again."

Marie, who had informed herself by listening to what was said in the crowd, thereupon exclaimed: "You were quite right, Pierre; it would be much better to go back yonder under the trees. I so much wish to see everything."

"Yes, certainly; we will seek a spot whence you may see it all," replied the priest. "The only difficulty lies in getting away from here."

Indeed, they were now inclosed within the mob of sight-seers; and, in order to secure a passage, Pierre with stubborn perseverance had to keep on begging a little room for a suffering girl.

M. de Guersaint meantime brought up the rear, screening the little conveyance so that it might not be upset by the jostling; whilst Marie turned her head, still endeavouring to see the sheet of flame spread out before the Grotto, that lake of little sparkling waves which never seemed to diminish, although the procession continued to flow from it without a pause.

At last they all three found themselves out of the crowd, near one of the arches, on a deserted spot where they were able to breathe for a moment. They now heard nothing but the distant canticle with its besetting refrain, and they only saw the reflection of the tapers, hovering like a luminous cloud in the neighbourhood of the Basilica.

"The best plan would be to climb to the Calvary," said M. de Guersaint. "The servant at the hotel told me so this morning. From up there, it seems, the scene is fairy-like."

But they could not think of making the ascent. Pierre at once enumerated the difficulties. "How could we hoist ourselves to such a height with Marie's conveyance?" he asked. "Besides, we should have to come down again, and that would be dangerous work in the darkness amidst all the scrambling."

Marie herself preferred to remain under the trees in the gardens, where it was very mild. So they started off, and reached the esplanade in front of the great crowned statue of the Virgin. It was illuminated by means of blue and yellow globes which encompassed it with a gaudy splendour; and despite all his piety M. de Guersaint could not help finding these decorations in execrable taste.

"There!" exclaimed Marie, "a good place would be near those shrubs yonder."

She was pointing to a shrubbery near the pilgrims' shelter-house; and the spot was indeed an excellent one for their purpose, as it enabled them to see the procession come down by the gradient way on the left, and watch it as it passed between the lawns to the new bridge and back again. Moreover, a delightful freshness prevailed there by reason of the vicinity of the Gave. There was nobody there as yet, and one could enjoy deep peacefulness in the dense shade which fell from the big plane-trees bordering the path.

In his impatience to see the first tapers reappear as soon as they should have passed behind the Basilica, M. de Guersaint had risen on tiptoe. "I see nothing as yet," he muttered, "so whatever the regulations may be I shall sit on the grass for a moment. I've no strength left in my legs." Then, growing anxious about his daughter, he inquired: "Shall I cover you up? It is very cool here."

"Oh, no! I'm not cold, father!" answered Marie; "I feel so happy. It is long since I breathed such sweet air. There must be some roses about—can't you smell that delicious perfume?" And turning to Pierre she asked: "Where are the roses, my friend? Can you see them?"

When M. de Guersaint had seated himself on the grass near the little vehicle, it occurred to Pierre to see if there was not some bed of roses near at hand. But is was in vain that he explored the dark lawns; he could only distinguish sundry clumps of evergreens. And, as he passed in front of the pilgrims' shelter-house on his way back, curiosity prompted him to enter it.

This building formed a long and lofty hall, lighted by large windows upon two sides. With bare walls and a stone pavement, it contained no other furniture than a number of benches, which stood here and there in haphazard fashion. There was neither table nor shelf, so that the homeless pilgrims who had sought refuge there had piled up their baskets, parcels, and valises in the window embrasures. Moreover, the place was apparently empty; the poor folk that it sheltered had no doubt joined the procession. Nevertheless, although the door stood wide open, an almost unbearable smell reigned inside. The very walls seemed impregnated with an odour of poverty, and in spite of the bright sunshine which had prevailed during the day, the flagstones were quite damp, soiled and soaked with expectorations, spilt wine, and grease. This mess had been made by the poorer pilgrims, who with their dirty skins and wretched rags lived in the hall, eating and sleeping in heaps on the benches. Pierre speedily came to the conclusion that the pleasant smell of roses must emanate from some other spot; still, he was making the round of the hall, which was lighted by four smoky lanterns, and which he believed to be altogether unoccupied, when, against the left-hand wall, he was surprised to espy the vague figure of a woman in black, with what seemed to be a white parcel lying on her lap. She was all alone in that solitude, and did not stir; however, her eyes were wide open.

He drew near and recognised Madame Vincent. She addressed him in a deep, broken voice: "Rose has suffered so dreadfully to-day! Since daybreak she has not ceased moaning. And so, as she fell asleep a couple of hours ago, I haven't dared to stir for fear lest she should awake and suffer again."

Thus the poor woman remained motionless, martyr-mother that she was, having for long months held her daughter in her arms in this fashion, in the stubborn hope of curing her. In her arms, too, she had brought her to Lourdes; in her arms she had carried her to the Grotto; in her arms she had rocked her to sleep, having neither a room of her own, nor even a hospital bed at her disposal.

"Isn't the poor little thing any better?" asked Pierre, whose heart ached at the sight.

"No, Monsieur l'Abbe; no, I think not."

"But you are very badly off here on this bench. You should have made an application to the pilgrimage managers instead of remaining like this, in the street, as it were. Some accommodation would have been found for your little girl, at any rate; that's certain."

"Oh! what would have been the use of it, Monsieur l'Abbe? She is all right on my lap. And besides, should I have been allowed to stay with her? No, no, I prefer to have her on my knees; it seems to me that it will end by curing her." Two big tears rolled down the poor woman's motionless cheeks, and in her stifled voice she continued: "I am not penniless. I had thirty sous when I left Paris, and I still have ten left. All I need is a little bread, and she, poor darling, can no longer drink any milk even. I have enough to last me till we go back, and if she gets well again, oh! we shall be rich, rich, rich!"

She had leant forward while speaking, and by the flickering light of a lantern near by, gazed at Rose, who was breathing faintly, with parted lips. "You see how soundly she is sleeping," resumed the unhappy mother. "Surely the Blessed Virgin will take pity on her and cure her, won't she, Monsieur l'Abbe? We only have one day left; still, I don't despair; and I shall again pray all night long without moving from here. She will be cured to-morrow; we must live till then."

Infinite pity was filling the heart of Pierre, who, fearing that he also might weep, now went away. "Yes, yes, my poor woman, we must hope, still hope," said he, as he left her there among the scattered benches, in that deserted, malodorous hall, so motionless in her painful maternal passion as to hold her own breath, fearful lest the heaving of her bosom should awaken the poor little sufferer. And in deepest grief, with closed lips, she prayed ardently.

On Pierre returning to Marie's side, the girl inquired of him: "Well, and those roses? Are there any near here?"

He did not wish to sadden her by telling her what he had seen, so he simply answered: "No, I have searched the lawns; there are none."

"How singular!" she rejoined, in a thoughtful way. "The perfume is both so sweet and penetrating. You can smell it, can't you? At this moment it is wonderfully strong, as though all the roses of Paradise were flowering around us in the darkness."

A low exclamation from her father interrupted her. M. de Guersaint had risen to his feet again on seeing some specks of light shine out above the gradient ways on the left side of the Basilica. "At last! Here they come!" said he.

It was indeed the head of the procession again appearing; and at once the specks of light began to swarm and extend in long, wavering double files. The darkness submerged everything except these luminous points, which seemed to be at a great elevation, and to emerge, as it were, from the black depths of the Unknown. And at the same time the everlasting canticle was again heard, but so lightly, for the procession was far away, that it seemed as yet merely like the rustle of a coming storm, stirring the leaves of the trees.

"Ah! I said so," muttered M. de Guersaint; "one ought to be at the Calvary to see everything." With the obstinacy of a child he kept on returning to his first idea, again and again complaining that they had chosen "the worst possible place."

"But why don't you go up to the Calvary, papa?" at last said Marie. "There is still time. Pierre will stay here with me." And with a mournful laugh she added: "Go; you know very well that nobody will run away with me."

He at first refused to act upon the suggestion, but, unable to resist his desire, he all at once fell in with it. And he had to hasten his steps, crossing the lawns at a run. "Don't move," he called; "wait for me under the trees. I will tell you of all that I may see up there."

Then Pierre and Marie remained alone in that dim, solitary nook, whence came such a perfume of roses, albeit no roses could be found. And they did not speak, but in silence watched the procession, which was now coming down from the hill with a gentle, continuous, gliding motion.

A double file of quivering stars leapt into view on the left-hand side of the Basilica, and then followed the monumental, gradient way, whose curve is gradually described. At that distance you were still unable to see the pilgrims themselves, and you beheld simply those well-disciplined travelling lights tracing geometrical lines amidst the darkness. Under the deep blue heavens, even the buildings at first remained vague, forming but blacker patches against the sky. Little by little, however, as the number of candles increased, the principal architectural lines—the tapering spire of the Basilica, the cyclopean arches of the gradient ways, the heavy, squat facade of the Rosary— became more distinctly visible. And with that ceaseless torrent of bright sparks, flowing slowly downward with the stubborn persistence of a stream which has overflowed its banks and can be stopped by nothing, there came as it were an aurora, a growing, invading mass of light, which would at last spread its glory over the whole horizon.

"Look, look, Pierre!" cried Marie, in an access of childish joy. "There is no end of them; fresh ones are ever shining out."

Indeed, the sudden appearances of the little lights continued with mechanical regularity, as though some inexhaustible celestial source were pouring forth all those solar specks. The head of the procession had just reached the gardens, near the crowned statue of the Virgin, so that as yet the double file of flames merely outlined the curves of the Rosary and the broad inclined way. However, the approach of the multitude was foretokened by the perturbation of the atmosphere, by the gusts of human breath coming from afar; and particularly did the voices swell, the canticle of Bernadette surging with the clamour of a rising tide, through which, with rhythmical persistence, the refrain of "Ave, ave, ave Maria!" rolled ever in a louder key.

"Ah, that refrain!" muttered Pierre; "it penetrates one's very skin. It seems to me as though my whole body were at last singing it."

Again did Marie give vent to that childish laugh of hers. "It is true," said she; "it follows me about everywhere. I heard it the other night whilst I was asleep. And now it is again taking possession of me, rocking me, wafting me above the ground." Then she broke off to say: "Here they come, just across the lawn, in front of us."

The procession had entered one of the long, straight paths; and then, turning round the lawn by way of the Breton's Cross, it came back by a parallel path. It took more than a quarter of an hour to execute this movement, during which the double file of tapers resembled two long parallel streams of flame. That which ever excited one's admiration was the ceaseless march of this serpent of fire, whose golden coils crept so gently over the black earth, winding, stretching into the far distance, without the immense body ever seeming to end. There must have been some jostling and scrambling every now and then, for some of the luminous lines shook and bent as though they were about to break; but order was soon re-established, and then the slow, regular, gliding movement set in afresh. There now seemed to be fewer stars in the heavens; it was as though a milky way had fallen from on high, rolling its glittering dust of worlds, and transferring the revolutions of the planets from the empyrean to earth. A bluish light streamed all around;

there was naught but heaven left; the buildings and the trees assumed a visionary aspect in the mysterious glow of those thousands of tapers, whose number still and ever increased.

A faint sigh of admiration came from Marie. She was at a loss for words, and could only repeat "How beautiful it is! *Mon Dieu*! how beautiful it is! Look, Pierre, is it not beautiful?"

However, since the procession had been going by at so short a distance from them it had ceased to be a rhythmic march of stars which no human hand appeared to guide, for amidst the stream of light they could distinguish the figures of the pilgrims carrying the tapers, and at times even recognise them as they passed. First they espied La Grivotte, who, exaggerating her cure, and repeating that she had never felt in better health, had insisted upon taking part in the ceremony despite the lateness of the hour; and she still retained her excited demeanour, her dancing gait in that cool night air, which often made her shiver. Then the Vignerons appeared; the father at the head of the party, raising his taper on high, and followed by Madame Vigneron and Madame Chaise, who dragged their weary legs; whilst little Gustave, quite worn out, kept on tapping the sanded path with his crutch, his right hand covered meantime with all the wax that had dripped upon it. Every sufferer who could walk was there, among others Elise Rouquet, who, with her bare red face, passed by like some apparition from among the damned. Others were laughing; Sophie Couteau, the little girl who had been miraculously healed the previous year, was quite forgetting herself, playing with her taper as though it were a switch. Heads followed heads without a pause, heads of women especially, more often with sordid, common features, but at times wearing an exalted expression, which you saw for a second ere it vanished amidst the fantastic illumination. And there was no end to that terrible march past; fresh pilgrims were ever appearing. Among them Pierre and Marie noticed yet another little black shadowy figure, gliding along in a discreet, humble way; it was Madame Maze, whom they would not have recognised if she had not for a moment raised her pale face, down which the tears were streaming.

"Look!" exclaimed Pierre; "the first tapers in the procession are reaching the Place du Rosaire, and I am sure that half of the pilgrims are still in front of the Grotto."

Marie had raised her eyes. Up yonder, on the left-hand side of the Basilica, she could see other lights incessantly appearing with that mechanical kind of movement which seemed as though it would never cease. "Ah!" she said, "how many, how many distressed souls there are! For each of those little flames is a suffering soul seeking deliverance, is it not?"

Pierre had to lean over in order to hear her, for since the procession had been streaming by, so near to them, they had been deafened by the sound of the endless canticle, the hymn of Bernadette. The voices of the pilgrims rang out more loudly than ever amidst the increasing vertigo; the couplets became jumbled together—each batch of processionists chanted a different one with the ecstatic voices of beings possessed, who can no longer hear themselves. There was a huge indistinct clamour, the distracted clamour of a multitude intoxicated by its ardent faith. And meantime the refrain of "Ave, ave, ave Maria!" was ever returning, rising, with its frantic, importunate rhythm, above everything else.

All at once Pierre and Marie, to their great surprise, saw M. de Guersaint before them again. "Ah! my children," he said, "I did not want to linger too long up there, I cut through the procession twice in order to get back to you. But what a sight, what a sight it is! It is certainly the first beautiful thing that I have seen since I have been here!" Thereupon he began to describe the procession as he had beheld it from the Calvary height. "Imagine," said he, "another heaven, a heaven down below reflecting that above, a heaven entirely filled by a single immense constellation. The swarming stars seem to be lost, to lie in dim faraway depths; and the trail of fire is in form like a monstrance—yes, a real monstrance, the base of which is outlined by the inclined ways, the stem by the two parallel paths, and the Host by the round lawn which crowns them. It is a monstrance of burning gold, shining out in the depths of the darkness with a perpetual sparkle of moving stars. Nothing else seems to exist; it is gigantic, paramount. I really never saw anything so extraordinary before!"

He was waving his arms, beside himself, overflowing with the emotion of an artist.

"Father dear," said Marie, tenderly, "since you have come back you ought to go to bed. It is nearly eleven o'clock, and you know that you have to start at two in the morning." Then, to render him compliant, she added: "I am so pleased that you are going to make that excursion! Only, come back early to-morrow evening, because you'll see, you'll see—" She stopped short, not daring to express her conviction that she would be cured.

"You are right; I will go to bed," replied M. de Guersaint, quite calmed. "Since Pierre will be with you I sha'n't feel anxious."

"But I don't wish Pierre to pass the night out here. He will join you by-and-by after he has taken me to the Grotto. I sha'n't have any further need of anybody; the first bearer who passes can take me back to the hospital to-morrow morning."

Pierre had not interrupted her, and now he simply said: "No, no, Marie, I shall stay. Like you, I shall spend the night at the Grotto."

She opened her mouth to insist and express her displeasure. But he had spoken those words so gently, and she had detected in them such a dolorous thirst for happiness, that, stirred to the depths of her soul, she stayed her tongue.

"Well, well, my children," replied her father, "settle the matter between you. I know that you are both very sensible. And now good-night, and don't be at all uneasy about me."

He gave his daughter a long, loving kiss, pressed the young priest's hands, and then went off, disappearing among the serried ranks of the procession, which he once more had to cross.

Then they remained alone in their dark, solitary nook under the spreading trees, she still sitting up in her box, and he kneeling on the grass, with his elbow resting on one of the wheels. And it was truly sweet to linger there while the tapers continued marching past, and, after a turning movement, assembled on the Place du Rosaire. What delighted Pierre was that nothing of all the daytime junketing remained. It seemed as though a purifying breeze had come down from the mountains, sweeping away all the odour of strong meats, the greedy Sunday delights, the scorching, pestilential, fair-field dust which, at an earlier hour, had hovered above the town. Overhead there was now only the vast sky, studded with pure stars, and the freshness of the Gave was delicious, whilst the wandering breezes were laden with the perfumes of wild flowers. The mysterious Infinite spread far around in the sovereign peacefulness of night, and nothing of materiality remained save those little candle-flames which the young priest's companion had compared to suffering souls seeking deliverance. All was now exquisitely restful, instinct with unlimited hope. Since Pierre had been there all the heart-rending memories of the afternoon, of the voracious appetites, the impudent simony, and the poisoning of the old town, had gradually left him, allowing him to savour the divine refreshment of that beautiful night, in which his whole being was steeped as in some revivifying water.

A feeling of infinite sweetness had likewise come over Marie, who murmured: "Ah! how happy Blanche would be to see all these marvels."

She was thinking of her sister, who had been left in Paris to all the worries of her hard profession as a teacher forced to run hither and thither giving lessons. And that simple mention of her sister, of whom Marie had not spoken since her arrival at Lourdes, but whose figure now unexpectedly arose in her mind's eye, sufficed to evoke a vision of all the past.

Then, without exchanging a word, Marie and Pierre lived their childhood's days afresh, playing together once more in the neighbouring gardens parted by the quickset hedge. But separation came on the day when he entered the seminary and when she kissed him on the cheeks, vowing that she would never forget him. Years went by, and they found themselves forever parted: he a priest, she prostrated by illness, no longer with any hope of ever being a woman. That was their whole story—an ardent affection of which they had long been ignorant, then absolute severance, as though they were dead, albeit they lived side by side. They again beheld the sorry lodging whence they had started to come to Lourdes after so much battling, so much discussion—his doubts and her passionate faith, which last had conquered. And it seemed to them truly delightful to find themselves once more quite alone together, in that dark nook on that lovely night, when there were as many stars upon earth as there were in heaven.

Marie had hitherto retained the soul of a child, a spotless soul, as her father said, good and pure among the purest. Stricken low in her thirteenth year, she had grown no older in mind. Although she was now three-and-twenty, she was still a child, a child of thirteen, who had retired within herself, absorbed in the bitter catastrophe which had annihilated her. You could tell this by the frigidity of her glance, by her absent expression, by the haunted air she ever wore, unable as she was to bestow a thought on anything but her calamity. And never was woman's soul more pure and candid, arrested as it had been in its development. She had had no other romance in life save that tearful farewell to her friend, which for ten long years had sufficed to fill her heart. During the endless days which she had spent on her couch of wretchedness, she had never gone beyond this dream—that if she had grown up in health, he doubtless would not have become a priest, in order to live near her. She never read any novels. The pious works which she was allowed to peruse maintained her in the excitement of a superhuman love. Even

　　　　　　　　　　　　　　　　　　ÉMILE ZOLA

the rumours of everyday life died away at the door of the room where she lived in seclusion; and, in past years, when she had been taken from one to the other end of France, from one inland spa to another, she had passed through the crowds like a somnambulist who neither sees nor hears anything, possessed, as she was, by the idea of the calamity that had befallen her, the bond which made her a sexless thing. Hence her purity and childishness; hence she was but an adorable daughter of suffering, who, despite the growth of her sorry flesh, harboured nothing in her heart save that distant awakening of passion, the unconscious love of her thirteenth year.

Her hand sought Pierre's in the darkness, and when she found it, coming to meet her own, she, for a long time, continued pressing it. Ah! how sweet it was! Never before, indeed, had they tasted such pure and perfect joy in being together, far from the world, amidst the sovereign enchantment of darkness and mystery. Around them nothing subsisted, save the revolving stars. The lulling hymns were like the very vertigo that bore them away. And she knew right well that after spending a night of rapture at the Grotto, she would, on the morrow, be cured. Of this she was, indeed, absolutely convinced; she would prevail upon the Blessed Virgin to listen to her; she would soften her, as soon as she should be alone, imploring her face to face. And she well understood what Pierre had wished to say a short time previously, when expressing his desire to spend the whole night outside the Grotto, like herself. Was it not that he intended to make a supreme effort to believe, that he meant to fall upon his knees like a little child, and beg the all-powerful Mother to restore his lost faith? Without need of any further exchange of words, their clasped hands repeated all those things. They mutually promised that they would pray for each other, and so absorbed in each other did they become that they forgot themselves, with such an ardent desire for one another's cure and happiness, that for a moment they attained to the depths of the love which offers itself in sacrifice. It was divine enjoyment.

"Ah!" murmured Pierre, "how beautiful is this blue night, this infinite darkness, which has swept away all the hideousness of things and beings, this deep, fresh peacefulness, in which I myself should like to bury my doubts!"

His voice died away, and Marie, in her turn, said in a very low voice: "And the roses, the perfume of the roses? Can't you smell them, my friend? Where can they be since you could not see them?"

"Yes, yes, I smell them, but there are none," he replied. "I should certainly have seen them, for I hunted everywhere."

"How can you say that there are no roses when they perfume the air around us, when we are steeped in their aroma? Why, there are moments when the scent is so powerful that I almost faint with delight in inhaling it! They must certainly be here, innumerable, under our very feet."

"No, no," said Pierre, "I swear to you I hunted everywhere, and there are no roses. They must be invisible, or they may be the very grass we tread and the spreading trees that are around us; their perfume may come from the soil itself, from the torrent which flows along close by, from the woods and the mountains that rise yonder."

For a moment they remained silent. Then, in an undertone, she resumed: "How sweet they smell, Pierre! And it seems to me that even our clasped hands form a bouquet."

"Yes, they smell delightfully sweet; but it is from you, Marie, that the perfume now ascends, as though the roses were budding from your hair."

Then they ceased speaking. The procession was still gliding along, and at the corner of the Basilica bright sparks were still appearing, flashing suddenly from out of the obscurity, as though spurting from some invisible source. The vast train of little flames, marching in double file, threw a riband of light across the darkness. But the great sight was now on the Place du Rosaire, where the head of the procession, still continuing its measured evolutions, was revolving and revolving in a circle which ever grew smaller, with a stubborn whirl which increased the dizziness of the weary pilgrims and the violence of their chants. And soon the circle formed a nucleus, the nucleus of a nebula, so to say, around which the endless riband of fire began to coil itself. And the brasier grew larger and larger—there was first a pool, then a lake of light. The whole vast Place du Rosaire changed at last into a burning ocean, rolling its little sparkling wavelets with the dizzy motion of a whirlpool that never rested. A reflection like that of dawn whitened the Basilica; while the rest of the horizon faded into deep obscurity, amidst which you only saw a few stray tapers journeying alone, like glowworms seeking their way with the help of their little lights. However, a straggling rear-guard of the procession must have climbed the Calvary height, for up there, against the sky, some moving stars could also be seen. Eventually the moment came when the last tapers appeared down below, marched round the lawns, flowed away, and were merged in the

ÉMILE ZOLA

sea of flame. Thirty thousand tapers were burning there, still and ever revolving, quickening their sparkles under the vast calm heavens where the planets had grown pale. A luminous glow ascended in company with the strains of the canticle which never ceased. And the roar of voices incessantly repeating the refrain of "Ave, ave, ave Maria!" was like the very crackling of those hearts of fire which were burning away in prayers in order that souls might be saved.

The candles had just been extinguished, one by one, and the night was falling again, paramount, densely black, and extremely mild, when Pierre and Marie perceived that they were still there, hand in hand, hidden away among the trees. In the dim streets of Lourdes, far off, there were now only some stray, lost pilgrims inquiring their way, in order that they might get to bed. Through the darkness there swept a rustling sound—the rustling of those who prowl and fall asleep when days of festivity draw to a close. But the young priest and the girl lingered in their nook forgetfully, never stirring, but tasting delicious happiness amidst the perfume of the invisible roses.

IV

The Vigil

When Pierre dragged Marie in her box to the front of the Grotto, and placed her as near as possible to the railing, it was past midnight, and about a hundred persons were still there, some seated on the benches, but the greater number kneeling as though prostrated in prayer. The Grotto shone from afar, with its multitude of lighted tapers, similar to the illumination round a coffin, though all that you could distinguish was a star-like blaze, from the midst of which, with visionary whiteness, emerged the statue of the Virgin in its niche. The hanging foliage assumed an emerald sheen, the hundreds of crutches covering the vault resembled an inextricable network of dead wood on the point of reflowering. And the darkness was rendered more dense by so great a brightness, the surroundings became lost in a deep shadow in which nothing, neither walls nor trees, remained; whilst all alone ascended the angry and continuous murmur of the Gave, rolling along beneath the gloomy, boundless sky, now heavy with a gathering storm.

"Are you comfortable, Marie?" gently inquired Pierre. "Don't you feel chilly?"

She had just shivered. But it was only at a breath from the other world, which had seemed to her to come from the Grotto.

"No, no, I am so comfortable! Only place the shawl over my knees. And—thank you, Pierre—don't be anxious about me. I no longer require anyone now that I am with her."

Her voice died away, she was already falling into an ecstasy, her hands clasped, her eyes raised towards the white statue, in a beatific transfiguration of the whole of her poor suffering face.

Yet Pierre remained a few minutes longer beside her. He would have liked to wrap her in the shawl, for he perceived the trembling of her little wasted hands. But he feared to annoy her, so confined himself to tucking her in like a child; whilst she, slightly raised, with her elbows on the edges of her box, and her eyes fixed on the Grotto, no longer beheld him.

A bench stood near, and he had just seated himself upon it, intending to collect his thoughts, when his glance fell upon a woman kneeling in the gloom. Dressed in black, she was so slim, so discreet, so unobtrusive, so wrapt in darkness, that at first he had not noticed her. After a while, however, he recognised her as Madame Maze. The thought of the letter which she had received during the day then recurred to him. And the sight of her filled him with pity; he could feel for the forlornness of this solitary woman, who had no physical sore to heal, but only implored the Blessed Virgin to relieve her heart-pain by converting her inconstant husband. The letter had no doubt been some harsh reply, for, with bowed head, she seemed almost annihilated, filled with the humility of some poor beaten creature. It was only at night-time that she readily forgot herself there, happy at disappearing, at being able to weep, suffer martyrdom, and implore the return of the lost caresses, for hours together, without anyone suspecting her grievous secret. Her lips did not even move; it was her wounded heart which prayed, which desperately begged for its share of love and happiness.

Ah! that inextinguishable thirst for happiness which brought them all there, wounded either in body or in spirit; Pierre also felt it parching his throat, in an ardent desire to be quenched. He longed to cast himself upon his knees, to beg the divine aid with the same humble faith as that woman. But his limbs were as though tied; he could not find the words he wanted, and it was a relief when he at last felt someone touch him on the arm. "Come with me, Monsieur l'Abbe, if you do not know the Grotto," said a voice. "I will find you a place. It is so pleasant there at this time!"

He raised his head, and recognised Baron Suire, the director of the Hospitality of Our Lady of Salvation. This benevolent and simple man no doubt felt some affection for him. He therefore accepted his offer, and followed him into the Grotto, which was quite empty. The Baron had a key, with which he locked the railing behind them.

"You see, Monsieur l'Abbe," said he, "this is the time when one can really be comfortable here. For my part, whenever I come to spend a few days at Lourdes, I seldom retire to rest before daybreak, as I have fallen into the habit of finishing my night here. The place is deserted, one is quite alone, and is it not pleasant? How well one feels oneself to be in the abode of the Blessed Virgin!"

He smiled with a kindly air, doing the honours of the Grotto like an old frequenter of the place, somewhat enfeebled by age, but full of genuine affection for this delightful nook. Moreover, in spite of his great piety, he was in no way ill at ease there, but talked on and explained matters with the familiarity of a man who felt himself to be the friend of Heaven.

"Ah! you are looking at the tapers," he said. "There are about two hundred of them which burn together night and day; and they end by making the place warm. It is even warm here in winter."

Indeed, Pierre was beginning to feel incommoded by the warm odour of the wax. Dazzled by the brilliant light into which he was penetrating, he gazed at the large, central, pyramidal holder, all bristling with little tapers, and resembling a luminous clipped yew glistening with stars. In the background, a straight holder, on a level with the ground, upheld the large tapers, which, like the pipes of an organ, formed a row of uneven height, some of them being as large as a man's thigh. And yet other holders, resembling massive candelabra, stood here and there on the jutting parts of the rock. The vault of the Grotto sank towards the left, where the stone seemed baked and blackened by the eternal flames which had been heating it for years. And the wax was perpetually dripping like fine snow; the trays of the holders were smothered with it, whitened by its ever-thickening dust. In fact, it coated the whole rock, which had become quite greasy to the touch; and to such a degree did it cover the ground that accidents had occurred, and it had been necessary to spread some mats about to prevent persons from slipping.

"You see those large ones there," obligingly continued Baron Suire. "They are the most expensive and cost sixty francs apiece; they will continue burning for a month. The smallest ones, which cost but five sous each, only last three hours. Oh! we don't husband them; we never run short. Look here! Here are two more hampers full, which there has not yet been time to remove to the storehouse."

Then he pointed to the furniture, which comprised a harmonium covered with a cloth, a substantial dresser with several large drawers in which the sacred vestments were kept, some benches and chairs reserved for the privileged few who were admitted during the ceremonies, and finally a very handsome movable altar, which was adorned with engraved silver plates, the gift of a great lady, and—for fear of injury from dampness—was only brought out on the occasions of remunerative pilgrimages.

Pierre was disturbed by all this well-meant chatter. His religious emotion lost some of its charm. In spite of his lack of faith, he had, on entering, experienced a feeling of agitation, a heaving of the soul, as though the mystery were about to be revealed to him. It was at the same time both an anxious and a delicious feeling. And he beheld things which deeply stirred him: bunches of flowers, lying in a heap at the Virgin's feet, with the votive offerings of children—little faded shoes, a tiny iron corselet, and a doll-like crutch which almost seemed to be a toy. Beneath the natural ogival cavity in which the apparition had appeared, at the spot where the pilgrims rubbed the chaplets and medals they wished to consecrate, the rock was quite worn away and polished. Millions of ardent lips had pressed kisses on the wall with such intensity of love that the stone was as though calcined, streaked with black veins, shining like marble.

However, he stopped short at last opposite a cavity in which lay a considerable pile of letters and papers of every description.

"Ah! I was forgetting," hastily resumed Baron Suire; "this is the most interesting part of it. These are the letters which the faithful throw into the Grotto through the railing every day. We gather them up and place them there; and in the winter I amuse myself by glancing through them. You see, we cannot burn them without opening them, for they often contain money—francs, half-francs, and especially postage-stamps."

He stirred up the letters, and, selecting a few at random, showed the addresses, and opened them to read. Nearly all of them were letters from illiterate persons, with the superscription, "To Our Lady of Lourdes," scrawled on the envelopes in big, irregular handwriting. Many of them contained requests or thanks, incorrectly worded and wondrously spelt; and nothing was more affecting than the nature of some of the petitions: a little brother to be saved, a lawsuit to be gained, a lover to be preserved, a marriage to be effected. Other letters, however, were angry ones, taking the Blessed Virgin to task for not having had the politeness to acknowledge a former communication by granting the writer's prayers. Then there were still others, written in a finer hand, with carefully worded phrases containing confessions and fervent entreaties; and these were from women who confided to the Queen of Heaven things which they dared not even say to a priest in the shadow of the confessional. Finally, one envelope, selected at random, merely contained a photograph; a young girl had sent her portrait to Our Lady of Lourdes, with this dedication: "To my good Mother." In short, they every day received the correspondence of a most powerful Queen, to whom both prayers and secrets were addressed, and who was expected to reply with favours and kindnesses of every kind. The franc and half-franc pieces were simple tokens of love to propitiate her; while, as for the postage-stamps, these could only be sent for convenience' sake, in lieu of coined money; unless, indeed, they were sent guilelessly, as in the case of a peasant woman who had added a postscript to her letter to say that she enclosed a stamp for the reply.

"I can assure you," concluded the Baron, "that there are some very nice ones among them, much less foolish than you might imagine. During a period of three years I constantly found some very interesting letters from a lady who did nothing without relating it to the Blessed Virgin. She was a married woman, and entertained a most dangerous passion for a friend of her husband's. Well, Monsieur l'Abbe, she overcame it; the Blessed Virgin answered her by sending her an armour for her chastity, an all-divine power to resist the promptings of her heart." Then he broke off to say: "But come and seat yourself here, Monsieur l'Abbe. You will see how comfortable you will be."

Pierre went and placed himself beside him on a bench on the left hand, at the spot where the rock sloped down. This was a deliciously reposeful corner, and neither the one nor the other spoke; a profound silence had ensued, when, behind him, Pierre heard an indistinct murmur, a light crystalline voice, which seemed to come from the Invisible. He gave a start, which Baron Suire understood.

"That is the spring which you hear," said he; "it is there, underground, below this grating. Would you like to see it?"

And without waiting for Pierre's reply, he at once bent down to open one of the iron plates protecting the spring, mentioning that it was thus closed up in order to prevent freethinkers from throwing poison into it. For a moment this extraordinary idea quite amazed the priest; but he ended by attributing it entirely to the Baron, who was, indeed, very childish. The latter, meantime, was vainly struggling with the padlock, which opened by a combination of letters, and refused to yield to his endeavours. "It is singular," he muttered; "the word is *Rome*, and I am positive that it hasn't been changed. The damp destroys everything. Every two years or so we are obliged to replace those crutches up there, otherwise they would all rot away. Be good enough to bring me a taper."

By the light of the candle which Pierre then took from one of the holders, he at last succeeded in unfastening the brass padlock, which was covered with *vert-de-gris*. Then, the plate having been raised, the spring appeared to view. Upon a bed of muddy gravel, in a fissure of the rock, there was a limpid stream, quite tranquil, but seemingly spreading over a rather large surface. The Baron explained that it had been necessary to conduct it to the fountains through pipes coated with cement; and he even admitted that, behind the piscinas, a large cistern had been dug in which the water was collected during the night, as otherwise the small output of the source would not suffice for the daily requirements.

"Will you taste it?" he suddenly asked. "It is much better here, fresh from the earth."

Pierre did not answer; he was gazing at that tranquil, innocent water, which assumed a moire-like golden sheen in the dancing light of the taper. The falling drops of wax now and again ruffled its surface. And, as he gazed at it, the young priest pondered upon all the mystery it brought with it from the distant mountain slopes.

"Come, drink some!" said the Baron, who had already dipped and filled a glass which was kept there handy. The priest had no choice but to empty it; it was good pure, water, fresh and transparent, like that which flows from all the lofty uplands of the Pyrenees.

After refastening the padlock, they both returned to the bench. Now and again Pierre could still hear the spring flowing behind him, with a music resembling the gentle warble of some unseen bird. And now the Baron again raised his voice, giving him the history of the Grotto at all times and seasons, in a pathetic babble, replete with puerile details.

The summer was the roughest season, for then came the great itinerant pilgrimage crowds, with the uproarious fervour of thousands of eager beings, all praying and vociferating together. But with the autumn came the rain, those diluvial rains which beat against the Grotto entrance for days together; and with them arrived the pilgrims from remote countries, small, silent, and ecstatic bands of Indians, Malays, and even Chinese, who fell upon their knees in the mud at the sign from the missionaries accompanying them. Of all the old provinces of France, it was Brittany that sent the most devout pilgrims, whole parishes arriving together, the men as numerous as the women, and all displaying a pious deportment, a simple and unostentatious faith, such as might edify the world. Then came the winter, December with its terrible cold, its dense snow-drifts blocking the mountain ways. But even then families put up at the hotels, and, despite everything, faithful worshippers—all those who, fleeing the noise of the world, wished to speak to the Virgin in the tender intimacy of solitude—still came every morning to the Grotto. Among them were some whom no one knew, who appeared directly they felt certain they would be alone there to kneel and love like jealous lovers; and who departed, frightened away by the first suspicion of a crowd. And how warm and pleasant the place was throughout the foul winter weather! In spite of rain and wind and snow, the Grotto still continued flaring. Even during nights of howling tempest, when not a soul was there, it lighted up the empty darkness, blazing like a brasier of love that nothing could extinguish. The Baron related that, at the time of the heavy snowfall of the previous winter, he had spent whole afternoons there, on the bench where they were then seated. A gentle warmth prevailed, although the spot faced the north and was never reached by a ray of sunshine. No doubt the circumstance of the burning tapers continually heating the rock explained this generous warmth; but might one not also believe in some charming kindness on the part of the Virgin, who endowed the spot with perpetual springtide? And the little birds were well aware of it; when the snow on the ground froze their feet, all the finches of the neighbourhood sought shelter there, fluttering about in the ivy around the holy statue. At length came the awakening of the real spring: the Gave, swollen with melted snow, and rolling on with a voice of thunder: the trees, under the action of their sap, arraying themselves in a mantle of greenery, whilst the crowds, once more returning, noisily invaded the sparkling Grotto, whence they drove the little birds of heaven.

"Yes, yes," repeated Baron Suire, in a declining voice, "I spent some most delightful winter days here all alone. I saw no one but a woman, who leant against the railing to avoid kneeling in the snow. She was quite young, twenty-five perhaps, and very pretty—dark, with magnificent blue eyes. She never spoke, and did not even seem to pray, but remained there for hours together, looking intensely sad. I do not know who she was, nor have I ever seen her since."

He ceased speaking; and when, a couple of minutes later, Pierre, surprised at his silence, looked at him, he perceived that he had fallen asleep. With his hands clasped upon his belly, his chin resting on his chest, he slept as peacefully as a child, a smile hovering the while about his mouth. Doubtless, when he said that he spent the night there, he meant that he came thither to indulge in the early nap of a happy old man, whose dreams are of the angels. And now Pierre tasted all the charms of the solitude. It was indeed true that a feeling of peacefulness and comfort permeated the soul in this rocky nook. It was occasioned by the somewhat stifling fumes of the burning wax, by the transplendent ecstasy into which one sank amidst the glare of the tapers. The young priest could no longer distinctly see the crutches on the roof, the votive offerings hanging from the sides, the altar of engraved silver, and the harmonium in its wrapper, for a slow intoxication seemed to be stealing over him, a gradual prostration of his whole being. And he particularly experienced the divine sensation of having left the living world, of having attained to the far realms of the marvellous and the superhuman, as though that simple iron railing yonder had become the very barrier of the Infinite.

However, a slight noise on his left again disturbed him. It was the spring flowing, ever flowing on, with its bird-like warble. Ah! how he would have liked to fall upon his knees and believe in the miracle, to acquire a certain conviction that that divine water had gushed from the rock solely for the healing of suffering humanity. Had he not come there to prostrate himself and implore the Virgin to restore the faith of his childhood? Why, then, did he not pray, why did he not beseech her to bring him back to grace? His feeling of suffocation increased, the burning tapers dazzled him almost to the point of giddiness. And, all at once, the recollection came to him that for two days past, amidst the great freedom which priests enjoyed at Lourdes, he had neglected to say his mass. He was in a state of sin, and perhaps it was the weight of this transgression which was oppressing his heart. He suffered so much that he was at last compelled to rise from his seat and walk away. He gently closed the gate behind him, leaving Baron Suire still asleep on the bench. Marie, he found, had not stirred, but was still raised on her elbows, with her ecstatic eyes uplifted towards the figure of the Virgin.

"How are you, Marie?" asked Pierre. "Don't you feel cold?"

She did not reply. He felt her hands and found them warm and soft, albeit slightly trembling. "It is not the cold which makes you tremble, is it, Marie?" he asked.

In a voice as gentle as a zephyr she replied: "No, no! let me be; I am so happy! I shall see her, I feel it. Ah! what joy!"

So, after slightly pulling up her shawl, he went forth into the night, a prey to indescribable agitation. Beyond the bright glow of the Grotto was a night as black as ink, a region of darkness, into which he plunged at random. Then, as his eyes became accustomed to this gloom, he found himself near the Gave, and skirted it, following a path shaded by tall trees, where he again came upon a refreshing obscurity. This shade and coolness, both so soothing, now brought him relief. And his only surprise was that he had not fallen on his knees in the Grotto, and prayed, even as Marie was praying, with all the power of his soul. What could be the obstacle within him? Whence came the irresistible revolt which prevented him from surrendering himself to faith even when his overtaxed, tortured being longed to yield? He understood well enough that it was his reason alone which protested, and the time had come when he would gladly have killed that voracious reason, which was devouring his life and preventing him from enjoying the happiness allowed to the ignorant and the simple. Perhaps, had he beheld a miracle, he might have acquired enough strength of will to believe. For instance, would he not have bowed himself down, vanquished at last, if Marie had suddenly risen up and walked before him. The scene which he conjured up of Marie saved, Marie cured, affected him so deeply that he stopped short, his trembling arms uplifted towards the star-spangled vault of heaven. What a lovely night it was!—so deep and mysterious, so airy and fragrant; and what joy rained down at the hope that eternal health might be restored, that eternal love might ever revive, even as spring returns! Then he continued his walk, following the path to the end. But his doubts were again coming back to him; when you need a miracle to gain belief, it means that you are incapable of believing. There is no need for the Almighty to prove His existence. Pierre also felt uneasy at the thought that, so long as he had not discharged his priestly duties by saying his mass, his prayers would not be answered. Why did he not go at once to the church of the Rosary, whose altars, from midnight till noon, are placed at the disposal of the priests who come from a distance? Thus thinking, he descended by another path, again finding himself beneath the trees, near the leafy spot whence he and Marie had watched the procession of tapers. Not a light now remained, there was but a boundless expanse of gloom.

Here Pierre experienced a fresh attack of faintness, and as though to gain time, he turned mechanically into the pilgrims' shelter-house. Its door had remained wide open; still this failed to sufficiently ventilate the spacious hall, which was now full of people. On the very threshold Pierre felt oppressed by the stifling heat emanating from the multitude of bodies, the dense pestilential smell of human breath and perspiration. The smoking lanterns gave out so bad a light that he had to pick his way with extreme care in order to avoid treading upon outstretched limbs; for the overcrowding was extraordinary, and many persons, unable to find room on the benches, had stretched themselves on the pavement, on the damp stone slabs fouled by all the refuse of the day.

ÉMILE ZOLA

And on all sides indescribable promiscuousness prevailed: prostrated by overpowering weariness, men, women, and priests were lying there, pell-mell, at random, open-mouthed and utterly exhausted. A large number were snoring, seated on the slabs, with their backs against the walls and their heads drooping on their chests. Others had slipped down, with limbs intermingled, and one young girl lay prostrate across an old country priest, who in his calm, childlike slumber was smiling at the angels. It was like a cattle-shed sheltering poor wanderers of the roads, all those who were homeless on that beautiful holiday night, and who had dropped in there and fallen fraternally asleep. Still, there were some who found no repose in their feverish excitement, but turned and twisted, or rose up to finish eating the food which remained in their baskets. Others could be seen lying perfectly motionless, their eyes wide open and fixed upon the gloom. The cries of dreamers, the wailing of sufferers, arose amidst general snoring. And pity came to the heart, a pity full of anguish, at sight of this flock of wretches lying there in heaps in loathsome rags, whilst their poor spotless souls no doubt were far away in the blue realm of some mystical dream. Pierre was on the point of withdrawing, feeling sick at heart, when a low continuous moan attracted his attention. He looked, and recognised Madame Vincent, on the same spot and in the same position as before, still nursing little Rose upon her lap. "Ah! Monsieur l'Abbe," the poor woman murmured, "you hear her; she woke up nearly an hour ago, and has been sobbing ever since. Yet I assure you I have not moved even a finger, I felt so happy at seeing her sleep."

The priest bent down, examining the little one, who had not even the strength to raise her eyelids. A plaintive cry no stronger than a breath was coming from her lips; and she was so white that he shuddered, for he felt that death was hovering near.

"Dear me! what shall I do?" continued the poor mother, utterly worn out. "This cannot last; I can no longer bear to hear her cry. And if you knew all that I have been saying to her: 'My jewel, my treasure, my angel, I beseech you cry no more. Be good; the Blessed Virgin will cure you!' And yet she still cries on."

With these words the poor creature burst out sobbing, her big tears falling on the face of the child, whose rattle still continued. "Had it been daylight," she resumed, "I would long ago have left this hall, the more especially as she disturbs the others. There is an old lady yonder who has already complained. But I fear it may be chilly outside; and besides, where could I go in the middle of the night? Ah! Blessed Virgin, Blessed Virgin, take pity upon us!"

Overcome by emotion, Pierre kissed the child's fair head, and then hastened away to avoid bursting into tears like the sorrowing mother. And he went straight to the Rosary, as though he were determined to conquer death.

He had already beheld the Rosary in broad daylight, and had been displeased by the aspect of this church, which the architect, fettered by the rockbound site, had been obliged to make circular and low, so that it seemed crushed beneath its great cupola, which square pillars supported. The worst was that, despite its archaic Byzantine style, it altogether lacked any religious appearance, and suggested neither mystery nor meditation. Indeed, with the glaring light admitted by the cupola and the broad glazed doors it was more like some brand-new corn-market. And then, too, it was not yet completed: the decorations were lacking, the bare walls against which the altars stood had no other embellishment than some artificial roses of coloured paper and a few insignificant votive offerings; and this bareness heightened the resemblance to some vast public hall. Moreover, in time of rain the paved floor became as muddy as that of a general waiting-room at a railway station. The high altar was a temporary structure of painted wood. Innumerable rows of benches filled the central rotunda, benches free to the public, on which people could come and rest at all hours, for night and day alike the Rosary remained open to the swarming pilgrims. Like the shelter-house, it was a cow-shed in which the Almighty received the poor ones of the earth.

On entering, Pierre felt himself to be in some common hall trod by the footsteps of an ever-changing crowd. But the brilliant sunlight no longer streamed on the pallid walls, the tapers burning at every altar simply gleamed like stars amidst the uncertain gloom which filled the building. A solemn high mass had been celebrated at midnight with extraordinary pomp, amidst all the splendour of candles, chants, golden vestments, and swinging, steaming censers; but of all this glorious display there now remained only the regulation number of tapers necessary for the celebration of the masses at each of the fifteen altars ranged around the edifice. These masses began at midnight and did not cease till noon. Nearly four hundred were said during those twelve hours at the Rosary alone. Taking the whole of Lourdes, where there were altogether some fifty altars, more than two thousand masses were celebrated daily. And so great was the abundance of priests, that many had extreme difficulty in fulfilling their duties, having to wait for hours together before they could find an altar unoccupied. What particularly struck Pierre that evening, was the sight of all the altars besieged by rows of priests patiently awaiting their turn in the dim light at the foot of the steps; whilst the officiating minister galloped through the Latin phrases, hastily punctuating them with the prescribed signs of the cross. And the weariness of all the waiting ones was so great, that most of them were seated on the flagstones, some even dozing on the altar steps in heaps, quite overpowered, relying on the beadle to come and rouse them.

For a moment Pierre walked about undecided. Was he going to wait like the others? However, the scene determined him against doing so. At every altar, at every mass, a crowd of pilgrims was gathered, communicating in all haste with a sort of voracious fervour. Each pyx was filled and emptied incessantly; the priests' hands grew tired in thus distributing the bread of life; and Pierre's surprise increased at the sight. Never before had he beheld a corner of this earth so watered by the divine blood, whence faith took wing in such a flight of souls. It was like a return to the heroic days of the Church, when all nations prostrated themselves beneath the same blast of credulity in their terrified ignorance which led them to place their hope of eternal happiness in an Almighty God. He could fancy himself carried back some eight or nine centuries, to the time of great public piety, when people believed in the approaching end of the world; and this he could fancy the more readily as the crowd of simple folk, the whole host that had attended high mass, was still seated on the benches, as much at ease in God's house as at home. Many had no place of refuge. Was not the church their home, the asylum where consolation awaited them both by day and by night? Those who knew not where to sleep, who had not found room even at the shelter place, came to the Rosary, where sometimes they succeeded in finding a vacant seat on a bench, at others sufficient space to lie down on the flagstones. And others who had beds awaiting them lingered there for the joy of passing a whole night in that divine abode, so full of beautiful dreams. Until daylight the concourse and promiscuity were extraordinary; every row of benches was occupied, sleeping persons were scattered in every corner and behind every pillar; men, women, children were leaning against each other, their heads on one another's shoulders, their breath mingling in calm unconsciousness. It was the break-up of a religious gathering overwhelmed by sleep, a church transformed into a chance hospital, its doors wide open to the lovely August night, giving access to all who were wandering in the darkness, the good and the bad, the weary and the lost. And all over the place, from each of the fifteen altars, the bells announcing the elevation of the Host incessantly sounded, whilst from among the mob of sleepers bands of believers now and again arose, went and received the sacrament, and then returned to mingle once more with the nameless, shepherdless flock which the semi-obscurity enveloped like a veil.

With an air of restless indecision, Pierre was still wandering through the shadowy groups, when an old priest, seated on the step of an altar, beckoned to him. For two hours he had been waiting there, and now that his turn was at length arriving he felt so faint that he feared he might not have strength to say the whole of his mass, and preferred, therefore, to surrender his place to another. No doubt the sight of Pierre, wandering so distressfully in the gloom, had moved him. He pointed the vestry out to him, waited until he returned with chasuble and chalice, and then went off and fell into a sound sleep on one of the neighbouring benches. Pierre thereupon said his mass in the same way as he said it at Paris, like a worthy man fulfilling a professional duty. He outwardly maintained an air of sincere faith. But, contrary to what he had expected from the two feverish days through which he had just gone, from the extraordinary and agitating surroundings amidst which he had spent the last few hours, nothing moved him nor touched his heart. He had hoped that a great commotion would overpower him at the moment of the communion, when the divine mystery is accomplished; that he would find himself in view of Paradise, steeped in grace, in the very presence of the Almighty; but there was no manifestation, his chilled heart did not even throb, he went on to the end pronouncing the usual words, making the regulation gestures, with the mechanical accuracy of the profession. In spite of his effort to be fervent, one single idea kept obstinately returning to his mind—that the vestry was far too small, since such an enormous number of masses had to be said. How could the sacristans manage to distribute the holy vestments and the cloths? It puzzled him, and engaged his thoughts with absurd persistency.

At length, to his surprise, he once more found himself outside. Again he wandered through the night, a night which seemed to him utterly void, darker and stiller than before. The town was lifeless, not a light was gleaming. There only remained the growl of the Gave, which his accustomed ears no longer heard. And suddenly, similar to a miraculous apparition, the Grotto blazed before him, illumining the darkness with its everlasting brasier, which burnt with a flame of inextinguishable love. He had returned thither unconsciously, attracted no doubt by thoughts of Marie. Three o'clock was about to strike, the benches before the Grotto were emptying, and only some twenty persons remained there, dark, indistinct forms, kneeling in slumberous ecstasy, wrapped in divine torpor. It seemed as though the night in progressing had increased the gloom, and imparted a remote visionary aspect to the Grotto. All faded away amidst delicious lassitude, sleep reigned supreme over the dim, far-spreading country side; whilst the voice of the invisible waters seemed to be merely the breathing of this pure slumber, upon which the Blessed Virgin, all white with her aureola of tapers, was smiling. And among the few unconscious women was Madame Maze, still kneeling, with clasped hands and bowed head, but so indistinct that she seemed to have melted away amidst her ardent prayer.

Pierre, however, had immediately gone up to Marie. He was shivering, and fancied that she must be chilled by the early morning air. "I beseech you, Marie, cover yourself up," said he. "Do you want to suffer still more?" And thereupon he drew up the shawl which had slipped off her, and endeavoured to fasten it about her neck. "You are cold, Marie," he added; "your hands are like ice."

She did not answer, she was still in the same attitude as when he had left her a couple of hours previously. With her elbows resting on the edges of her box, she kept herself raised, her soul still lifted towards the Blessed Virgin and her face transfigured, beaming with a celestial joy. Her lips moved, though no sound came from them. Perhaps she was still carrying on some mysterious conversation in the world of enchantments, dreaming wide awake, as she had been doing ever since he had placed her there. He spoke to her again, but still she answered not. At last, however, of her own accord, she murmured in a far-away voice: "Oh! I am so happy, Pierre! I have seen her; I prayed to her for you, and she smiled at me, slightly nodding her head to let me know that she heard me and would grant my prayers. And though she did not speak to me, Pierre, I understood what she wished me to know. 'Tis to-day, at four o'clock in the afternoon, when the Blessed Sacrament passes by, that I shall be cured!"

He listened to her in deep agitation. Had she been sleeping with her eyes wide open? Was it in a dream that she had seen the marble figure of the Blessed Virgin bend its head and smile? A great tremor passed through him at the thought that this poor child had prayed for him. And he walked up to the railing, and dropped upon his knees, stammering: "O Marie! O Marie!" without knowing whether this heart-cry were intended for the Virgin or for the beloved friend of his childhood. And he remained there, utterly overwhelmed, waiting for grace to come to him.

Endless minutes went by. This was indeed the superhuman effort, the waiting for the miracle which he had come to seek for himself, the sudden revelation, the thunderclap which was to sweep away his unbelief and restore him, rejuvenated and triumphant, to the faith of the simple-minded. He surrendered himself, he wished that some mighty power might ravage his being and transform it. But, even as before whilst saying his mass, he heard naught within him but an endless silence, felt nothing but a boundless vacuum. There was no divine intervention, his despairing heart almost seemed to cease beating. And although he strove to pray, to fix his mind wholly upon that powerful Virgin, so compassionate to poor humanity, his thoughts none the less wandered, won back by the outside world, and again turning to puerile trifles. Within the Grotto, on the other side of the railing, he had once more caught sight of Baron Suire, still asleep, still continuing his pleasant nap with his hands clasped in front of him. Other things also attracted his attention: the flowers deposited at the feet of the Virgin, the letters cast there as though into a heavenly letter-box, the delicate lace-like work of wax which remained erect around the flames of the larger tapers, looking like some rich silver ornamentation. Then, without any apparent reason, his thoughts flew away to the days of his childhood, and his brother Guillaume's face rose before him with extreme distinctness. He had not seen him since their mother's death. He merely knew that he led a very secluded life, occupying himself with scientific matters, in a little house in which he had buried himself with a mistress and two big dogs; and he would have known nothing more about him, but for having recently read his name in a newspaper in connection with some revolutionary attempt. It was stated that he was passionately devoting himself to the study of explosives, and in constant intercourse with the leaders of the most advanced parties. Why, however, should Guillaume appear to him in this wise, in this ecstatic spot, amidst the mystical light of the tapers,—appear to him, moreover, such as he had formerly known him, so good, affectionate, and brotherly, overflowing with charity for every affliction! The thought haunted him for a moment, and filled him with painful regret for that brotherliness now dead and gone. Then, with hardly a moment's pause, his mind reverted to himself, and he realised that he might stubbornly remain there for hours without regaining faith. Nevertheless, he felt a sort of tremor pass through him, a final hope, a feeling that if the Blessed Virgin should perform the great miracle of curing Marie, he would at last believe. It was like a final delay which he allowed himself, an appointment with Faith for that very day, at four o'clock in the afternoon, when, according to what the girl had told him, the Blessed Sacrament would pass by. And at this thought his anguish at once ceased, he remained kneeling, worn out with fatigue and overcome by invincible drowsiness.

The hours passed by, the resplendent illumination of the Grotto was still projected into the night, its reflection stretching to the neighbouring hillsides and whitening the walls of the convents there. However, Pierre noticed it grow paler and paler, which surprised him, and he roused himself, feeling thoroughly chilled; it was the day breaking, beneath a leaden sky overcast with clouds. He perceived that one of those storms, so sudden in mountainous regions, was rapidly rising from the south. The thunder could already be heard rumbling in the distance, whilst gusts of wind swept along the roads. Perhaps he also had been sleeping, for he no longer beheld Baron Suire, whose departure he did not remember having witnessed. There were scarcely ten persons left before the Grotto, though among them he again recognised Madame Maze with her face hidden in her hands. However, when she noticed that it was daylight and that she could be seen, she rose up, and vanished at a turn of the narrow path leading to the convent of the Blue Sisters.

Feeling anxious, Pierre went up to Marie to tell her she must not remain there any longer, unless she wished to get wet through. "I will take you back to the hospital," said he.

She refused and then entreated: "No, no! I am waiting for mass; I promised to communicate here. Don't trouble about me, return to the hotel at once, and go to bed, I implore you. You know very well that covered vehicles are sent here for the sick whenever it rains."

And she persisted in refusing to leave, whilst on his side he kept on repeating that he did not wish to go to bed. A mass, it should be mentioned, was said at the Grotto early every morning, and it was a divine joy for the pilgrims to be able to communicate, amidst the glory of the rising sun, after a long night of ecstasy. And now, just as some large drops of rain were beginning to fall, there came the priest, wearing a chasuble and accompanied by two acolytes, one of whom, in order to protect the chalice, held a large white silk umbrella, embroidered with gold, over him.

Pierre, after pushing Marie's little conveyance close to the railing, so that the girl might be sheltered by the overhanging rock, under which the few other worshippers had also sought refuge, had just seen her receive the sacrament with ardent fervour, when his attention was attracted by a pitiful spectacle which quite wrung his heart.

Beneath a dense, heavy deluge of rain, he caught sight of Madame Vincent, still with that precious, woeful burden, her little Rose, whom with outstretched arms she was offering to the Blessed Virgin. Unable to stay any longer at the shelter-house owing to the complaints caused by the child's constant moaning, she had carried her off into the night, and during two hours had roamed about in the darkness, lost, distracted, bearing this poor flesh of her flesh, which she pressed to her bosom, unable to give it any relief. She knew not what road she had taken, beneath what trees she had strayed, so absorbed had she been in her revolt against the unjust sufferings which had so sorely stricken this poor little being, so feeble and so pure, and as yet quite incapable of sin. Was it not abominable that the grip of disease should for weeks have been incessantly torturing her child, whose cry she knew not how to quiet? She carried her about, rocking her in her arms as she went wildly along the paths, obstinately hoping that she would at last get her to sleep, and so hush that wail which was rending her heart. And suddenly, utterly worn-out, sharing each of her daughter's death pangs, she found herself opposite the Grotto, at the feet of the miracle-working Virgin, she who forgave and who healed.

"O Virgin, Mother most admirable, heal her! O Virgin, Mother of Divine Grace, heal her!"

She had fallen on her knees, and with quivering, outstretched arms was still offering her expiring daughter, in a paroxysm of hope and desire which seemed to raise her from the ground. And the rain, which she never noticed, beat down behind her with the fury of an escaped torrent, whilst violent claps of thunder shook the mountains. For one moment she thought her prayer was granted, for Rose had slightly shivered as though visited by the archangel, her face becoming quite white, her eyes and mouth opening wide; and with one last little gasp she ceased to cry.

"O Virgin, Mother of Our Redeemer, heal her! O Virgin, All-powerful Mother, heal her!"

But the poor woman felt her child become even lighter in her extended arms. And now she became afraid at no longer hearing her moan, at seeing her so white, with staring eyes and open mouth, without a sign of life. How was it that she did not smile if she were cured? Suddenly a loud heart-rending cry rang out, the cry of the mother, surpassing even the din of the thunder in the storm, whose violence was increasing. Her child was dead. And she rose up erect, turned her back on that deaf Virgin who let little children die, and started off like a madwoman beneath the lashing downpour, going straight before her without knowing whither, and still and ever carrying and nursing that poor little body which she had held in her arms during so many days and nights. A thunderbolt fell, shivering one of the neighbouring trees, as though with the stroke of a giant axe, amidst a great crash of twisted and broken branches.

Pierre had rushed after Madame Vincent, eager to guide and help her. But he was unable to follow her, for he at once lost sight of her behind the blurring curtain of rain. When he returned, the mass was drawing to an end, and, as soon as the rain fell less violently, the officiating priest went off under the white silk umbrella embroidered with gold. Meantime a kind of omnibus awaited the few patients to take them back to the hospital.

Marie pressed Pierre's hands. "Oh! how happy I am!" she said. "Do not come for me before three o'clock this afternoon."

On being left amidst the rain, which had now become an obstinate fine drizzle, Pierre re-entered the Grotto and seated himself on the bench near the spring. He would not go to bed, for in spite of his weariness he dreaded sleep in the state of nervous excitement in which he had been plunged ever since the day before. Little Rose's death had increased his fever; he could not banish from his mind the thought of that heart-broken mother, wandering along the muddy paths with the dead body of her child. What could be the reasons which influenced the Virgin? He was amazed that she could make a choice. Divine Mother as she was, he wondered how her heart could decide upon healing only ten out of a hundred sufferers—that ten per cent. of miracles which Doctor Bonamy had proved by statistics. He, Pierre, had already asked himself the day before which ones he would have chosen had he possessed the power of saving ten. A terrible power in all truth, a formidable selection, which he would never have had the courage to make. Why this one, and not that other? Where was the justice, where the compassion? To be all-powerful and heal every one of them, was not that the desire which rose from each heart? And the Virgin seemed to him to be cruel, badly informed, as harsh and indifferent as even impassible nature, distributing life and death at random, or in accordance with laws which mankind knew nothing of.

The rain was at last leaving off, and Pierre had been there a couple of hours when he felt that his feet were damp. He looked down, and was greatly surprised, for the spring was overflowing through the gratings. The soil of the Grotto was already covered; whilst outside a sheet of water was flowing under the benches, as far as the parapet against the Gave. The late storms had swollen the waters in the neighbourhood. Pierre thereupon reflected that this spring, in spite of its miraculous origin, was subject to the laws that governed other springs, for it certainly communicated with some natural reservoirs, wherein the rain penetrated and accumulated. And then, to keep his ankles dry, he left the place.

V

THE TWO VICTIMS

Pierre walked along thirsting for fresh air, his head so heavy that he took off his hat to relieve his burning brow. Despite all the fatigue of that terrible night of vigil, he did not think of sleeping. He was kept erect by that rebellion of his whole being which he could not quiet. Eight o'clock was striking, and he walked at random under the glorious morning sun, now shining forth in a spotless sky, which the storm seemed to have cleansed of all the Sunday dust.

All at once, however, he raised his head, anxious to know where he was; and he was quite astonished, for he found that he had already covered a deal of ground, and was now below the station, near the municipal hospital. He was hesitating at a point where the road forked, not knowing which direction to take, when a friendly hand was laid on his shoulder, and a voice inquired: "Where are you going at this early hour?"

It was Doctor Chassaigne who addressed him, drawing up his lofty figure, clad in black from head to foot. "Have you lost yourself?" he added; "do you want to know your way?"

"No, thanks, no," replied Pierre, somewhat disturbed. "I spent the night at the Grotto with that young patient to whom I am so much attached, and my heart was so upset that I have been walking about in the hope it would do me good, before returning to the hotel to take a little sleep."

The doctor continued looking at him, clearly detecting the frightful struggle which was raging within him, the despair which he felt at being unable to sink asleep in faith, the suffering which the futility of all his efforts brought him. "Ah, my poor child!" murmured M. Chassaigne; and in a fatherly way he added: "Well, since you are walking, suppose we take a walk together? I was just going down yonder, to the bank of the Gave. Come along, and on our way back you will see what a lovely view we shall have."

For his part, the doctor took a walk of a couple of hours' duration each morning, ever alone, seeking, as it were, to tire and exhaust his grief. First of all, as soon as he had risen, he repaired to the cemetery, and knelt on the tomb of his wife and daughter, which, at all seasons, he decked with flowers. And afterwards he would roam along the roads, with tearful eyes, never returning home until fatigue compelled him.

With a wave of the hand, Pierre accepted his proposal, and in perfect silence they went, side by side, down the sloping road. They remained for a long time without speaking; the doctor seemed more overcome than was his wont that morning; it was as though his chat with his dear lost ones had made his heart bleed yet more copiously. He walked along with his head bowed; his face, round which his white hair streamed, was very pale, and tears still blurred his eyes. And yet it was so pleasant, so warm in the sunlight on that lovely morning. The road now followed the Gave on its right bank, on the other side of the new town; and you could see the gardens, the inclined ways, and the Basilica. And, all at once, the Grotto appeared, with the everlasting flare of its tapers, now paling in the broad light.

Doctor Chassaigne, who had turned his head, made the sign of the cross, which Pierre did not at first understand. And when, in his turn, he had perceived the Grotto, he glanced in surprise at his old friend, and once more relapsed into the astonishment which had come over him a couple of days previously on finding this man of science, this whilom atheist and materialist, so overwhelmed by grief that he was now a believer, longing for the one delight of meeting his dear ones in another life. His heart had swept his reason away; old and lonely as he was, it was only the illusion that he would live once more in Paradise, where loving souls meet again, that prolonged his life on earth. This thought increased the young priest's discomfort. Must he also wait until he had grown old and endured equal sufferings in order to find a refuge in faith?

Still walking beside the Gave, leaving the town farther and farther behind them, they were lulled as it were by the noise of those clear waters rolling over the pebbles between banks shaded by trees. And they still remained silent, walking on with an equal step, each, on his own side, absorbed in his sorrows.

"And Bernadette," Pierre suddenly inquired; "did you know her?"

The doctor raised his head. "Bernadette? Yes, yes," said he. "I saw her once—afterwards." He relapsed into silence for a moment, and then began chatting: "In 1858, you know, at the time of the apparitions, I was thirty years of age. I was in Paris, still young in my profession, and opposed to all supernatural notions, so that I had no idea of returning to my native mountains to see a girl suffering from hallucinations. Five or six years later, however, some time about 1864, I passed through Lourdes, and was inquisitive enough to pay Bernadette a visit. She was then still at the asylum with the Sisters of Nevers."

Pierre remembered that one of the reasons of his journey had been his desire to complete his inquiry respecting Bernadette. And who could tell if grace might not come to him from that humble, lovable girl, on the day when he should be convinced that she had indeed fulfilled a mission of divine love and forgiveness? For this consummation to ensue it would perhaps suffice that he should know her better and learn to feel that she was really the saint, the chosen one, as others believed her to have been.

"Tell me about her, I pray you," he said; "tell me all you know of her."

A faint smile curved the doctor's lips. He understood, and would have greatly liked to calm and comfort the young priest whose soul was so grievously tortured by doubt. "Oh! willingly, my poor child!" he answered. "I should be so happy to help you on the path to light. You do well to love Bernadette—that may save you; for since all those old-time things I have deeply reflected on her case, and I declare to you that I never met a more charming creature, or one with a better heart."

Then, to the slow rhythm of their footsteps along the well-kept, sunlit road, in the delightful freshness of morning, the doctor began to relate his visit to Bernadette in 1864. She had then just attained her twentieth birthday, the apparitions had taken place six years previously, and she had astonished him by her candid and sensible air, her perfect modesty. The Sisters of Nevers, who had taught her to read, kept her with them at the asylum in order to shield her from public inquisitiveness. She found an occupation there, helping them in sundry petty duties; but she was very often taken ill, and would spend weeks at a time in her bed. The doctor had been particularly struck by her beautiful eyes, pure, candid, and frank, like those of a child. The rest of her face, said he, had become somewhat spoilt; her complexion was losing its clearness, her features had grown less delicate, and her general appearance was that of an ordinary servant-girl, short, puny, and unobtrusive. Her piety was still keen, but she had not seemed to him to be the ecstatical, excitable creature that many might have supposed; indeed, she appeared to have a rather positive mind which did not indulge in flights of fancy; and she invariably had some little piece of needlework, some knitting, some embroidery in her hand. In a word, she appeared to have entered the common path, and in nowise resembled the intensely passionate female worshippers of the Christ. She had no further visions, and never of her own accord spoke of the eighteen apparitions which had decided her life. To learn anything it was necessary to interrogate her, to address precise questions to her. These she would briefly answer, and then seek to change the conversation, as though she did not like to talk of such mysterious things. If wishing to probe the matter further, you asked her the nature of the three secrets which the Virgin had confided to her, she would remain silent, simply averting her eyes. And it was impossible to make her contradict herself; the particulars she gave invariably agreed with her original narrative; and, indeed, she always seemed to repeat the same words, with the same inflections of the voice.

"I had her in hand during the whole of one afternoon," continued Doctor Chassaigne, "and there was not the variation of a syllable in her story. It was disconcerting. Still, I am prepared to swear that she was not lying, that she never lied, that she was altogether incapable of falsehood."

Pierre boldly ventured to discuss this point. "But won't you admit, doctor, the possibility of some disorder of the will?" he asked. "Has it not been proved, is it not admitted nowadays, that when certain degenerate creatures with childish minds fall into an hallucination, a fancy of some kind or other, they are often unable to free themselves from it, especially when they remain in the same environment in which the phenomenon occurred? Cloistered, living alone with her fixed idea, Bernadette, naturally enough, obstinately clung to it."

The doctor's faint smile returned to his lips, and vaguely waving his arm, he replied: "Ah! my child, you ask me too much. You know very well that I am now only a poor old man, who prides himself but little on his science, and no longer claims to be able to explain anything. However, I do of course know of that famous medical-school example of the young girl who allowed herself to waste away with hunger at home, because she imagined that she was suffering from a serious complaint of the digestive organs, but who nevertheless began to eat when she was taken elsewhere. However, that is but one circumstance, and there are so many contradictory cases."

For a moment they became silent, and only the rhythmical sound of their steps was heard along the road. Then the doctor resumed: "Moreover, it is quite true that Bernadette shunned the world, and was only happy in her solitary corner. She was never known to have a single intimate female friend, any particular human love for anybody. She was kind and gentle towards all, but it was only for children that she showed any lively affection. And as, after all, the medical man is not quite dead within me, I will confess to you that I have sometimes wondered if she remained as pure in mind, as, most undoubtedly, she did remain in body. However, I think it quite possible, given her sluggish, poor-blooded temperament, not to speak of the innocent sphere in which she grew up, first Bartres, and then the convent. Still, a doubt came to me when I heard of the tender interest which she took in the orphan asylum built by the Sisters of Nevers, farther along this very road. Poor little girls are received into it, and shielded from the perils of the highways. And if Bernadette wished it to be extremely large, so as to lodge all the little lambs in danger, was it not because she herself remembered having roamed the roads with bare feet, and still trembled at the idea of what might have become of her but for the help of the Blessed Virgin?"

Then, resuming his narrative, he went on telling Pierre of the crowds that flocked to see Bernadette and pay her reverence in her asylum at Lourdes. This had proved a source of considerable fatigue to her. Not a day went by without a stream of visitors appearing before her. They came from all parts of France, some even from abroad; and it soon proved necessary to refuse the applications of those who were actuated by mere inquisitiveness, and to grant admittance only to the genuine believers, the members of the clergy, and the people of mark on whom the doors could not well have been shut. A Sister was always present to protect Bernadette against the excessive indiscretion of some of her visitors, for questions literally rained upon her, and she often grew faint through having to repeat her story so many times. Ladies of high position fell on their knees, kissed her gown, and would have liked to carry a piece of it away as a relic. She also had to defend her chaplet, which in their excitement they all begged her to sell to them for a fabulous amount. One day a certain marchioness endeavoured to secure it by giving her another one which she had brought with her—a chaplet with a golden cross and beads of real pearls. Many hoped that she would consent to work a miracle in their presence; children were brought to her in order that she might lay her hands upon them; she was also consulted in cases of illness, and attempts were made to purchase her influence with the Virgin. Large sums were offered to her. At the slightest sign, the slightest expression of a desire to be a queen, decked with jewels and crowned with gold, she would have been overwhelmed with regal presents. And while the humble remained on their knees on her threshold, the great ones of the earth pressed round her, and would have counted it a glory to act as her escort. It was even related that one among them, the handsomest and wealthiest of princes, came one clear sunny April day to ask her hand in marriage.

"But what always struck and displeased me," said Pierre, "was her departure from Lourdes when she was two-and-twenty, her sudden disappearance and sequestration in the convent of Saint Gildard at Nevers, whence she never emerged. Didn't that give a semblance of truth to those spurious rumours of insanity which were circulated? Didn't it help people to suppose that she was being shut up, whisked away for fear of some indiscretion on her part, some naive remark or other which might have revealed the secret of a prolonged fraud? Indeed, to speak plainly, I will confess to you that for my own part I still believe that she was spirited away."

Doctor Chassaigne gently shook his head. "No, no," said he, "there was no story prepared in advance in this affair, no big melodrama secretly staged and afterwards performed by more or less unconscious actors. The developments came of themselves, by the sole force of circumstances; and they were always very intricate, very difficult to analyse. Moreover, it is certain that it was Bernadette herself who wished to leave Lourdes. Those incessant visits wearied her, she felt ill at ease amidst all that noisy worship. All that *she* desired was a dim nook where she might live in peace, and so fierce was she at times in her disinterestedness, that when money was handed to her, even with the pious intent of having a mass said or a taper burnt, she would fling it upon the floor. She never accepted anything for herself or for her family, which remained in poverty. And with such pride as she possessed, such natural simplicity, such a desire to remain in the background, one can very well understand that she should have wished to disappear and cloister herself in some lonely spot so as to prepare herself to make a good death. Her work was accomplished; she had initiated this great movement scarcely knowing how or why; and she could really be of no further utility. Others were about to conduct matters to an issue and insure the triumph of the Grotto."

"Let us admit, then, that she went off of her own accord," said Pierre; "still, what a relief it must have been for the people you speak of, who thenceforth became the real masters, whilst millions of money were raining down on Lourdes from the whole world."

ÉMILE ZOLA

"Oh! certainly; I don't pretend that any attempt was made to detain her here!" exclaimed the doctor. "Frankly, I even believe that she was in some degree urged into the course she took. She ended by becoming somewhat of an incumbrance. It was not that any annoying revelations were feared from her; but remember that with her extreme timidity and frequent illnesses she was scarcely ornamental. Besides, however small the room which she took up at Lourdes, however obedient she showed herself, she was none the less a power, and attracted the multitude, which made her, so to say, a competitor of the Grotto. For the Grotto to remain alone, resplendent in its glory, it was advisable that Bernadette should withdraw into the background, become as it were a simple legend. Such, indeed, must have been the reasons which induced Monseigneur Laurence, the Bishop of Tarbes, to hasten her departure. The only mistake that was made was in saying that it was a question of screening her from the enterprises of the world, as though it were feared that she might fall into the sin of pride, by growing vain of the saintly fame with which the whole of Christendom re-echoed. And this was doing her a grave injury, for she was as incapable of pride as she was of falsehood. Never, indeed, was there a more candid or more modest child."

The doctor was growing impassioned, excited. But all at once he became calm again, and a pale smile returned to his lips. "'Tis true," said he, "I love her; the more I have thought of her, the more have I learned to love her. But you must not think, Pierre, that I am completely brutified by belief. If I nowadays acknowledge the existence of an unseen power, if I feel a need of believing in another, better, and more just life, I nevertheless know right well that there are men remaining in this world of ours; and at times, even when they wear the cowl or the cassock, the work they do is vile."

There came another interval of silence. Each was continuing his dream apart from the other. Then the doctor resumed: "I will tell you of a fancy which has often haunted me. Suppose we admit that Bernadette was not the shy, simple child we knew her to be; let us endow her with a spirit of intrigue and domination, transform her into a conqueress, a leader of nations, and try to picture what, in that case, would have happened. It is evident that the Grotto would be hers, the Basilica also. We should see her lording it at all the ceremonies, under a dais, with a gold mitre on her head. She would distribute the miracles; with a sovereign gesture her little hand would lead the multitudes to heaven. All the lustre and glory would come from her, she being the saint, the chosen one, the only one that had been privileged to see the Divinity face to face. And indeed nothing would seem more just, for she would triumph after toiling, enjoy the fruit of her labour in all glory. But you see, as it happens, she is defrauded, robbed. The marvellous harvests sown by her are reaped by others. During the twelve years which she lived at Saint Gildard, kneeling in the gloom, Lourdes was full of victors, priests in golden vestments chanting thanksgivings, and blessing churches and monuments erected at a cost of millions. She alone did not behold the triumph of the new faith, whose author she had been. You say that she dreamt it all. Well, at all events, what a beautiful dream it was, a dream which has stirred the whole world, and from which she, dear girl, never awakened!"

They halted and sat down for a moment on a rock beside the road, before returning to the town. In front of them the Gave, deep at this point of its course, was rolling blue waters tinged with dark moiré-like reflections, whilst, farther on, rushing hurriedly over a bed of large stones, the stream became so much foam, a white froth, light like snow. Amidst the gold raining from the sun, a fresh breeze came down from the mountains.

Whilst listening to that story of how Bernadette had been exploited and suppressed, Pierre had simply found in it all a fresh motive for revolt; and, with his eyes fixed on the ground, he began to think of the injustice of nature, of that law which wills that the strong should devour the weak. Then, all at once raising his head, he inquired: "And did you also know Abbe Peyramale?"

The doctor's eyes brightened once more, and he eagerly replied: "Certainly I did! He was an upright, energetic man, a saint, an apostle. He and Bernadette were the great makers of Our Lady of Lourdes. Like her, he endured frightful sufferings, and, like her, he died from them. Those who do not know his story can know nothing, understand nothing, of the drama enacted here."

Thereupon he related that story at length. Abbe Peyramale was the parish priest of Lourdes at the time of the apparitions. A native of the region, tall, broad-shouldered, with a powerful leonine head, he was extremely intelligent, very honest and goodhearted, though at times violent and domineering. He seemed built for combat. An enemy of all pious exaggerations, discharging the duties of his ministry in a broad, liberal spirit, he regarded the apparitions with distrust when he first heard of them, refused to believe in Bernadette's stories, questioned her, and demanded proofs. It was only at a later stage, when the blast of faith became irresistible, upsetting the most rebellious minds and mastering the multitude, that he ended, in his turn, by bowing his head; and when he was finally conquered, it was more particularly by his love for the humble and the oppressed which he could not restrain when he beheld Bernadette threatened with imprisonment. The civil authorities were persecuting one of his flock; at this his shepherd's heart awoke, and, in her defence, he gave full reign to his ardent passion for justice. Moreover, the charm which the child diffused had worked upon him; he felt her to be so candid, so truthful, that he began to place a blind faith in her and love her even as everybody else loved her. Moreover, why should he have curtly dismissed all questions of miracles, when miracles abound in the pages of Holy Writ? It was not for a minister of religion, whatever his prudence, to set himself up as a sceptic when entire populations were falling on their knees and the Church seemed to be on the eve of another great triumph. Then, too, he had the nature of one who leads men, who stirs up crowds, who builds, and in this affair he had really found his vocation, the vast field in which he might exercise his energy, the great cause to which he might wholly devote himself with all his passionate ardour and determination to succeed.

From that moment, then, Abbe Peyramale had but one thought, to execute the orders which the Virgin had commissioned Bernadette to transmit to him. He caused improvements to be carried out at the Grotto. A railing was placed in front of it; pipes were laid for the conveyance of the water from the source, and a variety of work was accomplished in order to clear the approaches. However, the Virgin had particularly requested that a chapel might be built; and he wished to have a church, quite a triumphal Basilica. He pictured everything on a grand scale, and, full of confidence in the enthusiastic help of Christendom, he worried the architects, requiring them to design real palaces worthy of the Queen of Heaven. As a matter of fact, offerings already abounded, gold poured from the most distant dioceses, a rain of gold destined to increase and never end. Then came his happy years: he was to be met among the workmen at all hours, instilling activity into them like the jovial, good-natured fellow he was, constantly on the point of taking a pick or trowel in hand himself, such was his eagerness to behold the realisation of his dream. But days of trial were in store for him: he fell ill, and lay in danger of death on the fourth of April, 1864, when the first procession started from his parish church to the Grotto, a procession of sixty thousand pilgrims, which wound along the streets amidst an immense concourse of spectators.

On the day when Abbe Peyramale rose from his bed, saved, a first time, from death, he found himself despoiled. To second him in his heavy task, Monseigneur Laurence, the Bishop, had already given him as assistant a former episcopal secretary, Father Sempe, whom he had appointed warden of the Missionaries of Geraison, a community founded by himself. Father Sempe was a sly, spare little man, to all appearance most disinterested and humble, but in reality consumed by all the thirst of ambition. At the outset he kept in his place, serving the parish priest of Lourdes like a faithful subordinate, attending to matters of all kinds in order to lighten the other's work, and acquiring information on every possible subject in his desire to render himself indispensable. He must soon have realised what a rich farm the Grotto was destined to become, and what a colossal revenue might be derived from it, if only a little skill were exercised. And thenceforth he no longer stirred from the episcopal residence, but ended by acquiring great influence over the calm, practical Bishop, who was in great need of money for the charities of his diocese. And thus it was that during Abbe Peyramale's illness Father Sempe succeeded in effecting a separation between the parish of Lourdes and the domain of the Grotto, which last he was commissioned to manage at the head of a few Fathers of the Immaculate Conception, over whom the Bishop placed him as Father Superior.

The struggle soon began, one of those covert, desperate, mortal struggles which are waged under the cloak of ecclesiastical discipline. There was a pretext for rupture all ready, a field of battle on which the longer purse would necessarily end by conquering. It was proposed to build a new parish church, larger and more worthy of Lourdes than the old one already in existence, which was admitted to have become too small since the faithful had been flocking into the town in larger and larger numbers. Moreover, it was an old idea of Abbe Peyramale, who desired to carry out the Virgin's orders with all possible precision. Speaking of the Grotto, she had said that people would go "thither in procession"; and the Abbe had always seen the pilgrims start in procession from the town, whither they were expected to return in the same fashion, as indeed had been the practice on the first occasions after the apparitions. A central point, a rallying spot, was therefore required, and the Abbe's dream was to erect a magnificent church, a cathedral of gigantic proportions, which would accommodate a vast multitude. Builder as he was by temperament, impassioned artisan working for the glory of Heaven, he already pictured this cathedral springing from the soil, and rearing its clanging belfry in the sunlight. And it was also his own house that he wished to build, the edifice which would be his act of faith and adoration, the temple where he would be the pontiff, and triumph in company with the sweet memory of Bernadette, in full view of the spot of which both he and she had been so cruelly dispossessed. Naturally enough, bitterly as he felt that act of spoliation, the building of this new parish church was in some degree his revenge, his share of all the glory, besides being a task which would enable him to utilise both his militant activity and the fever that had been consuming him ever since he had ceased going to the Grotto, by reason of his soreness of heart.

At the outset of the new enterprise there was again a flash of enthusiasm. At the prospect of seeing all the life and all the money flow into the new city which was springing from the ground around the Basilica, the old town, which felt itself thrust upon one side, espoused the cause of its priest. The municipal council voted a sum of one hundred thousand francs, which, unfortunately, was not to be paid until the new church should be roofed in. Abbe Peyramale had already accepted the plans of his architect—plans which, he had insisted, should be on a grand scale—and had also treated with a contractor of Chartres, who engaged to complete the church in three or four years if the promised supplies of funds should be regularly forthcoming. The Abbe believed that offerings would assuredly continue raining down from all parts, and so he launched into this big enterprise without any anxiety, overflowing with a careless bravery, and fully expecting that Heaven would not abandon him on the road. He even fancied that he could rely upon the support of Monseigneur Jourdan, who had now succeeded Monseigneur Laurence as Bishop of Tarbes, for this prelate, after blessing the foundation-stone of the new church, had delivered an address in which he admitted that the enterprise was necessary and meritorious. And it seemed, too, as though Father Sempe, with his customary humility, had bowed to the inevitable and accepted this vexatious competition, which would compel him to relinquish a share of the plunder; for he now pretended to devote himself entirely to the management of the Grotto, and even allowed a collection-box for contributions to the building of the new parish church to be placed inside the Basilica.

Then, however, the secret, rageful struggle began afresh. Abbe Peyramale, who was a wretched manager, exulted on seeing his new church so rapidly take shape. The work was being carried on at a fast pace, and he troubled about nothing else, being still under the delusion that the Blessed Virgin would find whatever money might be needed. Thus he was quite stupefied when he at last perceived that the offerings were falling off, that the money of the faithful no longer reached him, as though, indeed, someone had secretly diverted its flow. And eventually the day came when he was unable to make the stipulated payments. In all this there had been so much skilfully combined strangulation, of which he only became aware later on. Father Sempe, however, had once more prevailed on the Bishop to grant his favour exclusively to the Grotto. There was even a talk of some confidential circulars distributed through the various dioceses, so that the many sums of money offered by the faithful should no longer be sent to the parish. The voracious, insatiable Grotto was bent upon securing everything, and to such a point were things carried that five hundred franc notes slipped into the collection-box at the Basilica were kept back; the box was rifled and the parish robbed. Abbe Peyramale, however, in his passion for the rising church, his child, continued fighting most desperately, ready if need were to give his blood. He had at first treated with the contractor in the name of the vestry; then, when he was at a loss how to pay, he treated in his own name. His life was bound up in the enterprise, he wore himself out in the heroic efforts which he made. Of the four hundred thousand francs that he had promised, he had only been able to pay two hundred thousand; and the municipal council still obstinately refused to hand over the hundred thousand francs which it had voted, until the new church should be covered in. This was acting against the town's real interests. However, it was said that Father Sempe was trying to bring influence to bear on the contractor. And, all at once, the work was stopped.

From that moment the death agony began. Wounded in the heart, the Abbe Peyramale, the broad-shouldered mountaineer with the leonine face, staggered and fell like an oak struck down by a thunderbolt. He took to his bed, and never left it alive. Strange stories circulated: it was said that Father Sempe had sought to secure admission to the parsonage under some pious pretext, but in reality to see if his much-dreaded adversary were really mortally stricken; and it was added, that it had been necessary to drive him from the sick-room, where his presence was an outrageous scandal. Then, when the unhappy priest, vanquished and steeped in bitterness, was dead, Father Sempe was seen triumphing at the funeral, from which the others had not dared to keep him away. It was affirmed that he openly displayed his abominable delight, that his face was radiant that day with the joy of victory. He was at last rid of the only man who had been an obstacle to his designs, whose legitimate authority he had feared. He would no longer be forced to share anything with anybody now that both the founders of Our Lady of Lourdes had been suppressed—Bernadette placed in a convent, and Abbe Peyramale lowered into the ground. The Grotto was now his own property, the alms would come to him alone, and he could do what he pleased with the eight hundred thousand francs* or so which were at his disposal every year. He would complete the gigantic works destined to make the Basilica a self-supporting centre, and assist in embellishing the new town in order to increase the isolation of the old one and seclude it behind its rock, like an insignificant parish submerged beneath the splendour of its all-powerful neighbour. All the money, all the sovereignty, would be his; he henceforth would reign.

However, although the works had been stopped, and the new parish church was slumbering inside its wooden fence, it was none the less more than half built. The vaulted aisles were already erected. And the imperfect pile remained there like a threat, for the town might some day attempt to finish it. Like Abbe Peyramale, therefore, it must be killed for good, turned into an irreparable ruin. The secret labour therefore continued, a work of refined cruelty and slow destruction. To begin with, the new parish priest, a simple-minded creature, was cowed to such a point that he no longer opened the envelopes containing remittances for the parish; all the registered letters were at once taken to the Fathers. Then the site selected for the new parish church was criticised, and the diocesan architect was induced to draw up a report stating that the old church was still in good condition and of ample size for the requirements of the community. Moreover, influence was brought to bear on the Bishop, and representations were made to him respecting the annoying features of the pecuniary difficulties which had arisen with the contractor. With a little imagination poor Peyramale was transformed into a violent, obstinate madman, through

---

* About 145,000 dollars.

whose undisciplined zeal the Church had almost been compromised. And, at last, the Bishop, forgetting that he himself had blessed the foundation-stone, issued a pastoral letter laying the unfinished church under interdict, and prohibiting all religious services in it. This was the supreme blow. Endless lawsuits had already begun; the contractor, who had only received two hundred thousand francs for the five hundred thousand francs' worth of work which had been executed, had taken proceedings against Abbe Peyramale's heir-at-law, the vestry, and the town, for the last still refused to pay over the amount which it had voted. At first the Prefect's Council declared itself incompetent to deal with the case, and when it was sent back to it by the Council of State, it rendered a judgment by which the town was condemned to pay the hundred thousand francs and the heir-at-law to finish the church. At the same time the vestry was put out of court. However, there was a fresh appeal to the Council of State, which quashed this judgment, and condemned the vestry, and, in default, the heir-at-law, to pay the contractor. Neither party being solvent, matters remained in this position. The lawsuits had lasted fifteen years. The town had now resignedly paid over the hundred thousand francs, and only two hundred thousand remained owing to the contractor. However, the costs and the accumulated interest had so increased the amount of indebtedness that it had risen to six hundred thousand francs; and as, on the other hand, it was estimated that four hundred thousand francs would be required to finish the church, a million was needed to save this young ruin from certain destruction. The Fathers of the Grotto were thenceforth able to sleep in peace; they had assassinated the poor church; it was as dead as Abbe Peyramale himself.

The bells of the Basilica rang out triumphantly, and Father Sempe reigned as a victor at the conclusion of that great struggle, that dagger warfare in which not only a man but stones also had been done to death in the shrouding gloom of intriguing sacristies. And old Lourdes, obstinate and unintelligent, paid a hard penalty for its mistake in not giving more support to its minister, who had died struggling, killed by his love for his parish, for now the new town did not cease to grow and prosper at the expense of the old one. All the wealth flowed to the former: the Fathers of the Grotto coined money, financed hotels and candle shops, and sold the water of the source, although a clause of their agreement with the municipality expressly prohibited them from carrying on any commercial pursuits.

The whole region began to rot and fester; the triumph of the Grotto had brought about such a passion for lucre, such a burning, feverish desire to possess and enjoy, that extraordinary perversion set in, growing worse and worse each day, and changing Bernadette's peaceful Bethlehem into a perfect Sodom or Gomorrah. Father Sempe had ensured the triumph of his Divinity by spreading human abominations all around and wrecking thousands of souls. Gigantic buildings rose from the ground, five or six millions of francs had already been expended, everything being sacrificed to the stern determination to leave the poor parish out in the cold and keep the entire plunder for self and friends. Those costly, colossal gradient ways had only been erected in order to avoid compliance with the Virgin's express desire that the faithful should come to the Grotto in procession. For to go down from the Basilica by the incline on the left, and climb up to it again by the incline on the right, could certainly not be called going to the Grotto in procession: it was simply so much revolving in a circle. However, the Fathers cared little about that; they had succeeded in compelling people to start from their premises and return to them, in order that they might be the sole proprietors of the affair, the opulent farmers who garnered the whole harvest. Abbe Peyramale lay buried in the crypt of his unfinished, ruined church, and Bernadette, who had long since dragged out her life of suffering in the depths of a convent far away, was now likewise sleeping the eternal sleep under a flagstone in a chapel.

Deep silence fell when Doctor Chassaigne had finished this long narrative. Then, with a painful effort, he rose to his feet again: "It will soon be ten o'clock, my dear child," said he, "and I want you to take a little rest. Let us go back."

Pierre followed him without speaking; and they retraced their steps toward the town at a more rapid pace.

"Ah! yes," resumed the doctor, "there were great iniquities and great sufferings in it all. But what else could you expect? Man spoils and corrupts the most beautiful things. And you cannot yet understand all the woeful sadness of the things of which I have been talking to you. You must see them, lay your hand on them. Would you like me to show you Bernadette's room and Abbe Peyramale's unfinished church this evening?"

"Yes, I should indeed," replied Pierre.

"Well, I will meet you in front of the Basilica after the four-o'clock procession, and you can come with me."

Then they spoke no further, each becoming absorbed in his reverie once more.

The Gave, now upon their right hand, was flowing through a deep gorge, a kind of cleft into which it plunged, vanishing from sight among the bushes. But at intervals a clear stretch of it, looking like unburnished silver, would appear to view; and, farther on, after a sudden turn in the road, they found it flowing in increased volume across a plain, where it spread at times into glassy sheets which must often have changed their beds, for the gravelly soil was ravined on all sides. The sun was now becoming very hot, and was already high in the heavens, whose limpid azure assumed a deeper tinge above the vast circle of mountains.

And it was at this turn of the road that Lourdes, still some distance away, reappeared to the eyes of Pierre and Doctor Chassaigne. In the splendid morning atmosphere, amid a flying dust of gold and purple rays, the town shone whitely on the horizon, its houses and monuments becoming more and more distinct at each step which brought them nearer. And the doctor, still silent, at last waved his arm with a broad, mournful gesture in order to call his companion's attention to this growing town, as though to a proof of all that he had been telling him. There, indeed, rising up in the dazzling daylight, was the evidence which confirmed his words.

The flare of the Grotto, fainter now that the sun was shining, could already be espied amidst the greenery. And soon afterwards the gigantic monumental works spread out: the quay with its freestone parapet skirting the Gave, whose course had been diverted; the new bridge connecting the new gardens with the recently opened boulevard; the colossal gradient ways, the massive church of the Rosary, and, finally, the slim, tapering Basilica, rising above all else with graceful pride. Of the new town spread all around the monuments, the wealthy city which had sprung, as though by enchantment, from the ancient impoverished soil, the great convents and the great hotels, you could, at this distance, merely distinguish a swarming of white facades and a scintillation of new slates; whilst, in confusion, far away, beyond the rocky mass on which the crumbling castle walls were profiled against the sky, appeared the humble roofs of the old town, a jumble of little time-worn roofs, pressing timorously against one another. And as a background to this vision of the life of yesterday and to-day, the little and the big Gers rose up beneath the splendour of the everlasting sun, and barred the horizon

ÉMILE ZOLA

with their bare slopes, which the oblique rays were tingeing with streaks of pink and yellow.

Doctor Chassaigne insisted on accompanying Pierre to the Hotel of the Apparitions, and only parted from him at its door, after reminding him of their appointment for the afternoon. It was not yet eleven o'clock. Pierre, whom fatigue had suddenly mastered, forced himself to eat before going to bed, for he realised that want of food was one of the chief causes of the weakness which had come over him. He fortunately found a vacant seat at the *table d' hote*, and made some kind of a *dejeuner*, half asleep all the time, and scarcely knowing what was served to him. Then he went up-stairs and flung himself on his bed, after taking care to tell the servant to awake him at three o'clock.

However, on lying down, the fever that consumed him at first prevented him from closing his eyes. A pair of gloves, forgotten in the next room, had reminded him of M. de Guersaint, who had left for Gavarnie before daybreak, and would only return in the evening. What a delightful gift was thoughtlessness, thought Pierre. For his own part, with his limbs worn out by weariness and his mind distracted, he was sad unto death. Everything seemed to conspire against his willing desire to regain the faith of his childhood. The tale of Abbe Peyramale's tragic adventures had simply aggravated the feeling of revolt which the story of Bernadette, chosen and martyred, had implanted in his breast. And thus he asked himself whether his search after the truth, instead of restoring his faith, would not rather lead him to yet greater hatred of ignorance and credulity, and to the bitter conviction that man is indeed all alone in the world, with naught to guide him save his reason.

At last he fell asleep, but visions continued hovering around him in his painful slumber. He beheld Lourdes, contaminated by Mammon, turned into a spot of abomination and perdition, transformed into a huge bazaar, where everything was sold, masses and souls alike! He beheld also Abbe Peyramale, dead and slumbering under the ruins of his church, among the nettles which ingratitude had sown there. And he only grew calm again, only tasted the delights of forgetfulness when a last pale, woeful vision had faded from his gaze—a vision of Bernadette upon her knees in a gloomy corner at Nevers, dreaming of her far-away work, which she was never, never to behold.

THE FOURTH DAY

I

The Bitterness of Death

At the Hospital of Our Lady of Dolours, that morning, Marie remained seated on her bed, propped up by pillows. Having spent the whole night at the Grotto, she had refused to let them take her back there. And, as Madame de Jonquiere approached her, to raise one of the pillows which was slipping from its place, she asked: "What day is it, madame?"

"Monday, my dear child."

"Ah! true. One so soon loses count of time. And, besides, I am so happy! It is to-day that the Blessed Virgin will cure me!"

She smiled divinely, with the air of a day-dreamer, her eyes gazing into vacancy, her thoughts so far away, so absorbed in her one fixed idea, that she beheld nothing save the certainty of her hope. Round about her, the Sainte-Honorine Ward was now quite deserted, all the patients, excepting Madame Vetu, who lay at the last extremity in the next bed, having already started for the Grotto. But Marie did not even notice her neighbour; she was delighted with the sudden stillness which had fallen. One of the windows overlooking the courtyard had been opened, and the glorious morning sunshine entered in one broad beam, whose golden dust was dancing over her bed and streaming upon her pale hands. It was indeed pleasant to find this room, so dismal at nighttime with its many beds of sickness, its unhealthy atmosphere, and its nightmare groans, thus suddenly filled with sunlight, purified by the morning air, and wrapped in such delicious silence! "Why don't you try to sleep a little?" maternally inquired Madame de Jonquiere. "You must be quite worn out by your vigil."

Marie, who felt so light and cheerful that she no longer experienced any pain, seemed surprised.

"But I am not at all tired, and I don't feel a bit sleepy. Go to sleep? Oh! no, that would be too sad. I should no longer know that I was going to be cured!"

At this the superintendent laughed. "Then why didn't you let them take you to the Grotto?" she asked. "You won't know what to do with yourself all alone here."

"I am not alone, madame, I am with her," replied Marie; and thereupon, her vision returning to her, she clasped her hands in ecstasy. "Last night, you know, I saw her bend her head towards me and smile. I quite understood her, I could hear her voice, although she never opened her lips. When the Blessed Sacrament passes at four o'clock I shall be cured."

Madame de Jonquiere tried to calm her, feeling rather anxious at the species of somnambulism in which she beheld her. However, the sick girl went on: "No, no, I am no worse, I am waiting. Only, you must surely see, madame, that there is no need for me to go to the Grotto this morning, since the appointment which she gave me is for four o'clock." And then the girl added in a lower tone: "Pierre will come for me at half-past three. At four o'clock I shall be cured."

The sunbeam slowly made its way up her bare arms, which were now almost transparent, so wasted had they become through illness; whilst her glorious fair hair, which had fallen over her shoulders, seemed like the very effulgence of the great luminary enveloping her. The trill of a bird came in from the courtyard, and quite enlivened the tremulous silence of the ward. Some child who could not be seen must also have been playing close by, for now and again a soft laugh could be heard ascending in the warm air which was so delightfully calm.

"Well," said Madame de Jonquiere by way of conclusion, "don't sleep then, as you don't wish to. But keep quite quiet, and it will rest you all the same."

Meantime Madame Vetu was expiring in the adjoining bed. They had not dared to take her to the Grotto, for fear they should see her die on the way. For some little time she had lain there with her eyes closed; and Sister Hyacinthe, who was watching, had beckoned to Madame Desagneaux in order to acquaint her with the bad opinion she had formed of the case. Both of them were now leaning over the dying woman, observing her with increasing anxiety. The mask upon her face had turned more yellow than ever, and now looked like a coating of mud; her eyes too had become more sunken, her lips seemed to have grown thinner, and the death rattle had begun, a slow, pestilential wheezing, polluted by the cancer which was finishing its destructive work. All at once she raised her eyelids, and was seized with fear on beholding those two faces bent over her own. Could her death be near, that they should thus be gazing at her? Immense sadness showed itself in her eyes, a despairing regret of life. It was not a vehement revolt, for she no longer had the strength to struggle; but what a frightful fate it was to have left her shop, her surroundings, and her husband, merely to come and die so far away; to have braved the abominable torture of such a journey, to have prayed both day and night, and then, instead of having her prayer granted, to die when others recovered!

However, she could do no more than murmur "Oh! how I suffer; oh! how I suffer. Do something, anything, to relieve this pain, I beseech you."

Little Madame Desagneaux, with her pretty milk-white face showing amidst her mass of fair, frizzy hair, was quite upset. She was not used to deathbed scenes, she would have given half her heart, as she expressed it, to see that poor woman recover. And she rose up and began to question Sister Hyacinthe, who was also in tears but already resigned, knowing as she did that salvation was assured when one died well. Could nothing really be done, however? Could not something be tried to ease the dying woman? Abbe Judaine had come and administered the last sacrament to her a couple of hours earlier that very morning. She now only had Heaven to look to; it was her only hope, for she had long since given up expecting aid from the skill of man.

"No, no! we must do something," exclaimed Madame Desagneaux. And thereupon she went and fetched Madame de Jonquiere from beside Marie's bed. "Look how this poor creature is suffering, madame!" she exclaimed. "Sister Hyacinthe says that she can only last a few hours longer. But we cannot leave her moaning like this. There are things which give relief. Why not call that young doctor who is here?"

"Of course we will," replied the superintendent. "We will send for him at once."

They seldom thought of the doctor in the wards. It only occurred to the ladies to send for him when a case was at its very worst, when one of their patients was howling with pain. Sister Hyacinthe, who herself felt surprised at not having thought of Ferrand, whom she believed to be in an adjoining room, inquired if she should fetch him.

"Certainly," was the reply. "Bring him as quickly as possible."

When the Sister had gone off, Madame de Jonquiere made Madame Desagneaux help her in slightly raising the dying woman's head, thinking that this might relieve her. The two ladies happened to be alone there that morning, all the other lady-hospitallers having gone to their devotions or their private affairs. However, from the end of the large deserted ward, where, amidst the warm quiver of the sunlight such sweet tranquillity prevailed, there still came at intervals the light laughter of the unseen child.

"Can it be Sophie who is making such a noise?" suddenly asked the lady-superintendent, whose nerves were somewhat upset by all the worry of the death which she foresaw. Then quickly walking to the end of the ward, she found that it was indeed Sophie Couteau—the young girl so miraculously healed the previous year—who, seated on the floor behind a bed, had been amusing herself, despite her fourteen years, in making a doll out of a few rags. She was now talking to it, so happy, so absorbed in her play, that she laughed quite heartily. "Hold yourself up, mademoiselle," said she. "Dance the polka, that I may see how you can do it! One! two! dance, turn, kiss the one you like best!"

Madame de Jonquiere, however, was now coming up. "Little girl," she said, "we have one of our patients here in great pain, and not expected to recover. You must not laugh so loud."

"Ah! madame, I didn't know," replied Sophie, rising up, and becoming quite serious, although still holding the doll in her hand. "Is she going to die, madame?"

"I fear so, my poor child."

Thereupon Sophie became quite silent. She followed the superintendent, and seated herself on an adjoining bed; whence, without the slightest sign of fear, but with her large eyes burning with curiosity, she began to watch Madame Vetu's death agony. In her nervous state, Madame Desagneaux was growing impatient at the delay in the doctor's arrival; whilst Marie, still enraptured, and resplendent in the sunlight, seemed unconscious of what was taking place about her, wrapt as she was in delightful expectancy of the miracle.

Not having found Ferrand in the small apartment near the linen-room which he usually occupied, Sister Hyacinthe was now searching for him all over the building. During the past two days the young doctor had become more bewildered than ever in that extraordinary hospital, where his assistance was only sought for the relief of death pangs. The small medicine-chest which he had brought with him proved quite useless; for there could be no thought of trying any course of treatment, as the sick were not there to be doctored, but simply to be cured by the lightning stroke of a miracle. And so he mainly confined himself to administering a few opium pills, in order to deaden the severer sufferings. He had been fairly amazed when accompanying Doctor Bonamy on a round through the wards. It had resolved itself into a mere stroll, the doctor, who had only come out of curiosity, taking no interest in the patients, whom he neither questioned nor examined. He solely concerned himself with the pretended cases of cure, stopping opposite those women whom he recognised from having seen them at his office where the miracles were verified. One of them had suffered from three complaints, only one of which the Blessed Virgin had so far deigned to cure; but great hopes were entertained respecting the other two. Sometimes, when a wretched woman, who the day before had claimed to be cured, was questioned with reference to her health, she would reply that her pains had returned to her. However, this never disturbed the doctor's serenity; ever conciliatory, the good man declared that Heaven would surely complete what Heaven had begun. Whenever there was an improvement in health, he would ask if it were not something to be thankful for. And, indeed, his constant saying was: "There's an improvement already; be patient!" What he most dreaded were the importunities of the lady-superintendents, who all wished to detain him to show him sundry extraordinary cases. Each prided herself on having the most serious illnesses, the most frightful, exceptional cases in her ward; so that she was eager to have them medically authenticated, in order that she might share in the triumph should cure supervene. One caught the doctor by the arm and assured him that she felt confident she had a leper in her charge; another entreated him to come and look at a young girl whose back, she said, was covered with fish's scales; whilst a third, whispering in his ear, gave him some terrible details about a married lady of the best society. He hastened away, however, refusing to see even one of them, or else simply promising to come back later on when he was not so busy. As he himself said, if he listened to all those ladies, the day would pass in useless consultations. However, he at last suddenly stopped opposite one of the miraculously cured inmates, and, beckoning Ferrand to his side, exclaimed: "Ah! now here is an interesting cure!" and Ferrand, utterly bewildered, had to listen to him whilst he described all the features of the illness, which had totally disappeared at the first immersion in the piscina.

At last Sister Hyacinthe, still wandering about, encountered Abbe Judaine, who informed her that the young doctor had just been summoned to the Family Ward. It was the fourth time he had gone thither to attend to Brother Isidore, whose sufferings were as acute as ever, and whom he could only fill with opium. In his agony, the Brother merely asked to be soothed a little, in order that he might gather together sufficient strength to return to the Grotto in the afternoon, as he had not been able to do so in the morning. However, his pains increased, and at last he swooned away.

When the Sister entered the ward she found the doctor seated at the missionary's bedside. "Monsieur Ferrand," she said, "come up-stairs with me to the Sainte-Honorine Ward at once. We have a patient there at the point of death."

He smiled at her; indeed, he never beheld her without feeling brighter and comforted. "I will come with you, Sister," he replied. "But you'll wait a minute, won't you? I must try to restore this poor man."

She waited patiently and made herself useful. The Family Ward, situated on the ground-floor, was also full of sunshine and fresh air which entered through three large windows opening on to a narrow strip of garden. In addition to Brother Isidore, only Monsieur Sabathier had remained in bed that morning, with the view of obtaining a little rest; whilst Madame Sabathier, taking advantage of the opportunity, had gone to purchase a few medals and pictures, which she intended for presents. Comfortably seated on his bed, his back supported by some pillows, the ex-professor was rolling the beads of a chaplet between his fingers. He was no longer praying, however, but merely continuing the operation in a mechanical manner, his eyes, meantime, fixed upon his neighbour, whose attack he was following with painful interest.

"Ah! Sister," said he to Sister Hyacinthe, who had drawn near, "that poor Brother fills me with admiration. Yesterday I doubted the Blessed Virgin for a moment, seeing that she did not deign to hear me, though I have been coming here for seven years past; but the example set me by that poor martyr, so resigned amidst his torments, has quite shamed me for my want of faith. You can have no idea how grievously he suffers, and you should see him at the Grotto, with his eyes glowing with divine hope! It is really sublime! I only know of one picture at the Louvre—a picture by some unknown Italian master—in which there is the head of a monk beatified by a similar faith."

The man of intellect, the ex-university-professor, reared on literature and art, was reappearing in this poor old fellow, whose life had been blasted, and who had desired to become a free patient, one of the poor of the earth, in order to move the pity of Heaven. He again began thinking of his own case, and with tenacious hopefulness, which the futility of seven journeys to Lourdes had failed to destroy, he added: "Well, I still have this afternoon, since we sha'n't leave till to-morrow.

The water is certainly very cold, but I shall let them dip me a last time; and all the morning I have been praying and asking pardon for my revolt of yesterday. When the Blessed Virgin chooses to cure one of her children, it only takes her a second to do so; is that not so, Sister? May her will be done, and blessed be her name!"

Passing the beads of the chaplet more slowly between his fingers, he again began saying his "Aves" and "Paters," whilst his eyelids drooped on his flabby face, to which a childish expression had been returning during the many years that he had been virtually cut off from the world.

Meantime Ferrand had signalled to Brother Isidore's sister, Marthe, to come to him. She had been standing at the foot of the bed with her arms hanging down beside her, showing the tearless resignation of a poor, narrow-minded girl whilst she watched that dying man whom she worshipped. She was no more than a faithful dog; she had accompanied her brother and spent her scanty savings, without being of any use save to watch him suffer. Accordingly, when the doctor told her to take the invalid in her arms and raise him up a little, she felt quite happy at being of some service at last. Her heavy, freckled, mournful face actually grew bright.

"Hold him," said the doctor, "whilst I try to give him this."

When she had raised him, Ferrand, with the aid of a small spoon, succeeded in introducing a few drops of liquid between his set teeth. Almost immediately the sick man opened his eyes and heaved a deep sigh. He was calmer already; the opium was taking effect and dulling the pain which he felt burning his right side, as though a red-hot iron were being applied to it. However, he remained so weak that, when he wished to speak, it became necessary to place one's ear close to his mouth in order to catch what he said. With a slight sign he had begged Ferrand to bend over him. "You are the doctor, monsieur, are you not?" he faltered. "Give me sufficient strength that I may go once more to the Grotto, this afternoon. I am certain that, if I am able to go, the Blessed Virgin will cure me."

"Why, of course you shall go," replied the young man. "Don't you feel ever so much better?"

"Oh! ever so much better—no! I know very well what my condition is, because I saw many of our Brothers die, out there in Senegal. When the liver is attacked and the abscess has worked its way outside, it means the end. Sweating, fever, and delirium follow. But the Blessed Virgin will touch the sore with her little finger and it will be healed. Oh! I implore you all, take me to the Grotto, even if I should be unconscious!"

Sister Hyacinthe had also approached, and leant over him. "Be easy, dear Brother," said she. "You shall go to the Grotto after *dejeuner*, and we will all pray for you."

At length, in despair at these delays and extremely anxious about Madame Vetu, she was able to get Ferrand away. Still, the Brother's state filled her with pity; and, as they ascended the stairs, she questioned the doctor, asking him if there were really no more hope. The other made a gesture expressive of absolute hopelessness. It was madness to come to Lourdes when one was in such a condition. However, he hastened to add, with a smile: "I beg your pardon, Sister. You know that I am unfortunate enough not to be a believer."

But she smiled in her turn, like an indulgent friend who tolerates the shortcomings of those she loves. "Oh! that doesn't matter," she replied. "I know you; you're all the same a good fellow. Besides, we see so many people, we go amongst such pagans that it would be difficult to shock us."

Up above, in the Sainte-Honorine Ward, they found Madame Vetu still moaning, a prey to most intolerable suffering. Madame de Jonquiere and Madame Desagneaux had remained beside the bed, their faces turning pale, their hearts distracted by that death-cry, which never ceased. And when they consulted Ferrand in a whisper, he merely replied, with a slight shrug of the shoulders, that she was a lost woman, that it was only a question of hours, perhaps merely of minutes. All he could do was to stupefy her also, in order to ease the atrocious death agony which he foresaw. She was watching him, still conscious, and also very obedient, never refusing the medicine offered her. Like the others, she now had but one ardent desire—to go back to the Grotto— and she gave expression to it in the stammering accents of a child who fears that its prayer may not be granted: "To the Grotto—will you? To the Grotto!"

"You shall be taken there by-and-by, I promise you," said Sister Hyacinthe. "But you must be good. Try to sleep a little to gain some strength."

The sick woman appeared to sink into a doze, and Madame de Jonquiere then thought that she might take Madame Desagneaux with her to the other end of the ward to count the linen, a troublesome business, in which they became quite bewildered, as some of the articles were missing. Meantime Sophie, seated on the bed opposite Madame Vetu, had not stirred. She had laid her doll on her lap, and was waiting for the lady's death, since they had told her that she was about to die. Sister Hyacinthe, moreover, had remained beside the dying woman, and, unwilling to waste her time, had taken a needle and cotton to mend some patient's bodice which had a hole in the sleeve.

"You'll stay a little while with us, won't you?" she asked Ferrand.

The latter, who was still watching Madame Vetu, replied: "Yes, yes. She may go off at any moment. I fear hemorrhage." Then, catching sight of Marie on the neighbouring bed, he added in a lower voice: "How is she? Has she experienced any relief?"

"No, not yet. Ah, dear child! we all pray for her very sincerely. She is so young, so sweet, and so sorely afflicted. Just look at her now! Isn't she pretty? One might think her a saint amid all this sunshine, with her large, ecstatic eyes, and her golden hair shining like an aureola!"

Ferrand watched Marie for a moment with interest. Her absent air, her indifference to all about her, the ardent faith, the internal joy which so completely absorbed her, surprised him. "She will recover," he murmured, as though giving utterance to a prognostic. "She will recover."

Then he rejoined Sister Hyacinthe, who had seated herself in the embrasure of the lofty window, which stood wide open, admitting the warm air of the courtyard. The sun was now creeping round, and only a narrow golden ray fell upon her white coif and wimple. Ferrand stood opposite to her, leaning against the window bar and watching her while she sewed. "Do you know, Sister," said he, "this journey to Lourdes, which I undertook to oblige a friend, will be one of the few delights of my life."

She did not understand him, but innocently asked: "Why so?"

"Because I have found you again, because I am here with you, assisting you in your admirable work. And if you only knew how grateful I am to you, what sincere affection and reverence I feel for you!"

She raised her head to look him straight in the face, and began jesting without the least constraint. She was really delicious, with her pure lily-white complexion, her small laughing mouth, and adorable blue eyes which ever smiled. And you could realise that she had grown up in all innocence and devotion, slender and supple, with all the appearance of a girl hardly in her teens.

"What! You are so fond of me as all that!" she exclaimed. "Why?"

"Why I'm fond of you? Because you are the best, the most consoling, the most sisterly of beings. You are the sweetest memory in my life, the memory I evoke whenever I need to be encouraged and sustained. Do you no longer remember the month we spent together, in my poor room, when I was so ill and you so affectionately nursed me?"

"Of course, of course I remember it! Why, I never had so good a patient as you. You took all I offered you; and when I tucked you in, after changing your linen, you remained as still as a little child."

So speaking, she continued looking at him, smiling ingenuously the while. He was very handsome and robust, in the very prime of youth, with a rather pronounced nose, superb eyes, and red lips showing under his black moustache. But she seemed to be simply pleased at seeing him there before her moved almost to tears.

"Ah! Sister, I should have died if it hadn't been for you," he said. "It was through having you that I was cured."

Then, as they gazed at one another, with tender gaiety of heart, the memory of that adorable month recurred to them. They no longer heard Madame Vetu's death moans, nor beheld the ward littered with beds, and, with all its disorder, resembling some infirmary improvised after a public catastrophe. They once more found themselves in a small attic at the top of a dingy house in old Paris, where air and light only reached them through a tiny window opening on to a sea of roofs. And how charming it was to be alone there together—he who had been prostrated by fever, she who had appeared there like a good angel, who had quietly come from her convent like a comrade who fears nothing! It was thus that she nursed women, children, and men, as chance ordained, feeling perfectly happy so long as she had something to do, some sufferer to relieve. She never displayed any consciousness of her sex; and he, on his side, never seemed to have suspected that she might be a woman, except it were for the extreme softness of her hands, the caressing accents of her voice, the beneficent gentleness of her manner; and yet all the tender love of a mother, all the affection of a sister, radiated from her person. During three weeks, as she had said, she had nursed him like a child, helping him in and out of bed, and rendering him every necessary attention, without the slightest embarrassment or repugnance, the holy purity born of suffering and charity shielding them both the while. They were indeed far removed from the frailties of life. And when he became convalescent, what a happy existence began, how joyously they laughed, like two old friends! She still watched over him, scolding

ÉMILE ZOLA

him and gently slapping his arms when he persisted in keeping them uncovered. He would watch her standing at the basin, washing him a shirt in order to save him the trifling expense of employing a laundress. No one ever came up there; they were quite alone, thousands of miles away from the world, delighted with this solitude, in which their youth displayed such fraternal gaiety.

"Do you remember, Sister, the morning when I was first able to walk about?" asked Ferrand. "You helped me to get up, and supported me whilst I awkwardly stumbled about, no longer knowing how to use my legs. We did laugh so."

"Yes, yes, you were saved, and I was very pleased."

"And the day when you brought me some cherries—I can see it all again: myself reclining on my pillows, and you seated at the edge of the bed, with the cherries lying between us in a large piece of white paper. I refused to touch them unless you ate some with me. And then we took them in turn, one at a time, until the paper was emptied; and they were very nice."

"Yes, yes, very nice. It was the same with the currant syrup: you would only drink it when I took some also."

Thereupon they laughed yet louder; these recollections quite delighted them. But a painful sigh from Madame Vetu brought them back to the present. Ferrand leant over and cast a glance at the sick woman, who had not stirred. The ward was still full of a quivering peacefulness, which was only broken by the clear voice of Madame Desagneaux counting the linen. Stifling with emotion, the young man resumed in a lower tone: "Ah! Sister, were I to live a hundred years, to know every joy, every pleasure, I should never love another woman as I love you!"

Then Sister Hyacinthe, without, however, showing any confusion, bowed her head and resumed her sewing. An almost imperceptible blush tinged her lily-white skin with pink.

"I also love you well, Monsieur Ferrand," she said, "but you must not make me vain. I only did for you what I do for so many others. It is my business, you see. And there was really only one pleasant thing about it all, that the Almighty cured you."

They were now again interrupted. La Grivotte and Elise Rouquet had returned from the Grotto before the others. La Grivotte at once squatted down on her mattress on the floor, at the foot of Madame Vetu's bed, and, taking a piece of bread from her pocket, proceeded to devour it. Ferrand, since the day before, had felt some interest in this consumptive patient, who was traversing such a curious phase of agitation, a prey to an inordinate appetite and a feverish need of motion. For the moment, however, Elise Rouquet's case interested him still more; for it had now become evident that the lupus, the sore which was eating away her face, was showing signs of cure. She had continued bathing her face at the miraculous fountain, and had just come from the Verification Office, where Doctor Bonamy had triumphed. Ferrand, quite surprised, went and examined the sore, which, although still far from healed, was already paler in colour and slightly desiccated, displaying all the symptoms of gradual cure. And the case seemed to him so curious, that he resolved to make some notes upon it for one of his old masters at the medical college, who was studying the nervous origin of certain skin diseases due to faulty nutrition.

"Have you felt any pricking sensation?" he asked.

"Not at all, monsieur," she replied. "I bathe my face and tell my beads with my whole soul, and that is all."

La Grivotte, who was vain and jealous, and ever since the day before had been going in triumph among the crowds, thereupon called to the doctor. "I say, monsieur, I am cured, cured, cured completely!"

He waved his hand to her in a friendly way, but refused to examine her. "I know, my girl. There is nothing more the matter with you."

Just then Sister Hyacinthe called to him. She had put her sewing down on seeing Madame Vetu raise herself in a frightful fit of nausea. In spite of her haste, however, she was too late with the basin; the sick woman had brought up another discharge of black matter, similar to soot; but, this time, some blood was mixed with it, little specks of violet-coloured blood. It was the hemorrhage coming, the near end which Ferrand had been dreading.

"Send for the superintendent," he said in a low voice, seating himself at the bedside.

Sister Hyacinthe ran for Madame de Jonquiere. The linen having been counted, she found her deep in conversation with her daughter Raymonde, at some distance from Madame Desagneaux, who was washing her hands.

Raymonde had just escaped for a few minutes from the refectory, where she was on duty. This was the roughest of her labours. The long narrow room, with its double row of greasy tables, its sickening smell of food and misery, quite disgusted her. And taking advantage of the half-hour still remaining before the return of the patients, she had hurried up-stairs, where, out of breath, with a rosy face and shining eyes, she had thrown her arms around her mother's neck.

"Ah! mamma," she cried, "what happiness! It's settled!"

Amazed, her head buzzing, busy with the superintendence of her ward, Madame de Jonquiere did not understand. "What's settled, my child?" she asked.

Then Raymonde lowered her voice, and, with a faint blush, replied: "My marriage!"

It was now the mother's turn to rejoice. Lively satisfaction appeared upon her face, the fat face of a ripe, handsome, and still agreeable woman. She at once beheld in her mind's eye their little lodging in the Rue Vaneau, where, since her husband's death, she had reared her daughter with great difficulty upon the few thousand francs he had left her. This marriage, however, meant a return to life, to society, the good old times come back once more.

"Ah! my child, how happy you make me!" she exclaimed.

But a feeling of uneasiness suddenly restrained her. God was her witness that for three years past she had been coming to Lourdes through pure motives of charity, for the one great joy of nursing His beloved invalids. Perhaps, had she closely examined her conscience, she might, behind her devotion, have found some trace of her fondness for authority, which rendered her present managerial duties extremely pleasant to her. However, the hope of finding a husband for her daughter among the suitable young men who swarmed at the Grotto was certainly her last thought. It was a thought which came to her, of course, but merely as something that was possible, though she never mentioned it. However, her happiness, wrung an avowal from her:

"Ah! my child, your success doesn't surprise me. I prayed to the Blessed Virgin for it this morning."

Then she wished to be quite sure, and asked for further information. Raymonde had not yet told her of her long walk leaning on Gerard's arm the day before, for she did not wish to speak of such things until she was triumphant, certain of having at last secured a husband. And now it was indeed settled, as she had exclaimed so gaily: that very morning she had again seen the young man at the Grotto, and he had formally become engaged to her. M. Berthaud would undoubtedly ask for her hand on his cousin's behalf before they took their departure from Lourdes.

"Well," declared Madame de Jonquiere, who was now convinced, smiling, and delighted at heart, "I hope you will be happy, since you are so sensible and do not need my aid to bring your affairs to a successful issue. Kiss me."

It was at this moment that Sister Hyacinthe arrived to announce Madame Vetu's imminent death. Raymonde at once ran off. And Madame Desagneaux, who was wiping her hands, began to complain of the lady-assistants, who had all disappeared precisely on the morning when they were most wanted. "For instance," said she, "there's Madame Volmar. I should like to know where she can have got to. She has not been seen, even for an hour, ever since our arrival."

"Pray leave Madame Volmar alone!" replied Madame de Jonquiere with some asperity. "I have already told you that she is ill."

They both hastened to Madame Vetu. Ferrand stood there waiting; and Sister Hyacinthe having asked him if there were indeed nothing to be done, he shook his head. The dying woman, relieved by her first emesis, now lay inert, with closed eyes. But, a second time, the frightful nausea returned to her, and she brought up another discharge of black matter mingled with violet-coloured blood. Then she had another short interval of calm, during which she noticed La Grivotte, who was greedily devouring her hunk of bread on the mattress on the floor.

"She is cured, isn't she?" the poor woman asked, feeling that she herself was dying.

La Grivotte heard her, and exclaimed triumphantly: "Oh, yes, madame, cured, cured, cured completely!"

For a moment Madame Vetu seemed overcome by a miserable feeling of grief, the revolt of one who will not succumb while others continue to live. But almost immediately she became resigned, and they heard her add very faintly, "It is the young ones who ought to remain."

Then her eyes, which remained wide open, looked round, as though bidding farewell to all those persons, whom she seemed surprised to see about her. She attempted to smile as she encountered the eager gaze of curiosity which little Sophie Couteau still fixed upon her: the charming child had come to kiss her that very morning, in her bed. Elise Rouquet, who troubled herself about nobody, was meantime holding her hand-glass, absorbed in the contemplation of her face, which seemed to her to be growing beautiful, now that the sore was healing. But what especially charmed the dying woman was the sight of Marie, so lovely in her ecstasy. She watched her for a long time, constantly attracted towards her, as towards a vision of light and joy. Perhaps she fancied that she already beheld one of the saints of Paradise amid the glory of the sun.

Suddenly, however, the fits of vomiting returned, and now she solely brought up blood, vitiated blood, the colour of claret. The rush was so great that it bespattered the sheet, and ran all over the bed. In vain did Madame de Jonquiere and Madame Desagneaux bring cloths; they were both very pale and scarce able to remain standing. Ferrand, knowing how powerless he was, had withdrawn to the window, to the very spot where he had so lately experienced such delicious emotion; and with an instinctive movement, of which she was surely unconscious, Sister Hyacinthe had likewise returned to that happy window, as though to be near him.

"Really, can you do nothing?" she inquired.

"No, nothing! She will go off like that, in the same way as a lamp that has burnt out."

Madame Vetu, who was now utterly exhausted, with a thin red stream still flowing from her mouth, looked fixedly at Madame de Jonquiere whilst faintly moving her lips. The lady-superintendent thereupon bent over her and heard these slowly uttered words:

"About my husband, madame—the shop is in the Rue Mouffetard—oh! it's quite a tiny one, not far from the Gobelins.—He's a clockmaker, he is; he couldn't come with me, of course, having to attend to the business; and he will be very much put out when he finds I don't come back.—Yes, I cleaned the jewelry and did the errands—" Then her voice grew fainter, her words disjointed by the death rattle, which began. "Therefore, madame, I beg you will write to him, because I haven't done so, and now here's the end.—Tell him my body had better remain here at Lourdes, on account of the expense.—And he must marry again; it's necessary for one in trade—his cousin—tell him his cousin—"

The rest became a confused murmur. Her weakness was too great, her breath was halting. Yet her eyes continued open and full of life, amid her pale, yellow, waxy mask. And those eyes seemed to fix themselves despairingly on the past, on all that which soon would be no more: the little clockmaker's shop hidden away in a populous neighbourhood; the gentle humdrum existence, with a toiling husband who was ever bending over his watches; the great pleasures of Sunday, such as watching children fly their kites upon the fortifications. And at last these staring eyes gazed vainly into the frightful night which was gathering.

A last time did Madame de Jonquiere lean over her, seeing that her lips were again moving. There came but a faint breath, a voice from far away, which distantly murmured in an accent of intense grief: "She did not cure me."

And then Madame Vetu expired, very gently.

As though this were all that she had been waiting for, little Sophie Couteau jumped from the bed quite satisfied, and went off to play with her doll again at the far end of the ward. Neither La Grivotte, who was finishing her bread, nor Elise Rouquet, busy with her mirror, noticed the catastrophe. However, amidst the cold breath which seemingly swept by, while Madame de Jonquiere and Madame Desagneaux—the latter of whom was unaccustomed to the sight of death—were whispering together in agitation, Marie emerged from the expectant rapture in which the continuous, unspoken prayer of her whole being had plunged her so long. And when she understood what had happened, a feeling of sisterly compassion—the compassion of a suffering companion, on her side certain of cure—brought tears to her eyes.

"Ah! the poor woman!" she murmured; "to think that she has died so far from home, in such loneliness, at the hour when others are being born anew!"

Ferrand, who, in spite of professional indifference, had also been stirred by the scene, stepped forward to verify the death; and it was on a sign from him that Sister Hyacinthe turned up the sheet, and threw it over the dead woman's face, for there could be no question of removing the corpse at that moment. The patients were now returning from the Grotto in bands, and the ward, hitherto so calm, so full of sunshine, was again filling with the tumult of wretchedness and pain—deep coughing and feeble shuffling, mingled with a noisome smell—a pitiful display, in fact, of well-nigh every human infirmity.

II

The Service at the Grotto

On that day, Monday, the crowd at the Grotto, was enormous. It was the last day that the national pilgrimage would spend at Lourdes, and Father Fourcade, in his morning address, had said that it would be necessary to make a supreme effort of fervour and faith to obtain from Heaven all that it might be willing to grant in the way of grace and prodigious cure. So, from two o'clock in the afternoon, twenty thousand pilgrims were assembled there, feverish, and agitated by the most ardent hopes. From minute to minute the throng continued increasing, to such a point, indeed, that Baron Suire became alarmed, and came out of the Grotto to say to Berthaud: "My friend, we shall be overwhelmed, that's certain. Double your squads, bring your men closer together."

The Hospitality of Our Lady of Salvation was alone entrusted with the task of keeping order, for there were neither guardians nor policemen, of any sort present; and it was for this reason that the President of the Association was so alarmed. However, Berthaud, under grave circumstances, was a leader whose words commanded attention, and who was endowed with energy that could be relied on.

"Be easy," said he; "I will be answerable for everything. I shall not move from here until the four-o'clock procession has passed by."

Nevertheless, he signalled to Gerard to approach.

"Give your men the strictest instructions," he said to him. "Only those persons who have cards should be allowed to pass. And place your men nearer each other; tell them to hold the cord tight."

Yonder, beneath the ivy which draped the rock, the Grotto opened, with the eternal flaring of its candles. From a distance it looked rather squat and misshapen, a very narrow and modest aperture for the breath of the Infinite which issued from it, turning all faces pale and bowing every head. The statue of the Virgin had become a mere white spot, which seemed to move amid the quiver of the atmosphere, heated by the small yellow flames. To see everything it was necessary to raise oneself; for the silver altar, the harmonium divested of its housing, the heap of bouquets flung there, and the votive offerings streaking the smoky walls were scarcely distinguishable from behind the railing. And the day was lovely; never yet had a purer sky expanded above the immense crowd; the softness of the breeze in particular seemed delicious after the storm of the night, which had brought down the over-oppressive heat of the two first days.

Gerard had to fight his way with his elbows in order to repeat the orders to his men. The crowd had already begun pushing. "Two more men here!" he called. "Come, four together, if necessary, and hold the rope well!"

The general impulse was instinctive and invincible; the twenty thousand persons assembled there were drawn towards the Grotto by an irresistible attraction, in which burning curiosity mingled with the thirst for mystery. All eyes converged, every mouth, hand, and body was borne towards the pale glitter of the candles and the white moving speck of the marble Virgin. And, in order that the large space reserved to the sick, in front of the railings, might not be invaded by the swelling mob, it had been necessary to inclose it with a stout rope which the bearers at intervals of two or three yards grasped with both hands. Their orders were to let nobody pass excepting the sick provided with hospital cards and the few persons to whom special authorisations had been granted. They limited themselves, therefore, to raising the cords and then letting them fall behind the chosen ones, without heeding the supplications of the others. In fact they even showed themselves somewhat rough, taking a certain pleasure in exercising the authority with which they were invested for a day. In truth, however, they were very much pushed about, and had to support each other and resist with all the strength of their loins to avoid being swept away.

While the benches before the Grotto and the vast reserved space were filling with sick people, handcarts, and stretchers, the crowd, the immense crowd, swayed about on the outskirts. Starting from the Place du Rosaire, it extended to the bottom of the promenade along the Gave, where the pavement throughout its entire length was black with people, so dense a human sea that all circulation was prevented. On the parapet was an interminable line of women—most of them seated, but some few standing so as to see the better—and almost all carrying silk parasols, which, with holiday-like gaiety, shimmered in the sunlight. The managers had wished to keep a path open in order that the sick might be brought along; but it was ever being invaded and obstructed, so that the carts and stretchers remained on the road, submerged and lost until a bearer freed them. Nevertheless, the great tramping was that of a docile flock, an innocent, lamb-like crowd; and it was only the involuntary pushing, the blind rolling towards the light of the candles that had to be contended against. No accident had ever happened there, notwithstanding the excitement, which gradually increased and threw the people into the unruly delirium of faith.

However, Baron Suire again forced his way through the throng. "Berthaud! Berthaud!" he called, "see that the *defile* is conducted less rapidly. There are women and children stifling."

This time Berthaud gave a sign of impatience. "Ah! hang it, I can't be everywhere! Close the gate for a moment if it's necessary."

It was a question of the march through the Grotto which went on throughout the afternoon. The faithful were permitted to enter by the door on the left, and made their exit by that on the right.

"Close the gate!" exclaimed the Baron. "But that would be worse; they would all get crushed against it!"

As it happened Gerard was there, thoughtlessly talking for an instant with Raymonde, who was standing on the other side of the cord, holding a bowl of milk which she was about to carry to a paralysed old woman; and Berthaud ordered the young fellow to post two men at the entrance gate of the iron railing, with instructions only to allow the pilgrims to enter by tens. When Gerard had executed this order, and returned, he found Berthaud laughing and joking with Raymonde. She went off on her errand, however, and the two men stood watching her while she made the paralysed woman drink.

"She is charming, and it's settled, eh?" said Berthaud. "You are going to marry her, aren't you?"

"I shall ask her mother to-night. I rely upon you to accompany me."

"Why, certainly. You know what I told you. Nothing could be more sensible. The uncle will find you a berth before six months are over."

A push of the crowd separated them, and Berthaud went off to make sure whether the march through the Grotto was now being accomplished in a methodical manner, without any crushing. For hours the same unbroken tide rolled in—women, men, and children from all parts of the world, all who chose, all who passed that way. As a result, the crowd was singularly mixed: there were beggars in rags beside neat *bourgeois*, peasants of either sex, well dressed ladies, servants with bare hair, young girls with bare feet, and others with pomatumed hair and foreheads bound with ribbons. Admission was free; the mystery was open to all, to unbelievers as well as to the faithful, to those who were solely influenced by curiosity as well as to those who entered with their hearts faint with love. And it was a sight to see them, all almost equally affected by the tepid odour of the wax, half stifling in the heavy tabernacle air which gathered beneath the rocky vault, and lowering their eyes for fear of slipping on the gratings. Many stood there bewildered, not even bowing, examining the things around with the covert uneasiness of indifferent folks astray amidst the redoubtable mysteries of a sanctuary. But the devout crossed themselves, threw letters, deposited candles and bouquets, kissed the rock below the Virgin's statue, or else rubbed their chaplets, medals, and other small objects of piety against it, as the contact sufficed to bless them. And the *defile* continued, continued without end during days and months as it had done for years; and it seemed as if the whole world, all the miseries and sufferings of humanity, came in turn and passed in the same hypnotic, contagious kind of round, through that rocky nook, ever in search of happiness.

When Berthaud had satisfied himself that everything was working well, he walked about like a mere spectator, superintending his men. Only one matter remained to trouble him: the procession of the Blessed Sacrament, during which such frenzy burst forth that accidents were always to be feared.

This last day seemed likely to be a very fervent one, for he already felt a tremor of exalted faith rising among the crowd. The treatment needed for miraculous care was drawing to an end; there had been the fever of the journey, the besetting influence of the same endlessly repeated hymns, and the stubborn continuation of the same religious exercises; and ever and ever the conversation had been turned on miracles, and the mind fixed on the divine illumination of the Grotto. Many, not having slept for three nights, had reached a state of hallucination, and walked about in a rageful dream. No repose was granted them, the continual prayers were like whips lashing their souls. The appeals to the Blessed Virgin never ceased; priest followed priest in the pulpit, proclaiming the universal dolour and directing the despairing supplications of the throng, during the whole time that the sick remained with hands clasped and eyes raised to heaven before the pale, smiling, marble statue.

At that moment the white stone pulpit against the rock on the right of the Grotto was occupied by a priest from Toulouse, whom Berthaud knew, and to whom he listened for a moment with an air of approval.

He was a stout man with an unctuous diction, famous for his rhetorical successes. However, all eloquence here consisted in displaying the strength of one's lungs in a violent delivery of the phrase or cry which the whole crowd had to repeat; for the addresses were nothing more than so much vociferation interspersed with "Ayes" and "Paters."

The priest, who had just finished the Rosary, strove to increase his stature by stretching his short legs, whilst shouting the first appeal of the litanies which he improvised, and led in his own way, according to the inspiration which possessed him.

"Mary, we love thee!" he called.

And thereupon the crowd repeated in a lower, confused, and broken tone: "Mary, we love thee!"

From that moment there was no stopping. The voice of the priest rang out at full swing, and the voices of the crowd responded in a dolorous murmur:

"Mary, thou art our only hope!"

"Mary, thou art our only hope!"

"Pure Virgin, make us purer, among the pure!"

"Pure Virgin, make us purer, among the pure!"

"Powerful Virgin, save our sick!"

"Powerful Virgin, save our sick!"

Often, when the priest's imagination failed him, or he wished to thrust a cry home with greater force, he would repeat it thrice; while the docile crowd would do the same, quivering under the enervating effect of the persistent lamentation, which increased the fever.

The litanies continued, and Berthaud went back towards the Grotto. Those who defiled through it beheld an extraordinary sight when they turned and faced the sick. The whole of the large space between the cords was occupied by the thousand or twelve hundred patients whom the national pilgrimage had brought with it; and beneath the vast, spotless sky on that radiant day there was the most heart-rending jumble of sufferers that one could behold. The three hospitals of Lourdes had emptied their chambers of horror. To begin with, those who were still able to remain seated had been piled upon the benches. Many of them, however, were propped up with cushions, whilst others kept shoulder to shoulder, the strong ones supporting the weak. Then, in front of the benches, before the Grotto itself, were the more grievously afflicted sufferers lying at full length; the flagstones disappearing from view beneath this woeful assemblage, which was like a large, stagnant pool of horror. There was an indescribable block of vehicles, stretchers, and mattresses. Some of the invalids in little boxes not unlike coffins had raised themselves up and showed above the others, but the majority lay almost on a level with the ground. There were some lying fully dressed on the check-patterned ticks of mattresses; whilst others had been brought with their bedding, so that only their heads and pale hands were seen outside the sheets. Few of these pallets were clean. Some pillows of dazzling whiteness, which by a last feeling of coquetry had been trimmed with embroidery, alone shone out among all the filthy wretchedness of all the rest—a fearful collection of rags, worn-out blankets, and linen splashed with stains. And all were pushed, squeezed, piled up by chance as they came, women, men, children, and priests, people in nightgowns beside people who were fully attired being jumbled together in the blinding light of day.

And all forms of disease were there, the whole frightful procession which, twice a day, left the hospitals to wend its way through horrified Lourdes. There were the heads eaten away by eczema, the foreheads crowned with roseola, and the noses and mouths which elephantiasis had transformed into shapeless snouts. Next, the dropsical ones, swollen out like leathern bottles; the rheumatic ones with twisted hands and swollen feet, like bags stuffed full of rags; and a sufferer from hydrocephalus, whose huge and weighty skull fell backwards. Then the consumptive ones, with livid skins, trembling with fever, exhausted by dysentery, wasted to skeletons. Then the deformities, the contractions, the twisted trunks, the twisted arms, the necks all awry; all the poor broken, pounded creatures, motionless in their tragic, marionette-like postures. Then the poor rachitic girls displaying their waxen complexions and slender necks eaten into by sores; the yellow-faced, besotted-looking women in the painful stupor which falls on unfortunate creatures devoured by cancer; and the others who turned pale, and dared not move, fearing as they did the shock of the tumours whose weighty pain was stifling them. On the benches sat bewildered deaf women, who heard nothing, but sang on all the same, and blind ones with heads erect, who remained for hours turned toward the statue of the Virgin which they could not see. And there was also the woman stricken with imbecility, whose nose was eaten away, and who laughed with a terrifying laugh, displaying the black, empty cavern of her mouth; and then the epileptic woman, whom a recent attack had left as pale as death, with froth still at the corners of her lips.

ÉMILE ZOLA

But sickness and suffering were no longer of consequence, since they were all there, seated or stretched with their eyes upon the Grotto. The poor, fleshless, earthy-looking faces became transfigured, and began to glow with hope. Anchylosed hands were joined, heavy eyelids found the strength to rise, exhausted voices revived as the priest shouted the appeals. At first there was nothing but indistinct stuttering, similar to slight puffs of air rising, here and there above the multitude. Then the cry ascended and spread through the crowd itself from one to the other end of the immense square.

"Mary, conceived without sin, pray for us!" cried the priest in his thundering voice.

And the sick and the pilgrims repeated louder and louder: "Mary, conceived without sin, pray for us!"

Then the flow of the litany set in, and continued with increasing speed:

"Most pure Mother, most chaste Mother, thy children are at thy feet!"

"Most pure Mother, most chaste Mother, thy children are at thy feet!"

"Queen of the Angels, say but a word, and our sick shall be healed!"

"Queen of the Angels, say but a word, and our sick shall be healed!"

In the second row of sufferers, near the pulpit, was M. Sabathier, who had asked to be brought there early, wishing to choose his place like an old *habitue* who knew the cosy corners. Moreover, it seemed to him that it was of paramount importance that he should be as near as possible, under the very eyes of the Virgin, as though she required to see her faithful in order not to forget them. However, for the seven years that he had been coming there he had nursed this one hope of being some day noticed by her, of touching her, and of obtaining his cure, if not by selection, at least by seniority. This merely needed patience on his part without the firmness of his faith being in the least shaken by his way of thinking. Only, like a poor, resigned man just a little weary of being always put off, he sometimes allowed himself diversions. For instance, he had obtained permission to keep his wife near him, seated on a camp-stool, and he liked to talk to her, and acquaint her with his reflections.

"Raise me a little, my dear," said he. "I am slipping. I am very uncomfortable."

Attired in trousers and a coarse woollen jacket, he was sitting upon his mattress, with his back leaning against a tilted chair.

"Are you better?" asked his wife, when she had raised him.

"Yes, yes," he answered; and then began to take an interest in Brother Isidore, whom they had succeeded in bringing in spite of everything, and who was lying upon a neighbouring mattress, with a sheet drawn up to his chin, and nothing protruding but his wasted hands, which lay clasped upon the blanket.

"Ah! the poor man," said M. Sabathier. "It's very imprudent, but the Blessed Virgin is so powerful when she chooses!"

He took up his chaplet again, but once more broke off from his devotions on perceiving Madame Maze, who had just glided into the reserved space—so slender and unobtrusive that she had doubtless slipped under the ropes without being noticed. She had seated herself at the end of a bench and, very quiet and motionless, did not occupy more room there than a child. And her long face, with its weary features, the face of a woman of two-and-thirty faded before her time, wore an expression of unlimited sadness, infinite abandonment.

"And so," resumed M. Sabathier in a low voice, again addressing his wife after attracting her attention by a slight movement of the chin, "it's for the conversion of her husband that this lady prays. You came across her this morning in a shop, didn't you?"

"Yes, yes," replied Madame Sabathier. "And, besides, I had some talk about her with another lady who knows her. Her husband is a commercial-traveller. He leaves her for six months at a time, and goes about with other people. Oh! he's a very gay fellow, it seems, very nice, and he doesn't let her want for money; only she adores him, she cannot accustom herself to his neglect, and comes to pray the Blessed Virgin to give him back to her. At this moment, it appears, he is close by, at Luchon, with two ladies—two sisters."

M. Sabathier signed to his wife to stop. He was now looking at the Grotto, again becoming a man of intellect, a professor whom questions of art had formerly impassioned. "You see, my dear," he said, "they have spoilt the Grotto by endeavouring to make it too beautiful. I am certain it looked much better in its original wildness. It has lost its characteristic features—and what a frightful shop they have stuck there, on the left!"

However, he now experienced sudden remorse for his thoughtlessness. Whilst he was chatting away, might not the Blessed Virgin be noticing one of his neighbours, more fervent, more sedate than himself? Feeling anxious on the point, he reverted to his customary modesty and patience, and with dull, expressionless eyes again began waiting for the good pleasure of Heaven.

Moreover, the sound of a fresh voice helped to bring him back to this annihilation, in which nothing was left of the cultured reasoner that he had formerly been. It was another preacher who had just entered the pulpit, a Capuchin this time, whose guttural call, persistently repeated, sent a tremor through the crowd.

"Holy Virgin of virgins, be blessed!"

"Holy Virgin of virgins, be blessed!"

"Holy Virgin of virgins, turn not thy face from thy children!"

"Holy Virgin of virgins, turn not thy face from thy children!"

"Holy Virgin of virgins, breathe upon our sores, and our sores shall heal!"

"Holy Virgin of virgins, breathe upon our sores, and our sores shall heal!"

At the end of the first bench, skirting the central path, which was becoming crowded, the Vigneron family had succeeded in finding room for themselves. They were all there: little Gustave, seated in a sinking posture, with his crutch between his legs; his mother, beside him, following the prayers like a punctilious *bourgeoise*; his aunt, Madame Chaise, on the other side, so inconvenienced by the crowd that she was stifling; and M. Vigneron, who remained silent and, for a moment, had been examining Madame Chaise attentively.

"What is the matter with you, my dear?" he inquired. "Do you feel unwell?"

She was breathing with difficulty. "Well, I don't know," she answered; "but I can't feel my limbs, and my breath fails me."

At that very moment the thought had occurred to him that all the agitation, fever, and scramble of a pilgrimage could not be very good for heart-disease. Of course he did not desire anybody's death, he had never asked the Blessed Virgin for any such thing. If his prayer for advancement had already been granted through the sudden death of his chief, it must certainly be because Heaven had already ordained the latter's death. And, in the same way, if Madame Chaise should die first, leaving her fortune to Gustave, he would only have to bow before the will of God, which generally requires that the aged should go off before the young. Nevertheless, his hope unconsciously became so keen that he could not help exchanging a glance with his wife, to whom had come the same involuntary thought.

"Gustave, draw back," he exclaimed; "you are inconveniencing your aunt." And then, as Raymonde passed, he asked; "Do you happen to have a glass of water, mademoiselle? One of our relatives here is losing consciousness."

But Madame Chaise refused the offer with a gesture. She was getting better, recovering her breath with an effort. "No, I want nothing, thank you," she gasped. "There, I'm better—still, I really thought this time that I should stifle!"

Her fright left her trembling, with haggard eyes in her pale face. She again joined her hands, and begged the Blessed Virgin to save her from other attacks and cure her; while the Vignerons, man and wife, honest folk both of them, reverted to the covert prayer for happiness that they had come to offer up at Lourdes: a pleasant old age, deservedly gained by twenty years of honesty, with a respectable fortune which in later years they would go and enjoy in the country, cultivating flowers. On the other hand, little Gustave, who had seen and noted everything with his bright eyes and intelligence sharpened by suffering, was not praying, but smiling at space, with his vague enigmatical smile. What could be the use of his praying? He knew that the Blessed Virgin would not cure him, and that he would die.

However, M. Vigneron could not remain long without busying himself about his neighbours. Madame Dieulafay, who had come late, had been deposited in the crowded central pathway; and he marvelled at the luxury about the young woman, that sort of coffin quilted with white silk, in which she was lying, attired in a pink dressing-gown trimmed with Valenciennes lace. The husband in a frock-coat, and the sister in a black gown of simple but marvellous elegance, were standing by; while Abbe Judaine, kneeling near the sufferer, finished offering up a fervent prayer.

When the priest had risen, M. Vigneron made him a little room on the bench beside him; and he then took the liberty of questioning him. "Well, Monsieur le Cure, does that poor young woman feel a little better?"

Abbe Judaine made a gesture of infinite sadness.

"Alas! no. I was full of so much hope! It was I who persuaded the family to come. Two years ago the Blessed Virgin showed me such extraordinary grace by curing my poor lost eyes, that I hoped to obtain another favour from her. However, I will not despair. We still have until to-morrow."

M. Vigneron again looked towards Madame Dieulafay and examined her face, still of a perfect oval and with admirable eyes; but it was expressionless, with ashen hue, similar to a mask of death, amidst the lace. "It's really very sad," he murmured.

"And if you had seen her last summer!" resumed the priest. "They have their country seat at Saligny, my parish, and I often dined with them. I cannot help feeling sad when I look at her elder sister, Madame Jousseur, that lady in black who stands there, for she bears a strong resemblance to her; and the poor sufferer was even prettier, one of the beauties of Paris. And now compare them together—observe that brilliancy, that sovereign grace, beside that poor, pitiful creature—it oppresses one's heart—ah! what a frightful lesson!"

He became silent for an instant. Saintly man that he was naturally, altogether devoid of passions, with no keen intelligence to disturb him in his faith, he displayed a naive admiration for beauty, wealth, and power, which he had never envied. Nevertheless, he ventured to express a doubt, a scruple, which troubled his usual serenity. "For my part, I should have liked her to come here with more simplicity, without all that surrounding of luxury, because the Blessed Virgin prefers the humble—But I understand very well that there are certain social exigencies. And, then, her husband and sister love her so! Remember that he has forsaken his business and she her pleasures in order to come here with her; and so overcome are they at the idea of losing her that their eyes are never dry, they always have that bewildered look which you can notice. So they must be excused for trying to procure her the comfort of looking beautiful until the last hour."

M. Vigneron nodded his head approvingly. Ah! it was certainly not the wealthy who had the most luck at the Grotto! Servants, country folk, poor beggars, were cured, while ladies returned home with their ailments unrelieved, notwithstanding their gifts and the big candles they had burnt. And, in spite of himself, Vigneron then looked at Madame Chaise, who, having recovered from her attack, was now reposing with a comfortable air.

But a tremor passed through the crowd and Abbe Judaine spoke again: "Here is Father Massias coming towards the pulpit. He is a saint; listen to him."

They knew him, and were aware that he could not make his appearance without every soul being stirred by sudden hope, for it was reported that the miracles were often brought to pass by his great fervour. His voice, full of tenderness and strength, was said to be appreciated by the Virgin.

All heads were therefore uplifted and the emotion yet further increased when Father Fourcade was seen coming to the foot of the pulpit, leaning on the shoulder of his well-beloved brother, the preferred of all; and he stayed there, so that he also might hear him. His gouty foot had been paining him more acutely since the morning, so that it required great courage on his part to remain thus standing and smiling. The increasing exaltation of the crowd made him happy, however; he foresaw prodigies and dazzling cures which would redound to the glory of Mary and Jesus.

Having ascended the pulpit, Father Massias did not at once speak. He seemed, very tall, thin, and pale, with an ascetic face, elongated the more by his discoloured beard. His eyes sparkled, and his large eloquent mouth protruded passionately.

"Lord, save us, for we perish!" he suddenly cried; and in a fever, which increased minute by minute, the transported crowd repeated: "Lord, save us, for we perish!"

Then he opened his arms and again launched forth his flaming cry, as if he had torn it from his glowing heart: "Lord, if it be Thy will, Thou canst heal me!"

"Lord, if it be Thy will, Thou canst heal me!"

"Lord, I am not worthy that Thou shouldst enter under my roof, but only say the word, and I shall be healed!"

"Lord, I am not worthy that Thou shouldst enter under my roof, but only say the word, and I shall be healed!"

Marthe, Brother Isidore's sister, had now begun to talk in a whisper to Madame Sabathier, near whom she had at last seated herself. They had formed an acquaintance at the hospital; and, drawn together by so much suffering, the servant had familiarly confided to the *bourgeoise* how anxious she felt about her brother; for she could plainly see that he had very little breath left in him. The Blessed Virgin must be quick indeed if she desired to save him. It was already a miracle that they had been able to bring him alive as far as the Grotto.

In her resignation, poor, simple creature that she was, she did not weep; but her heart was so swollen that her infrequent words came faintly from her lips. Then a flood of past memories suddenly returned to her; and with her utterance thickened by prolonged silence, she began to relieve her heart: "We were fourteen at home, at Saint Jacut, near Vannes. He, big as he was, has always been delicate, and that was why he remained with our priest, who ended by placing him among the

Christian Brothers. The elder ones took over the property, and, for my part, I preferred going out to service. Yes, it was a lady who took me with her to Paris, five years ago already. Ah! what a lot of trouble there is in life! Everyone has so much trouble!"

"You are quite right, my girl," replied Madame Sabathier, looking the while at her husband, who was devoutly repeating each of Father Massias's appeals.

"And then," continued Marthe, "there I learned last month that Isidore, who had returned from a hot climate where he had been on a mission, had brought a bad sickness back with him. And, when I ran to see him, he told me he should die if he did not leave for Lourdes, but that he couldn't make the journey, because he had nobody to accompany him. Then, as I had eighty francs saved up, I gave up my place, and we set out together. You see, madame, if I am so fond of him, it's because he used to bring me gooseberries from the parsonage, whereas all the others beat me."

She relapsed into silence for a moment, her countenance swollen by grief, and her poor eyes so scorched by watching that no tears could come from them. Then she began to stutter disjointed words: "Look at him, madame. It fills one with pity. Ah! my God, his poor cheeks, his poor chin, his poor face—"

It was, in fact, a lamentable spectacle. Madame Sabathier's heart was quite upset when she observed Brother Isidore so yellow, cadaverous, steeped in a cold sweat of agony. Above the sheet he still only showed his clasped hands and his face encircled with long scanty hair; but if those wax-like hands seemed lifeless, if there was not a feature of that long-suffering face that stirred, its eyes were still alive, inextinguishable eyes of love, whose flame sufficed to illumine the whole of his expiring visage—the visage of a Christ upon the cross. And never had the contrast been so clearly marked between his low forehead and unintelligent, loutish, peasant air, and the divine splendour which came from his poor human mask, ravaged and sanctified by suffering, sublime at this last hour in the passionate radiance of his faith. His flesh had melted, as it were; he was no longer a breath, nothing but a look, a light.

Since he had been set down there his eyes had not strayed from the statue of the Virgin. Nothing else existed around him. He did not see the enormous multitude, he did not even hear the wild cries of the priests, the incessant cries which shook this quivering crowd. His eyes alone remained to him, his eyes burning with infinite tenderness, and they were fixed upon the Virgin, never more to turn from her. They drank her in, even unto death; they made a last effort of will to disappear, die out in her. For an instant, however, his mouth half opened and his drawn visage relaxed as an expression of celestial beatitude came over it. Then nothing more stirred, his eyes remained wide open, still obstinately fixed upon the white statue.

A few seconds elapsed. Marthe had felt a cold breath, chilling the roots of her hair. "I say, madame, look!" she stammered.

Madame Sabathier, who felt anxious, pretended that she did not understand. "What is it, my girl?"

"My brother! look! He no longer moves. He opened his mouth, and has not stirred since." Then they both shuddered, feeling certain he was dead. He had, indeed, just passed away, without a rattle, without a breath, as if life had escaped in his glance, through his large, loving eyes, ravenous with passion. He had expired gazing upon the Virgin, and nothing could have been so sweet; and he still continued to gaze upon her with his dead eyes, as though with ineffable delight.

"Try to close his eyes," murmured Madame Sabathier. "We shall soon know then."

Marthe had already risen, and, leaning forward, so as not to be observed, she endeavoured to close the eyes with a trembling finger. But each time they reopened, and again looked at the Virgin with invincible obstinacy. He was dead, and Marthe had to leave his eyes wide open, steeped in unbounded ecstasy.

"Ah! it's finished, it's quite finished, madame!" she stuttered.

Two tears then burst from her heavy eyelids and ran down her cheeks; while Madame Sabathier caught hold of her hand to keep her quiet. There had been whisperings, and uneasiness was already spreading. But what course could be adopted? It was impossible to carry off the corpse amidst such a mob, during the prayers, without incurring the risk of creating a disastrous effect. The best plan would be to leave it there, pending a favourable moment. The poor fellow scandalised no one, he did not seem any more dead now than he had seemed ten minutes previously, and everybody would think that his flaming eyes were still alive, ardently appealing to the divine compassion of the Blessed Virgin.

Only a few persons among those around knew the truth. M. Sabathier, quite scared, had made a questioning sign to his wife, and on being answered by a prolonged affirmative nod, he had returned to his prayers without any rebellion, though he could not help turning

ÉMILE ZOLA

pale at the thought of the mysterious almighty power which sent death when life was asked for. The Vignerons, who were very much interested, leaned forward, and whispered as though in presence of some street accident, one of those petty incidents which in Paris the father sometimes related on returning home from the Ministry, and which sufficed to occupy them all, throughout the evening. Madame Jousseur, for her part, had simply turned round and whispered a word or two in M. Dieulafay's ear, and then they had both reverted to the heart-rending contemplation of their own dear invalid; whilst Abbe Judaine, informed by M. Vigneron, knelt down, and in a low, agitated voice recited the prayers for the dead. Was he not a Saint, that missionary who had returned from a deadly climate, with a mortal wound in his side, to die there, beneath the smiling gaze of the Blessed Virgin? And Madame Maze, who also knew what had happened, suddenly felt a taste for death, and resolved that she would implore Heaven to suppress her also, in unobtrusive fashion, if it would not listen to her prayer and give her back her husband.

But the cry of Father Massias rose into a still higher key, burst forth with a strength of terrible despair, with a rending like that of a sob: "Jesus, son of David, I am perishing, save me!"

And the crowd sobbed after him in unison "Jesus, son of David, I am perishing, save me!"

Then, in quick succession, and in higher and higher keys, the appeals went on proclaiming the intolerable misery of the world:

"Jesus, son of David, take pity on Thy sick children!"

"Jesus, son of David, take pity on Thy sick children!"

"Jesus, son of David, come, heal them, that they may live!"

"Jesus, son of David, come, heal them, that they may live!"

It was delirium. At the foot of the pulpit Father Fourcade, succumbing to the extraordinary passion which overflowed from all hearts, had likewise raised his arms, and was shouting the appeals in his thundering voice as though to compel the intervention of Heaven. And the exaltation was still increasing beneath this blast of desire, whose powerful breath bowed every head in turn, spreading even to the young women who, in a spirit of mere curiosity, sat watching the scene from the parapet of the Gave; for these also turned pale under their sunshades.

Miserable humanity was clamouring from the depths of its abyss of suffering, and the clamour swept along, sending a shudder down every spine, for one and all were plunged in agony, refusing to die, longing to compel God to grant them eternal life. Ah! life, life! that was what all those unfortunates, who had come so far, amid so many obstacles, wanted—that was the one boon they asked for in their wild desire to live it over again, to live it always! O Lord, whatever our misery, whatever the torment of our life may be, cure us, grant that we may begin to live again and suffer once more what we have suffered already. However unhappy we may be, to be is what we wish. It is not heaven that we ask Thee for, it is earth; and grant that we may leave it at the latest possible moment, never leave it, indeed, if such be Thy good pleasure. And even when we no longer implore a physical cure, but a moral favour, it is still happiness that we ask Thee for; happiness, the thirst for which alone consumes us. O Lord, grant that we may be happy and healthy; let us live, ay, let us live forever!

This wild cry, the cry of man's furious desire for life, came in broken accents, mingled with tears, from every breast.

"O Lord, son of David, heal our sick!"

"O Lord, son of David, heal our sick!"

Berthaud had twice been obliged to dash forward to prevent the cords from giving way under the unconscious pressure of the crowd. Baron Suire, in despair, kept on making signs, begging someone to come to his assistance; for the Grotto was now invaded, and the march past had become the mere trampling of a flock rushing to its passion. In vain did Gerard again leave Raymonde and post himself at the entrance gate of the iron railing, so as to carry out the orders, which were to admit the pilgrims by tens. He was hustled and swept aside, while with feverish excitement everybody rushed in, passing like a torrent between the flaring candles, throwing bouquets and letters to the Virgin, and kissing the rock, which the pressure of millions of inflamed lips had polished. It was faith run wild, the great power that nothing henceforth could stop.

And now, whilst Gerard stood there, hemmed in against the iron railing, he heard two countrywomen, whom the advance was bearing onward, raise loud exclamations at sight of the sufferers lying on the stretchers before them. One of them was so greatly impressed by the pallid face of Brother Isidore, whose large dilated eyes were still fixed on the statue of the Virgin, that she crossed herself, and, overcome by devout admiration, murmured: "Oh! look at that one; see how he is praying with his whole heart, and how he gazes on Our Lady of Lourdes!"

ÉMILE ZOLA

The other peasant woman thereupon replied "Oh! she will certainly cure him, he is so beautiful!"

Indeed, as the dead man lay there, his eyes still fixedly staring whilst he continued his prayer of love and faith, his appearance touched every heart. No one in that endless, streaming throng could behold him without feeling edified.

III

MARIE'S CURE

It was good Abbe Judaine who was to carry the Blessed Sacrament in the four-o'clock procession. Since the Blessed Virgin had cured him of a disease of the eyes, a miracle with which the Catholic press still resounded, he had become one of the glories of Lourdes, was given the first place, and honoured with all sorts of attentions.

At half-past three he rose, wishing to leave the Grotto, but the extraordinary concourse of people quite frightened him, and he feared he would be late if he did not succeed in getting out of it. Fortunately help came to him in the person of Berthaud. "Monsieur le Cure," exclaimed the superintendent of the bearers, "don't attempt to pass out by way of the Rosary; you would never arrive in time. The best course is to ascend by the winding paths—and come! follow me; I will go before you."

By means of his elbows, he thereupon parted the dense throng and opened a path for the priest, who overwhelmed him with thanks. "You are too kind. It's my fault; I had forgotten myself. But, good heavens! how shall we manage to pass with the procession presently?"

This procession was Berthaud's remaining anxiety. Even on ordinary days it provoked wild excitement, which forced him to take special measures; and what would now happen, as it wended its way through this dense multitude of thirty thousand persons, consumed by such a fever of faith, already on the verge of divine frenzy? Accordingly, in a sensible way, he took advantage of this opportunity to give Abbe Judaine the best advice.

"Ah! Monsieur le Cure, pray impress upon your colleagues of the clergy that they must not leave any space between their ranks; they should come on slowly, one close behind the other. And, above all, the banners should be firmly grasped, so that they may not be overthrown. As for yourself, Monsieur le Cure, see that the canopy-bearers are strong, tighten the cloth around the monstrance, and don't be afraid to carry it in both hands with all your strength."

A little frightened by this advice, the priest went on expressing his thanks. "Of course, of course; you are very good," said he. "Ah! monsieur, how much I am indebted to you for having helped me to escape from all those people!"

Then, free at last, he hastened towards the Basilica by the narrow serpentine path which climbs the hill; while his companion again plunged into the mob, to return to his post of inspection.

At that same moment Pierre, who was bringing Marie to the Grotto in her little cart, encountered on the other side, that of the Place du Rosaire, the impenetrable wall formed by the crowd. The servant at the hotel had awakened him at three o'clock, so that he might go and fetch the young girl at the hospital. There seemed to be no hurry; they apparently had plenty of time to reach the Grotto before the procession. However, that immense throng, that resisting, living wall, through which he did not know how to break, began to cause him some uneasiness. He would never succeed in passing with the little car if the people did not evince some obligingness. "Come, ladies, come!" he appealed. "I beg of you! You see, it's for a patient!"

The ladies, hypnotised as they were by the spectacle of the Grotto sparkling in the distance, and standing on tiptoe so as to lose nothing of the sight, did not move, however. Besides, the clamour of the litanies was so loud at this moment that they did not even hear the young priest's entreaties.

Then Pierre began again: "Pray stand on one side, gentlemen; allow me to pass. A little room for a sick person. Come, please, listen to what I am saying!"

But the men, beside themselves, in a blind, deaf rapture, would stir no more than the women.

Marie, however, smiled serenely, as if ignorant of the impediments, and convinced that nothing in the world could prevent her from going to her cure. However, when Pierre had found an aperture, and begun to work his way through the moving mass, the situation became more serious. From all parts the swelling human waves beat against the frail chariot, and at times threatened to submerge it. At each step it became necessary to stop, wait, and again entreat the people. Pierre had never before felt such an anxious sensation in a crowd. True, it was not a threatening mob, it was as innocent as a flock of sheep; but he found a troubling thrill in its midst, a peculiar atmosphere that upset him. And, in spite of his affection for the humble, the ugliness of the features around him, the common, sweating faces, the evil breath, and the old clothes, smelling of poverty, made him suffer even to nausea.

"Now, ladies, now, gentlemen, it's for a patient," he repeated. "A little room, I beg of you!"

Buffeted about in this vast ocean, the little vehicle continued to advance by fits and starts, taking long minutes to get over a few yards of ground. At one moment you might have thought it swamped, for no sign of it could be detected. Then, however, it reappeared near the piscinas. Tender sympathy had at length been awakened for this sick girl, so wasted by suffering, but still so beautiful. When people had been compelled to give way before the priest's stubborn pushing, they turned round, but did not dare to get angry, for pity penetrated them at sight of that thin, suffering face, shining out amidst a halo of fair hair. Words of compassion and admiration were heard on all sides: "Ah, the poor child!"—"Was it not cruel to be infirm at her age?"—"Might the Blessed Virgin be merciful to her!" Others, however, expressed surprise, struck as they were by the ecstasy in which they saw her, with her clear eyes open to the spheres beyond, where she had placed her hope. She beheld Heaven, she would assuredly be cured. And thus the little car left, as it were, a feeling of wonder and fraternal charity behind it, as it made its way with so much difficulty through that human ocean.

Pierre, however, was in despair and at the end of his strength, when some of the stretcher-bearers came to his aid by forming a path for the passage of the procession—a path which Berthaud had ordered them to keep clear by means of cords, which they were to hold at intervals of a couple of yards. From that moment the young priest was able to drag Marie along in a fairly easy manner, and at last place her within the reserved space, where he halted, facing the Grotto on the left side. You could no longer move in this reserved space, where the crowd seemed to increase every minute. And, quite exhausted by the painful journey he had just accomplished, Pierre reflected what a prodigious concourse of people there was; it had seemed to him as if he were in the midst of an ocean, whose waves he had heard heaving around him without a pause.

Since leaving the hospital Marie had not opened her lips. He now realised, however, that she wished to speak to him, and accordingly bent over her. "And my father," she inquired, "is he here? Hasn't he returned from his excursion?"

Pierre had to answer that M. de Guersaint had not returned, and that he had doubtless been delayed against his will. And thereupon she merely added with a smile: "Ah I poor father, won't he be pleased when he finds me cured!"

Pierre looked at her with tender admiration. He did not remember having ever seen her looking so adorable since the slow wasting of sickness had begun. Her hair, which alone disease had respected, clothed her in gold. Her thin, delicate face had assumed a dreamy expression, her eyes wandering away to the haunting thought of her sufferings, her features motionless, as if she had fallen asleep in a fixed thought until the expected shock of happiness should waken her. She was absent from herself, ready, however, to return to consciousness whenever God might will it. And, indeed, this delicious infantile creature, this little girl of three-and-twenty, still a child as when an accident had struck her, delaying her growth, preventing her from becoming a woman, was at last ready to receive the visit of the angel, the miraculous shock which would draw her out of her torpor and set her upright once more. Her morning ecstasy continued; she had clasped her hands, and a leap of her whole being had ravished her from earth as soon as she had perceived the image of the Blessed Virgin yonder. And now she prayed and offered herself divinely.

It was an hour of great mental trouble for Pierre. He felt that the drama of his priestly life was about to be enacted, and that if he did not recover faith in this crisis, it would never return to him. And he was without bad thoughts, without resistance, hoping with fervour, he also, that they might both be healed! Oh! that he might be convinced by her cure, that he might believe like her, that they might be saved together! He wished to pray, ardently, as she herself did. But in spite of himself he was preoccupied by the crowd, that limitless crowd, among which he found it so difficult to drown himself, disappear, become nothing more than a leaf in the forest, lost amidst the rustle of all the leaves. He could not prevent himself from analysing and judging it. He knew that for four days past it had been undergoing all the training of suggestion; there had been the fever of the long journey, the excitement of the new landscapes, the days spent before the splendour of the Grotto, the sleepless nights, and all the exasperating suffering, ravenous for illusion. Then, again, there had been the all-besetting prayers, those hymns, those litanies, which agitated it without a pause. Another priest had followed Father Massias in the pulpit, a little thin, dark Abbe, whom Pierre heard hurling appeals to the Virgin and Jesus in a lashing voice which resounded like a whip. Father Massias and Father Fourcade had remained at the foot of the pulpit, and were now directing the cries of the crowd, whose lamentations rose in louder and louder tones beneath the limpid sunlight. The general exaltation had yet increased; it was the hour when the violence done to Heaven at last produced the miracles.

All at once a paralytic rose up and walked towards the Grotto, holding his crutch in the air; and this crutch, waving like a flag above the swaying heads, wrung loud applause from the faithful. They were all on the look-out for prodigies, they awaited them with the certainty that they would take place, innumerable and wonderful. Some eyes seemed to behold them, and feverish voices pointed them out. Another woman had been cured! Another! Yet another! A deaf person had heard, a mute had spoken, a consumptive had revived! What, a consumptive? Certainly, that was a daily occurrence! Surprise was no longer possible; you might have certified that an amputated leg was growing again without astonishing anyone. Miracle-working became the actual state of nature, the usual thing, quite commonplace, such was its abundance. The most incredible stories seemed quite simple to those overheated imaginations, given what they expected from the Blessed Virgin. And you should have heard the tales that went about, the quiet affirmations, the expressions of absolute certainty which were exchanged whenever a delirious patient cried out that she was cured. Another! Yet another! However, a piteous voice would at times exclaim: "Ah! she's cured; that one; she's lucky, she is!"

Already, at the Verification Office, Pierre had suffered from this credulity of the folk among whom he lived. But here it surpassed everything he could have imagined; and he was exasperated by the extravagant things he heard people say in such a placid fashion, with the open smiles of children. Accordingly he tried to absorb himself in his thoughts and listen to nothing. "O God!" he prayed, "grant that my reason may be annihilated, that I may no longer desire to understand, that I may accept the unreal and impossible." For a moment he thought the spirit of inquiry dead within him, and allowed the cry of supplication to carry him away: "Lord, heal our sick! Lord, heal our sick!" He repeated this appeal with all his charity, clasped his hands, and gazed fixedly at the statue of the Virgin, until he became quite giddy, and imagined that the figure moved. Why should he not return to a state of childhood like the others, since happiness lay in ignorance and falsehood? Contagion would surely end by acting; he would become nothing more than a grain of sand among innumerable other grains, one of the humblest among the humble ones under the millstone, who trouble not about the power that crushes them. But just at that second, when he hoped that he had killed the old man in him, that he had annihilated himself along with his will and intelligence, the stubborn work of thought, incessant and invincible, began afresh in the depths of his brain. Little by little, notwithstanding his efforts to the contrary, he returned to his inquiries, doubted, and sought the truth. What was the unknown force thrown off by this crowd, the vital fluid powerful enough to work the few cures that really occurred? There was here a phenomenon that no physiologist had yet studied. Ought one to believe that a multitude became a single being, as it were, able to increase the power of auto-suggestion tenfold upon itself? Might one admit that, under certain circumstances of extreme exaltation, a multitude became an agent of sovereign will compelling the obedience of matter? That would have explained how sudden cure fell at times upon the most sincerely excited of the throng. The breaths of all of them united in one breath, and the power that acted was a power of consolation, hope, and life.

This thought, the outcome of his human charity, filled Pierre with emotion. For another moment he was able to regain possession of himself, and prayed for the cure of all, deeply touched by the belief that he himself might in some degree contribute towards the cure of Marie. But all at once, without knowing what transition of ideas led to it, a recollection returned to him of the medical consultation which he had insisted upon prior to the young girl's departure for Lourdes. The scene rose before him with extraordinary clearness and precision; he saw the room with its grey, blue-flowered wall-paper, and he heard the three doctors discuss and decide. The two who had given certificates diagnosticating paralysis of the marrow spoke discreetly, slowly, like esteemed, well-known, perfectly honourable practitioners; but Pierre still heard the warm, vivacious voice of his cousin Beauclair, the third doctor, a young man of vast and daring intelligence, who was treated coldly by his colleagues as being of an adventurous turn of mind. And at this supreme moment Pierre was surprised to find in his memory things which he did not know were there; but it was only an instance of that singular phenomenon by which it sometimes happens that words scarce listened to, words but imperfectly heard, words stored away in the brain almost in spite of self, will awaken, burst forth, and impose themselves on the mind after they have long been forgotten. And thus it now seemed to him that the very approach of the miracle was bringing him a vision of the conditions under which—according to Beauclair's predictions—the miracle would be accomplished.

In vain did Pierre endeavour to drive away this recollection by praying with an increase of fervour. The scene again appeared to him, and the old words rang out, filling his ears like a trumpet-blast. He was now again in the dining-room, where Beauclair and he had shut themselves up after the departure of the two others, and Beauclair recapitulated the history of the malady: the fall from a horse at the age of fourteen; the dislocation and displacement of the organ, with doubtless a slight laceration of the ligaments, whence the weight which the sufferer had felt, and the weakness of the legs leading to paralysis. Then, a slow healing of the disorder, everything returning to its place of itself, but without the pain ceasing. In fact this big, nervous child, whose mind had been so grievously impressed by her accident, was unable to forget it; her attention remained fixed on the part where she suffered, and she could not divert it, so that, even after cure, her sufferings had continued—a neuropathic state, a consecutive nervous exhaustion, doubtless aggravated by accidents due to faulty nutrition as yet imperfectly understood. And further, Beauclair easily explained the contrary and erroneous diagnosis of the numerous doctors who had attended her, and who, as she would not submit to examination, had groped in the dark, some believing in a tumour, and the others, the more numerous, convinced of some lesion of the marrow. He alone, after inquiring into the girl's parentage, had just begun to suspect a simple state of auto-suggestion, in which she had obstinately remained ever since the first violent shock of pain; and among the reasons which he gave for this belief were the contraction of her visual field, the fixity of her eyes, the absorbed, inattentive expression of her face, and above all the nature of the pain she felt, which, leaving the organ, had borne to the left, where it continued in the form of a crushing, intolerable weight, which sometimes rose to the breast in frightful fits of stifling. A sudden determination to throw off the false notion she had formed of her complaint, the will to rise, breathe freely, and suffer no more, could alone place her on her feet again, cured, transfigured, beneath the lash of some intense emotion.

A last time did Pierre endeavour to see and hear no more, for he felt that the irreparable ruin of all belief in the miraculous was in him. And, in spite of his efforts, in spite of the ardour with which he began to cry, "Jesus, son of David, heal our sick!" he still saw, he still heard Beauclair telling him, in his calm, smiling manner how the miracle would take place, like a lightning flash, at the moment of extreme emotion, under the decisive circumstance which would complete the loosening of the muscles. The patient would rise and walk in a wild transport of joy, her legs would all at once be light again, relieved of the weight which had so long made them like lead, as though this weight had melted, fallen to the ground. But above all, the weight which bore upon the lower part of the trunk, which rose, ravaged the breast, and strangled the throat, would this time depart in a prodigious soaring flight, a tempest blast bearing all the evil away with it. And was it not thus that, in the Middle Ages, possessed women had by the mouth cast up the Devil, by whom their flesh had so long been tortured? And Beauclair had added that Marie would at last become a woman, that in that moment of supreme joy she would cease to be a child, that although seemingly worn out by her prolonged dream of suffering, she would all at once be restored to resplendent health, with beaming face, and eyes full of life.

Pierre looked at her, and his trouble increased still more on seeing her so wretched in her little cart, so distractedly imploring health, her whole being soaring towards Our Lady of Lourdes, who gave life. Ah! might she be saved, at the cost even of his own damnation! But she was too ill; science lied like faith; he could not believe that this child, whose limbs had been dead for so many years, would indeed return to life. And, in the bewildered doubt into which he again relapsed, his bleeding heart clamoured yet more loudly, ever and ever repeating with the delirious crowd: "Lord, son of David, heal our sick!—Lord, son of David, heal our sick!"

At that moment a tumult arose agitating one and all. People shuddered, faces were turned and raised. It was the cross of the four-o'clock procession, a little behind time that day, appearing from beneath one of the arches of the monumental gradient way. There was such applause and such violent, instinctive pushing that Berthaud, waving his arms, commanded the bearers to thrust the crowd back by pulling strongly on the cords. Overpowered for a moment, the bearers had to throw themselves backward with sore hands; however, they ended by somewhat enlarging the reserved path, along which the procession was then able to slowly wend its way. At the head came a superb beadle, all blue and gold, followed by the processional cross, a tall cross shining like a star. Then followed the delegations of the different pilgrimages with their banners, standards of velvet and satin, embroidered with metal and bright silk, adorned with painted figures, and bearing the names of towns: Versailles, Rheims, Orleans, Poitiers, and Toulouse.

One, which was quite white, magnificently rich, displayed in red letters the inscription "Association of Catholic Working Men's Clubs." Then came the clergy, two or three hundred priests in simple cassocks, about a hundred in surplices, and some fifty clothed in golden chasubles, effulgent like stars. They all carried lighted candles, and sang the "Laudate Sion Salvatorem" in full voices. And then the canopy appeared in royal pomp, a canopy of purple silk, braided with gold, and upheld by four ecclesiastics, who, it could be seen, had been selected from among the most robust. Beneath it, between two other priests who assisted him, was Abbe Judaine, vigorously clasping the Blessed Sacrament with both hands, as Berthaud had recommended him to do; and the somewhat uneasy glances that he cast on the encroaching crowd right and left showed how anxious he was that no injury should befall the heavy divine monstrance, whose weight was already straining his wrists. When the slanting sun fell upon him in front, the monstrance itself looked like another sun. Choir-boys meantime were swinging censers in the blinding glow which gave splendour to the entire procession; and, finally, in the rear, there was a confused mass of pilgrims, a flock-like tramping of believers and sightseers all aflame, hurrying along, and blocking the track with their ever-rolling waves.

Father Massias had returned to the pulpit a moment previously; and this time he had devised another pious exercise. After the burning cries of faith, hope, and love that he threw forth, he all at once commanded absolute silence, in order that one and all might, with closed lips, speak to God in secret for a few minutes. These sudden spells of silence falling upon the vast crowd, these minutes of mute prayer, in which all souls unbosomed their secrets, were deeply, wonderfully impressive. Their solemnity became formidable; you heard desire, the immense desire for life, winging its flight on high. Then Father Massias invited the sick alone to speak, to implore God to grant them what they asked of His almighty power. And, in response, came a pitiful lamentation, hundreds of tremulous, broken voices rising amidst a concert of sobs. "Lord Jesus, if it please Thee, Thou canst cure me!"—"Lord Jesus take pity on Thy child, who is dying of love!"—"Lord Jesus, grant that I may see, grant that I may hear, grant that I may walk!" And, all at once, the shrill voice of a little girl, light and vivacious as the notes of a flute, rose above the universal sob, repeating in the distance: "Save the others, save the others, Lord Jesus!" Tears streamed from every eye; these supplications upset all hearts, threw the hardest into the frenzy

ÉMILE ZOLA

of charity, into a sublime disorder which would have impelled them to open their breasts with both hands, if by doing so they could have given their neighbours their health and youth. And then Father Massias, not letting this enthusiasm abate, resumed his cries, and again lashed the delirious crowd with them; while Father Fourcade himself sobbed on one of the steps of the pulpit, raising his streaming face to heaven as though to command God to descend on earth.

But the procession had arrived; the delegations, the priests, had ranged themselves on the right and left; and, when the canopy entered the space reserved to the sick in front of the Grotto, when the sufferers perceived Jesus the Host, the Blessed Sacrament, shining like a sun, in the hands of Abbe Judaine, it became impossible to direct the prayers, all voices mingled together, and all will was borne away by vertigo. The cries, calls, entreaties broke, lapsing into groans. Human forms rose from pallets of suffering; trembling arms were stretched forth; clenched hands seemingly desired to clutch at the miracle on the way. "Lord Jesus, save us, for we perish!"—"Lord Jesus, we worship Thee; heal us!"— "Lord Jesus, Thou art the Christ, the Son of the living God; heal us!" Thrice did the despairing, exasperated voices give vent to the supreme lamentation in a clamour which rushed up to Heaven; and the tears redoubled, flooding all the burning faces which desire transformed. At one moment, the delirium became so great, the instinctive leap toward the Blessed Sacrament seemed so irresistible, that Berthaud placed the bearers who were there in a chain about it. This was the extreme protective manoeuvre, a hedge of bearers drawn up on either side of the canopy, each placing an arm firmly round his neighbour's neck, so as to establish a sort of living wall. Not the smallest aperture was left in it; nothing whatever could pass. Still, these human barriers staggered under the pressure of the unfortunate creatures who hungered for life, who wished to touch, to kiss Jesus; and, oscillating and recoiling, the bearers were at last thrust against the canopy they were defending, and the canopy itself began swaying among the crowd, ever in danger of being swept away like some holy bark in peril of being wrecked.

Then, at the very climax of this holy frenzy, the miracles began amidst supplications and sobs, as when the heavens open during a storm, and a thunderbolt falls on earth. A paralytic woman rose and cast aside her crutches. There was a piercing yell, and another woman appeared erect on her mattress, wrapped in a white blanket as in a winding sheet; and people said it was a half-dead consumptive who had thus been resuscitated. Then grace fell upon two others in quick succession: a blind woman suddenly perceived the Grotto in a flame; a dumb woman fell on both her knees, thanking the Blessed Virgin in a loud, clear voice. And all in a like way prostrated themselves at the feet of Our Lady of Lourdes, distracted with joy and gratitude.

But Pierre had not taken his eyes off Marie, and he was overcome with tender emotion at what he saw. The sufferer's eyes were still expressionless, but they had dilated, while her poor, pale face, with its heavy mask, was contracted as if she were suffering frightfully. She did not speak in her despair; she undoubtedly thought that she was again in the clutches of her ailment. But all at once, when the Blessed Sacrament passed by, and she saw the star-like monstrance sparkling in the sun, a sensation of dizziness came over her. She imagined herself struck by lightning. Her eyes caught fire from the glare which flashed upon her, and at last regained their flame of life, shining out like stars. And under the influence of a wave of blood her face became animated, suffused with colour, beaming with a smile of joy and health. And, suddenly, Pierre saw her rise, stand upright in her little car, staggering, stuttering, and finding in her mind only these caressing words: "Oh, my friend! Oh, my friend!"

He hurriedly drew near in order to support her. But she drove him back with a gesture. She was regaining strength, looking so touching, so beautiful, in the little black woollen gown and slippers which she always wore; tall and slender, too, and crowned as with a halo of gold by her beautiful flaxen hair, which was covered with a simple piece of lace. The whole of her virgin form was quivering as if some powerful fermentation had regenerated her. First of all, it was her legs that were relieved of the chains that bound them; and then, while she felt the spirit of life—the life of woman, wife, and mother—within her, there came a final agony, an enormous weight that rose to her very throat. Only, this time, it did not linger there, did not stifle her, but burst from her open mouth, and flew away in a cry of sublime joy.

"I am cured!—I am cured!"

Then there was an extraordinary sight. The blanket lay at her feet, she was triumphant, she had a superb, glowing face. And her cry of cure had resounded with such rapturous delight that the entire crowd was distracted by it. She had become the sole point of interest, the others saw none but her, erect, grown so radiant and so divine.

"I am cured!—I am cured!"

Pierre, at the violent shock his heart had received, had begun to weep. Indeed, tears glistened again in every eye. Amidst exclamations of gratitude and praise, frantic enthusiasm passed from one to another, throwing the thousands of pilgrims who pressed forward to see into a state of violent emotion. Applause broke out, a fury of applause, whose thunder rolled from one to the other end of the valley.

However, Father Fourcade began waving his arms, and Father Massias was at last able to make himself heard from the pulpit: "God has visited us, my dear brothers, my dear sisters!" said he. "*Magnificat anima mea Dominum*, My soul doth magnify the Lord, and my spirit hath rejoiced in God my Saviour."

And then all the voices, the thousands of voices, began the chant of adoration and gratitude. The procession found itself at a stand-still. Abbe Judaine had been able to reach the Grotto with the monstrance, but he patiently remained there before giving the Benediction. The canopy was awaiting him outside the railings, surrounded by priests in surplices and chasubles, all a glitter of white and gold in the rays of the setting sun.

Marie, however, had knelt down, sobbing; and, whilst the canticle lasted, a burning prayer of faith and love ascended from her whole being. But the crowd wanted to see her walk, delighted women called to her, a group surrounded her, and swept her towards the Verification Office, so that the miracle might be proved true, as patent as the very light of the sun. Her box was forgotten, Pierre followed her, while she, stammering and hesitating, she who for seven years had not used her legs, advanced with adorable awkwardness, the uneasy, charming gait of a little child making its first steps; and it was so affecting, so delicious, that the young priest thought of nothing but the immense happiness of seeing her thus return to her childhood. Ah! the dear friend of infancy, the dear tenderness of long ago, so she would at last be the beautiful and charming woman that she had promised to be as a young girl when, in the little garden at Neuilly, she had looked so gay and pretty beneath the tall trees flecked with sunlight!

The crowd continued to applaud her furiously, a huge wave of people accompanied her; and all remained awaiting her egress, swarming in a fever before the door, when she had entered the office, whither Pierre only was admitted with her.

That particular afternoon there were few people at the Verification Office. The small square room, with its hot wooden walls and rudimentary furniture, its rush-bottomed chairs, and its two tables of unequal height, contained, apart from the usual staff only some five or six doctors, seated and silent. At the tables were the inspector of the piscinas and two young Abbes making entries in the registers, and consulting the sets of documents; while Father Dargeles, at one end, wrote a paragraph for his newspaper. And, as it happened, Doctor Bonamy was just then examining Elise Rouquet, who, for the third time, had come to have the increasing cicatrisation of her sore certified.

"Anyhow, gentlemen," exclaimed the doctor, "have you ever seen a lupus heal in this way so rapidly? I am aware that a new work has appeared on faith healing in which it is stated that certain sores may have a nervous origin. Only that is by no means proved in the case of lupus, and I defy a committee of doctors to assemble and explain mademoiselle's cure by ordinary means."

He paused, and turning towards Father Dargeles, inquired: "Have you noted, Father, that the suppuration has completely disappeared, and that the skin is resuming its natural colour?"

However, he did not wait for the reply, for just then Marie entered, followed by Pierre; and by her beaming radiance he immediately guessed what good-fortune was befalling him. She looked superb, admirably fitted to transport and convert the multitude. He therefore promptly dismissed Elise Rouquet, inquired the new arrival's name, and asked one of the young priests to look for her papers. Then, as she slightly staggered, he wished to seat her in the arm-chair.

"Oh no! oh no!" she exclaimed. "I am so happy to be able to use my legs!"

Pierre, with a glance, had sought for Doctor Chassaigne, whom he was sorry not to see there. He remained on one side, waiting while they rummaged in the untidy drawers without being able to place their hands on the required papers. "Let's see," repeated Dr. Bonamy; "Marie de Guersaint, Marie de Guersaint. I have certainly seen that name before."

At last Raboin discovered the documents classified under a wrong letter; and when the doctor had perused the two medical certificates he became quite enthusiastic. "Here is something very interesting, gentlemen," said he. "I beg you to listen attentively. This young lady, whom you see standing here, was afflicted with a very serious lesion of the marrow. And, if one had the least doubt of it, these two certificates would suffice to convince the most incredulous, for they are signed by two doctors of the Paris faculty, whose names are well known to us all."

Then he passed the certificates to the doctors present, who read them, wagging their heads the while. It was beyond dispute; the medical men who had drawn up these documents enjoyed the reputation of being honest and clever practitioners.

"Well, gentlemen, if the diagnosis is not disputed—and it cannot be when a patient brings us documents of this value—we will now see what change has taken place in the young lady's condition."

However, before questioning her he turned towards Pierre. "Monsieur l'Abbé," said he, "you came from Paris with Mademoiselle de Guersaint, I think. Did you converse with the doctors before your departure?"

The priest shuddered amidst all his great delight.

"I was present at the consultation, monsieur," he replied.

And again the scene rose up before him. He once more saw the two doctors, so serious and rational, and he once more saw Beauclair smiling, while his colleagues drew up their certificates, which were identical. And was he, Pierre, to reduce these certificates to nothing, reveal the other diagnosis, the one that allowed of the cure being explained scientifically? The miracle had been predicted, shattered beforehand.

"You will observe, gentlemen," now resumed Dr. Bonamy, "that the presence of the Abbé gives these proofs additional weight. However, mademoiselle will now tell us exactly what she felt."

He had leant over Father Dargeles's shoulder to impress upon him that he must not forget to make Pierre play the part of a witness in the narrative.

"*Mon Dieu!* gentlemen, how can I tell you?" exclaimed Marie in a halting voice, broken by her surging happiness. "Since yesterday I had felt certain that I should be cured. And yet, a little while ago, when the pins and needles seized me in the legs again, I was afraid it might only be another attack. For an instant I doubted. Then the feeling stopped. But it began again as soon as I recommenced praying. Oh! I prayed, I prayed with all my soul! I ended by surrendering myself like a child. 'Blessed Virgin, Our Lady of Lourdes, do with me as thou wilt,' I said. But the feeling did not cease, it seemed as if my blood were boiling; a voice cried to me: 'Rise! Rise!' And I felt the miracle fall on me in a cracking of all my bones, of all my flesh, as if I had been struck by lightning."

Pierre, very pale, listened to her. Beauclair had positively told him that the cure would come like a lightning flash, that under the influence of extreme excitement a sudden awakening of will so long somnolent would take place within her.

"It was my legs which the Holy Virgin first of all delivered," she continued. "I could well feel that the iron bands which bound them were gliding along my skin like broken chains. Then the weight which still suffocated me, there, in the left side, began to ascend; and I thought I was going to die, it hurt me so. But it passed my chest, it passed my throat, and I felt it there in my mouth, and spat it out violently. It was all over, I no longer had any pain, it had flown away!"

She had made a gesture expressive of the motion of a night bird beating its wings, and, lapsing into silence, stood smiling at Pierre, who was bewildered. Beauclair had told him all that beforehand, using almost the same words and the same imagery. Point by point, his prognostics were realised, there was nothing more in the case than natural phenomena, which had been foreseen.

Raboin, however, had followed Marie's narrative with dilated eyes and the passion of a pietist of limited intelligence, ever haunted by the idea of hell. "It was the devil," he cried; "it was the devil that she spat out!"

Doctor Bonamy, who was more wary, made him hold his tongue. And turning towards the doctors he said: "Gentlemen, you know that we always avoid pronouncing the big word of miracle here. Only here is a fact, and I am curious to know how any of you can explain it by natural means. Seven years ago this young lady was struck with serious paralysis, evidently due to a lesion of the marrow. And that cannot be denied; the certificates are there, irrefutable. She could no longer walk, she could no longer make a movement without a cry of pain, she had reached that extreme state of exhaustion which precedes but by little an unfortunate issue. All at once, however, here she rises, walks, laughs, and beams on us. The paralysis has completely disappeared, no pain remains, she is as well as you and I. Come, gentlemen, approach, examine her, and tell me what has happened."

He triumphed. Not one of the doctors spoke. Two, who were doubtless true Catholics, had shown their approval of his speech by their vigorous nods, while the others remained motionless, with a constrained air, not caring to mix themselves up in the business. However, a little thin man, whose eyes shone behind the glasses he was wearing, ended by rising to take a closer look at Marie. He caught hold of her hand, examined the pupils of her eyes, and merely seemed preoccupied by the air of transfiguration which she wore. Then, in a very courteous manner, without even showing a desire to discuss the matter, he came back and sat down again.

"The case is beyond science, that is all I can assume," concluded Doctor Bonamy, victoriously. "I will add that we have no convalescence here; health is at once restored, full, entire. Observe the young lady. Her eyes are bright, her colour is rosy, her physiognomy has recovered its lively gaiety. Without doubt, the healing of the tissues will proceed somewhat slowly, but one can already say that mademoiselle has been born again. Is it not so, Monsieur l'Abbe, you who have seen her so frequently; you no longer recognise her, eh?"

"That's true, that's true," stammered Pierre.

And, in fact, she already appeared strong to him, her cheeks full and fresh, gaily blooming. But Beauclair had also foreseen this sudden joyful change, this straightening and resplendency of her invalid frame, when life should re-enter it, with the will to be cured and be happy. Once again, however, had Doctor Bonamy leant over Father Dargeles, who was finishing his note, a brief but fairly complete account of the affair. They exchanged a few words in low tones, consulting together, and the doctor ended by saying: "You have witnessed these marvels, Monsieur l'Abbe, so you will not refuse to sign the careful report which the reverend Father has drawn up for publication in the 'Journal de la Grotte.'"

He—Pierre—sign that page of error and falsehood! A revolt roused him, and he was on the point of shouting out the truth. But he felt the weight of his cassock on his shoulders; and, above all, Marie's divine joy filled his heart. He was penetrated with deep happiness at seeing her saved. Since they had ceased questioning her she had come and leant on his arm, and remained smiling at him with eyes full of enthusiasm.

"Oh, my, friend, thank the Blessed Virgin!" she murmured in a low voice. "She has been so good to me; I am now so well, so beautiful, so young! And how pleased my father, my poor father, will be!"

Then Pierre signed. Everything was collapsing within him, but it was enough that she should be saved; he would have thought it sacrilegious to interfere with the faith of that child, the great pure faith which had healed her.

When Marie reappeared outside the office, the applause began afresh, the crowd clapped their hands. It now seemed that the miracle was official. However, certain charitable persons, fearing that she might again fatigue herself and again require her little car, which she had abandoned before the Grotto, had brought it to the office, and when she found it there she felt deeply moved. Ah! that box in which she had lived so many years, that rolling coffin in which she had sometimes imagined herself buried alive, how many tears, how much despair, how many bad days it had witnessed! And, all at once, the idea occurred to her that it had so long been linked with her sufferings, it ought also to share her triumph. It was a sudden inspiration, a kind of holy folly, that made her seize the handle.

At that moment the procession passed by, returning from the Grotto, where Abbe Judaine had pronounced the Benediction. And thereupon Marie, dragging the little car, placed herself behind the canopy. And, in her slippers, her head covered with a strip of lace, her bosom heaving, her face erect, glowing, and superb, she walked on behind the clergy, dragging after her that car of misery, that rolling coffin, in which she had endured so much agony. And the crowd which acclaimed her, the frantic crowd, followed in her wake.

IV

Triumph—Despair

Pierre also had followed Marie, and like her was behind the canopy, carried along as it were by the blast of glory which made her drag her little car along in triumph. Every moment, however, there was so much tempestuous pushing that the young priest would assuredly have fallen if a rough hand had not upheld him.

"Don't be alarmed," said a voice; "give me your arm, otherwise you won't be able to remain on your feet."

Pierre turned round, and was surprised to recognise Father Massias, who had left Father Fourcade in the pulpit in order to accompany the procession. An extraordinary fever was sustaining him, throwing him forward, as solid as a rock, with eyes glowing like live coals, and an excited face covered with perspiration.

"Take care, then!" he again exclaimed; "give me your arm."

A fresh human wave had almost swept them away. And Pierre now yielded to the support of this terrible enthusiast, whom he remembered as a fellow-student at the seminary. What a singular meeting it was, and how greatly he would have liked to possess that violent faith, that mad faith, which was making Massias pant, with his throat full of sobs, whilst he continued giving vent to the ardent entreaty "Lord Jesus, heal our sick! Lord Jesus, heal our sick!"

There was no cessation of this cry behind the canopy, where there was always a crier whose duty it was to accord no respite to the slow clemency of Heaven. At times a thick voice full of anguish, and at others a shrill and piercing voice, would arise. The Father's, which was an imperious one, was now at last breaking through sheer emotion.

"Lord Jesus, heal our sick! Lord Jesus, heal our sick!"

The rumour of Marie's wondrous cure, of the miracle whose fame would speedily fill all Christendom, had already spread from one to the other end of Lourdes; and from this had come the increased vertigo of the multitude, the attack of contagious delirium which now caused it to whirl and rush toward the Blessed Sacrament like the resistless flux of a rising tide. One and all yielded to the desire of beholding the Sacrament and touching it, of being cured and becoming happy. The Divinity was passing; and now it was not merely a question of ailing beings glowing with a desire for life, but a longing for happiness which consumed all present and raised them up with bleeding, open hearts and eager hands.

Berthaud, who feared the excesses of this religious adoration, had decided to accompany his men. He commanded them, carefully watching over the double chain of bearers beside the canopy in order that it might not be broken.

"Close your ranks—closer—closer!" he called, "and keep your arms firmly linked!"

These young men, chosen from among the most vigorous of the bearers, had an extremely difficult duty to discharge. The wall which they formed, shoulder to shoulder, with arms linked at the waist and the neck, kept on giving way under the involuntary assaults of the throng. Nobody, certainly, fancied that he was pushing, but there was constant eddying, and deep waves of people rolled towards the procession from afar and threatened to submerge it.

When the canopy had reached the middle of the Place du Rosaire, Abbe Judaine really thought that he would be unable to go any farther. Numerous conflicting currents had set in over the vast expanse, and were whirling, assailing him from all sides, so that he had to halt under the swaying canopy, which shook like a sail in a sudden squall on the open sea. He held the Blessed Sacrament aloft with his numbed hands, each moment fearing that a final push would throw him over; for he fully realised that the golden monstrance, radiant like a sun, was the one passion of all that multitude, the Divinity they demanded to kiss, in order that they might lose themselves in it, even though they should annihilate it in doing so. Accordingly, while standing there, the priest anxiously turned his eyes on Berthaud.

"Let nobody pass!" called the latter to the bearers—"nobody! The orders are precise; you hear me?"

Voices, however, were rising in supplication on all sides, wretched beings were sobbing with arms outstretched and lips protruding, in the wild desire that they might be allowed to approach and kneel at the priest's feet. What divine grace it would be to be thrown upon the ground and trampled under foot by the whole procession!* An infirm

---

* One is here irresistibly reminded of the car of Juggernaut, and of the Hindoo fanatics throwing themselves beneath its wheels in the belief that they would thus obtain an entrance into Paradise.—Trans.

old man displayed his withered hand in the conviction that it would be made sound again were he only allowed to touch the monstrance. A dumb woman wildly pushed her way through the throng with her broad shoulders, in order that she might loosen her tongue by a kiss. Others were shouting, imploring, and even clenching their fists in their rage with those cruel men who denied cure to their bodily sufferings and their mental wretchedness. The orders to keep them back were rigidly enforced, however, for the most serious accidents were feared.

"Nobody, nobody!" repeated Berthaud; "let nobody whatever pass!"

There was a woman there, however, who touched every heart with compassion. Clad in wretched garments, bareheaded, her face wet with tears, she was holding in her arms a little boy of ten years or so, whose limp, paralysed legs hung down inertly. The lad's weight was too great for one so weak as herself, still she did not seem to feel it. She had brought the boy there, and was now entreating the bearers with an invincible obstinacy which neither words nor hustling could conquer.

At last, as Abbe Judaine, who felt deeply moved, beckoned to her to approach, two of the bearers, in deference to his compassion, drew apart, despite all the danger of opening a breach, and the woman then rushed forward with her burden, and fell in a heap before the priest. For a moment he rested the foot of the monstrance on the child's head, and the mother herself pressed her eager, longing lips to it; and, as they started off again, she wished to remain behind the canopy, and followed the procession, with streaming hair and panting breast, staggering the while under the heavy burden, which was fast exhausting her strength.

They managed, with great difficulty, to cross the remainder of the Place du Rosaire, and then the ascent began, the glorious ascent by way of the monumental incline; whilst upon high, on the fringe of heaven, the Basilica reared its slim spire, whence pealing bells were winging their flight, sounding the triumphs of Our Lady of Lourdes. And now it was towards an apotheosis that the canopy slowly climbed, towards the lofty portal of the high-perched sanctuary which stood open, face to face with the Infinite, high above the huge multitude whose waves continued soaring across the valley's squares and avenues. Preceding the processional cross, the magnificent beadle, all blue and silver, was already rearing the level of the Rosary cupola, the spacious esplanade formed by the roof of the lower church, across which the pilgrimage deputations began to wind, with their bright-coloured silk and velvet banners waving in the ruddy glow of the sunset. Then came the clergy, the priests in snowy surplices, and the priests in golden chasubles, likewise shining out like a procession of stars. And the censers swung, and the canopy continued climbing, without anything of its bearers being seen, so that it seemed as though a mysterious power, some troop of invisible angels, were carrying it off in this glorious ascension towards the open portal of heaven.

A sound of chanting had burst forth; the voices in the procession no longer called for the healing of the sick, now that the *cortege* had extricated itself from amidst the crowd. The miracle had been worked, and they were celebrating it with the full power of their lungs, amidst the pealing of the bells and the quivering gaiety of the atmosphere.

"*Magnificat anima mea Dominum*"—they began. "My soul doth magnify the Lord."

'Twas the song of gratitude, already chanted at the Grotto, and again springing from every heart: "*Et exsultavit spiritus meus in Deo salutari meo.*" "And my spirit hath rejoiced in God my Saviour."

Meantime it was with increasing, overflowing joy that Marie took part in that radiant ascent, by the colossal gradient way, towards the glowing Basilica. It seemed to her, as she continued climbing, that she was growing stronger and stronger, that her legs, so long lifeless, became firmer at each step. The little car which she victoriously dragged behind her was like the earthly tenement of her illness, the *inferno* whence the Blessed Virgin had extricated her, and although its handle was making her hands sore, she nevertheless wished to pull it up yonder with her, in order that she might cast it at last at the feet of the Almighty. No obstacle could stay her course, she laughed through the big tears which were falling on her cheeks, her bosom was swelling, her demeanour becoming warlike. One of her slippers had become unfastened, and the strip of lace had fallen from her head to her shoulders. Nevertheless, with her lovely fair hair crowning her like a helmet and her face beaming brightly, she still marched on and on with such an awakening of will and strength that, behind her, you could hear her car leap and rattle over the rough slope of the flagstones, as though it had been a mere toy.

Near Marie was Pierre, still leaning on the arm of Father Massias, who had not relinquished his hold. Lost amidst the far-spreading emotion, the young priest was unable to reflect. Moreover his companion's sonorous voice quite deafened him.

"*Deposuit potentes de sede et exaltavit humiles.*" "He hath put down the mighty from their seat, and hath exalted the humble."

On Pierre's other side, the right, Berthaud, who no longer had any cause for anxiety, was now also following the canopy. He had given his bearers orders to break their chain, and was gazing with an expression of delight on the human sea through which the procession had lately passed. The higher they the incline, the more did the Place du Rosaire and the avenues and paths of the gardens expand below them, black with the swarming multitude. It was a bird's-eye view of a whole nation, an ant-hill which ever increased in size, spreading farther and farther away. "Look!" Berthaud at last exclaimed to Pierre. "How vast and how beautiful it is! Ah! well, the year won't have been a bad one after all."

Looking upon Lourdes as a centre of propaganda, where his political rancour found satisfaction, he always rejoiced when there was a numerous pilgrimage, as in his mind it was bound to prove unpleasant to the Government. Ah! thought he, if they had only been able to bring the working classes of the towns thither, and create a Catholic democracy. "Last year we scarcely reached the figure of two hundred thousand pilgrims," he continued, "but we shall exceed it this year, I hope." And then, with the gay air of the jolly fellow that he was, despite his sectarian passions, he added: "Well, 'pon my word, I was really pleased just now when there was such a crush. Things are looking up, I thought, things are looking up."

Pierre, however, was not listening to him; his mind had been struck by the grandeur of the spectacle. That multitude, which spread out more and more as the procession rose higher and higher above it, that magnificent valley which was hollowed out below and ever became more and more extensive, displaying afar off its gorgeous horizon of mountains, filled him with quivering admiration. His mental trouble was increased by it all, and seeking Marie's glance, he waved his arm to draw her attention to the vast circular expanse of country. And his gesture deceived her, for in the purely spiritual excitement that possessed her she did not behold the material spectacle he pointed at, but thought that he was calling earth to witness the prodigious favours which the Blessed Virgin had heaped upon them both; for she imagined that he had had his share of the miracle, and that in the stroke of grace which had set her erect with her flesh healed, he, so near to her that their hearts mingled, had felt himself enveloped and raised by the same divine power, his soul saved from doubt, conquered by faith once more. How could he have witnessed her wondrous cure, indeed, without being convinced? Moreover, she had prayed so fervently for him outside the Grotto on the previous night. And now, therefore, to her excessive delight, she espied him transfigured like herself, weeping and laughing, restored to God again. And this lent increased force to her blissful fever; she dragged her little car along with unwearying hands, and—as though it were their double cross, her own redemption and her friend's redemption which she was carrying up that incline with its resounding flagstones—she would have liked to drag it yet farther, for leagues and leagues, ever higher and higher, to the most inaccessible summits, to the transplendent threshold of Paradise itself.

"O Pierre, Pierre!" she stammered, "how sweet it is that this great happiness should have fallen on us together—yes, together! I prayed for it so fervently, and she granted my prayer, and saved you even in saving me. Yes, I felt your soul mingling with my own. Tell me that our mutual prayers have been granted, tell me that I have won your salvation even as you have won mine!"

He understood her mistake and shuddered.

"If you only knew," she continued, "how great would have been my grief had I thus ascended into light alone. Oh! to be chosen without you, to soar yonder without you! But with you, Pierre, it is rapturous delight! We have been saved together, we shall be happy forever! I feel all needful strength for happiness, yes, strength enough to raise the world!"

And in spite of everything, he was obliged to answer her and lie, revolting at the idea of spoiling, dimming that great and pure felicity. "Yes, yes, be happy, Marie," he said, "for I am very happy myself, and all our sufferings are redeemed."

But even while he spoke he felt a deep rending within him, as though a brutal hatchet-stroke were parting them forever. Amidst their common sufferings, she had hitherto remained the little friend of childhood's days, the first artlessly loved woman, whom he knew to be still his own, since she could belong to none. But now she was cured, and he remained alone in his hell, repeating to himself that she would never more be his! This sudden thought so upset him that he averted his eyes, in despair at reaping such suffering from the prodigious felicity with which she exulted.

However the chant went on, and Father Massias, hearing nothing and seeing nothing, absorbed as he was in his glowing gratitude to God, shouted the final verse in a thundering voice: "*Sicut locutus est ad patres nostros, Abraham, et semini ejus in saecula.*" "As He spake to our fathers, to Abraham, and to his seed for ever!"

Yet another incline had to be climbed, yet another effort had to be made up that rough acclivity, with its large slippery flagstones. And the procession rose yet higher, and the ascent still went on in the full, bright light. There came a last turn, and the wheels of Marie's car grated against a granite curb. Then, still higher, still and ever higher, did it roll until it finally reached what seemed to be the very fringe of heaven.

And all at once the canopy appeared on the summit of the gigantic inclined ways, on the stone balcony overlooking the stretch of country outside the portal of the Basilica. Abbe Judaine stepped forward holding the Blessed Sacrament aloft with both hands. Marie, who had pulled her car up the balcony steps, was near him, her heart beating from her exertion, her face all aglow amidst the gold of her loosened hair. Then all the clergy, the snowy surplices, and the dazzling chasubles ranged themselves behind, whilst the banners waved like bunting decking the white balustrades. And a solemn minute followed.

From on high there could have been no grander spectacle. First, immediately below, there was the multitude, the human sea with its dark waves, its heaving billows, now for a moment stilled, amidst which you only distinguished the small pale specks of the faces uplifted towards the Basilica, in expectation of the Benediction; and as far as the eye could reach, from the place du Rosaire to the Gave, along the paths and avenues and across the open spaces, even to the old town in the distance; those little pale faces multiplied and multiplied, all with lips parted, and eyes fixed upon the august heaven was about to open to their gaze.

Then the vast amphitheatre of slopes and hills and mountains surged aloft, ascended upon all sides, crests following crests, until they faded away in the far blue atmosphere. The numerous convents among the trees on the first of the northern slopes, beyond the torrent—those of the Carmelites, the Dominicans, the Assumptionists, and the Sisters of Nevers—were coloured by a rosy reflection from the fire-like glow of the sunset. Then wooded masses rose one above the other, until they reached the heights of Le Buala, which were surmounted by the Serre de Julos, in its turn capped by the Miramont.

Deep valleys opened on the south, narrow gorges between piles of gigantic rocks whose bases were already steeped in lakes of bluish shadow, whilst the summits sparkled with the smiling farewell of the sun. The hills of Visens upon this side were empurpled, and shewed like a promontory of coral, in front of the stagnant lake of the ether, which was bright with a sapphire-like transparency. But, on the east, in front of you, the horizon again spread out to the very point of intersection of the seven valleys. The castle which had formerly guarded them still stood with its keep, its lofty walls, its black outlines—the outlines of a fierce fortress of feudal time,—upon the rock whose base was watered by the Gave; and upon this side of the stern old pile was the new town, looking quite gay amidst its gardens, with its swarm of white house-fronts, its large hotels, its lodging-houses, and its fine shops, whose windows were glowing like live embers; whilst, behind the castle, the discoloured roofs of old Lourdes spread out in confusion, in a ruddy light which hovered over them like a cloud of dust. At this late hour, when the declining luminary was sinking in royal splendour behind the little Gers and the big Gers, those two huge ridges of bare rock, spotted with patches of short herbage, formed nothing but a neutral, somewhat violet, background, as though, indeed, they were two curtains of sober hue drawn across the margin of the horizon.

And higher and still higher, in front of this immensity, did Abbe Judaine with both hands raise the Blessed Sacrament. He moved it slowly from one to the other horizon, causing it to describe a huge sign of the cross against the vault of heaven. He saluted the convents, the heights of Le Buala, the Serre de Julos, and the Miramont, upon his left; he saluted the huge fallen rocks of the dim valleys, and the empurpled hills of Visens, on his right; he saluted the new and the old town, the castle bathed by the Gave, the big and the little Gers, already drowsy, in front of him; and he saluted the woods, the torrents, the mountains, the faint chains linking the distant peaks, the whole earth, even beyond the visible horizon: Peace upon earth, hope and consolation to mankind! The multitude below had quivered beneath that great sign of the cross which enveloped it. It seemed as though a divine breath were passing, rolling those billows of little pale faces which were as numerous as the waves of an ocean. A loud murmur of adoration ascended; all those parted lips proclaimed the glory of God when, in the rays of the setting sun, the illumined monstrance again shone forth like another sun, a sun of pure gold, describing the sign of the cross in streaks of flame upon the threshold of the Infinite.

The banners, the clergy, with Abbe Judaine under the canopy, were already returning to the Basilica, when Marie, who was also entering it, still dragging her car by the handle, was stopped by two ladies, who kissed her, weeping. They were Madame de Jonquiere and her daughter Raymonde, who had come thither to witness the Benediction, and had been told of the miracle.

"Ah! my dear child, what happiness!" repeated the lady-hospitaller; "and how proud I am to have you in my ward! It is so precious a favour for all of us that the Blessed Virgin should have been pleased to select you."

Raymonde, meanwhile, had kept one of the young girl's hands in her own. "Will you allow me to call you my friend, mademoiselle?" said she. "I felt so much pity for you, and I am now so pleased to see you walking, so strong and beautiful already. Let me kiss you again. It will bring me happiness."

"Thank you, thank you with all my heart," Marie stammered amidst her rapture. "I am so happy, so very happy!"

"Oh! we will not leave you," resumed Madame de Jonquiere. "You hear me, Raymonde? We must follow her, and kneel beside her, and we will take her back after the ceremony."

Thereupon the two ladies joined the *cortege*, and, following the canopy, walked beside Pierre and Father Massias, between the rows of chairs which the deputations already occupied, to the very centre of the choir. The banners alone were allowed on either side of the high altar; but Marie advanced to its steps, still dragging her car, whose wheels resounded over the flagstones. She had at last brought it to the spot whither the sacred madness of her desire had longingly impelled her to drag it. She had brought it, indeed, woeful, wretched-looking as it was, into the splendour of God's house, so that it might there testify to the truth of the miracle. The threshold had scarcely been crossed when the organs burst into a hymn of triumph, the sonorous acclamation of a happy people, from amidst which there soon arose a celestial, angelic voice, of joyful shrillness and crystalline purity. Abbe Judaine had placed the Blessed Sacrament upon the altar, and the crowd was streaming into the nave, each taking a seat, installing him or herself in a corner, pending the commencement of the ceremony. Marie had at once fallen on her knees between Madame de Jonquiere and Raymonde, whose eyes were moist with tender emotion; whilst Father Massias, exhausted by the extraordinary tension of the nerves which had been sustaining him ever since his departure from the Grotto, had sunk upon the ground, sobbing, with his head between his hands. Behind him

Pierre and Berthaud remained standing, the latter still busy with his superintendence, his eyes ever on the watch, seeing that good order was preserved even during the most violent outbursts of emotion.

Then, amidst all his mental confusion, increased by the deafening strains of the organ, Pierre raised his head and examined the interior of the Basilica. The nave was narrow and lofty, and streaked with bright colours, which numerous windows flooded with light. There were scarcely any aisles; they were reduced to the proportions of a mere passage running between the side-chapels and the clustering columns, and this circumstance seemed to increase the slim loftiness of the nave, the soaring of the stonework in perpendicular lines of infantile, graceful slenderness. A gilded railing, as transparent as lace, closed the choir, where the high altar, of white marble richly sculptured, arose in all its lavish chasteness. But the feature of the building which astonished you was the mass of extraordinary ornamentation which transformed the whole of it into an overflowing exhibition of embroidery and jewellery. What with all the banners and votive offerings, the perfect river of gifts which had flowed into it and remained clinging to its walls in a stream of gold and silver, velvet and silk, covering it from top to bottom, it was, so to say, the ever-glowing sanctuary of gratitude, whose thousand rich adornments seemed to be chanting a perpetual canticle of faith and thankfulness.

The banners, in particular, abounded, as innumerable as the leaves of trees. Some thirty hung from the vaulted roof, whilst others were suspended, like pictures, between the little columns around the triforium. And others, again, displayed themselves on the walls, waved in the depths of the side-chapels, and encompassed the choir with a heaven of silk, satin, and velvet. You could count them by hundreds, and your eyes grew weary of admiring them. Many of them were quite celebrated, so renowned for their skilful workmanship that talented embroideresses took the trouble to come to Lourdes on purpose to examine them. Among these were the banner of our Lady of Fourvieres, bearing the arms of the city of Lyons; the banner of Alsace, of black velvet embroidered with gold; the banner of Lorraine, on which you beheld the Virgin casting her cloak around two children; and the white and blue banner of Brittany, on which bled the sacred heart of Jesus in the midst of a halo. All empires and kingdoms of the earth were represented; the most distant lands—Canada, Brazil, Chili, Haiti—

here had their flags, which, in all piety, were being offered as a tribute of homage to the Queen of Heaven.

Then, after the banners, there were other marvels, the thousands and thousands of gold and silver hearts which were hanging everywhere, glittering on the walls like stars in the heavens. Some were grouped together in the form of mystical roses, others described festoons and garlands, others, again, climbed up the pillars, surrounded the windows, and constellated the deep, dim chapels. Below the triforium somebody had had the ingenious idea of employing these hearts to trace in tall letters the various words which the Blessed Virgin had addressed to Bernadette; and thus, around the nave, there extended a long frieze of words, the delight of the infantile minds which busied themselves with spelling them. It was a swarming, a prodigious resplendency of hearts, whose infinite number deeply impressed you when you thought of all the hands, trembling with gratitude, which had offered them. Moreover, the adornments comprised many other votive offerings, and some of quite an unexpected description. There were bridal wreaths and crosses of honour, jewels and photographs, chaplets, and even spurs, in glass cases or frames. There were also the epaulets and swords of officers, together with a superb sabre, left there in memory of a miraculous conversion.

But all this was not sufficient; other riches, riches of every kind, shone out on all sides—marble statues, diadems enriched with brilliants, a marvellous carpet designed at Blois and embroidered by ladies of all parts of France, and a golden palm with ornaments of enamel, the gift of the sovereign pontiff. The lamps suspended from the vaulted roof, some of them of massive gold and the most delicate workmanship, were also gifts. They were too numerous to be counted, they studded the nave with stars of great price. Immediately in front of the tabernacle there was one, a masterpiece of chasing, offered by Ireland. Others—one from Lille, one from Valence, one from Macao in far-off China—were veritable jewels, sparkling with precious stones. And how great was the resplendency when the choir's score of chandeliers was illumined, when the hundreds of lamps and the hundreds of candles burned all together, at the great evening ceremonies! The whole church then became a conflagration, the thousands of gold and silver hearts reflecting all the little flames with thousands of fiery scintillations. It was like a huge and wondrous brasier; the walls streamed with live flakes of light; you seemed to be entering into the blinding glory of

Paradise itself; whilst on all sides the innumerable banners spread out their silk, their satin, and their velvet, embroidered with sanguifluous sacred hearts, victorious saints, and Virgins whose kindly smiles engendered miracles.

Ah! how many ceremonies had already displayed their pomp in that Basilica! Worship, prayer, chanting, never ceased there. From one end of the year to the other incense smoked, organs roared, and kneeling multitudes prayed there with their whole souls. Masses, vespers, sermons, were continually following one upon another; day by day the religious exercises began afresh, and each festival of the Church was celebrated with unparalleled magnificence. The least noteworthy anniversary supplied a pretext for pompous solemnities. Each pilgrimage was granted its share of the dazzling resplendency. It was necessary that those suffering ones and those humble ones who had come from such long distances should be sent home consoled and enraptured, carrying with them a vision of Paradise espied through its opening portals. They beheld the luxurious surroundings of the Divinity, and would forever remain enraptured by the sight. In the depths of bare, wretched rooms, indeed, by the side of humble pallets of suffering throughout all Christendom, a vision of the Basilica with its blazing riches continually arose like a vision of fortune itself, like a vision of the wealth of that life to be, into which the poor would surely some day enter after their long, long misery in this terrestrial sphere.

Pierre, however, felt no delight; no consolation, no hope, came to him as he gazed upon all the splendour. His frightful feeling of discomfort was increasing, all was becoming black within him, with that blackness of the tempest which gathers when men's thoughts and feelings pant and shriek. He had felt immense desolation rising in his soul ever since Marie, crying that she was healed, had risen from her little car and walked along with such strength and fulness of life. Yet he loved her like a passionately attached brother, and had experienced unlimited happiness on seeing that she no longer suffered. Why, therefore, should her felicity bring him such agony? He could now no longer gaze at her, kneeling there, radiant amidst her tears, with beauty recovered and increased, without his poor heart bleeding as from some mortal wound. Still he wished to remain there, and so, averting his eyes, he tried to interest himself in Father Massias, who was still shaking with violent sobbing on the flagstones, and whose prostration and annihilation, amidst the consuming illusion of divine love, he sorely envied. For a moment, moreover, he questioned Berthaud, feigning to admire some banner and requesting information respecting it.

"Which one?" asked the superintendent of the bearers; "that lace banner over there?"

"Yes, that one on the left."

"Oh! it is a banner offered by Le Puy. The arms are those of Le Puy and Lourdes linked together by the Rosary. The lace is so fine that if you crumpled the banner up, you could hold it in the hollow of your hand."

However, Abbe Judaine was now stepping forward; the ceremony was about to begin. Again did the organs resound, and again was a canticle chanted, whilst, on the altar, the Blessed Sacrament looked like the sovereign planet amidst the scintillations of the gold and silver hearts, as innumerable as stars. And then Pierre lacked the strength to remain there any longer. Since Marie had Madame de Jonquiere and Raymonde with her, and they would accompany her back, he might surely go off by himself, vanish into some shadowy corner, and there, at last, vent his grief. In a few words he excused himself, giving his appointment with Doctor Chassaigne as a pretext for his departure. However, another fear suddenly came to him, that of being unable to leave the building, so densely did the serried throng of believers bar the open doorway. But immediately afterwards he had an inspiration, and, crossing the sacristy, descended into the crypt by the narrow interior stairway.

Deep silence and sepulchral gloom suddenly succeeded to the joyous chants and prodigious radiance of the Basilica above. Cut in the rock, the crypt formed two narrow passages, parted by a massive block of stone which upheld the nave, and conducting to a subterranean chapel under the apse, where some little lamps remained burning both day and night. A dim forest of pillars rose up there, a mystic terror reigned in that semi-obscurity where the mystery ever quivered. The chapel walls remained bare, like the very stones of the tomb, in which all men must some day sleep the last sleep. And along the passages, against their sides, covered from top to bottom with marble votive offerings, you only saw a double row of confessionals; for it was here, in the lifeless tranquillity of the bowels of the earth, that sins were confessed; and there were priests, speaking all languages, to absolve the sinners who came thither from the four corners of the world.

At that hour, however, when the multitude was thronging the Basilica above, the crypt had become quite deserted. Not a soul, save

Pierre's, throbbed there ever so faintly; and he, amidst that deep silence, that darkness, that coolness of the grave, fell upon his knees. It was not, however, through any need of prayer and worship, but because his whole being was giving way beneath his crushing mental torment. He felt a torturing longing to be able to see clearly within himself. Ah! why could he not plunge even more deeply into the heart of things, reflect, understand, and at last calm himself.

And it was a fearful agony that he experienced. He tried to remember all the minutes that had gone by since Marie, suddenly springing from her pallet of wretchedness, had raised her cry of resurrection. Why had he even then, despite his fraternal joy in seeing her erect, felt such an awful sensation of discomfort, as though, indeed, the greatest of all possible misfortunes had fallen upon him? Was he jealous of the divine grace? Did he suffer because the Virgin, whilst healing her, had forgotten him, whose soul was so afflicted? He remembered how he had granted himself a last delay, fixed a supreme appointment with Faith for the moment when the Blessed Sacrament should pass by, were Marie only cured; and she was cured, and still he did not believe, and henceforth there was no hope, for never, never would he be able to believe. Therein lay the bare, bleeding sore. The truth burst upon him with blinding cruelty and certainty—she was saved, he was lost. That pretended miracle which had restored her to life had, in him, completed the ruin of all belief in the supernatural. That which he had, for a moment, dreamed of seeking, and perhaps finding, at Lourdes,—naive faith, the happy faith of a little child,—was no longer possible, would never bloom again after that collapse of the miraculous, that cure which Beauclair had foretold, and which had afterwards come to pass, exactly as had been predicted. Jealous! No—he was not jealous; but he was ravaged, full of mortal sadness at thus remaining all alone in the icy desert of his intelligence, regretting the illusion, the lie, the divine love of the simpleminded, for which henceforth there was no room in his heart.

A flood of bitterness stifled him, and tears started from his eyes. He had slipped on to the flagstones, prostrated by his anguish. And, by degrees, he remembered the whole delightful story, from the day when Marie, guessing how he was tortured by doubt, had become so passionately eager for his conversion, taking hold of his hand in the gloom, retaining it in her own, and stammering that she would pray for him—oh! pray for him with her whole soul. She forgot herself, she entreated the Blessed Virgin to save her friend rather than herself if there were but one grace that she could obtain from her Divine Son. Then came another memory, the memory of the delightful hours which they had spent together amid the dense darkness of the trees during the night procession. There, again, they had prayed for one another, mingled one in the other with so ardent a desire for mutual happiness that, for a moment, they had attained to the very depths of the love which gives and immolates itself. And now their long, tear-drenched tenderness, their pure idyl of suffering, was ending in this brutal separation; she on her side saved, radiant amidst the hosannas of the triumphant Basilica; and he lost, sobbing with wretchedness, bowed down in the depths of the dark crypt in an icy, grave-like solitude. It was as though he had just lost her again, and this time forever and forever.

All at once Pierre felt the sharp stab which this thought dealt his heart. He at last understood his pain—a sudden light illumined the terrible crisis of woe amidst which he was struggling. He had lost Marie for the first time on the day when he had become a priest, saying to himself that he might well renounce his manhood since she, stricken in her sex by incurable illness, would never be a woman. But behold! she *was* cured. Behold! she *had* become a woman. She had all at once appeared to him very strong, very beautiful, living, and desirable. He, who was dead, however, could not become a man again. Never more would he be able to raise the tombstone which crushed and imprisoned his flesh. She fled away alone, leaving him in the cold grave. The whole wide world was opening before her with smiling happiness, with the love which laughs in the sunlit paths, with the husband, with children, no doubt. Whereas he, buried, as it were to his shoulders, had naught of his body free, save his brain, and that remained free, no doubt, in order that he might suffer the more. She had still been his so long as she had not belonged to another; and if he had been enduring such agony during the past hour, it was only through this final rending which, this time, parted her from him forever and forever.

Then rage shook Pierre from head to foot. He was tempted to return to the Basilica, and cry the truth aloud to Marie. The miracle was a lie! The helpful beneficence of an all-powerful Divinity was but so much illusion! Nature alone had acted, life had conquered once again. And he would have given proofs: he would have shown how life, the only sovereign, worked for health amid all the sufferings of this terrestrial sphere. And then they would have gone off together; they would have fled far, far away, that they might be happy. But a sudden terror took possession of him. What! lay hands upon that little spotless soul, kill all belief in it, fill it with the ruins which worked such havoc in his own soul? It all at once occurred to him that this would be odious sacrilege. He would afterwards become horrified with himself, he would look upon himself as her murderer were he some day to realise that he was unable to give her a happiness equal to that which she would have lost. Perhaps, too, she would not believe him. And, moreover, would she ever consent to marry a priest who had broken his vows? She who would always retain the sweet and never-to be-forgotten memory of how she had been healed in ecstasy! His design then appeared to him insane, monstrous, polluting. And his revolt rapidly subsided, until he only retained a feeling of infinite weariness, a sensation of a burning, incurable wound—the wound of his poor, bruised, lacerated heart.

Then, however, amidst his abandonment, the void in which he was whirling, a supreme struggle began, filling him again with agony. What should he do? His sufferings made a coward of him, and he would have liked to flee, so that he might never see Marie again. For he understood very well that he would now have to lie to her, since she thought that he was saved like herself, converted, healed in soul, even as she had been healed in body. She had told him of her joy while dragging her car up the colossal gradient way. Oh! to have had that great happiness together, together; to have felt their hearts melt and mingle one in the other! And even then he had already lied, as he would always be obliged to lie in order that he might not spoil her pure and blissful illusion. He let the last throbbings of his veins subside, and vowed that he would find sufficient strength for the sublime charity of feigning peacefulness of soul, the rapture of one who is redeemed. For he wished her to be wholly happy—without a regret, without a doubt—in the full serenity of faith, convinced that the blessed Virgin had indeed given her consent to their purely mystical union. What did his torments matter? Later on, perhaps, he might recover possession of himself. Amidst his desolate solitude of mind would there not always be a little joy to sustain him, all that joy whose consoling falsity he would leave to her?

Several minutes again elapsed, and Pierre, still overwhelmed, remained on the flagstones, seeking to calm his fever. He no longer thought, he no longer lived; he was a prey to that prostration of the entire being which follows upon great crises. But, all at once, he fancied he could hear a sound of footsteps, and thereupon he painfully rose to his feet, and feigned to be reading the inscriptions graven in the marble votive slabs along the walls. He had been mistaken—nobody was there; nevertheless, seeking to divert his mind, he continued perusing the inscriptions, at first in a mechanical kind of way, and then, little by little, feeling a fresh emotion steal over him.

The sight was almost beyond imagination. Faith, love, and gratitude displayed themselves in a hundred, a thousand ways on these marble slabs with gilded lettering. Some of the inscriptions were so artless as to provoke a smile. A colonel had sent a sculptured representation of his foot with the words: "Thou hast preserved it; grant that it may serve Thee." Farther on you read the line: "May Her protection extend to the glass trade." And then, by the frankness of certain expressions of thanks, you realised of what a strange character the appeals had been. "To Mary the Immaculate," ran one inscription, "from a father of a family, in recognition of health restored, a lawsuit won, and advancement gained." However, the memory of these instances faded away amidst the chorus of soaring, fervent cries. There was the cry of the lovers: "Paul and Anna entreat Our Lady of Lourdes to bless their union." There was the cry of the mothers in various forms: "Gratitude to Mary, who has thrice healed my child."—"Gratitude to Mary for the birth of Antoinette, whom I dedicate, like myself and all my kin, to Her."—"P. D., three years old, has been preserved to the love of his parents." And then came the cry of the wives, the cry, too, of the sick restored to health, and of the souls restored to happiness: "Protect my husband; grant that my husband may enjoy good health."—"I was crippled in both legs, and now I am healed."—"We came, and now we hope."—"I prayed, I wept, and She heard me." And there were yet other cries, cries whose veiled glow conjured up thoughts of long romances: "Thou didst join us together; protect us, we pray Thee."—"To Mary, for the greatest of all blessings." And the same cries, the same words—gratitude, thankfulness, homage, acknowledgment,—occurred again and again, ever with the same passionate fervour. All! those hundreds, those thousands of cries which were forever graven on that marble, and from the depths of the crypt rose clamorously to the Virgin, proclaiming the everlasting devotion of the unhappy beings whom she had succoured.

Pierre did not weary of reading them, albeit his mouth was bitter and increasing desolation was filling him. So it was only he who had no succour to hope for! When so many sufferers were listened to, he alone had been unable to make himself heard! And he now began to think of the extraordinary number of prayers which must be said at Lourdes from one end of the year to the other. He tried to cast them up; those said during the days spent at the Grotto and during the nights spent at the Rosary, those said at the ceremonies at the Basilica, and those said at the sunlight and the starlight processions. But this continual entreaty of every second was beyond computation. It seemed as if the faithful were determined to weary the ears of the Divinity, determined to extort favours and forgiveness by the very multitude, the vast multitude of their prayers. The priests said that it was necessary to offer to God the acts of expiation which the sins of France required, and that when the number of these acts of expiation should be large enough, God would smite France no more. What a harsh belief in the necessity of chastisement! What a ferocious idea born of the gloomiest pessimism! How evil life must be if it were indeed necessary that such imploring cries, such cries of physical and moral wretchedness, should ever and ever ascend to Heaven!

In the midst of all his sadness, Pierre felt deep compassion penetrate his heart. He was upset by the thought that mankind should be so wretched, reduced to such a state of woe, so bare, so weak, so utterly forsaken, that it renounced its own reason to place the one sole possibility of happiness in the hallucinatory intoxication of dreams. Tears once more filled his eyes; he wept for himself and for others, for all the poor tortured beings who feel a need of stupefying and numbing their pains in order to escape from the realities of the world. He again seemed to hear the swarming, kneeling crowd of the Grotto, raising the glowing entreaty of its prayer to Heaven, the multitude of twenty and thirty thousand souls from whose midst ascended such a fervour of desire that you seemed to see it smoking in the sunlight like incense. Then another form of the exaltation of faith glowed, beneath the crypt, in the Church of the Rosary, where nights were spent in a paradise of rapture, amidst the silent delights of the communion, the mute appeals in which the whole being pines, burns, and soars aloft. And as though the cries raised before the Grotto and the perpetual adoration of the Rosary were not sufficient, that clamour of ardent entreaty burst forth afresh on the walls of the crypt around him; and here it was eternised in marble, here it would continue shrieking the sufferings of humanity even into the far-away ages. It was the marble, it was the walls themselves praying, seized by that shudder of universal woe which penetrated even the world's stones. And, at last, the prayers ascended yet higher, still higher, soared aloft from the radiant Basilica, which was humming and buzzing above him, full as it now was of a frantic multitude, whose mighty voice, bursting into a canticle of hope, he fancied he could hear through the flagstones of the nave. And it finally seemed to him that he was being whirled away, transported, as though he were indeed amidst the very vibrations of that huge wave of prayer, which, starting from the dust of the earth, ascended the tier of superposed churches, spreading from tabernacle to tabernacle, and filling even the walls with such pity that they sobbed aloud, and that the supreme cry of wretchedness pierced its way into heaven with the white spire, the lofty golden cross, above the steeple. O Almighty God, O Divinity, Helpful Power, whoever, whatever Thou mayst be, take pity upon poor mankind and make human suffering cease!

All at once Pierre was dazzled. He had followed the left-hand passage, and was coming out into broad daylight, above the inclined ways, and two affectionate arms at once caught hold of him and clasped him. It was Doctor Chassaigne, whose appointment he had forgotten, and who had been waiting there to take him to visit Bernadette's room and Abbe Peyramale's church. "Oh! what joy must be yours, my child!" exclaimed the good old man. "I have just learnt the great news, the extraordinary favour which Our Lady of Lourdes has granted to your young friend. Recollect what I told you the day before yesterday. I am now at ease—you are saved!"

A last bitterness came to the young priest who was very pale. However, he was able to smile, and he gently answered: "Yes, we are saved, we are very happy."

It was the lie beginning; the divine illusion which in a spirit of charity he wished to give to others.

And then one more spectacle met Pierre's eyes. The principal door of the Basilica stood wide open, and a red sheet of light from the setting sun was enfilading the nave from one to the other end. Everything was flaring with the splendour of a conflagration—the gilt railings of the choir, the votive offerings of gold and silver, the lamps enriched with precious stones, the banners with their bright embroideries, and the swinging censers, which seemed like flying jewels. And yonder, in the depths of this burning splendour, amidst the snowy surplices and the golden chasubles, he recognised Marie, with hair unbound, hair of gold like all else, enveloping her in a golden mantle. And the organs burst into a hymn of triumph; and the delirious people acclaimed God; and Abbe Judaine, who had again just taken the Blessed Sacrament from off the altar, raised it aloft and presented it to their gaze for the last time; and radiantly magnificent it shone out like a glory amidst the streaming gold of the Basilica, whose prodigious triumph all the bells proclaimed in clanging, flying peals.

V

CRADLE AND GRAVE

Immediately afterwards, as they descended the steps, Doctor Chassaigne said to Pierre: "You have just seen the triumph; I will now show you two great injustices."

And he conducted him into the Rue des Petits-Fosses to visit Bernadette's room, that low, dark chamber whence she set out on the day the Blessed Virgin appeared to her.

The Rue des Petits-Fosses starts from the former Rue des Bois, now the Rue de la Grotte, and crosses the Rue du Tribunal. It is a winding lane, slightly sloping and very gloomy. The passers-by are few; it is skirted by long walls, wretched-looking houses, with mournful facades in which never a window opens. All its gaiety consists in an occasional tree in a courtyard.

"Here we are," at last said the doctor.

At the part where he had halted, the street contracted, becoming very narrow, and the house faced the high, grey wall of a barn. Raising their heads, both men looked up at the little dwelling, which seemed quite lifeless, with its narrow casements and its coarse, violet pargeting, displaying the shameful ugliness of poverty. The entrance passage down below was quite black; an old light iron gate was all that closed it; and there was a step to mount, which in rainy weather was immersed in the water of the gutter.

"Go in, my friend, go in," said the doctor. "You have only to push the gate."

The passage was long, and Pierre kept on feeling the damp wall with his hand, for fear of making a false step. It seemed to him as if he were descending into a cellar, in deep obscurity, and he could feel a slippery soil impregnated with water beneath his feet. Then at the end, in obedience to the doctor's direction, he turned to the right.

"Stoop, or you may hurt yourself," said M. Chassaigne; "the door is very low. There, here we are."

The door of the room, like the gate in the street, stood wide open, as if the place had been carelessly abandoned; and Pierre, who had stopped in the middle of the chamber, hesitating, his eyes still full of the bright daylight outside, could distinguish absolutely nothing. He had fallen into complete darkness, and felt an icy chill about the shoulders similar to the sensation that might be caused by a wet towel.

But, little by little, his eyes became accustomed to the dimness. Two windows of unequal size opened on to a narrow, interior courtyard, where only a greenish light descended, as at the bottom of a well; and to read there, in the middle of the day, it would be necessary to have a candle. Measuring about fifteen feet by twelve, the room was flagged with large uneven stones; while the principal beam and the rafters of the roof, which were visible, had darkened with time and assumed a dirty, sooty hue. Opposite the door was the chimney, a miserable plaster chimney, with a mantelpiece formed of a rotten old plank. There was a sink between this chimney and one of the windows. The walls, with their decaying, damp-stained plaster falling off by bits, were full of cracks, and turning a dirty black like the ceiling. There was no longer any furniture there; the room seemed abandoned; you could only catch a glimpse of some confused, strange objects, unrecognisable in the heavy obscurity that hung about the corners.

After a spell of silence, the doctor exclaimed "Yes, this is the room; all came from here. Nothing has been changed, with the exception that the furniture has gone. I have tried to picture how it was placed: the beds certainly stood against this wall, opposite the windows; there must have been three of them at least, for the Soubirouses were seven—the father, mother, two boys, and three girls. Think of that! Three beds filling this room! Seven persons living in this small space! All of them buried alive, without air, without light, almost without bread! What frightful misery! What lowly, pity-awaking poverty!"

But he was interrupted. A shadowy form, which Pierre at first took for an old woman, entered. It was a priest, however, the curate of the parish, who now occupied the house. He was acquainted with the doctor.

"I heard your voice, Monsieur Chassaigne, and came down," said he. "So there you are, showing the room again?"

"Just so, Monsieur l' Abbe; I took the liberty. It does not inconvenience you?"

"Oh! not at all, not at all! Come as often as you please, and bring other people."

He laughed in an engaging manner, and bowed to Pierre, who, astonished by this quiet carelessness, observed: "The people who come, however, must sometimes plague you?"

The curate in his turn seemed surprised. "Indeed, no! Nobody comes. You see the place is scarcely known. Every one remains over there at the Grotto. I leave the door open so as not to be worried. But days and days often pass without my hearing even the sound of a mouse."

Pierre's eyes were becoming more and more accustomed to the obscurity; and among the vague, perplexing objects which filled the corners, he ended by distinguishing some old barrels, remnants of fowl cages, and broken tools, a lot of rubbish such as is swept away and thrown to the bottom of cellars. Hanging from the rafters, moreover, were some provisions, a salad basket full of eggs, and several bunches of big pink onions.

"And, from what I see," resumed Pierre, with a slight shudder, "you have thought that you might make use of the room?"

The curate was beginning to feel uncomfortable. "Of course, that's it," said he. "What can one do? The house is so small, I have so little space. And then you can't imagine how damp it is here; it is altogether impossible to occupy the room. And so, *mon Dieu*, little by little all this has accumulated here by itself, contrary to one's own desire."

"It has become a lumber-room," concluded Pierre.

"Oh no! hardly that. An unoccupied room, and yet in truth, if you insist on it, it is a lumber-room!"

His uneasiness was increasing, mingled with a little shame. Doctor Chassaigne remained silent and did not interfere; but he smiled, and was visibly delighted at his companion's revolt against human ingratitude. Pierre, unable to restrain himself, now continued: "You must excuse me, Monsieur l'Abbe, if I insist. But just reflect that you owe everything to Bernadette; but for her Lourdes would still be one of the least known towns of France. And really it seems to me that out of mere gratitude the parish ought to have transformed this wretched room into a chapel."

"Oh! a chapel!" interrupted the curate. "It is only a question of a human creature: the Church could not make her an object of worship."

"Well, we won't say a chapel, then; but at all events there ought to be some lights and flowers—bouquets of roses constantly renewed by the piety of the inhabitants and the pilgrims. In a word, I should like some little show of affection—a touching souvenir, a picture of Bernadette—something that would delicately indicate that she deserves to have a place in all hearts. This forgetfulness and desertion are shocking. It is monstrous that so much dirt should have been allowed to accumulate!"

The curate, a poor, thoughtless, nervous man, at once adopted Pierre's views: "In reality, you are a thousand times right," said he; "but I myself have no power, I can do nothing. Whenever they ask me for the room, to set it to rights, I will give it up and remove my barrels, although I really don't know where else to put them. Only, I repeat, it does not depend on me. I can do nothing, nothing at all!" Then, under the pretext that he had to go out, he hastened to take leave and run away again, saying to Doctor Chassaigne: "Remain, remain as long as you please; you are never in my way."

When the doctor once more found himself alone with Pierre he caught hold of both his hands with effusive delight. "Ah, my dear child," said he, "how pleased you have made me! How admirably you expressed to him all that has been boiling in my own heart so long! Like you, I thought of bringing some roses here every morning. I should have simply had the room cleaned, and would have contented myself with placing two large bunches of roses on the mantelpiece; for you know that I have long felt deep affection for Bernadette, and it seemed to me that those roses would be like the very flowering and perfume of her memory. Only—only—" and so saying he made a despairing gesture, "only courage failed me. Yes, I say courage, no one having yet dared to declare himself openly against the Fathers of the Grotto. One hesitates and recoils in the fear of stirring up a religious scandal. Fancy what a deplorable racket all this would create. And so those who are as indignant as I am are reduced to the necessity of holding their tongues—preferring a continuance of silence to anything else." Then, by way of conclusion, he added: "The ingratitude and rapacity of man, my dear child, are sad things to see. Each time I come into this dim wretchedness, my heart swells and I cannot restrain my tears."

He ceased speaking, and neither of them said another word, both being overcome by the extreme melancholy which the surroundings fostered. They were steeped in gloom. The dampness made them shudder as they stood there amidst the dilapidated walls and the dust of the old rubbish piled upon either side. And the idea returned to them that without Bernadette none of the prodigies which had made Lourdes a town unique in the world would have existed. It was at her voice that the miraculous spring had gushed forth, that the Grotto, bright with candles, had opened. Immense works were executed, new churches rose from the ground, giant-like causeways led up to God. An entire new city was built, as if by enchantment, with gardens, walks, quays, bridges, shops, and hotels. And people from the uttermost parts of the earth flocked thither in crowds, and the rain of millions fell with such force and so abundantly that the young city seemed likely to increase indefinitely—to fill the whole valley, from one to the other end of the mountains. If Bernadette had been suppressed none of those things would have existed, the extraordinary story would have relapsed into nothingness, old unknown Lourdes would still have been plunged in the sleep of ages at the foot of its castle. Bernadette was the sole labourer and creatress; and yet this room, whence she had set out on the day she beheld the Virgin, this cradle, indeed, of the miracle and of all the marvellous fortune of the town, was disdained, left a prey to vermin, good only for a lumber-room, where onions and empty barrels were put away.

Then the other side of the question vividly appeared in Pierre's mind, and he again seemed to see the triumph which he had just witnessed, the exaltation of the Grotto and Basilica, while Marie, dragging her little car, ascended behind the Blessed Sacrament, amidst the clamour of the multitude. But the Grotto especially shone out before him. It was no longer the wild, rocky cavity before which the child had formerly knelt on the deserted bank of the torrent; it was a chapel, transformed and enriched, a chapel illumined by a vast number of candles, where nations marched past in procession. All the noise, all the brightness, all the adoration, all the money, burst forth there in a splendour of constant victory. Here, at the cradle, in this dark, icy hole, there was not a soul, not a taper, not a hymn, not a flower. Of the infrequent visitors who came thither, none knelt or prayed. All that a few tender-hearted pilgrims had done in their desire to carry away a souvenir had been to reduce to dust, between their fingers, the half-rotten plank serving as a mantelshelf. The clergy ignored the existence of this spot of misery, which the processions ought to have visited as they might visit a station of glory. It was there that the poor child had begun her dream, one cold night, lying in bed between her two sisters, and seized with a fit of her ailment while the whole family was fast asleep. It was thence, too, that she had set out, unconsciously carrying along with her that dream, which was again to be born within her in the broad daylight and to flower so prettily in a vision such as those of the legends. And no one now followed in her footsteps. The manger was forgotten, and left in darkness—that manger where had germed the little humble seed which over yonder was now yielding such prodigious harvests, reaped by the workmen of the last hour amidst the sovereign pomp of ceremonies.

Pierre, whom the great human emotion of the story moved to tears, at last summed up his thoughts in three words, saying in a low voice, "It is Bethlehem."

"Yes," remarked Doctor Chassaigne, in his turn, "it is the wretched lodging, the chance refuge, where new religions are born of suffering and pity. And at times I ask myself if all is not better thus: if it is not better that this room should remain in its actual state of wretchedness and abandonment. It seems to me that Bernadette has nothing to lose by it, for I love her all the more when I come to spend an hour here."

He again became silent, and then made a gesture of revolt: "But no, no! I cannot forgive it—this ingratitude sets me beside myself. I told you I was convinced that Bernadette had freely gone to cloister herself at Nevers. But although no one smuggled her away, what a relief it was for those whom she had begun to inconvenience here! And they are the same men, so anxious to be the absolute masters, who at the present time endeavour by all possible means to wrap her memory in silence. Ah! my dear child, if I were to tell you all!"

Little by little he spoke out and relieved himself. Those Fathers of the Grotto, who showed such greed in trading on the work of Bernadette, dreaded her still more now that she was dead than they had done whilst she was alive. So long as she had lived, their great terror had assuredly been that she might return to Lourdes to claim a portion of the spoil; and her humility alone reassured them, for she was in nowise of a domineering disposition, and had herself chosen the dim abode of renunciation where she was destined to pass away. But at present their fears had increased at the idea that a will other than theirs might bring the relics of the visionary back to Lourdes; that, thought had, indeed, occurred to the municipal council immediately after her death; the town had wished to raise a tomb, and there had been talk of opening a subscription. The Sisters of Nevers, however, formally refused to give up the body, which they said belonged to them. Everyone felt that the Sisters were acting under the influence of the Fathers, who were very uneasy, and energetically bestirred themselves to prevent by all means in their power the return of those venerated ashes, in whose presence at Lourdes they foresaw a possible competition with the Grotto itself. Could they have imagined some such threatening occurrence as this—a monumental tomb in the cemetery, pilgrims proceeding thither in procession, the sick feverishly kissing the marble, and miracles being worked there amidst a holy fervour? This would have been disastrous rivalry, a certain displacement of all the present devotion and prodigies. And the great, the sole fear, still and ever returned to them, that of having to divide the spoils, of seeing the money go elsewhere should the town, now taught by experience, know how to turn the tomb to account.

The Fathers were even credited with a scheme of profound craftiness. They were supposed to have the secret idea of reserving Bernadette's remains for themselves; the Sisters of Nevers having simply undertaken to keep it for them within the peaceful precincts of their chapel. Only, they were waiting, and would not bring it back until the affluence of the pilgrims should decrease. What was the use of a solemn return at present, when crowds flocked to the place without interruption and in increasing numbers? Whereas, when the extraordinary success of Our Lady of Lourdes should decline, like everything else in this world, one could imagine what a reawakening of faith would attend the solemn, resounding ceremony at which Christendom would behold the relics of the chosen one take possession of the soil whence she had made so many marvels spring. And the miracles would then begin again on the marble of her tomb before the Grotto or in the choir of the Basilica.

"You may search," continued Doctor Chassaigne, "but you won't find a single official picture of Bernadette at Lourdes. Her portrait is sold, but it is hung no where, in no sanctuary. It is systematic forgetfulness, the same sentiment of covert uneasiness as that which has wrought silence and abandonment in this sad chamber where we are. In the same way as they are afraid of worship at her tomb, so are they afraid of crowds coming and kneeling here, should two candles burn or a couple of bouquets of roses bloom upon this chimney. And if a paralytic woman were to rise shouting that she was cured, what a scandal would arise, how disturbed would be those good traders of the Grotto on seeing their monopoly seriously threatened! They are the masters, and the masters they intend to remain; they will not part with any portion of the magnificent farm that they have acquired and are working. Nevertheless they tremble—yes, they tremble at the memory of the workers of the first hour, of that little girl who is still so great in death, and for whose huge inheritance they burn with such greed that after having sent her to live at Nevers, they dare not even bring back her corpse, but leave it imprisoned beneath the flagstones of a convent!"

Ah! how wretched was the fate of that poor creature, who had been cut off from among the living, and whose corpse in its turn was condemned to exile! And how Pierre pitied her, that daughter of misery, who seemed to have been chosen only that she might suffer in her life and in her death! Even admitting that an unique, persistent will had not compelled her to disappear, still guarding her even in her tomb, what a strange succession of circumstances there had been—how it seemed as if someone, uneasy at the idea of the immense power she might grasp, had jealously sought to keep her out of the way! In Pierre's eyes she remained the chosen one, the martyr; and if he could no longer believe, if the history of this unfortunate girl sufficed to complete within him the ruin of his faith, it none the less upset him in all his brotherly love for mankind by revealing a new religion to him, the only one which might still fill his heart, the religion of life, of human sorrow.

Just then, before leaving the room, Doctor Chassaigne exclaimed: "And it's here that one must believe, my dear child. Do you see this obscure hole, do you think of the resplendent Grotto, of the triumphant Basilica, of the town built, of the world created, the crowds that flock to Lourdes! And if Bernadette was only hallucinated, only an idiot, would not the outcome be more astonishing, more inexplicable still? What! An idiot's dream would have sufficed to stir up nations like this! No! no! The Divine breath which alone can explain prodigies passed here."

Pierre was on the point of hastily replying "Yes!" It was true, a breath had passed there, the sob of sorrow, the inextinguishable yearning towards the Infinite of hope. If the dream of a suffering child had sufficed to attract multitudes, to bring about a rain of millions and raise a new city from the soil, was it not because this dream in a measure appeased the hunger of poor mankind, its insatiable need of being deceived and consoled? She had once more opened the Unknown, doubtless at a favourable moment both socially and historically; and the crowds had rushed towards it. Oh! to take refuge in mystery, when reality is so hard, to abandon oneself to the miraculous, since cruel nature seems merely one long injustice! But although you may organise the Unknown, reduce it to dogmas, make revealed religions of it, there is never anything at the bottom of it beyond the appeal of suffering, the cry of life, demanding health, joy, and fraternal happiness, and ready to accept them in another world if they cannot be obtained on earth. What use is it to believe in dogmas? Does it not suffice to weep and love?

Pierre, however, did not discuss the question. He withheld the answer that was on his lips, convinced, moreover, that the eternal need of the supernatural would cause eternal faith to abide among sorrowing mankind. The miraculous, which could not be verified, must be a food necessary to human despair. Besides, had he not vowed in all charity that he would not wound anyone with his doubts?

"What a prodigy, isn't it?" repeated the doctor.

"Certainly," Pierre ended by answering. "The whole human drama has been played, all the unknown forces have acted in this poor room, so damp and dark."

They remained there a few minutes more in silence; they walked round the walls, raised their eyes toward the smoky ceiling, and cast a final glance at the narrow, greenish yard. Truly it was a heart-rending sight, this poverty of the cobweb level, with its dirty old barrels, its worn-out tools, its refuse of all kinds rotting in the corners in heaps. And without adding a word they at last slowly retired, feeling extremely sad.

It was only in the street that Doctor Chassaigne seemed to awaken. He gave a slight shudder and hastened his steps, saying: "It is not finished, my dear child; follow me. We are now going to look at the other great iniquity." He referred to Abbe Peyramale and his church.

They crossed the Place du Porche and turned into the Rue Saint Pierre; a few minutes would suffice them. But their conversation had again fallen on the Fathers of the Grotto, on the terrible, merciless war waged by Father Sempe against the former Cure of Lourdes. The latter had been vanquished, and had died in consequence, overcome by feelings of frightful bitterness; and, after thus killing him by grief, they had completed the destruction of his church, which he had left unfinished, without a roof, open to the wind and to the rain. With what a glorious dream had that monumental edifice filled the last year of the Cure's life! Since he had been dispossessed of the Grotto, driven from the work of Our Lady of Lourdes, of which he, with Bernadette, had been the first artisan, his church had become his revenge, his protestation, his own share of the glory, the House of the Lord where he would triumph in his sacred vestments, and whence he would conduct endless processions in compliance with the formal desire of the Blessed Virgin. Man of authority and domination as he was at bottom, a pastor of the multitude, a builder of temples, he experienced a restless delight in hurrying on the work, with the lack of foresight of an eager man who did not allow indebtedness to trouble him, but was perfectly contented so long as he always had a swarm of workmen busy on the scaffoldings. And thus he saw his church rise up, and pictured it finished, one bright summer morning, all new in the rising sun.

Ah! that vision constantly evoked gave him courage for the struggle, amidst the underhand, murderous designs by which he felt himself to be enveloped. His church, towering above the vast square, at last rose in all its colossal majesty. He had decided that it should be in the Romanesque style, very large, very simple, its nave nearly three hundred feet long, its steeple four hundred and sixty feet high. It shone out resplendently in the clear sunlight, freed on the previous day of the last scaffolding, and looking quite smart in its newness, with its broad courses of stone disposed with perfect regularity. And, in thought, he sauntered around it, charmed with its nudity, its stupendous candour, its chasteness recalling that of a virgin child, for there was not a piece of sculpture, not an ornament that would have uselessly loaded it. The roofs of the nave, transept, and apse were of equal height above the entablature, which was decorated with simple mouldings. In the same way the apertures in the aisles and nave had no other adornments than archivaults with mouldings, rising above the piers. He stopped in thought before the great coloured glass windows of the transept, whose roses were sparkling; and passing round the building he skirted the semicircular apse against which stood the vestry building with its two rows of little windows; and then he returned, never tiring of his contemplation of that regal ordonnance, those great lines standing out against the blue sky, those superposed roofs, that enormous mass of stone, whose solidity promised to defy centuries. But, when he closed his eyes he, above all else, conjured up, with rapturous pride, a vision of the facade and steeple; down below, the three portals, the roofs of the two lateral ones forming terraces, while from the central one, in the very middle of the facade, the steeple boldly sprang. Here again columns resting on piers supported archivaults with simple mouldings. Against the gable, at a point where there was a pinnacle, and between the two lofty windows lighting the nave, was a statue of Our Lady of Lourdes under a canopy. Up above, were other bays with freshly painted luffer-boards. Buttresses started from the ground at the four corners of the steeple-base, becoming less and less massive from storey to storey, till they reached the spire, a bold, tapering spire in stone, flanked by four turrets and adorned with pinnacles, and soaring upward till it vanished in the sky. And to the parish priest of Lourdes it seemed as if it were his own fervent soul which had grown and flown aloft with this spire, to testify to his faith throughout the ages, there on high, quite close to God.

At other times another vision delighted him still more. He thought he could see the inside of his church on the day of the first solemn mass he would perform there. The coloured windows threw flashes of fire brilliant like precious stones; the twelve chapels, the aisles, were beaming with lighted candles. And he was at the high altar of marble and gold; and the fourteen columns of the nave in single blocks of Pyrenean marble, magnificent marble purchased with money that had come from the four corners of Christendom, rose up supporting the vaulted roof, while the sonorous voices of the organs filled the whole building with a hymn of joy. A multitude of the faithful was gathered there, kneeling on the flags in front of the choir, which was screened by ironwork as delicate as lace, and covered with admirably carved wood. The pulpit, the regal present of a great lady, was a marvel of art cut in massive oak. The baptismal fonts had been hewn out of hard stone by an artist of great talent. Pictures by masters ornamented the walls. Crosses, pyxes, precious monstrances, sacred vestments, similar to suns, were piled up in the vestry cupboards. And what a dream it was to be the pontiff of such a temple, to reign there after having erected it with passion, to bless the crowds who hastened to it from the entire earth, while the flying peals from the steeple told the Grotto and Basilica that they had over there, in old Lourdes, a rival, a victorious sister, in whose great nave God triumphed also!

After following the Rue Saint Pierre for a moment, Doctor Chassaigne and his companion turned into the little Rue de Langelle.

"We are coming to it," said the doctor. But though Pierre looked around him he could see no church. There were merely some wretched hovels, a whole district of poverty, littered with foul buildings. At length, however, at the bottom of a blind alley, he perceived a remnant of the half-rotten palings which still surrounded the vast square site bordered by the Rue Saint Pierre, the Rue de Bagneres, the Rue de Langelle, and the Rue des Jardins.

"We must turn to the left," continued the doctor, who had entered a narrow passage among the rubbish. "Here we are!"

And the ruin suddenly appeared amidst the ugliness and wretchedness that masked it.

The whole great carcase of the nave and the aisles, the transept and the apse was standing. The walls rose on all sides to the point where the vaulting would have begun. You entered as into a real church, you could walk about at ease, identifying all the usual parts of an edifice of this description. Only when you raised your eyes you saw the sky; the roofs were wanting, the rain could fall and the wind blow there freely. Some fifteen years previously the works had been abandoned, and things had remained in the same state as the last workman had left them. What struck you first of all were the ten pillars of the nave and the four pillars of the choir, those magnificent columns of Pyrenean marble, each of a single block, which had been covered with a casing of planks in order to protect them from damage. The bases and capitals were still in the rough, awaiting the sculptors. And these isolated columns, thus cased in wood, had a mournful aspect indeed. Moreover, a dismal sensation filled you at sight of the whole gaping enclosure, where grass had sprung up all over the ravaged, bumpy soil of the aisles and the nave, a thick cemetery grass, through which the women of the neighbourhood had ended by making paths. They came in to spread out their washing there. And even now a collection of poor people's washing—thick sheets, shirts in shreds, and babies' swaddling clothes—was fast drying in the last rays of the sun, which glided in through the broad, empty bays.

Slowly, without speaking, Pierre and Doctor Chassaigne walked round the inside of the church. The ten chapels of the aisles formed a species of compartments full of rubbish and remnants. The ground of the choir had been cemented, doubtless to protect the crypt below against infiltrations; but unfortunately the vaults must be sinking; there was a hollow there which the storm of the previous night had transformed into a little lake. However, it was these portions of the transept and the apse which had the least suffered. Not a stone had moved; the great central rose windows above the triforium seemed to be awaiting their coloured glass, while some thick planks, forgotten atop of the walls of the apse, might have made anyone think that the workmen would begin covering it the next day. But, when Pierre and the doctor had retraced their steps, and went out to look at the facade, the lamentable woefulness of the young ruin was displayed to their gaze. On this side, indeed, the works had not been carried forward to anything like the same extent: the porch with its three portals alone was built, and fifteen years of abandonment had sufficed for the winter weather to eat into the sculptures, the small columns and the archivaults, with a really singular destructive effect, as though the stones, deeply penetrated, destroyed, had melted away beneath tears. The heart grieved at the sight of the decay which had attacked the work before it was even finished. Not yet to be, and nevertheless to crumble away in this fashion under the sky! To be arrested in one's colossal growth, and simply strew the weeds with ruins!

They returned to the nave, and were overcome by the frightful sadness which this assassination of a monument provoked. The spacious plot of waste ground inside was littered with the remains of scaffoldings, which had been pulled down when half rotten, in fear lest their fall might crush people; and everywhere amidst the tall grass were boards, put-logs, moulds for arches, mingled with bundles of old cord eaten away by damp. There was also the long narrow carcase of a crane rising up like a gibbet. Spade-handles, pieces of broken wheelbarrows, and heaps of greenish bricks, speckled with moss and wild convolvuli in bloom, were still lying among the forgotten materials. In the beds of nettles you here and there distinguished the rails of a little railway laid down for the trucks, one of which was lying overturned in a corner. But the saddest sight in all this death of things was certainly the portable engine which had remained in the shed that sheltered it. For fifteen years it had been standing there cold and lifeless. A part of the roof of the shed had ended by falling in upon it, and now the rain drenched it at every shower. A bit of the leather harness by which the crane was worked hung down, and seemed to bind the engine like a thread of some gigantic spider's web. And its metal-work, its steel and copper, was also decaying, as if rusted by lichens, covered with the vegetation of old age, whose yellowish patches made it look like a very ancient, grass-grown machine which the winters had preyed upon. This lifeless engine, this cold engine with its empty firebox and its silent boiler, was like the very soul of the departed labour vainly awaiting the advent of some great charitable heart, whose coming through the eglantine and the brambles would awaken this sleeping church in the wood from its heavy slumber of ruin.

At last Doctor Chassaigne spoke: "Ah!" he said, "when one thinks that fifty thousand francs would have sufficed to prevent such a disaster! With fifty thousand francs the roof could have been put on, the heavy work would have been saved, and one could have waited patiently. But they wanted to kill the work just as they had killed the man." With a gesture he designated the Fathers of the Grotto, whom he avoided naming. "And to think," he continued, "that their annual receipts are eight hundred thousand francs. However, they prefer to send presents to Rome to propitiate powerful friends there."

In spite of himself, he was again opening hostilities against the adversaries of Cure Peyramale. The whole story caused a holy anger of justice to haunt him. Face to face with those lamentable ruins, he returned to the facts—the enthusiastic Cure starting on the building of his beloved church, and getting deeper and deeper into debt, whilst Father Sempe, ever on the lookout, took advantage of each of his mistakes, discrediting him with the Bishop, arresting the flow of offerings, and finally stopping the works. Then, after the conquered man was dead, had come interminable lawsuits, lawsuits lasting fifteen years, which gave the winters time to devour the building. And now it was in such a woeful state, and the debt had risen to such an enormous figure, that all seemed over. The slow death, the death of the stones, was becoming irrevocable. The portable engine beneath its tumbling shed would fall to pieces, pounded by the rain and eaten away by the moss.

"I know very well that they chant victory," resumed the doctor; "that they alone remain. It is just what they wanted—to be the absolute masters, to have all the power, all the money for themselves alone. I may tell you that their terror of competition has even made them intrigue against the religious Orders that have attempted to come to Lourdes. Jesuits, Dominicans, Benedictines, Capuchins, and Carmelites have made applications at various times, and the Fathers of the Grotto have always succeeded in keeping them away. They only tolerate the female Orders, and will only have one flock. And the town belongs to them; they have opened shop there, and sell God there wholesale and retail!"

Walking slowly, he had while speaking returned to the middle of the nave, amidst the ruins, and with a sweeping wave of the arm he pointed to all the devastation surrounding him. "Look at this sadness, this frightful wretchedness! Over yonder the Rosary and Basilica cost them three millions of francs."*

Then, as in Bernadette's cold, dark room, Pierre saw the Basilica rise before him, radiant in its triumph. It was not here that you found the realisation of the dream of Cure Peyramale, officiating and blessing kneeling multitudes while the organs resounded joyfully. The Basilica, over yonder, appeared, vibrating with the pealing of its bells, clamorous

---

* About 580,000 dollars.

with the superhuman joy of an accomplished miracle, all sparkling with its countless lights, its banners, its lamps, its hearts of silver and gold, its clergy attired in gold, and its monstrance akin to a golden star. It flamed in the setting sun, it touched the heavens with its spire, amidst the soaring of the milliards of prayers which caused its walls to quiver. Here, however, was the church that had died before being born, the church placed under interdict by a mandamus of the Bishop, the church falling into dust, and open to the four winds of heaven. Each storm carried away a little more of the stones, big flies buzzed all alone among the nettles which had invaded the nave; and there were no other devotees than the poor women of the neighbourhood, who came thither to turn their sorry linen, spread upon the grass.

It seemed amidst the mournful silence as though a low voice were sobbing, perhaps the voice of the marble columns weeping over their useless beauty under their wooden shirts. At times birds would fly across the deserted apse uttering a shrill cry. Bands of enormous rats which had taken refuge under bits of the lowered scaffoldings would fight, and bite, and bound out of their holes in a gallop of terror. And nothing could have been more heart-rending than the sight of this pre-determined ruin, face to face with its triumphant rival, the Basilica, which beamed with gold.

Again Doctor Chassaigne curtly said, "Come."

They left the church, and following the left aisle, reached a door, roughly fashioned out of a few planks nailed together; and, when they had passed down a half-demolished wooden staircase, the steps of which shook beneath their feet, they found themselves in the crypt.

It was a low vault, with squat arches, on exactly the same plan as the choir. The thick, stunted columns, left in the rough, also awaited their sculptors. Materials were lying about, pieces of wood were rotting on the beaten ground, the whole vast hall was white with plaster in the abandonment in which unfinished buildings are left. At the far end, three bays, formerly glazed, but in which not a pane of glass remained, threw a clear, cold light upon the desolate bareness of the walls.

And there, in the middle, lay Cure Peyramale's corpse. Some pious friends had conceived the touching idea of thus burying him in the crypt of his unfinished church. The tomb stood on a broad step and was all marble. The inscriptions, in letters of gold, expressed the feelings of the subscribers, the cry of truth and reparation that came from the monument itself. You read on the face: "This tomb has been erected by the aid of pious offerings from the entire universe to the blessed memory of the great servant of Our Lady of Lourdes." On the right side were these words from a Brief of Pope Pius IX: "You have entirely devoted yourself to erecting a temple to the Mother of God." And on the left were these words from the New Testament: "Happy are they who suffer persecution for justice' sake." Did not these inscriptions embody the true plaint, the legitimate hope of the vanquished man who had fought so long in the sole desire of strictly executing the commands of the Virgin as transmitted to him by Bernadette? She, Our Lady of Lourdes, was there personified by a slender statuette, standing above the commemorative inscription, against the naked wall whose only decorations were a few bead wreaths hanging from nails. And before the tomb, as before the Grotto, were five or six benches in rows, for the faithful who desired to sit down.

But with another gesture of sorrowful compassion, Doctor Chassaigne had silently pointed out to Pierre a huge damp spot which was turning the wall at the far end quite green. Pierre remembered the little lake which he had noticed up above on the cracked cement flooring of the choir—quite a quantity of water left by the storm of the previous night. Infiltration had evidently commenced, a perfect stream ran down, invading the crypt, whenever there was heavy rain. And they both felt a pang at their hearts when they perceived that the water was trickling along the vaulted roof in narrow threads, and thence falling in large, regular rhythmical drops upon the tomb. The doctor could not restrain a groan. "Now it rains," he said; "it rains on him!"

Pierre remained motionless, in a kind of awe. In the presence of that falling water, at the thought of the blasts which must rush at winter time through the glassless windows, that corpse appeared to him both woeful and tragic. It acquired a fierce grandeur, lying there alone in its splendid marble tomb, amidst all the rubbish, at the bottom of the crumbling ruins of its own church. It was the solitary guardian, the dead sleeper and dreamer watching over the empty spaces, open to all the birds of night. It was the mute, obstinate, eternal protest, and it was expectation also. Cure Peyramale, stretched in his coffin, having all eternity before him to acquire patience, there, without weariness, awaited the workmen who would perhaps return thither some fine April morning. If they should take ten years to do so, he would be there, and if it should take them a century, he would be there still. He was waiting for the rotten scaffoldings up above, among the grass of the nave, to be resuscitated like the dead, and by the force of some miracle to stand upright once more, along the walls. He was waiting, too, for the moss-covered engine to become all at once burning hot, recover its breath, and raise the timbers for the roof. His beloved enterprise, his gigantic building, was crumbling about his head, and yet with joined hands and closed eyes he was watching over its ruins, watching and waiting too.

In a low voice, the doctor finished the cruel story, telling how, after persecuting Cure Peyramale and his work, they persecuted his tomb. There had formerly been a bust of the Cure there, and pious hands had kept a little lamp burning before it. But a woman had one day fallen with her face to the earth, saying that she had perceived the soul of the deceased, and thereupon the Fathers of the Grotto were in a flutter. Were miracles about to take place there? The sick already passed entire days there, seated on the benches before the tomb. Others knelt down, kissed the marble, and prayed to be cured. And at this a feeling of terror arose: supposing they should be cured, supposing the Grotto should find a competitor in this martyr, lying all alone, amidst the old tools left there by the masons! The Bishop of Tarbes, informed and influenced, thereupon published the mandamus which placed the church under interdict, forbidding all worship there and all pilgrimages and processions to the tomb of the former priest of Lourdes. As in the case of Bernadette, his memory was proscribed, his portrait could be found, officially, nowhere. In the same manner as they had shown themselves merciless against the living man, so did the Fathers prove merciless to his memory. They pursued him even in his tomb. They alone, again nowadays, prevented the works of the church from being proceeded with, by raising continual obstacles, and absolutely refusing to share their rich harvest of alms. And they seemed to be waiting for the winter rains to fall and complete the work of destruction, for the vaulted roof of the crypt, the walls, the whole gigantic pile to crumble down upon the tomb of the martyr, upon the body of the defeated man, so that he might be buried beneath them and at last pounded to dust!

"Ah!" murmured the doctor, "I, who knew him so valiant, so enthusiastic in all noble labour! Now, you see it, it rains, it rains on him!"

Painfully, he set himself on his knees and found relief in a long prayer.

Pierre, who could not pray, remained standing. Compassionate sorrow was overflowing from his heart. He listened to the heavy drops from the roof as one by one they broke on the tomb with a slow rhythmical pit-a-pat, which seemed to be numbering the seconds of eternity, amidst the profound silence. And he reflected on the eternal misery of this world, on the choice which suffering makes in always falling on the best. The two great makers of Our Lady of Lourdes, Bernadette and Cure Peyramale, rose up in the flesh again before him, like woeful victims, tortured during their lives and exiled after their deaths. That alone, indeed, would have completed within him the destruction of his faith; for the Bernadette, whom he had just found at the end of his researches, was but a human sister, loaded with every dolour. But none the less he preserved a tender brotherly veneration for her, and two tears slowly trickled down his cheeks.

THE FIFTH DAY

I

Egotism and Love

Again that night Pierre, at the Hotel of the Apparitions, was unable to obtain a wink of sleep. After calling at the hospital to inquire after Marie, who, since her return from the procession, had been soundly enjoying the delicious, restoring sleep of a child, he had gone to bed himself feeling anxious at the prolonged absence of M. de Guersaint. He had expected him at latest at dinner-time, but probably some mischance had detained him at Gavarnie; and he thought how disappointed Marie would be if her father were not there to embrace her the first thing in the morning. With a man like M. de Guersaint, so pleasantly heedless and so hare-brained, everything was possible, every fear might be realised.

Perhaps this anxiety had at first sufficed to keep Pierre awake in spite of his great fatigue; but afterwards the nocturnal noises of the hotel had really assumed unbearable proportions. The morrow, Tuesday, was the day of departure, the last day which the national pilgrimage would spend at Lourdes, and the pilgrims no doubt were making the most of their time, coming from the Grotto and returning thither in the middle of the night, endeavouring as it were to force the grace of Heaven by their commotion, and apparently never feeling the slightest need of repose. The doors slammed, the floors shook, the entire building vibrated beneath the disorderly gallop of a crowd. Never before had the walls reverberated with such obstinate coughs, such thick, husky voices. Thus Pierre, a prey to insomnia, tossed about on his bed and continually rose up, beset with the idea that the noise he heard must have been made by M. de Guersaint who had returned. For some minutes he would listen feverishly; but he could only hear the extraordinary sounds of the passage, amid which he could distinguish nothing precisely. Was it the priest, the mother and her three daughters, or the old married couple on his left, who were fighting with the furniture? or was it rather the larger family, or the single gentleman, or the young single woman on his right, whom some incomprehensible occurrences were leading into adventures? At one moment he jumped from his bed, wishing to explore his absent friend's empty room, as he felt certain that some deeds of violence were taking place in it. But although he listened very attentively when he got there, the only sound he could distinguish was the tender caressing murmur of two voices. Then a sudden recollection of Madame Volmar came to him, and he returned shuddering to bed.

At length, when it was broad daylight and Pierre had just fallen asleep, a loud knocking at his door awoke him with a start. This time there could be no mistake, a loud voice broken by sobs was calling "Monsieur l'Abbe! Monsieur l'Abbe! for Heaven's sake wake up!"

Surely it must be M. de Guersaint who had been brought back dead, at least. Quite scared, Pierre ran and opened the door, in his night-shirt, and found himself in the presence of his neighbour, M. Vigneron.

"Oh! for Heaven's sake, Monsieur l'Abbe, dress yourself at once!" exclaimed the assistant head-clerk. "Your holy ministry is required." And he began to relate that he had just got up to see the time by his watch on the mantelpiece, when he had heard some most frightful sighs issuing from the adjoining room, where Madame Chaise slept. She had left the communicating door open in order to be more with them, as she pleasantly expressed it. Accordingly he had hastened in, and flung the shutters open so as to admit both light and air. "And what a sight, Monsieur l'Abbe!" he continued. "Our poor aunt lying on her bed, nearly purple in the face already, her mouth wide open in a vain effort to breathe, and her hands fumbling with the sheet. It's her heart complaint, you know. Come, come at once, Monsieur l'Abbe, and help her, I implore you!"

Pierre, utterly bewildered, could find neither his breeches nor his cassock. "Of course, of course I'll come with you," said he. "But I have not what is necessary for administering the last sacraments."

M. Vigneron had assisted him to dress, and was now stooping down looking for his slippers. "Never mind," he said, "the mere sight of you will assist her in her last moments, if Heaven has this affliction in store for us. Here! put these on your feet, and follow me at once—oh! at once!"

He went off like a gust of wind and plunged into the adjoining room. All the doors remained wide open. The young priest, who followed him, noticed nothing in the first room, which was in an incredible state of disorder, beyond the half-naked figure of little Gustave, who sat on the sofa serving him as a bed, motionless, very pale, forgotten, and shivering amid this drama of inexorable death. Open bags littered the floor, the greasy remains of supper soiled the table, the parents' bed seemed devastated by the catastrophe, its coverlets torn off and lying on the floor. And almost immediately afterwards he caught sight of the mother, who had hastily enveloped herself in an old yellow dressing-gown, standing with a terrified look in the inner room.

"Well, my love, well, my love?" repeated M. Vigneron, in stammering accents.

With a wave of her hand and without uttering a word Madame Vigneron drew their attention to Madame Chaise, who lay motionless, with her head sunk in the pillow and her hands stiffened and twisted. She was blue in the face, and her mouth gaped, as though with the last great gasp that had come from her.

Pierre bent over her. Then in a low voice he said: "She is dead!"

Dead! The word rang through the room where a heavy silence reigned, and the husband and wife looked at each other in amazement, bewilderment. So it was over? The aunt had died before Gustave, and the youngster inherited her five hundred thousand francs. How many times had they dwelt on that dream; whose sudden realisation dumfounded them? How many times had despair overcome them when they feared that the poor child might depart before her? Dead! Good heavens! was it their fault? Had they really prayed to the Blessed Virgin for this? She had shown herself so good to them that they trembled at the thought that they had not been able to express a wish without its being granted. In the death of the chief clerk, so suddenly carried off so that they might have his place, they had already recognised the powerful hand of Our Lady of Lourdes. Had she again loaded them with favours, listening even to the unconscious dreams of their desire? Yet they had never desired anyone's death; they were worthy people incapable of any bad action, loving their relations, fulfilling their religious duties, going to confession, partaking of the communion like other people without any ostentation. Whenever they thought of those five hundred thousand francs, of their son who might be the first to go, and of the annoyance it would be to them to see another and far less worthy nephew inherit that fortune, it was merely in the innermost recesses of their hearts, in short, quite innocently and naturally. Certainly they *had* thought of it when they were at the Grotto, but was not the Blessed Virgin wisdom itself? Did she not know far better than ourselves what she ought to do for the happiness of both the living and the dead?

Then Madame Vigneron in all sincerity burst into tears and wept for the sister whom she loved so much. "Ah! Monsieur l'Abbe," she said, "I saw her expire; she passed away before my eyes. What a misfortune that you were not here sooner to receive her soul! She died without a priest; your presence would have consoled her so much."

A prey also to emotion, his eyes full of tears, Vigneron sought to console his wife. "Your sister was a saint," said he; "she communicated again yesterday morning, and you need have no anxiety concerning her; her soul has gone straight to heaven. No doubt, if Monsieur l'Abbe had been here in time she would have been glad to see him. But what would you? Death was quicker. I went at once, and really there is nothing for us to reproach ourselves with."

Then, turning towards the priest, he added "Monsieur l'Abbe, it was her excessive piety which certainly hastened her end. Yesterday, at the Grotto, she had a bad attack, which was a warning. And in spite of her fatigue she obstinately followed the procession afterwards. I thought then that she could not last long. Yet, out of delicacy, one did not like to say anything to her, for fear of frightening her."

Pierre gently knelt down and said the customary prayers, with that human emotion which was his nearest approach to faith in the presence of eternal life and eternal death, both so pitiful. Then, as he remained kneeling a little longer, he overheard snatches of the conversation around him.

Little Gustave, forgotten on his couch amid the disorder of the other room, must have lost patience, for he had begun to cry and call out, "Mamma! mamma! mamma!"

At length Madame Vigneron went to quiet him, and it occurred to her to carry him in her arms to kiss his poor aunt for the last time. But at first he struggled and refused, crying so much that M. Vigneron was obliged to interfere and try to make him ashamed of himself. What! he who was never frightened of anything! who bore suffering with the courage of a grown-up man! And to think it was a question of kissing his poor aunt, who had always been so kind, whose last thought must most certainly have been for him!

"Give him to me," said he to his wife; "he's going to be good."

Gustave ended by clinging to his father's neck. He came shivering in his night-shirt, displaying his wretched little body devoured by scrofula. It seemed indeed as though the miraculous water of the piscinas, far from curing him, had freshened the sore on his back; whilst his scraggy leg hung down inertly like a dry stick.

"Kiss her," resumed M. Vigneron.

The child leant forward and kissed his aunt on the forehead. It was not death which upset him and caused him to struggle. Since he had been in the room he had been looking at the dead woman with an air of quiet curiosity. He did not love her, he had suffered on her account so long. He had the ideas and feelings of a man, and the weight of them was stifling him as, like his complaint, they developed and became more acute. He felt full well that he was too little, that children ought not to understand what only concerns their elders.

However, his father, seating himself out of the way, kept him on his knee, whilst his mother closed the window and lit the two candles on the mantelpiece. "Ah! my poor dear," murmured M. Vigneron, feeling that he must say something, "it's a cruel loss for all of us. Our trip is now completely spoilt; this is our last day, for we start this afternoon. And the Blessed Virgin, too, was showing herself so kind to us."

However, seeing his son's surprised look, a look of infinite sadness and reproach, he hastened to add: "Yes, of course, I know that she hasn't yet quite cured you. But we must not despair of her kindness. She loves us so well, she shows us so many favours that she will certainly end by curing you, since that is now the only favour that remains for her to grant us."

Madame Vigneron, who was listening, drew near and said: "How happy we should have been to have returned to Paris all three hale and hearty! Nothing is ever perfect!"

"I say!" suddenly observed Monsieur Vigneron, "I sha'n't be able to leave with you this afternoon, on account of the formalities which have to be gone through. I hope that my return ticket will still be available to-morrow!"

They were both getting over the frightful shock, feeling a sense of relief in spite of their affection for Madame Chaise; and, in fact, they were already forgetting her, anxious above all things to leave Lourdes as soon as possible, as though the principal object of their journey had been attained. A decorous, unavowed delight was slowly penetrating them.

"When I get back to Paris there will be so much for me to do," continued M. Vigneron. "I, who now only long for repose! All the same I shall remain my three years at the Ministry, until I can retire, especially now that I am certain of the retiring pension of chief clerk. But afterwards—oh! afterwards I certainly hope to enjoy life a bit. Since this money has come to us I shall purchase the estate of Les Billottes, that superb property down at my native place which I have always been dreaming of. And I promise you that I sha'n't find time hanging heavy on my hands in the midst of my horses, my dogs, and my flowers!"

Little Gustave was still on his father's knee, his night-shirt tucked up, his whole wretched misshapen body shivering, and displaying the scragginess of a slowly dying child. When he perceived that his father, now full of his dream of an opulent life, no longer seemed to notice that he was there, he gave one of his enigmatical smiles, in which melancholy was tinged with malice. "But what about me, father?" he asked.

M. Vigneron started, like one aroused from sleep, and did not at first seem to understand. "You, little one? You'll be with us, of course!"

But Gustave gave him a long, straight look, without ceasing to smile with his artful, though woeful lips. "Oh! do you think so?" he asked.

"Of course I think so! You'll be with us, and it will be very nice to be with us."

Uneasy, stammering, unable to find the proper words, M. Vigneron felt a chill come over him when his son shrugged his skinny shoulders with an air of philosophical disdain and answered: "Oh, no! I shall be dead."

And then the terrified father was suddenly able to detect in the child's deep glance the glance of a man who was very aged, very knowing in all things, acquainted with all the abominations of life through having gone through them. What especially alarmed him was the abrupt conviction that this child had always seen into the innermost recesses of his heart, even farther than the things he dared to acknowledge to himself. He could recall that when the little sufferer had been but a baby in his cradle his eyes would frequently be fixed upon his own—and even then those eyes had been rendered so sharp by suffering, endowed, too, with such an extraordinary power of divination, that they had seemed able to dive into the unconscious thoughts buried in the depths of his brain. And by a singular counter-effect all the things that he had never owned to himself he now found in his child's eyes—he beheld them, read them there, against his will. The story of his cupidity lay unfolded before him, his anger at having such a sorry son, his anguish at the idea that Madame Chaise's fortune depended upon such a fragile existence, his eager desire that she might make haste and die whilst the youngster was still there, in order that he might finger the legacy. It was simply a question of days, this duel as to which should go off first. And then, at the end, it still meant death—the youngster must in his turn disappear, whilst he, the father, alone pocketed the cash, and lived joyfully to a good old age. And these frightful things shone forth so clearly from the keen, melancholy, smiling eyes of the poor condemned child, passed from son to father with such evident distinctness, that for a moment it seemed to them that they were shouting them aloud.

However, M. Vigneron struggled against it all, and, averting his head, began energetically protesting: "How! You'll be dead? What an idea! It's absurd to have such ideas as that!"

Meantime, Madame Vigneron was sobbing. "You wicked child," she gasped; "how can you make us so unhappy, when we already have such a cruel loss to deplore?"

Gustave had to kiss them, and to promise them that he would live for their sakes. Yet he did not cease smiling, conscious as he was that a lie is necessary when one does not wish to be too miserable, and quite prepared, moreover, to leave his parents happy behind him, since even the Blessed Virgin herself was powerless to grant him in this world the little happy lot to which each creature should be born.

His mother took him back to bed, and Pierre at length rose up, just as M. Vigneron had finished arranging the chamber of death in a suitable manner. "You'll excuse me, won't you, Monsieur l'Abbe?" said he, accompanying the young priest to the door. "I'm not quite myself. Well, it's an unpleasant time to go through. I must get over it somehow, however."

When Pierre got into the passage he stopped for a moment, listening to a sound of voices which was ascending the stairs. He had just been thinking of M. de Guersaint again, and imagined that he could recognise his voice. However, whilst he stood there waiting, an incident occurred which caused him intense discomfort. The door of the room next to M. de Guersaint's softly opened and a woman, clad in black, slipped into the passage. As she turned, she found herself face to face with Pierre, in such a fashion that it was impossible for them to pretend not to recognise each other.

The woman was Madame Volmar. Six o'clock had not yet struck, and she was going off, hoping that nobody would notice her, with the intention of showing herself at the hospital, and there spending this last morning, in order, in some measure, to justify her journey to Lourdes. When she perceived Pierre, she began to tremble, and, at first, could only stammer: "Oh, Monsieur l'Abbe, Monsieur l'Abbe!"

Then, noticing that the priest had left his door wide open, she seemed to give way to the fever consuming her, to a need of speaking out, explaining things and justifying herself. With her face suffused by a rush of blood she entered the young man's room, whither he had to follow her, greatly disturbed by this strange adventure. And, as he still left the door open, it was she who, in her desire to confide her sorrow and her sin to him, begged that he would close it.

"Oh! I pray you, Monsieur l'Abbe," said she, "do not judge me too harshly."

He made a gesture as though to reply that he did not allow himself the right to pass judgment upon her.

"But yes, but yes," she responded; "I know very well that you are acquainted with my misfortune. You saw me once in Paris behind the church of La Trinite, and the other day you recognised me on the balcony here! You were aware that I was there—in that room. But if you only knew—ah, if you only knew!"

Her lips were quivering, and tears were welling into her eyes. As he looked at her he was surprised by the extraordinary beauty transfiguring her face. This woman, invariably clad in black, extremely simple, with never a jewel, now appeared to him in all the brilliancy of her passion; no longer drawing back into the gloom, no longer seeking to bedim the lustre of her eyes, as was her wont. She, who at first sight did not seem pretty, but too dark and slender, with drawn features, a large mouth and long nose, assumed, as he now examined her, a troubling charm, a powerful, irresistible beauty. Her eyes especially—her large, magnificent eyes, whose brasiers she usually sought to cover with a veil of indifference—were flaring like torches; and he understood that she should be loved, adored, to madness.

"If you only knew, Monsieur l'Abbe," she continued. "If I were only to tell you all that I have suffered. Doubtless you have suspected something of it, since you are acquainted with my mother-in-law and my husband. On the few occasions when you have called on us you cannot but have understood some of the abominable things which go on in my home, though I have always striven to appear happy in my silent little corner. But to live like that for ten years, to have no existence—never to love, never to be loved—no, no, it was beyond my power!"

And then she related the whole painful story: her marriage with the diamond merchant, a disastrous, though it seemed an advantageous one; her mother-in-law, with the stern soul of a jailer or an executioner, and her husband, a monster of physical ugliness and mental villainy. They imprisoned her, they did not even allow her to look out of a window. They had beaten her, they had pitilessly assailed her in her tastes, her inclinations, in all her feminine weaknesses. She knew that her husband wandered in his affections, and yet if she smiled to a relative, if she had a flower in her corsage on some rare day of gaiety, he would tear it from her, enter into the most jealous rage, and seize and bruise her wrists whilst shouting the most fearful threats. For years and years she had lived in that hell, hoping, hoping still, having within her such a power of life, such an ardent need of affection, that she continued waiting for happiness, ever thinking, at the faintest breath, that it was about to enter.

"I swear to you, Monsieur l'Abbe," said she, "that I could not do otherwise than I have done. I was too unhappy: my whole being longed for someone who would care for me. And when my friend the first time told me that he loved me it was all over—I was his forever. Ah! to be loved, to be spoken to gently, to have someone near you who is always solicitous and amiable; to know that in absence he thinks of you, that there is a heart somewhere in which you live. . . Ah! if it be a crime, Monsieur l'Abbe, I cannot, cannot feel remorse for it. I will not even say that I was urged to it; I simply say that it came to me as naturally as my breath, because it was as necessary to my life!"

She had carried her hand to her lips as though to throw a kiss to the world, and Pierre felt deeply disturbed in presence of this lovely woman, who personified all the ardour of human passion, and at the same time a feeling of deep pity began to arise within him.

"Poor woman!" he murmured.

"It is not to the priest that I am confessing," she resumed; "it is to the man that I am speaking, to a man by whom I should greatly like to be understood. No, I am not a believer: religion has not sufficed me. It is said that some women find contentment in it, a firm protection even against all transgressions. But I have ever felt cold in church, weary unto death. Oh! I know very well that it is wrong to feign piety, to mingle religion with my heart affairs. But what would you? I am forced to it. If you saw me in Paris behind La Trinite it was because that church is the only place to which I am allowed to go alone; and if you find me here at Lourdes it is because, in the whole long year, I have but these three days of happiness and freedom."

Again she began to tremble. Hot tears were coursing down her cheeks. A vision of it all arose in Pierre's mind, and, distracted by the thought of the ardent earthly love which possessed this unhappy creature, he again murmured: "Poor woman!"

"And, Monsieur l'Abbe," she continued, "think of the hell to which I am about to return! For weeks and months I live my life of martyrdom without complaint. Another year, another year must go by without a day, an hour of happiness! Ah! I am indeed very unhappy, Monsieur l'Abbe, yet do you not think all the same that I am a good woman?"

He had been deeply moved by her sincere display of mingled grief and passion. He felt in her the breath of universal desire—a sovereign flame. And his compassion overflowed from his heart, and his words were words of pardon. "Madame," he said, "I pity you and respect you infinitely."

Then she spoke no further, but looked at him with her large tear-blurred eyes. And suddenly catching hold of both his hands, she grasped them tightly with her burning fingers. And then she went off, vanishing down the passage as light, as ethereal, as a shadow.

However, Pierre suffered from her presence in that room even more acutely after she had departed. He opened the window wide that the fresh air might carry off the breath of passion which she had left there. Already on the Sunday when he had seen her on the balcony he had been seized with terror at the thought that she personified the revenge of the world and the flesh amidst all the mystical exaltation of immaculate Lourdes. And now his terror was returning to him. Love seemed stronger than faith, and perhaps it was only love that was divine. To love, to belong to one another, to create and continue life—was not that the one sole object of nature outside of all social and religious policies? For a moment he was conscious of the abyss before him: his chastity was his last prop, the very dignity of his spoilt life; and he realised that, if after yielding to his reason he also yielded to his flesh, he would be utterly lost. All his pride of purity, all his strength which he had placed in professional rectitude, thereupon returned to him, and he again vowed that he would never be a man, since he had voluntarily cut himself off from among men.

Seven o'clock was striking, and Pierre did not go back to bed, but began to wash himself, thoroughly enjoying the cool water, which ended by calming his fever. As he finished dressing, the anxious thought of M. de Guersaint recurred to him on hearing a sound of footsteps in the passage. These steps stopped outside his room and someone knocked. With a feeling of relief he went to open the door, but on doing so

ÉMILE ZOLA

exclaimed in great surprise "What, it's you! How is it that you're already up, running about to see people?"

Marie stood on the threshold smiling, whilst behind her was Sister Hyacinthe, who had come with her, and who also was smiling, with her lovely, candid eyes.

"Ah! my friend," said the girl, "I could not remain in bed. I sprang out directly I saw the sunshine. I had such a longing to walk, to run and jump about like a child, and I begged and implored so much that Sister was good enough to come with me. I think I should have got out through the window if the door had been closed against me."

Pierre ushered them in, and an indescribable emotion oppressed him as he heard her jest so gaily and saw her move about so freely with such grace and liveliness. She, good heavens! she whom he had seen for years with lifeless legs and colourless face! Since he had left her the day before at the Basilica she had blossomed into full youth and beauty. One night had sufficed for him to find again, developed it is true, the sweet creature whom he had loved so tenderly, the superb, radiant child whom he had embraced so wildly in the by-gone days behind the flowering hedge, beneath the sun-flecked trees.

"How tall and lovely you are, Marie!" said he, in spite of himself.

Then Sister Hyacinthe interposed: "Hasn't the Blessed Virgin done things well, Monsieur l'Abbé? When she takes us in hand, you see, she turns us out as fresh as roses and smelling quite as sweet."

"Ah!" resumed Marie, "I'm so happy; I feel quite strong and well and spotless, as though I had just been born!"

All this was very delicious to Pierre. It seemed to him that the atmosphere was now truly purified of Madame Volmar's presence. Marie filled the room with her candour, with the perfume and brightness of her innocent youth. And yet the joy he felt at the sight of pure beauty and life reflowering was not exempt from sadness. For, after all, the revolt which he had felt in the crypt, the wound of his wrecked life, must forever leave him a bleeding heart. As he gazed upon all that resuscitated grace, as the woman he loved thus reappeared before him in the flower of her youth, he could not but remember that she would never be his, that he belonged no longer to the world, but to the grave. However, he no longer lamented; he experienced a boundless melancholy—a sensation of utter nothingness as he told himself that he was dead, that this dawn of beauty was rising on the tomb in which his manhood slept. It was renunciation, accepted, resolved upon amidst all the desolate grandeur attaching to those lives which are led contrary to nature's law. Then, like the other woman, the impassioned one, Marie took hold of Pierre's hands. But hers were so soft, so fresh, so soothing! She looked at him with so little confusion and a great longing which she dared not express. After a while, however, she summoned up her courage and said: "Will you kiss me, Pierre? It would please me so much."

He shuddered, his heart crushed by this last torture. Ah! the kisses of other days—those kisses which had ever lingered on his lips! Never since had he kissed her, and to-day she was like a sister flinging her arms around his neck. She kissed him with a loud smack on both his cheeks, and offering her own, insisted on his doing likewise to her. So twice, in his turn, he embraced her.

"I, too, Marie," said he, "am pleased, very pleased, I assure you." And then, overcome by emotion, his courage exhausted, whilst at the same time filled with delight and bitterness, he burst into sobs, weeping with his face buried in his hands, like a child seeking to hide its tears.

"Come, come, we must not give way," said Sister Hyacinthe, gaily. "Monsieur l'Abbe would feel too proud if he fancied that we had merely come on his account. M. de Guersaint is about, isn't he?"

Marie raised a cry of deep affection. "Ah! my dear father! After all, it's he who'll be most pleased!"

Thereupon Pierre had to relate that M. de Guersaint had not returned from his excursion to Gavarnie. His increasing anxiety showed itself while he spoke, although he sought to explain his friend's absence, surmising all sorts of obstacles and unforeseen complications. Marie, however, did not seem afraid, but again laughed, saying that her father never could be punctual. Still she was extremely eager for him to see her walking, to find her on her legs again, resuscitated, in the fresh blossoming of her youth.

All at once Sister Hyacinthe, who had gone to lean over the balcony, returned to the room, saying "Here he comes! He's down below, just alighting from his carriage."

"Ah!" cried Marie, with the eager playfulness of a school-girl, "let's give him a surprise. Yes, we must hide, and when he's here we'll show ourselves all of a sudden."

With these words, she hastily dragged Sister Hyacinthe into the adjoining room.

Almost immediately afterwards, M. de Guersaint entered like a whirlwind from the passage, the door communicating with which had been quickly opened by Pierre, and, shaking the young priest's hand, the belated excursionist exclaimed: "Here I am at last! Ah! my friend, you can't have known what to think since four o'clock yesterday, when you expected me back, eh? But you have no idea of the adventures we have had. To begin with, one of the wheels of our landau came off just as we reached Gavarnie; then, yesterday evening—though we managed to start off again—a frightful storm detained us all night long at Saint-Sauveur. I wasn't able to sleep a wink." Then, breaking off, he inquired, "And you, are you all right?"

"I wasn't able to sleep either," said the priest; "they made such a noise in the hotel."

But M. de Guersaint had already started off again: "All the same, it was delightful. I must tell you; you can't imagine it. I was with three delightful churchmen. Abbe des Hermoises is certainly the most charming man I know. Oh! we did laugh—we did laugh!"

Then he again stopped, to inquire, "And how's my daughter?"

Thereupon a clear laugh behind him caused him to turn round, and he remained with his mouth wide open. Marie was there, and was walking, with a look of rapturous delight upon her face, which was beaming with health. He had never for a moment doubted the miracle, and was not in the least surprised that it had taken place, for he had returned with the conviction that everything would end well, and that he would surely find her cured. But what so utterly astounded him was the prodigious spectacle which he had not foreseen: his daughter, looking so beautiful, so divine, in her little black gown!—his daughter, who had not even brought a hat with her, and merely had a piece of lace tied over her lovely fair hair!—his daughter, full of life, blooming, triumphant, similar to all the daughters of all the fathers whom he had envied for so many years!

"O my child! O my child!" he exclaimed.

And, as she had flown into his arms, he pressed her to his heart, and then they fell upon their knees together. Everything disappeared from before them in a radiant effusion of faith and love. This heedless, hare-brained man, who fell asleep instead of accompanying his daughter to the Grotto, who went off to Gavarnie on the day the Blessed Virgin was to cure her, overflowed with such paternal affection, with such Christian faith so exalted by thankfulness, that for a moment he appeared sublime.

"O Jesus! O Mary! let me thank you for having restored my child to me! O my child, we shall never have breath enough, soul enough, to render thanks to Mary and Jesus for the great happiness they have vouchsafed us! O my child, whom they have resuscitated, O my child, whom they have made so beautiful again, take my heart to offer it to them with your own! I am yours, I am theirs eternally, O my beloved child, my adored child!"

Kneeling before the open window they both, with uplifted eyes, gazed ardently on heaven. The daughter had rested her head on her father's shoulder; whilst he had passed an arm round her waist. They had become one. Tears slowly trickled down their enraptured faces, which were smiling with superhuman felicity, whilst they stammered together disconnected expressions of gratitude.

"O Jesus, we give Thee thanks! O Holy Mother of Jesus, we give thee thanks! We love you, we adore you both. You have rejuvenated the best blood in our veins; it is yours, it circulates only for you. O All-powerful Mother, O Divine and Well-beloved Son, behold a daughter and a father who bless you, who prostrate themselves with joy at your feet."

So affecting was this mingling of two beings, happy at last after so many dark days, this happiness, which could but stammer as though still tinged with suffering, that Pierre was again moved to tears. But this time they were soothing tears which relieved his heart. Ah! poor pitiable humanity! how pleasant it was to see it somewhat consoled and enraptured! and what did it matter, after all, if its great joys of a few seconds' duration sprang from the eternal illusion! Was not the whole of humanity, pitiable humanity, saved by love, personified by that poor childish man who suddenly became sublime because he found his daughter resuscitated?

Standing a little aside, Sister Hyacinthe was also weeping, her heart very full, full of human emotion which she had never before experienced, she who had known no other parents than the Almighty and the Blessed Virgin. Silence had now fallen in this room full of so much tearful fraternity. And it was she who spoke the first, when the father and the daughter, overcome with emotion, at length rose up.

"Now, mademoiselle," she said, "we must be quick and get back to the hospital."

But they all protested. M. de Guersaint wished to keep his daughter with him, and Marie's eyes expressed an eager desire, a longing to enjoy life, to walk and ramble through the whole vast world.

"Oh! no, no!" said the father, "I won't give her back to you. We'll each have a cup of milk, for I'm dying of thirst; then we'll go out and walk about. Yes, yes, both of us! She shall take my arm, like a little woman!"

Sister Hyacinthe laughed again. "Very well!" said she, "I'll leave her with you, and tell the ladies that you've stolen her from me. But for my own part I must be off. You've no idea what an amount of work we have to get through at the hospital if we are to be ready in time to leave: there are all the patients and things to be seen to; and all is in the greatest confusion!"

"So to-day's really Tuesday, and we leave this afternoon?" asked Monsieur de Guersaint, already absent-minded again.

"Of course we do, and don't forget! The white train starts at 3.40. And if you're sensible you'll bring your daughter back early so that she may have a little rest."

Marie walked with the Sister to the door, saying "Be easy, I will be very good. Besides, I want to go back to the Grotto, to thank the Blessed Virgin once more."

When they found themselves all three alone in the little room full of sunshine, it was delicious. Pierre called the servant and told her to bring them some milk, some chocolate, and cakes, in fact the nicest things he could think of. And although Marie had already broken her fast, she ate again, so great an appetite had come upon her since the night before. They drew the table to the window and made quite a feast amidst the keen air from the mountains, whilst the hundred bells of Lourdes, proclaimed with flying peals the glory of that radiant day. They chattered and laughed, and the young woman told her father the story of the miracle, with all the oft-repeated details. She related, too, how she had left her box at the Basilica, and how she had slept twelve hours without stirring. Then M. de Guersaint on his side wished to relate his excursion, but got mixed and kept coming back to the miracle. Finally, it appeared that the Cirque de Gavarnie was something colossal. Only, when you looked at it from a distance it seemed small, for you lost all sense of proportion. The gigantic snow-covered tiers of cliffs, the topmost ridge standing out against the sky with the outlines of some cyclopean fortress with razed keep and jagged ramparts, the great cascade, whose ceaseless jet seemed so slow when in reality it must have rushed down with a noise like thunder, the whole immensity, the forests on right and left, the torrents and the landslips, looked as though they might have been held in the palm of one's hand, when one gazed upon them from the village market-place. And what had impressed him most, what he repeatedly alluded to, were the strange figures described by the snow, which had remained up there amongst the rocks. Amongst others was a huge crucifix, a white cross, several thousand yards in length, which you might have thought had been thrown across the amphitheatre from one end to the other.

However, all at once M. de Guersaint broke off to inquire: "By the way, what's happening at our neighbour's? As I came up-stairs a little while ago I met Monsieur Vigneron running about like a madman; and, through the open doorway of their room, I fancied I saw Madame Vigneron looking very red. Has their son Gustave had another attack?"

Pierre had quite forgotten Madame Chaise lying dead on the other side of the partition. He seemed to feel a cold breath pass over him. "No, no," he answered, "the child is all right." And he said no more, preferring to remain silent. Why spoil this happy hour of new life and reconquered youth by mingling with it the image of death? However, from that moment he himself could not cease thinking of the proximity of nothingness. And he thought, too, of that other room where Madame Volmar's friend was now alone, stifling his sobs with his lips pressed upon a pair of gloves which he had stolen from her. All the sounds of the hotel were now becoming audible again—the coughs, the sighs, the indistinct voices, the continual slamming of doors, the creaking of the floors beneath the great accumulation of travellers, and all the stir in the passages, along which flying skirts were sweeping, and families galloping distractedly amidst the hurry-scurry of departure.

"On my word! you'll do yourself an injury," all at once cried Monsieur de Guersaint, on seeing his daughter take up another cake.

Marie was quite merry too. But at a sudden thought tears came into her eyes, and she exclaimed: "Ah! how glad I am! but also how sorry when I think that everybody is not as pleased as myself."

II

Pleasant Hours

It was eight o'clock, and Marie was so impatient that she could not keep still, but continued going to the window, as if she wished to inhale all the air of the vast, expanse and the immense sky. Ah! what a pleasure to be able to run about the streets, across the squares, to go everywhere as far as she might wish. And to show how strong she was, to have the pride of walking leagues in the presence of everyone, now that the Blessed Virgin had cured her! It was an irresistible impulsion, a flight of her entire being, her blood, and her heart.

However, just as she was setting out she made up her mind that her first visit with her father ought to be to the Grotto, where both of them had to thank Our Lady of Lourdes. Then they would be free; they would have two long hours before them, and might walk wherever they chose, before she returned to lunch and pack up her few things at the hospital.

"Well, is everyone ready?" repeated M. de Guersaint. "Shall we make a move?"

Pierre took his hat, and all three went down-stairs, talking very loud and laughing on the staircase, like boisterous school-boys going for their holidays. They had almost reached the street, when at the doorway Madame Majeste rushed forward. She had evidently been waiting for them to go out.

"Ah! mademoiselle; ah! gentlemen, allow me to congratulate you," she said. "We have heard of the extraordinary favour that has been granted you; we are so happy, so much flattered, when the Blessed Virgin is pleased to select one of our customers!"

Her dry, harsh face was melting with amiability, and she observed the miraculously healed girl with the fondest of eyes. Then she impulsively called her husband, who was passing: "Look, my dear! It's mademoiselle; it's mademoiselle."

Majeste's clean-shaven face, puffed out with yellow fat, assumed a happy and grateful expression. "Really, mademoiselle, I cannot tell you how honoured we feel," said he. "We shall never forget that your papa put up at our place. It has already excited the envy of many people."

While he spoke Madame Majeste stopped the other travellers who were going out, and with a sign summoned the families already seated in the dining-room; indeed, she would have called in the whole street if they had given her time, to show that she had in her house the miracle at which all Lourdes had been marvelling since the previous day. People ended by collecting there, a crowd gathered little by little, while she whispered in the ear of each "Look! that's she; the young party, you know, the young party who—"

But all at once she exclaimed: "I'll go and fetch Apolline from the shop; I must show mademoiselle to Apolline."

Thereupon, however, Majeste, in a very dignified way, restrained her. "No," he said, "leave Apolline; she has three ladies to serve already. Mademoiselle and these gentlemen will certainly not leave Lourdes without making a few purchases. The little souvenirs that one carries away with one are so pleasant to look at later on! And our customers make a point of never buying elsewhere than here, in the shop which we have annexed to the hotel."

"I have already offered my services," added Madame Majeste, "and I renew them. Apolline will be so happy to show mademoiselle all our prettiest articles, at prices, too, which are incredibly low! Oh! there are some delightful things, delightful!"

Marie was becoming impatient at being detained in this manner, and Pierre was suffering from the increasing curiosity which they were arousing. As for M. de Guersaint, he enjoyed this popularity and triumph of his daughter immensely, and promised to return.

"Certainly," said he, "we will purchase a few little knick-knacks. Some souvenirs for ourselves, and some presents that we shall have to make, but later on, when we come back."

At last they escaped and descended the Avenue de la Grotte. The weather was again superb after the storms of the two preceding nights. Cooled by the rain, the morning air was delicious amidst the gaiety which the bright sun shed around. A busy crowd, well pleased with life, was already hurrying along the pavements. And what pleasure it all was for Marie, to whom everything seemed new, charming, inappreciable! In the morning she had had to allow Raymonde to lend her a pair of boots, for she had taken good care not to put any in her portmanteau, superstitiously fearing that they might bring her bad luck. However, Raymonde's boots fitted her admirably, and she listened with childish delight to the little heels tapping merrily on the flagstones. And she did not remember having ever seen houses so white, trees so green, and passers-by so happy. All her senses seemed holiday-making, endowed with a marvellously delicate sensibility; she heard music, smelt distant perfumes, savoured the air greedily, as though it were some delicious fruit. But what she considered, above all, so nice, so charming, was to walk along in this wise on her father's arm. She had never done so before, although she had felt the desire for years, as for one of those impossible pleasures with which people occupy their minds when invalided. And now her dream was realised and her heart beat with joy. She pressed against her father, and strove to walk very upright and look very handsome, so as to do him honour. And he was quite proud, as happy as she was, showing, exhibiting her, overcome with joy at the thought that she belonged to him, that she was his blood, his flesh, his daughter, henceforth beaming with youth and health.

As they were all three crossing the Plateau de la Merlasse, already obstructed by a band of candle and bouquet sellers running after the pilgrims, M. de Guersaint exclaimed, "We are surely not going to the Grotto empty-handed!"

Pierre, who was walking on the other side of Marie, himself brightened by her merry humour, thereupon stopped, and they were at once surrounded by a crowd of female hawkers, who with eager fingers thrust their goods into their faces. "My beautiful young lady! My good gentleman! Buy of me, of me, of me!" Such was the onslaught that it became necessary to struggle in order to extricate oneself. M. de Guersaint ended by purchasing the largest nosegay he could see—a bouquet of white marguerites, as round and hard as a cabbage—from a handsome, fair-haired, well developed girl of twenty, who was extremely bold both in look and manner. It only cost twenty sons, and he insisted on paying for it out of his own little purse, somewhat abashed meantime by the girl's unblushing effrontery. Then Pierre in his turn settled for the three candles which Marie had taken from an old woman, candles at two francs each, a very reasonable price, as she repeatedly said. And on being paid, the old creature, who had an angular face, covetous eyes, and a nose like the beak of a bird of prey, returned profuse and mellifluous thanks: "May Our Lady of Lourdes bless you, my beautiful young lady! May she cure you of your complaints, you and yours!" This enlivened them again, and they set out once more, all three laughing, amused like children at the idea that the good woman's wish had already been accomplished.

At the Grotto Marie wished to file off at once, in order to offer the bouquet and candles herself before even kneeling down. There were not many people there as yet, and having gone to the end of the line their turn came after waiting some three or four minutes. And with what enraptured glances did she then examine everything—the altar of engraved silver, the harmonium-organ, the votive offerings, the candle-holders, streaming with wax blazing in broad daylight. She was now inside that Grotto which she had hitherto only seen from her box of misery; she breathed there as in Paradise itself, steeped rapturously in a pleasant warmth and odour, which slightly oppressed her. When she had placed the tapers at the bottom of the large basket, and had raised herself on tiptoe to fix the bouquet on one of the spears of the iron railing, she imprinted a long kiss upon the rock, below the statue of the Blessed Virgin, at the very spot, indeed, which millions of lips had already polished. And the stone received a kiss of love in which she put forth all the strength of her gratitude, a kiss with which her heart melted.

When she was once more outside, Marie prostrated and humbled herself in an almost endless act of thanksgiving. Her father also had knelt down near her, and mingled the fervour of his gratitude with hers. But he could not remain doing the same thing for long. Little by little he became uneasy, and ended by bending down to his daughter's ear to tell her that he had a call to make which he had previously forgotten. Assuredly the best course would be for her to remain where she was, praying, and waiting for him. While she completed her devotions he would hurry along and get his troublesome errand over; and then they might walk about at ease wheresoever they liked. She did not understand him, did not even hear him, but simply nodded her head, promising that she would not move, and then such tender faith again took possession of her that her eyes, fixed on the white statue of the Virgin, filled with tears.

When M. de Guersaint had joined Pierre, who had remained a short distance off, he gave him the following explanation. "My dear fellow," he said, "it's a matter of conscience; I formally promised the coachman who drove us to Gavarnie that I would see his master and tell him the real cause of our delay. You know whom I mean—the hairdresser on the Place du Marcadal. And, besides, I want to get shaved."

Pierre, who felt uneasy at this proposal, had to give way in face of the promise that they would be back within a quarter of an hour. Only, as the distance seemed long, he on his side insisted on taking a trap which was standing at the bottom of the Plateau de la Merlasse. It was a sort of greenish cabriolet, and its driver, a fat fellow of about thirty, with the usual Basque cap on his head, was smoking a cigarette whilst waiting to be hired. Perched sideways on the seat with his knees wide apart, he drove them on with the tranquil indifference of a well-fed man who considers himself the master of the street.

"We will keep you," said Pierre as he alighted, when they had reached the Place du Marcadal.

"Very well, very well, Monsieur l'Abbe! I'll wait for you!" And then, leaving his lean horse in the hot sun, the driver went to chat and laugh with a strong, dishevelled servant-girl who was washing a dog in the basin of the neighbouring fountain.

Cazaban, as it happened, was just then on the threshold of his shop, the lofty windows and pale green painting of which enlivened the dull Place, which was so deserted on week-days. When he was not pressed with work he delighted to parade in this manner, standing between his two windows, which pots of pomatum and bottles of perfumery decorated with bright shades of colour.

He at once recognised the gentlemen. "Very flattered, very much honoured. Pray walk in, I beg of you," he said.

Then, at the first words which M. de Guersaint said to him to excuse the man who had driven him to Gavarnie, he showed himself well disposed. Of course it was not the man's fault; he could not prevent wheels coming to pieces, or storms falling. So long as the travellers did not complain all was well.

"Oh!" thereupon exclaimed M. de Guersaint, "it's a magnificent country, never to be forgotten."

"Well, monsieur, as our neighbourhood pleases you, you must come and see us again; we don't ask anything better," said Cazaban; and, on the architect seating himself in one of the arm-chairs and asking to be shaved, he began to bustle about.

His assistant was still absent, running errands for the pilgrims whom he lodged, a whole family, who were taking a case of chaplets, plaster Virgins, and framed engravings away with them. You heard a confused tramping of feet and violent bursts of conversation coming from the first floor, all the helter-skelter of people whom the approaching departure and the packing of purchases lying hither and thither drove almost crazy. In the adjoining dining-room, the door of which had remained open, two children were draining the dregs of some cups of chocolate which stood about amidst the disorder of the breakfast service. The whole of the house had been let, entirely given over, and now had come the last hours of this invasion which compelled the hairdresser and his wife to seek refuge in the narrow cellar, where they slept on a small camp-bed.

While Cazaban was rubbing M. de Guersaint's cheeks with soap-suds, the architect questioned him. "Well, are you satisfied with the season?"

"Certainly, monsieur, I can't complain. As you hear, my travellers are leaving to-day, but I am expecting others to-morrow morning; barely sufficient time for a sweep out. It will be the same up to October."

Then, as Pierre remained standing, walking about the shop and looking at the walls with an air of impatience, he turned round politely and said: "Pray be seated, Monsieur l'Abbe; take a newspaper. It will not be long."

The priest having thanked him with a nod, and refusing to sit down, the hairdresser, whose tongue was ever itching to talk, continued: "Oh! as for myself, I am always busy, my house is renowned for the cleanliness of the beds and the excellence of the fare. Only the town is not satisfied. Ah, no! I may even say that I have never known so much discontent here."

He became silent for a moment, and shaved his customer's left cheek; then again pausing in his work he suddenly declared with a cry, wrung from him by conviction, "The Fathers of the Grotto are playing with fire, monsieur, that is all I have to say."

From that moment, however, the vent-plug was withdrawn, and he talked and talked and talked again. His big eyes rolled in his long face with prominent cheek-bones and sunburnt complexion sprinkled with red, while the whole of his nervous little body continued on the jump, agitated by his growing exuberance of speech and gesture. He returned to his former indictment, and enumerated all the many grievances that the old town had against the Fathers. The hotel-keepers complained; the dealers in religious fancy articles did not take half the amount they ought to have realised; and, finally, the new town monopolised both the pilgrims and the cash; there was now no possibility for anyone but the keepers of the lodging-houses, hotels, and shops open in the neighbourhood of the Grotto to make any money whatever. It was a merciless struggle, a deadly hostility increasing from day to day, the old city losing a little of its life each season, and assuredly destined to disappear,—to be choked, assassinated, by the young town. Ah! their dirty Grotto! He would rather have his feet cut off than tread there. Wasn't it heart-rending, that knick-knack shop which they had stuck beside it? A shameful thing, at which a bishop had shown himself so indignant that it was said he had written to the Pope! He, Cazaban, who flattered himself with being a freethinker and a Republican of the old days, who already under the Empire had voted for the Opposition candidates, assuredly had the right to declare that he did not believe in their dirty Grotto, and that he did not care a fig for it!

"Look here, monsieur," he continued; "I am going to tell you a fact. My brother belongs to the municipal council, and it's through him that I know it. I must tell you first of all that we now have a Republican municipal council, which is much worried by the demoralisation of the town. You can no longer go out at night without meeting girls in the streets—you know, those candle hawkers! They gad about with the drivers who come here when the season commences, and swell the suspicious floating population which comes no one knows whence. And I must also explain to you the position of the Fathers towards the town. When they purchased the land at the Grotto they signed an agreement by which they undertook not to engage in any business there. Well, they have opened a shop in spite of their signature. Is not that an unfair rivalry, unworthy of honest people? So the new council decided on sending them a deputation to insist on the agreement being respected, and enjoining them to close their shop at once. What do you think they answered, monsieur? Oh! what they have replied twenty times before, what they will always answer, when they are reminded of their engagements: 'Very well, we consent to keep them, but we are masters at our own place, and we'll close the Grotto!'"

He raised himself up, his razor in the air, and, repeating his words, his eyes dilated by the enormity of the thing, he said, "'We'll close the Grotto.'"

Pierre, who was continuing his slow walk, suddenly stopped and said in his face, "Well! the municipal council had only to answer, 'Close it.'"

At this Cazaban almost choked; the blood rushed to his face, he was beside himself, and stammered out "Close the Grotto?—Close the Grotto?"

"Certainly! As the Grotto irritates you and rends your heart; as it's a cause of continual warfare, injustice, and corruption. Everything would be over, we should hear no more about it. That would really be a capital solution, and if the council had the power it would render you a service by forcing the Fathers to carry out their threat."

As Pierre went on speaking, Cazaban's anger subsided. He became very calm and somewhat pale, and in the depths of his big eyes the priest detected an expression of increasing uneasiness. Had he not gone too far in his passion against the Fathers? Many ecclesiastics did not like them; perhaps this young priest was simply at Lourdes for the purpose of stirring-up an agitation against them. Then who knows?—it might possibly result in the Grotto being closed later on. But it was by the Grotto that they all lived. If the old city screeched with rage at only picking up the crumbs, it was well pleased to secure even that windfall; and the freethinkers themselves, who coined money with the pilgrims, like everyone else, held their tongues, ill at ease, and even frightened, when they found people too much of their opinion with regard to the objectionable features of new Lourdes. It was necessary to be prudent.

Cazaban thereupon returned to M. de Guersaint, whose other cheek he began shaving, murmuring the while in an off-hand manner: "Oh! what I say about the Grotto is not because it troubles me much in reality, and, besides, everyone must live."

In the dining-room, the children, amidst deafening shouts, had just broken one of the bowls, and Pierre, glancing through the open doorway, again noticed the engravings of religious subjects and the plaster Virgin with which the hairdresser had ornamented the apartment in order to please his lodgers. And just then, too, a voice shouted from the first floor that the trunk was ready, and that they would be much obliged if the assistant would cord it as soon as he returned.

However, Cazaban, in the presence of these two gentlemen whom, as a matter of fact, he did not know, remained suspicious and uneasy, his brain haunted by all sorts of disquieting suppositions. He was in despair at the idea of having to let them go away without learning anything about them, especially after having exposed himself. If he had only been able to withdraw the more rabid of his biting remarks about the Fathers. Accordingly, when M. de Guersaint rose to wash his chin, he yielded to a desire to renew the conversation.

"Have you heard talk of yesterday's miracle? The town is quite upside down with it; more than twenty people have already given me an account of what occurred. Yes, it seems they obtained an extraordinary

ÉMILE ZOLA

miracle, a paralytic young lady got up and dragged her invalid carriage as far as the choir of the Basilica."

M. de Guersaint, who was about to sit down after wiping himself, gave a complacent laugh. "That young lady is my daughter," he said.

Thereupon, under this sudden and fortunate flash of enlightenment, Cazaban became all smiles. He felt reassured, and combed M. de Guersaint's hair with a masterly touch, amid a returning exuberance of speech and gesture. "Ah! monsieur, I congratulate you, I am flattered at having you in my hands. Since the young lady your daughter is cured, your father's heart is at ease. Am I not right?"

And he also found a few pleasant words for Pierre. Then, when he had decided to let them go, he looked at the priest with an air of conviction, and remarked, like a sensible man, desirous of coming to a conclusion on the subject of miracles: "There are some, Monsieur l'Abbe, which are good fortunes for everybody. From time to time we require one of that description."

Outside, M. de Guersaint had to go and fetch the coachman, who was still laughing with the servant-girl, while her dog, dripping with water, was shaking itself in the sun. In five minutes the trap brought them back to the bottom of the Plateau de la Merlasse. The trip had taken a good half-hour. Pierre wanted to keep the conveyance, with the idea of showing Marie the town without giving her too much fatigue. So, while the father ran to the Grotto to fetch his daughter, he waited there beneath the trees.

The coachman at once engaged in conversation with the priest. He had lit another cigarette and showed himself very familiar. He came from a village in the environs of Toulouse, and did not complain, for he earned good round sums each day at Lourdes. You fed well there, said he, you amused yourself, it was what you might call a good neighbourhood. He said these things with the *abandon* of a man who was not troubled with religious scruples, but yet did not forget the respect which he owed to an ecclesiastic.

At last, from the top of his box, where he remained half lying down, dangling one of his legs, he allowed this remark to fall slowly from his lips: "Ah! yes, Monsieur l'Abbe, Lourdes has caught on well, but the question is whether it will all last long!"

Pierre, who was very much struck by the remark, was pondering on its involuntary profundity, when M. de Guersaint reappeared, bringing Marie with him. He had found her kneeling on the same spot, in the same act of faith and thankfulness, at the feet of the Blessed Virgin; and it seemed as if she had brought all the brilliant light of the Grotto away in her eyes, so vividly did they sparkle with divine joy at her cure. She would not entertain a proposal to keep the trap. No, no! she preferred to go on foot; she did not care about seeing the town, so long as she might for another hour continue walking on her father's arm through the gardens, the streets, the squares, anywhere they pleased! And, when Pierre had paid the driver, it was she who turned into a path of the Esplanade garden, delighted at being able to saunter in this wise beside the turf and the flower beds, under the great trees. The grass, the leaves, the shady solitary walks where you heard the everlasting rippling of the Gave, were so sweet and fresh! But afterwards she wished to return by way of the streets, among the crowd, that she might find the agitation, noise, and life, the need of which possessed her whole being.

In the Rue St. Joseph, on perceiving the panorama, where the former Grotto was depicted, with Bernadette kneeling down before it on the day of the miracle of the candle, the idea occurred to Pierre to go in. Marie became as happy as a child; and even M. de Guersaint was full of innocent delight, especially when he noticed that among the batch of pilgrims who dived at the same time as themselves into the depths of the obscure corridor, several recognised in his daughter the girl so miraculously healed the day before, who was already famous, and whose name flew from mouth to mouth. Up above, on the circular platform, when they came out into the diffuse light, filtering through a vellum, there was a sort of ovation around Marie; soft whispers, beatifical glances, a rapture of delight in seeing, following, and touching her. Now glory had come, she would be loved in that way wherever she went, and it was not until the showman who gave the explanations had placed himself at the head of the little party of visitors, and begun to walk round, relating the incident depicted on the huge circular canvas, nearly five hundred feet in length, that she was in some measure forgotten. The painting represented the seventeenth apparition of the Blessed Virgin to Bernadette, on the day when, kneeling before the Grotto during her vision, she had heedlessly left her hand on the flame of the candle without burning it. The whole of the old primitive landscape of the Grotto was shown, the whole scene was set out with all its historical personages: the doctor verifying the miracle watch in hand, the Mayor, the Commissary of Police, and the Public Prosecutor, whose names the showman gave out, amidst the amazement of the public following him.

Then, by an unconscious transition of ideas, Pierre recalled the remark which the driver of the cabriolet had made a short time previously: "Lourdes has caught on well, but the question is whether it will all last long." That, in fact, was the question. How many venerated sanctuaries had thus been built already, at the bidding of innocent chosen children, to whom the Blessed Virgin had shown herself! It was always the same story beginning afresh: an apparition; a persecuted shepherdess, who was called a liar; next the covert propulsion of human misery hungering after illusion; then propaganda, and the triumph of the sanctuary shining like a star; and afterwards decline, and oblivion, when the ecstatic dream of another visionary gave birth to another sanctuary elsewhere. It seemed as if the power of illusion wore away; that it was necessary in the course of centuries to displace it, set it amidst new scenery, under fresh circumstances, in order to renew its force. La Salette had dethroned the old wooden and stone Virgins that had healed; Lourdes had just dethroned La Salette, pending the time when it would be dethroned itself by Our Lady of to-morrow, she who will show her sweet, consoling features to some pure child as yet unborn. Only, if Lourdes had met with such rapid, such prodigious fortune, it assuredly owed it to the little sincere soul, the delightful charm of Bernadette. Here there was no deceit, no falsehood, merely the blossoming of suffering, a delicate sick child who brought to the afflicted multitude her dream of justice and equality in the miraculous. She was merely eternal hope, eternal consolation. Besides, all historical and social circumstances seem to have combined to increase the need of this mystical flight at the close of a terrible century of positivist inquiry; and that was perhaps the reason why Lourdes would still long endure in its triumph, before becoming a mere legend, one of those dead religions whose powerful perfume has evaporated.

Ah! that ancient Lourdes, that city of peace and belief, the only possible cradle where the legend could come into being, how easily Pierre conjured it up before him, whilst walking round the vast canvas of the Panorama! That canvas said everything; it was the best lesson of things that could be seen. The monotonous explanations of the showman were not heard; the landscape spoke for itself. First of all there was the Grotto, the rocky hollow beside the Gave, a savage spot suitable for reverie—bushy slopes and heaps of fallen stone, without a path among them; and nothing yet in the way of ornamentation—no monumental quay, no garden paths winding among trimly cut shrubs; no Grotto set in order, deformed, enclosed with iron railings; above all, no shop for the sale of religious articles, that simony shop which was the scandal of all pious souls. The Virgin could not have selected a more solitary and charming nook wherein to show herself to the chosen one of her heart, the poor young girl who came thither still possessed by the dream of her painful nights, even whilst gathering dead wood. And on the opposite side of the Gave, behind the rock of the castle, was old Lourdes, confident and asleep. Another age was then conjured up; a small town, with narrow pebble-paved streets, black houses with marble dressings, and an antique, semi-Spanish church, full of old carvings, and peopled with visions of gold and painted flesh. Communication with other places was only kept up by the Bagneres and Cauterets *diligences*, which twice a day forded the Lapaca to climb the steep causeway of the Rue Basse. The spirit of the century had not breathed on those peaceful roofs sheltering a belated population which had remained childish, enclosed within the narrow limits of strict religious discipline. There was no debauchery; a slow antique commerce sufficed for daily life, a poor life whose hardships were the safeguards of morality. And Pierre had never better understood how Bernadette, born in that land of faith and honesty, had flowered like a natural rose, budding on the briars of the road.

"It's all the same very curious," observed M. de Guersaint when they found themselves in the street again. "I'm not at all sorry I saw it."

Marie was also laughing with pleasure. "One would almost think oneself there. Isn't it so, father? At times it seems as if the people were going to move. And how charming Bernadette looks on her knees, in ecstasy, while the candle flame licks her fingers without burning them."

"Let us see," said the architect; "we have only an hour left, so we must think of making our purchases, if we wish to buy anything. Shall we take a look at the shops? We certainly promised Majeste to give him the preference; but that does not prevent us from making a few inquiries. Eh! Pierre, what do you say?"

"Oh! certainly, as you like," answered the priest. "Besides, it will give us a walk."

And he thereupon followed the young girl and her father, who returned to the Plateau de la Merlasse. Since he had quitted the Panorama

ÉMILE ZOLA

he felt as though he no longer knew where he was. It seemed to him as if he had all at once been transported from one to another town, parted by centuries. He had left the solitude, the slumbering peacefulness of old Lourdes, which the dead light of the vellum had increased, to fall at last into new Lourdes, sparkling with brightness and noisy with the crowd. Ten o'clock had just struck, and extraordinary animation reigned on the footways, where before breakfast an entire people was hastening to complete its purchases, so that it might have nothing but its departure to think of afterwards. The thousands of pilgrims of the national pilgrimage streamed along the thoroughfares and besieged the shops in a final scramble. You would have taken the cries, the jostling, and the sudden rushes for those at some fair just breaking up amidst a ceaseless roll of vehicles. Many, providing themselves with provisions for the journey, cleared the open-air stalls where bread and slices of sausages and ham were sold. Others purchased fruit and wine; baskets were filled with bottles and greasy parcels until they almost burst. A hawker who was wheeling some cheeses about on a small truck saw his goods carried off as if swept away by the wind. But what the crowd more particularly purchased were religious articles, and those hawkers whose barrows were loaded with statuettes and sacred engravings were reaping golden gains. The customers at the shops stood in strings on the pavement; the women were belted with immense chaplets, had Blessed Virgins tucked under their arms, and were provided with cans which they meant to fill at the miraculous spring. Carried in the hand or slung from the shoulder, some of them quite plain and others daubed over with a Lady of Lourdes in blue paint, these cans held from one to ten quarts apiece; and, shining with all the brightness of new tin, clashing, too, at times with the sharp jingle of stew-pans, they added a gay note to the aspect of the noisy multitude. And the fever of dealing, the pleasure of spending one's money, of returning home with one's pockets crammed with photographs and medals, lit up all faces with a holiday expression, transforming the radiant gathering into a fair-field crowd with appetites either beyond control or satisfied.

On the Plateau de la Merlasse, M. de Guersaint for a moment felt tempted to enter one of the finest and most patronised shops, on the board over which were these words in large letters: "Soubirous, Brother of Bernadette."

"Eh! what if we were to make our purchases there? It would be more appropriate, more interesting to remember."

However, he passed on, repeating that they must see everything first of all.

Pierre had looked at the shop kept by Bernadette's brother with a heavy heart. It grieved him to find the brother selling the Blessed Virgin whom the sister had beheld. However, it was necessary to live, and he had reason to believe that, beside the triumphant Basilica resplendent with gold, the visionary's relatives were not making a fortune, the competition being so terrible. If on the one hand the pilgrims left millions behind them at Lourdes, on the other there were more than two hundred dealers in religious articles, to say nothing of the hotel and lodging-house keepers, to whom the largest part of the spoils fell; and thus the gain, so eagerly disputed, ended by being moderate enough after all. Along the Plateau on the right and left of the repository kept by Bernadette's brother, other shops appeared, an uninterrupted row of them, pressing one against the other, each occupying a division of a long wooden structure, a sort of gallery erected by the town, which derived from it some sixty thousand francs a year. It formed a regular bazaar of open stalls, encroaching on the pavements so as to tempt people to stop as they passed along. For more than three hundred yards no other trade was plied: a river of chaplets, medals, and statuettes streamed without end behind the windows; and in enormous letters on the boards above appeared the venerated names of Saint Roch, Saint Joseph, Jerusalem, The Immaculate Virgin, The Sacred Heart of Mary, all the names in Paradise that were most likely to touch and attract customers.

"Really," said M. de Guersaint, "I think it's the same thing all over the place. Let us go anywhere." He himself had had enough of it, this interminable display was quite exhausting him.

"But as you promised to make the purchases at Majeste's," said Marie, who was not, in the least tired, "the best thing will be to go back."

"That's it; let's return to Majeste's place."

But the rows of shops began again in the Avenue de la Grotte. They swarmed on both sides; and among them here were jewellers, drapers, and umbrella-makers, who also dealt in religious articles. There was even a confectioner who sold boxes of pastilles *a l'eau de Lourdes*, with a figure of the Virgin on the cover. A photographer's windows were crammed with views of the Grotto and the Basilica, and portraits of Bishops and reverend Fathers of all Orders, mixed up with views of famous sites in the neighbouring mountains. A bookseller displayed the last Catholic publications, volumes bearing devout titles, and among them the innumerable works published on Lourdes during the last twenty years, some of which had had a wonderful success, which was still fresh in memory. In this broad, populous thoroughfare the crowd streamed along in more open order; their cans jingled, everyone was in high spirits, amid the bright sunrays which enfiladed the road from one end to the other. And it seemed as if there would never be a finish to the statuettes, the medals, and the chaplets; one display followed another; and, indeed, there were miles of them running through the streets of the entire town, which was ever the same bazaar selling the same articles.

In front of the Hotel of the Apparitions M. de Guersaint again hesitated. "Then it's decided, we are going to make our purchases there?" he asked.

"Certainly," said Marie. "See what a beautiful shop it is!"

And she was the first to enter the establishment, which was, in fact, one of the largest in the street, occupying the ground-floor of the hotel on the left hand. M. de Guersaint and Pierre followed her.

Apolline, the niece of the Majestes, who was in charge of the place, was standing on a stool, taking some holy-water vases from a top shelf to show them to a young man, an elegant bearer, wearing beautiful yellow gaiters. She was laughing with the cooing sound of a dove, and looked charming with her thick black hair and her superb eyes, set in a somewhat square face, which had a straight forehead, chubby cheeks, and full red lips. Jumping lightly to the ground, she exclaimed: "Then you don't think that this pattern would please madame, your aunt?"

"No, no," answered the bearer, as he went off. "Obtain the other pattern. I shall not leave until to-morrow, and will come back."

When Apolline learnt that Marie was the young person visited by the miracle of whom Madame Majeste had been talking ever since the previous day, she became extremely attentive. She looked at her with her merry smile, in which there was a dash of surprise and covert incredulity. However, like the clever saleswoman that she was, she was profuse in complimentary remarks. "Ah, mademoiselle, I shall be so happy to sell to you! Your miracle is so beautiful! Look, the whole shop is at your disposal. We have the largest choice."

Marie was ill at ease. "Thank you," she replied, "you are very good. But we have only come to buy a few small things."

"If you will allow us," said M. de Guersaint, "we will choose ourselves."

"Very well. That's it, monsieur. Afterwards we will see!"

And as some other customers now came in, Apolline forgot them, returned to her duties as a pretty saleswoman, with caressing words and seductive glances, especially for the gentlemen, whom she never allowed to leave until they had their pockets full of purchases.

M. de Guersaint had only two francs left of the louis which Blanche, his eldest daughter, had slipped into his hand when he was leaving, as pocket-money; and so he did not dare to make any large selection. But Pierre declared that they would cause him great pain if they did not allow him to offer them the few things which they would like to take away with them from Lourdes. It was therefore understood that they would first of all choose a present for Blanche, and then Marie and her father should select the souvenirs that pleased them best.

"Don't let us hurry," repeated M. de Guersaint, who had become very gay. "Come, Marie, have a good look. What would be most likely to please Blanche?"

All three looked, searched, and rummaged. But their indecision increased as they went from one object to another. With its counters, show-cases, and nests of drawers, furnishing it from top to bottom, the spacious shop was a sea of endless billows, overflowing with all the religious knick-knacks imaginable. There were the chaplets: skeins of chaplets hanging along the walls, and heaps of chaplets lying in the drawers, from humble ones costing twenty sons a dozen, to those of sweet-scented wood, agate, and lapis-lazuli, with chains of gold or silver; and some of them, of immense length, made to go twice round the neck or waist, had carved beads, as large as walnuts, separated by death's-heads. Then there were the medals: a shower of medals, boxes full of medals, of all sizes, of all metals, the cheapest and the most precious. They bore different inscriptions, they represented the Basilica, the Grotto, or the Immaculate Conception; they were engraved, *repoussees*, or enamelled, executed with care, or made by the gross, according to the price. And next there were the Blessed Virgins, great and small, in zinc, wood, ivory, and especially plaster; some entirely white, others tinted in bright colours, in accordance with the description given by Bernadette; the amiable and smiling face, the extremely long veil, the blue sash, and the golden roses on the feet, there being, however, some slight modification in each model so as to guarantee the copyright. And there was another flood of other religious objects: a hundred varieties of scapularies, a thousand different sorts of sacred pictures: fine engravings, large chromo-lithographs in glaring colours, submerged beneath a mass of smaller pictures, which were coloured, gilded, varnished, decorated with bouquets of flowers, and bordered with lace paper. And there was also jewellery: rings, brooches, and bracelets, loaded with stars and crosses, and ornamented with saintly figures. Finally, there was the Paris article, which rose above and submerged all the rest: pencil-holders, purses, cigar-holders, paperweights, paper-knives, even snuff-boxes; and innumerable other objects on which the Basilica, Grotto, and Blessed Virgin ever and ever appeared, reproduced in every way, by every process that is known. Heaped together pell-mell in one of the cases reserved to articles at fifty centimes apiece were napkin-rings, egg-cups, and wooden pipes, on which was carved the beaming apparition of Our Lady of Lourdes.

Little by little, M. de Guersaint, with the annoyance of a man who prides himself on being an artist, became disgusted and quite sad. "But all this is frightful, frightful!" he repeated at every new article he took up to look at.

Then he relieved himself by reminding Pierre of the ruinous attempt which he had made to improve the artistic quality of religious prints. The remains of his fortune had been lost in that attempt, and the thought made him all the more angry, in presence of the wretched productions with which the shop was crammed. Had anyone ever seen things of such idiotic, pretentious, and complicated ugliness! The vulgarity of the ideas and the silliness of the expressions portrayed rivalled the commonplace character of the composition. You were reminded of fashion-plates, the covers of boxes of sweets, and the wax dolls' heads that revolve in hairdressers' windows; it was an art abounding in false prettiness, painfully childish, with no really human touch in it, no tone, and no sincerity. And the architect, who was wound up, could not stop, but went on to express his disgust with the buildings of new Lourdes, the pitiable disfigurement of the Grotto, the colossal monstrosity of the inclined ways, the disastrous lack of symmetry in the church of the Rosary and the Basilica, the former looking too heavy, like a corn market, whilst the latter had an anaemical structural leanness with no kind of style but the mongrel.

"Ah! one must really be very fond of God," he at last concluded, "to have courage enough to come and adore Him amidst such horrors! They have failed in everything, spoilt everything, as though out of pleasure. Not one of them has experienced that moment of true feeling, of real naturalness and sincere faith, which gives birth to masterpieces.

They are all clever people, but all plagiarists; not one has given his mind and being to the undertaking. And what must they not require to inspire them, since they have failed to produce anything grand even in this land of miracles?"

Pierre did not reply, but he was very much struck by these reflections, which at last gave him an explanation of a feeling of discomfort that he had experienced ever since his arrival at Lourdes. This discomfort arose from the difference between the modern surroundings and the faith of past ages which it sought to resuscitate. He thought of the old cathedrals where quivered that faith of nations; he pictured the former attributes of worship—the images, the goldsmith's work, the saints in wood and stone—all of admirable power and beauty of expression. The fact was that in those ancient times the workmen had been true believers, had given their whole souls and bodies and all the candour of their feelings to their productions, just as M. de Guersaint said. But nowadays architects built churches with the same practical tranquillity that they erected five-storey houses, just as the religious articles, the chaplets, the medals, and the statuettes were manufactured by the gross in the populous quarters of Paris by merrymaking workmen who did not even follow their religion. And thus what slopwork, what toymakers', ironmongers' stuff it all was! of a prettiness fit to make you cry, a silly sentimentality fit to make your heart turn with disgust! Lourdes was inundated, devastated, disfigured by it all to such a point as to quite upset persons with any delicacy of taste who happened to stray through its streets. It clashed jarringly with the attempted resuscitation of the legends, ceremonies, and processions of dead ages; and all at once it occurred to Pierre that the social and historical condemnation of Lourdes lay in this, that faith is forever dead among a people when it no longer introduces it into the churches it builds or the chaplets it manufactures.

However, Marie had continued examining the shelves with the impatience of a child, hesitating, and finding nothing which seemed to her worthy of the great dream of ecstasy which she would ever keep within her.

"Father," she said, "it is getting late; you must take me back to the hospital; and to make up my mind, look, I will give Blanche this medal with the silver chain. After all it's the most simple and prettiest thing here. She will wear it; it will make her a little piece of jewellery. As for myself, I will take this statuette of Our Lady of Lourdes, this small one, which is rather prettily painted. I shall place it in my room and surround it with fresh flowers. It will be very nice, will it not?"

M. de Guersaint approved of her idea, and then busied himself with his own choice. "O dear! oh dear! how embarrassed I am!" said he.

He was examining some ivory-handled penholders capped with pea-like balls, in which were microscopic photographs, and while bringing one of the little holes to his eye to look in it he raised an exclamation of mingled surprise and pleasure. "Hallo! here's the Cirque de Gavarnie! Ah! it's prodigious; everything is there; how can that colossal panorama have been got into so small a space? Come, I'll take this penholder; it's curious, and will remind me of my excursion."

Pierre had simply chosen a portrait of Bernadette, the large photograph which represents her on her knees in a black gown, with a handkerchief tied over her hair, and which is said to be the only one in existence taken from life. He hastened to pay, and they were all three on the point of leaving when Madame Majeste entered, protested, and positively insisted on making Marie a little present, saying that it would bring her establishment good-fortune. "I beg of you, mademoiselle, take a scapulary," said she. "Look among those there. The Blessed Virgin who chose you will repay me in good luck."

She raised her voice and made so much fuss that the purchasers filling the shop were interested, and began gazing at the girl with envious eyes. It was popularity bursting out again around her, a popularity which ended even by reaching the street when the landlady went to the threshold of the shop, making signs to the tradespeople opposite and putting all the neighbourhood in a flutter.

"Let us go," repeated Marie, feeling more and more uncomfortable.

But her father, on noticing a priest come in, detained her. "Ah! Monsieur l'Abbe des Hermoises!"

It was in fact the handsome Abbe, clad in a cassock of fine cloth emitting a pleasant odour, and with an expression of soft gaiety on his fresh-coloured face. He had not noticed his companion of the previous day, but had gone straight to Apolline and taken her on one side. And Pierre overheard him saying in a subdued tone: "Why didn't you bring me my three-dozen chaplets this morning?"

Apolline again began laughing with the cooing notes of a dove, and looked at him sideways, roguishly, without answering.

"They are for my little penitents at Toulouse. I wanted to place them at the bottom of my trunk; and you offered to help me pack my linen."

She continued laughing, and her pretty eyes sparkled.

"However, I shall not leave before to-morrow. Bring them me to-night, will you not? When you are at liberty. It's at the end of the street, at Duchene's."

Thereupon, with a slight movement of her red lips, and in a somewhat bantering way, which left him in doubt as to whether she would keep her promise, she replied: "Certainly, Monsieur l'Abbe, I will go."

They were now interrupted by M. de Guersaint, who came forward to shake the priest's hand. And the two men at once began talking again of the Cirque de Gavarnie: they had had a delightful trip, a most pleasant time, which they would never forget. Then they enjoyed a laugh at the expense of their two companions, ecclesiastics of slender means, good-natured fellows, who had much amused them. And the architect ended by reminding his new friend that he had kindly promised to induce a personage at Toulouse, who was ten times a millionaire, to interest himself in his studies on navigable balloons. "A first advance of a hundred thousand francs would be sufficient," he said.

"You can rely on me," answered Abbe des Hermoises. "You will not have prayed to the Blessed Virgin in vain."

However, Pierre, who had kept Bernadette's portrait in his hand, had just then been struck by the extraordinary likeness between Apolline and the visionary. It was the same rather massive face, the same full thick mouth, and the same magnificent eyes; and he recollected that Madame Majeste had already pointed out to him this striking resemblance, which was all the more peculiar as Apolline had passed through a similar poverty-stricken childhood at Bartres before her aunt had taken her with her to assist in keeping the shop. Bernadette! Apolline! What a strange association, what an unexpected reincarnation at thirty years' distance! And, all at once, with this Apolline, who was so flightily merry and careless, and in regard to whom there were so many odd rumours, new Lourdes rose before his eyes: the coachmen, the candle-girls, the persons who let rooms and waylaid tenants at the railway station, the hundreds of furnished houses with discreet little lodgings, the crowd of free priests, the lady hospitallers, and the simple passers-by, who came there to satisfy their appetites. Then, too, there was the trading mania excited by the shower of millions, the entire town given up to lucre, the shops transforming the streets into bazaars which devoured one another, the hotels living gluttonously on the pilgrims, even to the Blue Sisters who kept a *table d'hote*, and the Fathers of the

Grotto who coined money with their God! What a sad and frightful course of events, the vision of pure Bernadette inflaming multitudes, making them rush to the illusion of happiness, bringing a river of gold to the town, and from that moment rotting everything. The breath of superstition had sufficed to make humanity flock thither, to attract abundance of money, and to corrupt this honest corner of the earth forever. Where the candid lily had formerly bloomed there now grew the carnal rose, in the new loam of cupidity and enjoyment. Bethlehem had become Sodom since an innocent child had seen the Virgin.

"Eh? What did I tell you?" exclaimed Madame Majeste, perceiving that Pierre was comparing her niece with the portrait. "Apolline is Bernadette all over!"

The young girl approached with her amiable smile, flattered at first by the comparison.

"Let's see, let's see!" said Abbe des Hermoises, with an air of lively interest.

He took the photograph in his turn, compared it with the girl, and then exclaimed in amazement: "It's wonderful; the same features. I had not noticed it before. Really I'm delighted—"

"Still I fancy she had a larger nose," Apolline ended by remarking.

The Abbe then raised an exclamation of irresistible admiration: "Oh! you are prettier, much prettier, that's evident. But that does not matter, anyone would take you for two sisters."

Pierre could not refrain from laughing, he thought the remark so peculiar. Ah! poor Bernadette was absolutely dead, and she had no sister. She could not have been born again; it would have been impossible for her to exist in the region of crowded life and passion which she had made.

At length Marie went off leaning on her father's arm, and it was agreed that they would both call and fetch her at the hospital to go to the station together. More than fifty people were awaiting her in the street in a state of ecstasy. They bowed to her and followed her; and one woman even made her infirm child, whom she was bringing back from the Grotto, touch her gown.

III

Departure

At half-past two o'clock the white train, which was to leave Lourdes at three-forty, was already in the station, alongside the second platform. For three days it had been waiting on a siding, in the same state as when it had come from Paris, and since it had been run into the station again white flags had been waving from the foremost and hindmost of its carriages, by way of preventing any mistakes on the part of the pilgrims, whose entraining was usually a very long and troublesome affair. Moreover, all the fourteen trains of the pilgrimage were timed to leave that day. The green train had started off at ten o'clock, followed by the pink and the yellow trains, and the others—the orange, the grey, and the blue—would start in turn after the white train had taken its departure. It was, indeed, another terrible day's work for the station staff, amidst a tumult and a scramble which altogether distracted them.

However, the departure of the white train was always the event of the day which provoked most interest and emotion, for it took away with it all the more afflicted patients, amongst whom were naturally those loved by the Virgin and chosen by her for the miraculous cures. Accordingly, a large, serried crowd was collected under the roofing of the spacious platform, a hundred yards in length, where all the benches were already covered with waiting pilgrims and their parcels. In the refreshment-room, at one end of the buildings, men were drinking beer and women ordering lemonade at the little tables which had been taken by assault, whilst at the other end bearers stood on guard at the goods entrance so as to keep the way clear for the speedy passage of the patients, who would soon be arriving. And all along the broad platform there was incessant coming and going, poor people rushing hither and thither in bewilderment, priests trotting along to render assistance, gentlemen in frock-coats looking on with quiet inquisitiveness: indeed, all the jumbling and jostling of the most mixed, most variegated throng ever elbowed in a railway station.

At three o'clock, however, the sick had not yet reached the station, and Baron Suire was in despair, his anxiety arising from the dearth of horses, for a number of unexpected tourists had arrived at Lourdes that morning and hired conveyances for Bareges, Cauterets, and Gavarnie. At last, however, the Baron espied Berthaud and Gerard arriving in all haste, after scouring the town; and when he had rushed up to them they soon pacified him by announcing that things were going splendidly. They had been able to procure the needful animals, and the removal of the patients from the hospital was now being carried out under the most favorable circumstances. Squads of bearers with their stretchers and little carts were already in the station yard, watching for the arrival of the vans, breaks, and other vehicles which had been recruited. A reserve supply of mattresses and cushions was, moreover, heaped up beside a lamp-post. Nevertheless, just as the first patients arrived, Baron Suire again lost his head, whilst Berthaud and Gerard hastened to the platform from which the train would start. There they began to superintend matters, and gave orders amidst an increasing scramble.

Father Fourcade was on this platform, walking up and down alongside the train, on Father Massias's arm. Seeing Doctor Bonamy approach, he stopped short to speak to him: "Ah, doctor," said he, "I am pleased to see you. Father Massias, who is about to leave us, was again telling me just now of the extraordinary favor granted by the Blessed Virgin to that interesting young person, Mademoiselle Marie de Guersaint. There has not been such a brilliant miracle for years! It is signal good-fortune for us—a blessing which should render our labours fruitful. All Christendom will be illumined, comforted, enriched by it."

He was radiant with pleasure, and forthwith the doctor with his clean-shaven face, heavy, peaceful features, and usually tired eyes, also began to exult: "Yes, your reverence, it is prodigious, prodigious! I shall write a pamphlet about it. Never was cure produced by supernatural means in a more authentic manner. Ah! what a stir it will create!"

Then, as they had begun walking to and fro again, all three together, he noticed that Father Fourcade was dragging his leg with increased difficulty, leaning heavily the while on his companion's arm. "Is your attack of gout worse, your reverence?" he inquired. "You seem to be suffering a great deal."

"Oh! don't speak of it; I wasn't able to close my eyes all night! It is very annoying that this attack should have come on me the very day of my arrival here! It might as well have waited. But there is nothing to be done, so don't let us talk of it any more. I am, at all events, very pleased with this year's result."

"Ah! yes, yes indeed," in his turn said Father Massias, in a voice which quivered with fervour; "we may all feel proud, and go away with our hearts full of enthusiasm and gratitude. How many prodigies there have been, in addition to the healing of that young woman you spoke of! There is no counting all the miracles: deaf women and dumb women have recovered their faculties, faces disfigured by sores have become as smooth as the hand, moribund consumptives have come to life again and eaten and danced! It is not a train of sufferers, but a train of resurrection, a train of glory, that I am about to take back to Paris!"

He had ceased to see the ailing creatures around him, and in the blindness of his faith was soaring triumphantly.

Then, alongside the carriages, whose compartments were beginning to fill, they all three continued their slow saunter, smiling at the pilgrims who bowed to them, and at times again stopping to address a kind word to some mournful woman who, pale and shivering, passed by upon a stretcher. They boldly declared that she was looking much better, and would assuredly soon get well.

However, the station-master, who was incessantly bustling about, passed by, calling in a shrill voice: "Don't block up the platform, please; don't block up the platform!" And on Berthaud pointing out to him that it was, at all events, necessary to deposit the stretchers on the platform before hoisting the patients into the carriages, he became quite angry: "But, come, come; is it reasonable?" he asked. "Look at that little hand-cart which has been left on the rails over yonder. I expect the train to Toulouse in a few minutes. Do you want your people to be crushed to death?"

Then he went off at a run to instruct some porters to keep the bewildered flock of pilgrims away from the rails. Many of them, old and simple people, did not even recognise the colour of their train, and this was the reason why one and all wore cards of some particular hue hanging from their necks, so that they might be led and entrained like marked cattle. And what a constant state of excitement it was, with the starting of these fourteen special trains, in addition to all the ordinary traffic, in which no change had been made.

Pierre arrived, valise in hand, and found some difficulty in reaching the platform. He was alone, for Marie had expressed an ardent desire to kneel once more at the Grotto, so that her soul might burn with gratitude before the Blessed Virgin until the last moment; and so he had left M. de Guersaint to conduct her thither whilst he himself settled the hotel bill. Moreover, he had made them promise that they would take a fly to the station, and they would certainly arrive within a quarter of an hour. Meantime, his idea was to seek their carriage, and there rid himself of his valise. This, however, was not an easy task, and he only recognised the carriage eventually by the placard which had been swinging from it in the sunlight and the storms during the last three days—a square of pasteboard bearing the names of Madame de Jonquiere and Sisters Hyacinthe and Claire des Anges. There could be no mistake, and Pierre again pictured the compartments full of his travelling companions. Some cushions already marked M. Sabathier's corner, and on the seat where Marie had experienced such suffering he still found some scratches caused by the ironwork of her box. Then, having deposited his valise in his own place, he remained on the platform waiting and looking around him, with a slight feeling of surprise at not perceiving Doctor Chassaigne, who had promised to come and embrace him before the train started.

Now that Marie was well again, Pierre had laid his bearer straps aside, and merely wore the red cross of the pilgrimage on his cassock. The station, of which he had caught but a glimpse, in the livid dawn amidst the anguish of the terrible morning of their arrival, now surprised him by its spacious platforms, its broad exits, and its clear gaiety. He could not see the mountains, but some verdant slopes rose up on the other side, in front of the waiting-rooms; and that afternoon the weather was delightfully mild, the sky of a milky whiteness, with light fleecy clouds veiling the sun, whence there fell a broad diffuse light, like a nacreous, pearly dust: "maiden's weather," as country folk are wont to say.

The big clock had just struck three, and Pierre was looking at it when he saw Madame Desagneaux and Madame Volmar arrive, followed by Madame de Jonquiere and her daughter. These ladies, who had driven from the hospital in a landau, at once began looking for their carriage, and it was Raymonde who first recognised the first-class compartment in which she had travelled from Paris. "Mamma, mamma, here; here it is!" she called. "Stay a little while with us; you have plenty of time to install yourself among your patients, since they haven't yet arrived."

Pierre now again found himself face to face with Madame Volmar, and their glances met. However, he gave no sign of recognition, and on her side there was but a slight sudden drooping of the eyelids. She had again assumed the air of a languid, indolent, black-robed woman, who modestly shrinks back, well pleased to escape notice. Her brasier-like eyes no longer glowed; it was only at long intervals that they kindled into a spark beneath the veil of indifference, the moire-like shade, which dimmed them.

"Oh! it was a fearful sick headache!" she was repeating to Madame Desagneaux. "And, you can see, I've hardly recovered the use of my poor head yet. It's the journey which brings it on. It's the same thing every year."

However, Berthaud and Gerard, who had just perceived the ladies, were hurrying up to them. That morning they had presented themselves at the Hospital of Our Lady of Dolours, and Madame de Jonquiere had received them in a little office near the linen-room. Thereupon, apologising with smiling affability for making his request amidst such a hurly-burly, Berthaud had solicited the hand of Mademoiselle Raymonde for his cousin, Gerard. They at once felt themselves at ease, the mother, with some show of emotion, saying that Lourdes would bring the young couple good luck. And so the marriage was arranged in a few words, amidst general satisfaction. A meeting was even appointed for the fifteenth of September at the Chateau of Berneville, near Caen, an estate belonging to Raymonde's uncle, the diplomatist, whom Berthaud knew, and to whom he promised to introduce Gerard. Then Raymonde was summoned, and blushed with pleasure as she placed her little hand in those of her betrothed.

Binding her now upon the platform, the latter began paying her every attention, and asking, "Would you like some pillows for the night? Don't make any ceremony about it; I can give you plenty, both for yourself and for these ladies who are accompanying you."

However, Raymonde gaily refused the offer, "No, no," said she, "we are not so delicate. Keep them for the poor sufferers."

All the ladies were now talking together. Madame de Jonquiere declared that she was so tired, so tired that she no longer felt alive; and yet she displayed great happiness, her eyes smiling as she glanced at her daughter and the young man she was engaged to. But neither Berthaud nor Gerard could remain there; they had their duties to perform, and accordingly took their leave, after reminding Madame de Jonquiere and Raymonde of the appointed meeting. It was understood, was it not, on September 15th, at the Chateau of Berneville? Yes, yes, it was understood! And then came fresh smiles and handshakes, whilst the eyes of the newly engaged couple—caressing, delighted eyes—added all that they dared not say aloud in the midst of such a throng.

"What!" exclaimed little Madame Desagneaux, "you will go to Berneville on the 15th? But if we stay at Trouville till the 10th, as my husband wishes to do, we will go to see you!" And then, turning towards Madame Volmar, who stood there silent, she added, "You ought to come as well, my dear. It would be so nice to meet there all together."

But, with a slow wave of the hand and an air of weary indifference, Madame Volmar answered, "Oh! my holiday is all over; I am going home."

Just then her eyes again met those of Pierre, who had remained standing near the party, and he fancied that she became confused, whilst an expression of indescribable suffering passed over her lifeless face.

The Sisters of the Assumption were now arriving, and the ladies joined them in front of the cantine van. Ferrand, who had come with the Sisters from the hospital, got into the van, and then helped Sister Saint-Francois to mount upon the somewhat high footboard. Then he remained standing on the threshold of the van—transformed into a kitchen and containing all sorts of supplies for the journey, such as bread, broth, milk, and chocolate,—whilst Sister Hyacinthe and Sister Claire des Anges, who were still on the platform, passed him his little medicine-chest and some small articles of luggage.

"You are sure you have everything?" Sister Hyacinthe asked him. "All right. Well, now you only have to go and lie down in your corner and get to sleep, since you complain that your services are not utilised."

Ferrand began to laugh softly. "I shall help Sister Saint-Francois," said he. "I shall light the oil-stove, wash the crockery, carry the cups of broth and milk to the patients whenever we stop, according to the time-table hanging yonder; and if, all the same, you *should* require a doctor, you will please come to fetch me."

Sister Hyacinthe had also begun to laugh. "But we no longer require a doctor since all our patients are cured," she replied; and, fixing her eyes on his, with her calm, sisterly air, she added, "Good-bye, Monsieur Ferrand."

He smiled again, whilst a feeling of deep emotion brought moisture to his eyes. The tremulous accents of his voice expressed his conviction that he would never be able to forget this journey, his joy at having seen her again, and the souvenir of divine and eternal affection which he was taking away with him. "Good-bye, Sister," said he.

Then Madame de Jonquiere talked of going to her carriage with Sister Claire des Anges and Sister Hyacinthe; but the latter assured her that there was no hurry, since the sick pilgrims were as yet scarcely arriving. She left her, therefore, taking the other Sister with her, and promising to see to everything. Moreover, she even insisted on ridding the superintendent of her little bag, saying that she would find it on her seat when it was time for her to come. Thus the ladies continued walking and chatting gaily on the broad platform, where the atmosphere was so pleasant.

Pierre, however, his eyes fixed upon the big clock, watched the minutes hasten by on the dial, and began to feel surprised at not seeing Marie arrive with her father. It was to be hoped that M. de Guersaint would not lose himself on the road!

The young priest was still watching, when, to his surprise, he caught sight of M. Vigneron, in a state of perfect exasperation, pushing his wife and little Gustave furiously before him.

"Oh, Monsieur l'Abbe," he exclaimed, "tell me where our carriage is! Help me to put our luggage and this child in it. I am at my wit's end! They have made me altogether lose my temper."

Then, on reaching the second-class compartment, he caught hold of Pierre's hands, just as the young man was about to place little Gustave inside, and quite an outburst followed. "Could you believe it? They insist on my starting. They tell me that my return-ticket will not be available if I wait here till to-morrow. It was of no use my telling them about the accident. As it is, it's by no means pleasant to have to stay with that corpse, watch over it, see it put in a coffin, and remove it to-morrow within the regulation time. But they pretend that it doesn't concern them, that they already make large enough reductions on the pilgrimage tickets, and that they can't enter into any questions of people dying."

Madame Vigneron stood all of a tremble listening to him, whilst Gustave, forgotten, staggering on his crutch with fatigue, raised his poor, inquisitive, suffering face.

"But at all events," continued the irate father, "as I told them, it's a case of compulsion. What do they expect me to do with that corpse? I can't take it under my arm, and bring it them to-day, like an article of luggage! I am therefore absolutely obliged to remain behind. But no! ah! how many stupid and wicked people there are!"

"Have you spoken to the station-master?" asked Pierre.

"The station-master! Oh! he's somewhere about, in the midst of the scramble. They were never able to find him. How could you have anything done properly in such a bear-garden? Still, I mean to rout him out, and give him a bit of my mind!"

Then, perceiving his wife standing beside him motionless, glued as it were to the platform, he cried: "What are you doing there? Get in, so that we may pass you the youngster and the parcels!"

With these words he pushed her in, and threw the parcels after her, whilst the young priest took Gustave in his arms. The poor little fellow, who was as light as a bird, seemingly thinner than before, consumed by sores, and so full of pain, raised a faint cry. "Oh, my dear child, have I hurt you?" asked Pierre.

"No, no, Monsieur l'Abbe, but I've been moved about so much to-day, and I'm very tired this afternoon." As he spoke, he smiled with his usual intelligent and mournful expression, and then, sinking back into his corner, closed his eyes, exhausted, indeed done for, by this fearful trip to Lourdes.

"As you can very well understand," now resumed M. Vigneron, "it by no means amuses me to stay here, kicking my heels, while my wife and my son go back to Paris without me. They have to go, however, for life at the hotel is no longer bearable; and besides, if I kept them with me, and the railway people won't listen to reason, I should have to pay three extra fares. And to make matters worse, my wife hasn't got much brains. I'm afraid she won't be able to manage things properly."

Then, almost breathless, he overwhelmed Madame Vigneron with the most minute instructions—what she was to do during the journey, how she was to get back home on arriving in Paris, and what steps she was to take if Gustave was to have another attack. Somewhat scared, she responded, in all docility, to each recommendation: "Yes, yes, dear—of course, dear, of course."

But all at once her husband's rage came back to him. "After all," he shouted, "what I want to know is whether my return ticket be good or not! I must know for certain! They must find that station-master for me!"

He was already on the point of rushing away through the crowd, when he noticed Gustave's crutch lying on the platform. This was disastrous, and he raised his eyes to heaven as though to call Providence to witness that he would never be able to extricate himself from such awful complications. And, throwing the crutch to his wife, he hurried off, distracted and shouting, "There, take it! You forget everything!"

The sick pilgrims were now flocking into the station, and, as on the occasion of their arrival, there was plenty of disorderly carting along the platform and across the lines. All the abominable ailments, all the sores, all the deformities, went past once more, neither their gravity nor their number seeming to have decreased; for the few cures which had been effected were but a faint inappreciable gleam of light amidst the general mourning. They were taken back as they had come. The little carts, laden with helpless old women with their bags at their feet, grated over the rails. The stretchers on which you saw inflated bodies and pale faces with glittering eyes, swayed amidst the jostling of the throng. There was wild and senseless haste, indescribable confusion, questions, calls, sudden running, all the whirling of a flock which cannot find the entrance to the pen. And the bearers ended by losing their heads, no longer knowing which direction to take amidst the warning cries of the porters, who at each moment were frightening people, distracting them with anguish. "Take care, take care over there! Make haste! No, no, don't cross! The Toulouse train, the Toulouse train!"

Retracing his steps, Pierre again perceived the ladies, Madame de Jonquiere and the others, still gaily chatting together. Lingering near them, he listened to Berthaud, whom Father Fourcade had stopped, to congratulate him on the good order which had been maintained throughout the pilgrimage. The ex-public prosecutor was now bowing his thanks, feeling quite flattered by this praise. "Is it not a lesson for their Republic, your reverence?" he asked. "People get killed in Paris when such crowds as these celebrate some bloody anniversary of their hateful history. They ought to come and take a lesson here."

He was delighted with the thought of being disagreeable to the Government which had compelled him to resign. He was never so happy as when women were just saved from being knocked over amidst the great concourse of believers at Lourdes. However, he did not seem to be satisfied with the results of the political propaganda which he came to further there, during three days, every year. Fits of impatience came over him, things did not move fast enough. When did Our Lady of Lourdes mean to bring back the monarchy?

"You see, your reverence," said he, "the only means, the real triumph, would be to bring the working classes of the towns here *en masse*. I shall cease dreaming, I shall devote myself to that entirely. Ah! if one could only create a Catholic democracy!"

Father Fourcade had become very grave. His fine, intelligent eyes filled with a dreamy expression, and wandered far away. How many times already had he himself made the creation of that new people the object of his efforts! But was not the breath of a new Messiah needed for the accomplishment of such a task? "Yes, yes," he murmured, "a Catholic democracy; ah! the history of humanity would begin afresh!"

But Father Massias interrupted him in a passionate voice, saying that all the nations of the earth would end by coming; whilst Doctor Bonamy, who already detected a slight subsidence of fervour among the pilgrims, wagged his head and expressed the opinion that the faithful ones of the Grotto ought to increase their zeal. To his mind, success especially depended on the greatest possible measure of publicity being given to the miracles. And he assumed a radiant air and laughed complacently whilst pointing to the tumultuous *defile* of the sick. "Look at them!" said he. "Don't they go off looking better? There are a great many who, although they don't appear to be cured, are nevertheless carrying the germs of cure away with them; of that you may be certain! Ah! the good people; they do far more than we do all together for the glory of Our Lady of Lourdes!"

However, he had to check himself, for Madame Dieulafay was passing before them, in her box lined with quilted silk. She was deposited in front of the door of the first-class carriage, in which a maid was already placing the luggage. Pity came to all who beheld the unhappy woman, for she did not seem to have awakened from her prostration during her three days' sojourn at Lourdes. What she had been when they had removed her from the carriage on the morning of her arrival, that she also was now when the bearers were about to place her inside it again— clad in lace, covered with jewels, still with the lifeless, imbecile face of a mummy slowly liquefying; and, indeed, one might have thought that she had become yet more wasted, that she was being taken back diminished, shrunken more and more to the proportions of a child, by the march of that horrible disease which, after destroying her bones, was now dissolving the softened fibres of her muscles. Inconsolable, bowed down by the loss of their last hope, her husband and sister, their eyes red, were following her with Abbe Judaine, even as one follows a corpse to the grave.

"No, no! not yet!" said the old priest to the bearers, in order to prevent them from placing the box in the carriage. "She will have time enough to roll along in there. Let her have the warmth of that lovely sky above her till the last possible moment."

Then, seeing Pierre near him, he drew him a few steps aside, and, in a voice broken by grief, resumed: "Ah! I am indeed distressed. Again this morning I had a hope. I had her taken to the Grotto, I said my mass for her, and came back to pray till eleven o'clock. But nothing came of it; the Blessed Virgin did not listen to me. Although she cured me, a poor, useless old man like me, I could not obtain from her the cure of this beautiful, young, and wealthy woman, whose life ought to be a continual *fete*. Undoubtedly the Blessed Virgin knows what she ought to do better than ourselves, and I bow and bless her name. Nevertheless, my soul is full of frightful sadness."

He did not tell everything; he did not confess the thought which was upsetting him, simple, childish, worthy man that he was, whose life had never been troubled by either passion or doubt. But his thought was that those poor weeping people, the husband and the sister, had too many millions, that the presents they had brought were too costly, that they had given far too much money to the Basilica. A miracle is not to be bought. The wealth of the world is a hindrance rather than an advantage when you address yourself to God. Assuredly, if the Blessed Virgin had turned a deaf ear to their entreaties, had shown them but a stern, cold countenance, it was in order that she might the more attentively listen to the weak voices of the lowly ones who had come to her with empty hands, with no other wealth than their love, and these she had loaded with grace, flooded with the glowing affection of her Divine Motherhood. And those poor wealthy ones, who had not been heard, that sister and that husband, both so wretched beside the sorry body they were taking away with them, they themselves felt like pariahs among the throng of the humble who had been consoled or healed; they seemed embarrassed by their very luxury, and recoiled, awkward and ill at ease, covered with shame at the thought that Our Lady of Lourdes had relieved beggars whilst never casting a glance upon that beautiful and powerful lady agonising unto death amidst all her lace!

All at once it occurred to Pierre that he might have missed seeing M. de Guersaint and Marie arrive, and that they were perhaps already in the carriage. He returned thither, but there was still only his valise on the seat. Sister Hyacinthe and Sister Claire des Anges, however, had begun to install themselves, pending the arrival of their charges, and as Gerard just then brought up M. Sabathier in a little handcart, Pierre helped to place him in the carriage, a laborious task which put both the young priest and Gerard into a perspiration. The ex-professor, who looked disconsolate though very calm, at once settled himself in his corner.

"Thank you, gentlemen," said he. "That's over, thank goodness. And now they'll only have to take me out at Paris."

After wrapping a rug round his legs, Madame Sabathier, who was also there, got out of the carriage and remained standing near the open door. She was talking to Pierre when all at once she broke off to say: "Ah! here's Madame Maze coming to take her seat. She confided in me the other day, you know. She's a very unhappy little woman."

Then, in an obliging spirit, she called to her and offered to watch over her things. But Madame Maze shook her head, laughed, and gesticulated as though she were out of her senses.

"No, no, I am not going," said she.

"What! you are not going back?"

"No, no, I am not going—that is, I am, but not with you, not with you!"

She wore such an extraordinary air, she looked so bright, that Pierre and Madame Sabathier found it difficult to recognise her. Her fair, prematurely faded face was radiant, she seemed to be ten years younger, suddenly aroused from the infinite sadness into which desertion had plunged her. And, at last, her joy overflowing, she raised a cry: "I am going off with him! Yes, he has come to fetch me, he is taking me with him. Yes, yes, we are going to Luchon together, together!"

Then, with a rapturous glance, she pointed out a dark, sturdy-looking young man, with gay eyes and bright red lips, who was purchasing some newspapers. "There! that's my husband," said she, "that handsome man who's laughing over there with the newspaper-girl. He turned up here early this morning, and he's carrying me off. We shall take the Toulouse train in a couple of minutes. Ah! dear madame, I told you of all my worries, and you can understand my happiness, can't you?"

However, she could not remain silent, but again spoke of the frightful letter which she had received on Sunday, a letter in which he had declared to her that if she should take advantage of her sojourn at Lourdes to come to Luchon after him, he would not open the door to her. And, think of it, theirs had been a love match! But for ten years he had neglected her, profiting by his continual journeys as a commercial traveller to take friends about with him from one to the other end of France. Ah! that time she had thought it all over, she had asked the Blessed Virgin to let her die, for she knew that the faithless one was at that very moment at Luchon with two friends. What was it then that had happened? A thunderbolt must certainly have fallen from heaven.

Those two friends must have received a warning from on high—perhaps they had dreamt that they were already condemned to everlasting punishment. At all events they had fled one evening without a word of explanation, and he, unable to live alone, had suddenly been seized with a desire to fetch his wife and keep her with him for a week. Grace must have certainly fallen on him, though he did not say it, for he was so kind and pleasant that she could not do otherwise than believe in a real beginning of conversion.

"Ah! how grateful I am to the Blessed Virgin," she continued; "she alone can have acted, and I well understood her last evening. It seemed to me that she made me a little sign just at the very moment when my husband was making up his mind to come here to fetch me. I asked him at what time it was that the idea occurred to him, and the hours fit in exactly. Ah! there has been no greater miracle. The others make me smile with their mended legs and their vanished sores. Blessed be Our Lady of Lourdes, who has healed my heart!"

Just then the sturdy young man turned round, and she darted away to join him, so full of delight that she forgot to bid the others good-bye. And it was at this moment, amidst the growing crowd of patients whom the bearers were bringing, that the Toulouse train at last came in. The tumult increased, the confusion became extraordinary. Bells rang and signals worked, whilst the station-master was seen rushing up, shouting with all the strength of his lungs: "Be careful there! Clear the line at once!"

A railway *employe* had to rush from the platform to push a little vehicle, which had been forgotten on the line, with an old woman in it, out of harm's way; however, yet another scared band of pilgrims ran across when the steaming, growling engine was only thirty yards distant. Others, losing their heads, would have been crushed by the wheels if porters had not roughly caught them by the shoulders. Then, without having pounded anybody, the train at last stopped alongside the mattresses, pillows, and cushions lying hither and thither, and the bewildered, whirling groups of people. The carriage doors opened and a torrent of travellers alighted, whilst another torrent climbed in, these two obstinately contending currents bringing the tumult to a climax. Faces, first wearing an inquisitive expression, and then overcome by stupefaction at the astonishing sight, showed themselves at the windows of the doors which remained closed; and, among them, one especially noticed the faces of two remarkably pretty girls, whose large candid eyes ended by expressing the most dolorous compassion.

Followed by her husband, however, Madame Maze had climbed into one of the carriages, feeling as happy and buoyant as if she were in her twentieth year again, as on the already distant evening of her honeymoon journey. And the doors having been slammed, the engine gave a loud whistle and began to move, going off slowly and heavily between the throng, which, in the rear of the train, flowed on to the lines again like an invading torrent whose flood-gates have been swept away.

"Bar the platform!" shouted the station-master to his men. "Keep watch when the engine comes up!"

The belated patients and pilgrims had arrived during this alert. La Grivotte passed by with her feverish eyes and excited, dancing gait, followed by Elise Rouquet and Sophie Couteau, who were very gay, and quite out of breath through running. All three hastened to their carriage, where Sister Hyacinthe scolded them. They had almost been left behind at the Grotto, where, at times, the pilgrims lingered forgetfully, unable to tear themselves away, still imploring and entreating the Blessed Virgin, when the train was waiting for them at the railway-station.

All at once Pierre, who likewise was anxious, no longer knowing what to think, perceived M. de Guersaint and Marie quietly talking with Abbe Judaine on the covered platform. He hastened to join them, and told them of his impatience. "What have you been doing?" he asked. "I was losing all hope."

"What have we been doing?" responded M. de Guersaint, with quiet astonishment. "We were at the Grotto, as you know very well. There was a priest there, preaching in a most remarkable manner, and we should still be there if I hadn't remembered that we had to leave. And we took a fly here, as we promised you we would do."

He broke off to look at the clock. "But hang it all!" he added, "there's no hurry. The train won't start for another quarter of an hour."

This was true. Then Marie, smiling with divine joy, exclaimed: "Oh! if you only knew, Pierre, what happiness I have brought away from that last visit to the Blessed Virgin. I saw her smile at me, I felt her giving me strength to live. Really, that farewell was delightful, and you must not scold us, Pierre."

He himself had begun to smile, somewhat ill at ease, however, as he thought of his nervous fidgeting. Had he, then, experienced so keen a desire to get far away from Lourdes? Had he feared that the Grotto might keep Marie, that she might never come away from it again? Now that she was there beside him, he was astonished at having indulged such thoughts, and felt himself to be very calm.

However, whilst he was advising them to go and take their seats in the carriage, he recognised Doctor Chassaigne hastily approaching. "Ah! my dear doctor," he said, "I was waiting for you. I should have been sorry indeed to have gone away without embracing you."

But the old doctor, who was trembling with emotion, interrupted him. "Yes, yes, I am late. But ten minutes ago, just as I arrived, I caught sight of that eccentric fellow, the Commander, and had a talk with him over yonder. He was sneering at the sight of your people taking the train again to go and die at home, when, said he, they ought to have done so before coming to Lourdes. Well, all at once, while he was talking like this, he fell on the ground before me. It was his third attack of paralysis; the one he had long been expecting."

"Oh! *mon Dieu*," murmured Abbe Judaine, who heard the doctor, "he was blaspheming. Heaven has punished him."

M. de Guersaint and Marie were listening, greatly interested and deeply moved.

"I had him carried yonder, into that shed," continued the doctor. "It is all over; I can do nothing. He will doubtless be dead before a quarter of an hour has gone by. But I thought of a priest, and hastened up to you."

Then, turning towards Abbe Judaine, M. Chassaigne added: "Come with me, Monsieur le Cure; you know him. We cannot let a Christian depart unsuccoured. Perhaps he will be moved, recognise his error, and become reconciled with God."

Abbe Judaine quickly followed the doctor, and in the rear went M. de Guersaint, leading Marie and Pierre, whom the thought of this tragedy impassioned. All five entered the goods shed, at twenty paces from the crowd which was still bustling and buzzing, without a soul in it expecting that there was a man dying so near by.

In a solitary corner of the shed, between two piles of sacks filled with oats, lay the Commander, on a mattress borrowed from the Hospitality reserve supply. He wore his everlasting frock-coat, with its buttonhole decked with a broad red riband, and somebody who had taken the precaution to pick up his silver-knobbed walking-stick had carefully placed it on the ground beside the mattress.

Abbe Judaine at once leant over him. "You recognise us, you can hear us, my poor friend, can't you?" asked the priest.

Only the Commander's eyes now appeared to be alive; but they *were* alive, still glittering brightly with a stubborn flame of energy. The attack had this time fallen on his right side, almost entirely depriving him of the power of speech. He could only stammer a few words, by which he succeeded in making them understand that he wished to die there, without being moved or worried any further. He had no relative at Lourdes, where nobody knew anything either of his former life or his family. For three years he had lived there happily on the salary attached to his little post at the station, and now he at last beheld his ardent, his only desire, approaching fulfilment—the desire that he might depart and fall into the eternal sleep. His eyes expressed the great joy he felt at being so near his end.

"Have you any wish to make known to us?" resumed Abbe Judaine. "Cannot we be useful to you in any way?"

No, no; his eyes replied that he was all right, well pleased. For three years past he had never got up in the morning without hoping that by night time he would be sleeping in the cemetery. Whenever he saw the sun shine he was wont to say in an envious tone: "What a beautiful day for departure!" And now that death was at last at hand, ready to deliver him from his hateful existence, it was indeed welcome.

"I can do nothing, science is powerless. He is condemned," said Doctor Chassaigne in a low, bitter tone to the old priest, who begged him to attempt some effort.

However, at that same moment it chanced that an aged woman, a pilgrim of fourscore years, who had lost her way and knew not whither she was going, entered the shed. Lame and humpbacked, reduced to the stature of childhood's days, afflicted with all the ailments of extreme old age, she was dragging herself along with the assistance of a stick, and at her side was slung a can full of Lourdes water, which she was taking away with her, in the hope of yet prolonging her old age, in spite of all its frightful decay. For a moment her senile, imbecile mind was quite scared. She stood looking at that outstretched, stiffened man, who was dying. Then a gleam of grandmotherly kindliness appeared in the depths of her dim, vague eyes; and with the sisterly feelings of one who was very aged and suffered very grievously she drew nearer, and, taking hold of her can with her hands, which never ceased shaking, she offered it to the man.

To Abbe Judaine this seemed like a sudden flash of light, an inspiration from on high. He, who had prayed so fervently and so often for the cure of Madame Dieulafay without being heard by the Blessed Virgin, now glowed with fresh faith in the conviction that if the Commander would only drink that water he would be cured.

The old priest fell upon his knees beside the mattress. "O brother!" he said, "it is God who has sent you this woman. Reconcile yourself with God, drink and pray, whilst we ourselves implore the divine mercy with our whole souls. God will prove His power to you; God will work the great miracle of setting you erect once more, so that you may yet spend many years upon this earth, loving Him and glorifying Him."

No, no! the Commander's sparkling eyes cried no! He, indeed, show himself as cowardly as those flocks of pilgrims who came from afar, through so many fatigues, in order to drag themselves on the ground and sob and beg Heaven to let them live a month, a year, ten years longer! It was so pleasant, so simple to die quietly in your bed. You turned your face to the wall and you died.

"Drink, O my brother, I implore you!" continued the old priest. "It is life that you will drink, it is strength and health, the very joy of living. Drink that you may become young again, that you may begin a new and pious life; drink that you may sing the praises of the Divine Mother, who will have saved both your body and your soul. She is speaking to me, your resurrection is certain."

But no! but no! The eyes refused, repelled the offer of life with growing obstinacy, and in their expression now appeared a covert fear of the miraculous. The Commander did not believe; for three years he had been shrugging his shoulders at the pretended cases of cure. But could one ever tell in this strange world of ours? Such extraordinary things did sometimes happen. And if by chance their water should really have a supernatural power, and if by force they should make him drink some of it, it would be terrible to have to live again—to endure once more the punishment of a galley-slave existence, that abomination which Lazarus—the pitiable object of the great miracle—had suffered twice. No, no, he would not drink; he would not incur the fearful risk of resurrection.

"Drink, drink, my brother," repeated Abbe Judaine, who was now in tears; "do not harden your heart to refuse the favours of Heaven."

And then a terrible thing was seen; this man, already half dead, raised himself, shaking off the stifling bonds of paralysis, loosening for a second his tied tongue, and stammering, growling in a hoarse voice: "No, no, No!"

Pierre had to lead the stupefied old woman away and put her in the right direction again. She had failed to understand that refusal of the water which she herself was taking home with her like an inestimable treasure, the very gift of God's eternity to the poor who did not wish to die. Lame of one leg, humpbacked, dragging the sorry remnants of her fourscore years along by the assistance of her stick, she disappeared among the tramping crowd, consumed by the passion of being, eager for space, air, sunshine, and noise.

Marie and her father had shuddered in presence of that appetite for death, that greedy hungering for the end which the Commander showed. Ah! to sleep, to sleep without a dream, in the infinite darkness forever and ever—nothing in the world could have seemed so sweet to him. He did not hope in a better life; he had no desire to become happy, at last, in Paradise where equality and justice would reign. His sole longing was for black night and endless sleep, the joy of being no more, of never, never being again. And Doctor Chassaigne also had shuddered, for he also nourished but one thought, the thought of the happy moment when he would depart. But, in his case, on the other side of this earthly existence he would find his dear lost ones awaiting him, at the spot where eternal life began; and how icy cold all would have seemed had he but for a single moment thought that he might not meet them there.

Abbe Judaine painfully rose up. It had seemed to him that the Commander was now fixing his bright eyes upon Marie. Deeply grieved that his entreaties should have been of no avail, the priest wished to show the dying man an example of that goodness of God which he repulsed.

"You recognise her, do you not?" he asked. "Yes, it is the young lady who arrived here on Saturday so ill, with both legs paralysed. And you see her now, so full of health, so strong, so beautiful. Heaven has taken pity on her, and now she is reviving to youth, to the long life she was born to live. Do you feel no regret in seeing her? Would you also like her to be dead? would you have advised her not to drink the water?"

The Commander could not answer; but his eyes no longer strayed from Marie's young face, on which one read such great happiness at having resuscitated, such vast hopes in countless morrows; and tears appeared in those fixed eyes of his, gathered under their lids, and rolled down his cheeks, which were already cold. He was certainly weeping for her; he must have been thinking of that other miracle which he had wished her—that if she should be cured, she might be happy. It was the tenderness of an old man, who knows the miseries of this world, stirred to pity by the thought of all the sorrows which awaited this young creature. Ah! poor woman, how many times; perhaps, might she regret that she had not died in her twentieth year!

Then the Commander's eyes grew very dim, as though those last pitiful tears had dissolved them. It was the end; coma was coming; the mind was departing with the breath. He slightly turned, and died.

Doctor Chassaigne at once drew Marie aside. "The train's starting," he said; "make haste, make haste!"

Indeed, the loud ringing of a bell was clearly resounding above the growing tumult of the crowd. And the doctor, having requested two bearers to watch the body, which would be removed later on when the train had gone, desired to accompany his friends to their carriage.

They hastened their steps. Abbe Judaine, who was in despair, joined them after saying a short prayer for the repose of that rebellious soul. However, while Marie, followed by Pierre and M. de Guersaint, was running along the platform, she was stopped once more, and this time by Doctor Bonamy, who triumphantly presented her to Father Fourcade. "Here is Mademoiselle de Guersaint, your reverence, the young lady who was healed so marvellously yesterday."

The radiant smile of a general who is reminded of his most decisive victory appeared on Father Fourcade's face. "I know, I know; I was there," he replied. "God has blessed you among all women, my dear daughter; go, and cause His name to be worshipped."

Then he congratulated M. de Guersaint, whose paternal pride savoured divine enjoyment. It was the ovation beginning afresh—the concert of loving words and enraptured glances which had followed the girl through the streets of Lourdes that morning, and which again surrounded her at the moment of departure. The bell might go on ringing; a circle of delighted pilgrims still lingered around her; it seemed as if she were carrying away in her person all the glory of the pilgrimage, the triumph of religion, which would echo and echo to the four corners of the earth.

And Pierre was moved as he noticed the dolorous group which Madame Jousseur and M. Dieulafay formed near by. Their eyes were fixed upon Marie; like the others, they were astonished by the resurrection of this beautiful girl, whom they had seen lying inert, emaciated, with ashen face. Why should that child have been healed?

Why not the young woman, the dear woman, whom they were taking home in a dying state? Their confusion, their sense of shame, seemed to increase; they drew back, uneasy, like pariahs burdened with too much wealth; and it was a great relief for them when, three bearers having with difficulty placed Madame Dieulafay in the first-class compartment, they themselves were able to vanish into it in company with Abbe Judaine.

The *employes* were already shouting, "Take your seats! take your seats," and Father Massias, the spiritual director of the train, had returned to his compartment, leaving Father Fourcade on the platform leaning on Doctor Bonamy's shoulder. In all haste Gerard and Berthaud again saluted the ladies, while Raymonde got in to join Madame Desagneaux and Madame Volmar in their corner; and Madame de Jonquiere at last ran off to her carriage, which she reached at the same time as the Guersaints. There was hustling, and shouting, and wild running from one to the other end of the long train, to which the engine, a copper engine, glittering like a star, had just been coupled.

Pierre was helping Marie into the carriage, when M. Vigneron, coming back at a gallop, shouted to him: "It'll be good to-morrow, it'll be good tomorrow!" Very red in the face, he showed and waved his ticket, and then galloped off again to the compartment where his wife and son had their seats, in order to announce the good news to them.

When Marie and her father were installed in their places, Pierre lingered for another moment on the platform with Doctor Chassaigne, who embraced him paternally. The young man wished to induce the doctor to return to Paris and take some little interest in life again. But M. Chassaigne shook his head. "No, no, my dear child," he replied. "I shall remain here. They are here, they keep me here." He was speaking of his dear lost ones. Then, very gently and lovingly, he said, "Farewell."

"Not farewell, my dear doctor; till we meet again."

"Yes, yes, farewell. The Commander was right, you know; nothing can be so sweet as to die, but to die in order to live again."

Baron Suire was now giving orders for the removal of the white flags on the foremost and hindmost carriages of the train; the shouts of the railway *employes* were ringing out in more and more imperious tones, "Take your seats! take your seats!" and now came the supreme scramble, the torrent of belated pilgrims rushing up distracted, breathless, and covered with perspiration. Madame de Jonquiere and Sister Hyacinthe were counting their party in the carriage. La Grivotte, Elise Rouquet, and Sophie Couteau were all three there. Madame Sabathier, too, had taken her seat in front of her husband, who, with his eyes half closed, was patiently awaiting the departure. However, a voice inquired, "And Madame Vincent, isn't she going back with us?"

Thereupon Sister Hyacinthe, who was leaning out of the window exchanging a last smile with Ferrand, who stood at the door of the cantine van, exclaimed: "Here she comes!"

Madame Vincent crossed the lines, rushed up, the last of all, breathless and haggard. And at once, by an involuntary impulse, Pierre glanced at her arms. They carried nothing now.

All the doors were being closed, slammed one after the other; the carriages were full, and only the signal for departure was awaited. Panting and smoking, the engine gave vent to a first loud whistle, shrill and joyous; and at that moment the sun, hitherto veiled from sight, dissipated the light cloudlets and made the whole train resplendent, gilding the engine, which seemed on the point of starting for the legendary Paradise. No bitterness, but a divine, infantile gaiety attended the departure. All the sick appeared to be healed. Though most of them were being taken away in the same condition as they had been brought, they went off relieved and happy, at all events, for an hour. And not the slightest jealousy tainted their brotherly and sisterly feelings; those who were not cured waxed quite gay, triumphant at the cure of the others. Their own turns would surely come; yesterday's miracle was the formal promise of to-morrow's. Even after those three days of burning entreaty their fever of desire remained within them; the faith of the forgotten ones continued as keen as ever in the conviction that the Blessed Virgin had simply deferred a cure for their souls' benefit. Inextinguishable love, invincible hope glowed within all those wretched ones thirsting for life. And so a last outburst of joy, a turbulent display of happiness, laughter and shouts, overflowed from all the crowded carriages. "Till next year! We'll come back, we'll come back again!" was the cry; and then the gay little Sisters of the Assumption clapped their hands, and the hymn of gratitude, the "Magnificat," began, sung by all the eight hundred pilgrims: "*Magnificat anima mea Dominum.*" "My soul doth magnify the Lord."

Thereupon the station-master, his mind at last at ease, his arms hanging beside him, caused the signal to be given. The engine whistled once again and then set out, rolling along in the dazzling sunlight as amidst a glory. Although his leg was causing him great suffering,

Father Fourcade had remained on the platform, leaning upon Doctor Bonamy's shoulder, and, in spite of everything, saluting the departure of his dear children with a smile. Berthaud, Gerard, and Baron Suire formed another group, and near them were Doctor Chassaigne and M. Vigneron waving their handkerchiefs. Heads were looking joyously out of the windows of the fleeing carriages, whence other handkerchiefs were streaming in the current of air produced by the motion of the train. Madame Vigneron compelled Gustave to show his pale little face, and for a long time Raymonde's small hand could be seen waving good wishes; but Marie remained the last, looking back on Lourdes as it grew smaller and smaller amidst the trees.

Across the bright countryside the train triumphantly disappeared, resplendent, growling, chanting at the full pitch of its eight hundred voices: *"Et exsultavit spiritus meus in Deo salutari meo."* "And my spirit hath rejoiced in God my Saviour!"

IV

Marie's Vow

O nce more was the white train rolling, rolling towards Paris on its way
home; and the third-class carriage, where the shrill voices singing
the "Magnificat" at full pitch rose above the growling of the wheels,
had again become a common room, a travelling hospital ward, full of
disorder, littered like an improvised ambulance. Basins and brooms and
sponges lay about under the seats, which half concealed them. Articles
of luggage, all the wretched mass of poor worn-out things, were heaped
together, a little bit everywhere; and up above, the litter began again,
what with the parcels, the baskets, and the bags hanging from the brass
pegs and swinging to and fro without a moment's rest. The same Sisters
of the Assumption and the same lady-hospitallers were there with their
patients, amidst the contingent of healthy pilgrims, who were already
suffering from the overpowering heat and unbearable odour. And at the
far end there was again the compartment full of women, the ten close-
packed female pilgrims, some young, some old, and all looking pitifully
ugly as they violently chanted the canticle in cracked and woeful voices.

"At what time shall we reach Paris?" M. de Guersaint inquired of
Pierre.

"To-morrow at about two in the afternoon, I think," the priest replied.

Since starting, Marie had been looking at the latter with an air of
anxious preoccupation, as though haunted by a sudden sorrow which
she could not reveal. However, she found her gay, healthful smile again
to say: "Twenty-two hours' journey! Ah! it won't be so long and trying
as it was coming."

"Besides," resumed her father, "we have left some of our people
behind. We have plenty of room now."

In fact Madame Maze's absence left a corner free at the end of the
seat which Marie, now sitting up like any other passenger, no longer
encumbered with her box. Moreover, little Sophie had this time been
placed in the next compartment, where there was neither Brother
Isidore nor his sister Marthe. The latter, it was said, had remained at
Lourdes in service with a pious lady. On the other side, Madame de
Jonquiere and Sister Hyacinthe also had the benefit of a vacant seat,

that of Madame Vetu; and it had further occurred to them to get rid of Elise Rouquet by placing her with Sophie, so that only La Grivotte and the Sabathier couple were with them in their compartment. Thanks to these new arrangements, they were better able to breathe, and perhaps they might manage to sleep a little.

The last verse of the "Magnificat" having been sung, the ladies finished installing themselves as comfortably as possible by setting their little household in order. One of the most important matters was to put the zinc water-can, which interfered with their legs, out of the way. All the blinds of the left-hand windows had been pulled down, for the oblique sunrays were falling on the train, and had poured into it in sheets of fire. The last storms, however, must have laid the dust, and the night would certainly be cool. Moreover, there was less suffering: death had carried off the most afflicted ones, and only stupefied ailments, numbed by fatigue and lapsing into a slow torpor, remained. The overpowering reaction which always follows great moral shocks was about to declare itself. The souls had made the efforts required of them, the miracles had been worked, and now the relaxing was beginning amidst a hebetude tinged with profound relief.

Until they got to Tarbes they were all very much occupied in setting things in order and making themselves comfortable. But as they left that station Sister Hyacinthe rose up and clapped her hands. "My children," said she, "we must not forget the Blessed Virgin who has been so kind to us. Let us begin the Rosary."

Then the whole carriage repeated the first chaplet—the five joyful mysteries, the Annunciation, the Visitation, the Nativity, the Purification, and the Finding of Jesus in the Temple. And afterwards they intoned the canticle, "Let us contemplate the heavenly Archangel," in such loud voices that the peasants working in the fields raised their heads to look at this singing train as it rushed past them at full speed.

Marie was at the window, gazing with admiration at the vast landscape and the immense stretch of sky, which had gradually freed itself of its mist and was now of a dazzling blue. It was the delicious close of a fine day. However, she at last looked back into the carriage, and her eyes were fixing themselves on Pierre with that mute sadness which had previously dimmed them, when all at once a sound of furious sobbing burst forth in front of her. The canticle was finished, and it was Madame Vincent who was crying, stammering confused words, half-choked by her tears: "Ah, my poor little one!" she gasped. "Ah, my jewel, my treasure, my life!"

She had previously remained in her corner, shrinking back into it as though anxious to disappear. With a fierce face, her lips tightly set, and her eyes closed, as though to isolate herself in the depths of her cruel grief, she had hitherto not said a word. But, chancing to open her eyes, she had espied the leathern window-strap hanging down beside the door, and the sight of that strap, which her daughter had touched, almost played with at one moment during the previous journey, had overwhelmed her with a frantic despair which swept away her resolution to remain silent.

"Ah! my poor little Rose," she continued. "Her little hand touched that strap, she turned it, and looked at it—ah, it was her last plaything! And we were there both together then; she was still alive, I still had her on my lap, in my arms. It was still so nice, so nice! But now I no longer have her; I shall never, never have her again, my poor little Rose, my poor little Rose!"

Distracted, sobbing bitterly, she looked at her knees and her arms, on which nothing now rested, and which she was at a loss how to employ. She had so long rocked her daughter on her knees, so long carried her in her arms, that it now seemed to her as if some portion of her being had been amputated, as if her body had been deprived of one of its functions, leaving her diminished, unoccupied, distracted at being unable to fulfil that function any more. Those useless arms and knees of hers quite embarrassed her.

Pierre and Marie, who were deeply moved, had drawn near, uttering kind words and striving to console the unhappy mother. And, little by little, from the disconnected sentences which mingled with her sobs, they learned what a Calvary she had ascended since her daughter's death. On the morning of the previous day, when she had carried the body off in her arms amidst the storm, she must have long continued walking, blind and deaf to everything, whilst the torrential rain beat down upon her. She no longer remembered what squares she had crossed, what streets she had traversed, as she roamed through that infamous Lourdes, that Lourdes which killed little children, that Lourdes which she cursed.

"Ah! I can't remember, I can't remember," she faltered. "But some people took me in, had pity upon me, some people whom I don't know, but who live somewhere. Ah! I can't remember where, but it was somewhere high up, far away, at the other end of the town. And they

ÉMILE ZOLA

were certainly very poor folk, for I can still see myself in a poor-looking room with my dear little one who was quite cold, and whom they laid upon their bed."

At this recollection a fresh attack of sobbing shook her, in fact almost stifled her.

"No, no," she at last resumed, "I would not part with her dear little body by leaving it in that abominable town. And I can't tell exactly how it happened, but it must have been those poor people who took me with them. We did a great deal of walking, oh! a great deal of walking; we saw all those gentlemen of the pilgrimage and the railway. 'What can it matter to you?' I repeated to them. 'Let me take her back to Paris in my arms. I brought her here like that when she was alive, I may surely take her back dead? Nobody will notice anything, people will think that she is asleep.'"

"And all of them, all those officials, began shouting and driving me away as though I were asking them to let me do something wicked. Then I ended by telling them my mind. When people make so much fuss, and bring so many agonising sick to a place like that, they surely ought to send the dead ones home again, ought they not? And do you know how much money they ended by asking of me at the station? Three hundred francs! Yes, it appears it is the price! Three hundred francs, good Lord! of me, who came here with thirty sous in my pocket and have only five left. Why, I don't earn that amount of money by six months' sewing. They ought to have asked me for my life; I would have given it so willingly. Three hundred francs! three hundred francs for that poor little bird-like body, which it would have consoled me so much to have brought away on my knees!"

Then she began stammering and complaining in a confused, husky voice: "Ah, if you only knew how sensibly those poor people talked to me to induce me to go back. A work-woman like myself, with work waiting, ought to return to Paris, they said; and, besides, I couldn't afford to sacrifice my return ticket; I must take the three-forty train. And they told me, too, that people are compelled to put up with things when they are not rich. Only the rich can keep their dead, do what they like with them, eh? And I can't remember—no, again I can't remember! I didn't even know the time; I should never have been able to find my way back to the station. After the funeral over there, at a place where there were two trees, it must have been those poor people who led me away, half out of my senses, and brought me to the station, and pushed me into the carriage just at the moment when the train was starting. But what a rending it was—as if my heart had remained there underground, and it is frightful, that it is, frightful, my God!"

"Poor woman!" murmured Marie. "Take courage, and pray to the Blessed Virgin for the succour which she never refuses to the afflicted."

But at this Madame Vincent shook with rage. "It isn't true!" she cried. "The Blessed Virgin doesn't care a rap about me. She doesn't tell the truth! Why did she deceive me? I should never have gone to Lourdes if I hadn't heard that voice in a church. My little girl would still be alive, and perhaps the doctors would have saved her. I, who would never set my foot among the priests formerly! Ah! I was right! I was right! There's no Blessed Virgin at all!"

And in this wise, without resignation, without illusion, without hope, she continued blaspheming with the coarse fury of a woman of the people, shrieking the sufferings of her heart aloud in such rough fashion that Sister Hyacinthe had to intervene: "Be quiet, you unhappy woman! It is God who is making you suffer, to punish you."

The scene had already lasted a long time, and as they passed Riscle at full speed the Sister again clapped her hands and gave the signal for the chanting of the "Laudate Mariam." "Come, come, my children," she exclaimed, "all together, and with all your hearts:

"In heav'n, on earth,
All voices raise,
In concert sing
My Mother's praise:
Laudate, laudate, laudate Mariam!"

Madame Vincent, whose voice was drowned by this canticle of love, now only sobbed, with her hands pressed to her face. Her revolt was over, she was again strengthless, weak like a suffering woman whom grief and weariness have stupefied.

After the canticle, fatigue fell more or less heavily upon all the occupants of the carriage. Only Sister Hyacinthe, so quick and active, and Sister Claire des Anges, so gentle, serious, and slight, retained, as on their departure from Paris and during their sojourn at Lourdes, the professional serenity of women accustomed to everything, amidst the bright gaiety of their white coifs and wimples. Madame de Jonquiere, who had scarcely slept for five days past, had to make an effort to keep her poor eyes open; and yet she was delighted with the journey, for her heart was full of joy at having arranged her daughter's marriage, and at bringing back with her the greatest of all the miracles, a *miraculee* whom everybody was talking of. She decided in her own mind that she would get to sleep that night, however bad the jolting might be; though on the other hand she could not shake off a covert fear with regard to La Grivotte, who looked very strange, excited, and haggard, with dull eyes, and cheeks glowing with patches of violet colour. Madame de Jonquiere had tried a dozen times to keep her from fidgeting, but had not been able to induce her to remain still, with joined hands and closed eyes. Fortunately, the other patients gave her no anxiety; most of them were either so relieved or so weary that they were already dozing off. Elise Rouquet, however, had bought herself a pocket mirror, a large round one, in which she did not weary of contemplating herself, finding herself quite pretty, and verifying from minute to minute the progress of her cure with a coquetry which, now that her monstrous face was becoming human again, made her purse her lips and try a variety of smiles. As for Sophie Couteau, she was playing very prettily; for finding that nobody now asked to examine her foot, she had taken off her shoe and stocking of her own accord, repeating that she must surely have a pebble in one or the other of them; and as her companions still paid no attention to that little foot which the Blessed Virgin had been pleased to visit, she kept it in her hands, caressing it, seemingly delighted to touch it and turn it into a plaything.

M. de Guersaint had meantime risen from his seat, and, leaning on the low partition between the compartments, he was glancing at M. Sabathier, when all of a sudden Marie called: "Oh! father, father, look at this notch in the seat; it was the ironwork of my box that made it!"

The discovery of this trace rendered her so happy that for a moment she forgot the secret sorrow which she seemed anxious to keep to herself. And in the same way as Madame Vincent had burst out sobbing on perceiving the leather strap which her little girl had touched, so she burst into joy at the sight of this scratch, which reminded her of her long martyrdom in this same carriage, all the abomination which had now disappeared, vanished like a nightmare. "To think that four days have scarcely gone by," she said; "I was lying there, I could not stir, and now, now I come and go, and feel so comfortable!"

Pierre and M. de Guersaint were smiling at her; and M. Sabathier, who had heard her, slowly said: "It is quite true. We leave a little of ourselves in things, a little of our sufferings and our hopes, and when we find them again they speak to us, and once more tell us the things which sadden us or make us gay."

He had remained in his corner silent, with an air of resignation, ever since their departure from Lourdes. Even his wife whilst wrapping up his legs had only been able to obtain sundry shakes of the head from him in response to her inquiries whether he was suffering. In point of fact he was not suffering, but extreme dejection was overcoming him.

"Thus for my own part," he continued, "during our long journey from Paris I tried to divert my thoughts by counting the bands in the roofing up there. There were thirteen from the lamp to the door. Well, I have just been counting them again, and naturally enough there are still thirteen. It's like that brass knob beside me. You can't imagine what dreams I had whilst I watched it shining at night-time when Monsieur l'Abbe was reading the story of Bernadette to us. Yes, I saw myself cured; I was making that journey to Rome which I have been talking of for twenty years past; I walked and travelled the world—briefly, I had all manner of wild and delightful dreams. And now here we are on our way back to Paris, and there are thirteen bands across the roofing there, and the knob is still shining—all of which tells me that I am again on the same seat, with my legs lifeless. Well, well, it's understood, I'm a poor, old, used-up animal, and such I shall remain."

Two big tears appeared in his eyes; he must have been passing through an hour of frightful bitterness. However, he raised his big square head, with its jaw typical of patient obstinacy, and added: "This is the seventh year that I have been to Lourdes, and the Blessed Virgin has not listened to me. No matter! It won't prevent me from going back next year. Perhaps she will at last deign to hear me."

For his part he did not revolt. And Pierre, whilst chatting with him, was stupefied to find persistent, tenacious credulity springing up once more, in spite of everything, in the cultivated brain of this man of intellect. What ardent desire of cure and life was it that had led to this refusal to accept evidence, this determination to remain blind? He stubbornly clung to the resolution to be saved when all human probabilities were against him, when the experiment of the miracle itself had failed so many times already; and he had reached such a point that he wished to explain his fresh rebuff, urging moments of inattention at the Grotto, a lack of sufficient contrition, and all sorts of little transgressions which must have displeased the Blessed Virgin.

Moreover, he was already deciding in his mind that he would perform a novena somewhere next year, before again repairing to Lourdes.

"Ah! by the way," he resumed, "do you know of the good-luck which my substitute has had? Yes, you must remember my telling you about that poor fellow suffering from tuberculosis, for whom I paid fifty francs when I obtained *hospitalisation* for myself. Well, he has been thoroughly cured."

"Really! And he was suffering from tuberculosis!" exclaimed M. de Guersaint.

"Certainly, monsieur, perfectly cured I had seen him looking so low, so yellow, so emaciated, when we started; but when he came to pay me a visit at the hospital he was quite a new man; and, dear me, I gave him five francs."

Pierre had to restrain a smile, for be had heard the story from Doctor Chassaigne. This miraculously healed individual was a feigner, who had eventually been recognised at the Medical Verification Office. It was, apparently, the third year that he had presented himself there, the first time alleging paralysis and the second time a tumour, both of which had been as completely healed as his pretended tuberculosis. On each occasion he obtained an outing, lodging and food, and returned home loaded with alms. It appeared that he had formerly been a hospital nurse, and that he transformed himself, "made-up" a face suited to his pretended ailment, in such an extremely artistic manner that it was only by chance that Doctor Bonamy had detected the imposition. Moreover, the Fathers had immediately required that the incident should be kept secret. What was the use of stirring up a scandal which would only have led to jocular remarks in the newspapers? Whenever any fraudulent miracles of this kind were discovered, the Fathers contented themselves with forcing the guilty parties to go away. Moreover, these feigners were far from numerous, despite all that was related of them in the amusing stories concocted by Voltairean humourists. Apart from faith, human stupidity and ignorance, alas! were quite sufficient to account for the miracles.

M. Sabathier, however, was greatly stirred by the idea that Heaven had healed this man who had gone to Lourdes at his expense, whereas he himself was returning home still helpless, still in the same woeful state. He sighed, and, despite all his resignation, could not help saying, with a touch of envy: "What would you, however? The Blessed Virgin must know very well what she's about. Neither you nor I can call her to account to us for her actions. Whenever it may please her to cast her eyes on me she will find me at her feet."

After the "Angelus" when they got to Mont-de-Marsan, Sister Hyacinthe made them repeat the second chaplet, the five sorrowful mysteries, Jesus in the Garden of Olives, Jesus scourged, Jesus crowned with thorns, Jesus carrying the cross, and Jesus crucified. Then they took dinner in the carriage, for there would be no stopping until they reached Bordeaux, where they would only arrive at eleven o'clock at night. All the pilgrims' baskets were crammed with provisions, to say nothing of the milk, broth, chocolate, and fruit which Sister Saint-Francois had sent from the cantine. Then, too, there was fraternal sharing: they sat with their food on their laps and drew close together, every compartment becoming, as it were, the scene of a picnic, to which each contributed his share. And they had finished their meal and were packing up the remaining bread again when the train passed Morceux.

"My children," now said Sister Hyacinthe, rising up, "the evening prayer!"

Thereupon came a confused murmuring made up of "Paters" and "Aves," self-examinations, acts of contrition and vows of trustful reliance in God, the Blessed Virgin, and the Saints, with thanksgivings for that happy day, and, at last, a prayer for the living and for the faithful departed.

"I warn you," then resumed the Sister, "that when we get to Lamothe, at ten o'clock, I shall order silence. However, I think you will all be very good and won't require any rocking to get to sleep."

This made them laugh. It was now half-past eight o'clock, and the night had slowly covered the country-side. The hills alone retained a vague trace of the twilight's farewell, whilst a dense sheet of darkness blotted out all the low ground. Rushing on at full speed, the train entered an immense plain, and then there was nothing but a sea of darkness, through which they ever and ever rolled under a blackish sky, studded with stars.

For a moment or so Pierre had been astonished by the demeanour of La Grivotte. While the other pilgrims and patients were already dozing off, sinking down amidst the luggage, which the constant jolting shook, she had risen to her feet and was clinging to the partition in a sudden spasm of agony. And under the pale, yellow, dancing gleam of the lamp she once more looked emaciated, with a livid, tortured face.

"Take care, madame, she will fall!" the priest called to Madame de Jonquiere, who, with eyelids lowered, was at last giving way to sleep.

She made all haste to intervene, but Sister Hyacinthe had turned more quickly and caught La Grivotte in her arms. A frightful fit of coughing, however, prostrated the unhappy creature upon the seat, and for five minutes she continued stifling, shaken by such an attack that her poor body seemed to be actually cracking and rending. Then a red thread oozed from between her lips, and at last she spat up blood by the throatful.

"Good heavens! good heavens! it's coming on her again!" repeated Madame de Jonquiere in despair. "I had a fear of it; I was not at ease, seeing her looking so strange. Wait a moment; I will sit down beside her."

But the Sister would not consent: "No, no, madame, sleep a little. I'll watch over her. You are not accustomed to it: you would end by making yourself ill as well."

Then she settled herself beside La Grivotte, made her rest her head against her shoulder, and wiped the blood from her lips. The attack subsided, but weakness was coming back, so extreme that the wretched woman was scarcely able to stammer: "Oh, it is nothing, nothing at all; I am cured, I am cured, completely cured!"

Pierre was thoroughly upset: This sudden, overwhelming relapse had sent an icy chill through the whole carriage. Many of the passengers raised themselves up and looked at La Grivotte with terror in their eyes. Then they dived down into their corners again, and nobody spoke, nobody stirred any further. Pierre, for his part, reflected on the curious medical aspect of this girl's case. Her strength had come back to her over yonder. She had displayed a ravenous appetite, she had walked long distances with a dancing gait, her face quite radiant the while; and now she had spat blood, her cough had broken out afresh, she again had the heavy ashen face of one in the last agony. Her ailment had returned to her with brutal force, victorious over everything. Was this, then, some special case of phthisis complicated by neurosis? Or was it some other malady, some unknown disease, quietly continuing its work in the midst of contradictory diagnosis? The sea of error and ignorance, the darkness amidst which human science is still struggling, again appeared to Pierre. And he once more saw Doctor Chassaigne shrugging his shoulders with disdain, whilst Doctor Bonamy, full of serenity, quietly continued his verification work, absolutely convinced that nobody would be able to prove to him the impossibility of his miracles any more than he himself could have proved their possibility.

"Oh! I am not frightened," La Grivotte continued, stammering. "I am cured, completely cured; they all told me so, over yonder."

Meantime the carriage was rolling, rolling along, through the black night. Each of its occupants was making preparations, stretching himself out in order to sleep more comfortably. They compelled Madame Vincent to lie down on the seat, and gave her a pillow on which to rest her poor pain-racked head; and then, as docile as a child, quite stupefied, she fell asleep in a nightmare-like torpor, with big, silent tears still flowing from her closed eyes. Elise Rouquet, who had a whole seat to herself, was also getting ready to lie down, but first of all she made quite an elaborate toilet, tying the black wrap which had served to hide her sore about her head, and then again peering into her glass to see if this headgear became her, now that the swelling of her lip had subsided. And again did Pierre feel astonished at sight of that sore, which was certainly healing, if not already healed—that face, so lately a monster's face, which one could now look at without feeling horrified. The sea of incertitude stretched before him once more. Was it even a real lupus? Might it not rather be some unknown form of ulcer of hysterical origin? Or ought one to admit that certain forms of lupus, as yet but imperfectly studied and arising from faulty nutrition of the skin, might be benefited by a great moral shock? At all events there here seemed to be a miracle, unless, indeed, the sore should reappear again in three weeks', three months', or three years' time, like La Grivotte's phthisis.

It was ten o'clock, and the people in the carriage were falling asleep when they left Lamothe. Sister Hyacinthe, upon whose knees La Grivotte was now drowsily resting her head, was unable to rise, and, for form's sake, merely said, "Silence, silence, my children!" in a low voice, which died away amidst the growling rumble of the wheels.

However, something continued stirring in an adjoining compartment; she heard a noise which irritated her nerves, and the cause of which she at last fancied she could understand.

"Why do you keep on kicking the seat, Sophie?" she asked. "You must get to sleep, my child."

"I'm not kicking, Sister. It's a key that was rolling about under my foot."

"A key!—how is that? Pass it to me."

Then she examined it. A very old, poor-looking key it was—blackened, worn away, and polished by long use, its ring bearing the mark of where it had been broken and resoldered. However, they all searched their pockets, and none of them, it seemed, had lost a key.

"I found it in the corner," now resumed Sophie; "it must have belonged to the man."

"What man?" asked Sister Hyacinthe.

"The man who died there."

They had already forgotten him. But it had surely been his, for Sister Hyacinthe recollected that she had heard something fall while she was wiping his forehead. And she turned the key over and continued looking at it, as it lay in her hand, poor, ugly, wretched key that it was, no longer of any use, never again to open the lock it belonged to—some unknown lock, hidden far away in the depths of the world. For a moment she was minded to put it in her pocket, as though by a kind of compassion for this little bit of iron, so humble and so mysterious, since it was all that remained of that unknown man. But then the pious thought came to her that it is wrong to show attachment to any earthly thing; and, the window being half-lowered, she threw out the key, which fell into the black night.

"You must not play any more, Sophie," she resumed. "Come, come, my children, silence!"

It was only after the brief stay at Bordeaux, however, at about half-past eleven o'clock, that sleep came back again and overpowered all in the carriage. Madame de Jonquiere had been unable to contend against it any longer, and her head was now resting against the partition, her face wearing an expression of happiness amidst all her fatigue. The Sabathiers were, in a like fashion, calmly sleeping; and not a sound now came from the compartment which Sophie Couteau and Elise Rouquet occupied, stretched in front of each other, on the seats. From time to time a low plaint would rise, a strangled cry of grief or fright, escaping from the lips of Madame Vincent, who, amidst her prostration, was being tortured by evil dreams. Sister Hyacinthe was one of the very few who still had their eyes open, anxious as she was respecting La Grivotte, who now lay quite motionless, like a felled animal, breathing painfully, with a continuous wheezing sound. From one to the other end of this travelling dormitory, shaken by the rumbling of the train rolling on at full speed, the pilgrims and the sick surrendered themselves to sleep, and limbs dangled and heads swayed under the pale, dancing gleams from the lamps. At the far end, in the compartment occupied by the ten female pilgrims, there was a woeful jumbling of poor, ugly faces, old and young, and all open-mouthed, as though sleep had suddenly fallen upon them at the moment they were finishing some hymn. Great pity came to the heart at the sight of all those mournful, weary beings, prostrated by five days of wild hope and infinite ecstasy, and destined to awaken, on the very morrow, to the stern realities of life.

And now Pierre once more felt himself to be alone with Marie. She had not consented to stretch herself on the seat—she had been lying down too long, she said, for seven years, alas! And in order that M. de Guersaint, who on leaving Bordeaux had again fallen into his childlike slumber, might be more at ease, Pierre came and sat down beside the girl. As the light of the lamp annoyed her he drew the little screen, and they thus found themselves in the shade, a soft and transparent shade. The train must now have been crossing a plain, for it glided through the night as in an endless flight, with a sound like the regular flapping of huge wings. Through the window, which they had opened, a delicious coolness came from the black fields, the fathomless fields, where not even any lonely little village lights could be seen gleaming. For a moment Pierre had turned towards Marie and had noticed that her eyes were closed. But he could divine that she was not sleeping, that she was savouring the deep peacefulness which prevailed around them amidst the thundering roar of their rush through the darkness, and, like her, he closed his eyelids and began dreaming.

Yet once again did the past arise before him: the little house at Neuilly, the embrace which they had exchanged near the flowering hedge under the trees flecked with sunlight. How far away all that already was, and with what perfume had it not filled his life! Then bitter thoughts returned to him at the memory of the day when he had become a priest. Since she would never be a woman, he had consented to be a man no more; and that was to prove their eternal misfortune, for ironical Nature was to make her a wife and a mother after all. Had he only been able to retain his faith he might have found eternal consolation in it. But all his attempts to regain it had been in vain. He had gone to Lourdes, he had striven his utmost at the Grotto, he had hoped for a moment that he would end by believing should Marie be miraculously healed; but total and irremediable ruin had come when the predicted cure had taken place even as science had foretold. And their idyl, so pure and so painful, the long story of their affection bathed in tears, likewise spread out before him. She, having penetrated his sad secret, had come to Lourdes to pray to Heaven for the miracle of his conversion. When they had remained alone under the trees amidst the perfume of the invisible roses, during the night procession, they had prayed one for the other, mingling one in the other, with an ardent desire for their mutual happiness. Before the Grotto, too, she had entreated the Blessed Virgin to forget her and to save him, if she could obtain but one favour from her Divine Son. Then, healed, beside herself, transported with love and gratitude, whirled with her little car up the inclined ways to the Basilica, she had thought her prayers granted, and had cried aloud the joy she felt that they should have both been saved, together, together! Ah! that lie which he, prompted by affection and charity, had told, that error in which he had from that moment suffered her to remain, with what a weight did it oppress his heart! It was the heavy slab which walled him in his voluntarily chosen sepulchre. He remembered the frightful attack of grief which had almost killed him in the gloom of the crypt, his sobs, his brutal revolt, his longing to keep her for himself alone, to possess her since he knew her to be his own—all that rising passion of his awakened manhood, which little by little had fallen asleep again, drowned by the rushing river of his tears; and in order that he might not destroy the divine illusion which possessed her, yielding to brotherly compassion, he had taken that heroic vow to lie to her, that vow which now filled him with such anguish.

Pierre shuddered amidst his reverie. Would he have the strength to keep that vow forever? Had he not detected a feeling of impatience in his heart even whilst he was waiting for her at the railway station, a jealous longing to leave that Lourdes which she loved too well, in the vague hope that she might again become his own, somewhere far away? If he had not been a priest he would have married her. And what rapture, what felicity would then have been his! He would have given himself wholly unto her, she would have been wholly his own, and he and she would have lived again in the dear child that would doubtless have been born to them. Ah! surely that alone was divine, the life which is complete, the life which creates life! And then his reverie strayed: he pictured himself married, and the thought filled him with such delight that he asked why such a dream should be unrealisable? She knew no more than a child of ten; he would educate her, form her mind. She would then understand that this cure for which she thought herself indebted to the Blessed Virgin, had in reality come to her from the

Only Mother, serene and impassive Nature. But even whilst he was thus settling things in his mind, a kind of terror, born of his religious education, arose within him. Could he tell if that human happiness with which he desired to endow her would ever be worth as much as the holy ignorance, the infantile candour in which she now lived? How bitterly he would reproach himself afterwards if she should not be happy. Then, too, what a drama it would all be; he to throw off the cassock, and marry this girl healed by an alleged miracle—ravage her faith sufficiently to induce her to consent to such sacrilege? Yet therein lay the brave course; there lay reason, life, real manhood, real womanhood. Why, then, did he not dare? Horrible sadness was breaking upon his reverie, he became conscious of nothing beyond the sufferings of his poor heart.

The train was still rolling along with its great noise of flapping wings. Beside Pierre and Marie, only Sister Hyacinthe was still awake amidst the weary slumber of the carriage; and just then, Marie leant towards Pierre, and softly said to him: "It's strange, my friend; I am so sleepy, and yet I can't sleep." Then, with a light laugh, she added: "I've got Paris in my head!"

"How is that—Paris?"

"Yes, yes. I'm thinking that it's waiting for me, that I am about to return to it—that Paris which I know nothing of, and where I shall have to live!"

These words brought fresh anguish to Pierre's heart. He had well foreseen it; she could no longer belong to him, she would belong to others. If Lourdes had restored her to him, Paris was about to take her from him again. And he pictured this ignorant little being fatally acquiring all the education of woman. That little spotless soul which had remained so candid in the frame of a big girl of three-and-twenty, that soul which illness had kept apart from others, far from life, far even from novels, would soon ripen, now that it could fly freely once more. He beheld her, a gay, healthy young girl, running everywhere, looking and learning, and, some day, meeting the husband who would finish her education.

"And so," said he, "you propose to amuse yourself in Paris?"

"Oh! what are you saying, my friend? Are we rich enough to amuse ourselves?" she replied. "No, I was thinking of my poor sister Blanche, and wondering what I should be able to do in Paris to help her a little. She is so good, she works so hard; I don't wish that she should have to continue earning all the money."

And, after a fresh pause, as he, deeply moved, remained silent, she added: "Formerly, before I suffered so dreadfully, I painted miniatures rather nicely. You remember, don't you, that I painted a portrait of papa which was very like him, and which everybody praised. You will help me, won't you? You will find me customers?"

Then she began talking of the new life which she was about to live. She wanted to arrange her room and hang it with cretonne, something pretty, with a pattern of little blue flowers. She would buy it out of the first money she could save. Blanche had spoken to her of the big shops where things could be bought so cheaply. To go out with Blanche and run about a little would be so amusing for her, who, confined to her bed since childhood, had never seen anything. Then Pierre, who for a moment had been calmer, again began to suffer, for he could divine all her glowing desire to live, her ardour to see everything, know everything, and taste everything. It was at last the awakening of the woman whom she was destined to be, whom he had divined in childhood's days—a dear creature of gaiety and passion, with blooming lips, starry eyes, a milky complexion, golden hair, all resplendent with the joy of being.

"Oh! I shall work, I shall work," she resumed; "but you are right, Pierre, I shall also amuse myself, because it cannot be a sin to be gay, can it?"

"No, surely not, Marie."

"On Sundays we will go into the country, oh very far away, into the woods where there are beautiful trees. And we will sometimes go to the theatre, too, if papa will take us. I have been told that there are many plays that one may see. But, after all, it's not all that. Provided I can go out and walk in the streets and see things, I shall be so happy; I shall come home so gay. It is so nice to live, is it not, Pierre?"

"Yes, yes, Marie, it is very nice."

A chill like that of death was coming over him; his regret that he was no longer a man was filling him with agony. But since she tempted him like this with her irritating candour, why should he not confess to her the truth which was ravaging his being? He would have won her, have conquered her. Never had a more frightful struggle arisen between his heart and his will. For a moment he was on the point of uttering irrevocable words.

But with the voice of a joyous child she was already resuming: "Oh! look at poor papa; how pleased he must be to sleep so soundly!"

On the seat in front of them M. de Guersaint was indeed slumbering with a comfortable expression on his face, as though he were in his bed, and had no consciousness of the continual jolting of the train. This monotonous rolling and heaving seemed, in fact, a lullaby rocking the whole carriage to sleep. All surrendered themselves to it, sinking powerless on to the piles of bags and parcels, many of which had also fallen; and the rhythmical growling of the wheels never ceased in the unknown darkness through which the train was still rolling. Now and again, as they passed through a station or under a bridge, there would be a loud rush of wind, a tempest would suddenly sweep by; and then the lulling, growling sound would begin again, ever the same for hours together.

Marie gently took hold of Pierre's hands; he and she were so lost, so completely alone among all those prostrated beings, in the deep, rumbling peacefulness of the train flying across the black night. And sadness, the sadness which she had hitherto hidden, had again come back to her, casting a shadow over her large blue eyes.

"You will often come with us, my good Pierre, won't you?" she asked.

He had started on feeling her little hand pressing his own. His heart was on his lips, he was making up his mind to speak. However, he once again restrained himself and stammered: "I am not always at liberty, Marie; a priest cannot go everywhere."

"A priest?" she repeated. "Yes, yes, a priest. I understand."

Then it was she who spoke, who confessed the mortal secret which had been oppressing her heart ever since they had started. She leant nearer, and in a lower voice resumed: "Listen, my good Pierre; I am fearfully sad. I may look pleased, but there is death in my soul. You did not tell me the truth yesterday."

He became quite scared, but did not at first understand her. "I did not tell you the truth—About what?" he asked.

A kind of shame restrained her, and she again hesitated at the moment of descending into the depths of another conscience than her own. Then, like a friend, a sister, she continued: "No, you let me believe that you had been saved with me, and it was not true, Pierre, you have not found your lost faith again."

Good Lord! she knew. For him this was desolation, such a catastrophe that he forgot his torments. And, at first, he obstinately clung to the falsehood born of his fraternal charity. "But I assure you, Marie. How can you have formed such a wicked idea?"

ÉMILE ZOLA

"Oh! be quiet, my friend, for pity's sake. It would grieve me too deeply if you were to speak to me falsely again. It was yonder, at the station, at the moment when we were starting, and that unhappy man had died. Good Abbe Judaine had knelt down to pray for the repose of that rebellious soul. And I divined everything, I understood everything when I saw that you did not kneel as well, that prayer did not rise to your lips as to his."

"But, really, I assure you, Marie—"

"No, no, you did not pray for the dead; you no longer believe. And besides, there is something else; something I can guess, something which comes to me from you, a despair which you can't hide from me, a melancholy look which comes into your poor eyes directly they meet mine. The Blessed Virgin did not grant my prayer, she did not restore your faith, and I am very, very wretched."

She was weeping, a hot tear fell upon the priest's hand, which she was still holding. It quite upset him, and he ceased struggling, confessing, in his turn letting his tears flow, whilst, in a very low voice, he stammered: "Ah! Marie, I am very wretched also. Oh! so very wretched."

For a moment they remained silent, in their cruel grief at feeling that the abyss which parts different beliefs was yawning between them. They would never belong to one another again, and they were in despair at being so utterly unable to bring themselves nearer to one another; but the severance was henceforth definitive, since Heaven itself had been unable to reconnect the bond. And thus, side by side, they wept over their separation.

"I who prayed so fervently for your conversion," she said in a dolorous voice, "I who was so happy. It had seemed to me that your soul was mingling with mine; and it was so delightful to have been saved together, together. I felt such strength for life; oh, strength enough to raise the world!"

He did not answer; his tears were still flowing, flowing without end.

"And to think," she resumed, "that I was saved all alone; that this great happiness fell upon me without you having any share in it. And to see you so forsaken, so desolate, when I am loaded with grace and joy, rends my heart. Ah! how severe the Blessed Virgin has been! Why did she not heal your soul at the same time that she healed my body?"

The last opportunity was presenting itself; he ought to have illumined this innocent creature's mind with the light of reason, have explained the miracle to her, in order that life, after accomplishing its healthful work in her body, might complete its triumph by throwing them into one another's arms. He also was healed, his mind was healthy now, and it was not for the loss of faith, but for the loss of herself, that he was weeping. However, invincible compassion was taking possession of him amidst all his grief. No, no, he would not trouble that dear soul; he would not rob her of her belief, which some day might prove her only stay amidst the sorrows of this world. One cannot yet require of children and women the bitter heroism of reason. He had not the strength to do it; he even thought that he had not the right. It would have seemed to him violation, abominable murder. And he did not speak out, but his tears flowed, hotter and hotter, in this immolation of his love, this despairing sacrifice of his own happiness in order that she might remain candid and ignorant and gay at heart.

"Oh, Marie, how wretched I am! Nowhere on the roads, nowhere at the galleys even, is there a man more wretched than myself! Oh, Marie, if you only knew; if you only knew how wretched I am!"

She was distracted, and caught him in her trembling arms, wishing to console him with a sisterly embrace. And at that moment the woman awaking within her understood everything, and she herself sobbed with sorrow that both human and divine will should thus part them. She had never yet reflected on such things, but suddenly she caught a glimpse of life, with its passions, its struggles, and its sufferings; and then, seeking for what she might say to soothe in some degree that broken heart, she stammered very faintly, distressed that she could find nothing sweet enough, "I know, I know—"

Then the words it was needful she should speak came to her; and as though that which she had to say ought only to be heard by the angels, she became anxious and looked around her. But the slumber which reigned in the carriage seemed more heavy even than before. Her father was still sleeping, with the innocent look of a big child. Not one of the pilgrims, not one of the ailing ones, had stirred amidst the rough rocking which bore them onward. Even Sister Hyacinthe, giving way to her overpowering weariness, had just closed her eyes, after drawing the lamp-screen in her own compartment. And now there were only vague shadows there, ill-defined bodies amidst nameless things, ghostly forms scarce visible, which a tempest blast, a furious rush, was carrying on and on through the darkness. And she likewise distrusted that black country-side whose unknown depths went by on either side of the train without one even being able to tell what forests, what rivers, what hills one was crossing. A short time back some bright sparks of light had appeared, possibly the lights of some distant forges, or the woeful lamps of workers or sufferers. Now, however, the night again streamed deeply all around, the obscure, infinite, nameless sea, farther and farther through which they ever went, not knowing where they were.

Then, with a chaste confusion, blushing amidst her tears, Marie placed her lips near Pierre's ear. "Listen, my friend; there is a great secret between the Blessed Virgin and myself. I had sworn that I would never tell it to anybody. But you are too unhappy, you are suffering too bitterly; she will forgive me; I will confide it to you."

And in a faint breath she went on: "During that night of love, you know, that night of burning ecstasy which I spent before the Grotto, I engaged myself by a vow: I promised the Blessed Virgin the gift of my chastity if she would but heal me. . . She has healed me, and never—you hear me, Pierre, never will I marry anybody."

Ah! what unhoped-for sweetness! He thought that a balmy dew was falling on his poor wounded heart. It was a divine enchantment, a delicious relief. If she belonged to none other she would always be a little bit his own. And how well she had known his torment and what it was needful she should say in order that life might yet be possible for him.

In his turn he wished to find happy words and promise that he also would ever be hers, ever love her as he had loved her since childhood, like the dear creature she was, whose one kiss, long, long ago, had sufficed to perfume his entire life. But she made him stop, already anxious, fearing to spoil that pure moment. "No, no, my friend," she murmured, "let us say nothing more; it would be wrong, perhaps. I am very weary; I shall sleep quietly now."

And, with her head against his shoulder, she fell asleep at once, like a sister who is all confidence. He for a moment kept himself awake in that painful happiness of renunciation which they had just tasted together. It was all over, quite over now; the sacrifice was consummated. He would live a solitary life, apart from the life of other men. Never would he know woman, never would any child be born to him. And there remained to him only the consoling pride of that accepted and desired suicide, with the desolate grandeur that attaches to lives which are beyond the pale of nature.

But fatigue overpowered him also; his eyes closed, and in his turn he fell asleep. And afterwards his head slipped down, and his cheek touched the cheek of his dear friend, who was sleeping very gently with her brow against his shoulder. Then their hair mingled. She had her golden hair, her royal hair, half unbound, and it streamed over his face, and he dreamed amidst its perfume. Doubtless the same blissful dream fell upon them both, for their loving faces assumed the same expression of rapture; they both seemed to be smiling to the angels. It was chaste and passionate abandon, the innocence of chance slumber placing them in one another's arms, with warm, close lips so that their breath mingled, like the breath of two babes lying in the same cradle. And such was their bridal night, the consummation of the spiritual marriage in which they were to live, a delicious annihilation born of extreme fatigue, with scarcely a fleeting dream of mystical possession, amidst that carriage of wretchedness and suffering, which still and ever rolled along through the dense night. Hours and hours slipped by, the wheels growled, the bags and baskets swung from the brass hooks, whilst from the piled-up, crushed bodies there only arose a sense of terrible fatigue, the great physical exhaustion brought back from the land of miracles when the overworked souls returned home.

At last, at five o'clock, whilst the sun was rising, there was a sudden awakening, a resounding entry into a large station, with porters calling, doors opening, and people scrambling together. They were at Poitiers, and at once the whole carriage was on foot, amidst a chorus of laughter and exclamations. Little Sophie Couteau alighted here, and was bidding everybody farewell. She embraced all the ladies, even passing over the partition to take leave of Sister Claire des Anges, whom nobody had seen since the previous evening, for, silent and slight of build, with eyes full of mystery, she had vanished into her corner. Then the child came back again, took her little parcel, and showed herself particularly amiable towards Sister Hyacinthe and Madame de Jonquiere.

"*Au revoir*, Sister! *Au revoir*, madame! I thank you for all your kindness."

"You must come back again next year, my child."

"Oh, I sha'n't fail, Sister; it's my duty."

"And be good, my dear child, and take care of your health, so that the Blessed Virgin may be proud of you."

"To be sure, madame, she was so good to me, and it amuses me so much to go to see her."

When she was on the platform, all the pilgrims in the carriage leaned out, and with happy faces watched her go off.

"Till next year!" they called to her; "till next year!"

"Yes, yes, thank you kindly. Till next year."

The morning prayer was only to be said at Chatelherault. After the stoppage at Poitiers, when the train was once more rolling on in the fresh breeze of morning, M. de Guersaint gaily declared that he had slept delightfully, in spite of the hardness of the seat. Madame de Jonquiere also congratulated herself on the good rest which she had had, and of which she had been in so much need; though, at the same time, she was somewhat annoyed at having left Sister Hyacinthe all alone to watch over La Grivotte, who was now shivering with intense fever, again attacked by her horrible cough. Meanwhile the other female pilgrims were tidying themselves. The ten women at the far end were fastening their *fichus* and tying their cap strings, with a kind of modest nervousness displayed on their mournfully ugly faces. And Elise Rouquet, all attention, with her face close to her pocket glass, did not cease examining her nose, mouth, and cheeks, admiring herself with the thought that she was really and truly becoming nice-looking.

And it was then that Pierre and Marie again experienced a feeling of deep compassion on glancing at Madame Vincent, whom nothing had been able to rouse from a state of torpor, neither the tumultuous stoppage at Poitiers, nor the noise of voices which had continued ever since they had started off again. Prostrate on the seat, she had not opened her eyes, but still and ever slumbered, tortured by atrocious dreams. And, with big tears still streaming from her closed eyes, she had caught hold of the pillow which had been forced upon her, and was closely pressing it to her breast in some nightmare born of her suffering. Her poor arms, which had so long carried her dying daughter, her arms now unoccupied, forever empty, had found this cushion whilst she slept, and had coiled around them, as around a phantom, with a blind and frantic embrace.

On the other hand, M. Sabathier had woke up feeling quite joyous. Whilst his wife was pulling up his rug, carefully wrapping it round his lifeless legs; he began to chat with sparkling eyes, once more basking in illusion. He had dreamt of Lourdes, said he, and had seen the Blessed Virgin leaning towards him with a smile of kindly promise. And then, although he had before him both Madame Vincent, that mother whose daughter the Virgin had allowed to die, and La Grivotte, the wretched woman whom she had healed and who had so cruelly relapsed into her mortal disease, he nevertheless rejoiced and made merry, repeating to

M. de Guersaint, with an air of perfect conviction: "Oh! I shall return home quite easy in mind, monsieur—I shall be cured next year. Yes, yes, as that dear little girl said just now: 'Till next year, till next year!'"

It was indestructible illusion, victorious even over certainty, eternal hope determined not to die, but shooting up with more life than ever, after each defeat, upon the ruins of everything.

At Chatelherault, Sister Hyacinthe made them say the morning prayer, the "Pater," the "Ave," the "Credo," and an appeal to God begging Him for the happiness of a glorious day: "O God, grant me sufficient strength that I may avoid all that is evil, do all that is good, and suffer without complaint every pain."

V

The Death of Bernadette— The New Religion

And the journey continued; the train rolled, still rolled along. At Sainte-Maure the prayers of the mass were said, and at Sainte-Pierre-des-Corps the "Credo" was chanted. However, the religious exercises no longer proved so welcome; the pilgrims' zeal was flagging somewhat in the increasing fatigue of their return journey, after such prolonged mental excitement. It occurred to Sister Hyacinthe that the happiest way of entertaining these poor worn-out folks would be for someone to read aloud; and she promised that she would allow Monsieur l'Abbe to read them the finish of Bernadette's life, some of the marvellous episodes of which he had already on two occasions related to them. However, they must wait until they arrived at Les Aubrais; there would be nearly two hours between Les Aubrais and Etampes, ample time to finish the story without being disturbed.

Then the various religious exercises followed one after the other, in a monotonous repetition of the order which had been observed whilst they crossed the same plains on their way to Lourdes. They again began the Rosary at Amboise, where they said the first chaplet, the five joyful mysteries; then, after singing the canticle, "O loving Mother, bless," at Blois, they recited the second chaplet, the five sorrowful mysteries, at Beaugency. Some little fleecy clouds had veiled the sun since morning, and the landscapes, very sweet and somewhat sad, flew by with a continuous fan-like motion. The trees and houses on either side of the line disappeared in the grey light with the fleetness of vague visions, whilst the distant hills, enveloped in mist, vanished more slowly, with the gentle rise and fall of a swelling sea. Between Beaugency and Les Aubrais the train seemed to slacken speed, though it still kept up its rhythmical, persistent rumbling, which the deafened pilgrims no longer even heard.

At length, when Les Aubrais had been left behind, they began to lunch in the carriage. It was then a quarter to twelve, and when they had said the "Angelus," and the three "Aves" had been thrice repeated, Pierre took from Marie's bag the little book whose blue cover was ornamented with an artless picture of Our Lady of Lourdes. Sister Hyacinthe clapped her hands as a signal for silence, and amidst general wakefulness and ardent curiosity like that of big children impassioned by the marvellous story, the priest was able to begin reading in his fine, penetrating voice. Now came the narrative of Bernadette's sojourn at Nevers, and then her death there. Pierre, however, as on the two previous occasions, soon ceased following the exact text of the little book, and added charming anecdotes of his own, both what he knew and what he could divine; and, for himself alone, he again evolved the true story, the human, pitiful story, that which none had ever told, but which he felt so deeply.

It was on the 8th July, 1866, that Bernadette left Lourdes. She went to take the veil at Nevers, in the convent of Saint-Gildard, the chief habitation of the Sisters on duty at the Asylum where she had learnt to read and had been living for eight years. She was then twenty-two years of age, and it was eight years since the Blessed Virgin had appeared to her. And her farewells to the Grotto, to the Basilica, to the whole town which she loved, were watered with tears. But she could no longer remain there, owing to the continuous persecution of public curiosity, the visits, the homage, and the adoration paid to her, from which, on account of her delicate health, she suffered cruelly. Her sincere humility, her timid love of shade and silence, had at last produced in her an ardent desire to disappear, to hide her resounding glory—the glory of one whom heaven had chosen and whom the world would not leave in peace—in the depth of some unknown darkness; and she longed only for simple-mindedness, for a quiet humdrum life devoted to prayer and petty daily occupations. Her departure was therefore a relief both to her and to the Grotto, which she was beginning to embarrass with her excessive innocence and burdensome complaints.

At Nevers, Saint-Gildard ought to have proved a paradise. She there found fresh air, sunshine, spacious apartments, and an extensive garden planted with fine trees. Yet she did not enjoy peace,—that utter forgetfulness of the world for which one flees to the far-away desert. Scarcely twenty days after her arrival, she donned the garb of the Order and assumed the name of Sister Marie-Bernard, for the time simply engaging herself by partial vows. However, the world still flocked around her, the persecution of the multitude began afresh. She was pursued even into the cloister through an irresistible desire to obtain favours from her saintly person. Ah! to see her, touch her, become lucky by gazing on her or surreptitiously rubbing some medal against her dress. It was the credulous passion of fetishism, a rush of believers pursuing this poor beatified being in the desire which each felt to secure a share of hope and divine illusion. She wept at it with very weariness, with impatient revolt, and often repeated: "Why do they torment me like this? What more is there in me than in others?" And at last she felt real grief at thus becoming "the raree-show," as she ended by calling herself with a sad, suffering smile. She defended herself as far as she could, refusing to see anyone. Her companions defended her also, and sometimes very sternly, showing her only to such visitors as were authorised by the Bishop. The doors of the Convent remained closed, and ecclesiastics almost alone succeeded in effecting an entrance. Still, even this was too much for her desire for solitude, and she often had to be obstinate, to request that the priests who had called might be sent away, weary as she was of always telling the same story, of ever answering the same questions. She was incensed, wounded, on behalf of the Blessed Virgin herself. Still, she sometimes had to yield, for the Bishop in person would bring great personages, dignitaries, and prelates; and she would then appear with her grave air, answering politely and as briefly as possible; only feeling at ease when she was allowed to return to her shadowy corner. Never, indeed, had distinction weighed more heavily on a mortal. One day, when she was asked if she was not proud of the continual visits paid her by the Bishop, she answered simply: "Monseigneur does not come to see me, he comes to show me." On another occasion some princes of the Church, great militant Catholics, who wished to see her, were overcome with emotion and sobbed before her; but, in her horror of being shown, in the vexation they caused her simple mind, she left them without comprehending, merely feeling very weary and very sad.

At length, however, she grew accustomed to Saint-Gildard, and spent a peaceful existence there, engaged in avocations of which she became very fond. She was so delicate, so frequently ill, that she was employed in the infirmary. In addition to the little assistance she rendered there, she worked with her needle, with which she became rather skilful, embroidering albs and altar-cloths in a delicate manner. But at times she, would lose all strength, and be unable to do even this light work. When she was not confined to her bed she spent long days in an easy-chair, her only diversion being to recite her rosary or to read some pious work. Now that she had learnt to read, books interested her, especially the beautiful stories of conversion, the delightful legends in which saints of both sexes appear, and the splendid and terrible dramas in which the devil is baffled and cast back into hell. But her great favourite, the book at which she continually marvelled, was the Bible, that wonderful New Testament of whose perpetual miracle she never wearied. She remembered the Bible at Bartres, that old book which had been in the family a hundred years, and whose pages had turned yellow; she could again see her foster-father slip a pin between the leaves to open the book at random, and then read aloud from the top of the right-hand page; and even at that time she had already known those beautiful stories so well that she could have continued repeating the narrative by heart, whatever might be the passage at which the perusal had ceased. And now that she read the book herself, she found in it a constant source of surprise, an ever-increasing delight. The story of the Passion particularly upset her, as though it were some extraordinary tragical event that had happened only the day before. She sobbed with pity; it made her poor suffering body quiver for hours. Mingled with her tears, perhaps, there was the unconscious dolour of her own passion, the desolate Calvary which she also had been ascending ever since her childhood.

When Bernadette was well and able to perform her duties in the infirmary, she bustled about, filling the building with childish liveliness. Until her death she remained an innocent, infantile being, fond of laughing, romping, and play. She was very little, the smallest Sister of the community, so that her companions always treated her somewhat like a child. Her face grew long and hollow, and lost its bloom of youth; but she retained the pure divine brightness of her eyes, the beautiful eyes of a visionary, in which, as in a limpid sky, you detected the flight of her dreams. As she grew older and her sufferings increased, she became somewhat sour-tempered and violent, cross-grained, anxious, and at times rough; little imperfections which after each attack filled her with remorse. She would humble herself, think herself damned, and beg pardon of everyone. But, more frequently, what a good little daughter of Providence she was! She became lively, alert, quick at repartee, full of mirth-provoking remarks, with a grace quite her own, which made her beloved. In spite of her great devotion, although she spent days in prayer, she was not at all bigoted or over-exacting with regard to others, but tolerant and compassionate. In fact, no nun was ever so much a woman, with distinct features, a decided personality, charming even in its puerility. And this gift of childishness which she had retained, the simple innocence of the child she still was, also made children love her, as though they recognised in her one of themselves. They all ran to her, jumped upon her lap, and passed their tiny arms round her neck, and the garden would then fill with the noise of joyous games, races, and cries; and it was not she who ran or cried the least, so happy was she at once more feeling herself a poor unknown little girl as in the far-away days of Bartres! Later on it was related that a mother had one day brought her paralysed child to the convent for the saint to touch and cure it. The woman sobbed so much that the Superior ended by consenting to make the attempt. However, as Bernadette indignantly protested whenever she was asked to perform a miracle, she was not forewarned, but simply called to take the sick child to the infirmary. And she did so, and when she stood the child on the ground it walked. It was cured.

Ah! how many times must Bartres and her free childhood spent watching her lambs—the years passed among the hills, in the long grass, in the leafy woods—have returned to her during the hours she gave to her dreams when weary of praying for sinners! No one then fathomed her soul, no one could say if involuntary regrets did not rend her wounded heart. One day she spoke some words, which her historians have preserved, with the view of making her passion more touching. Cloistered far away from her mountains, confined to a bed of sickness, she exclaimed: "It seems to me that I was made to live, to act, to be ever on the move, and yet the Lord will have me remain motionless." What a revelation, full of terrible testimony and immense sadness! Why should the Lord wish that dear being, all grace and gaiety, to remain motionless? Could she not have honoured Him equally well by living the free, healthy life that she had been born to live? And would she not have done more to increase the world's happiness and her own if, instead of praying for sinners, her constant occupation, she had given her love to the husband who might have been united to her and to the children who might have been born to her? She, so gay and so active, would, on certain evenings, become extremely depressed. She turned gloomy and remained wrapped in herself, as though overcome by excess of pain. No doubt the cup was becoming too bitter. The thought of her life's perpetual renunciation was killing her.

Did Bernadette often think of Lourdes whilst she was at Saint-Gildard? What knew she of the triumph of the Grotto, of the prodigies which were daily transforming the land of miracles? These questions were never thoroughly elucidated. Her companions were forbidden to talk to her of such matters, which remained enveloped in absolute, continual silence. She herself did not care to speak of them; she kept silent with regard to the mysterious past, and evinced no desire to know the present, however triumphant it might be. But all the same did not her heart, in imagination, fly away to the enchanted country of her childhood, where lived her kith and kin, where all her life-ties had been formed, where she had left the most extraordinary dream that ever human being dreamt? Surely she must have sometimes travelled the beautiful journey of memory, she must have known the main features of the great events that had taken place at Lourdes. What she most dreaded was to go there herself, and, she always refused to do so, knowing full well that she could not remain unrecognised, and fearful of meeting the crowds whose adoration awaited her. What glory would have been hers had she been headstrong, ambitious, domineering! She would have returned to the holy spot of her visions, have worked miracles there, have become a priestess, a female pope, with the infallibility and sovereignty of one of the elect, a friend of the Blessed Virgin. But the Fathers never really feared this, although express orders had been given to withdraw her from the world for her salvation's sake. In reality they were easy, for they knew her, so gentle and so humble in her fear of becoming divine, in her ignorance of the colossal machine which she had put in motion, and the working of which would have made her recoil with affright had she understood it. No, no! that was no longer her land, that place of crowds, of violence and trafficking. She would have suffered too much there, she would have been out of her element, bewildered, ashamed. And so, when pilgrims bound thither asked her with a smile, "Will you come with us?" she shivered slightly, and then hastily replied, "No, no! but how I should like to, were I a little bird!"

Her reverie alone was that little travelling bird, with rapid flight and noiseless wings, which continually went on pilgrimage to the Grotto. In her dreams, indeed, she must have continually lived at Lourdes, though in the flesh she had not even gone there for either her father's or her mother's funeral. Yet she loved her kin; she was anxious to procure work for her relations who had remained poor, and she had insisted on seeing her eldest brother, who, coming to Nevers to complain, had been refused admission to the convent. However, he found her weary and resigned, and she did not ask him a single question about New Lourdes, as though that rising town were no longer her own. The year of the crowning of the Virgin, a priest whom she had deputed to pray for her before the Grotto came back and told her of the never-to-be forgotten wonders of the ceremony, the hundred thousand pilgrims who had flocked to it, and the five-and-thirty bishops in golden vestments who had assembled in the resplendent Basilica. Whilst listening, she trembled with her customary little quiver of desire and anxiety. And when the priest exclaimed, "Ah! if you had only seen that pomp!" she answered: "Me! I was much better here in my little corner in the infirmary." They had robbed her of her glory; her work shone forth resplendently amidst a continuous hosanna, and she only tasted joy in forgetfulness, in the gloom of the cloister, where the opulent farmers of the Grotto forgot her. It was never the re-echoing solemnities that prompted her mysterious journeys; the little bird of her soul only winged its lonesome flight to Lourdes on days of solitude, in the peaceful hours when no one could there disturb its devotions. It was before the wild primitive Grotto that she returned to kneel, amongst the bushy eglantine, as in the days when the Gave was not walled in by a monumental quay. And it was the old town that she visited at twilight, when the cool, perfumed breezes came down from the mountains, the old painted and gilded semi-Spanish church where she had made her first communion, the old Asylum so full of suffering where during eight years she had grown accustomed to solitude—all that poor, innocent old town, whose every paving-stone awoke old affections in her memory's depths.

And did Bernadette ever extend the pilgrimage of her dreams as far as Bartres? Probably, at times when she sat in her invalid-chair and let some pious book slip from her tired hands, and closed her eyes, Bartres did appear to her, lighting up the darkness of her view. The little antique Romanesque church with sky-blue nave and blood-red altar screens stood there amidst the tombs of the narrow cemetery. Then she would find herself once more in the house of the Lagues, in the large room on the left, where the fire was burning, and where, in winter-time, such wonderful stories were told whilst the big clock gravely ticked the hours away. At times the whole countryside spread out before her, meadows without end, giant chestnut-trees beneath which you lost yourself, deserted table-lands whence you descried the distant mountains, the Pic du Midi and the Pic de Viscos soaring aloft as airy and as rose-coloured as dreams, in a paradise such as the legends have depicted. And afterwards, afterwards came her free childhood, when she scampered off whither she listed in the open air, her lonely, dreamy thirteenth year, when with all the joy of living she wandered through the immensity of nature. And now, too, perhaps, she again beheld herself roaming in the tall grass among the hawthorn bushes beside the streams on a warm sunny day in June. Did she not picture herself grown, with a lover of her own age, whom she would have loved with all the simplicity and affection of her heart? Ah! to be a child again, to be free, unknown, happy once more, to love afresh, and to love differently! The vision must have passed confusedly before her—a husband who worshipped her, children gaily growing up around her, the life that everybody led, the joys and sorrows that her own parents had known, and which her children would have had to know in their turn. But little by little all vanished, and she again found herself in her chair of suffering, imprisoned between four cold walls, with no other desire than a longing one for a speedy death, since she had been denied a share of the poor common happiness of this world.

Bernadette's ailments increased each year. It was, in fact, the commencement of her passion, the passion of this new child-Messiah, who had come to bring relief to the unhappy, to announce to mankind the religion of divine justice and equality in the face of miracles which flouted the laws of impassible nature. If she now rose it was only to drag herself from chair to chair for a few days at a time, and then she would have a relapse and be again forced to take to her bed. Her sufferings became terrible. Her hereditary nervousness, her asthma, aggravated by cloister life, had probably turned into phthisis. She coughed frightfully, each fit rending her burning chest and leaving her half dead. To complete her misery, caries of the right knee-cap supervened, a gnawing disease, the shooting pains of which caused her to cry aloud. Her poor body, to which dressings were continually being applied, became one great sore, which was irritated by the warmth of her bed, by her prolonged sojourn between sheets whose friction ended by breaking her skin. One and all pitied her; those who beheld her martyrdom said that it was impossible to suffer more, or with greater fortitude. She tried some of the Lourdes water, but it brought her no relief. Lord, Almighty King, why cure others and not cure her? To save her soul? Then dost Thou not save the souls of the others? What an inexplicable selection! How absurd that in the eternal evolution of worlds it should be necessary for this poor being to be tortured! She sobbed, and again and again said in order to keep up her courage: "Heaven is at the end, but how long the end is in coming!" There was ever the idea that suffering is the test, that it is necessary to suffer upon earth if one would triumph elsewhere, that suffering is indispensable, enviable, and blessed. But is this not blasphemous, O Lord? Hast Thou not created youth and joy? Is it Thy wish that Thy creatures should enjoy neither the sun, nor the smiling Nature which Thou hast created, nor the human affections with which Thou hast endowed their flesh? She dreaded the feeling of revolt which maddened her at times, and wished also to strengthen herself against the disease which made her groan, and she crucified herself in thought, extending her arms so as to form a cross and unite herself to Jesus, her limbs against His limbs, her mouth against His mouth, streaming the while with blood like Him, and steeped like Him in bitterness! Jesus died in three hours, but a longer agony fell to her, who again brought redemption by pain, who died to give others life. When her bones ached with agony she would sometimes utter complaints, but she reproached herself immediately. "Oh! how I suffer, oh! how I suffer! but what happiness it is to bear this pain!" There can be no more frightful words, words pregnant with a blacker pessimism. Happy to suffer, O Lord! but why, and to what unknown and senseless end? Where is the reason in this useless cruelty, in this revolting glorification of suffering, when from the whole of humanity there ascends but one desperate longing for health and happiness?

In the midst of her frightful sufferings, however, Sister Marie-Bernard took the final vows on September 22, 1878. Twenty years had gone by since the Blessed Virgin had appeared to her, visiting her as the Angel had visited the Virgin, choosing her as the Virgin had been chosen, amongst the most lowly and the most candid, that she might hide within her the secret of King Jesus. Such was the mystical explanation of that election of suffering, the *raison d'etre* of that being who was so harshly separated from her fellows, weighed down by disease, transformed into the pitiable field of every human affliction. She was the "garden inclosed"* that brings such pleasure to the gaze of the Spouse. He had chosen her, then buried her in the death of her hidden life. And even when the unhappy creature staggered beneath the weight of her cross, her companions would say to her: "Do you forget that the Blessed Virgin promised you that you should be happy, not in this world, but in the next?" And with renewed strength, and striking her forehead, she would answer: "Forget? no, no! it is here!" She only recovered temporary

---

* Song of Solomon iv. 12.

energy by means of this illusion of a paradise of glory, into which she would enter escorted by seraphims, to be forever and ever happy. The three personal secrets which the Blessed Virgin had confided to her, to arm her against evil, must have been promises of beauty, felicity, and immortality in heaven. What monstrous dupery if there were only the darkness of the earth beyond the grave, if the Blessed Virgin of her dream were not there to meet her with the prodigious guerdons she had promised! But Bernadette had not a doubt; she willingly undertook all the little commissions with which her companions naively entrusted her for Heaven: "Sister Marie-Bernard, you'll say this, you'll say that, to the Almighty." "Sister Marie-Bernard, you'll kiss my brother if you meet him in Paradise." "Sister Marie-Bernard, give me a little place beside you when I die." And she obligingly answered each one: "Have no fear, I will do it!" Ah! all-powerful illusion, delicious repose, power ever reviving and consolatory!

And then came the last agony, then came death.

On Friday, March 28, 1879, it was thought that she would not last the night. She had a despairing longing for the tomb, in order that she might suffer no more, and live again in heaven. And thus she obstinately refused to receive extreme unction, saying that twice already it had cured her. She wished, in short, that God would let her die, for it was more than she could bear; it would have been unreasonable to require that she should suffer longer. Yet she ended by consenting to receive the sacraments, and her last agony was thereby prolonged for nearly three weeks. The priest who attended her frequently said: "My daughter, you must make the sacrifice of your life"; and one day, quite out of patience, she sharply answered him: "But, Father, it is no sacrifice." A terrible saying, that also, for it implied disgust at *being*, furious contempt for existence, and an immediate ending of her humanity, had she had the power to suppress herself by a gesture. It is true that the poor girl had nothing to regret, that she had been compelled to banish everything from her life, health, joy, and love, so that she might leave it as one casts off a soiled, worn, tattered garment. And she was right; she condemned her useless, cruel life when she said: "My passion will finish only at my death; it will not cease until I enter into eternity." And this idea of her passion pursued her, attaching her more closely to the cross with her Divine Master. She had induced them to give her a large crucifix; she pressed it vehemently against her poor maidenly breast, exclaiming that she would like to thrust it into her bosom and leave it there. Towards

ÉMILE ZOLA

the end, her strength completely forsook her, and she could no longer grasp the crucifix with her trembling hands. "Let it be tightly tied to me," she prayed, "that I may feel it until my last breath!" The Redeemer upon that crucifix was the only spouse that she was destined to know; His bleeding kiss was to be the only one bestowed upon her womanhood, diverted from nature's course. The nuns took cords, passed them under her aching back, and fastened the crucifix so roughly to her bosom that it did indeed penetrate it.

At last death took pity upon her. On Easter Monday she was seized with a great fit of shivering. Hallucinations perturbed her, she trembled with fright, she beheld the devil jeering and prowling around her. "Be off, be off, Satan!" she gasped; "do not touch me, do not carry me away!" And amidst her delirium she related that the fiend had sought to throw himself upon her, that she had felt his mouth scorching her with all the flames of hell. The devil in a life so pure, in a soul without sin! what for, O Lord! and again I ask it, why this relentless suffering, intense to the very last, why this nightmare-like ending, this death troubled with such frightful fancies, after so beautiful a life of candour, purity, and innocence? Could she not fall asleep serenely in the peacefulness of her chaste soul? But doubtless so long as breath remained in her body it was necessary to leave her the hatred and dread of life, which is the devil. It was life which menaced her, and it was life which she cast out, in the same way that she denied life when she reserved to the Celestial Bridegroom her tortured, crucified womanhood. That dogma of the Immaculate Conception, which her dream had come to strengthen, was a blow dealt by the Church to woman, both wife and mother. To decree that woman is only worthy of worship on condition that she be a virgin, to imagine that virgin to be herself born without sin, is not this an insult to Nature, the condemnation of life, the denial of womanhood, whose true greatness consists in perpetuating life? "Be off, be off, Satan! let me die without fulfilling Nature's law." And she drove the sunshine from the room and the free air that entered by the window, the air that was sweet with the scent of flowers, laden with all the floating germs which transmit love throughout the whole vast world.

On the Wednesday after Easter (April 16th), the death agony commenced. It is related that on the morning of that day one of Bernadette's companions, a nun attacked with a mortal illness and lying in the infirmary in an adjoining bed, was suddenly healed upon drinking a glass of Lourdes water. But she, the privileged one, had drunk of it in vain. God at last granted her the signal favour which she desired by sending her into the good sound sleep of the earth, in which there is no more suffering. She asked pardon of everyone. Her passion was consummated; like the Saviour, she had the nails and the crown of thorns, the scourged limbs, the pierced side. Like Him she raised her eyes to heaven, extended her arms in the form of a cross, and uttered a loud cry: "My God!" And, like Him, she said, towards three o'clock: "I thirst." She moistened her lips in the glass, then bowed her head and expired.

Thus, very glorious and very holy, died the Visionary of Lourdes, Bernadette Soubirous, Sister Marie-Bernard, one of the Sisters of Charity of Nevers. During three days her body remained exposed to view, and vast crowds passed before it; a whole people hastened to the convent, an interminable procession of devotees hungering after hope, who rubbed medals, chaplets, pictures, and missals against the dead woman's dress, to obtain from her one more favour, a fetish bringing happiness. Even in death her dream of solitude was denied her: a mob of the wretched ones of this world rushed to the spot, drinking in illusion around her coffin. And it was noticed that her left eye, the eye which at the time of the apparitions had been nearest to the Blessed Virgin, remained obstinately open. Then a last miracle amazed the convent: the body underwent no change, but was interred on the third day, still supple, warm, with red lips, and a very white skin, rejuvenated as it were, and smelling sweet. And to-day Bernadette Soubirous, exiled from Lourdes, obscurely sleeps her last sleep at Saint Gildard, beneath a stone slab in a little chapel, amidst the shade and silence of the old trees of the garden, whilst yonder the Grotto shines resplendently in all its triumph.

Pierre ceased speaking; the beautiful, marvellous story was ended. And yet the whole carriage was still listening, deeply impressed by that death, at once so tragic and so touching. Compassionate tears fell from Marie's eyes, while the others, Elise Rouquet, La Grivotte herself, now calmer, clasped their hands and prayed to her who was in heaven to intercede with the Divinity to complete their cure. M. Sabathier made a big sign of the cross, and then ate a cake which his wife had bought him at Poitiers.

M. de Guersaint, whom sad things always upset, had fallen asleep again in the middle of the story. And there was only Madame Vincent, with her face buried in her pillow, who had not stirred, like a deaf and blind creature, determined to see and hear nothing more.

Meanwhile the train rolled, still rolled along. Madame de Jonquiere, after putting her head out of the window, informed them that they were approaching Etampes. And, when they had left that station behind them, Sister Hyacinthe gave the signal, and they recited the third chaplet of the Rosary, the five glorious mysteries—the Resurrection of Our Lord, the Ascension of Our Lord, the Mission of the Holy Ghost, the Assumption of the Most Blessed Virgin, and the Crowning of the Most Blessed Virgin. And afterwards they sang the canticle:

"O Virgin, in thy help I put my trust."

Then Pierre fell into a deep reverie. His glance had turned towards the now sunlit landscape, the continual flight of which seemed to lull his thoughts. The noise of the wheels was making him dizzy, and he ended by no longer recognising the familiar horizon of this vast suburban expanse with which he had once been acquainted. They still had to pass Bretigny and Juvisy, and then, in an hour and a half at the utmost, they would at last be at Paris. So the great journey was finished! the inquiry, which he had so much desired to make, the experiment which he had attempted with so much passion, were over! He had wished to acquire certainty, to study Bernadette's case on the spot, and see if grace would not come back to him in a lightning flash, restoring him his faith. And now he had settled the point—Bernadette had dreamed through the continual torments of her flesh, and he himself would never believe again. And this forced itself upon his mind like a brutal fact: the simple faith of the child who kneels and prays, the primitive faith of young people, bowed down by an awe born of their ignorance, was dead. Though thousands of pilgrims might each year go to Lourdes, the nations were no longer with them; this attempt to bring about the resurrection of absolute faith, the faith of dead-and-gone centuries, without revolt or examination, was fatally doomed to fail. History never retraces its steps, humanity cannot return to childhood, times have too much changed, too many new inspirations have sown new harvests for the men of to-day to become once more like the men of olden time. It was decisive; Lourdes was only an explainable accident, whose reactionary violence was even a proof of the extreme agony in which belief under the antique form of Catholicism was struggling. Never again, as in the cathedrals of the twelfth century, would the entire nation kneel like a docile flock in the hands of the Master. To blindly, obstinately cling to the attempt to bring that to pass would mean to dash oneself against the impossible, to rush, perhaps, towards great moral catastrophes.

And of his journey there already only remained to Pierre an immense feeling of compassion. Ah! his heart was overflowing with pity; his poor heart was returning wrung by all that he had seen. He recalled the words of worthy Abbe Judaine; and he had seen those thousands of unhappy beings praying, weeping, and imploring God to take pity on their suffering; and he had wept with them, and felt within himself, like an open wound, a sorrowful fraternal feeling for all their ailments. He could not think of those poor people without burning with a desire to relieve them. If it were true that the faith of the simple-minded no longer sufficed; if one ran the risk of going astray in wishing to turn back, would it become necessary to close the Grotto, to preach other efforts, other sufferings? However, his compassion revolted at that thought. No, no! it would be a crime to snatch their dream of Heaven from those poor creatures who suffered either in body or in mind, and who only found relief in kneeling yonder amidst the splendour of tapers and the soothing repetition of hymns. He had not taken the murderous course of undeceiving Marie, but had sacrificed himself in order to leave her the joy of her fancy, the divine consolation of having been healed by the Virgin. Where was the man hard enough, cruel enough, to prevent the lowly from believing, to rob them of the consolation of the supernatural, the hope that God troubled Himself about them, that He held a better life in His paradise in reserve for them? All humanity was weeping, desperate with anguish, like some despairing invalid, irrevocably condemned, and whom only a miracle could save. He felt mankind to be unhappy indeed, and he shuddered with fraternal affection in the presence of such pitiable humility, ignorance, poverty in its rags, disease with its sores and evil odour, all the lowly sufferers, in hospital, convent, and slums, amidst vermin and dirt, with ugliness and imbecility written on their faces, an immense protest against health, life, and Nature, in the triumphal name of justice, equality, and benevolence. No, no! it would never do to drive the wretched to despair. Lourdes must be tolerated, in the same way that you tolerate a falsehood which makes life possible. And, as he had already said in Bernadette's chamber, she remained the martyr, she it was who revealed to him the only religion which still filled his heart, the religion of human suffering. Ah! to be good and kindly, to alleviate all ills, to lull pain, to sleep in a dream, to lie even, so that no one might suffer any more!

The train passed at full speed through a village, and Pierre vaguely caught sight of a church nestling amidst some large apple trees. All the pilgrims in the carriage crossed themselves. But he was now becoming uneasy, scruples were tingeing his reverie with anxiety. This religion of human suffering, this redemption by pain, was not this yet another lure, a continual aggravation of pain and misery? It is cowardly and dangerous to allow superstition to live. To tolerate and accept it is to revive the dark evil ages afresh. It weakens and stupefies; the sanctimoniousness bequeathed by heredity produces humiliated, timorous generations, decadent and docile nations, who are an easy prey to the powerful of the earth. Whole nations are imposed upon, robbed, devoured, when they have devoted the whole effort of their will to the mere conquest of a future existence. Would it not, therefore, be better to cure humanity at once by boldly closing the miraculous Grottos whither it goes to weep, and thus restore to it the courage to live the real life, even in the midst of tears? And it was the same prayer, that incessant flood of prayer which ascended from Lourdes, the endless supplication in which he had been immersed and softened: was it not after all but puerile lullaby, a debasement of all one's energies? It benumbed the will, one's very being became dissolved in it and acquired disgust for life and action. Of what use could it be to will anything, do anything, when you totally resigned yourself to the caprices of an unknown almighty power? And, in another respect, what a strange thing was this mad desire for prodigies, this anxiety to drive the Divinity to transgress the laws of Nature established by Himself in His infinite wisdom! Therein evidently lay peril and unreasonableness; at the risk even of losing illusion, that divine comforter, only the habit of personal effort and the courage of truth should have been developed in man, and especially in the child.

Then a great brightness arose in Pierre's mind and dazzled him. It was Reason, protesting against the glorification of the absurd and the deposition of common-sense. Ah! reason, it was through her that he had suffered, through her alone that he was happy. As he had told Doctor Chassaigne, his one consuming longing was to satisfy reason ever more and more, although it might cost him happiness to do so. It was reason, he now well understood it, whose continual revolt at the Grotto, at the Basilica, throughout entire Lourdes, had prevented him from believing. Unlike his old friend—that stricken old man, who was afflicted with such dolorous senility, who had fallen into second childhood since the shipwreck of his affections,—he had been unable to kill reason and humiliate and annihilate himself. Reason remained his sovereign mistress, and she it was who buoyed him up even amidst the obscurities and failures of science. Whenever he met with a thing which he could not understand, it was she who whispered to him, "There is certainly a natural explanation which escapes me." He repeated that there could be no healthy ideal outside the march towards the discovery of the unknown, the slow victory of reason amidst all the wretchedness of body and mind. In the clashing of the twofold heredity which he had derived from his father, all brain, and his mother, all faith, he, a priest, found it possible to ravage his life in order that he might keep his vows. He had acquired strength enough to master his flesh, but he felt that his paternal heredity had now definitely gained the upper hand, for henceforth the sacrifice of his reason had become an impossibility; this he would not renounce and would not master. No, no, even human suffering, the hallowed suffering of the poor, ought not to prove an obstacle, enjoining the necessity of ignorance and folly. Reason before all; in her alone lay salvation. If at Lourdes, whilst bathed in tears, softened by the sight of so much affliction, he had said that it was sufficient to weep and love, he had made a dangerous mistake. Pity was but a convenient expedient. One must live, one must act; reason must combat suffering, unless it be desired that the latter should last forever.

However, as the train rolled on and the landscape flew by, a church once more appeared, this time on the fringe of heaven, some votive chapel perched upon a hill and surmounted by a lofty statue of the Virgin. And once more all the pilgrims made the sign of the cross, and once more Pierre's reverie strayed, a fresh stream of reflections bringing his anguish back to him. What was this imperious need of the things beyond, which tortured suffering humanity? Whence came it? Why should equality and justice be desired when they did not seem to exist in impassive nature? Man had set them in the unknown spheres of the Mysterious, in the supernatural realms of religious paradises, and there contented his ardent thirst for them. That unquenchable thirst for happiness had ever consumed, and would consume him always. If the Fathers of the Grotto drove such a glorious trade, it was simply because they made motley out of what was divine. That thirst for the Divine, which nothing had quenched through the long, long ages, seemed to have returned with increased violence at the close of our century of science. Lourdes was a resounding and undeniable proof that man could never live without the dream of a Sovereign Divinity, re-establishing equality and re-creating happiness by dint of miracles. When man has reached the depths of life's misfortunes, he returns to the divine illusion, and the origin of all religions lies there. Man, weak and bare, lacks the strength to live through his terrestrial misery without the everlasting lie of a paradise. To-day, thought Pierre, the experiment had been made; it seemed that science alone could not suffice, and that one would be obliged to leave a door open on the Mysterious.

All at once in the depths of his deeply absorbed mind the words rang out, A new religion! The door which must be left open on the Mysterious was indeed a new religion. To subject mankind to brutal amputation, lop off its dream, and forcibly deprive it of the Marvellous, which it needed to live as much as it needed bread, would possibly kill it. Would it ever have the philosophical courage to take life as it is, and live it for its own sake, without any idea of future rewards and penalties? It certainly seemed that centuries must elapse before the advent of a society wise enough to lead a life of rectitude without the moral control of some cultus and the consolation of superhuman equality and justice. Yes, a new religion! The call burst forth, resounded within Pierre's brain like the call of the nations, the eager, despairing desire of the modern soul. The consolation and hope which Catholicism had brought the world seemed exhausted after eighteen hundred years full of so many tears, so much blood, so much vain and barbarous agitation. It was an illusion departing, and it was at least necessary that the illusion should be changed. If mankind had long ago darted for refuge into the Christian paradise, it was because that paradise then opened before it like a fresh hope. But now a new religion, a new hope, a new paradise, yes, that was what the world thirsted for, in the discomfort in which it was struggling. And Father Fourcade, for his part, fully felt such to be the case; he had not meant to imply anything else when he had given rein to his anxiety, entreating that the people of the great towns, the dense mass of the humble which forms the nation, might be brought to Lourdes. One hundred thousand, two hundred thousand pilgrims at Lourdes each year, that was, after all, but a grain of sand. It was the people, the whole people, that was required. But the people has forever deserted the churches, it no longer puts any soul in the Blessed Virgins which it manufactures, and nothing nowadays could restore its lost faith. A Catholic democracy—yes, history would then begin afresh;

only were it possible to create a new Christian people, would not the advent of a new Saviour, the mighty breath of a new Messiah, have been needed for such a task?

However, the words still sounded, still rang out in Pierre's mind with the growing clamour of pealing bells. A new religion; a new religion. Doubtless it must be a religion nearer to life, giving a larger place to the things of the world, and taking the acquired truths into due account. And, above all, it must be a religion which was not an appetite for death—Bernadette living solely in order that she might die, Doctor Chassaigne aspiring to the tomb as to the only happiness—for all that spiritualistic abandonment was so much continuous disorganisation of the will to live. At bottom of it was hatred to life, disgust with and cessation of action. Every religion, it is true, is but a promise of immortality, an embellishment of the spheres beyond, an enchanted garden to be entered on the morrow of death. Could a new religion ever place such a garden of eternal happiness on earth? Where was the formula, the dogma, that would satisfy the hopes of the mankind of to-day? What belief should be sown to blossom forth in a harvest of strength and peace? How could one fecundate the universal doubt so that it should give birth to a new faith? and what sort of illusion, what divine falsehood of any kind could be made to germinate in the contemporary world, ravaged as it had been upon all sides, broken up by a century of science?

At that moment, without any apparent transition, Pierre saw the face of his brother Guillaume arise in the troublous depths of his mind. Still, he was not surprised; some secret link must have brought that vision there. Ah! how fond they had been of one another long ago, and what a good brother that elder brother, so upright and gentle, had been! Henceforth, also, the rupture was complete; Pierre no longer saw Guillaume, since the latter had cloistered himself in his chemical studies, living like a savage in a little suburban house, with a mistress and two big dogs. Then Pierre's reverie again diverged, and he thought of that trial in which Guillaume had been mentioned, like one suspected of having compromising friendships amongst the most violent revolutionaries. It was related, too, that the young man had, after long researches, discovered the formula of a terrible explosive, one pound of which would suffice to blow up a cathedral. And Pierre then thought of those Anarchists who wished to renew and save the world by destroying it. They were but dreamers, horrible dreamers; yet dreamers in the same way as those innocent pilgrims whom he had seen kneeling at the Grotto in an enraptured flock. If the Anarchists, if the extreme Socialists, demanded with violence the equality of wealth, the sharing of all the enjoyments of the world, the pilgrims on their side demanded with tears equality of health and an equitable sharing of moral and physical peace. The latter relied on miracles, the former appealed to brute force. At bottom, however, it was but the same exasperated dream of fraternity and justice, the eternal desire for happiness—neither poor nor sick left, but bliss for one and all. And, in fact, had not the primitive Christians been terrible revolutionaries for the pagan world, which they threatened, and did, indeed, destroy? They who were persecuted, whom the others sought to exterminate, are to-day inoffensive, because they have become the Past. The frightful Future is ever the man who dreams of a future society; even as to-day it is the madman so wildly bent on social renovation that he harbours the great black dream of purifying everything by the flame of conflagrations. This seemed monstrous to Pierre. Yet, who could tell? Therein, perchance, lay the rejuvenated world of to-morrow.

Astray, full of doubts, he nevertheless, in his horror of violence, made common cause with old society now reduced to defend itself, unable though he was to say whence would come the new Messiah of Gentleness, in whose hands he would have liked to place poor ailing mankind. A new religion, yes, a new religion. But it is not easy to invent one, and he knew not to what conclusion to come between the ancient faith, which was dead, and the young faith of to-morrow, as yet unborn. For his part, in his desolation, he was only sure of keeping his vow, like an unbelieving priest watching over the belief of others, chastely and honestly discharging his duties, with the proud sadness that he had been unable to renounce his reason as he had renounced his flesh. And for the rest, he would wait.

However, the train rolled on between large parks, and the engine gave a prolonged whistle, a joyful flourish, which drew Pierre from his reflections. The others were stirring, displaying emotion around him. The train had just left Juvisy, and Paris was at last near at hand, within a short half-hour's journey. One and all were getting their things together: the Sabathiers were remaking their little parcels, Elise Rouquet was giving a last glance at her mirror. For a moment Madame de Jonquiere again became anxious concerning La Grivotte, and decided that as the girl was in such a pitiful condition she would have her taken straight to a hospital on arriving; whilst Marie endeavoured to rouse Madame Vincent from the torpor in which she seemed determined to remain. M. de Guersaint, who had been indulging in a little siesta, also had to be awakened. And at last, when Sister Hyacinthe had clapped her hands, the whole carriage intonated the "Te Deum," the hymn of praise and thanksgiving. "*Te Deum, laudamus, te Dominum confitemur*." The voices rose amidst a last burst of fervour. All those glowing souls returned thanks to God for the beautiful journey, the marvellous favours that He had already bestowed on them, and would bestow on them yet again.

At last came the fortifications. The two o'clock sun was slowly descending the vast, pure heavens, so serenely warm. Distant smoke, a ruddy smoke, was rising in light clouds above the immensity of Paris like the scattered, flying breath of that toiling colossus. It was Paris in her forge, Paris with her passions, her battles, her ever-growling thunder, her ardent life ever engendering the life of to-morrow. And the white train, the woeful train of every misery and every dolour, was returning into it all at full speed, sounding in higher and higher strains the piercing flourishes of its whistle-calls. The five hundred pilgrims, the three hundred patients, were about to disappear in the vast city, fall again upon the hard pavement of life after the prodigious dream in which they had just indulged, until the day should come when their need of the consolation of a fresh dream would irresistibly impel them to start once more on the everlasting pilgrimage to mystery and forgetfulness.

Ah! unhappy mankind, poor ailing humanity, hungering for illusion, and in the weariness of this waning century distracted and sore from having too greedily acquired science; it fancies itself abandoned by the physicians of both the mind and the body, and, in great danger of succumbing to incurable disease, retraces its steps and asks the miracle of its cure of the mystical Lourdes of a past forever dead! Yonder, however, Bernadette, the new Messiah of suffering, so touching in her human reality, constitutes the terrible lesson, the sacrifice cut off from the world, the victim condemned to abandonment, solitude, and death, smitten with the penalty of being neither woman, nor wife, nor mother, because she beheld the Blessed Virgin.

ÉMILE ZOLA

A Note About the Author

Émile Zola (1840–1902) was a French novelist, journalist, and playwright. Born in Paris to a French mother and Italian father, Zola was raised in Aix-en-Provence. At 18, Zola moved back to Paris, where he befriended Paul Cézanne and began his writing career. During this early period, Zola worked as a clerk for a publisher while writing literary and art reviews as well as political journalism for local newspapers. Following the success of his novel *Thérèse Raquin* (1867), Zola began a series of twenty novels known as *Les Rougon-Macquart*, a sprawling collection following the fates of a single family living under the Second Empire of Napoleon III. Zola's work earned him a reputation as a leading figure in literary naturalism, a style noted for its rejection of Romanticism in favor of detachment, rationalism, and social commentary. Following the infamous Dreyfus affair of 1894, in which a French-Jewish artillery officer was falsely convicted of spying for the German Embassy, Zola wrote a scathing open letter to French President Félix Faure accusing the government and military of antisemitism and obstruction of justice. Having sacrificed his reputation as a writer and intellectual, Zola helped reverse public opinion on the affair, placing pressure on the government that led to Dreyfus' full exoneration in 1906. Nominated for the Nobel Prize in Literature in 1901 and 1902, Zola is considered one of the most influential and talented writers in French history.

A Note from the Publisher

Spanning many genres, from non-fiction essays to literature classics to children's books and lyric poetry, Mint Edition books showcase the master works of our time in a modern new package. The text is freshly typeset, is clean and easy to read, and features a new note about the author in each volume. Many books also include exclusive new introductory material. Every book boasts a striking new cover, which makes it as appropriate for collecting as it is for gift giving. Mint Edition books are only printed when a reader orders them, so natural resources are not wasted. We're proud that our books are never manufactured in excess and exist only in the exact quantity they need to be read and enjoyed.

Discover more of your favorite classics with Bookfinity™.

- Track your reading with custom book lists.
- Get great book recommendations for your personalized Reader Type.
- Add reviews for your favorite books.
- AND MUCH MORE!

Visit **bookfinity.com** and take the fun Reader Type quiz to get started.

Enjoy our classic and modern companion pairings!

Printed in the USA
CPSIA information can be obtained
at www.ICGtesting.com
JSHW022202140824
68134JS00018B/817